Praise for the Lavender Road novels:

'A delightful experience. The large cast of memorable characters and the great sense of time and place are a credit to the author. I can thoroughly recommend it' Ellie Dean

'Funny, poignant, emotional and unputdownable' *London Evening Standard*

'A tale of ordinary people living extraordinary lives' *Inside Soap*

'Written with a lightness of touch, an emotional integrity and an historical accuracy which has brought her respect from critics and readers alike' Louis de Bernières

'An incredible tale of bravery, love and trust . . . a must read' ★★★★★ whisperingstories.com

'An exciting, action-packed book, which makes a very enjoyable, satisfying read' *Western Telegraph*

'This book simply absorbed me . . . left me hooked and interested till the las^

527 831 32 0

HELEN CAREY

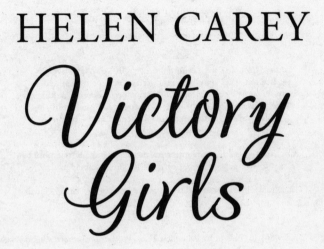

Victory Girls

HEADLINE

First published in 2018 by
HEADLINE PUBLISHING GROUP

First published in paperback in 2018 by
HEADLINE PUBLISHING GROUP

1

Cataloguing in Publication Data is available from the British Library

ISBN 978 1 4722 3156 7

Typeset in Bembo Std 11/13.8 pt by Palimpsest Book Production Limited, Falkirk, Stirlingshire

Printed and bound by CPI Group (UK) Ltd, Croydon CR0 4YY

Headline's policy is to use papers that are natural, renewable and recyclable
products and made from wood grown in well-managed forests and other
controlled sources. The logging and manufacturing processes are expected to
conform to the environmental regulations of the country of origin.

HEADLINE PUBLISHING GROUP
An Hachette UK Company
Carmelite House
50 Victoria Embankment
London EC4Y 0DZ

www.headline.co.uk
www.hachette.co.uk

To my wonderful husband Marc
for his unfailing support and enthusiasm.

Prologue

15 August 1944

Lost in her own thoughts, Molly Coogan didn't immediately notice the small crowd of people standing on the bridge over the railway on St John's Hill in south London. It was a hot August afternoon and she was revelling in the feel of the sun on her skin. There was a scent of geraniums in the air, and a blackbird was singing in one of the trees adjacent to the railway line. In other, happier times it would have been a perfect day for a picnic up on Clapham Common, but that was out of the question at the moment. Hitler's beastly V-1 rockets had seen to that.

When, just over a month ago, Molly had returned to London from a six-month nursing stint in newly liberated Tunisia, she had expected everyone to be delighted that the Allied forces were finally beginning to make some headway in France. But no, after the brief excitement of D-Day, all hopes of an early end to the war had been overshadowed by the daily threat of rocket attacks.

So when one of the people on the railway bridge shouted, 'Look! Here it comes!' her instinct was to run for cover. But as the bystanders craned forward expectantly, she realised that it wasn't a rocket they had spotted, it was a train. She could hear it approaching now, and she could see the thick plume of smoke pumping out into the still air as it chugged along the side of Wandsworth Common towards them. It wouldn't be long before it passed underneath the bridge. She heard the grating squeal of brakes as it began to slow up to cross the points, and suddenly the people on the bridge started shouting and jeering.

Molly stared, aghast. She couldn't imagine what was going on. Then she spotted someone she knew, George Nelson, the eleven-year-old adopted son of her landlady. He was armed with a catapult and was clearly taking aim at the approaching train.

Without pausing for thought, she ran forward. 'George!' she shouted. 'What on earth are you doing?' But he didn't hear her. In any case, she was too late. A pellet of inky blotting paper was already sailing down towards the windows of the train.

It wasn't the only projectile to find its mark. Other people were spitting, and two women were emptying buckets of dirty water over the balustrade. Insults and abuse were flying around too. 'Filthy Nazis! Rotten Kraut bastards! Murdering cowards!'

Molly felt her flesh creep. But she knew now what had caused the rumpus. It must be a trainload of German prisoners of war, presumably on its way up from one of the Channel ports, heading for a POW camp somewhere further north. How members of the public found out about these transfers she had no idea, but somehow they had, and were clearly bent on making their feelings known.

Barging through the crowd, she reached George just in time to stop him firing a second pellet.

'No.' She grasped his arm. 'You mustn't do that. It's wrong.'

George flinched back in alarm, and the unused pellet plopped off the catapult onto Molly's shoe. As she tried to flick it off, fearing that it would leave a permanent stain on her thick regulation Red Cross stocking, a burly man swung round towards her.

'Wrong?' he bawled at her. 'What do you mean, wrong? They deserve everything they bloody get.' Then, leaning over the balustrade, he let rip with a vitriolic suggestion as to what the occupants of the train might like to do to their mothers.

'They're Germans,' George explained helpfully, as Molly drew him hastily out of the crowd. 'Nazis.'

2

'I know what they are,' Molly muttered grimly, trying to wipe the ink off her foot. 'But you still shouldn't throw things at them.'

George seemed surprised. 'Why not?' he asked. 'I hate them. Everybody hates them.'

Molly looked at him and sighed. With his blond hair and delicate features, George Nelson had the looks of an angel, but she knew of old that he was a bloodthirsty little devil and, to be fair, he had more cause than most to hate the Germans. His father had died at Dunkirk, his younger brother had been killed by a car in the blackout and his mother had lost her life during the Blitz. It was hardly surprising he wanted to fire ink pellets at enemy prisoners.

'We are meant to be better than that,' Molly said as they walked back down the road. 'If we do things like that, we sink to their level.'

But was it really so very wrong? She had good reasons of her own for hating the Germans.

Like George, Molly had been orphaned at a young age. Even now she could remember that glorious day at the children's home when she had been told that there was a family who wanted to adopt her. They had taken her in when she was ten years old, and she had lost them eight years later in 1940, when a Nazi bomb landed on the block of flats where they had lived.

Then this time last year, on her way to the nursing job in Tunisia, the troopship she had been travelling on had been torpedoed, and she had spent several unpleasant months in a German POW camp in Italy. That hadn't endeared the Nazis to her either. But in an odd way, she was grateful for that experience, because it was attempting to administer medical aid to the other inmates that had given her the idea of training to be a doctor. One of the reasons she had come back to England now was to study for a Higher School Certificate in sciences, with a view to applying to medical school next year.

The other reason she had left Tunisia was that she had fallen in love with a man she could never hope to marry.

Callum Frazer was the twenty-year-old son of a wealthy Canadian businessman. At the moment he was a pilot in the Royal

3

Canadian Air Force, stationed near Tunis, but after the war he would be going to go back to Canada to take up his place in the family business. His parents were expecting him to marry someone of his own class and background, and even though she and Callum had spent some fun off-duty days together in Tunisia, Molly knew he would never defy his father and marry a penniless back-street orphan from Clapham.

So she had come back to London with the intention of making a new life for herself. Thanks to the recommendation of the matron of the Red Cross hospital where she had worked in Tunisia, she had managed to find a paid nursing post in one of the new first-aid units set up to deal with V-1 casualties. When she wasn't on duty there, she worked at her friend Katy's pub, the Flag and Garter in Lavender Road. All she needed now was a good teacher. But with so many teachers enrolled in the services, and so many schools currently evacuated from London, finding somewhere to study was proving more difficult than she had envisaged. In fact everything was more difficult than she had envisaged. It had all seemed so straightforward from the comfortable safety of liberated Tunisia. But the reality of grey, weary, war-torn London was very different. Especially without a family to fall back on.

'What did that man mean about the prisoners' mothers?' George asked.

Jerked out of her reverie, Molly eyed him suspiciously. She knew that innocent look too well.

'Never you mind,' she said. As it happened, she wasn't quite sure she had understood the vulgar comment herself, and she certainly wasn't going to enter into a discussion about it with Master George.

George giggled, then wrinkled his nose. 'Did you ever know my real mother?' he asked.

Molly shook her head. 'No,' she said. 'I didn't live here in those days.'

'I wish I remembered her better,' he said. 'But it's all a bit of a blur.'

Molly knew what he meant. She had a blur too. Just a faint

recollection of someone. Not someone at the children's home. Someone else. Someone pretty and fragrant. She didn't think of it much. It had always been too painful. She knew, because the staff at the children's home had told her when she was old enough to understand, that her mother had died when she was three years old. But apart from that, she had no idea of her heritage. Questions of that nature had been discouraged, and once she had been adopted by such a kind family, it had no longer seemed important.

'Are you all right, Molly?' George asked as they walked up the hill towards Lavender Road. 'You've gone all quiet.'

Molly stared at him blankly for a moment, then gave a slightly self-conscious laugh. 'Yes, I'm fine,' she said. 'I was just wondering how to get that ink stain out of my stocking, that's all.'

But that wasn't all, and she hadn't been thinking about her stocking. She had been thinking about her mother. And now, suddenly, she too wished her memory was more than a blur.

George had the grace to look apologetic, but not for long. 'Can we stop at Mrs Carter's café?' he asked.

'No,' Molly said. Much as she loved Mrs Carter's cakes, she couldn't afford to splurge her hard-earned pay on unnecessary treats. Medical school wasn't going to come cheap.

'Oh go on, Molly,' George wheedled. 'Please.'

'No,' she said. 'We'll call in at the pub instead. I'm sure Katy will let you have a lemonade. But only if you promise not to fire your catapult at any more German prisoners.'

But when they got to the pub, the lemonade was forgotten, because Katy had just turned on the wireless for the daily war report. People in the bar generally stopped to listen to the news, but today's unexpected announcement today caused even the most chatty of the Flag and Garter's regulars to fall silent.

'Early this morning, large numbers of American and Free French troops, supported by Allied naval forces, landed on the beaches of the south-east Mediterranean coast of France between Toulon and

Nice. Despite enemy resistance, our troops have already established a firm beachhead on French soil. The operation is being hailed as a second D–Day.'

As the BBC newsreader's clipped tones died away, there was a moment's silence, then spontaneous applause broke out in the bar.

'A second front,' someone said in satisfaction. 'They must have brought all our troops up from Tunisia and Egypt, and all them other North African places. I wonder what old Adolf will make of that.'

Katy put her hand to her mouth. 'Oh my goodness,' she said.

Molly looked at her in alarm. 'What is it?'

'I got a letter from Helen this morning,' Katy said.

Molly nodded. 'And?' Their friend Helen de Burrel was still in Tunisia. Due to security considerations and the risk of being censored, her letters were more chatty than newsy, but Molly and Katy could sometimes read between the lines.

Katy was looking troubled. 'She said she was hoping to see André soon. I assumed she meant he had managed to get out of France to meet her somewhere in North Africa, but now . . .' She glanced at the wireless and then at Molly. 'I think she must have meant she was hoping to go to France.'

'Oh my goodness indeed,' Molly said. It was nearly two years since Helen had seen her fiancé, the handsome French resistance fighter André Cabillard. Helen had been in France on a top-secret mission for the Special Operations Executive when she had been betrayed by an SOE double agent in the pay of the Nazis. She had been shot and seriously injured and it was only thanks to André that she had got out of France alive.

That experience would have put most people off the idea of ever going back in occupied Europe. But Molly knew Katy was right. Helen would risk anything to see André again. If she'd got wind of Allied troops leaving Tunisia for an invasion of the south of France, she would certainly have moved heaven and earth to wangle herself a passage. Toulon was exactly where André's father's extensive wine estates were situated.

Molly met Katy's eye and smiled reassuringly. 'Lucky Helen,' she whispered. But even as she said the words she was conscious of an unwelcome stab of envy for her intrepid friend. With her impeccable lineage and elegant blond good looks, nobody was likely to think Helen de Burrel wasn't good enough for glamorous, aristocratic André Cabillard. It had been obvious from the moment the two of them had first met in London that they were made for each other. And now it sounded as though they at least, Adolf Hitler permitting, were going to get the fairy-tale ending they so deserved.

Part One

Chapter One

Seven hundred miles away as the crow flew, on the tranquil waters of perhaps the most beautiful sea in the world, the northern Mediterranean, Helen de Burrel stood at the rail of the USS *Catoctin*, waiting impatiently for her moment to disembark. The previous day, steaming in from all directions – Naples, Sicily, Malta and North Africa – ten huge convoys had congregated off the coast of Corsica: great hulking American battleships, sleek British corvettes camouflaged in greys and blues, Norwegian cargo vessels, Italian cruisers, Polish trawlers, Greek tankers. It was truly an international armada.

Early in the morning, under a light mist, the thousand or so vessels of the Operation Dragoon Allied fleet had crept stealthily northwards, behind the minesweepers, under the protective umbrella of anti-aircraft balloons. It had been a moving sight, made more so when, with the faint blue coastline of France already in sight, Helen's attention had been drawn to a small Royal Navy destroyer, the *Kimberley*, displaying the white flag of the commander-in-chief of the Mediterranean, Sir John Cunningham. As the British ship ploughed past, a young French signalman standing near her on the deck read off the message that was displayed on the double halyard of flags. 'Good luck! Good luck to all you who are on the sea today.'

The decks of the *Catoctin* were full of soldiers, sailors and airmen, and Helen had been lucky to get a spot by the rail. But not as lucky as she had been to get aboard in the first place. It had taken all her ingenuity to wangle a role for herself among the invasion forces.

Despite her French surname, Helen was actually more English than French, but she had spent some of her childhood in France and as a result spoke the language fluently. Having volunteered for the FANYs, one of the British Women's Army services, at the beginning of the war, she had quickly been selected for intelligence work.

For the last six months, since recovering from the injuries she had received on her earlier mission to Toulon, she had been working in an admin capacity for the Special Operations Executive in Tunisia. Her job had been to liaise between the headquarters of the various international clandestine organisations based there, principally the British and American intelligence services and General de Gaulle's exiled Free French army. But despite her requests, her SOE employers – perhaps concerned about the risk of her getting captured when she knew so much, or more likely because she was a woman – had been reluctant to include her in their plans for Operation Dragoon.

In the end, however, her language skills had secured her the role of liaison interpreter to assist the top brass of the British and American forces with their dealings with the French. Helen had no idea what the job would involve, or how she would carry it out, but she didn't really care. All she wanted was the chance to get back to France, to be with her beloved André Cabillard once again.

It had been so long since she had seen him. Since she had left France, at death's door, on an escaping French submarine, André had been operating independently, running sabotage missions with trusted henchmen against the German occupation forces under the cover of his family's respected wine business. Because of the collapse of the SOE network due to the treachery of one of the British agents, his position was precarious, to say the least. The risk of another betrayal was ever present and, as a result, correspondence had been almost impossible. All Helen had received from him in the last nine months were two brief relayed messages via the only SOE agent André trusted, Katy's husband Ward Frazer.

But Ward Frazer had long since left the Mediterranean theatre. He was working undercover in Paris now, paving the way for the D-Day forces in northern France to reach the Nazi-occupied French capital. Since he had gone, Helen had been unable to communicate with André at all. But now that a second invasion was under way so close to where he lived, she was sure André would be expecting her. Waiting for her. He would know that she would come.

And here she was. It was late afternoon. The aerial and naval bombardment of the German positions on the cliffs and beaches was over, thousands upon thousands of paratroopers had been dropped from Allied planes, sappers had cleared the beaches of mines and the first wave of assault troops had been ashore since dawn. Now, finally, the *Catoctin* landing craft were being lowered and Helen's boarding number was being called. Wild animals, even the Waffen-SS, who had been occupying a wing of the Cabillards' chateau for the last two years, were not going to be able to keep her away.

In London, news of the second invasion of France spread fast, and the Flag and Garter was crowded that evening. While Katy put her two children, Malcolm and baby Caroline, to bed in the relative safety of the cellar, Molly and Elsa, Katy's barmaid, manned the two bars. In the kitchen, fifteen-year-old Bella James was busy with the washing-up. Glasses, especially pint beer glasses, were in short supply these days, and if they weren't going to run out, they had to have a quick turnaround.

Bella was yet another orphan of the war. Her mother, the local lady of the night, had been killed when a V-1 had landed on her house two months ago. Bella hadn't uttered a single word since. In the absence of any other family, Katy had taken the girl in, but it wasn't easy housing a silent, traumatised teenager in a busy pub, and it was made worse by Bella's startling beauty. There was hardly a man in the bar tonight who failed to salivate each time she brought the clean glasses through from the pantry.

Molly had still been in Tunisia when the V-1 had hit Lavender

Road, and she had been shocked on her return to find half the street demolished, and the other half uninhabitable.

It wasn't just Lavender Road that had suffered. Altogether Molly had been away from London for over a year. In the rosy glow of nostalgia, she had forgotten the grey, bomb-damaged buildings, the flapping tarpaulins, the taped-up windows, the ubiquitous sandbags, the endless delays, the queues and the swingeing ration system, and that was before the vicious doodlebugs had begun to add to the misery.

It wasn't just the buildings that were grey and battle scarred. Despite the summer weather, Londoners seemed drab and weary too in their patched-up clothes and worn-out shoes. It all seemed a million miles away from the gay frivolity, colour and exoticism of Tunisia, and although Molly's high hopes about her immediate future hadn't exactly been dashed, they had certainly diminished.

Tonight, however, the mood in the pub was optimistic. Over the top of the rousing marching-band music blaring out of the wireless on the bar, Molly could hear the prevailing chit-chat. 'Hitler will be on the run now . . . With another front opened up in Froggyland, I reckon as it will all be over by Christmas.'

'I wonder what will happen to us once it *is* all over,' Katy murmured, appearing up the cellar steps and taking her place beside Molly behind the bar.

What indeed? Molly thought,

Molly hadn't told Katy about Callum. She had mentioned that she had seen him in Tunisia, of course; she could hardly conceal that. Callum was Ward Frazer's cousin, after all. But that was all she had said. It was partly shyness, and partly because she didn't want Katy to confirm her fears.

The Frazer family hadn't approved of Katy either. Molly had met Callum's father when he came to London last year to try to persuade Ward to break off their relationship. Maurice Frazer was a terrifying man, stern, unbending and crushingly superior. But Ward and Katy had held their ground. Ward was older and tougher than Callum,

14

and Katy, albeit like Molly only in her early twenties, was already a respectable businesswoman running a successful pub. In any case, by that time, it was a fait accompli. Ward and Katy were married with a child, and little Caroline, now eight months old, on the way.

But Maurice Frazer and his wife were hardly likely to let the same thing happen to Callum. They weren't going to allow him to hitch up with someone who had spent the first ten years of her life in a residential Home for Waifs and Strays. And Molly wouldn't blame them.

Nor would she blame Callum. Yes, by enlisting as a pilot and joining the war in Europe, he had defied his parents' desire for him to stay safely in Canada. But the same sense of duty that had made him do that would also surely make him unwilling to defy them in the matter of his post-war life.

Not only were Callum and Ward heirs to a huge aeronautical business; the Frazers were also fabulously wealthy members of Canadian high society. Callum would be mad to give all that up to marry a complete nobody. Even if he did, it would just make everyone cross and miserable, and Molly couldn't bear the thought of causing him pain. He deserved better, better than her, even though they'd had fun together in Tunisia, even though Callum had kissed her a couple of times, just small light kisses, once at the end of a moonlit camel ride across the desert, and again during a lazy picnic among the beautiful ruins of Thurburbo Maius. Both times, he had apologised, and in her effort to make light of it, Molly had been unable to tell him that it had been the most wonderful thing that had ever happened to her.

Sometimes in the dark hours of the night, she asked herself if that was why she had fallen for him. Because he was the only man she had known who had ever wanted to kiss her.

'Molly! Watch out, the glass is overflowing!'

Molly jumped and hastily pushed back the beer lever. Then, realising that Katy was still waiting for her to respond to her earlier comment, she forced a smile. 'Well, you'll be all right,' she said lightly.

'You and Ward will finally be able to settle down and live happily ever after.'

It was Katy's turn to be silent. 'What is it?' Molly asked. 'What's the matter?'

Katy dropped some coins into the till and closed the wooden drawer with a snap. 'I'm not sure that Ward is going to want to settle down,' she said.

Molly knew she had a point. It wasn't going to be easy for a man like Ward Frazer, who had lived life on the edge for the last five years, to settle back into run-of-the-mill civilian life.

'He doesn't really like working in the pub,' Katy added, and Molly saw the anxiety in her eyes. All Katy had ever wanted was a quiet life in which to bring up her children. Ward Frazer, with all his derring-do behind enemy lines, was the complete opposite. He thrived on danger and adventure. Molly could understand why Katy was scared. Not so much of losing him, but of him being bored and unhappy, and perhaps deciding after all that he wanted to go back to Canada.

'Then he can find something else to do,' Molly said reassuringly.

Katy made a face. 'I hope so,' she said. Then, picking up a fresh glass from the batch Bella had just delivered to them, she shook her head as though to dismiss her unwelcome thoughts. 'What about you?' she asked. 'Have you made any progress with finding some-where to study?'

Molly sighed. 'No,' she said. 'Most of the local colleges have moved out of London or even closed down completely. The ones that are left aren't offering the courses I need.'

'Why don't you try and find a private tutor?' Katy said. 'Then you could time your lessons round your other commitments. It would be much better than trundling all over town to some distant college.' She was clearly pleased with her idea. 'You could use the cellar here,' she went on eagerly. 'So you'd be safe from the blasted doodlebugs.'

Molly couldn't help smiling at her enthusiasm. 'I suppose it might be worth at least finding out if there are any suitable tutors around.'

'Exactly,' Katy said with satisfaction. 'We'll write out an advertisement and you can drop it in at the *Wandsworth Gazette* tomorrow morning on your way to the Red Cross.' Wiping her hands on a tea towel, she nodded over towards the door, where Angie, Mrs Carter's daughter, was just pushing in through the blackout curtain with her plump little Italian husband. 'There's someone else who needs a tutor,' she whispered with a giggle. 'If you find somebody suitable, maybe they could drum some English into Gino Moretti at the same time.'

Katy wasn't the only person who wished Gino Moretti could speak better English. His mother-in-law, Joyce Carter, had been wishing it for some considerable time. Gino was a former Italian prisoner of war. He was also, in Joyce's opinion, a bit of a waste of space, but Angie had unaccountably fallen in love with him, and in the end Joyce had been forced to give in and let them get married. They both now worked in the café Joyce ran with her boss, Mrs Rutherford, and since the V-1 attack on Lavender Road, they had all been lodging in Mrs Rutherford's big house at the top of the road while they waited for Joyce's own house to be repaired.

Staying with the frightfully posh and oh-so-correct Rutherfords had been stressful enough for Joyce, but having her sex-mad daughter and the linguistically challenged Gino there as well had made it all much worse. There had been numerous awkward incidents, such as when Angie and Gino had somehow managed to break the legs of the bed in their room, and another when Mrs Rutherford's husband had come home unexpectedly from his Home Guard duties on the south coast to find them frolicking stark naked in his bathroom. It was only the placid good sense of Albert Lorenz, Joyce's own soon-to-be husband, that had prevented her from packing her bags and going back to the WVS shelter in the church hall.

Now, as she sat in the saloon bar of the Flag and Garter, watching her intended limp up to the counter to fetch the drinks, she was conscious of a sudden constriction around her heart, because concealed in her handbag was a letter from her eldest son Bob, objecting to the idea of her marrying again.

It wasn't clear whether Bob was anti Albert Lorenz because he was the local pawnbroker, or because he was Jewish, but either way he clearly didn't approve. Joyce hadn't told Albert, of course. She was determined that the wedding would go ahead. But now, tonight, with all this talk of a second invasion of France, she couldn't help wondering what would happen when Bob came home. As presumably he would, as soon as the war was over. Unlike her other sons Paul and Pete, who were both now fighting in France, and Mick, who was serving in the merchant navy, Bob had spent almost the entire war in POW camps, first in Italy and now in Germany.

She felt sorry for him being incarcerated like that, of course she did, but she did feel that it was a bit much for him to be laying down the law from the safety of a POW camp when the rest of them had been living in daily fear of their lives for five long years.

Albert himself had very nearly lost his life in the recent V-1 attack. He had been dragged from the wreckage of his house more dead than alive, and it was only then, realising how desperately she didn't want him to die, that Joyce had finally given in to his long and patient courtship and agreed to marry him.

He was back on his feet now, just about, and the wedding was all set for 25 August, ten days from now. Joyce was jittery enough about it as it was. The last thing she needed was Bob putting a spanner in the works. None of her three other boys minded her marrying again. On the contrary, they were pleased for her. As was Angie.

The person most likely to have expressed disapproval, Joyce thought, had been her elder daughter, Jen. Jen was an actress, working for ENSA, the forces entertainment organisation, and liked nothing better than to throw her weight around and play the prima donna. But Jen liked Albert, and was even deigning to come home from her current ENSA tour for the occasion.

But Bob seemed to be labouring under some kind of misplaced

loyalty to his father. It didn't seem to bother him that the man had been a nasty drunk, a violent husband and crooked to boot. The day she had received the news that Stanley had died in prison had been one of the best of Joyce's life.

She cast a quick glance over at the counter, where Albert was now in earnest discussion with Katy Frazer. Guessing that they were discussing the plans for the wedding party, which they were holding in the pub, Joyce felt her heartbeat accelerate slightly. The only good thing about Bob's letter was that it had taken her mind off the wedding, or more precisely, the honeymoon, the moment when she and Albert Lorenz would find themselves alone in a bedroom together for the very first time.

It had also taken her mind off the daunting thought of Angie and Gino holding the fort in the café for the three days that she and Albert would be away. It was a worrying prospect, and even more worrying was that in a moment of madness a few weeks ago, she had given them permission to open the café in the evenings, to serve Italian food cooked by Gino. They had been waiting for the licence to come through, but it had arrived yesterday, in the same post as Bob's letter, and Angie and Gino had decided to have their opening night the day she and Albert returned from honeymoon. Joyce suspected it wasn't going to be quite the homecoming she might have wished for. If it was anything like their practice sessions, she would be coming back to a kitchen full of steam, Angie with her hair plastered to her face, Gino stripped to the waist, and soggy pasta dough adhering to every surface.

'There you are.' Albert spoke suddenly beside her, making her jump. 'I'm afraid Katy has run out of sherry, so I took the liberty of getting you a small brandy. Or would you have preferred a Guinness?'

'No, no,' Joyce said hastily. 'The brandy is fine.' She could do with a brandy. With any luck, it might settle her jangling nerves.

Catching the flinch of pain that crossed Albert's face as he lowered himself into his chair, Joyce suddenly wondered if there might be a reprieve. Perhaps he wasn't fit enough yet to do the other business, the hanky-panky, as Angie called it. She wouldn't want to cause him any additional damage, after all. She would be more than happy to delay that side of things until . . .

Albert lifted his glass. 'Cheers,' he said. His kindly eyes twinkled behind his spectacles. 'I can't wait for next weekend. I do hope you are looking forward to it too?'

'Oh yes,' Joyce said faintly. She lifted the brandy to her lips and took a fortifying slug. 'Very much so.'

In the South of France Helen de Burrel could have done with a brandy too, but she had to make do with a tin mug of NAAFI tea. It was almost midnight, and she was sitting on the garden steps of a rambling Provençal house, formerly the country residence of the wealthy magazine tycoon and manager of the Tour de France, Henri Desgrange, and now requisitioned as the staff HQ. As she waited for the tea to cool, she looked back over the last few hours and decided that it had been one of the most extraordinary evenings of her life.

She could hardly believe she was back in France after all this time. It was only as they had been queuing up to board the landing craft that she had become aware that the salty tang of the sea and the stench of cordite and machine oil had suddenly gained a new overtone, the warm fragrance of land, the pine-scented and herb-encrusted cliffs and headlands of Provence, and had felt a surge of excitement.

She wasn't the only one.

'La belle France,' one of the French soldiers standing beside her had murmured as he breathed in the scented air. Helen could see the emotion on his face. And when half an hour later they disembarked, wading up the shallows onto a shell-cratered white beach somewhere not far from Sainte-Maxime, she saw the same man fall to his knees and kiss the sand. He was home again after four long years of exile.

Somehow, in the melee on the beach, on legs wobbly after six days at sea, Helen had managed to locate the driver and the Jeep she had been promised. But to her initial surprise, and subsequent dismay, she found she wasn't the only person allocated to that vehicle. Already aboard was a British Army colonel dressed in a pair of extraordinarily wide outdated military jodhpurs, and wearing on his head what looked like a pith helmet. To add to the impression of coming from a different century, and certainly a different war, he sported a wide handlebar moustache with waxed points and spoke in a hearty colonial drawl. The only missing attribute of the bygone era he seemed to represent was a monocle.

'Jolly good show,' he said approvingly as Helen lifted her small suitcase into the back of the Jeep. Helen couldn't help noticing that his own luggage comprised a large wooden trunk, bounded by metal stays and secured by an ornate lock. He shot a hand out over the side of the vehicle. 'Izzard-Lane,' he said. 'The beach master told me I'd have the company of a pretty FANY girl. Can't think of anything nicer. Gather you speak the lingo. Couldn't be better, as I haven't a single word. Learned a little Pashtu on the frontier, don't you know, but I don't suppose that will be much use here.'

Gathering from this that her companion had in some former life served in India as an officer of the Raj, Helen bit back an unruly giggle, shook hands, mumbled a polite greeting and climbed into the back of the Jeep beside him.

It turned out that the bizarrely named Colonel Izzard-Lane had, for some equally bizarre reason to do with 'knowing a frightfully useful chap in the War Office', also been given the job of liaising with the French, which seemed to Helen to be a perfect example of the army's ability to put square pegs in round holes. And nobody could be more square, or indeed less knowledgeable about France, let alone modern warfare, than Colonel Izzard-Lane.

Somewhat to her relief, however, their American driver, Sergeant Maxwell, was clearly a seasoned campaigner. He had come ashore earlier in the day and seemed to have a pretty good idea of how things were going.

'The Jerries are well on the run,' he shouted over his shoulder, when Helen leaned forward to enquire if he knew the current state of play. 'Seems they weren't expecting us. That's not to say they haven't put up a good fight,' he added grudgingly as they followed a half-track up off the beach, sticking to the line of small sapper flags that indicated a mine-free route through the sand dunes. 'We need to keep a bit of an eye out, though,' he warned casually. 'Just in case there are any stragglers.'

Colonel Izzard-Lane gave a grunt of satisfaction, and after grappling for a moment with the flap of his jacket, he produced a fearsome-looking long-muzzled pistol, which, somewhat unwisely, Helen thought, as they bucked and skidded up through the rutted dunes towards the coast road, he proceeded to cradle in his lap.

They were headed for the newly established staff HQ, but it took rather longer than expected to get there because the road to Beauvallon was chock-a-block with traffic. They had to queue for ages behind a column of armoured vehicles before they could even get onto it. When they were finally signalled forward by a US navy rating dressed in white cap and gaiters, Helen could hardly believe her eyes.

She'd known warfare wasn't nice — how could it be? — but she had never imagined anything like the scene that greeted them now. On either side of the slow-moving convoy of Allied vehicles, the highway and adjacent crater-riddled fields were strewn with discarded vehicles — farm carts, wagons and even bicycles — presumably requisitioned by the Wehrmacht and cast off in their haste to flee the might of the Allied invasion forces. Among the abandoned vehicles lay numerous dead horses together with dozens of lifeless bodies, some burnt to a mangled frazzle, others identifiable by their uniforms as Wehrmacht or SS, and some just hapless French civilians caught in the wrong place at the wrong time.

There were horrible fat flies everywhere and, fighting a sudden wave of nausea, Helen turned her head the other way and caught sight of a long column of miserable-looking, dust-covered German prisoners being forced to march along the verge, shepherded by

22

some hard-faced US marines, while at the roadside, moaning and sweating under the merciless evening sun, lay dozens of injured Wehrmacht solders waiting for medical assistance.

'Oh my God,' she whispered.

'Yes, very bad form to abandon one's wounded,' Colonel Izzard-Lane agreed jovially. 'Buggers deserve everything they get.'

'We're never going to get there at this rate,' Sergeant Maxwell remarked suddenly. He nodded off to the right. 'What do you reckon we take a side road, sir?'

Helen stared at the back of his head incredulously. From beyond the high tree-lined ridge to the north came the spine-chilling sound of booming guns, the screeching wail of shells and the clattering of machine guns, interspersed with the explosive crashes of grenades.

But before she could object, Colonel Izzard-Lane waved airily. 'Certainly, Sergeant. Whatever you think best. We are, after all, entirely in your hands.'

No we're not, Helen wanted to shout at him. It's up to us where we go. But she was too late. Sergeant Maxwell had already swung off the road, and soon they were bowling along a straight and completely empty country lane, bordered on both sides by small fields of vines behind which the ground rose steeply to wooded hills.

If only these were André's vines, Helen thought longingly. But they were a long way from the Cabillard wine estates at Domaine Saint-Jean, and she knew she would have to wait until the Germans had been thoroughly routed from the coastal zone before she could make her way to find him.

In the meantime, there was a small village ahead, and as Sergeant Maxwell approached with a degree of caution, Colonel Izzard-Lane sat up even straighter and fingered his weapon hopefully. But the only sign of the Germans they encountered was a slogan scrawled in white paint on the wall of the first house: *Ein Reich, ein Volk, ein Führer.*

'Not for much longer,' Sergeant Maxwell muttered. 'With any luck.' But even as he spoke the words, he screeched the Jeep to a halt, almost unseating the colonel and causing his pistol to clatter down into the footwell under Helen's feet.

'For goodness' sake,' she muttered irritably as she gingerly retrieved it for him. 'You might have blown my leg off.'

Sergeant Maxwell had pulled up by a gateway and was peering at some wide, churned-up indentations in the dry soil. 'Tank tracks,' he said shortly.

Colonel Izzard-Lane's moustache bristled with excitement. Taking firm hold of his gun, he climbed stiffly out of the Jeep and inspected the ruts. Then, with the air of a man more used to hunting tigers than German panzers, he straightened up eagerly. 'Spoor's recent,' he pronounced. 'We'd better get after him.'

'I think it's one of ours, sir,' Sergeant Maxwell said politely. He pointed at the hill on the far side of the field to their right. 'I can see them up there on the high ground. Challengers, I believe.'

Disappointed, the colonel clambered back into the Jeep, but he had barely taken his seat when an elderly man came hobbling down the road towards them from the village.

'*Bienvenue!*' the ancient fellow shouted in a wheezing voice. 'You are our liberators, and we are grateful, but please make haste. This afternoon we made a small token of resistance and the Boches have taken some of our people to the woods.' He gesticulated wildly towards the forested slopes on their left. 'I fear they are going to shoot them. I fear for their lives.'

He was speaking some kind of local patois, and even Helen found it difficult to understand exactly what he was saying, though it wasn't hard to get the gist. With the best will in the world, however, she didn't feel that she, the colonel and Sergeant Maxwell were the right people to go chasing about in the woods in an attempt to rescue hostages from the clutches of the Nazis.

But Colonel Izzard-Lane apparently couldn't wait to engage the enemy, and the next thing she knew, with the elderly gentleman now installed in the front seat of the vehicle, they were careering off up a track through the vines, heading for the distant trees.

This bloody colonel is going to be the end of me, Helen thought, as she clung on for dear life. I'm not going to be at all pleased if he gets us killed just as I'm finally about to be reunited with André.

Colonel Izzard-Lane didn't get them killed, but it was a close-run thing. Suddenly, without any warning, there was a tremendous explosion behind them. At the same moment, Helen was conscious of something screaming past overhead. There was a rending crash, and a tree less than a hundred yards ahead of them split in half in front of their eyes. Stunned, and with her ears ringing, it took a moment for her to grasp the fact that the tanks on the ridge behind them were firing. A moment later, the same thing happened again, except this time clods of grass, branches and foliage flew in all directions as the shell landed at the edge of the forest.

Thinking that the tanks must be German after all, and aiming at them, she screamed at Sergeant Maxwell to take evasive action, but then belatedly she realised that the guns were firing over their heads at something or someone in the woods.

They never discovered exactly who or what it was that had caught the British tank commander's attention, because just then, further along the treeline, a motley group of people emerged from the woods and started running across the field towards them.

'*Mon dieu*,' the elderly gentleman gasped. 'It is the villagers.' Leaping like a stag out of the now stationary Jeep, he went staggering off towards them.

'By Jove,' Colonel Izzard-Lane remarked rather shakily. 'That was a close shave. Another minute and we'd have been blown to kingdom come.'

Within seconds, the straggle of villagers were upon them. They comprised several middle-aged men, a dozen or so youngish women and three children, and nothing Helen could say would convince them that she, Colonel Izzard-Lane and Sergeant Maxwell were not in any way responsible for saving their lives. Apparently their vengeful German kidnappers had lined them up and had been just about to shoot them when the volley of tank fire had come crashing through the woods yards from their position, causing everyone to run for their lives.

As one of the escaped hostages leaned into the Jeep to embrace her, Helen smelt the acrid sweat on the woman's skin, the smell of recent abject terror and panic still evident in her convulsively clutching fingers.

The old man was almost faint with relief. '*Sacré bleu*,' he said, clinging to the side of the vehicle for support. He insisted that they all return to the village so that their saviours could be toasted with wine from his cellar, which had been hidden from the Germans for four long years.

Everyone was smiling now, but behind the smiles Helen could see the strain that these people had been under, and not just that afternoon, but for the preceding few years. Their thin, drawn faces, threadbare clothes and inadequate shoes, and the lack of any young men, told an unhappy story. Times had clearly been very tough in the south of France under Nazi occupation.

The celebration had gone on for some considerable time before the liberators were allowed to get on their way, and by that time, Colonel Izzard-Lane was somewhat the worse for wear.

'What a marvellous country,' he mumbled as Sergeant Maxwell drove off rather unsteadily, followed by a gaggle of cheering barefoot children. 'Jolly nice people, too. Can't imagine why I haven't been here before.'

An hour later, they finally reached the rather sumptuous HQ, just in time for the evening briefing.

The military situation was still somewhat confused, but after a full day of fighting, it seemed that most of the German units were indeed pulling back, making for the valley of the Rhône, while others were attempting to hold off the chasing Allied advance units with dangerous rearguard actions. The Nazis had also left do-or-die units in the docks at Toulon, Marseilles and Nice to try to deny their use to the Allies as long as possible.

But all in all, the Allied commanders' objectives for the first day of action had been more than met. Local resistance groups had played a major part by blowing up bridges, attacking railway lines and cutting telephone cables to hamper the enemy's retreat. As a result, even though some divisions had managed to get away, thousands of German prisoners had been taken.

The briefing officer was confident that within two days or so, the entire coastal area, apart perhaps from the major cities, would be secure, and the Nazis routed.

Two days, Helen thought as she sipped her tea in the cool, scented, cicada-filled garden. Just two more days to wait.

Chapter Two

Molly's boss at the Wandsworth Red Cross detachment was a man called Mr Sparrow. He was a fussy, pedantic middle-aged despot who bore a striking resemblance to Adolf Hitler.

If Molly had been Mr Sparrow, she certainly wouldn't have grown a tightly clipped pencil moustache, nor would she have allowed her hair to drape rather greasily over her scalp exactly like the Führer. She couldn't imagine why his friends, or indeed Mrs Sparrow, if such a person existed, hadn't pointed out the uncanny resemblance. But she certainly wasn't going to mention it, because Mr Sparrow still resented the fact that Molly had been foisted upon him by some higher Red Cross authority.

'I had no choice in the matter,' he had grumbled on her first day, when she had thanked him for taking her on. 'What's more, I've already done my rotas for this month, and now I'm going to have to do them all again.'

The discovery that she had trained as a nurse at the Wilhelmina Hospital at Clapham Junction had mollified him somewhat, and when they had subsequently attended a V-1 incident together, he had told her afterwards, albeit grudgingly, that he had been impressed by her calm efficiency. So she was surprised when he appeared at the first-aid post on Wednesday morning with a peeved expression on his face.

'Nurse Coogan,' he barked, 'I need to have a private word.'

Wondering what she had done wrong, Molly obediently put down the bandage she was rolling and followed him out of the heavily sandbagged hut into the street.

'I've just been sorting out your documentation,' he said. 'And I can't find your birth certificate.'

'That's probably because I never gave you one,' Molly said.

'Well, you should have done,' he said. 'It states quite clearly on the registration form that it needs to be handed in for inspection.'

'But I don't have a birth certificate,' Molly said.

'Of course you have a birth certificate; everyone has one.'

Ridiculously, Molly felt herself colouring. She disliked discussing her family history, especially with someone who looked like Adolf Hitler. 'I was adopted,' she said in the end. 'All I ever had was an adoption certificate.'

If Mr Sparrow was discomfited by the confession, he hid it well. 'Well, I suppose I'll have to make do with that then,' he said.

'But I'm afraid I don't have that either,' Molly said. 'It was lost with everything else when my adoptive parents' flat was bombed in the Blitz.' She thought she caught a flicker of compassion in his eyes and rushed on quickly. She didn't want his sympathy. She didn't want anything from him except this very satisfactory job. 'Won't my ID card do?' she asked. 'I've used that for everything else.'

'Well, you can't use it for this,' he said irritably. 'I need to see an original document. You'll have to go to the General Register Office at Somerset House and get a replacement.' Then, perhaps thinking he had been unduly harsh, he gave her a thin smile. 'If things are quiet tomorrow, you can go then. It shouldn't take long. I believe it's quite a simple process.'

But the following morning, things were far from quiet. The new V-1 klaxons, operated by rooftop spotters, started blaring almost as soon as Molly arrived at the Red Cross post. Thankfully, as far as the residents of Clapham were concerned at least, the first two doodlebugs that came into sight continued on their noisy trajectory. But at 3.30 in the afternoon, only moments after the klaxons started up once again, a third rocket approached, and this time it didn't continue on its way. Its engine cut out, and it dropped right on to Lavender Hill with a massive explosion.

The Red Cross team were at the scene within fifteen minutes. The incident had taken place quite near to the Lavender Road turning, and Molly dreaded that she would find someone she knew among the casualties. Even as she busied herself with assessing and treating the most urgent of the wounded, her eyes, smarting from the smoke and dust, were flicking to the line of corpses at the side of the road already pulled out of the wreckage of a number 77 bus by the rescue workers.

It really was no wonder people hated the Germans, she thought. She knew Hitler claimed that these rocket attacks were revenge for the relentless Allied bombing of Germany, but whether that was true or not, this kind of indiscriminate killing of innocent people seemed a very cheap and nasty way to try to win a war.

She was just risking another glance at the bodies when an imperious female voice spoke behind her. 'I don't want to be a nuisance, Nurse. I'm sure there are others more needy than myself, but I wonder if you could just have a quick look at my hand.'

Swinging round, Molly did now find herself confronting someone she knew. At least by sight. A tall, wild-haired woman, wearing only one high-heeled shoe and dressed in what had once been a long, glamorously off-the-shoulder summer frock.

It was Mrs d'Arcy Billière, who owned the big house at the top end of Lavender Road where Katy's barmaid Elsa and her husband, the young wheeler-dealer Aaref Hoch, lived with their various relatives, having been taken in by the eccentric woman as Jewish refugees. Even without the exotic turban with which she usually bound her long curly hair, Molly recognised her at once. In fact, as she looked more closely, she saw that Mrs d'Arcy Billière was using the long swathe of material to try to stem the gush of blood streaming from her wrist.

Taking the other woman by the elbow, Molly cautiously drew

back the material, but before she could inspect the injury properly, Mr Sparrow was bustling officiously onto the scene. 'A few stitches will sort that out,' he said. 'Will you see to it, Nurse Coogan? We don't want to burden the hospital unnecessarily.'

Molly hesitated. She was reluctant to contradict him, but she could see that Mrs d'Arcy Billière, despite her brave words, was beginning to look rather faint. 'I think it's a severed artery, sir,' she said. 'I think she's going to need surgery. And urgently.'

'No, no, quite unnecessary,' he said. 'You are being overcautious, Nurse. Even if one of the arteries is damaged, there'll be quite enough remaining blood vessels to compensate.'

He was already turning away, and, gritting her teeth, Molly waited for him to move off before escorting the increasingly wobbly Mrs d'Arcy Billière to a waiting ambulance. 'Make sure this lady is seen as soon as possible,' she muttered to the driver as she bundled her inside. 'Tell them she has a severed artery, possibly two, and I think the tendons are damaged as well.' Turning back to Mrs d'Arcy Billière, she took her hand and showed her where to apply pressure to the injured arm. 'Try to keep your arm elevated until they see you,' she said. 'And remember to keep breathing.'

Then she slammed the ambulance door and ran back to see who needed dealing with next.

'I heard that,' Mr Sparrow snapped. 'How dare you defy me?'

Molly met his angry gaze bravely. 'I'm sorry, Mr Sparrow, but it was too much of a risk. If the arteries are severed, she could lose her hand. She lives in the same street as me, and I don't want her on my conscience.'

He glared at her, in the same way Molly imagined Adolf Hitler might glare at his generals, the ones who had, according to the BBC, failed to comply with his instructions to hold out at all costs against yesterday's invasion of southern France.

'Well, I suppose you did what you thought was best,' he said finally. 'But another time, you listen to what I say, all right?'

Feeling she had got off lightly, Molly nodded. 'Of course.'

31

However, Mr Sparrow hadn't quite finished. 'And I want to see that adoption certificate as soon as possible. But I'm no longer inclined to give you the time off. So you'll have to do it on your day off.'

'All right,' Molly said. Unexpectedly, she felt her skin prickle slightly. For a second she didn't know why, and then suddenly she knew that she was going to take the opportunity of visiting Somerset House to see if she could find out who her real mother had been. If it really was as easy as Mr Sparrow thought to find original documents, she would be crazy not to try.

After all, if, by some miracle, she discovered that she came from a posh family, it might make all the difference to her application to medical school. And to her relationship with Callum Frazer.

By Friday morning, Helen was getting excited. The rout of the Germans from the Var, aided by local resistance fighters, had continued apace; meanwhile, the newly disembarked Free French troops under the command of General Jean de Lattre de Tassigny had started to head for Toulon and Marseilles. The original plan had apparently been to capture the two German-held ports in succession, but the unexpectedly quick Allied advance had allowed General de Lattre de Tassigny to attack both cities simultaneously.

Helen had once briefly met the general, a close friend of the Free French leader, General de Gaulle, at a dinner in Tunisia with her father, who was one of Winston Churchill's advisers. Her father was normally based in Washington, where his principal role was to smooth relations with the Americans, but on that occasion he had been travelling with the prime minister on one of the Middle Eastern diplomatic missions.

Helen had never met General de Gaulle, but General de Lattre de Tassigny had struck her as a tough, temperamental sort of man. He had certainly not gone down well with the PM. Perhaps because of that, the Free French forces had been kept out of the first thrust of invasion, but now that the forceful general had finally arrived,

Helen was relying on his men to clear the way through to the area where André's family home, the Domaine Saint-Jean, was situated.

Some of the soldiers who made up the French divisions were from North Africa. Used to the sight of endless motorised convoys, long lines of tanks, troop carriers, artillery, trucks, Jeeps and scout cars trundling their way inland, Helen had been astonished on one of her sorties with Sergeant Maxwell to see on a distant cliff a completely different style of fighting column: a pack train of mules. The uniforms of the copper-coloured men who accompanied them bore very little resemblance to regulation army issue. They consisted of heavy woollen robes with dark striped hoods with bearded fringes, and the men sported thick twists of wool wound round their shaven heads. The whole troop, mules and all, was moving fast across terrain totally inaccessible to motorised transport, with the obvious intention of making an unexpected approach on the German defenders of Marseilles.

'Wow,' Sergeant Maxwell remarked drily as they lost sight of them in a turn of a hill. 'I've never seen anything like that before.'

'No,' Helen agreed. 'Let's hope they take the Nazis by surprise too.'

Most of Helen's work since arriving in France had involved acting as an interpreter between American military commanders and local French dignitaries keen to offer the liberators the freedom of their villages and other hospitality. Sergeant Maxwell's Jeep had been equipped with a radio, and he and Helen had spent much of their time speeding from one area to another in response to various summonses.

Colonel Izzard-Lane, in the meantime, had attached himself to a group of British journalists who were buzzing around the recently liberated areas looking for real-life feel-good stories, and using the intervals in between to accept the offered wares, both culinary and alcoholic, of numerous grateful restaurateurs.

Helen wasn't quite sure about the ethics of this, but when later on in the afternoon, hot and dusty after hours of driving under the scorching Mediterranean sun in the open Jeep, they passed through a small coastal village flying a plethora of newly erected *tricolore* flags and spotted the colonel sitting at a table outside a small café with a glass in his hand, she suggested to Sergeant Maxwell that they stop for some refreshment.

'Ah,' Colonel Izzard-Lane said rather blearily as Helen approached his table. 'Jolly glad to see you chaps. I seem to have mislaid my newspaper pals. Can't imagine what's happened to them. They were here one minute and gone the next.' He waved an expansive hand towards the café's open door, nearly knocking the bottle off the table. 'What would you like to drink? I can recommend the local wine, slips down a treat.'

Seeing the bottle of Cabillard wine on the table, Helen was about to accept when she saw Sergeant Maxwell beckoning to her. Having parked the Jeep in a patch of shade, he was now listening intently to his radio headset.

'Are we needed?' Helen called over.

'No,' he replied. 'But it sounds as though the French have punched through the area to the north of Toulon. I think the way might now be clear to your friend's vineyard.'

Helen felt her heart jolt. She had told the obliging Sergeant Maxwell that her fiancé lived nearby, and pointed out the position of the Domaine Saint-Jean on his map. She knew he had been listening out on the radio frequencies for news, but now that the moment had come, she didn't know what to say. In any case, her voice seemed to have deserted her.

Unfortunately, Colonel Izzard-Lane had no such inhibitions. 'A vineyard?' he said, his eyes lighting up. 'That sounds well worth a visit, my dear. I'll come along if you don't mind.'

Helen looked at him in dismay. She had waited an eternity for this chance to be reunited with André. The last thing she wanted was to have the precious moment spoiled by an inebriated old buffer from a bygone age.

But she could hardly abandon the poor man, even though that

34

was clearly what the journalists had done, so she had to wait impatiently while he finished his glass of wine, bade a ponderous farewell to *le patron* and veered unsteadily across the dusty road to the Jeep.

Somerset House turned out to be a huge, impressive neoclassical building occupying most of the space between London's Aldwych and the river. The massive central courtyard alone was the size of a football pitch. When Molly had looked it up in the library, she hadn't been able to find anything much about how to search for family records, but she had found a quote in an old history book: *In these damp, black and comfortless recesses, the clerks of the nation grope about like moles, immersed in Tartarean gloom, where they stamp, sign, examine, indite, doze, and swear.*

She had no idea what Tartarean gloom was, but the dark, silent interior of the General Register Office that Friday morning gave her a pretty fair idea.

By the time the black-suited man who answered her tentative ping on the bell had explained the process of the filling-out of the request form, the payment of one shilling for permission to search, the numbering system and the requirement to wait while the records were brought up from the archives, Molly was feeling pretty gloomy herself.

Of course, it wasn't easy at all. She should have known that pedantic British officialdom would thwart her. After hours of searching, she was eventually able to locate her adoption certificate, but that was all.

The sepulchral clerk was unable to help her. 'Adoptions are by their very nature confidential,' he said. 'Once an adoption has taken place, the original birth certificate is removed from the public records. The whole system would break down if adopted children were allowed to find their birth parents willy-nilly. Think how the parents would feel.'

'Both my adoptive parents and my mother are dead,' Molly said sourly. 'So presumably they won't feel anything.' She glared at him.

'And what about adopted children? People like me. Don't we have a right to know our heritage?'

'I don't make the rules,' he said stiffly. 'Presumably the people who do believe that adopted children should feel themselves lucky to have found a family to take them in. And should therefore refrain from rocking the boat.'

Molly had a sudden urge to rock *his* boat. But it wasn't his fault; he was only doing his job.

'You know, he's right in a way,' Katy said later, when Molly eventually got back to the pub, having waited four hours for her original adoption certificate to be brought up from the archives by a man in a brown overall and then laboriously copied out by hand. It hadn't told her anything she didn't already know, but at least it would pacify Mr Sparrow.

'What do you mean?' Molly asked crossly.

Katy made a face as she wiped a cloth over the counter, sticky from a busy lunchtime session. 'Well,' she said. 'Things are going well for you at the moment: you've got a nice job with the Red Cross, you've got extra work here, you've got your dream of becoming a doctor, you've got good friends like me and Ward, and the Nelsons, and Jen Carter, and Helen de Burrel. Do you really need to know who your mother was? Maybe it's better to let sleeping dogs lie. You never know, you might find out something you didn't want to know. Something upsetting.' Catching Molly's sudden flinch, she shrugged. 'I'm just saying. The blasted war is bad enough. Do you really need anything else to get anxious about?'

There was no time for Molly to reply, because at that moment they heard a rumpus behind them, and a second later, little Malcolm erupted up the cellar steps closely followed by Lucky the large mongrel pub dog.

'Lucky wants to play ball on the common,' Malcolm said. 'And he wants Molly to take us. And we want George to come too.'

Molly caught Katy's eye and knew what she was thinking. It was perfectly normal that Malcolm wanted to go and play on the common. What wasn't perfectly normal was the likelihood that a V-1 could easily come crashing down and blast him to smithereens. It simply wasn't safe.

'Not now,' Katy said. 'Maybe later Molly will take you over to George's house to play there.'

It seemed a reasonable compromise. There was at least an Anderson shelter in Pam Nelson's back yard. But Malcolm clearly wasn't feeling reasonable. Nor was he in the mood for compromise. His little face was already darkening ominously 'I don't want to go to George's house,' he said, stamping his foot petulantly. 'I want to go to the common. And so does Lucky.'

It seemed he was right about that, because at the sound of his name, Lucky started barking. Malcolm began to scream and Katy took his arm, making him wriggle and kick, and that made Lucky bark even more.

Or perhaps he had heard someone outside, because at that precise moment the pub door swung open, and after a brief tussle with the blackout curtain, into the maelstrom came an extremely tall man wearing an unseasonably heavy tweed suit and an incongruously large bowler hat.

'Good afternoon,' he said tentatively, as they all stopped in astonishment to stare at him. He took off the hat and gave a slight bow. 'My name is Bartholemew Howe. I hope I'm in the right place. I saw an advertisement in the newspaper for a science tutor.'

It was quite a long drive over to the area where André's family vineyards were, and all along the way was the evidence of war. As well as the debris of abandoned vehicles, and the occasional inadequately wired enclosure full of demoralised prisoners, there were canvas Red Cross posts with queues of wounded Allied soldiers outside, and German skull-and-crossbone signs warning of mines in the adjacent fields. Further on they saw a soldier perched on a broken wagon, shaving with water from his tin helmet, and American military policemen manning a vehicle control point at a trestle table hung with girlie pictures torn from a magazine. Everywhere, caught on the scrubby bushes that bordered the road or stirred up from the gutters by passing vehicles like old confetti, were flimsy yellow leaflets, dropped from Allied planes prior to the invasion, now already fading in the relentless sunshine, informing the local civilian population that '*la victoire est certaine*', and that it would be a great help if they remained calm and stayed out of the way.

In the villages the Jeep passed through, tricolour flags and Union Jacks were flying, and people sometimes cheered and clapped as they went by. Mostly the mood was good. Only once did they witness a nasty scene: a young woman being dragged kicking and screaming across a village square while a small group of people stood by watching with grim expressions on their faces.

'Wait,' Helen said urgently to Sergeant Maxwell. 'We ought to stop, what's going on?'

But Maxwell didn't stop. 'I've heard about this,' he said. 'She's probably one of the girls who consorted with the enemy. We've been told not to intervene.'

Helen was craning back in her seat to see what was going on in the square. 'But what will they do to her?'

'If that's all she's been up to, they'll shave her hair,' he said. He saw Helen's shocked expression and shrugged. 'Unless she's a collaborator, and then goodness knows . . .'

Helen forced herself to look away. After all, this kind of vengeful retaliation was nothing compared to what the Germans got up to. She'd known the danger when she had parachuted into France in 1942 as an SOE agent. It was only thanks to André that she hadn't been captured or killed. Since then countless agents, both English and French, had been betrayed by informers and collaborators. Most had since disappeared, along with hundreds of resistance fighters, some perhaps into Nazi prison camps, others probably into unmarked graves. It was a dirty war, and it was hard to blame these patriotic locals for taking their anger out on people they considered traitors.

Curious to know what the dyed-in-the-wool traditionalist Colonel

Izzard-Lane would make of it all, Helen glanced over her shoulder and saw that he was fast asleep.

Sergeant Maxwell winked. 'We're not far off now,' he said quietly. 'I've been thinking, when we get there, why don't I drop you off? I daresay you'd rather be on your own anyway.' He jerked his head towards the slumbering colonel. 'I'll take him back to HQ to sleep it off, and come back for you later.'

Touched by his thoughtfulness, Helen looked at him gratefully. For a second she couldn't quite trust herself to speak.

'Unless you'd rather I stayed,' he added. 'It's up to you. Whichever you'd prefer.'

Helen wouldn't have minded Sergeant Maxwell staying, but she certainly didn't want Colonel Izzard-Lane. 'No,' she said. 'I'll be fine on my own.'

It was nearly two years since André had rescued her from the perfidious SOE double agent in Toulon and brought her to the vineyard for sanctuary, but Helen remembered the pillared gates, the long avenue of silver poplars. And at the far end, on slightly higher ground, the long, low, creeper-covered sixteenth-century *manoir*, with its pink-roofed outbuildings, the arched cobbled courtyard and adjacent small chapel, all overlooking the rolling vine-covered countryside.

She wasn't the only person André and his father had sheltered here. Her friends Molly Coogan and Jen Carter from Lavender Road had also come here when they had escaped from their Nazi POW camp in Italy, after which André had spirited them away to safety in newly liberated Corsica. There had been countless others too: downed airmen, fleeing Jews, anti-fascist politicians, and young local men desperate to avoid transportation to German labour camps or wanting to escape France to join the Free French forces overseas.

As she stood at the end of the driveway, feasting her eyes on the tranquil beauty, Helen noticed a small pall of smoke drifting over one of the distant buildings. A bonfire, perhaps? It was surely too hot for anyone to wish to light a fire indoors. Suddenly she felt a frisson of unease. Had she come too soon? The SS had been occupying a wing of the house for two years. What if the Allied soldiers had passed by unknowingly and the SS were still there even now, burning incriminating papers, or preparing to mount a last stand or some kind of rearguard action?

Feeling suddenly stupid for letting Sergeant Maxwell go, she moved swiftly into the protective shade of the first poplar and began to walk cautiously down the track.

She hadn't gone far, barely ten yards in fact, when she heard the scuff of a boot behind her. The next thing, someone had grabbed her arms.

They had appeared from nowhere. Two men in rough working clothes, both smelling strongly of French cigarettes. Gauloises, Helen thought. The same brand André sometimes smoked. But her relief that they weren't German was short lived, because before she could speak, they were manhandling her towards the nearest tree.

Helen had been trained in unarmed combat by the SOE, but she had been expecting the danger to lie in the vicinity of the house, not on the avenue leading up to it, so she was caught unawares. Nevertheless, her training kicked in and she used the brief moment before they secured their grip on her to deliver a well-aimed knee into the groin of one of her assailants. He gave a grunt of pain, but even as his hold on her loosened, the other man weighed in and pinned her unceremoniously hard up against the tree trunk.

'Who are you?' he grunted in French as he frisked her efficiently for weapons. 'Why are you spying on us?'

'I'm not spying on you,' Helen said. 'I came to visit André Cabillard. My name is Helen de Burrel. I am with the liberation forces, and if you don't get your filthy hands off me pretty damn soon, I'm going to be very angry.'

She had expected them to back off at the mention of André's name, even to apologise, but they just regarded her in stony silence. She looked angrily from one to the other. One of them was dark and swarthy; the other, the man she had assaulted, was older, with thinning hair and blank, inexpressive eyes. It wasn't a pleasant face, but there was something vaguely familiar about that stony expression.

'I know you,' she said to him. 'I met you when I was here two years ago with André. I think your name is Raoul. Listen, I'm sorry I kicked you, but I want to see André. And I want to see him now.'

But Raoul clearly wasn't in a conciliatory mood. Or perhaps his pride had been wounded, in more ways than one. Eventually he muttered something unintelligible, at which point the other man loosened his grip and gestured in the direction of the house.

They walked in silence, but the silence was different now, less aggressive. The men seemed ill at ease, almost apprehensive, and Helen suspected they were wondering how André would react to the news of their violence towards her.

But a few minutes later, when they reached the house, she realised that that wasn't what they had been thinking at all. Because André wasn't there. He hadn't been seen for two days, and no one, not even his father, had any idea where he was.

Of all the scenarios that Helen had envisaged prior to her arrival at the Domaine Saint-Jean, this was one she hadn't considered.

Monsieur Cabillard, André's father, had greeted her with the same well-mannered courtesy she remembered from her previous visit, but his evident pleasure in seeing her again was tempered by the look of apprehension in his eyes.

'I am so sorry, Hélène,' he said. And for an awful moment Helen thought he was going to tell her that André had run off with someone else. But it wasn't that. It was much worse.

'I am sorry the men were rough with you,' he went on. 'But just a couple of days ago our SS house guests found out about André's involvement in the resistance. Or so we believe. Due to the rapid advance of the Allies, they didn't have time to do much more than try to set fire to the house before they left, and we feared they might come back to finish the job. Or to wreak further revenge.'

Drawing her through the stone-flagged hallway to the spacious kitchen, he poured her a glass of wine from an unlabelled bottle and waved her to a chair at the long wooden table. As Helen sat down, she noticed a rangy rough-coated mongrel lying on a ragged mat in front of the empty fireplace. It had raised its head as they came in; now it gave a mournful sigh and rested its nose back on its front paws.

Monsieur's Cabillard's eyes rested briefly on the dog too. Then he lifted his glass and took a sip of his wine. 'Perhaps luckily, for myself at least, I wasn't here,' he went on. 'Nor was André. He had been to Nice, and from what I can gather from the men, he was already angry. When he saw what had happened here, he only stayed long enough to satisfy himself that the fire was out before leaving again, and that was the last any of us have heard of him.'

Perhaps misunderstanding her stricken expression, he smiled faintly. 'Of course if he had known you were coming, I'm sure he would have stayed to await your arrival.'

'I wish I could have let him know,' Helen said. 'But I couldn't. There was too much risk that such a message would have been intercepted.'

Monsieur Cabillard nodded. 'But don't be downcast, Hélène. André will come home soon. He has often disappeared for a few days before.'

He was obviously making an effort to reassure her. But it wasn't very successful. The strain and weariness on his handsome patrician face wasn't something he could shake off in a moment.

Somehow his brave attempt to look on the bright side made it all seem much worse. 'But this time you are more worried than usual?' Helen suggested.

He gave a Gallic shrug, so reminiscent of André that Helen had to press her teeth together to stop her lips trembling. 'André has always taken such pains to be careful,' he said after a moment. 'He was calm, precise and vigilant. He trained the men to be so too. With the SS Boches right here, in the house, the danger was very great. But this time he was so angry . . .'

42

'But he must have often been angry before,' Helen said as he tailed off uneasily. 'So many awful things have happened.'

'Yes, yes, of course.' He hesitated. 'But I think this was a little different. And when André is angry, perhaps he forgets to be so careful.'

Helen shivered and hugged her FANY jacket round her more closely. She knew André had a temper. She had witnessed it herself two years ago when he had found out that the SOE suspected him of being a traitor. But she also knew how clever he had been in outwitting his unwelcome SS guests, and she couldn't bring herself to believe that he would have let his guard down now. Not just when she had come to find him.

'I'm sorry to burden you with my concern,' Monsieur Cabillard said suddenly. 'It is wrong of me when, after all, thanks to your Allies we have every reason to hope for the best.' He put his glass down on the table with a snap and smiled. 'My dear Hélène, it is so very good to see you. André and I have talked about this moment so often. Both of the liberation, and of your return. I have already asked the men to spread the word. When André hears that you have come, I know he will make every effort to return. How long can you stay? At least for dinner, I hope. And perhaps the night? Or longer if your duties permit? You know you are most welcome.'

She was about to refuse, to explain that Sergeant Maxwell would be coming back for her shortly, when she stopped herself. Why shouldn't she stay for the night? After all, Monsieur Cabillard would hopefully soon be her father-in law. The very least she could do was keep him company in his hour of need.

'Are the telephone lines working?' she asked.

Monsieur Cabillard looked surprised. 'Locally, yes, perhaps; further afield, no.'

'And would you by any chance know the number for the house of Henri Desgrange?'

Monsieur Cabillard nodded. 'Of course,' he said. 'We know the family well.'

43

A few minutes later, Helen found herself leaving a message with one of the aides-de-camp asking Colonel Izzard-Lane to arrange for Sergeant Maxwell to pick her up from the Domaine Saint-Jean first thing the following morning, unless she was needed before.

And after a dinner of rabbit and lentils served by an elderly lady from the local village, and a luxuriantly long hot bath in a tub with faded golden claws, she found herself settling down for the night in André's bedroom. Monsieur Cabillard had offered to have the house-keeper make up a fresh room for her, but Helen asked if he'd mind if she slept in André's bed. She wanted to lie where he usually lay. To revel in the faint residual scent of him. And to wait, in hope.

And if he did reappear, then . . . She smiled to herself, and closed her eyes.

Chapter Three

André didn't reappear. And, tired after several nights on a camp bed in the servants' quarters of Monsieur Desgrange's house in the company of two QA nurses and a WAAF map girl, the only thing that disturbed Helen's sleep was when the dog scratched on the door, wanting to be let in.

Climbing back into André's big bed while the hound slumped down on the Persian rug, Helen recalled that there had been two dogs at the Domaine last time she had been there. As she sank back into sleep, she found herself wondering if perhaps André had taken the other one with him on whatever mission he was on, and crossed her fingers, hoping that if he had, the dog would look after him.

But in the morning, she discovered from the surly Raoul, who grudgingly served her breakfast at the kitchen table while Monsieur Cabillard was engaged with some wine business on the telephone, that the truth was considerably less palatable.

The other dog, Raoul told her bluntly, André's favourite, the one that followed him everywhere, had been shot in the head by one of the departing SS officers.

Helen didn't know what to say. She barely knew what to think. For some reason this callous act of violence shocked her more than all the reports of Nazi persecution and murder. It was so specific, so unwarranted. So cold blooded. And she realised that cocooned in Sergeant Maxwell's Jeep, or in the Allied staff HQ, in her neat, clean FANY uniform, with her mind set on her own romantic future, she had been a long way from understanding the brutal horror of war.

But now, reeling inwardly from the effect of Raoul's brusque, unsparing words, the reality was beginning to sink in. And with it came a renewed anxiety about André. Last night, under the influence of several glasses of the delicious Cabillard wine, she had been so sure he was OK, so sure that he would reappear in time for the long-awaited happy reunion. But in the bright, unforgiving light of day, nothing seemed certain any more, and when André's father came back into the room, she looked at him with fear in her eyes.

'Raoul told me about André's dog,' she said.

Catching the quick admonishing look he threw at Raoul, she realised that Monsieur Cabillard had deliberately withheld that information last night, perhaps trying to spare her unnecessary pain, and wondered briefly if there was anything else he had concealed from her. 'Does André know?' she asked.

Monsieur Cabillard glanced again at Raoul, who shrugged. 'We don't know,' he said. 'We only found the dog after he had gone.'

Hearing a vehicle pulling up outside, Helen stood up. To her dismay, her knees suddenly felt rather weak, and she had to put a hand on the table to steady herself. 'I think that will be my transport,' she said. She looked at Monsieur Cabillard helplessly. 'I have to go, but you will promise to let me know . . .'

She couldn't quite finish the sentence, and he took her hands. '*Bien sûr*,' he said. 'Of course. I know where you are.' He kissed her politely on both cheeks in the French way and smiled reassuringly. '*Courage*, Hélène. All is not yet lost. And in the meantime, the news from Paris is good. Workers are striking. Parisians are putting up barricades. The Allies are closing fast. We just have to hope that the Boches don't destroy the city as they withdraw.'

The talk in London was of the advance on Paris too, and of the successful invasion in the south of France. *Germans on the run in*

Provence, screamed the headlines on Saturday morning. *Thousands of prisoners taken. Fewer than 1,000 Allied casualties so far. Toulon, Marseilles and Nice surrounded.*

Sitting on the top deck of a number 77 bus heading towards Tooting, Molly thought it all sounded hopeful, apart from the casualties. She knew all too well that 'casualties', reported so breezily in the newspapers, were in fact real people, and she found herself giving a silent prayer, to a God she no longer believed in, that Callum's name would never feature on one of those awful lists in the back of the paper. Nor Helen de Burrel's, nor André Cabillard's, nor Ward Frazer's, nor any of the other young men she knew currently fighting in France and Italy.

When, a moment later, someone behind her shouted that a V-1 was approaching, she suddenly had a nasty premonition that it might be her name on a list instead. But as the bus swerved to a halt, the rocket passed overhead, and although she felt guilty wishing it on its way to distant death and destruction, she was even more glad than usual, because she hadn't told anyone where she was going, and if she was blown to kingdom come, as so many people were with these beastly weapons, nobody would know about it for some considerable time.

And why hadn't she told anyone where she was going? Because she felt silly about it. Nobody seemed to understand the sudden compulsion that had come over her to find out about her mother. Even her friend and landlady Pam Nelson seemed to think she might be opening a can of worms. 'It's not always easy to revisit your past,' she had said.

George was the only person who was enthusiastic. 'Wouldn't it be brilliant if you found out your mother had left you a million pounds in her will?' he said. 'Or even better, if you were the daughter of a footballer, or a spy.'

So for the first time since she had walked out of the gates in the company of her newly adoptive parents, Molly was on her way back to the children's home where she had spent seven years of her life.

She didn't remember arriving there at the age of three, but she certainly remembered leaving at the age of ten.

That had been twelve years ago, and it occurred to Molly, as she got off the bus and turned down the road from the church where she had fidgeted through so many long Sunday sermons, that for all she knew, the Home for Waifs and Strays might have been bombed in the meantime. But, no, there it was, exactly the same as ever, a squat, drab building crouched behind a high red-brick wall. She drew a sharp breath. Perhaps Katy was right. Perhaps it would be upsetting. But now that she had spent the time getting here, she couldn't just run away again, even though that was what she had wanted to do so many times during the period she had lived behind that austere wall.

The gate had changed. It was wooden now; perhaps the imposing heavy metal barricade of her childhood had been put to use for the war effort. Or perhaps it had just rusted beyond repair. Either way, the new gate stood open now, and with a faintly sinking feeling in the region of her heart, she entered.

The matron had changed too. Unlike the grim-faced harridan who had been in charge in Molly's time, the post was now occupied by a pleasant-looking woman wearing court shoes and a navy-blue twinset. Molly herself was dressed in a smart little suit that Helen de Burrel had persuaded her to have made in Tunisia. She had hesitated about wearing it today, but now she was glad she had. It gave her confidence.

'Yes, Miss Coogan, what can I do for you?' the matron asked when Molly was shown into her office by a member of the kindergarten staff wearing one of the unattractive pale green protective overalls Molly suddenly remembered so well.

As succinctly as she could, Molly explained her mission, using the ruse of the medical school application. But she knew before she was halfway through that it was going to be hopeless. As soon as she said that she had spent time at the home and was hoping to find out how she came to be there, she saw the helpful, open

48

expression on the matron's face change to one of regret. The woman looked weary, and Molly wondered how often she had to deal with supplicants like her. She was clearly well practised in her response.

'I'm sorry,' she said. 'The regulations are very clear. We aren't allowed to divulge any information about the provenance of our children. The rules have been arranged that way to protect parents who feel the need to offer their children for adoption. If they wish to stay in touch, the choice is theirs. If not, they have a right to be shielded from importunate approaches from their former offspring.'

'But I don't want to make an importunate approach,' Molly said. 'I just want to know who my mother was. And why she died.'

The woman laid her hands flat on her desk. 'I understand,' she said, 'I really do. But it is not just the parents. It's the grandparents and wider families too. Often they have no idea that an unwanted child has even been born. How do you think they would feel if such a person suddenly jumped out of the woodwork claiming to be a family member?'

Molly wanted to respond, but she couldn't. Somehow her brain had got stuck on the word 'unwanted'. And for the first time, she allowed herself to wonder why, if her mother had died so suddenly, as she had always been led to believe, her father or some other family member, or even a friend, hadn't stepped in. After all, when George's mother had been killed when a bomb fell on her house in Lavender Road, Pam and Alan Nelson had taken the boy in. And Katy Frazer had taken in Bella. Nobody had thought of sending either of them to a children's home.

She stood up. 'I see,' she said. 'Well, thank you for your time.'

The matron stood up too. 'I'm sorry I can't be of more help,' she said.

Molly looked at her coldly. 'I'm sorry too.'

Perhaps taking pity on her, the woman came round the desk to shake hands. 'I wish you all the best with your future plans,' she said. 'I'm glad to hear that your life has turned out well. It would be quite something if one of our former pupils became a doctor.' As she opened the door, she smiled. 'I imagine things here have changed quite a lot since your day. Would you like to have a quick look round?'

'No, it's all right,' Molly said. But then, sensing an opportunity, she backtracked slightly. 'Unless there are any of the staff still here that I might have known?'

The matron frowned. 'Let me think. Of course we've had quite a turnover of staff due to the war and National Service and so on. I think Miss Webb might be the only person you might remember?'

Molly felt a surge of hope. She remembered Miss Webb all right. Short, plump and good tempered, she had been one of the few people Molly had liked. She had a vague recollection that the woman might even have written to her after she had left to ask how she was getting on. She couldn't remember if she had written back.

'Oh yes,' she said. 'Miss Webb was very kind to me while I was here. I'd love to see her.'

But even in that she was thwarted. 'Yes, that would have been nice for both of you,' the matron said. 'But unfortunately Miss Webb has hurt her back and is off sick at the moment.'

Molly looked at her suspiciously, but the matron sounded genuinely regretful. 'Perhaps another time?'

And that seemed to be that. Five minutes later, Molly was back at the bus stop. But although she was cross, she wasn't entirely downcast. Her experience at Somerset House and at the Home for Waifs and Strays had taught her a valuable lesson. Playing it straight clearly wasn't going to work. She had been too honest. If she was going to get anywhere in her quest, she would have to be much more devious.

'I'm afraid we aren't going to be able to get your house ready in time, Mrs Carter,' Mr Poole the builder said. He sucked his teeth and eyed the crack in her corridor wall with thoughtful concern. 'We'll do what we can, but with building materials in such short supply, it's not going to be easy.'

Nor was it easy for Joyce to restrain herself from losing her temper. You've had three weeks since the permission came through from the council, she wanted to shout at him. Three weeks in which you could have dug out the hallway, put in the underpinning prop and the new reinforced brace and rebuilt the corridor wall a dozen times.

But she couldn't say it. Mr Poole was a nice man, and he was after all doing his best, or what passed for his best in these difficult times. He had lost all his young builders to conscription, and the somewhat unimpressive workmen he was left with were never going to win any prizes for speed and efficiency. Most of them had been pulled out of retirement, and looking at them now as they stood about on the pavement outside her house, smoking and coughing, Joyce sighed. It was over two months now since her house had been declared unfit for habitation. It wasn't as unfit as Mr Lorenz's, of course, on the other side of the road. His house, together with Bella's mother's, was no longer fit for anything at all.

Now that the bulldozers had finished off the job already done by the V-1, all that remained of the devastated houses opposite was the bleak, jagged brick outline of the ground floor and a patch of cracked bloodstained concrete where Mrs James's front room had once been.

It must be hard for young Bella, Joyce thought now, to see the harsh evidence of her mother's demise every time she stepped out into the street. It was no wonder the poor child wouldn't talk.

'We'll do our best, won't we, lads?' Mr Poole said, and his team of workers nodded obligingly.

I suppose I ought to feel lucky, Joyce thought. When all's said and done, I *am* lucky. I'm alive, my children are alive, Albert is alive. Even my tortoise is alive. But she had set her heart on being back in her own place before the wedding. Not that it wasn't comfortable at Mrs Rutherford's house, because it was. Much more comfortable in fact than in her own, not least because it had an indoor bathroom and two separate lavatories. But living in her posh, prudish boss's house wasn't the same as being at home. She didn't want to start her new married life having to endlessly watch her Ps and Qs. What she wanted was to be able to spend cosy evenings with Albert in the front room with her feet up, listening to the radio and not worrying constantly that Angie and Gino were about to cause her some new embarrassment.

Aware that her best hope was to keep Mr Poole sweet, Joyce forced a smile. 'Well, finished or not, I hope you'll all join us in the pub for a quick drink on Thursday afternoon,' she said. 'We should get back from the registry office about three o'clock.'

'Oh yes.' Mr Poole nodded enthusiastically. 'We'll certainly be happy to down tools for that.'

I bet you will, Joyce thought sourly, as she hurried back to the café. It had been Albert's suggestion that they hold the reception in the pub instead of the café. 'It's your day,' he had said. 'And I don't want you to have to do all the cooking and organising.'

Now, as the fateful day drew near, she was grateful. She was tense enough as it was, what with Bob disapproving, and the thought of the honeymoon. And now, to add to her concerns, Jen had written to say that she had decided to go to drama school and wanted to come and live back at home while she was there.

It wasn't that Joyce didn't want her elder daughter to come home, but why Jen wanted to waste her time with drama school when she was due to marry the glamorous, well-to-do theatrical producer Henry Keller as soon as he came back from France was anyone's guess. But the girl insisted on ploughing her own furrow. She had always been strong willed, and that didn't make her the easiest person to live with.

When Joyce had tentatively broached the subject with Albert, however, he had been enthusiastic. 'So she got in, did she? Good for her. RADA no less. It's quite an honour to go there, I believe.'

Joyce had looked at him in surprise. 'You never said she had talked to you about it. When was that?'

For someone so precise and attentive, suddenly he had seemed unusually vague. 'Oh, I don't know,' he said. 'Sometime earlier in the year, I think.' But then he had taken her hand and, lifting it to his mouth, kissed her fingers. 'Of course we must let her stay with us,' he said. 'I'm very fond of Jen. It will be a pleasure.'

Flustered, Joyce had snatched her hand away in case anyone saw. 'Well, if the house isn't ready, she won't be able to,' she had said crossly.

And now the house clearly wasn't going to be ready, which would be sure to put Jen in a bad mood, and having Jen in a bad mood was the last thing anyone would want at their wedding.

The mood in the staff HQ in the south of France was buoyant. Although battles were still raging in Nice and Marseilles, Allied forces were already thrusting north in the direction of Montélimar and Grenoble.

Knowing that some of the key Operation Dragoon commanders had gone forward in pursuit of their troops, Helen was startled one morning, as she sat translating some notes into French for one of the American intelligence captains, when the door of the briefing room flew open and General de Lattre de Tassigny erupted into the room. He was clearly in a furious temper.

'Is it true?' he snarled at the captain. 'Is it true that the Germans have murdered my cousin? In cold blood?'

The intelligence officer stood up sharply and saluted. 'I'm afraid so, sir. In Nice. The Ariane quarter. We don't know who gave the order, but it happened on the day of the invasion. He was taken there with twenty-two other prisoners of the Gestapo. They were all shot.' He fumbled with his papers. 'I have the list of victims from our local agent here.'

General de Lattre de Tassigny snatched the scribbled note from his hand. 'Who is this Hélène Vagliano?' he asked. 'I've heard the name before.'

The captain shuffled his feet uneasily. 'She was the daughter of some wealthy Anglo-French ship owners,' he said. He hesitated, then lowered his voice almost as though he thought Helen wouldn't be able to hear. 'I'm afraid she was badly tortured before she died. I gather she worked for the French Secret Service, the Bureau Central de Renseignements et d'Action, operating out of London. Her codename was Veilleuse. She is known to have been a close colleague of the resistance fighter who severed the railways on the eve of the invasion. The man we know only as Renard.'

Helen felt her mouth fall open. But before she could fully take in what he had said, the captain went on. 'I understand it is thanks to this Renard that the people of Nice are now rising up against the Germans. In revenge for the shootings.'

'But he was not shot himself?'

'It seems not.'

General de Lattre de Tassigny glared at the captain and then swung angrily round to his own aides, who had followed him into the room and were now standing silently behind him. 'Everywhere I go I hear the name Renard,' he snapped. 'Who is this man? Why doesn't someone bring him to me? I would like to shake him by the hand.'

The men looked at each other and then rather anxiously at the captain. But nobody answered. They clearly had no idea who Renard was. But Helen knew. She knew only too well.

Straightening up slowly, she cleared her throat. 'His real name is André Cabillard,' she said.

In his fury, General de Lattre de Tassigny had clearly not noticed her presence in the room. Now he stared at her in utter astonishment. 'Cabillard?' he said. His expression told her that he was familiar with the name. 'Cabillard?'

Helen blinked. 'Do you know him, sir?'

'No, but I know the Cabillard wine,' he said. 'Are you telling me that this Renard is a Cabillard?'

'Yes, sir,' Helen said. 'He is also my fiancé.'

The general gave a sharp laugh. 'Is he indeed? In that case, *you* can bring him to me.'

'I can't, sir,' she said. 'He hasn't been seen for several days. Nobody knows where he is.'

General de Lattre de Tassigny stared at her for a moment, then swung back to his aides. 'Then for God's sake find him,' he shouted, waving the piece of paper. 'Perhaps he can tell us which of these Kraut bastards was responsible for this. Whoever it was has gone too far this time. This isn't war. This is downright murder.'

But it wasn't General de Lattre de Tassigny's aides who first got wind of André's possible whereabouts; it was Monsieur Cabillard's man Raoul, via the underground network. The Cabillard wine van that André had been driving had been discovered parked in a side street in Grenoble. But as there was now fierce fighting going on there, the city was currently inaccessible.

'*Alors*, I will send Raoul there as soon as it is possible,' Monsieur Cabillard said to Helen on the telephone.

'I'm going to go there as soon as possible too,' Helen said. Monsieur Cabillard might trust the surly Raoul to track down André and tell him that she was waiting for him here, but she certainly didn't. Raoul seemed to have his own agenda, and she was pretty sure she didn't feature on it.

'*Non, non*,' Monsieur Cabillard protested at once. 'I do not want you to put yourself in danger. Raoul knows what to do.'

'But how will he communicate with you?' she asked. Whatever resistance contacts Raoul had in Grenoble, it wasn't going to be easy to let Monsieur Cabillard know how he was getting on. The Germans would be sure to destroy the telephone lines in their retreat.

'He will take a box of pigeons,' Monsieur Cabillard said.

Even this line was bad, and Helen wondered if she had heard him correctly. '*Pigeons?*'

'*Mais oui, bien sûr*,' he said with a slight laugh. 'We have used them many times over the last years. Raoul's father trains them. They always come back to his loft.'

For the next two days, Helen was on tenterhooks. Perhaps luckily, she was increasingly busy with translation. Twice she had even had to use her rusty German to help interpret for the American captain during the interrogation of some of the captured Wehrmacht senior officers. These were proud men, professional soldiers who had done their best to carry out Hitler's orders, and who now clearly felt betrayed by his refusal to let them withdraw to regroup. As a result, they had been encircled by American forces and forced to surrender.

So many German soldiers had been captured, it was impossible to question them all. As soon as the ports were cleared, they would be loaded up on troopships and transported back to the UK. In the meantime, they stood about looking weary and defeated, in hastily erected barbed-wire enclosures.

Some Waffen-SS officers had been taken too, but these were very different men, arrogant and aloof, their all-consuming loyalty to the Führer apparently entirely undimmed by the rout. They did not believe that the military situation was as bad as they were told. Nor were they prepared to share any information, other than their rank and number. They certainly weren't going to confess to any atrocities. Looking into their ice-cold, indifferent eyes, Helen felt a new sense of unease. If these were the kind of men André had pitted himself against, she feared for his safety.

'My God,' the captain murmured as they left the makeshift camp after an abortive attempt to get a particularly objectionable SS-Standartenführer to explain why he was in France when his unit was still reported to be in Italy. 'I'm beginning to wonder if these guys are actually human. They don't show much sign of it, do they?'

Helen knew what he meant. She remembered Molly telling her that she and Jen had come up against a particularly unpleasant member of the SS while they had been in Italy. She didn't know the precise details, but she knew that the man had given them a nasty scare. Now that she had seen the species for herself, she could well believe it, and was even more glad that Molly and Jen had managed to escape his clutches.

Then suddenly news came that, thanks to the valiant efforts of the local Maquis resistance fighters, the Germans had been forced out of Grenoble. Leaving General de Lattre de Tassigny's French forces battling it out at Toulon, Marseilles and Nice, the whole Allied staff HQ was now about to move forward, and Helen with it. The only disappointment was that due to the lack of resupply, the US 45th Infantry Division had been unable to cut off the German retreat, and as a result there were fears that the Germans would call in reinforcements and make a major stand further up the Rhône valley.

Two days later, on 24 August, after an interminably long drive in the wake of a column of troop carriers, Helen, Sergeant Maxwell and Colonel Izzard-Lane finally arrived in the bruised and battered city of Grenoble.

As she climbed wearily out of the Jeep in front of the Fountain of the Three Orders in Place Notre Dame, Helen was astonished to see Raoul materialise out of a small crowd. She had no idea how he'd known she would be there. He was obviously brighter than he looked. But he hadn't found André.

'He was here,' he said in his lugubrious way. 'But then he disappeared.'

'I think he might have been chasing after the man who ordered the execution of the agent Veilleuse and some others in Nice on the day of the invasion,' Helen said.

She expected Raoul to look surprised or shocked, or even mildly interested, but he just jutted his chin slightly in acknowledgement, and she realised that he already knew all about the murders in Nice.

'I wish you had told me,' she said irritably. 'I might have been able to do something sooner.'

He raised his eyebrows. 'What?' he asked insolently. 'What could you have done? Your SOE has already caused enough damage. Hundreds of our people have died because of your incompetence.'

So that was it. That was the cause of his resentment towards her. He was right to be angry. The SOE French section had indeed been incompetent. Their refusal to accept that some of their agents had gone bad, or had been captured and were reporting under duress, had caused untold damage to the resistance networks.

'The Maquis leaders here believe he must have been taken,' Raoul went on in his deadpan voice.

'No,' Helen said. She refused to believe it. 'No, please don't say that.'

Raoul's face hardened. 'It would not be the first time,' he said. 'I think you do not know that Monsieur André was held in the Gestapo headquarters in Paris earlier this year.'

Helen stared at him. For a moment the noise of the square, the playing of the fountain faded to silence. 'No,' she said. 'I didn't know. What happened?'

'He escaped,' Raoul said. 'Perhaps he will escape again.' He took half a cigarette from his pocket and lit it with an old-fashioned taper amadou spark-wheel lighter. 'If he is not already dead. It is believed that some prisoners from the Gestapo prison here in Grenoble were taken away, but it is also believed that some were executed in the last few days before the Boches pulled out.' He shrugged. 'Unfortunately the bodies have not yet been found.'

Helen suddenly hated this Raoul with a bitter loathing. Why did he have to be so brutally blunt? He must know the effect his words were having on her. Maybe he didn't care. Maybe he felt she deserved the pain for daring to be in love with his master.

'I can't stay here in the city,' she said. She saw his eyes flicker with a scornful I-told-you-so kind of look. 'I am needed at the new American field HQ this evening. But if you find out anything, will you get a message to me?'

'*Bien sûr*,' he said. 'I will try to keep you informed.' But Helen didn't think he would try very hard, and she could feel her heart trembling. By coming to Grenoble she had thought she was getting nearer to André, but somehow he seemed to be slipping further and further away.

To be honest, Molly had not had very high hopes of Mr Bartholemew Howe, her new tutor, but there was something about his awkward manner, his slightly unfocused eyes and shaky hands that made her feel sorry for him. And his credentials certainly seemed to be good; a graduate of Cambridge University, he had taught physics and chemistry at a private boys' school in the north of England before the war. For some reason that job had come to an end, and he was currently employed in the Ministry of Agriculture and Fisheries, being too old for conscription into the armed forces and having failed on grounds of poor health to make the grade to serve as a volunteer.

In any case, as he had been the only person to answer her advertisement, she could hardly turn him down. Especially as the fee he suggested for the weekly tutorials she felt she required seemed very reasonable.

At first everything had gone well. He had arrived promptly at the appointed time, armed with some textbooks, and seemed pleased with the table and chair that Molly and Katy had with difficulty manhandled down into the pub cellar for him to sit at.

But as they started to discuss the curriculum she needed to study, Molly began to wonder if Mr Howe suffered from claustrophobia. They had only been in the cellar for twenty minutes when he asked if she would mind if he popped upstairs for a bit of fresh air. Molly of course didn't mind at all, and while he was gone she took the opportunity to inspect the dauntingly dense textbooks he had brought with him.

When he reappeared five minutes later, he seemed considerably more relaxed and informative, and Molly began to feel that she had misjudged him.

A quarter of an hour later, he said he needed fresh air again. He was back quite soon, coming somewhat cautiously down the cellar steps like an ungainly spider. And so the evening progressed.

It was during his fifth visit to the upstairs world that Molly began to get slightly worried. Immersed in the intricacies of the periodic table, it was some time before she realised that he hadn't reappeared. Just as she was about to go and see what had happened to him, she heard raised voices up in the bar, a scream and a heavy thump.

Running upstairs, she was horrified to see her teacher slumped at the top of the cellar steps, his hand clutching the hem of fifteen-year-old Bella's skirt.

'Oh my God,' Molly said. 'What on earth happened?'

Katy was trying to prise open the comatose Mr Howe's fingers. 'The bloody man suddenly started trying to kiss Bella,' she muttered. 'Of course he was blind drunk, but even so . . . Thank God he passed out at the crucial moment.'

'Drunk?' Molly stared at her in astonishment. 'But he told me he was coming upstairs for fresh air.'

Katy straightened up and smiled reassuringly at Bella. 'It's all right,' she said. 'No harm done. But perhaps you'd better go upstairs and check on the children while we sort things out down here.'

She turned to Molly. 'Every time he came upstairs, he ordered a whisky. I could hardly refuse to serve him. He seemed quite compos mentis. But then he spotted Bella, and went absolutely berserk.' She grimaced. 'It would have been funny if it had been anyone other than Bella. I'd better go and check she's all right.'

But before she could move, a voice spoke behind her.

'Good lord, who on earth's that? Whoever he is, I hope he hasn't drunk the place dry. I'm dying for a gin and tonic. And I need a bed for the night too, because I gather Mum's house isn't ready, and I'm damned if I'm going to stay at awful old Mrs Rutherford's.'

Swinging round, Molly gave a choke of laughter. There on the other side of the bar, looking like a film star in a chic little summer evening dress, carrying a suitcase and a bunch of flowers, was her former partner in crime in Italy, the up-and-coming actress Jen Carter.

Chapter Four

'All right, Mum,' Angie called up the stairs. 'They've gone. The coast's clear.'

Joyce, dressed in the smartest dress and shoes she had ever owned in her life, bought with winnings on a horse at Windsor earlier in the year, together with carefully saved-up clothing coupons, emerged from her bedroom. Angie had decreed that it would be unlucky for the bride to see her groom on the wedding morning, so Joyce and Albert had had to box-and-cox it over breakfast and getting ready for the ceremony.

Now Albert had finally left with Gino in a taxi for the Clapham register office, and Joyce suddenly realised that this was really going to happen. She was going to marry Albert Lorenz.

Angie was waiting at the bottom of the stairs. She was honouring the occasion with a jaunty straw boater with a tasteful pale pink band, borrowed without permission from Mrs Rutherford's daughter Louise's wardrobe. Louise was away somewhere in Wales doing something important with the ATS, so thankfully wasn't there to complain. Angie had set off the boater with a self-dyed shocking-pink dress that hugged her voluptuous figure considerably too tightly.

'Blimey, Mum,' she said. 'You look amazing. Mr Lorenz won't know himself when he claps eyes on you!'

'Oh stop it,' Joyce said gruffly. She felt self-conscious enough as it was. She had never been one for the limelight. Having to be the centre of attention for the day was one of the many things that had scared her about getting married. But it was too late now. Celia Rutherford was bustling in from the driveway.

'Your taxi is here,' she said, her eyes widening at the sight of Angie's outfit. She herself was wearing a staid tweed skirt and jacket, with a wide-brimmed felt hat trimmed with green gauze. 'I've put the suitcases in. We'll drop them off at the pub so you won't have to waste time coming back here before leaving for your honeymoon.' She paused and peered at Joyce in concern. 'You look rather pale, Mrs Carter, are you feeling quite all right? Or is it just nerves?'

'Just nerves,' Joyce said rather tautly.

Angie squeezed her arm. 'Don't worry,' she said. 'I felt nervous too, about the you-know-what, but as soon as me and Gino were alone in the hotel, it was as though I'd died and gone to heaven. I'm sure it will be the same with you and Mr Lorenz.'

As well as the two taxis from Cedars House, Mr Lorenz had also arranged for yet another to take the small contingent from the pub to the register office. Jen was glad, because she was wearing high heels and hadn't wanted to walk, especially if it was raining.

It wasn't raining, but it was overcast. The lovely weather of the last few weeks had given way to grey skies and the odd sharp shower.

'It's awfully generous of him,' Katy remarked as they waited outside the Flag and Garter for the cab to arrive. 'And there's to be no expense spared on the drinks later on either,' she added in considerable awe. 'We're to put it all on a tab and he's going to settle up at the end.'

Katy had seemed surprised at Mr Lorenz's largesse; she had after all known him for years as one of her most frugal and sober customers, rarely buying himself more than half a pint. But Jen, sitting in the back of the cab with Malcolm on her knee, was well aware what a generous man Mr Lorenz was.

Because what no one knew, not even her mother, was that Mr Lorenz had offered to pay for her course at RADA. Jen would never have been able to afford it otherwise. Fifteen guineas a term was well beyond her meagre means, especially as the RADA students were not allowed to accept professional work while they were attending the course. Even with Mr Lorenz's help, it was going to be a push. But a place at the highly prestigious Royal Academy of Dramatic Art was worth any amount of sacrifice.

In any case, Jen was glad to be back in London. It was a relief after being endlessly away on tour with ENSA. Until she and Henry got married, she could live at home, in her own room, and would no longer have to share with one or more of the other soubrettes in her troupe. She could hardly wait. She was a very light sleeper and hated sharing. Sleeping in the same room as Malcolm, Bella and baby Caroline at the pub last night had been a nightmare.

It had been late by the time they had managed to get rid of Molly's inebriated tutor. Malcolm had woken up while Jen was getting undressed, and excited to find her in the room, had taken ages to go back to sleep. And Bella, while still refusing to utter a single word by day, had mumbled endlessly in her sleep, and even shouted out once or twice, causing Jen to jerk awake with a racing heart, and leaving her feeling heavy eyed and jaded this morning.

Malcolm, however, seemed none the worse for his late night. Even now he was wriggling round on her lap. 'When are you going to marry Captain Keller?' he asked.

Jen shivered. Henry was in France. For all she knew, he was even now facing a German machine gun, or some vicious bayonet-wielding Nazi storm-trooper. Jen didn't have much idea of how battles were fought, but she knew first hand from her experiences with Molly in Europe last year how ruthless the Nazis could be.

'As soon as he gets home from France,' she said firmly.

It had taken Jen a long time to admit to herself how deeply she was in love with Henry Keller, her former boss at ENSA. She knew everyone was wondering why she was bothering with RADA when Henry, as a celebrated theatre producer, was soon going to be able not only to provide for her, but presumably find her good acting jobs too. But she didn't want to have to rely on Henry for decent roles. Nor did she want her fellow thespians whispering behind their hands that it was only because of him that she had got them.

Sometimes Jen wished that Henry wasn't quite so celebrated. It was all right for him to hobnob with the likes of Ivor Novello and Laurence Olivier; he had been brought up in those circles and was used to it. But for Jen it was different. She was a back-street girl from Clapham, and whatever anyone else thought, she knew she would feel a hell of a lot more confident rubbing shoulders with those sorts of people if she had a RADA qualification behind her.

'We're here!' Malcolm shouted. 'And look, everyone is waving flags at Mrs Carter.'

'What?' Craning forward, Jen saw her mother and Mrs Rutherford and Angie standing on the steps of the town hall surrounded by a group of people waving red, white and blue flags. As the taxi drew up, the crowd broke into a rousing version of 'La Marseillaise'. Jen started laughing. 'I think we must have taken Paris,' she said to Katy. 'Or do you think Mr Lorenz laid this on as well?'

The Allies had indeed taken Paris, and although it made no difference to the wedding ceremony itself, it caused the party in the pub afterwards to go with an extra swing.

'Wasn't it romantic?' Molly said to Jen as she notched yet another drink onto Mr Lorenz's tab. 'Your mother looks so happy.'

Jen laughed. 'I think she looks petrified,' she said.

Molly giggled. 'It'll be you and Henry next.' She lowered her voice. 'Will you be petrified? Or have you and Henry already . . . ?'

'Molly!' Jen said, mock aghast. 'What do you think I am?'

'Well, he is so gorgeous,' Molly said. 'I just thought . . .'

'Goodness,' Jen said. 'What's come over you? It must be all that hot sunshine in Tunisia. You never used to think thoughts like that.' Her eyes sparkled with amusement. 'Or only about Ward Frazer . . .'

'Shh!' Even as the heat flooded into her cheeks, Molly looked around the room, terrified that someone might have overheard. Jen was the only person in the world who knew she'd once had a painful crush on Katy's husband. And Molly wanted it to stay that way.

But being Jen, she couldn't leave it at that. 'Now that Paris has fallen, presumably he'll soon be home. How will you cope with that?'

'I'll be fine,' Molly said dismissively. 'That was just a stupid infatuation. I know that now.' But there must have been something in her voice, because Jen's ears pricked up immediately.

'Oho,' she said. 'Are you telling me there's someone else?'

'No,' Molly said at once.

But Jen wasn't having any of that. They hadn't spent several difficult months together in Nazi-occupied Italy without learning each other's defence mechanisms. 'Who is it?' she asked. 'Come on, Molly. Tell me. Why are you being so coy?'

'It's nobody,' Molly said rather frantically. 'I'm not being coy.'

But Jen was on the scent now. 'It's Callum Frazer, isn't it?' she said. Seeing Molly's confusion, she burst out laughing. 'Katy mentioned that you'd bumped into him in Tunisia. I might have known. That's hilarious! How ironic that the only person able to replace Ward in your affections is his cousin. Tell me, is he as heart-stoppingly good looking as Ward?'

It was too late to deny it. 'Jen, please,' Molly muttered. 'Please don't say anything. I don't want anyone to know.'

Jen raised her finely plucked eyebrows. 'Why not?'

Molly gritted her teeth. For all her quick-wittedness, Jen was sometimes remarkably dim. Once again Molly glanced round the bar to make sure nobody was listening. 'Because it's hopeless,' she said. 'Yes, Callum is nice looking. Maybe not quite as good looking as Ward, but still far too good looking for someone like me. No,' she saw Jen was going to interrupt and put up her hand to stop her, 'no, it's true. Not only that, he's younger than me, and about a squillion times more wealthy. The Frazers are one of the top families in Canada. I don't stand a chance.'

Jen frowned. 'Is that why you want to find out about your family history?' She saw Molly's start of surprise. 'Katy told me about that last night too. She's worried about it, you know.'

'I know,' Molly said. 'But I need to know.'

'But do you really?' Jen asked. 'Look at me. Henry is posh as you like, and he doesn't care about me coming from the back streets of Clapham.'

'It's different for you,' Molly said. 'You're an actress. You're glamorous. You've got pizzazz. But I haven't got anything to recommend me. Nothing at all.' She groaned. 'As of last night, I haven't even got a tutor to coach me into medical school.'

Jen had been looking serious, but at that she laughed again. 'No, that was a bit of a disaster,' she said. 'But you can hardly blame the poor man. It's not every day you come into a pub and see one of the prettiest girls in London standing behind the counter.'

'Of course I blame him,' Molly said hotly. 'We all know it's not perfect for Bella to be living in the pub, but even so . . .'

But Jen wasn't interested in Bella. 'So how far have you got?' she asked. 'In finding out about your heritage, I mean.'

'Not very far.' Molly felt suddenly despondent. 'Everywhere I go, the authorities slam the door in my face.'

Jen shrugged. 'That's what authorities always do.' She saw Katy approaching and lowered her voice. 'OK, I'll make a deal with you. I can't live in the pub for ever. I'm going to need my sleep when I get started at RADA. If you help me persuade Mr Poole to get a move on with Mum's house, I'll help you with your search.'

Molly stared at her. 'Would you? That would be brilliant. But what on earth can I do to hurry Mr Poole up?'

'Judging by the way he's knocking back the booze,' Jen said, 'I reckon the offer of a couple of free beers each evening might do the trick.' She saw Molly's expression and chuckled as she moved away. 'Surely you can swing it that they somehow go on Mr Lorenz's wedding tab? He'd never know, and even if he did find out, I'm sure he'd be grateful. I can't believe he wants to start married life with Mrs Rutherford breathing down his neck, any more than Mum does.'

'What have you two been whispering about?' Katy asked as she passed behind Molly carrying a tray of empties a minute or two later.

Molly hoped the dim lighting would hide her guilty flush. 'Jen seems to be under the impression that she can persuade Mr Poole to hurry up and finish Mrs Carter's house,' she said.

Katy glanced across the bar to where Jen was even now perched provocatively on a bar stool right next to the builder's elbow and gave a wry laugh. 'I know from experience that Mr Poole is not easily motivated,' she said. 'But if anyone can, Jen can.'

For Joyce, both the ceremony and the wedding party passed in a complete blur, which might have been due to the rather large tumbler of brandy she had pinched from the Rutherfords' drinks cabinet after breakfast. She would never have dared do such a thing if Mr Rutherford had been at home, but thankfully he was away with his Home Guard squadron, trying to shoot down the beastly V-1s as they came in over the Channel.

But despite her state of inebriation, she was aware that, apart from the pub dog Lucky escaping from the back yard and polishing off a plate of sandwiches, and George Nelson catching her rather wildly aimed bouquet when it should have gone to Jen, the whole thing had passed off surprisingly well. Now, boosted by a glass of champagne from a bottle that Albert had somehow procured for the toasts, she found herself in the back of a taxi on the way to Paddington station. And sitting next to her was her new husband.

'Well, well,' he said. 'We've done it. We've actually done it.'

Joyce tried to smile, she really did, but there was something unsettling about the motion of the cab. As she put out a hand to try to steady herself, she felt the unpleasant sensation of her throat tightening. followed by a cramping pain in her stomach.

As she uttered a slight groan, she heard Albert's concerned voice. 'Joyce, my dear, are you all right?'

'No,' she said. 'I'm awfully sorry, but I think I'm going to be sick.'

It wasn't a good start. And the taxi driver wasn't very pleased. But Albert couldn't have been nicer about it. 'It's entirely my fault,' he said, after they had mopped up as best they could and proceeded on their way to the station. 'I've failed in my husbandly duties already. I should have made sure you had something to eat. I don't suppose you had any breakfast, and—'

'Please don't talk about food,' Joyce muttered through clenched teeth. She had never felt so mortified in all her life. She felt like some stupid teenager, unable to hold their drink. She was starting her honeymoon reeking of vomit, hardly very romantic. If she had wanted to take his mind off the forthcoming hanky-panky, she had certainly gone the right way about it. But Albert just smiled and took her clammy hand, patting it reassuringly.

'You can sleep on the train,' he said. 'I'm sure by the time we get to Bath, you'll feel much more like it.'

He was right. Two hours' sleep in the first-class carriage did help to restore at least part of her equilibrium, and the sight of the beautiful Georgian terraces and pretty parks as they drove in yet another taxi to the boarding house Albert had booked in elegant Great Pulteney Street did the rest. If the kindly female proprietor noticed the unpleasant aroma that accompanied the middle-aged newly-weds into her smart Regency town house, she didn't mention it. And Joyce was able to face the dainty tray of tea and biscuits she brought them in the lounge with a certain amount of pleasure.

'Perhaps when you've had a cup of tea, you'd like to go and freshen up?' Mr Lorenz suggested tactfully. 'And then shall we go out and stretch our legs before dinner?'

Unlike neighbouring Bristol, Bath had mostly been spared the relentless devastating air raids of the Blitz, but in April 1942, Hitler had selected the beautiful city as the place to suffer retaliation for the devastating RAF raids on Lübeck. According to their landlady, the first raid had struck just before 11 p.m. one Saturday night, and by Monday morning over four hundred people had been killed. Nineteen thousand buildings were damaged, several houses in the famous Royal Crescent were totally destroyed, and the historic Assembly Rooms were burnt out.

Some of the bomb damage was still evident as Joyce and Albert took that first short walk over the bridge to look at the abbey and the Roman baths, but it was nothing like as bad as London, and there was a sense of calm gentility about the place that Joyce found oddly soothing.

But as night time approached, her new-found tranquillity wore off. Her previous husband had not given her a very positive view of things in the bed department. Stanley's lovemaking, if you could call it that, had not been gentle, especially, as was very often the case, if it had been preceded by a long evening at the Flag and Garter.

As she followed Albert up the elegant staircase, Joyce was wondering what on earth had induced her to get married again.

But then, noticing that Albert was fumbling unsuccessfully with the lock on the door, she sensed she wasn't the only one who was nervous. Albert of course had never been married before. So unless he had gained experience elsewhere, which seemed unlikely, he was probably in an even worse state than she was. Especially as he could hardly have failed to be aware of Angie and Gino's noisy, overenthusiastic antics at Cedars House. If nothing else, they had set the bar very high.

'Oh dear,' Albert said, looking up. 'The key has jammed in the lock. I'll have to get the landlady to help us. That's not a very good start, is it?' His expression was so comically bashful that all Joyce could do was giggle like a schoolgirl.

Suddenly he was chuckling too, and without quite knowing how, she was in his arms, and he was kissing her right there on the landing, in full view of anyone coming up the stairs. And as she threw caution to the winds and kissed him back, she knew it was going to be all right. She loved him, and he loved her, and somehow they would muddle through together.

The liberation of Paris was cause for great celebration among the Free French troops surging up the Rhône valley from the landings in the south of France. In every recently freed town and village they listened with glee to the wireless broadcast of General de Gaulle's speech. 'The enemy totters, but he is not yet beaten,' he declared. 'He remains on our soil. We will keep fighting until the last day, until the day of total and complete victory.'

At the new American field HQ just north of Grenoble, his words were greeted by a rousing cheer. But Helen wasn't in the mood to celebrate. Yes, of course she was pleased that after four years of German occupation, Paris was free again. But neither that nor the news the following morning that General de Lattre de Tassigny's troops had finally taken Toulon was enough to put a smile on her face. Several days had passed since she'd seen Raoul, and she had received no word from him, or indeed from anyone else, about André.

Then, on the morning of the 28th, the American intelligence officer told her that two mass graves had been discovered in Grenoble.

'Oh no,' Helen whispered. Ever since Raoul had told her about the shooting of the Gestapo prisoners, this was what she had feared.

'The bodies have not yet all been identified,' the captain said. 'I am going there this afternoon, and if you feel up to it, I'd like you to come with me. It's not going to be pleasant, but . . . well I guess I might need a translator.'

Helen dug her nails into her palms. She knew what he really meant. That he might need her to identify André's body. But she didn't know if she would be able to bear it.

For three hours before they set off she felt icy cold and sick with fear. Oddly it was Colonel Izzard-Lane who helped stiffen her nerve.

'There's no point getting yourself in a state about something that might not have happened,' he said. 'In my experience, things rarely turn out as one expects. Look at me. I thought I'd be a fish out of water in this liaison role, but thanks to you, I'm rather enjoying it. I'll come with you this afternoon if you like. Give you some moral support, what?'

It was a kind offer, even if Helen secretly suspected that his ulterior motive was to test out some of the watering holes in Grenoble. The current HQ was a tented camp in the middle of nowhere, and opportunities for savouring the local wines were limited.

But perhaps she maligned him, because instead of wandering off to find a hostelry as soon as they arrived near the Polygone arsenal where the fifty or so mutilated corpses had been found in adjacent bomb craters, he stuck to her side like glue, and she was grateful, because a noisy crowd had gathered and tensions were running high. Grenoble had already suffered terribly under German hands, and here was evidence of yet one more atrocity. The enormous arsenal on the western outskirts of the city had been attacked by resistance fighters earlier in the war, and this more recent atrocity was clearly German revenge.

As they pushed through the throng in the wake of the intelligence officer, Helen could hear names of the victims being bandied about: members of the local Maquis, other resisters and their relatives, agents of the Free French, and other individuals mistrusted by the Gestapo and SS, including a well-respected Jesuit theologian and a famous rugby player. She didn't hear the name of André Cabillard, or Renard, and when she tried to ask if anyone knew if he was one of the victims, her questions were met with apologetic shrugs and shaken heads. But that wasn't surprising; this wasn't André's area, he wouldn't have been well known here.

Then, once again, Raoul materialised out of the crowd. As the Frenchman grabbed Helen's arm, Colonel Izzard-Lane tried to intervene. 'I say,' he exclaimed. 'Get your hands off her.' Manfully he tried to interpose his stately person between them, but failed. 'Who is this ruffian?' he asked, somewhat discomposed. 'Do you know him?'

'Yes, I know him,' Helen said grimly. She wrenched her arm out of Raoul's grasp. 'What do you want?' she hissed at him in French. She jerked her head towards the front of the crowd, where the intelligence officer was already ducking under the improvised barrier erected to protect the site. 'I was on my way to see if André is one of the victims, and now, thanks to you, I've lost the officer who has permission to go in.'

'Monsieur André is not one of the victims,' Raoul said impassively.

For a second, as the import of his words sank in, Helen's world seemed to stop in its tracks. She raised her eyes momentarily to the sheer grey face of the rock that towered ominously over them on the other side of the Isère river. 'How do you know?'

Raoul gave one of his indifferent shrugs. 'I have seen the bodies,' he said.

Helen put her hand to her heart. 'Are you sure?'

He didn't bother to answer; just tilted his chin in an impatient gesture of confirmation. Helen reeled in relief, first that André wasn't among the dead, and second that she wouldn't after all have to inspect the corpses.

Colonel Izzard-Lane rubbed his hands together awkwardly. 'Do I gather that your fiancé's not in there?' he asked. 'Well, I must say, that is jolly good news.'

Catching the flicker of insolence in the curl of Raoul's lips, Helen frowned. She wasn't sure how much English, if any, Raoul spoke, but she felt oddly protective towards the colonel and didn't want him belittled.

'Yes,' she said in English. 'It is good news. But we are still none the wiser about where he might be.' Turning to Raoul, she tried to smile. '*Merci*,' she said. 'I hope you have let Monsieur Cabillard know?'

'Of course,' Raoul said.

Before she could respond to this curt retort, some angry shouting erupted on the other side of the crowd. Raoul's head spun round instantly, and Helen realised that, despite his unforthcoming manner, his reactions were lightning quick.

Following his gaze, she saw two young men being dragged through the shouting throng by their feet, their flailing arms trying to protect their faces.

'Good lord,' Colonel Izzard-Lane expostulated. 'What on earth's going on?'

Raoul didn't respond, and Helen looked uneasily at him. 'Who are they?' she asked.

He spat. 'Milice,' he said.

Helen blinked. She knew that the Milice Française was a vicious right-wing French paramilitary organisation formed to help the Nazis round up Jews and *résistants* in France. But she'd had no idea such young men would be part of it. They were barely more than boys.

'What's going to happen to them?'

'They will be shot,' Raoul said.

She stared at him in horror. 'But surely they should be tried first?'

He inclined his head. 'They will be tried, then they will be shot.'

Helen glanced back over the crowd, but the incident was over; the wretched little group had passed out of sight and people were already turning back to their previous conversations. It had left her feeling distinctly shaken.

Conscious that Raoul was watching her scornfully, daring her to express her feelings, she gritted her teeth and vowed not to give him the pleasure of mocking her British liberality. Instead she took a steadying breath. 'And what will you do now?' she asked. 'About André, I mean.'

If he was surprised by her restraint, he didn't show it. 'I will continue to make enquiries,' he said.

'I can't understand why we can't find news of him.' Helen hesitated for a moment, biting her lip. 'Do you think he's still alive?' She hardly dared ask the question, but she was desperate for some kind of reassurance.

Raoul, however, was not the person to give it to her. 'I don't know,' he replied. 'As I said, I will continue to make enquiries.'

'So will I,' Helen said stiffly. She could tell he wanted to get away, and added, 'Where can I find you, if I do discover anything?'

She thought he wasn't going to answer, but then he lifted his shoulders negligently. 'If necessary, you can leave a message at La Table Ronde café,' he said.

'What a disagreeable fellow,' Colonel Izzard-Lane remarked as, without bothering to say goodbye, the Frenchman took a step back and disappeared into the milling crowd. 'Couldn't understand a word he said, of course, but nevertheless, not at all the sort of chap I'd have thought you'd be friendly with.'

'I know,' Helen said despairingly. 'But there's nothing I can do about it. He's one of Monsieur Cabillard's most trusted men.'

But the colonel's mind was already moving on to more important matters. 'I don't know about you, dear girl,' he said, glancing around hopefully. 'But after all that, I wouldn't say no to a quick snifter.'

Against all expectations, by the following Thursday, Mr Poole had finished the repairs on Joyce's house.

'There you are,' Jen said smugly to Molly as they shared a celebratory slice of cake in the café. 'I told you a bit of flattery goes a long way.'

Molly laughed. 'And a few free pints of beer,' she said.

'You know what you should do now,' Angie said. 'As a surprise. You should move all Mum and Mr Lorenz's stuff back from Mrs Rutherford's before they get home.'

Jen eyed her sister beadily. 'What do you mean, "you"? Why can't you and Gino do it?'

Angie tossed her head. 'Because we're busy here,' she said. 'It's our big night tonight and we need to get ready.' She turned to Molly eagerly. 'I hope you're coming, Molly? Gino's cooking something called ravelioli, and we've got a fruit jelly for pudding.'

'Well . . .' Molly began doubtfully.

But Angie was persuasive. 'Oh go on,' she said. 'It'll only cost you two bob. And can't you persuade the Nelsons to come too? Gino will be so disappointed if we don't get any customers.'

So instead of using her free afternoon to go back to Tooting to try to track down her former dormitory mistress, Miss Webb, Molly found herself helping Jen to carry Joyce's bits and pieces back from Mrs Rutherford's house.

Once that was done, Jen collected her own things from the pub. 'It's going to be *so* nice to have a room to myself,' she said, sitting down on one of the kitchen chairs and pulling up her feet so Molly could mop the dusty kitchen floor. 'All I need now is some cotton wool to stick in my ears to block out the noise of Angie and Gino's frolicking.' She gave a sudden giggle. 'And maybe Mum and Mr Lorenz's, come to that . . .'

Aware that Jen had stopped mid sentence, Molly looked round from her mopping and saw Mrs Carter – or rather, Mrs Lorenz, as she was now – standing in the kitchen door. She almost laughed out loud as the colour rushed into Jen's cheeks.

Joyce eyed her daughter beadily. 'I'll ignore that last comment,' she said. 'Because I'm grateful to you and Molly for getting the house ready for us. But don't get too excited about having a room to yourself, because you're going to be sharing it with Bella James.'

'What?' The scarlet faded from Jen's face as quickly as it had appeared. 'But I don't want to share with Bella.'

Molly quailed at the tone of Jen's voice, but Joyce seemed oblivious. 'Albert 'and I have been talking it over while we've been away,' she said. 'Katy told me what happened with Molly's tutor, and we've all agreed the pub is no place for Bella to be. What that child needs is a safe, secure home. It's what Dr Goodacre has been saying all along. And it's what Bella wants. So she's going to come and live with us here. Albert is over at the pub now, arranging things with Katy.'

Jen's mouth had fallen open, but her eyes were sparkling with anger. 'Katy never said anything.'

I don't suppose she dared, Molly thought. But Joyce continued to be impervious.

'Well, it's take it or leave it,' she said calmly. 'Albert and I would like you to stay, and it would be nice for Bella not to have to sleep alone. But if you don't want to share, then I'm afraid you'll have to sort yourself out somewhere else. There is a war on, you know. We all have to make sacrifices.'

But this apparently was one sacrifice Jen wasn't prepared to make. 'Then I'll go elsewhere,' she snapped. 'It would have been nice if you'd thought to consult me before offering up my room to someone else. But as you clearly don't care about me, or my needs, I'd rather not stay.'

And with that, she picked up her suitcase and marched out of the kitchen.

Molly and Joyce stood in frozen silence until the front door slammed.

'Oh dear,' Joyce said. She pulled out a chair and sat down rather heavily. 'And to think I was looking forward to a happy homecoming.'

Molly felt awkward. She tried to think of something to say in her friend's defence. There was no doubt that Bella needed a better place to live. But she couldn't help feeling sorry for Jen. She had been so looking forward to having a room to herself.

But Joyce was already back on her feet. 'I'd almost forgotten,' she said. 'I need to get back to the café. When Albert and I popped in just now, it looked like a bomb had hit it.'

Chapter Five

'*Yuck!*' George said. He was sitting at a table in the café with Pam, Alan and Molly, staring in wide-eyed horror at the plate of ravioli that Angie had set before him. 'I can't eat that. It looks like dead slugs.'

'Shh,' Pam admonished him.

George looked at Molly reproachfully. 'You said Italian food was nice.'

Molly thought back to the little hill farm in Tuscany where she and Jen had hidden out after their escape from the Germans. The food the farmer's wife had provided had been simple but very tasty. Jen hadn't liked it, of course. But then Jen hated all things Italian. Almost as much as she hated all things German. There was no way Jen would have come to the café tonight to support Angie and Gino's new venture, even if she hadn't lost her temper with her mother.

'It is nice, and I'm sure this will be too,' Molly said, manfully putting a lump of pasta into her mouth. But actually it wasn't nice at all. It was entirely tasteless and had an unpleasant texture – half slimy, half powdery – that made her wonder how on earth she was going to swallow it.

Glancing across at Pam, she saw that she was similarly afflicted. Alan Nelson had yet to put his fork to his mouth. Catching his desperate look, Molly gave a guilty giggle. It was entirely due to her that they were here. She had thought it would be a treat to go out for a meal. She had even arranged for Pam's toddler, Nellie, to spend the evening in the relative safety of the pub cellar with Katy's children. The number of V-1 attacks had tailed off recently, but nobody was confident the threat was over.

With a heroic effort, Molly managed to force the lump of pasta down her throat, but she knew she couldn't eat any more.

'I've got a paper bag in my handbag,' Pam murmured.

In a minute, it was done. While Alan kept an eye on the kitchen door, Pam discreetly scooped the pasta from their plates into the paper bag, which she then quickly replaced in her handbag.

'We'll give it to Katy for Lucky,' she muttered. 'I expect he'll enjoy it.'

George thought the whole thing was hilarious. 'Look,' he whispered, nudging Molly gleefully. 'Those people over there have wrapped theirs in their handkerchiefs and put it in their pockets.'

But there was no time for Molly to look, because Joyce had come out of the kitchen and was heading in their direction. She stopped abruptly at their table, and stared in astonishment at the gleamingly clean plates.

'Goodness,' she said. 'You've eaten that up quickly. I was just coming out to say that Gino thinks something went wrong with the pasta. He forgot to put the salt in.'

Catching Alan Nelson's eye, Molly bit her lip. Something had certainly gone wrong with the pasta, but it had needed something rather more drastic than salt to put it right. But clearly too embarrassed to admit what they had done with it, Pam was already politely saying how much she had enjoyed it.

And now Angie was there too, sweating and red faced, but beaming with pleasure. 'There,' she said triumphantly to Joyce, 'I told you they'd eat it.' She turned to George. 'What about you, George?' she asked eagerly. 'Did you like the ravelioli?'

Sensing that George might be a bit too honest, Molly kicked him hard on the shin under the table, and in the ensuing commotion, his lack of enthusiasm went unnoticed.

'Sit tight,' Angie said as she removed their plates. 'I'll bring you the jelly. I'm afraid it hasn't set very well, but it's quite tasty.'

At least she was right about that, even though they more or less had to drink it.

'What are we going to do now?' George asked as he licked the last smear off his spoon.

'We are going to pay our bill and thank Angie and Gino for a lovely evening,' Pam said firmly. 'Then we are going to pick Nellie up from the pub and go home.'

'But I'm starving,' George complained.

Alan glanced at Pam, and then at his watch. 'I have a suggestion,' he murmured. 'Why don't we take a detour via the fish and chip shop on the way home?'

It was as they stood up to go that Molly noticed Mrs d'Arcy Billière sitting with three other people at a table near the door. Molly hadn't seen her since the incident on Lavender Hill, and was surprised when the woman put her hand out as they passed by.

'You're the girl who sent me to the hospital the other day, aren't you?' she said in her autocratic, oddly accented voice.

Aware that almost everyone in the café had stopped talking to listen, Molly nodded self-consciously. 'Yes, that's right,' she muttered.

Mrs d'Arcy Billière showed her bandaged wrist to her dining companions. With her other hand, she pointed at Molly. 'If it wasn't for this girl,' she declared loudly, 'I'd have bled to death.'

'No, no.' Molly tried to demur. She could feel the heat flooding to her cheeks, and she was also very conscious of George standing goggle eyed beside her. She didn't entirely blame him. Mrs d'Arcy Billière always dressed in a somewhat eccentric manner, but tonight her off-the-shoulder silver evening gown and ermine stole seemed positively conservative in comparison to the extraordinary attire of her dining companions. The only other lady of the group, an elderly raven-haired woman, was wearing a flamboyant voluminous floor-length robe in bright orange. The two men, who to Molly's considerable dismay had risen to their feet and bowed courteously as soon as she stopped at the table, were wearing high-necked black jackets, covered right up the front in gold braid. On their shoulders were gold epaulettes with tassels so long and thick that they wouldn't have looked out of place on the mane of a performing circus pony.

Suddenly Molly wished Helen de Burrel was there with them. Helen had been brought up among smart, wealthy foreigners and would have known exactly what to say. Not for the first time, Molly wished she had her friend's poise. As it was, she felt ridiculously tongue-tied.

But Mrs d'Arcy didn't seem to notice. 'I realised as soon as I got to the hospital who you were,' she said. 'I've seen you once or twice in Lavender Road and I know you are a friend of Aaref's. It is very rude of me not to have thanked you before.'

Molly tried to mumble that no thanks were necessary, but Mrs d'Arcy barely paused for breath. 'I understand from Aaref that you have an ambition to go to medical school, and I wanted to say that if there's anything I can do to help you, I do hope you will let me know.'

Molly blinked. She wondered rather wildly what Mrs d'Arcy Billière had in mind. 'That's very kind,' she stammered. 'But I can't think of anything I need . . .'

'Yes you can,' George said. Ignoring Molly's startled glance, he smiled appealingly at Mrs d'Arcy Billière. 'She needs a new science teacher to help her pass the exams. Because the last one she had got drunk and tried to—'

'George!' Pam interrupted sharply.

But Mrs d'Arcy Billière was looking amused. 'Science, you say?' She frowned thoughtfully and turned to the lady in the orange dress. 'What's Feodor doing these days?'

The lady gave an expressive shrug of her thin shoulders. 'Nothing,' she said. 'Apart from moaning about the Bolsheviks.'

'Well, there you are,' said Mrs d'Arcy Billière. She opened her hands in a gesture of munificence. 'I know the perfect person to help you. Feodor Nikolai Markov. He was a professor of natural sciences at the University of St Petersburg. Prior to the Revolution, of course.' She gave a short, sour laugh. 'Like the rest of us, when that happened, he had to run for his life.'

'Oh no, I couldn't possibly,' Molly said, appalled. 'Really, I . . .'

'No, no.' Mrs d'Arcy Billière waved away her objection. 'I will bring him to you. It will do him good to teach again. He has been idle too long.'

Molly had no idea how to respond. But luckily Pam took pity on her and stepped in, smiling at Mrs d'Arcy Billière and her guests. 'I hope you have enjoyed your evening?' she asked.

'Oh yes, very much,' Mrs d'Arcy Billière said. 'Shocking food, of course. Not going to say anything, though. Don't want to hurt young Angie's feelings.' She laughed. 'So we took our lead from you. Luckily Prince Anatoly here has very deep pockets.'

The older of the two men gave another solemn bow, which made George giggle. Then thankfully Alan put his hand under Molly's elbow, and they were finally moving away.

As soon as they were out in the street, Molly rounded on George. 'You've put the cat right among the pigeons now,' she said.

'I was only trying to be helpful,' George said indignantly. 'Anyway, it was your fault for saving Mrs d'Arcy Billière's life.'

'I didn't know Mrs d'Arcy Billière was Russian,' Pam said. 'I always thought she was French.'

And suddenly they were all laughing. 'What a terrible evening,' Molly said. 'I'm so sorry for making you go.'

'Oh, I really enjoyed it,' George replied. He giggled and did a ridiculous imitation of Mrs d'Arcy Billière's accent. 'Shocking food, of course. But luckily Princess Pam here has a very deep handbag.'

'I can't understand it,' Joyce said to Albert as she climbed into bed that night. 'I tried that ravelioli or whatever it was called, and it was absolutely repulsive. But all Angie's customers claimed to have loved it.'

'Then it can't have been quite as bad as you thought,' Albert said. Joyce turned her head to look at him, thinking how odd it was that he was sitting up in bed next to her in his striped flannel pyjamas, as though he'd been there all his life. She wished that he could have seen for himself the extraordinary muck Angie and Gino had served their customers, but he had wanted to check on his shop, which had been closed while they had been away on honeymoon, and by the time he arrived at the café, the customers had left and Angie and Gino had been triumphant about their opening night.

'Well, credit where credit's due,' Albert said now as he switched off the light and drew her comfortably into his arms. 'They made a nice little profit on it by all accounts.'

But Joyce remained suspicious.

The following morning, she discovered the truth. She had popped into the pub to make the arrangements for Bella's move over the road, and while she was there, Lucky the dog was copiously sick on the floor. She stepped hastily away, but not before noticing that the unpleasant deposit consisted almost entirely of ravioli.

'Look what Lucky's done, Mummy,' Malcolm said. He poked at it with his foot. 'It's not very nice. It looks like slugs.'

'I can see what it looks like,' Katy said hastily. 'Now come away and let me clear it up.'

'I can see what it looks like too,' Joyce said. 'I'm just wondering where Lucky got it.'

Katy gave a comical grimace. 'Please don't tell Angie, but Pam dropped it off last night when she came to collect Nellie. I don't think George liked it very much.'

'I don't think anyone liked it very much,' Joyce said. 'But they can't all have taken it home.'

Joyce didn't mention Lucky's indiscretion to Angie, nor to Gino, not that he would have understood, and when she told Albert later, he seemed to think it was funny.

'Either way it does them credit,' he said. 'Either people really did like the food, or they like Angie and Gino so much that they didn't want to hurt their feelings.' He patted her hand. 'They'll do better next time. You'll see.'

Joyce wasn't sure that she wanted to see. She felt the reputation of her café was at stake. But just at the moment she had more important things to worry about. Because Albert was concerned about Jen.

'Where's she going to live now?' he asked.

'I don't know,' Joyce said. 'At the pub, I imagine. Let's just hope Henry comes home soon and then they'll get married and we won't have to worry about her any more.'

'But what's she going to live on until then?' Albert said. 'She's got no income while she's at RADA. We can't expect Katy to feed her.'

'Then she can work for her keep,' Joyce said. 'I'm sure Katy could use some help. Especially as she'll no longer have Bella.'

'But—'

'I'd have fed her if she'd been here,' Joyce interrupted. 'But if she's too proud to share . . . Well, she's made her bed, and now she can damn well lie on it. It won't do her any harm, and it might do her some good.' She glared at him severely. 'I'm fed up with her tantrums. So don't you go offering to help her out.'

'No, no, of course not,' he murmured obediently.

Joyce smiled. She was enjoying being married. Not just the hanky-panky, although that had been surprisingly nice; mainly she liked the feeling of having someone on her side. Plus, of course, the fact that Albert was paying the bills now made things much easier financially.

In fact, if Pete and Paul hadn't been in France, and Mick braving Nazi submarines somewhere on the high seas, Joyce might even have felt comfortable. She had pushed the worry about Bob to the back of her mind. In her next letter, which she would put in with the quarterly parcel she was allowed to send via the Red Cross, she would tell him that the wedding had gone ahead and everyone was happy for her, and she hoped in time he would be too.

Bella was a worry, of course. Joyce's heart had ached when she saw the few pitiful possessions the girl had brought with her. Luckily she seemed to have settled in with relative ease, although that didn't solve the problem of what to do with her day to day. Her school had been evacuated to the country due to the V-1 attacks. But there was no way she could go with them, not until she could speak again. Until then it was hard to know how to keep her occupied.

Dr Goodacre was sure her speech would come back eventually. He called her condition selective mutism. It was induced by trauma, apparently currently quite common among bomb victims, even adults.

Apart from refusing to speak, Bella was an amenable girl and on the whole seemed happy to amuse herself. Luckily she loved reading, and sometimes Joyce left her in the library under the care of the rather frosty librarian. Sometimes Angie and Gino took her to the pictures. And sometimes she went up to the common with George Nelson to collect food for his rabbit and Joyce's tortoise.

The problem came when she was confronted by strangers. Most people were kind enough, but some treated her like a moron, or a mad person, as though, because she couldn't speak, she must be deficient in brain cells or common sense.

Joyce felt she needed to protect her, but she couldn't guard her all day long.

Then one evening Albert noticed Bella watching him doing his accounts in the front room and asked if she wanted to help. She nodded and seemed to grasp quickly what he wanted her to do.

'She's smart,' he said to Joyce later. 'She can come down to my shop a couple of mornings a week if she fancies it. After being out of action for so long, I've got very behind with my bookkeeping. I can give her some pocket money for doing it. It would be nice for her to have a little bit of money of her own to spend.'

Bella seemed to fancy it. And Joyce was grateful. For those few hours she could relax. Bella was safe with Albert. And now she could spend a bit more time supervising Angie and Gino in her precious café.

★ ★ ★

Jen was already regretting having stormed out of her mother's house. For two nights she'd slept on one of the camp beds Katy kept in the cellar for emergencies. It wasn't very salubrious, but it was blissfully quiet, apart from the occasional gurgle from the beer barrels. And there was at least an indoor bathroom, albeit upstairs, unlike at her mother's house, where calls of nature involved a freezing-cold trip to the lavatory in the back yard. But after a short lull, the damned V-1s had started coming over again, and now Katy and the children and the dog had joined her in the cellar too. And that wasn't salubrious at all.

It was just as bad by day. There was no peace and quiet for her to study the plays and books on the reading list RADA had sent her, so she had decided to take refuge in the public library, only to discover that Bella was there too. The first time, the girl had looked up and smiled shyly. Thankfully the hushed silence and presence of the frosty-faced librarian meant that Jen didn't need to talk to her. So she just waved casually, and then felt bad when Bella came across and slid a note in front of her saying, *I'm sorry I took your room.*

Jen groaned. The blasted girl was clearly on the ball, even if she refused to talk. So, braving the librarian's ire, she smiled at Bella and whispered that she didn't mind, that she was fine at the pub.

But she wasn't fine. And, having for so long been nervous about the idea of marrying Henry, and fitting into his elevated circle, she longed for him to come home so she could move into his flat. Oddly, she had never been there. After all the nervousness, prevarication and misunderstandings, they had made the decision to get engaged moments before he had left for France. There had been no time for visiting his flat. But she knew it was in Knightsbridge, and the thought of living in a smart apartment in central London was extremely appealing. The idea of living with Henry was appealing too, and she regretted that it had taken her so long to make up her mind.

She also regretted offering to help Molly find out her family history. It had seemed an easy thing to say, but now Molly wanted her to go trundling over to Tooting to visit some woman who had worked at the orphanage while she was there.

'Oh go on, Jen, please,' Molly had said. 'I thought you could pretend to be a journalist doing an article about you and me escaping from the POW camp in Italy, and wanting to check my background and so on. People are always happy to talk to the newspapers.'

'But I don't know anything about newspapers,' Jen complained.

'Well, you're an actress,' Molly said. 'Surely you can pretend.'

'But you don't even know where this blasted woman lives.'

'No,' Molly agreed. 'But I've thought of a way to find out. You can go to the orphanage pretending to be from a flower shop delivering a bouquet to her from some distant cousin or something. Because of her injury. They're bound to direct you to her home.'

So on Saturday, Jen found herself sitting on the bus to Tooting clutching a bunch of flowers. Molly had been intending to come with her, but then her boss had asked her to do an extra shift.

'You don't mind, Jen, do you?' she'd said. 'It's just that I need the money.'

Of course Jen minded. She had much better things to do than go on some wild goose chase round Tooting. But seeing Molly's eager face, she'd had to agree.

She had eyed the bouquet sourly when Molly had handed it over. 'These must have cost a fortune,' she said. 'You should have pinched them from Mrs Rutherford's garden.'

'They needed to be properly wrapped,' Molly said. 'Otherwise they wouldn't have believed you.'

Jen was pretty sure they wouldn't believe her anyway.

But astonishingly, they did.

'Oh, but I'm afraid Miss Webb is off sick,' the woman who answered the door of the orphanage said. 'Come in a moment and I'll find her address for you.'

As she waited in the hallway while the woman disappeared down a long corridor, her shoes squeaking on the drab green linoleum, Jen was immediately conscious of the distinctive institutional smell of floor polish, chalk and carbolic soap, and for the first time she realised what Molly must have lived through as a child. Jen's own family had never been much to write home about; her father had been drunk and violent, her mother too weak to stand up to him, and her brothers stupid and annoying. Nevertheless, this grim place must have been a hundred times worse.

The woman was already returning. In her hand she had a piece of paper with an address written on it. And within a minute, Jen was back out of the gate.

Molly had also equipped her with a shorthand notebook that she had bought from Woolworth's, and a pair of black-rimmed reading glasses borrowed from Alan Nelson. Five minutes later, Jen had changed her identity from an eager flower-shop girl to a serious-looking newspaper reporter. Unsure what to do with the flowers, she had thrust them into the arms of an astonished-looking old lady who happened to be standing at a nearby bus stop.

Phase one of Molly's plan had been remarkably simple, but as Jen rang the bell of Miss Webb's apartment in a neat block just off Tooting High Road, she had a feeling this was going to be a bit trickier.

When the door opened, she found herself facing a round-cheeked woman perched on a pair of crutches. 'Hello,' Jen said. 'Are you Miss Webb? I'm so sorry to bother you. My name is Jennifer Carter. I work for the *London Weekly News*. I believe you used to know a girl called Molly Coogan at the Home for Waifs and Strays?'

The woman blinked in surprise. 'Yes, yes, I do remember her,' she said doubtfully after a moment. 'But I haven't seen her for years.'

Jen smiled encouragingly. 'Well, the thing is, I've been asked to do an article about her. You may not have heard, but Molly Coogan escaped from a POW camp in Italy last year, and my editor wants me to write a feature about it. So I am trying to dig up some details about her past. What she was like as a child, that sort of thing.'

'Goodness,' the woman said. She looked both flustered and flattered. 'I had no idea. Well, of course, I will try to help if I can. I suppose you had better come in. But how did you find me?'

'Oh, the orphanage gave me your address,' Jen said blandly. Ha, she thought, as Miss Webb hobbled back across the small hallway, beckoning her to follow, RADA would be proud of me.

Miss Webb lowered herself painfully into an easy chair and waved Jen to one on the opposite side of the empty fireplace 'So tell me what happened,' she said. 'What on earth was Molly doing in Italy?'

'She was on her way to North Africa,' Jen said. 'She had trained as a nurse and was going to work there. But her ship was torpedoed and she ended up in a prison camp run by the Nazis.'

'And she escaped?'

'Yes.' Jen nodded. 'She and . . . some other women escaped from a train.'

Even now she could remember that heart-stopping moment when she and Molly had broken the window and . . .

'Where were they going on the train?'

The question caught Jen unawares. Suddenly she felt very peculiar. Shaky and cold. She knew she had to answer. But she could hardly bear to say the words. She could feel her hand trembling and knew she would have to get a grip on herself before going on. 'We were . . .' She coughed hastily to cover her mistake. 'They were being transported to Germany to work in an SS brothel,' she said.

Luckily the woman was so shocked, she didn't notice Jen's discomfort.

'Molly was terribly brave,' Jen hurried on. 'And that's why my . . . editor wants to do the story.'

She opened the notebook and sat with the tip of her pencil resting on the page, trying to breathe calmly. She had thought she was over the trauma of those awful days in Italy, but now she wondered if that was why she slept so badly. Perhaps all those horrendous nights crammed with countless other women into the camp dormitory had affected her more than she had thought.

Belatedly she realised that Miss Webb was burbling on about Molly as a child. 'She was a funny little thing. Not nearly as pretty as . . .'

Jen looked up from her pad. 'I'm sorry, I think I missed what you were saying. How old was she when she came to you?'

Miss Webb frowned in thought. 'Three or thereabouts.'

'And that was because her mother had died?'

Miss Webb was trying to adjust a cushion behind her back. 'Yes,' she muttered. 'That's what we were told.'

'Do you remember anything about her mother?' Jen asked casually when the woman had settled down again. 'Her name, perhaps? Or how she died?'

Miss Webb shook her head. 'No,' she said. 'I never knew her name.' But there seemed to be a hesitation there.

Laying her pencil down calmly on the pad, Jen put on a persuasive, confiding smile. 'I don't have to put everything in my article,' she said. 'But it would be awfully useful for me to know, just as background . . .'

But still the woman wouldn't speak. She was fidgeting with the cushion again.

'Molly showed such amazing courage and resourcefulness in Italy,' Jen said. 'I suppose I'm wondering where that came from.' She smiled. 'Or perhaps she developed it at the children's home. I imagine that it's not always easy growing up in a place like that.'

'No, it's not,' Miss Webb said. 'But we do our best for our children.'

'Oh, I'm sure you do,' Jen said warmly. 'Molly spoke of you with great affection.'

The woman looked pleased. 'I don't know what happened to Molly's mother,' she said. 'But I think she came from a good family. Molly was a quiet little thing, but her accent was definitely a cut above the other children. It was probably more like your own.'

'Oh, I see,' Jen said. She felt ridiculously flattered and was hard pushed not to flush. She had been trying for years to get rid of her south London accent. Now that she was about to enter the refined portals of RADA, she was trying even harder. 'Then I'm slightly surprised that some other family member didn't take her in when her mother died. What about her father?'

Miss Webb moved uncomfortably. 'I think I can explain that,' she said. She lowered her voice slightly, as though there was someone else in the room. 'Just between you and me. The lady who arranged for Molly to come to us was from the NCUMC.' She saw Jen's blank expression. 'It's a charity. It stands for the National Council for the Unmarried Mother and her Child,' she said.

'Oh,' Jen said. 'Oh, I see.'

But she didn't really see, and it must have been obvious on her face.

'The NCUMC believe that it is not beneficial for unwed mothers to give up their illegitimate babies,' Miss Webb said. It was clear from her tone that she didn't entirely approve of this policy. Or perhaps she just disapproved of women giving birth to illegitimate children in the first place. She certainly wouldn't be alone in that. There was still an enormous amount of stigma about unmarried mothers. That was partly why Jen's mother had allowed Angie to marry the gormless Gino, because she was so terrified of her daughter falling pregnant and producing an illegitimate child.

'They provide accommodation where the mothers can look after their fatherless babies themselves if their own families are not willing or able to support them,' Miss Webb explained. 'They believe that this often prevents a second fall from grace.'

Jen grimaced. 'And having fallen from grace, as you put it, and with no family support, and no husband, if one of their mothers dies, then presumably there's nowhere for the child to go but to an orphanage?'

Miss Webb gave an uneasy nod. 'Pending adoption. Which, as you know, didn't happen for Molly until she was quite a bit older.'

And apart from some reminiscences about Molly's quiet competence in the classroom, her dogged refusal to perform in the Christmas nativity play, and how poor she had been at gymnastics, that was all Jen could get out of her. She was sure there was something the woman was holding back, but without giving the game away, she couldn't see any way of getting her to reveal it. Perhaps it was just that Miss Webb felt she had said too much already.

In the end, all Jen could do was thank her for her time and trundle her way back to Clapham, hoping Molly wouldn't be too upset to discover that she was the illegitimate daughter of a deceased middle-class woman who had suffered a 'fall from grace'.

'I have a name for you,' the intelligence captain said, and Helen felt her heart give an uncomfortable jolt. She had just come into the briefing tent carrying a translation of some German documents that had been captured when the last remaining German troops in Montélimar had surrendered the previous week. The ten-day battle had been bloody, made worse by the fact that the majority of the German 19th Army had managed to break through the American cordon and escape, leaving behind 4,000 burnt-out vehicles and 1,500 dead horses.

Helen had been feeling slightly sick already. Now, seeing the grim expression on the intelligence officer's face, she felt even worse. 'What sort of name?'

'The name of the SS officer responsible for the killings at Nice,' he said. 'Hauptsturmführer Klaus Wessel.'

Helen took a breath. 'I've never heard of him,' she said. 'Who is he?'

'I don't know. All my informant knows is that he was quite recently arrived from Italy.'

'Where is he now?'

The captain made a regretful face. 'We don't know. We don't think we captured him. But we have so many POWs now, it is hard to keep track of them.'

'But you are looking for him?'

'Yes,' he said grimly.

'And if you find him, presumably he will be tried for war crimes?'

'I guess,' he said.

Helen heard the doubt in his voice. 'What do you mean?' she asked. 'Surely he's a prime candidate?'

He shrugged. 'You'd think so. But identifying these guys and bringing them to trial is going to be tough. We reckon quite a few are giving us false names. Plus killing twenty-three prisoners isn't exactly going to put him at the top of the list.'

'But it was cold-blooded murder,' Helen objected. 'General de Lattre de Tassigny said so himself.'

The captain sighed and shoved a printout of a decrypted signal message across the table. 'I just got this. It's an intercept via the Russians. They have overrun a place called Majdanek in Poland, where they found some kind of Nazi extermination camp.' He paused. 'Their current estimate is that maybe eighty thousand people have been killed there.'

He saw her flinch and lifted his hands helplessly. 'I know. Even the Russians sound shocked, and they aren't exactly known for sweetness and light where prisoners are concerned. But you see what I mean. I doubt this is a one-off. There's going to be a lot more nasty stuff uncovered before we're through. So it won't be surprising if some of the lesser guys get off the hook.'

Suddenly Helen knew he was right. Eighty thousand people. The scale of it was beyond comprehension. And if there were more such extermination camps, as there were rumoured to be, sheer logistics made it unlikely that every culprit would be brought to trial. André had probably worked that out too, and he certainly wouldn't want Hauptsturmführer Klaus Wessel to wriggle off the hook.

And now, after a moment's reprieve, she felt sick again. She just prayed that André would get to Wessel before Wessel got to him.

Part Two

Chapter Six

September brought heavy rain to London. Molly, with a few hours off in the afternoon one day, had promised to take George up to the common while Pam took little Nellie to the welfare clinic to collect her ration of orange juice, cod liver oil and 'priority' milk. Unfortunately, it was too wet for the common, so they had to stay indoors instead. However, even though the weather was depressing, at least the news from the various Allied fronts was good. The Russians had captured Bucharest in Romania, with all its rich oilfields. In Italy, a new offensive had begun against the German defensive 'Gothic' line north of Florence. In northern France, British troops under the command of the newly promoted Field Marshal Montgomery had reached the Belgian frontier, and in the south, the Germans were retreating up through Lyons, with Allied forces in hot pursuit.

'I wonder how Helen's getting on,' Molly said to George as she watched him try unsuccessfully to train his pet rabbit to sit quietly in a top hat for a magic trick he was trying to perfect. 'With any luck she'll have met up with André by now.'

She was longing to hear about their reunion. She remembered so clearly the utter relief on André Cabillard's handsome face when she and Jen had told him that Helen had not died from her wounds after the battle at Toulon harbour, as he had feared, but was alive and well and waiting impatiently for the moment when they could be together again.

But George was less interested in Helen's romantic prospects. 'I hope she's killing lots of Germans,' he said. He sat back on his heels and watched in frustration as Bunny hopped away across the room. Then he stood up and headed for the door. 'I'll have to go and get another couple of Mrs Rutherford's carrots.'

Molly put out a hand to stop him. 'No,' she said. 'You know you're not allowed to go into Mrs Rutherford's garden. And you are definitely not allowed to steal her carrots. What if she catches you climbing over the wall?'

He looked surprised. 'She won't catch me climbing over the wall,' he said. 'I've already stolen them. I've got them hidden behind the Anderson shelter.'

Molly wanted to laugh, but she knew she mustn't encourage him. He was naughty enough as it was. The problem was, of course, that he was bored. In normal times he would be going back to school next week after the summer holidays. But with the local schools all evacuated, there was nowhere for him to go. He had run away from his school earlier in the summer, and had threatened to do the same thing again if he was sent away once more. And he would, too. Charming though he was in many ways, he was a slippery little devil, and virtually impossible to control.

Molly knew Pam and Alan were worried about him. He couldn't be allowed to run wild in London for ever, but with little Nellie to look after as well, it was difficult for Pam to find ways of keeping him out of trouble.

'I wonder if Mrs d'Arcy Billière's Russian professor might be prepared to take George on too,' Pam had murmured in exasperation yesterday evening after George had made a fuss about going to bed. 'A bit of Russian discipline might do him good.'

'Don't!' Molly had cried. 'Thankfully I haven't heard a squeak from Mrs d'Arcy Billière since that evening in the café. I'm hoping she's forgotten.'

'Oh, I hope she hasn't,' Pam said. 'I think he sounds wonderful.'

Molly had groaned. That was all very well for Pam to say, but

Molly didn't want to be taught by some terrifying Russian professor; she just wanted some nice person who knew about science and could teach her what she needed to know without getting drunk. But now Mrs blasted d'Arcy Billière had put her in an awkward situation. Until she heard from her, she could hardly advertise for someone else.

Maybe it was a stupid idea anyway. She wasn't very confident about her ability to learn at all, let alone absorb two years' syllabus in one year, especially a year in which she was going to be juggling so many commitments. But at least being busy kept her mind off other things, like the fact that she was an illegitimate child. She should have known. It would have been a reasonably obvious conclusion to have drawn. But no, naively, she had been hoping for something more romantic. Something that would make her feel better about herself. And even the suggestion that her mother might have come from a well-to-do family didn't help. Who cared about a well-to-do family if they hadn't the heart to look after a motherless child?

George came back into the room brandishing an enormous carrot. 'I think this will do the trick,' he said.

Jerked out of her uncomfortable thoughts, Molly glanced nervously at the window, hoping that nobody passing down the street would choose that moment to look in, because as both she and George knew perfectly well, under war regulations it was illegal to feed human food to animals. The last thing she needed was some officious busybody reporting them to the authorities. Not that George would care two hoots.

Molly wondered suddenly where George had got his rebellious streak from. She had never met his real parents, but from what she had heard about them, they had been a perfectly normal young couple. As she watched him eagerly trying to lure Bunny out from under one of the armchairs, she thought how sad it was that they hadn't had the chance to see him growing up.

Then, feeling an odd prickling sensation on her skin, she realised that she had been so absorbed in self-pity, it hadn't occurred to her to feel sorry for her own dead mother. She hadn't ever thought about that side of the equation. Nor the fact that prior to her death, her mother must have felt abandoned too. Not only, presumably, by the man to whom she had fallen pregnant, but also by her family. After all, she could have given her baby up for adoption at birth, like so many young mothers did in that situation. But no, despite the inevitable stigma, the priggish small-mindedness of British society, her mother had opted to keep her, albeit with charitable support.

'Are you all right, Molly?' George asked. 'You look a bit peculiar.'

Molly looked up. He was standing in front of her now, holding Bunny in his arms, concern wrinkling his brow. She had to smile. Despite his naughty ways, he really was an angelic-looking child. 'I'm fine,' she said. 'I was just thinking about something.'

'Was it about lunch?' he asked hopefully.

Molly laughed. 'No,' she said. 'Although the others will be back soon, so we could start thinking about it.'

It wasn't all about her, she thought, as she stood up slowly and walked down the narrow corridor to the kitchen. It was about her mother, too. Even if the outcome did prove to be uncomfortable or upsetting, in some strange way she felt she owed it to her unknown mother to continue her quest. And that meant that in due course, she would have to face up to an encounter with the National Council for the Unmarried Mother and her Child.

Helen was sitting in the sun outside the mess tent, having a cup of A-ration tea with Colonel Izzard-Lane, when an orderly came up to their table and told her that someone was asking for her at the gate of the camp.

'At least I think it's you he wants,' he said. A slight flush stained his cheeks. 'He's asking for a pretty girl with blond hair in a green uniform with a brown belt and a red patch on her hat. And, well, there aren't many of those, not here at least.'

Helen was intrigued. Leaving Colonel Izzard-Lane at the table chuckling delightedly, she followed the young soldier through the lines of tents to the guard post.

Waiting for her was a nervous, narrow-faced young man she had never seen before in her life. He was wearing clean but patched clothes and a worn navy beret. As soon as he saw her, he snatched the beret off his head and began to knead it in his hands.

Helen spoke in polite French. '*Bonjour, monsieur.* I think you wanted to see me?'

He nodded but seemed unsure how to begin. 'My mother told me to come,' he said. 'She thinks I have information that might be of interest to you, but I don't know if I am doing the right thing.'

'I'm sure you are,' Helen said. 'Information is always useful.'

The boy looked doubtful and Helen smiled encouragingly. 'Perhaps you can start by telling me why your mother told you to ask for me?'

'My mother heard you, or someone like you, asking questions in the Polygone some days ago,' he said. He paused and looked at her, and realising that he expected a response, Helen nodded, confirming that she had indeed been there. He ran his tongue over his lips and went on. 'You said a name. A name she thought she recognised. But she wasn't sure. She wanted to check. She didn't want to raise a false hope, you understand?'

'I think so,' Helen said. She spoke as calmly as she could, but inside she was buzzing. She was pretty sure that the only name she had mentioned that afternoon had been André's. 'But perhaps you know something that can raise my hopes now?'

The boy looked around uneasily, as though nervous of being overheard. 'I don't know,' he muttered. 'This man, he told me not to tell anyone.'

Helen's heart was hammering now. 'What didn't he want you to tell?'

'That he had taken my car.'

Helen blinked. 'Your car?' This boy didn't look old enough to drive a car.

'I work for the *télégraphique*,' he explained. 'For the mountainous district we are given a small car. A Citroën. This is the car the man took. He told me to say that the Germans had stolen it. I believe he was nervous that the information might fall into the wrong hands.'

I'm sure he was, Helen thought.

'I have to ask you,' she said. She took a slow breath. 'Was this person called André Cabillard?'

He shook his head. 'He didn't give me his name.'

She stared at him in bewilderment. 'Then . . .' She knew she was stammering. 'Your mother . . . How . . .?'

'He gave me a crate of wine,' he said. 'And this is the name my mother thought she recognised. The label was Cabillard. This is not a wine we generally drink here, you understand. It is expensive, and in this area, in any case, we prefer the local Côtes du Rhône. So she was not familiar with it. This is why she had to go home to check.'

If the boy's mother had been there at that moment, Helen would have kissed her. She would have liked to kiss the boy too, but felt it might overpower him. André is alive, she thought. He's alive. After all this time, she could hardly believe it. And she realised that for the last few days, since hearing about the SS Hauptsturmführer, she had been bracing herself for bad news even more than she had before.

But then it occurred to her that this news wasn't as current as she might have liked. 'When was this?' she asked.

'Just over one week ago. Before the liberation.'

'And do you know where he went in your car?'

'He went north,' he said.

Helen frowned. There was no direct route north out of Grenoble; the mountains were in the way.

'Towards Chambéry?' she asked. 'Or Lyons?' Either meant Nazi-held territory. Even now that Grenoble itself had been liberated, the 11th German Panzer Division wasn't far away. In the quiet of the night it was still possible to hear the tanks and artillery firing further north as the Allied forces struggled to cut off their retreat.

The boy thought about it. 'I think Lyons,' he said. 'The route to Chambéry is mountainous, and I don't think he would have chosen my small Citroën for this purpose.'

He might not have had much choice, Helen thought grimly. A car with fuel was presumably not an easy thing to come by in the dying moments of a German occupation. Monsieur Cabillard had told her that the only reason the vineyard had sufficient fuel for the delivery vans was because on dark nights, little by little, André and his men had siphoned it off from the SS vehicles parked in the Domaine courtyard.

So for some reason, perhaps indeed lack of fuel, André had abandoned the wine van and 'liberated' the post office van instead.

'Did he by any chance mention the name of an officer in the SS?' she asked as she noted down the number of the van's licence plate.

The boy recoiled. Once again he looked around, this time very much more nervously. 'No,' he said. 'He mentioned nobody. But I think he was in some haste.'

'Thank you,' she said. 'Thank you for bringing me this news. And thank you for helping my friend. Please pass my thanks to your mother too. You have done a very good thing.'

The boy straightened his shoulders slightly and inclined his head. 'We are proud to have been of service,' he said. He gave a small shy smile. 'And when you find your friend, please tell him we enjoy very much his Provençal wine.'

'Miss Carter!' The sharp voice cut through the odd low humming noise Jen's fellow students were making. The room they were in was small and airless, and Jen had only closed her eyes for a moment. Now she jerked awake to find the RADA voice coach staring at her through narrowed eyes. 'I'm sorry if we are boring you,' he said sarcastically.

'No, no, you aren't,' Jen said hastily. 'I'm just really tired. I'm staying in a pub, and there are two noisy young children there, and a dog that keeps trying to get on my bed, and . . . well, basically I'm not getting enough sleep.'

The man looked at her for a moment. 'Drama training is a complex emotional and physical reworking of yourself,' he said. 'Here at RADA we take it very seriously indeed. As in the profession itself, we cannot make allowances for tiredness, illness or absence, for any but the most catastrophic of reasons. Do you understand what I am saying?'

'Yes,' Jen muttered. 'I understand.' She also understood that she had received her first black mark.

'In that case, I suggest that you leave us for a moment to freshen up. And while you do so, you can decide whether you are prepared to put your body and soul into this course or not.'

'I do want to put my body and soul into it,' Jen said. 'I really do.' If only the blasted man knew how hard she had struggled to get a place on the damn course, he would know that. But she wasn't going to tell him that, not in front of all the other students, who were already looking at her with shocked expressions on their smug, self-righteous faces, as though they had discovered an imposter in their midst.

The voice coach eyed her unsmilingly. 'In that case,' he said. 'I recommend that you find yourself a better place to live.'

Jen groaned. If only it was that easy. Because of the relentless bombing over the last few years, accommodation was hard to find in London. It was all right for the other students. Most of them had rich parents who were happy to pay through the nose for lodgings in the vicinity. One was even staying at a hotel. And as soon as the Allied advance overran the V-1 launch sites, the situation would get even worse, because all the people who had fled London in fear for their lives would start coming back.

Only yesterday Katy had received a letter from Ward's aunts, who had been living in Somerset ever since their house in Lavender

Road had been bombed during the Blitz, asking if there was any hope of getting it rebuilt, as they were longing to return to London. And if they came back, so would Katy's mother, who had been staying with them for the last year or so, and that would make the pub even more crowded, and Ward would presumably be back from Paris any day now too. Jen smiled to herself. She didn't mind the thought of sharing her accommodation with lovely Ward Frazer, but the thought of sharing it with Katy's nervous, highly strung mother made her feel quite queasy.

If only Henry would come home, she thought. Then all her problems would be solved.

But although she had had a couple of lovely letters from him, there was no word of him getting leave to come back to London. She had wondered about asking if she could use his flat while he was away, but somehow it seemed too mercenary. Too pushy. Their relationship had been fraught enough as it was without him thinking she only wanted him for his money and his fancy Knightsbridge home.

No, she thought, as she splashed cold water on her face in the RADA ladies' powder room. I'll just have to stick it out in the pub. If I shove some extra cotton wool into my ears, and wrap a towel round my head, maybe that will help.

'Well, I never really thought I'd say it,' Mrs Rutherford said to Joyce in the café one afternoon as she cashed up the till. 'But I really miss having you and Mr Lorenz and Angie and Gino in the house. It seems awfully empty now that you've gone.'

Joyce laughed. 'And mine seems awfully full,' she said. Not that Mr Lorenz took up much actual physical space, or Bella come to that – unlike Gino and Angie, they were both very quiet and unobtrusive – but the mere fact of having five people living there, using the outside toilet, and cramming into the kitchen for meals, made the place seem crowded. Goodness only knew what would happen when the boys were demobbed. Perhaps by then Angie and Gino might have found somewhere of their own, although that seemed unlikely. Despite their good intentions, they were never going to make a fortune out of their Italian evenings. Only five people had come to the second one yesterday, and Joyce had to assume that word had got round about the inedible ravioli.

Angie had been disappointed by the poor turnout, but had consoled herself, and presumably Gino, if he was able to understand such things with his poor English, with the fact that earlier in the day there had been a huge unexplained explosion in Chiswick. A massive double bang had been heard, and people all over London had seen a reddish flash. As usual, the government were hushing it up.

'They're saying it was a gas main,' Joyce said.

But Angie had shaken her head. 'That's exactly what they said about the first V-1s. I expect people were nervous to go out in case it was some new kind of rocket.'

Joyce had a nasty feeling she might be right, and her heart sank. Hadn't London been through enough already? Not quite as much as Hamburg or Berlin perhaps, thanks to the RAF. But it would be a cruel irony if, having survived everything the Luftwaffe had thrown at them, and the V-1s, they were now, just as the war was surely finally drawing to a close, to be obliterated by yet another of Hitler's fiendish weapons of destruction.

'Anyway,' Mrs Rutherford went on, 'I gather Jen is living in the cellar of the pub, which can't be very comfortable for her, and I wondered if she would rather come and stay at Cedars House. Greville is still down on the south coast and we haven't seen sight or sound of Louise for several weeks now.' She lowered her voice conspiratorially. 'Which is a shame, because there's this frightfully grand chap who keeps ringing up for her. I haven't met him yet, but I gather he's a lord. And I don't want her to let him slip through the net. After all, lords don't grow on trees.'

'Goodness,' Joyce said. So Mrs Rutherford was setting her sights high, was she? Not that she wasn't posh enough as it was. Joyce couldn't help wondering what was wrong with this lord that had stopped Louise snapping him up. Mrs Rutherford's daughter wasn't normally one to let an opportunity like that pass her by.

Joyce looked at her employer uneasily. 'I don't know about Jen,' she said. 'It's a kind offer, but are you sure you'd want her? She's such a prima donna.'

Mrs Rutherford gave a wry laugh. 'Oh, I'm well used to that,' she said. 'Although give Louise her due, since she joined the army, she's become much easier to deal with.'

'Then I wish Jen would join the army,' Joyce said sourly. 'Because it seems to me that since she started this RADA malarkey, she's got significantly worse.'

Helen was getting tired of living in a field camp. After the relative luxury of the original HQ, she found it annoying to have to wait her turn to wash, to eat, and even to go to the lavatory. More than anything, she longed for a bath. The most she'd managed was a makeshift shower, and that was only after mustering the three other girls in the camp, and persuading an engineer sergeant to divert some water from the men's ablution tent to a screened-off area away from inquisitive eyes. In desperation, the girls had washed their undergarments at the same time, causing great hilarity when they draped them over nearby lavender bushes to dry in the sun.

But there was little time for anything more permanent to be arranged. Operation Dragoon was proceeding much faster than expected. Lyons had been taken on 3 September, seventy-seven days ahead of the original schedule. The French 2nd Corps, commanded by General de Lattre de Tassigny, had liberated Avignon and was now moving north up the Rhône valley towards Mâcon and Dijon. By the end of the week, the Americans were fighting in the outskirts of Besançon.

It wasn't all good news, of course. Some of the German rearguard action was fierce and there were heavy losses on both sides. For example, having eventually managed to take Montreval, the US 117th Cavalry had become re-encircled by the 11th Panzer Division and had been almost annihilated, allowing the remaining German units to escape north once again.

But overall things were proceeding well, and as a result of the rapid forward advances, the field camp was about to move north too, which worried Helen as she hadn't managed to make contact with Raoul to tell him about André purloining the post van. She had twice visited La Table Ronde in the appropriately named Place Saint-André in the old quarter of Grenoble. But neither time had Raoul been there. She had left messages for him asking him to convey the information, presumably by pigeon post, to André's father, and had to trust that he had done what she asked, because when she sweet-talked a corporal in the signals unit into trying to telephone the Domaine Saint-Jean, the French operator had told her that the lines were down and the call could not be connected.

Now she was back in the Jeep again, with Sergeant Maxwell and Colonel Izzard-Lane, heading north, leapfrogging past Lyons and Montreval to a new HQ some way short of the embattled city of Besançon.

All along the way was evidence of rapid troop movements. Thousands of empty American cigarette packets lay scattered like giant confetti over the pretty countryside. And in some places, presumably where longer halts had been called, K-ration boxes and tin cans littered the roadsides. It was a slow journey. The stopping and starting of ambulances and repair trucks ahead of them frequently brought the whole straggling convoy to a halt, as did the long columns of German prisoners trudging wearily in the opposite direction, marshalled by white-helmeted military policemen on motorbikes.

The following day, Helen's translation skills were once again in demand. General Patch, the American commander, angry to learn that the French had stopped at Chalons-sur-Saône instead of continuing their thrust north in pursuit of the retreating Germans, dispatched one of his colonels to find out what was causing the delay, and the colonel asked Helen to accompany him.

'I've learnt over the past couple of weeks that when the Froggies don't want to answer a question, they start pretending they can't speak English,' he said. 'But if you're with me, they won't be able to use that excuse.' He winked. 'Plus, being French, they always respond to a pretty face.'

Whether they responded to a pretty face or not, it quickly became clear to Helen when they arrived at General de Monsabert's field HQ at Chalons that the French were indeed dragging their feet. At first she thought they must be waiting for resupply. But then, as she stood with the American colonel and one of the French intelligence officers in the map tent, waiting for a briefing, she noticed that one of the maps pinned on the wall was a page torn from the French wine atlas, the *Atlas de la France Vinicole*.

Following her astonished gaze, the intelligence officer shrugged. 'Between here and Dijon stretches the heart of Burgundy,' he explained. 'What we call the Côte d'Or. We do not wish to find ourselves fighting through the vineyards of the *grand crus*. France would never forgive us if these vineyards were destroyed. We are trying to work out another route to pursue the Boches, through vineyards of inferior quality.'

Helen didn't know whether to laugh or cry. It seemed so typical of the French. Even with so much at stake, they hadn't forgotten where their priorities lay.

But when she translated what he had said to the colonel, the poor man was almost apoplectic.

'What in God's name am I going to tell General Patch?' he said.

But neither he nor General Patch needed to worry. A route through lesser vineyards was evidently found, because within hours the French were pushing forward again.

No wonder General de Monsabert had looked happy, Helen thought when she caught sight of him in his Jeep, setting off up Route Nationale 74 in hot pursuit of his advancing tanks. Not only had the *grand crus* been saved, the Free French forces were now in the process of jumping ahead of the Americans.

She, however, was not feeling happy at all. Nobody, not the Americans, nor the British, nor the French, had been able to give her any news about the likely whereabouts of Hauptsturmführer Wessel, let alone André. Despite perusing all the reports, and asking endless questions, she had been unable to discover one single mention of either of them in any of the liberated towns and villages since Grenoble. Even bearing in mind the chaotic conditions of war, it was as though they had both disappeared off the face of the earth.

Then she heard that American troops had entered the Citadel at Besançon and discovered that it had been yet another of the SS prisons. Hundreds of prisoners held in the dungeons without trial were freed. But to Helen's disappointment, when she finally managed to lay hands on the list, André's name was not on it. The following day it transpired that once again Nazi firing squads had been at work, and once again she had a long, horrible wait while bodies were identified.

It was while she prowled restlessly through the newly liberated city, waiting for news to come through on Sergeant Maxwell's radio, that she spotted the distinctive Cabillard wine van. It was parked among a group of armoured vehicles adjacent to one of the broken bridges, and there, not far away, sitting outside a shabby café called Le Café de Cercle, with a cloudy glass of Pernod on the table in front of him, was Raoul.

For once the Frenchman looked mildly pleased to see her. He even went so far as to stand up as she approached. But any words of welcome he might have produced were drowned out by two American M24 Chaffee tanks that came grinding round the corner and rumbled noisily past over the cobbles, belching noxious fumes as they went. Two young French girls were riding up on the turret of the second tank, next to a beaming Yankee tank commander; they waved as they passed, and Helen waved back.

Raoul barely glanced at them. He just sat down again and took a sip of his Pernod. '*Eh bien*,' he said when he could be heard again. 'I got your message.'

'And what do you think?' Helen asked as she took the spare chair beside him.

Raoul lifted his shoulders. 'I do not know what to think,' he said. He jerked his chin up in the direction of the Citadel on Mont Saint-Etienne. '*Dieu merci*, I don't think he is one of the dead up there. I have spoken with some of the released *maquisards* and nobody knew him.'

The relief hit her like a punch in the chest. She put a hand to her head and closed her eyes. When she reopened them, Raoul was watching her.

'Until we know for certain he is dead, then I suppose we still have hope,' he said.

Helen tried to smile. It was the first kind thing he had said to her. 'I still have hope,' she said. 'And I will not rest until I find him. Dead or alive.'

Raoul didn't smile back, and Helen caught a flicker of emotion as his jaw clenched. For the first time, she realised just how much he cared.

But his voice, when he spoke again, was laconic. 'Then I fear you will have no rest for some time,' he said. 'Because if you are right and he is chasing your SS officer, the only place they could have gone from here is Germany.'

Helen gaped at him. *Germany?* But of course, he was right. She had looked at enough maps over the last few weeks. The German border was only a hundred miles away to the east, through the narrow passage of low-lying land known as the Belfort Gap, between the Vosges and the Jura. With the Operation Overlord D-Day troops now thundering across from Paris, cutting off any chance of escape to the north, and Operation Dragoon troops advancing rapidly from the south, any Germans left in this area had nowhere else to go. It was where the Allied generals expected them to make a last stand. After that, it was Germany.

'Oh my God,' she whispered. But before she could say more, she heard a shout and looked round to see Colonel Izzard-Lane hurrying across the road.

'Thank goodness I've found you,' he said, giving Raoul a wary look. He took out a huge maroon handkerchief, lifted his pith helmet and mopped his brow. 'Bad news, I'm afraid.'

Helen leaped to her feet. 'Not about André?'

'What?' He looked startled. 'No, nothing like that. No, it's just that a signal has come through for you. Nobody knew where you were, so I offered to come and find you. I'm afraid you're being reassigned.'

'Reassigned?' Helen stared at him blankly. 'Reassigned to where?'

'London,' he said. 'Apparently some organisation called the Inter Services Research Bureau needs you there.'

Helen felt the ground move beneath her feet and grasped the edge of the table to steady herself. The Inter Services Research Bureau was the cover name for the SOE. 'No,' she said.

Colonel Izzard-Lane gave a slight harrumph. 'Well, orders are orders,' he said. 'I'm not sure you have any choice.'

Helen sensed Raoul move beside her, and swung wildly towards him. There was an expression in his eyes she couldn't quite read. Pity? Relief? Dismay?

'No,' she said. 'I can't go back to London. I need to be here.'

'There's nothing more you can do here,' he said.

She stared at him in dismay. 'But . . .'

He gave his usual negligent shrug and drained his Pernod. 'If Monsieur André is already in Germany, there is nothing any of us can do. If he is not . . .' He paused, and tucked a couple of notes under the empty glass. 'Then perhaps he will come home.'

He didn't sound very hopeful, and Helen rounded on him angrily. 'You think he's dead, don't you? And now you're going to give up looking for him.'

'I told you,' he said. 'I don't know what to think.'

Helen didn't know what to think either. But she felt bad for shouting at him. After all, he had done more than she had. A lot more. 'I'm sorry, Raoul,' she said. 'I really am. I just so wanted to find him. I just so want him to be all right.'

Raoul held her eyes for a long moment, then, to her astonishment, he extended his hand. '*Bonne chance*, Mademoiselle Hélène,' he said. 'I hope we meet again.'

'I hope so too,' Helen said. She knew exactly what he meant. If they met again, it would mean that André was alive.

'Odd fellow, that,' Colonel Izzard-Lane remarked as they walked back to where he had left Sergeant Maxwell and the Jeep. 'I wouldn't trust him as far as I could throw him.'

Helen glanced back at the café, but Raoul was no longer there. Nor was there any sign of him anywhere in the street. Only the empty glass and the few franc notes on the table showed that he had ever been there.

'I would,' Helen said. 'I'd trust him with my life.'

Chapter Seven

'I've had a telegram from Ward in Paris,' Katy said. 'He's hoping to be home soon.'

She looked absolutely thrilled, and Molly was delighted for her. Katy had been through agonies over the last five years since she had met Ward Frazer. Every time he had gone away, on one of his secret missions into Nazi-occupied France, she had thought it would be the last time she ever saw him. But now, with the rapid Allied advance across France, Molly knew that Katy was hoping that those dangerous missions behind enemy lines would no longer be needed.

'I do so hope the war will be over soon,' Katy said. 'So everyone can come back safely: Helen and André, Henry, and all the Carter boys, and—' Interrupted by a wail, she glanced sharply over to the corner by the fireplace, where Malcolm was teasing baby Caroline by poking a feather duster through the bars of her playpen and pulling it back when she tried to catch it.

And Callum, Molly thought. But she didn't say it. Instead she picked up a glass and started polishing it with a tea towel. Jen was the only person to whom she had confided her feelings for Ward's cousin. Much as Molly would have liked to tell Katy, so far she hadn't dared, in case Katy told Ward. And Molly couldn't bear the thought of seeing the pity in his eyes, the knowledge that his glamorous pilot cousin had probably had nothing more in mind than a bit of fun, a mild flirtation with one of few available Western girls in Tunisia.

'Goodness knows what he's going to do, though,' Katy remarked.

Molly jumped. 'Who?'

Katy looked at her in surprise. 'Ward,' she said. 'I can't imagine what he's going to do when the war's over. I'm sure he's not going to want us to go on living here.'

Molly cast her eyes round the empty bar. The Flag and Garter was Katy's pride and joy, and it was a popular pub, but it never looked its best without customers. With a rancid smell of old cigarettes and beer lingering in the air, the chairs upended on the tables, and the swept-up piles of damp sawdust on the floor, it looked bleak and dingy and not at all the kind of place a man like Ward Frazer, however adaptable and easy-going, would want to spend his life.

'Do you think he'll want to go back to Canada?' Molly asked, and as she said the words, she had a sudden rosy vision of her and Callum and Katy and Ward living next door to each other as neighbours in some lovely, clean, wholesome Canadian city.

But Katy looked appalled. 'I hope not,' she said. 'I don't want to go to Canada. I don't want to leave all my friends. And Ward's parents sound so stuffy and disapproving. Just think what his uncle was like. I can't think of anything worse.'

Molly's dream evaporated like a puff of smoke in a high wind. Stop it, she berated herself. Just stop kidding yourself. Callum has probably forgotten all about you by now, and even if he hasn't . . .

A sudden cacophony of barking broke into her thoughts. Katy's dog, Lucky, was racing up the cellar steps in full cry. He must have heard someone approaching the door. He didn't mind customers coming in during opening hours, but he always objected vociferously to anyone daring to step onto his terrain at any other time.

But even Lucky quailed at the sight of Mrs d'Arcy Billière, dressed in a long belted lime-green mackintosh and matching turban, sweeping into the pub accompanied by a man with unusually bushy eyebrows and thick straggling white whiskers, carrying a cane with an ornate silver knob and wearing a shabby, old-fashioned double-breasted suit with a moth-eaten fur-collared greatcoat slung over his shoulders.

'Oh my goodness,' Katy whispered.

'Ha,' Mrs d'Arcy Billière shouted in satisfaction as she spied Molly cowering in the gloom behind the bar. 'I was hoping you would be here. I'd like to introduce you to Professor Feodor Nikolai Markov.'

As she made the introductions, Lucky sniffed tentatively at the Russian's heels, while Malcolm, the feather duster forgotten, stood with one hand on the playpen, his eyes popping out of his head. Even baby Caroline was staring at the stranger.

But Professor Markov didn't seem to notice them; he was peering at Molly with bright, beady eyes. 'So,' he said in a strongly accented voice, 'you wish to be a doctor, yes?'

Molly nodded nervously, but before she could speak, he turned back to Mrs d'Arcy Billière. 'She is very small. And young, I think. Does she have what it takes?'

Mrs d'Arcy Billière laughed and spread her hands. 'Don't ask me, ask her.'

The man swung back to Molly. 'Will you work hard and diligently?'

'Well, yes,' Molly stammered. 'I'll have to if I want to pass the exams.' She saw his thick brows draw together sharply, and regarded him doubtfully. 'I've already looked at the curriculum.'

He made a sharp, dismissive gesture. 'I am not interested in your curriculum,' he said. 'But I know what a person needs to embark on a course of medical training. This is what I will teach you.'

'But—'

'And when I have finished with you, there is not a medical school in the world that will not wish to admit you.'

Molly felt as though things were spinning out of control. Dragging her gaze away from the scary professor, she glanced at Katy and saw to her irritation that she was biting her lip in an effort not to laugh. But despite her disloyal amusement, at least Katy realised that something was expected of her.

'Well, that sounds perfect,' she said brightly, albeit in a slightly wobbly voice. 'Can I offer either of you a drink?'

Mercifully, Mrs d'Arcy shook her head, murmuring something about Feodor needing to catch a train.

But the Russian was still glaring at Molly. 'Where will we work?'

'Well, Katy has offered me the cellar,' Molly said, pointing down the steep stone steps behind the bar.

'A cellar?' His eyes bulged alarmingly. 'I can't work in a cellar.' He waved a hand towards the taped-up windows of the bar. 'We need light, we need fresh air. We need the stimulation of the outside world. All these things will contribute to our studies.'

As Molly looked at him helplessly, this time Mrs d'Arcy stepped in. 'You are welcome to use my house, Feodor,' she said.

He nodded happily at Molly. 'You see, it all falls into place. When will we begin?'

'I have a day off on Wednesday next week,' Molly murmured. Perhaps by then she would have thought of an excuse.

'We will need more than one day,' he said. 'I will come three times in the week. And you will pay me one pound for each time.'

'One pound?' Molly gaped.

'I live in north London. It is a long way for me to travel. At least one and a half hours in each direction.'

With considerable relief, she saw a way out. 'Oh dear,' she said regretfully. 'I don't think I can afford—'

He raised his hand authoritatively. 'If this is too much, then you will find some other students to share the cost of the time it takes me to travel here. But I will first come on Wednesday and we will see whether you have the ability to succeed.'

As the professor moved away, he belatedly noticed Malcolm standing transfixed by the playpen. He eyed him for a moment, then turned back to Molly. 'Is this boy yours?'

'No, he's Katy's,' Molly stammered.

To everyone's astonishment, the professor crouched down

ponderously in front of Malcolm and offered his hand. 'You are a fine-looking young man,' he barked at him. 'How old are you?'

If Molly had been Malcolm, she would have burst into tears. But Malcolm was made of sterner stuff. 'I'm two and three quarters,' he said stoutly as he put his tiny hand into the professor's enormous one.

'And where do you go to school?' the professor asked.

Malcolm shook his head and kicked the bars of the playpen. 'I'm not old enough to go to school.'

'Nonsense,' the professor said. 'One is never too young or too old to learn.' With some difficulty he straightened up again and, leaning heavily on his cane, addressed Katy. 'You bring him to me,' he said. 'I will open his mind to numbers.'

It was Katy's turn to prevaricate. 'Well, that's very kind,' she stammered. 'But I don't think . . .'

'I like numbers,' Malcolm said. 'I know up to ten.'

'Ha!' Professor Markov looked down at him with approval. 'A man after my own heart. Through numbers we can explain the world.'

But then, thankfully, Mrs d'Arcy was drawing him away with some muttered comment about being late.

'Oh my God,' Molly said as the door closed behind them. 'What a terrifying man.'

To her surprise, Katy started laughing. 'I liked him,' she said.

'It's all right for you,' Molly said. 'He's not coming next Wednesday to see if *you* have the ability to succeed.'

But for some reason, that just made Katy laugh even more.

Helen was both disappointed and furious at being recalled. It seemed the cruellest blow, and the worst possible timing. But she knew that as far as the SOE were concerned, her involvement with Operation Dragoon had always been a waste of time. Of course they had no idea she was trying to find André. Not that they would care. They had written him off a long time ago, when they had misguidedly believed he was a traitor, and had never been prepared to admit they had been wrong. Instead, as Raoul had so forcibly pointed out, they had continued to put their faith in agents who really were traitors.

Helen assumed she would have to travel all the way back down to Toulon or Marseilles and return to England by ship that way. But then news came that at a tiny place called Nod-sur-Seine, thirty miles north-east of recently fallen Dijon, a forward detachment of General de Lattre de Tassigny's troops had encountered an Allied armoured column moving eastwards across France. It was an extraordinary achievement. In less than a month, weeks ahead of schedule, the troops involved in Operation Dragoon had advanced 500 miles.

Despite continued fighting further north, the convergence of the two armies meant Helen could travel back via Paris and the Brittany coast. Even though she didn't want to leave, at least she might be able to stop off in Paris in the hope of finding out more about SS Hauptsturmführer Wessel. It was even conceivable that André might have gone to Paris for the same purpose.

It took a few days for the arrangements to be made, but eventually she was told to pack and be standing by for the morning of 15 September.

The officers of the field camp threw a small party for her the night before.

'We'll miss you,' the intelligence captain said as he raised his glass of Burgundy in a farewell toast. 'I guess we've all gotten used to having such a charming translator. The next guy is sure going to have a lot to live up to.'

Helen laughed. 'I'll miss you all too,' she said. 'Thank you for putting up with me.'

She was sad to say goodbye to Colonel Izzard-Lane, too. She had become fond of him, and his disappointment at losing her company was touching. Sergeant Maxwell also seemed sorry to see her go. 'It's been a pleasure, ma'am,' he said when, at daybreak the following morning, she sought him out in the motor pool to thank him for all his help. 'I hope you find that feller of yours. I really do.'

It was with swimming eyes that Helen picked up her suitcase

and climbed aboard the supply truck that was to take her on the first leg of her journey, to Châtillon-sur-Seine.

The long drive was slow and uncomfortable. Mostly they travelled in convoy with Medical Corps ambulances taking the wounded back to hospitals in England. The two-and-a-half-ton truck was a noisy, ponderous vehicle, but the high cab did at least give Helen a good vantage point to see the unfolding terrain of central France; first the bumpy tree-lined roads of La Bresse, then the fertile plains of the Doubs valley, the distant red-roofed villages, the dilapidated houses and farms clustered at crossroads. Ahead of them, on the horizon, the long line of well-tended, and undamaged, vine-clad hills of the Côte d'Or, and the flat, wide expanses of parched stubble as they approached Dijon.

As always, there were signs of war, but here the armies had moved through so quickly that, on the surface at least, the countryside seemed mostly untouched. Somewhere near Selongey, they passed one huge compound of German prisoners, thousands of men sitting despondently behind barbed wire in a field of stubble. Another time they passed some kind of sorting centre where hundreds of vehicles, tanks, field guns and sundry other German items were laid out in great lines and piles, like a huge military market.

'Blimey,' Helen exclaimed. It was a side of war she had not previously considered: what happened to all the captured paraphernalia.

'You wanna stop and take a look?' the driver shouted across the grinding of the engine as he changed gear and slowed down.

Helen shook her head. She found the sight of all that abandoned equipment depressing. It had been used to tyrannise, to kill and to maim, and seeing it all there, discarded, abandoned, made the whole occupation, the whole German brutal war effort, seem such a horrible, pointless waste, both of time and of lives.

'No, it's OK,' she said. 'Let's press on.' And now they were travelling through the thick wooded hills and dark forests north of Dijon, where it was only the occasional Nazi scrawl on some of the buildings that showed the area had ever been occupied.

Then at Châtillon-sur-Seine, everything changed. Here was the bulk of the army advancing from the west, the army that had fought on the D-Day beaches, through Normandy, and for Paris. Many of these men had been on the go since the beginning of June, and unlike most of the troops Helen had met from Operation Dragoon, they were weary and battle scarred. Thousands of their number had fallen along the way, and behind their current jubilation was a grim, gritty determination to give the retreating Hun a taste of his own medicine.

As Châtillon was principally an American camp, Helen had not expected to see General de Lattre de Tassigny, let alone be recognised by him. But on the morning of her departure, as she stood by the tented guardroom awaiting her transport, an enormous car, a Packard Clipper, pulled up alongside her. To her surprise, the rear window was wound down and she found herself staring at the familiar gold-braided cap and epaulettes of the French general.

Straightening up sharply, she saluted, but he was already addressing her. 'I knew I recognised you,' he said. 'You're the girl who knows the Cabillards.'

'Yes, sir,' Helen said.

'And have you found your Renard yet?'

'No, sir, I'm afraid not. But we have found out who ordered the executions in Nice. And I believe that André may be in the process of chasing him back into Germany.'

The general's eyes narrowed sharply. 'I see,' he said. He nodded to the suitcase and the crate of K-rations standing at Helen's feet. 'And you, *mademoiselle*, where are you going?'

'I've been recalled to England, sir.' She hesitated a fraction. 'But if I can get permission, I am hoping to visit Paris on the way, to see if I can find out anything there about your cousin's killer.'

General de Lattre de Tassigny regarded her thoughtfully for a moment, then withdrew his head and spoke to the aide who was sitting next to him. As Helen waited awkwardly by the open window, aware that her onward transport had pulled up behind the limousine, the aide scribbled a hasty note, to which the general added a scrawled signature.

'You have my permission,' he said, handing the piece of headed notepaper out of the window. '*Bonne chance, mademoiselle*. I hope that by the next time we meet, this war will be over, you will be reunited with your fiancé, and my cousin's killer will have received the justice he deserves.'

When Molly presented herself at the National Council for the Unmarried Mother and her Child, the woman on the desk did at least give the impression of being helpful.

'What was the name again?' she asked.

'Coogan,' Molly said. She had already explained that she was looking for some details about her mother, whom the charity had helped some years ago. 'She, or rather we, must have been in one of your hostels from 1922 to 1925.'

'I see,' the woman said. 'And what is it exactly that you wish to find out?'

'I just want to know who she was,' Molly said. 'And where she came from. She died in 1925, when I was only three years old, so I never had the chance to find out.'

The woman stood up. 'If you'd like to wait,' she said, 'I'll go and check our records.'

But of course when she came back, she said there was no record of anyone of that name.

'But there must be,' Molly said.

'I'm afraid not,' the woman replied. 'Although I should mention that we lost some of our archived material during a bombing raid in 1942.'

'How convenient,' Molly said.

The woman bristled. 'I beg your pardon?'

Molly sighed. 'I'm sorry. I didn't mean to be rude. But everywhere I go, I feel I'm banging my head against a brick wall. Nobody will tell me anything. I really don't see why I should be kept in the dark. I can hardly cause her trouble when she is already dead, can I?'

The woman was silent for a moment. Then she laid her hands on the table. 'I am not trying to keep you in the dark,' she said. 'I spoke the truth when I said that there was no one in our records of that name.' She paused for a second. 'Is it possible that you were renamed?'

'Renamed?' Molly stared at her. 'Why would I be renamed?'

The woman lifted her shoulders. 'It's not unheard of. Women who consign their children to orphanages are often reluctant to be traced. Changing the child's name is one way of avoiding that.'

'But my mother died,' Molly objected. 'She wasn't avoiding anything . . .' But then she stopped. The woman was right. She had no idea if Coogan had been her original name. Suddenly she wondered if that was the information Miss Webb had been hiding from Jen.

'But if my mother had a different name, there's no way I'll be able to find her,' she said despondently. The woman didn't respond, and Molly looked up suspiciously. 'Or do you know what it was? From the dates?'

'No,' she said. 'In any case, I'm sure you will understand that divulging information about someone who might not be your mother would be most unprofessional.'

'Yes, I understand that,' Molly said wearily. 'But surely there's some way you can help me?'

The woman looked at her for a moment, then stood up. 'I'm sorry,' she said. 'I've already done all I can. Of necessity, we take confidentiality very seriously. But it is nice to know that we have helped to produce an intelligent, well-mannered young woman like yourself, and I wish you luck with all your endeavours.' Opening a filing cabinet by the wall, she withdrew a thin pamphlet, which she handed to Molly with a faint smile. 'This is one of our annual reports. I'm afraid it's a little out of date, but there may be one or two things in it you might find interesting.'

Out on the street, Molly glanced irritably at the leaflet in her hand. She couldn't imagine why the woman thought she might find it interesting. She was about to drop in a litter bin when she recalled the woman's farewell smile. Had it held a slight hint of something complicit?

She flicked through the leaflet again, and this time she noticed something: a list of five London addresses. Could they be the locations of the accommodation run by the NCUMC to house their unmarried mothers? She stared at them blankly. None of them rang a bell. But was it possible that one of them might be the place where she had lived for the first three years of her life? Was that what the woman had been trying to hint at, without actually saying the forbidden words? Or had she just been trying to fob her off?

It was impossible to know. But Molly was going to make every effort to find out.

Jen had been shocked when her mother had passed on Mrs Rutherford's invitation to come and stay at Cedars House. And when she had refused out of hand, Joyce had been typically huffy about it. 'Well, you can tell her yourself,' she said. 'And make sure you're polite about it, because when all's said and done, she is my boss, and it was a kind offer.'

'I can't possibly go and stay there,' Jen said to Katy. 'Mrs R would be bound to complain to Mum that I hadn't tidied up or something. And imagine if awful old Mr Rutherford came home?' She gave a theatrical shudder. 'He's even worse than her.'

Mr Rutherford was the owner of the brewery, and everyone knew how mean he had been to Katy when she had first taken over the lease of the pub.

'You're certainly right there,' Katy agreed. Then she giggled. 'Plus he's got an eye for the ladies. When Helen stayed there at the beginning of the war, he tried to touch her up in the kitchen.'

'Oh my God!' The thought of being assaulted by Greville Rutherford made Jen feel rather queasy. And then she remembered that Douglas Rutherford, Louise's brother, had once tried to touch Angie up in the back yard of the pub. It must run in the family. 'Well, that decides it,' she said. 'I'm not going there. Do you mind if I stay here for another week?'

Katy said she didn't mind, but Jen knew that she had to find somewhere better as soon as possible. She still wasn't sleeping well, and it was a struggle getting through the day at RADA. Having worked so hard to win a place there, she didn't want to be thrown out for lack of concentration.

'What about Mrs d'Arcy Billière's?' Katy suggested suddenly. 'Aaref's brothers have gone away to the country with their school. Maybe you could have their room?'

Jen felt a flicker of hope. 'But I don't know Mrs d'Arcy Billière,' she said.

'No,' Katy said. 'But Molly seems to be on very good terms with her. Why don't you get her to ask her for you?'

But when Jen broached the subject in the pub the following evening, Molly flinched away. 'Oh no, please don't make me ask her,' she said. 'I'm already trying to think of ways to get out of being taught by her Russian professor.'

'But I thought you wanted a teacher,' Jen said.

'I did,' Molly wailed. 'I do. But not one like him. He scares the living daylights out of me.'

Jen laughed. 'Nonsense,' she said. 'Don't forget you are the person who broke us out of a prison train and evaded that beastly SS officer. I'm not listening to any rubbish about you being scared of some ancient professor.'

Molly had gone rather pink. 'You evaded the SS officer too,' she said. 'It wasn't just me.'

Jen felt a sudden, unexpected shiver of remembered fear, and wished she hadn't brought the subject up. 'It was mainly you,' she said firmly.

'Oh, all right,' Molly said. 'I'll ask her. But only if you help me with something.'

123

Jen eyed her warily. 'What is it this time?' she said. 'Something else to do with your mother?'

Molly nodded. 'The lady at the NCUMC gave me a list of hostels where my mother might have lived. I want to visit them to try and find out which of them, if any, is the right one. But it's going to take me ages to work through them all on my own. I just don't have the time.'

Jen groaned. She didn't have the time either, let alone the inclination to go traipsing round London looking for some hostel Molly's mother might or might not have lived in twenty years ago. But she could see the anxious, eager expression on Molly's face and knew she couldn't refuse.

'Oh, all right,' she said. 'It's a bargain. But only if you swear you're not going to get too upset if we can't find anything.'

'I swear,' Molly said happily. 'And thanks. It'll be much easier with two of us. The only slight problem is that the lady at the NCUMC thinks my mother might have been using a different name.'

Helen arrived in Paris in the early evening of 17 September, just over three weeks after the city had been liberated.

General de Lattre de Tassigny's note had worked wonders for her. Having travelled with the ambulances from Châtillon as far as a base hospital near Fontainebleau, from there she was able to cadge a lift with a Free French reconnaissance officer into Paris itself in a battered grey Renault. The car, which sported a line of bullet holes all down one wing, had clearly seen some exciting action, as had its driver, who insisted on describing to her in gory detail how his small band of renegades had single-handedly captured and killed a German army patrol in the Bois de Boulogne shortly before the liberation.

When she enquired if he knew where the HQ of the SS and Gestapo had been, the young man spat out of the broken window.

'Eighty-four Avenue Foch,' he said. 'This was where they brought and interrogated the Allied spies and resistance saboteurs. And after they had interrogated them, they sent them to prisons in Germany.'

He lifted his shoulders in a typical Gallic shrug as he swerved dangerously round a decrepit donkey laden with sheaves of corn, led by an elderly woman dressed in black. 'Or so we believe. Certainly they have not, so far, been seen again. Perhaps when we advance into Germany we will find them . . .' He tailed off. Clearly he wasn't holding out much hope.

Helen winced. It wasn't just André who was missing. Even before she had left London for her own mission in France, she had known that countless British SOE agents and French resistance fighters had disappeared. And many more had vanished since then.

'*Voilà*,' her driver said suddenly. 'Not so far now.'

And then, there through a gap in the trees, she caught a glimpse of the distant Paris skyline. Although she had visited several times as a child before her mother died, and once as a young teenager with her father, Helen didn't know the city well, but it was easy to make out the distinctive metal structure of the Eiffel Tower, and there, to the north, was that the white dome of the Sacré-Coeur?

'Where are you staying?' the young man asked her, as they passed through an FFI checkpoint on the Quai de Bercy and drove on past the ugly suburbs into the heart of the city alongside the Seine. 'Where shall I take you?'

This was a problem. With long-distance communications still so poor, Helen hadn't managed to make any arrangements. There might well be some SOE people still in Paris, but she had no idea who or where they might be. Her options were therefore either to throw herself on the mercy of the French military, or to check into a hotel, which might be problematic as she had very little cash, and none at all of the new *monnaie drapeau*, the post-liberation 'flag money' introduced by the Americans. The only other possibility was to see whether her mother's aunt was still living in her apartment in the Passy district of the 16th arrondissement.

Helen hadn't seen her great-aunt for many years, and had certainly had no contact since the beginning of the war. She had no idea if the old lady would even still be alive. But she remembered the name of her street, the Avenue de Camoëns, and it was there that she directed her helpful chauffeur.

He raised his eyebrows, clearly impressed. 'Passy? *Oh là là,*' he said. '*Très snob.*'

Helen laughed uneasily. The Passy district might indeed still prove to be *très snob*, but despite the plethora of tricolour flags and bunting that adorned every lamp and railing, the rest of the city was much shabbier than she remembered. And smellier. Through the Renault's empty windows wafted the odour of drains, pissoirs, cats and coffee. Next to rusting balconies and broken shutters were hoardings with torn and peeling posters, German posters mostly, now daubed with red, white and blue paint and freedom slogans: *Vive la France, Vive la libération*, and less politely, *Rentrez chez vous, porcs.* Go home, you pigs.

Avenue de Camoëns was just as Helen had remembered. A short dead-end street of tall, impressive large-windowed buildings adorned with ornate metalwork balconies, it was blocked at the south end by marble steps that descended to the level below and a statue of the famous Portuguese poet who gave the avenue its name. From the parapet was a marvellous view straight across the river to the Eiffel Tower, standing in solitary splendour on the Champ de Mars.

'*Comme j'ai dit,*' the officer said with satisfaction. '*Très snob.*'

But it wasn't so *snob* that the bell worked. And it was only by banging on the ground-floor window until she thought it was going to break that Helen was able to alert the concierge to her presence.

It wasn't the same kindly concierge Helen remembered from her childhood visits; this one was surly, and clearly annoyed to have been disturbed in the middle of the evening, and when Helen gave the name of her great-aunt, she grunted and pointed up the stairs.

'Second floor,' she said. 'The lift isn't working. We have no electricity.'

But when, having climbed the dark marble staircase and knocked repeatedly at the second-floor apartment, the door finally opened, Helen didn't recognise the tiny, birdlike lady who stood there. The old lady peered at her equally blankly. There was a hint of defiance in her expression, and perhaps of nervousness too. She obviously couldn't imagine why a young woman in a foreign service uniform was knocking at her door, and, after four years of military occupation, she didn't like it.

But despite the emaciated body and the wrinkled skin, there was something in those feisty, almost insolent eyes that seemed familiar.

'Tante Isabelle?' Helen ventured tentatively. '*C'est moi*, Hélène. Celine and Eduard's daughter.'

At once, a look of delighted amazement lit the old lady's face.

'Hélène?' she gasped. '*La fille de* Celine? Can it be true?'

One tiny wizened hand stretched out towards her, but before it got to her, the old lady's knees gave way, and she sank gracefully to the ground in a dead faint.

Chapter Eight

If Helen had needed to be convinced of how much people in Paris had suffered at the hands of the Germans, she only had to look at her aunt. When she lifted the old lady off the floor and carried her to a faded armchair in the spacious salon, she could hardly believe how little she weighed. Leaving her there for a moment, she went to the drinks cabinet to see if she could find something to revive her, but it was bare of anything except an empty wine bottle and a few glasses. The kitchen wasn't much better. In a store cupboard she found some packets of rice and some dried haricot beans, half a stale baguette and a jar of home-made strawberry jam, and on the cold marble slab in the pantry, two pieces of soft cheese in a yellow skin and a small tub of pâté. She stared at it in dismay. It was hardly enough to keep a flea alive.

Even the water was short, coming from the tap in an unnervingly slow trickle. But for now, that was the best Helen could do. And in fact by the time she carried the glass back into the salon, Aunt Isabelle had already come round.

Once she had made sure that the old lady's claw of a hand was strong enough to hold the glass, Helen opened one of the tall French windows that led onto the balcony.

The FFI officer was standing next to his battered Renault, apparently admiring the view as he smoked a leisurely cigarette. He looked up at once when Helen called to him. She explained that her aunt wasn't well and asked if he would mind leaving her suitcase and the box of K-rations in the lobby. She would go down to collect them later.

But to her surprise, a few minutes later he arrived at her aunt's door, having obligingly carried everything upstairs for her.

'Oh, that's so kind of you,' she said. 'Especially as the lift has broken down.'

'Everything in Paris has broken down,' he said bitterly. 'The Boches took everything – our food, our coal, our petrol, even our water.' He shrugged and lifted his chin. 'But they haven't taken our spirit. And soon, you will see, the city will be back on its feet.'

It could hardly be soon enough her for aunt, Helen reflected, as she waved him goodbye. If she hadn't come when she had, Tante Isabelle would probably have starved to death. She had been used to eating out most evenings, but as the German stranglehold on the city increased, that had become more difficult. Not only were the restaurants and cafés short of food, but the lift only operated when they had electricity. In the last few months the supply had dwindled to twenty minutes a day, and by the time the lift broke down completely, her aunt had been too weak to manage the stairs. A neighbour had brought her provisions from time to time, but she was elderly too and a month ago she had decided to abandon ship and go to live with her daughter in the country.

'What about the concierge?' Helen asked. 'Couldn't she help you?'

'*Pah*.' Her aunt made a gesture of distaste. 'She was far too busy toadying to the two German officers who lived upstairs.' She gave a sharp cackle of angry laughter. 'I believe they call it horizontal collaboration.'

Having seen the concierge with her own eyes, Helen thought this somewhat unlikely, but she realised that despite her weakened condition, her aunt still had a fierce patriotic pride. She would rather die of starvation than seek assistance from someone prepared to consort with the enemy.

But she was happy enough to allow Helen to help her, and over the next two days Helen did what she could to get her back on her feet. What the FFI officer had said was true. The Germans might have spared the beautiful Parisian buildings, there might be bunting and flags up everywhere, the girls might be wearing pretty dresses and flirting with the liberators, but there was still very little food in the shops. Luckily, she had the K-rations, and although her aunt, in typical Parisian fashion, disliked the idea of American food, when Helen fried some dinner-unit luncheon meat during the twenty minutes of evening electricity and served it with a bouillon soup made from an American stock cube, she tucked in with considerable alacrity.

She wasn't quite so keen on the oatmeal cereal and reconstituted malted-milk tablets Helen served her in bed the following morning, but by the time she had eaten a mid-morning snack of biscuits, a lump of processed cheese and a D-ration emergency chocolate bar, she was beginning to look a bit more perky.

But it wasn't just food Aunt Isabelle was lacking. Over the next few days, Helen scoured the local area for life's essentials, specifically soap and toilet paper, which, in the end, she had to buy at vast expense from a shifty-looking man, almost certainly a black-marketeer, with a handcart near Les Halles. She also managed to track down her aunt's doctor and forced him to visit, only to be told that there was nothing the matter with Isabelle that some good-quality red wine and decent food wouldn't cure. Helen wished she had brought a crate of wine with her from newly liberated Burgundy.

Thinking of wine inevitably made her think of André, although in fact she rarely thought of anything else. Even her aunt, weak and debilitated though she was, had noticed her occasional lapses in concentration. And when on the second evening Helen found herself telling her about André's disappearance and her abortive hunt for him, the old lady nodded knowingly.

'I didn't want to pry,' she said. 'But I could see it in your worried eyes. Something bad. More than just me, more than the war.'

Her sympathetic understanding made Helen choke up slightly. 'I am worried,' she said, when she could speak again. 'But I know I'm not alone. There must be thousands of women worrying about their men. It's just that I really thought I was going to see him again. And then when he wasn't there . . .' She stopped and turned her head to look out of the window.

Her aunt took a sip of her K-ration 'extra-vitamin grape-flavour powdered beverage'. 'Tell me about him,' she said. 'Would I approve of him? What does your father think?'

Helen managed a small laugh. 'My father has never met him,' she said. 'But I think you would both approve.' She shook her head and wondered how to describe André to her aunt. It was so long since she had seen him. Instead she spoke of how they had met, in London, after he had escaped France to join de Gaulle's Free French; his impatience with the bureaucracy, his determination to get back to France to fight the Germans making him instead join the SOE. And then when she met him again in France, in such dangerous circumstances, his unbelievable courage, his selfless efficiency in getting her away to safety.

It was all so hard to say, and to her ears it sounded flat, unreal, like she was describing some hero of a film she had once seen. Not the oh-so-vibrantly alive, gorgeous, tough yet tender, elemental man that was André Cabillard. In the end she went to get a photo from her suitcase. It was the only one she had of him, and it had become pretty dog-eared now. It showed him standing behind her, his hands folded round her shoulders, leaning back against a tree in one of the London parks.

Her aunt took up a pince-nez and studied the faded photograph carefully. 'Ah,' she said. 'Now I see. Any man who can make you look so happy, *ma chère* Hélène, will receive my approval.'

Perhaps aware that emotion was once again threatening Helen's composure, Isabelle leaned over and patted her arm. 'Whether you find him or not,' she said. 'You are lucky. You have tasted true love. Not many people in this world have this privilege. And it is a knowledge you can treasure for ever.'

★   ★   ★

Molly had never set foot in Mrs d'Arcy Billière's house. As she lifted the big brass knocker on the impressive front door, she took a steadying breath and reminded herself that she had two objectives for this visit. The first was to ask if there was any chance Jen could stay there for a while, and the second was to try to explain that she didn't think Professor Markov was quite the right person to tutor her for the Higher Certificate exam.

She had a nasty feeling that the first objective would be easier than the second. Not only had Mrs d'Arcy Billière taken in Aaref and his family as refugees at the beginning of the war, and now his new wife Elsa's family as well, but she had also housed posh, flighty Louise Rutherford for a while when she was newly married and hadn't wanted to live at home.

And now here was Jen not wanting to live in her parental home either. It was ironic, Molly thought, as she waited for someone to answer the door, that even as she longed to find out about her mother, all Louise and Jen wanted to do was get away from theirs. Even Katy dreaded the thought of her own highly strung mother returning from Somerset with Ward's aunts. And for a long time Ward himself had been estranged from his parents. They had never wanted him to leave Canada, let alone marry an English girl.

Lost in her thoughts, Molly jumped as the door swung open to reveal Mrs d'Arcy Billière swathed in scarlet silk and wearing a pair of matching high-heeled sandals that exposed remarkably shapely feet and a set of clashing bright-red toenails.

'Ah, Molly,' she said, as Molly's astonished gaze jerked up to her face. 'How nice of you to call. Do come in. I've been wanting to tell you how much Professor Markov is looking forward to next week. He was very taken with you, you know. Between you and me, he had got very low recently, the progress of the war, you understand. It will be good for him to think about something else.'

Molly was conscious of a sinking sensation in the pit of her stomach. 'But the war is going better now,' she said as Mrs d'Arcy Billière beckoned her indoors. 'With the Red Army advancing on one side of Germany, and us on the other, they're saying it might even be over by Christmas.'

Mrs d'Arcy drew her through a wide tiled hall into an enormous lounge with French windows open onto the garden. The taped-up glass in the windows in no way detracted from the glamour of the room, and the scent of roses drifted in on a light breeze that stirred the dangling glass beads of an enormous chandelier, making them clink softly against each other.

Using her bandaged hand, Mrs d'Arcy waved Molly into a huge sofa upholstered in some kind of thick purple patterned material that would have looked more at home on the floor.

'Hm,' she said. 'We pre-Revolution Russians are none of us quite so thrilled by the advance of the Red Army. We know what it will mean for the countries they have won back from the Germans. The iron fist of Bolshevik communism will suffocate them and all the people in them. And Stalin will not stop there. He is a megalomaniac, just like Hitler. He will take everything he can. Churchill knows it, even if the stupid Americans don't. But whether he has the power to stop him remains to be seen.'

Uneasily aware that the sofa she was now ensconced in was so deep she couldn't quite imagine how she was ever going to get out of it, Molly tried to make suitably concerned noises, but she knew very little about Stalin, and even less about Bolshevism. Up until today, she had been under the impression, like most of the British population, that the Russians were thoroughly good eggs, and that their valiant defence against Hitler's brutal attacks on their country, and their recent advances across Poland and Romania towards him, was one of the reasons the war would soon be at an end.

It was rather daunting to be faced with a completely different interpretation. Nearly as daunting, in fact, as the thought of the depressed, war-weary Professor Markov looking forward to meeting her next week. But before she could summon the words to explain that he might not be quite the teacher she was looking for, Mrs d'Arcy Billière had disappeared in a swirl of scarlet and a clack of heels on the polished wooden floor to make tea.

During her sojourn in Tunisia, Molly had got used to drinking some pretty odd types of tea, but she had never drunk anything quite as unpleasant as the strong black brew Mrs d'Arcy Billière carried back into the room in an ornate silver teapot. Luckily it was boiling hot, and while she let it cool, Molly managed to draw the conversation away from Stalin's inadequacies to the less contentious subject of Aaref's absent younger brothers, and how much Katy was missing their help in the pub. From there it was an easy step to ask if Mrs d'Arcy Billière had thought of offering their room to anyone else, i.e. Jen Carter.

And even though she clearly had no idea who Jen was, Mrs d'Arcy Billière had been delighted by the idea. 'An actress? At RADA? How marvellous. I love the arts. And a fiancé serving in France? Yes, I would be very happy to put her up for a few weeks. But she needn't use the boys' room; she can have the spare guest room. I have friends staying next weekend, but after that I'm not expecting any visitors. Talking of which . . .'

She put down her empty cup and stood up gracefully. 'Come,' she said. 'I'll show you the room Feodor thought would be the most suitable for your lessons.'

Misinterpreting Molly's start of dismay, she raised her hands in apology. 'Oh, I'm sorry. You haven't finished your tea. No, no, bring it with you. You don't want it to get cold.'

The room the professor had chosen was a large dining room also with French doors opening onto the garden. On the walls were hung a number of portraits of fierce-looking men in heavily brocaded formal jackets like the one the prince and his friend had worn to Angie and Gino's pasta dinner. The huge ornate round table in the centre of the room must have been eight feet in diameter and was made up of thin tapering pieces of different-coloured wood, all meeting with miraculous precision in the centre. The whole thing stood on enormous legs intricately carved as dragons. Molly had never seen anything like it in her life. The thought of sitting at such a table, in such a room, made her feel quite faint. And that was before the terrifying professor came into the picture with his piercing eyes and gold epaulettes. Suddenly she knew the whole thing was out of the question.

'Mrs d'Arcy Billière,' she began. 'The thing is, I really—'

But Mrs d'Arcy Billière waved an imperious hand. 'No, no,' she said. 'And please, Molly, do call me Lael. We're obviously going to be seeing a lot of each other, and we don't stand on ceremony here. So you must say at once if there's anything that doesn't suit you.'

Her smile was so charming that all Molly could do was smile helplessly back. 'Thank you,' she said, wishing she wasn't so British. She knew that never in a million years would she be able to call this extraordinary woman Lael, any more than she would be able to say that the whole thing suited her about as much as a punch in the solar plexus. 'It's a beautiful room. You are very kind.'

'Not at all, not at all,' Mrs d'Arcy Billière responded. 'After all, what is life for, if not to help others when we can?'

What indeed, Molly thought as she took a deep breath and swallowed the remaining tea in the dainty cup in her hand. Under all her flamboyance and strange exotic ways, Mrs d'Arcy Billière was obviously a very kind woman. Molly just wished she had chosen a different way to help her.

'I've had marvellous news this morning,' Mrs Rutherford said as she swept into the café kitchen. She smiled as Joyce looked up expectantly from chopping vegetables. 'Douglas is being posted back to England.'

'Oh,' Joyce said. She knew it wasn't quite the response her employer was hoping for, but it was the best she could do. Because as far as she was concerned, Douglas Rutherford, Mrs Rutherford's son, was a cocky little bugger. He had been bad enough as a schoolboy, but when he had joined the army as an officer in the Coldstream Guards, he had got far too big for his boots. Once, before he had been sent off to Tunisia, he had tried to have his way with Angie in the back yard of the pub, and it was only thanks to Molly Coogan, who had realised what was going on, that he had been thwarted.

'Yes, he's going to be undertaking some sort of ceremonial duty,' Mrs Rutherford went on blithely. 'I know I shouldn't say it to you when your boys are serving in France, but it's such a relief to know that he will be out of danger for a while.'

No, Joyce thought, you shouldn't say it to me. Especially as they both knew that Douglas had somehow managed to steer well clear of any danger for the entire war. The fighting in North Africa had already been over when he was posted to Tunisia, and an injury sustained there had prevented him from being sent to fight in Italy. And now, Joyce thought sourly, the little blighter had obviously wangled his way back to some cushy job in England.

Angie, when Joyce mentioned the news to her, seemed in her usual big-hearted fashion to have forgiven Douglas for the incident at the pub. But Katy, when she popped into the café with Malcolm and Caroline the following morning, was considerably less sanguine. 'Oh, bugger,' she said to Joyce. 'That's all we need.' She lowered her voice and cast a quick glance towards the kitchen. 'Let's just hope he doesn't clap eyes on Bella.'

'What does bugger mean?' Malcolm asked.

'It doesn't mean anything,' Katy said hastily. 'Now do you want a slice of Mrs Lorenz's cake? Or shall we go and see if George is at home?'

But young Malcolm was no fool. Joyce could almost see the cogs turning in his little brain as he weighed up whether to accept his mother's diversionary tactic, or to press for a better answer to his question. 'I want cake,' he said at last. 'And then I want to go George's house.'

'What does Angie think?' Katy asked Joyce as she settled Malcolm at a table with a slice of Victoria sponge.

Joyce watched him tucking in. Light as a feather, she thought proudly, despite it being made with National Flour, powdered egg, and fat scraped off the sides of a can of American corned beef. 'Oh, she doesn't care,' she said. 'You know what she's like. Anyway, she's got Gino now.' Not that tubby, peace-loving Gino would be much of a match for a vindictive little sod like Douglas Rutherford, she added silently to herself.

Katy gave a rueful smile. 'I don't think Molly will be quite so magnanimous,' she said. 'Douglas made her life a misery after that incident. I don't know whether he blamed her for catching him at it, or for making him look like a fool. Either way, I know she steered well clear of him in Tunisia.'

Several days elapsed before Helen finally made it to number 84 Avenue Foch, the former HQ of Hitler's counter-intelligence organisation, the vicious Sicherheitsdienst. It had taken that long to try to get things organised for her aunt. Despite the liberation, or perhaps because of it, Paris seemed to be on a go-slow. The Métro was barely functioning, and there were very few buses on the roads. Helen soon learnt that it was quicker to walk everywhere, but even when she eventually found the offices, banks and government departments she needed, she discovered that they were all in complete disarray, as numerous members of staff had left the capital to join the Free French in the battle to rid the country of the Nazis, while others, suspected of collaboration with the Germans, had been thrown out.

But by 20 September, the day Boulogne was finally won back from the diehard German troops, who, like those in Marseilles and Toulon, had been ordered by Hitler to fight to the death before letting invaluable ports fall into Allied hands, Helen felt she had done as much as she could for her aunt, for now. She had withdrawn some of her substantial savings from the bank, paid her outstanding bills, set things in train for her telephone to be reconnected, and taken a mound of washing to the laundry. She had also written a stiff letter to the absent landlord of the apartment, complaining both about the broken lift and the inadequacies of the concierge.

She felt mildly guilty about the time it had all taken, but consoled herself with the thought that if she had been trying to return to England via the south of France as the SOE had originally suggested, she would still probably be sitting in Toulon waiting for a ship.

The Sicherheitsdienst had chosen their headquarters well. The huge, imposing nineteenth-century villa, set back from the thickly tree-lined boulevard, had presumably been sufficiently secluded for their nefarious purposes, but yet near enough to the fancy restaurants of the Etoile and the Place des Ternes for the comfort of their senior staff.

And the most senior staff member of all, the man in charge of hunting down Allied spies and saboteurs, Helen learned, when she managed to gain access after a slight wrangle with the FFI guard at the door, had been a man called Hans Kieffer.

A few minutes later, she was standing in Sturmbannführer Kieffer's office, staring in stunned amazement at the charts on the elegantly papered wall. Charts that listed, in unbelievable detail, not only the ultra-secret address and chain of command of the SOE, but also their various training schools in both the UK and other parts of the world. At the top was the name of the head of F (French) Section, Maurice Buckmaster, and fanned out below him those of the men who worked for him, including Helen's former boss in London, the smooth-talking chauvinist Angus McNaughton. And there, way down the list in the Tunisian section, was her own name, with a tiny pencilled star against it, which she assumed indicated that she had once been an active agent.

'Oh my God,' she breathed. She couldn't believe it. They knew all this? They knew her *name*? Suddenly realising afresh what a lucky escape she had had in 1942, she felt her knees shaking and put her hand on the beautiful Louis XV desk for support. But she had only rested there for a second before she heard a noise behind her, and swung round in alarm.

'Oh my God, indeed,' a low voice murmured in English from the doorway. And there, looking clean and fresh in well-cut Parisian jacket and trousers, was Katy's husband, Ward Frazer.

Helen had a sudden desire to throw herself into his arms, but managed to restrain herself. 'Ward,' she gasped instead. 'You made me jump out of my skin. What on earth are you doing here? I knew you were in Paris before the liberation, but I'd assumed you'd be long gone by now.'

He laughed and came across the room to kiss her on both cheeks, in true Continental fashion. 'I've been tasked with finding out how much the SD knew about our operations,' he said. He gave a wry smile and waved a hand at the wall charts. 'As you see, that was kind of easy. What's not so easy is working out which of the many SOE guys and girls who passed through here spilled the beans.' He paused for a moment, and then added grimly, 'And why.'

Helen shuddered. 'Torture?'

He shrugged. 'And coercion. Hans Kieffer was clearly a very clever man.' He made a face. 'And our top brass didn't even know who he was. Mainly because they never made the effort to find out. It never seemed to occur to them that the Hun might have a brain.' He ran a hand through his hair. 'He knew everything,' he said. 'All the meeting places, all the airfields. He knew exactly when new agents were coming over. He had a man in every café in Paris and scooped them up like flies.'

'But he didn't scoop you up,' Helen said.

'He wanted to,' Ward said. 'My name is on that list, just like yours. But thank God I came in via a different route last time, a last-minute change due to the weather. Otherwise I guess I would just be another name on the SOE "missing" list. Plus the fact that I was extra careful. I never trusted anyone.'

'Nor did André,' Helen said. She bit her lip. 'But even he's missing now.'

She saw Ward's grey eyes widen in dismay. She felt her throat tighten and tried desperately to fight the threatening emotion. She had done so well for so long. But Ward had been her friend for many years, and the look on his handsome face was so compassionate, so concerned, that she couldn't hold back another moment. The floodgates broke, and the next thing she knew, she was in his arms, sobbing her heart out.

Her tears didn't last long. The feel of Ward's arms round her gave her strength. Yes, it was horrible, this not knowing, this silence, this constant dread, but now at least she was no longer alone. Ward would help her. She knew that without even asking him.

And she was right. The first thing he did was take her out of the building for a reviving coffee in a café he had found in one of the roads leading off Avenue Foch. As they walked down the road, she gave him the bare bones of her story. But Ward Frazer was not an experienced spy for nothing, and once they were sitting at a small metal table in the sun, with two wonderfully aromatic freshly ground coffees in front of them, he soon teased out the detail. And he didn't like what he heard.

He was particularly shocked to learn of the torture and murder of Hélène Vagliano.

'Veilleuse,' he murmured, bowing his head slightly. 'I knew her when I was working in Corsica. She was a good girl. Brave as hell.' When he looked up again, Helen could see the anger in his eyes. 'Do you know who did it?'

Helen nodded. 'An SS officer. According to American intelligence, his name is Hauptsturmführer Klaus Wessel, and—'

'What?' Ward's dark brows snapped together. He stared at her for a moment as though transfixed. 'Good God,' he said. 'No wonder André has gone after him. I'll need to check, but I'm pretty sure that's the same guy who gave Jen and Molly such a rough time in Italy.'

It was Helen's turn to stare. She had forgotten it had been Ward who had debriefed Molly and Jen about their experiences in Italy. Her mind was reeling, but not so much that she didn't catch the odd expression on Ward's face as he sat back in his chair. 'Why are you looking at me like that?' she asked. 'What do you mean, it's no wonder André's gone after him?'

Ward lifted his shoulders slightly. 'Because Molly told me that André had promised to kill him if he ever got the chance.'

'Oh my God,' Helen whispered. But it wasn't as much of a shock as it might have been. She had already guessed that André wanted to bring the Hauptsturmführer to account for Hélène Vagliano's death.

'Even so,' she said, 'he wouldn't follow him into Germany, would he?'

Ward hesitated. 'No,' he said. 'André Cabillard is not stupid. On the contrary. Over the last couple of years, he has proved to be one of the very best agents there is.'

He lifted his coffee cup, drained it and put it back on the table. His handsome face was serious and Helen knew he was going to say something she didn't want to hear. Ward Frazer was a nice man, but he had never been one to pussyfoot around, or to shelter her from the truth just because she was a woman. Nor did he do it now.

'I guess we have to face facts,' he said. 'André knew that the south of France was in the process of being liberated. Even if he didn't know you were going to be able to get there as soon as you did, he surely knew you would try to get in touch with him. So why hasn't he at the very least let his father know where he is?'

He paused, and Helen clenched her fingers under the table. 'You think he's been killed, don't you?' she said.

Ward's eyes narrowed. 'Or captured,' he said. 'In which case he will almost certainly be in Germany by now.' He took out some money, tucked it under his empty cup and stood up. 'Come on,' he said briskly. He reached out a hand to pull her to her feet. 'Let's go back to Avenue Foch and see what we can find out.'

'Molly?' George shouted up the stairs. 'You've got a letter. I think it's from Tunisia. Do you want me to bring it up?'

Molly had been about to put on her shoes, but at George's words she froze, then quickly straightened up. 'No,' she called back. 'It's all right, I'll come down.'

But she was too late; he was already thumping up the stairs and pushing open her door.

Molly took the flimsy airmail lettercard with a shaking hand. There were only two or three people in Tunisia who knew she was living at the Nelsons'. And one of them was Callum Frazer. She had written to him as soon as she got back to England, a friendly little note saying she had arrived safely and thanking him for the farewell dinner he had treated her to in a fancy restaurant in Tunis on the eve of her departure. But although she'd hoped he might write back, so far he hadn't. Unless . . .

She slit open the edge with her nail.

She had never seen his writing before. It was strong and slightly slanted, as though he'd been writing in a hurry.

Dear Molly, he began. And at once, in her head, she heard the way he pronounced her name in his lovely Canadian accent, the slightly swallowed double L making it sound more like 'Marly' than 'Molly'.

It was great to get your letter. I was real glad to hear that you had made it back to England in good shape, even though it was a kind of shame you felt you had to go. Not that I'd have had much chance to see you, as soon after you left I was posted to Italy for a while. That's why I didn't get your letter until now. I guess the censors won't let me say why I was there, but I can say that I got to fly over Mount Etna, the volcano in Sicily, which was quite something. I could see right down the crater and there was red-hot molten lava heaving about inside. I was all set to go see Rome on one of my days off, but in true air-force fashion I was posted back to Tunis before I got the chance. And now it looks like I may be on the move again. Who knows where, but I'll let you know when I can . . .

142

'Who's it from?' George asked.

Molly jumped. She had completely forgotten he was there. Ridiculously, she could feel herself flushing. She didn't want to tell him, because she didn't want him to tell anyone else. But if she didn't tell him, it might make it worse. She could already see the speculative gleam in his eye.

'It's from someone called Callum,' she said casually. 'He's Ward Frazer's cousin. He's a pilot in the Canadian Air Force. I saw him a few times in Tunisia.'

'I know who he is,' George said. 'I met him in the pub once. Is he your boyfriend?'

Molly forced herself to give a jolly laugh. 'Of course not,' she said. 'Why on earth would you think that?'

'Because you've gone red,' he said.

Molly picked up one of her shoes. 'You'll be going red if I get my hands on you,' she said grimly, advancing towards the door in a threatening manner. 'Now buzz off, because I'm going out and I need to get ready.'

George prudently retreated onto the landing at the top of the stairs. 'Where are you going?' he called as Molly closed the door behind him. 'Can I come?'

'No,' Molly called back.

'Why not?'

'Because I'm going up to town to see if I can find out where my mother was living when I was born.'

'Oh go on, Molly, please. I'm so bored having to stay here all the time.' There was a slight pause as he waited for a response. When one didn't come, he giggled. 'And if you let me come, I promise I won't tell anyone about Callum.'

Molly closed her eyes for a second, then marched to the door and flung it open. 'OK. You can come with me,' she said. 'But only if Pam says it's all right. And for your information, there isn't anything to tell about Callum. He's just a friend, that's all.'

She could tell from George's sly look that he wasn't convinced.

But nor was he going to push it when he had the rare chance of a jaunt into central London. Delightedly he ran off downstairs, shouting the news of the outing to his mother in the kitchen.

Finally Molly was left in peace to finish the letter.

And hey, Molly, if you don't hear from me, don't worry, it doesn't mean I've forgotten you. Because I haven't. We had some fun times, didn't we? Let's just hope that we get a chance to have some more real soon.

With love (and some very chaste Molly-style kisses!),
Callum

What did it mean? The fact that he'd written at all seemed hopeful, *love* was surely hopeful, but *chaste Molly-style kisses* less so. Or did he mean he would have preferred them to be less chaste? Whatever he meant, Molly was glad that George had left the room. She really was blushing now, and her fingers were trembling so much it took her quite a while to tie her shoelaces.

Chapter Nine

While Molly had been tied up with work all week, both at the Red Cross and at the pub, Jen, true to her word, had spent a couple of her evenings visiting the hostels listed in the NCUMC leaflet. But even though she had been greeted perfectly civilly, and had even been allowed to look through their record books, she had found no trace of a woman and baby bearing the name Coogan, or indeed any other name that matched the dates Molly had given her.

'It's been a complete waste of time,' she had complained last night. 'I'm absolutely exhausted, I've worn my shoe leather to shreds, and I'm damned if I'm going to do the other two.'

Which was why Molly, accompanied by George, was now walking briskly along Marylebone Road looking for the side street that contained the next hostel on the list.

'That'll be it.' George pointed ahead. 'Look, just beyond that church.'

Molly felt a sudden surge of excitement. With only two establishments left, statistically there was a good chance that this one might bear fruit. And now, as she looked around, she began to think that everything looked faintly familiar.

But as soon as they turned the corner, she knew that her optimism had been misplaced.

The church was intact, but beyond it, the rest of the short street was in ruins. Not recent ruins, either. The lush growth of rosebay willowherb, buddleia and other weeds that had invaded the empty spaces inside the blackened shells of the buildings indicated that this was a bombsite left over from the Blitz.

'Oh no,' Molly groaned. She knew she should feel sorry for the former occupants of the burnt-out houses, but actually she just felt sorry for herself. She was never going to get anywhere at this rate. Jen was right, she thought dejectedly. This was a hopeless quest. She might as well give up now and forget all about it.

But George wasn't prepared to give up yet. 'Did your mother go to church?' he asked suddenly.

'How on earth should I know?' Molly said impatiently. 'I was only three years old when she died.'

But George wasn't put off. 'Everyone went to church in the old days,' he said firmly, and despite her despondency, Molly couldn't help smiling. He made it sound as though she had been born in the time of the Reformation. 'We could ask the vicar,' George went on. 'If he's really old, like most vicars are, he might even have known your mother.'

But disappointingly, the vicar, when they eventually tracked him down in the vestry, turned out to be a youngish man. Less disappointingly, as far as George was concerned at least, he had a missing arm. Noticing the boy staring with fascination at his empty black sleeve, the vicar explained that he had been serving in the Army Chaplains' Department and had lost his arm when a German shell had hit a makeshift tented church in North Africa in 1942, just prior to the battle of El Alamein.

He winked at George. 'The Lord was looking after me that day.'

George wrinkled his nose. 'Yes, but not very well,' he pointed out. 'Or you wouldn't have lost your—'

'We were wondering if you knew anything about the mother-and-child hostel,' Molly interrupted hastily. 'The one that used to be in this street.'

'I'm afraid not,' the vicar said. 'The bomb fell in 1941, before I took up my ministry here. But I do know that a number of the women and children living in that building were killed. One of my parishioners used to work there, and she told me that they had failed to go to the shelter.' He hesitated for a moment. 'I suppose you might call it divine retribution.'

Molly stared at him in disbelief. 'Divine retribution?'

'What's divine retribution?' George asked.

The vicar smiled at him kindly. 'It is when our Lord punishes people for their sins.'

George looked slightly taken aback. 'What sort of sins?' he asked uneasily, perhaps thinking of his own numerous transgressions. 'What had they done?'

'They hadn't done anything,' Molly said. 'They were just—'

'They were fallen women,' the vicar interrupted her firmly. 'And I'm sure you appreciate that is not something the Church, or indeed society, condones.'

'What's a fallen woman?' George asked.

Molly ignored him. 'And what about their children?' she said. 'Did they deserve to die too?'

'Of course not,' the vicar said calmly. 'Children are innocent of sin. Nevertheless, we have to believe that the Lord, in his infinite wisdom, knew best. It is a sad fact that misbegotten children always struggle to—'

'I was a misbegotten child,' Molly said grittily. 'And I am struggling to accept your beliefs.' Grasping George's arm, she tried to draw him away.

'No, wait,' George objected. He wriggled free of her clutching fingers. 'You haven't asked about the parishioner.'

Molly glared at him. She wanted to get away before she exploded in fury. 'What parishioner?' she snapped.

'The one who knew about the women not going to the shelter,' George said. He turned to the vicar. 'Is she quite old? Had she worked there a long time? Like twenty years?'

The vicar had clearly taken umbrage at Molly's outburst. 'I have no idea how long she worked there,' he said stiffly. 'But she is a middle-aged woman, so I suppose it's possible.'

George threw an I-told-you-so-look over his shoulder to Molly, then smiled appealingly at the vicar. 'Can you tell us where she lives?' he asked eagerly. 'Because we'd like to go and talk to her.'

'Her name is Mrs Bridges,' the vicar said. 'But I don't know her address, as I have not had any call to visit her.'

Outside on the street, Molly stood still for a moment trying to regain her equilibrium, while George watched her with interest. 'I've never seen you look so cross,' he said.

She let out a slow breath and shook her head. 'I don't think I've ever been so cross,' she said. 'And the galling thing is that, in the end, it was all for nothing.'

'No it wasn't,' George said as they turned back onto busy Marylebone Road. 'We found out about Mrs Bridges.'

Molly felt the despondency wash over her again. 'Yes,' she said. 'But we've no means of getting in touch with her.'

George looked surprised. 'Yes we do,' he said. 'If she's one of his parishioners, that means she goes to his church. All you have to do is go on Sunday and find her in the congregation.'

'If you think I'm going to sit through a service taken by that objectionable man, then you've got another think coming,' Molly said. 'Anyway, I'm on duty next Sunday.' But his optimism had revived her slightly. 'Maybe I can get Jen to go.'

George nodded in satisfaction. 'I bet you're glad you brought me with you,' he said. 'When you find out your mother left you a million pounds in her will, I hope you'll give me some.'

Molly had to laugh. 'Of course I will,' she said. 'You've been a great help.'

'I know,' he said happily. He cast her a cheeky sideways glance. 'And now that you aren't so cross any more, will you tell me what a fallen women is? And a misbegotten child?'

Molly groaned inwardly. But thankfully, before she could embark on an explanation, his attention was diverted by a rumpus further up the street.

Newspapers were being unloaded from a van at a news-stand and a noisy queue was already forming. 'I wonder what's happened,' George said.

It didn't take them long to find out. As they approached the crowd, they heard the vendor screaming out the headlines. 'Arnhem disaster. Arnhem disaster. News just in. Only one in four rescued from hell in Arnhem.'

'Oh no,' Molly said. 'Oh no.'

For the last week, the newspapers had been full of the dramatic developments in Holland. After sweeping through France and Belgium, Field Marshal Montgomery had decided to make a sudden thrust northwards through Holland with the aim of bypassing the well-defended Siegfried Line on the German border. To that end, British and Polish airborne troops had been dropped to secure key Dutch bridges and towns. The British XXX Corps had been expected to reach the airborne forces within two to three days, but the entire operation had come up against unexpectedly fierce German resistance, specifically from two SS panzer divisions.

Not only had the fighting been fiercer than anticipated, but for several days a group of British soldiers from the Parachute Regiment had been valiantly holding the bridge at Arnhem, and everyone in England had been on tenterhooks waiting for news that reinforcements had arrived.

But now it sounded as though that hadn't happened.

Molly bought a paper and they read it on the bus on the way home.

The whole debacle made her recent despondency seem misplaced. The ground forces had failed to break through German lines to reach the bridge. The parachutists had held on as long as they could. The last anyone had heard of them was a radio message sent from the bridge during the final hours of the struggle: 'Out of ammunition. God save the King.'

Without access to the crucial bridges across the Rhine, and with their own numbers decimated, the rest of the Allied force had been forced to fall back. Despite the fact that at least 2,000 of the original 12,000 soldiers of the British 1st Airborne Division were known to have been killed, and another 7,000 listed as missing, astonishingly the ever-optimistic Montgomery was hailing the battle a success. Even though it had failed to achieve its original objective, it had apparently driven a wedge through the German defensive line and 'would stand for ever in history as an example of courage and endurance'.

Even George, normally so buoyant, was brought down by the news of the defeat. 'We will still win in the end, though, won't we?' he asked anxiously as the bus trundled its way back across the river towards Clapham.

'Of course we will,' Molly said firmly. 'But it might take a bit longer than we thought.'

She thought of those soldiers trapped on that bridge, others lying dead and abandoned in the Dutch countryside. They didn't give up, she told herself, and nor must I. She just needed to find a bit more courage and endurance.

Due to security considerations and censorship, parents and wives of serving soldiers never knew exactly where they were, which meant that when terrible news came in, like that of the Arnhem fiasco, nobody was sure whether their loved ones were involved.

Joyce had been desperately trying to work out if either Pete or Paul might have been anywhere near Arnhem. But as all the various battalions, corps, divisions, brigades and units the newspapers talked about seemed to contain a mishmash of regiments and bits of regiments, it was impossible to work out what was what, or more importantly, who was where.

The first thing most people knew about the death or capture of a son or husband was a telegram, but that wasn't always the case. Poor Mrs Freeman at the post office had waited two months before being told that her boy Frank had copped it on D-Day. Some of the local newspapers published lists of casualties, but although Joyce and Albert pored over the papers each evening, so far, thank goodness, her boys' names hadn't been there.

'I wish they'd write and let us know they're all right,' Joyce said, as once again she ran her finger down the dreadful list of names and ID numbers. Albert's distant cousin Leszek, who was also serving in France, was a much better correspondent; Albert received a letter from him almost every month.

'Why are my children so uncommunicative?' Joyce grumbled. 'Jen's just as bad. I found out earlier that she's going to go and live in Mrs d'Arcy Billière's house. And never a word to me about it. Goodness knows how she's going to afford it when she's already paying through the nose for that daft acting course of hers.'

Albert didn't respond, and Joyce looked across at him. She saw his finger was still on the page of newsprint and her blood ran cold. 'Have you found something?' she asked.

'No,' he said. 'No, they're not listed here.' He folded the newspaper neatly and rested it on the arm of his chair. 'But there is something I need to tell you.'

Joyce stared at him in alarm. 'What?' she said. 'What is it?'

'It's about Jen,' he said.

In a flash, Joyce's panic turned to anger. 'Don't tell me she's asked you to pay her rent?' she said.

He shook his head. 'No, it's not that.' He gave an awkward cough. 'I should have told you before we got married, but it was all agreed a long time ago, and I never quite got round to it.'

'What are you talking about?' Joyce said crossly. 'What was agreed a long time ago?'

There was a slight pause. 'That I would pay for her drama course at RADA,' he said.

'*What?*' Joyce gaped at him.

She could hardly believe it. He had gone behind her back. It didn't matter that it was a generous thing to do. Or that it was as much Jen's fault as his. What mattered was that he hadn't told her. He knew she wouldn't approve, and he had done it anyway.

151

'But why?' she stammered.

'Because I thought she deserved some help,' he said. 'And she couldn't have afforded it otherwise.'

'No,' Joyce snapped. 'I didn't mean that. I meant why didn't you tell me?'

He looked at her fondly and tried to take her hand. But she snatched it away angrily.

'I didn't tell you because I knew you would be cross,' he said. 'And I didn't want you to be cross before we got married in case you changed your mind. And before you say anything,' he went on quickly, as she went to interrupt, 'Jen didn't ask me for the money. I offered it. And she was reluctant to accept, because she knew you wouldn't like it.'

Joyce gave a sceptical sniff. 'But she did accept, didn't she?' she said.

'Yes,' he said. 'But only because I persuaded her to. I know you and Jen don't always see eye to eye, my darling. But she had a bad time in Italy last year, and I thought she needed a bit of help.'

Once again he reached over and tried to take her hand. This time she let him. 'Don't be cross,' he murmured as he kissed her fingers. 'I know you're worried about the boys, and about Bella, and about Angie and Gino making a mess of their pasta evenings.' He glanced up briefly with a twinkle in his eyes. 'But I don't want you to take it out on Jen. She must be just as worried as we are at the moment. Both about her brothers, and about Henry.'

'Well, she doesn't show it,' Joyce said. 'Jaunting into London every day, looking like a million dollars.'

Albert didn't reply, just continued to kiss her fingers gently one by one, and as she looked at his head, with its dark, slightly thinning hair, bowed over her fingers, she felt the anger drain out of her, to be replaced by a warm rush of emotion. Albert Lorenz might not be pin-up handsome like Henry Keller or Ward Frazer, but you'd be hard pushed to find a nicer, kinder, more considerate man. He didn't mind that she got ratty and cross. He didn't mind that she snapped at him. He understood her, and that was all that mattered.

I love him, she thought. And I can't imagine how I ever managed without him.

'Well, you're not to give her any more,' she said gruffly. 'Or any of the others. They need to learn to stand on their own feet.'

'No, no, of course I won't,' he said placatingly. She felt his smile against the skin on her knuckles. 'At least not without checking with you first.'

On Wednesday, feeling that she needed moral support before presenting herself at Mrs d'Arcy Billière's house for her ten o'clock appointment with the Russian professor, Molly popped into the pub to see Katy. She found her standing behind the bar in a state of excitement, having just received a telegram from Ward.

'Look,' she said, pushing it eagerly across the bar. 'I was just about to come over to show you.'

Molly picked up the yellow paper with its single line of jerky typewritten script: *Sorry re delay. H de B here now. Home soon. All love W*

'Goodness,' she said. 'So we were right. Helen's obviously been in France all this time.' She paused and frowned. 'Paris is a long way from Toulon though. I hope she met up with André all right.' She glanced at the telegram again, wishing Ward hadn't been so skimpy with his information. It was typical of a man to miss out the important bit, she thought, and wondered briefly why Helen hadn't sent her own message.

But Katy was excited that they would be back in London soon. She gave a happy sigh. 'And with any luck the war will be over before either of them gets sent away again.'

'Let's hope so,' Molly agreed, but even as she said the words, she superstitiously crossed her fingers behind her back. In her experience, it was all too easy to tempt fate.

Catching sight of the clock behind Katy's head, she recoiled in alarm. It was nearly ten o'clock and the moment of doom was almost upon her.

'Wish me luck,' she said. 'If I'm not back by lunchtime, you'd better tell them to start dredging the river.'

But to her surprise, instead of her first lesson being the excruciating ordeal she had anticipated, Molly found herself utterly enthralled by Professor Markov's enthusiasm for his subject.

'So,' he had barked as he balanced his cane against a huge sideboard. He flung his moth-eaten fur-collared coat over the back of a chair and sat down at the huge round table. 'Tell me, what is chemistry?'

For a second, Molly's mind had gone completely blank. Close up, she could see that his thick white moustache and beard were yellowing slightly at the edges, and he gave off a strange, rather tangy smell. But it was his eyes that unnerved her most. Deep set, and almost lost under the wildly luxuriant eyebrows, they were small, round and extraordinarily intense.

'Well, I'm not really sure,' she had stammered eventually. 'Is it something to do with combinations of substances? I've looked at some textbooks, but I don't really understand them.'

It was a pitiful start and she had half expected him to dismiss her out of hand. But instead of looking displeased or exasperated at her lack of mental ability, he had laughed delightedly, displaying, somewhat to her surprise, bearing in mind the unkemptness of the rest of him, a set of very even white teeth. It took her a moment to realise that they must be false.

'Yes, yes,' he had said. 'Now we will take an example. Chlorine is a deadly poison gas that was employed on European battlefields in the Great War. Sodium is a corrosive metal that burns upon contact with water. But if we combine poisonous chlorine with corrosive sodium, together they make a useful, harmless material called table salt. Why and how this happens is the subject of chemistry.'

He reached into a battered leather briefcase and drew out a somewhat faded chart of the periodic table. He pointed at the vertical line on the left-hand side. 'All of the alkali metals react vigorously with chlorine gas. The reaction gets more violent as you move down the group. For example, if a piece of hot lithium is lowered into a jar of chlorine, white powder is produced and settles on the sides of the jar. This is lithium chloride.' He scribbled a formula on the side of the chart. 'If a piece of hot sodium is lowered into a jar of chlorine, clouds of white powder settle on the sides of the jar. This is salt, sodium chloride.' He handed her the pen. 'Now you write the formula for that.'

And miraculously, perhaps because he had made it sound so simple, Molly found she could.

When the somewhat unorthodox lesson came to an end exactly an hour later, she was almost disappointed.

'Thank you so much, Professor Markov,' she said. 'It has been really interesting.'

'You sound surprised,' he said. 'Next time, we will talk about atoms. As the ancient philosopher Democritus said, "We think there is colour, we think there is sweet, we think there is bitter, but in reality all we have is atoms."'

Walking back to the Nelsons' house ten minutes later, having arranged another session for the following Monday, Molly found herself facing a dilemma. Despite his unusual aroma and his disconcertingly blunt manner, she rather liked Professor Markov, but she had no idea if his unconventional style of teaching would get her through the rigidly conservative examination system of the Higher Certificate. Nor could she imagine how she was going to afford him. He was insistent on seeing her at least twice a week. 'To help the brain learn efficiently, we need to have frequent reinforcement,' he had declared. 'Seven days makes too long a gap.' He had given one of his gleamingly white smiles. 'Even for the brightest young brains like yours.'

Molly had glowed with pleasure at the compliment, but it was clear to her that the only way to afford the 'reinforcement' she apparently needed would be to do as the professor had suggested the first time they had met and try to find some other students to help share the cost of his travel time from North London.

But who? She wondered about putting a notice up in the bar, but it was a bit of a risk; she didn't want to get a lot of drunkards applying for a joke. The only other person she could think of was George. But although George could certainly do with some schooling, the thought of letting him loose in Mrs d'Arcy Billière's antique-filled house made her feel quite queasy, let alone what effect he might have on Professor Markov.

But beggars couldn't be choosers, and when, a couple of days later, she asked Pam if she had been serious about asking the professor to tutor George, Pam jumped at the idea.

'Do you think he would?' she said. 'It would be just the thing for George, otherwise he's going to be terribly behind when he eventually gets back to school.'

George, however, wasn't quite so keen. 'Oh no,' he said at once when the idea was put to him. His face took on a mulish expression. 'I don't need lessons. I hate science and I don't want to be taught by some boring old professor. And if you make me, I'll run away.'

Pam met Molly's eyes and gave a slightly desperate grimace. Molly knew how she felt. For all his angelic looks and undoubted charm, George was one of the most intransigent children she had ever met.

'Well,' she said, turning back to him with a calm smile. 'For your information, Professor Markov is not at all boring. But he is Russian and rather scary. So maybe it's for the best. Maybe Pam can find someone more used to dealing with young boys.'

George bristled, but he was too smart to be lured into her trap. 'I know what you're trying to do,' he said. 'I'm not scared of Russians, or your stupid professor. But that doesn't mean I want him to give me lessons.'

'All right then,' Molly said unconcernedly. 'I'll ask Katy if Malcolm would like to come instead.'

George looked at her incredulously. 'Malcolm's too young for science lessons!'

Molly gave a careless shrug. 'Not according to the professor,' she said over her shoulder as she hurried off upstairs to put on her Red Cross uniform. 'He seemed very impressed with Malcolm's intellect.'

Jen finally moved into Mrs d'Arcy Billière's on the afternoon of Sunday 1 October. At Molly's request, and much against her will, she had spent both that morning and the previous Sunday attending long and unbelievably tedious services at the church on the corner of Marylebone Road. But to no avail.

Despite bearding various members of the congregation as they left the church, they found no one who knew of a Mrs Bridges who had worked at the mother-and-baby home, let alone where such a person might live. To Jen, used to Clapham, where everyone knew everyone else's business, this seemed odd. But someone explained to her that St Mary's was a big church with a wide catchment area, and unless Mrs Bridges attended the more intimate weekly prayer groups, or helped with parish good works, then the chances were that nobody would know her.

The vicar, when Jen accosted him, was equally unhelpful. At first, misguidedly assuming that she might be thinking of joining his flock, he had put on an ingratiating smile, but as soon as he realised the purpose of her visit, he had become distinctly frosty. 'As I told your friend the other day,' he said, 'I don't know where Mrs Bridges lives. All I know is that she used to come to church regularly. If her attendance has dropped off, then that is her problem, not mine, and it is up to her to make her peace with the Lord.'

Staggered by his smug pomposity, Jen was hard pushed not to laugh in his face. If his sermons were as boring as the two she had endured, she wasn't at all surprised that Mrs Bridges' attendance had dropped off. She had nearly dropped off herself.

On the way home, she called at the Red Cross first-aid post to give Molly the bad news, only to find that she wasn't there. A man with greasy hair and a little black moustache told her that Molly had been dispatched to Southampton to meet a ship carrying wounded soldiers back from France, and wouldn't be back until much later that evening. So Jen left a message and went back to the pub to pack up her things.

Like Molly, Jen had never previously set foot in Mrs d'Arcy Billière's house. But unlike Molly, she had not spent several months living in Tunisia, and the foreign exoticism of the household came as quite a shock.

'Do come in,' Mrs d'Arcy Billière had shouted from an upstairs window when Jen knocked tentatively at the front door. 'I'm just changing, but the door's open. Your room is at the top of the stairs on the right.'

Having made her way across the huge tiled hallway and up the wide staircase, flanked with portraits that looked like Old Masters, Jen found herself in a huge room decorated in scarlet and gold. She could only think that Mrs d'Arcy Billière had modelled it on some kind of bordello, and wished that there was someone around with whom she could share the joke. Henry, for example, would have found it highly amusing. Not that Jen had ever shared a room with Henry. Despite the somewhat turbulent nature of their relationship, the physical side of things had been limited. Jen was not a prude – she had in fact lost her virginity to a sexy young Irishman at the beginning of the war – but there was something about the cool, suave confidence of Henry Keller that had made her shy. The closest they had got to sex was a long, knee-tremblingly intimate kiss on the Rifle Brigade parade ground before he had left for France.

She was just reliving that kiss when Mrs d'Arcy Billière appeared in the doorway wearing pointed slippers and a somewhat revealing black silk dressing gown embroidered up the front with a bright-red fire-breathing dragon.

'My dear girl,' she said, advancing on Jen with open arms as though to embrace her. 'Oh, I'm sorry, did I startle you? We don't stand on ceremony here. Let me look at you. Yes, of course, I have seen you in the street. I gather from Molly that you're an actress, and a singer. So please, do feel free to use the piano in the drawing room whenever you want.' She waved carelessly towards the staircase.

'It is a Steinway, one of the best, I believe. We are all very fond of music. I myself trained briefly at the Conservatoire in Paris, and I frequently hold musical soirées here for my friends. Perhaps you will entertain us all one evening? What fun that would be.'

Oh my God, Jen thought. It might be fun for Mrs d'Arcy Billière, but it certainly wouldn't be fun for her. She could hardly think of anything more awful than having to sing for this extraordinary woman and her mad foreign friends.

'Well, I . . .' she began, but that was far as she got, because at that moment they heard footsteps running up the stairs and Aaref Hoch appeared in the doorway. Jen knew him, of course; he was always in and out of the pub, supplying Katy with under-the-counter bits and pieces.

'Supper is ready,' he said to Mrs d'Arcy Billière. 'Oh, hello, Jen. I didn't hear you arrive. Will you be joining us for dinner? I expect Lael has explained that we all take it in turns to prepare the evening meal. It is the turn of my mother-in-law tonight. She is cooking a Jewish rice dish called *tahdig*. I think you will like it. It is very nice.'

Jen stared at him in considerable dismay. Lael had not explained any such thing. Jen hated foreign food, nor had she any interest in cooking. It was as much as she could do to make a cup of tea. Now she would have to hand over her ration book in return for food she wouldn't be able to eat. Suddenly she had an overwhelming desire to run away. More than anything, she wanted to kill Katy and Molly for ever suggesting that she come to this madhouse. Why on earth hadn't she accepted Mrs Rutherford's offer of a room instead? The Rutherfords might be stuffy, but at least they were British.

Putting her acting skills to good use, she forced her lips into a polite regretful smile. 'It sounds delicious,' she lied. 'But unfortunately I've promised to go back and help Katy in the pub tonight.'

Ward Frazer had been due to leave Paris for London a few days after he and Helen had met up, but he gave the SOE some excuse about needing to carry out further interviews, and stayed on to help her try to find some trace of André. And Helen was very glad, because without him she wouldn't have known where to begin.

As it was, with the extra advantage of General de Lattre de Tassigny's letter of authority, they were able to inspect the cells on the fifth floor of the Avenue Foch where the SD prisoners had been kept, and read the scratched inscriptions on the walls, the bleak messages of distress and defiance. They were also allowed to read through the transcripts of post-liberation interviews with collaborators, now themselves prisoners of the Free French; cleaners, drivers and interpreters who had worked for the SD, and the thuggish bully boys who had acted as guards and escorts and intimidators. They were even allowed to visit some of them in jail to ask if they had ever heard any mention of André's name.

The people they really wanted to question, of course, were the SD themselves, but that was impossible, because the ruthlessly efficient Sturmbannführer Hans Kieffer and his entire staff had miraculously vanished from Paris days before the liberation, taking most of their incriminating paperwork with them.

Luckily, in the haste of their departure, some documents had been overlooked, but even so, the only trace Ward and Helen could find of André was from when he had been captured by chance after a railway line had been blown up somewhere near Lyons in early 1943. Referred to only as Renard, his SOE code name, he had been brought to Avenue Hoch with a number of other resistance fighters and interrogated. But somehow – it wasn't clear how – he had managed to escape out of a window on the third floor before his real identity could be discovered.

There were plenty of others who had not been so lucky. Numerous F Section agents and radio operators, both men and women, some of whom Helen and Ward had met in the past, had been held at Avenue Hoch, sometimes for months on end, before eventually being shipped off by train to unknown destinations in Germany.

'I guess we're the lucky ones,' Ward said, looking up from a report written by a young French girl who had occasionally acted as a courier for the SOE. 'At least we could speak the language. This girl says here that some of the British agents arrived in France brandishing huge-denomination notes, talking schoolboy French and imagining the Germans were comic-book baddies who drove around in swastika-bedecked cars shouting *Heil Hitler!* at every turn.' He put the report down on the table and sat back in his chair. 'What were they thinking back in SOE HQ? And why the hell didn't they realise what was going on?'

Why not indeed, Helen thought. Everyone knew that being a secret agent was dangerous work. But there was no need to make it worse. Poorly trained, inadequately equipped young men and women had been sent across the Channel like lambs to the slaughter. There was evidence that several agents had died within hours of arriving in France. It clearly hadn't occurred to anyone that Sturmbannführer Kieffer and his well-trained thugs were going to be waiting for them.

Suddenly Helen felt angry. Furiously angry. She knew from her own experience that some of the spymasters in London had run their operations with a ridiculously imprudent gung-ho attitude. But now, sitting here in Hans Kieffer's office, with his neat lists on the walls, their lack of concern for the welfare of their agents seemed almost criminal.

She stood up and went over to the window. It opened out onto a narrow iron balcony with a rusting drainpipe running down to the sloping roof of an adjacent building below. For all she knew it was the window André had climbed out of. For a moment she rested her forehead against the pane and closed her eyes.

Behind her, Ward was silent. When she turned round, he was watching her with a concerned expression on his handsome face. 'War is a messy business,' he said. 'Bad things happen.'

Helen sighed. 'I know,' she said. 'And I'm sorry to be grouchy. You've been such a help.'

He stretched his shoulders. 'You know what I think?'

'What?'

'I think we should go back to London. I don't think we can spin

161

out the excuses any longer. There's not much more we can do here anyway. But we may be able to find out something from Bletchley.' He saw her sceptical look. He knew as well as she did that top-secret Bletchley Park was notoriously tight. 'We can at least ask them to run a check to see if André's name has cropped up in any intercepted signals,' he said. 'We can't do that from here.'

Helen turned back to the window. Deep down, although she was reluctant to leave France, and put even more distance between herself and André, wherever he was – if he was even still alive – she knew Ward was right.

There were no more excuses. Even her aunt was back on her feet now.

Ward had been helpful with that as well. Twice Helen had invited him round for supper, and he had got on famously with the old lady. Discovering that, due to the power shortages, Helen was having a job finding anywhere that would wash and set Aunt Isabelle's hair, he had recommended Salon Gervais, where the hairdryers were powered by a team of fit young men stripped to the waist pedalling a stationary tandem bicycle in the basement.

Her aunt was a true Parisian, and having clean, properly styled hair for the first time in months had done wonders for her morale.

But there was one more thing Helen had to do before she left Paris, and that was to write to André's father.

It was a difficult letter, mainly because there was so little to tell. All she really wanted to say was how terribly, terribly sorry she was that, so far at least, she had failed to find any clues as to the whereabouts of his wonderful son.

Even more difficult was knowing how to sign off. All the usual French salutations seemed wrong. Sending love seemed presumptuous. 'Best wishes' seemed too bland; *tendresse* too intimate.

In the end she put: *Bien à vous, avec l'espoir constant et sans fin.*

Yours, with constant and never-ending hope.

Chapter Ten

'Oh go on, Jen,' Molly pleaded. 'Please.'

Jen yawned and pulled her dressing gown round her more tightly. It was early on Sunday morning, and Molly had called in on her way to the Red Cross post to ask her to make one more attempt to find Mrs Bridges at the church in Marylebone.

But Jen had a difficult piece to learn for the following week. Or at least that was the excuse she gave Molly. 'They've given me the leading role,' she said. 'It's only a read-through, but it's a chance to prove myself.' That at least was true. Even though she wasn't much enjoying living at Mrs d'Arcy Billière's house, she was enjoying RADA, and wanted to excel. She certainly didn't want to waste her morning sitting through yet another Sunday service.

Molly looked disappointed, but thankfully didn't have time to argue the toss because she was already running late. Muttering something about trying to arrange to go herself the following week, she dashed off. But after she had gone, Jen felt guilty. And later, when she bumped into George Nelson on her way to the pub, he made her feel even guiltier.

He and Bella were heading up to the common to collect dandelions for his rabbit and Joyce's tortoise. As soon as he saw her, George stopped in his tracks. 'Molly said you were going up to the church,' he said accusingly.

'No,' Jen replied. 'I can't today. I don't have time. Molly's going to go next week instead.'

George frowned. 'But what happens if Mrs Bridges only goes to church once a month, and today is the day?'

Jen groaned silently. 'Then it's just bad luck,' she said. 'We'll find her sooner or later.'

'Well, Molly wants to find her sooner,' George said sullenly. 'And I think you're mean not to go.'

'And I think you're a precocious brat,' Jen said, peeved. But as she turned away towards the Flag and Garter, she glanced at her watch, wondering if there would be time to get up to Marylebone before the congregation as they left the church.

As soon as she opened the door of the pub, though, all thoughts of going to find Mrs Bridges were forgotten, because standing talking to Katy at the bar was a Rifle Brigade officer.

Jen recognised the uniform at once. It was the same uniform Henry had worn the last time she had seen him. As she took in the distinctive purple and black beret under the officer's arm, the three gold pips on his shoulder, the breath caught in her throat. A visit from a regimental officer generally meant bad news. The worst news, in fact.

Hearing the door, Katy swung round. In the dingy morning light filtering through the taped-up pub windows, she looked pale, and her eyes seemed to be watering. 'Here she is now,' she said in a slightly choked voice. 'You can tell her yourself.'

Suddenly the bar seemed very silent. Jen wondered where Malcolm and Caroline were, and guessed that Katy had tactfully sent them away. She felt her stomach clench. She didn't want to hear bad news. She didn't want to have to face up to some new horrible reality. She wanted things to stay exactly as they were.

In fact she was so busy resisting the thought that something awful had happened to Henry that she almost missed what the officer was saying.

'I'm a friend of Henry's. I've just arrived back from Belgium. My unit was pretty much wiped out at Arnhem, and the survivors have been sent home for a bit of R and R.' His face worked for a moment and Jen felt goose bumps prickle her skin. But then he took a breath and tried to smile. 'Anyway, I happened to see Henry just before I left, and he asked me to come and see you.'

Jen stared at him blankly. 'Are you telling me Henry is alive?' she said.

He looked startled. 'Oh yes. Very much so. In fact he wanted me to tell you that he is expecting to get leave sometime soon, and is hoping to get back to London for long enough to get married.'

He stopped and looked at her expectantly, but Jen was still taking in the news that Henry was alive. 'Married?' she said in a faint voice.

The officer glanced at her uneasily, and then at Katy, as though for reassurance.

Katy nodded eagerly. 'Isn't it brilliant news?' she said.

And finally Jen realised that Katy's eyes were shining with excitement, not tears. Excitement for her. Because Henry was coming home. Coming home to get married.

Jen could hardly believe it. She had been so sure it was going to be bad news.

'I'm sorry,' she said to the officer. 'I thought you were going to tell me he was dead.'

'Good lord, no,' he said. He gave an embarrassed cough. 'Well, of course a lot of other poor fellows are. But not Henry. He has seen some action, but so far he's come through unscathed.' He flushed faintly. 'He told me to send you his love.'

Jen felt herself blushing too, and was glad when Katy once again intervened.

'I know it's only eleven o'clock,' she said brightly. 'But I think this calls for a celebratory brandy.'

It was Albert who brought the news to Joyce. He had been over to the pub for a quick pint with Gino and Angie while Joyce cooked Sunday lunch.

'I hope you don't mind,' he remarked mildly as he took off his coat. 'But I asked Jen to join us for lunch.'

Yesterday Joyce had finally received letters from Pete and Paul in response to her enquiries as to whether they were all right. It turned out that neither of them had been involved in the action at Arnhem, and as they both sounded pretty cheerful, Joyce had decided to make a celebratory roast lunch with a bit of unused brisket that she had smuggled out of the café.

'What?' She almost dropped the knife she was holding. 'But . . .'

Albert took the knife and laid it carefully on the table. 'I know you're still cross with her,' he said. 'But perhaps it's time now to let bygones be bygones. If Henry is coming home soon, then I assume we'll be celebrating her marriage, and it would be a pity if you let a couple of small niggles spoil our happiness for her.'

Joyce glared at him. The thought of Jen secretly accepting money from Albert constituted rather more than a small niggle in her book, but deep down she knew he was right. Her daughter had always been a bit of a madam, and she was hardly going to change now.

And she was pleased that Jen would soon be getting married, although she couldn't quite imagine becoming Henry Keller's mother-in-law. Henry was an extremely nice man and had always been very polite towards her. But when all was said and done, he was far too posh for the likes of her and Albert. But if he wanted to marry Jen, which he clearly did, then she supposed she would have to get used to it.

'Oh, all right,' she said. 'I'll let her off. What time is she coming over?'

Albert smiled, clearly pleased with her capitulation, but before he could reply, Angie came in.

'Where's Bella?' she asked.

Joyce glanced at the kitchen clock and felt a sudden flicker of alarm. 'She went up to the common with George Nelson,' she said. 'But she should have been home by now. She's probably upstairs reading her book?'

'No she's not,' Angie said.

Nor was she in the back yard feeding the tortoise.

'Perhaps she stopped off at the Nelsons' on the way home,' Albert said.

'Shall I go and see?' Angie asked.

'Yes,' Joyce said.

As soon as Angie had gone, Joyce put her hand to her head. She should have noticed that Bella hadn't come home, but she had been busy with her cooking. And Bella was so silent, it was easy to overlook her.

'She'll be all right as long as she's with George,' Albert said.

Joyce wasn't so sure about that. An unruly schoolboy was hardly the ideal escort for a beautiful but silent teenage girl. Why on earth had she let them go out together? What had she been thinking of? How could she have been so complacent? Goodness only knew what trouble they might have got into, and . . .

She jumped as Albert put his hand reassuringly on her arm. 'It'll be all right,' he said. 'If necessary, we can send out a search party. But let's see what Mrs Nelson says first.'

Ten minutes later, Angie came bursting back through the door.

'George is missing too,' she panted. 'Mrs Nelson is worried to death. She thinks he's taken some money out of her purse. Anyway, I called in at the pub on the way back to see if anyone had seen them, and Jen was there, and guess what, she reckons they might have gone to church.'

'To church?' Joyce repeated incredulously. She couldn't think of anything more unlikely. What was Jen thinking? That George had stolen money for the collection?

And now here was Jen, strolling unconcernedly in through the open front door. 'Yes,' she said. 'I'm afraid it may be partly my fault. Molly asked me to go and meet someone at a church in Marylebone, but I couldn't be bothered. And I'm guessing George has gone instead.'

Joyce stared at her. 'Taking Bella with him?'

Jen shrugged. 'Presumably.'

'And aren't you worried?'

Jen looked surprised. 'Not particularly. They're both old enough to be able to get to Marylebone and back without too much difficulty.'

Joyce was aware of a surge of hot fury making its way up her body. That was so typical of Jen. She didn't care about anyone except herself. She didn't care that she had let Molly down. She didn't care that her laziness had put everyone in a state of panic, or that George and Bella were on the loose in central London. All she cared about was looking pretty, and doing her stupid acting. God help Henry Keller, she thought suddenly. He had no idea what he was taking on.

She was about to give Jen the full force of her fury when she felt Albert's restraining hand on her arm. Glancing angrily at him, she saw the little warning smile on his lips, and realised that he didn't want her to let rip. He didn't want her to fall out with her daughter all over again.

And for his sake, rather than Jen's, she bit back the angry words. 'Well, if you're right, hopefully they'll be back soon,' she muttered, turning back to the kitchen. 'Someone had better go and tell the Nelsons.'

George and Bella were indeed back quite soon. One look at their faces told Joyce they knew they were going to be in trouble. But they also looked somewhat gleeful, or at least George did, until he caught sight of Pam standing anxiously in Joyce's kitchen.

'George!' Pam cried. 'Where on earth have you been?'

George lifted his chin with a hint of defiance. 'We went to Marylebone,' he said. He turned accusingly to Jen, who was sitting at the kitchen table with a glass in her hand. 'Well, you said you weren't going to go, and—'

'But why didn't you tell me where you were going?' Pam demanded.

He looked back at her as though she was mad. 'Because I knew you'd tell me I couldn't go.'

'So instead you stole money out of my purse?' Pam said grimly.

And now he did look slightly shamefaced. 'I only borrowed it,' he said. 'I didn't steal it. I'm sure Molly will pay you back.'

Bella meanwhile had been standing silently just inside the door, a self-conscious flush on her pretty face. Joyce could tell from her start of surprise that she hadn't known where the money had come from, but that didn't mean she didn't deserve a reprimand too.

'You at least should have known better,' she said. 'We were very worried about you.'

Bella bit her lip. Quickly, gracefully, she moved over to the sideboard, where the newspaper was lying next to the rapidly cooling brisket. *He was going anyway*, she wrote across the top of the page above the headline. *I thought it was better not to let him go alone.*

'Well, that's as may be,' Joyce said. 'But it was still very wrong. Of both of you.'

George wasn't deterred. 'We were perfectly safe,' he said. 'And what's more, we found the lady.' He looked round eagerly, as though expecting applause. 'I can't wait to tell Molly, but she wasn't there when we called at the first-aid post. A man there told us that a gas main had exploded and she had gone to help.'

Joyce flinched. She knew what that meant. It must be another of Hitler's beastly new rockets. The government kept pretending they were exploding gas mains so as not to let the enemy know where they had landed.

'Who is this lady Molly wanted to find?' Angie asked.

George was about to answer, but then shifted his feet. He glanced uneasily at Jen. 'I don't know if she would want me to tell,' he said.

But Jen, being Jen, apparently had no qualms about confidentiality. 'It's just some woman who might have known Molly when she was a baby,' she said. She looked at George. 'And did she?'

He nodded. 'Well, sort of. She's quite old, but she thought she remembered a baby called Molly. And she gave me her address so Molly can go and visit her.' He drew out a scribbled bit of paper from his pocket. Unfortunately, attached to it was a half-chewed piece of toffee. Joyce bit back a smile. It was clear to her that not all Pam's stolen money had been used on bus fares.

Pam saw it too. 'You'd better give that to me before you lose it,' she said. 'And I'll have the toffees too, if you don't mind. I suppose you "borrowed" one of my sweet coupons for those?'

George did mind, but as he clearly didn't have a leg to stand on, he gave way with good grace and, having handed over a small bag of broken toffee, meekly followed his mother out of the house.

After they had gone, Joyce turned to Bella. 'Go and wash your hands,' she said. 'And then we'll have lunch. You've kept us waiting long enough as it is.'

'You can't really blame her,' Albert said when Bella had left the room. 'Young George is very persuasive.'

'Of course I can blame her,' Joyce said. 'And I blame Jen too.'

Typically, Jen flared up at once at that. 'How was I to know that George was going to take it upon himself—' she began.

'How indeed?' Albert said peaceably. 'Well, well, they had their little adventure, and thankfully there's no harm done. But it does make me think Bella has too much time on her hands. I'm sure she is bored to death helping with my accounts and doing a bit of washing-up in the café. She needs something to occupy her mind.'

'Why don't you send her to Molly's new tutor?' Jen said. 'She's looking for people to help share the cost.'

Joyce stared at her. And then at Albert. Her first instinct, since it was Jen who had made the suggestion, was to pooh-pooh the idea. But then she began to wonder. 'But she still can't talk,' she said.

Jen shrugged. 'You don't have to talk to learn.'

'And she is a clever little thing,' Albert said.

Angie nodded eagerly. 'She's always got her nose in a book,' she said. She giggled and nudged Gino, who was sitting next to her, looking bemused. Despite being in the country for over two years, his English still wasn't good enough to follow a conversation. 'She's certainly a lot cleverer than me and Gino.'

'You can say that again,' Jen murmured.

Joyce glared at her. 'But the cost . . .'

'I'd be happy to pay for her,' Albert said easily. 'I tell you what, let's speak to Molly later on and see what she thinks.' He glanced at the sideboard and winked at Angie. 'But first of all I suggest we get this delicious-looking brisket carved up, before we all die of starvation.'

Molly was shocked to hear that George and Bella had taken it upon themselves to venture up to Marylebone on her behalf. But although she apologised to Pam and to Joyce for causing them such worry, she was thrilled to discover that Mrs Bridges claimed to remember her. Thrilled, but oddly apprehensive. So much so that she found herself putting off the moment when she would go and visit her.

'I haven't had time yet,' she said to George when he asked later in the week why she hadn't been.

He eyed her doubtfully. 'I thought you'd be pleased I found her for you.'

'I am pleased,' Molly said. 'But I'm awfully busy at the moment.'

It was true. Not only was she working long hours at the Red Cross and the pub, she also now had Professor Markov to deal with. She had begun to realise that, despite his unconventional approach to teaching, her new tutor was going to be a hard taskmaster. When he told her something, he expected her to remember it. His own mind was razor sharp, and he was so enthusiastic about his subject, and looked so disheartened when she failed to recite the periodic table correctly, or got confused between protons and electrons, she found herself studying at all hours of the day and night in order not to disappoint him.

And now she had to ask him if he wanted to take on George and Bella too. One of the outcomes of George's visit to Marylebone had been that Pam and Alan had decided that, whether he wanted to or not, the moment had come for him to resume his studies, and in the absence of a suitable local school, some lessons with Professor Markov seemed the best option.

Bella, in her silent way, had seemed excited by the idea, but George had not. And, feeling oddly protective of the professor's sensibilities, Molly was worried that George might somehow upset him. What the exuberant man would make of wordless little Bella was anyone's guess.

In addition, Molly found she had another problematic student to deal with. Earlier in the week, an agitated-looking woman called Mrs Powell had come into the pub. She had heard on the grapevine that somebody was offering science lessons and wanted to arrange some for her son. 'He would have been at university now if it hadn't been for the war,' she said. 'But he's home now and I think it might do him good to get out occasionally.' To Molly's dismay, she had broken down at that point, and had been unable to speak for a few minutes. She was clearly in a state of considerable distress.

It had taken some tactful questioning, and a small medicinal brandy, to elicit the information that Mrs Powell's son had been very badly injured during the battle for Monte Cassino and, having spent some considerable time in hospital, had recently been demobbed on medical grounds.

'He was always such a good boy, funny and clever,' Mrs Powell said, dabbing her eyes. 'And ever so handsome, too. But now . . . well, he's not the same.'

When Molly finally met the unfortunate young man, she could see what his mother had meant. Confined to a wheelchair, Graham Powell had clearly been through the wars in more ways than one. Not only was he apparently paralysed from the waist down, but the skin between his left eye and his chin, and on the back of his right hand, was bright red and distorted from severe burns. He had a look of such self-conscious despair on his damaged face that Molly could hardly bear to meet his eyes.

Knowing from her experience of nursing injured soldiers that he wouldn't want to see her sympathy, she tried to keep her welcoming smile as bland as possible. But she needn't have bothered. He made no effort to smile back. Nor did it seem that he was remotely interested in lessons with the professor. 'What's the point,' he snapped irritably when his mother muttered something about preparing for university. 'I'm never going to get to university now, am I?'

Catching Mrs Powell's agonised glance, Molly felt her heart sink. She had been on the brink of saying that maybe they should leave it until he felt a bit better. But the poor woman was clearly at the end of her tether. She needed help almost as much as her son did. She certainly needed a break. And even if he was depressed, the young man was obviously no fool.

'Oh well,' she said to him brightly. 'Whether you want to go to university or not, I suppose there'd be no harm in you meeting Professor Markov. He's a very interesting man. He fled Russia during the Revolution. I don't think life has been easy for him either, but he seems to know everything there is to know about science.'

For a fleeting second she thought she saw a glimmer of interest in Graham Powell's eyes. But it was swiftly gone. He glanced at his mother and lifted his thin, muscle-wasted shoulders. 'Oh, all right,' he said with a long-suffering sigh. 'After all, it's not as though I've got anything else to do.'

'Those bloody Nazis,' Katy murmured to Molly after Mrs Powell had wheeled him out of the pub. 'Just now I could quite happily kill them all.'

Molly thought about all the young soldiers she'd nursed at the Wilhelmina Hospital earlier on in the war, and in North Africa, and the ones she had escorted to London hospitals from Southampton last week. Some would recover, but others, like Graham Powell, would probably be maimed for life. It made a dreadful tally. And that wasn't even counting the countless thousands who had died on the battlefields. 'I suppose we are inflicting the same kind of injuries on them,' she said.

'Yes,' Katy agreed grimly. 'But they started it.'

Professor Markov seemed delighted at the idea of taking on some more students. 'Ah,' he said, rubbing his hands in pleasure. 'There is nothing more enjoyable than introducing young minds to the wonders of science.' And when Molly ventured to warn him that at least two of his prospective new pupils might not be quite as receptive as he thought, he just bared his perfect teeth in a jolly guffaw. 'Young minds are always receptive,' he said. 'Tell them all to come in one day next week, and we'll go from there.'

Mrs d'Arcy Billière, when consulted, was equally undaunted by the thought of opening her house to the daughter of the recently deceased local prostitute, a rumbustious schoolboy and an invalided ex-soldier in a wheelchair. 'Everyone is welcome here,' she said expansively. 'After all, what damage can they do that Hitler hasn't already tried to do with his bombs and his rockets? Not to mention these new flying gas mains? One of my friends was woken up by one of the damn things exploding in Wanstead the other morning. When she went to look, the crater was nearly fifty yards across.'

Molly had to laugh; nobody believed the government's gas explosion excuses any more. But secret or not, Hitler's new weapon was no laughing matter. Rumour had it that most of the hits so far had been in the countryside north-west of London, but if the Nazis improved their aim, life was once again going to become very unpleasant for Londoners.

Oddly, it was the thought of the flying gas mains that finally prompted Molly to travel up to Marylebone the following afternoon during a bit of precious time off. Mrs Bridges represented her only chance of finding out anything about her mother, and it would be an awful shame if she was killed before Molly got to talk to her.

* * *

Mrs Bridges lived in a very small apartment in a very large tenement block overlooking Regent's Park.

'You can see the zoo from the window,' she said chattily to Molly as she ushered her into her tiny front room. 'But there are no wild animals there nowadays. They were all moved away during the Blitz in case their enclosures got bombed and they escaped. And lucky they were, because the zoo was hit by a V-1 back in June.'

'Oh dear,' Molly said. 'I hope nobody was killed.'

Mrs Bridges shook her head. 'Only two pheasants and an adder.' She picked up a pair of spectacles from a side table. 'Now let me look at you. That lad you sent to find me said you think you might have been born at the mother-and-baby home? In 1922, wasn't it?'

Molly suddenly felt rather breathless. 'Yes, that's right,' she stammered. 'Is that when you were working there?'

Mrs Bridges nodded comfortably. 'I worked there on and off for years,' she said. 'They found it hard to get staff. People didn't want to work among what they called loose women. But I didn't mind. As far as I was concerned, they were just girls who had got into a spot of trouble and needed somewhere to live.'

Molly shivered. 'And George said you remembered a baby called Molly?'

'Yes, I do,' Mrs Bridges said. 'I was just about to get married and I can remember thinking it was a nice name and I might use it for my own daughter if I ever had one.' She stopped and glanced fondly at a silver-framed photograph of two young men in uniform that stood on the mantelpiece. 'As it happened, I only had sons.'

Fearing she was about to veer off into a proud description of her sons, Molly leaned forward, ready to steer her back onto her reminiscences, but Mrs Bridges just gave a slight regretful sigh and continued where she had left off. 'She was a funny little thing, that baby,' she said. 'Not much to look at, and that made me feel sorry for her because her mother was so pretty.' Sitting back in her chair with an air of satisfaction, she smiled at Molly. 'Looking at you now, even though you've grown into quite a nice-looking girl, I reckon you're that same Molly.'

Ridiculously, Molly felt herself colouring up. She wasn't at all surprised to learn that she had been an ugly baby; it made her more certain that the child Mrs Bridges was talking about had indeed been her. She had never been a beauty, and although she no longer thought of herself as ugly, she knew perfectly well that she still wasn't much to look at. But she was grateful to Mrs Bridges for pretending otherwise. It wasn't often that she received compliments about her looks.

However, she hadn't come here to find out about herself.

'Do you by any chance remember my mother's name?' she asked.

Mrs Bridges frowned. 'I knew you would ask me that,' she said. 'But I didn't know her well and I can't for the life of me remember her surname. Prissy was what everyone called her, but I can't even remember if that was because her name was Priscilla, or just because she was a bit prissy.' She saw Molly's startled glance. 'You know,' she put on a comical hoity-toity look, 'a bit posh, and not wanting to get her hands dirty and that.' She gave a quick chuckle. 'Although come to think of it, she can't have been that prissy if she got herself up the duff, can she?'

Molly didn't know what to think. She was no prude, but she was slightly shocked at Mrs Bridges' rough-and-ready humour. Perhaps that was what came of working in a home for unmarried mothers.

She took a breath. 'Do you know how she died?' she asked. 'I mean, was it an illness, or some kind of accident?'

Mrs Bridges looked surprised. 'I didn't know she died,' she said. 'When was that?'

Molly frowned. 'Well I think it must have been in 1925, because that's when I was put in the orphanage.'

'Oh well,' Mrs Bridges said. 'Perhaps that explains it. I was married by then and I'd stopped working because I was pregnant with my first son. I didn't go back until my second son was at primary school, and that was a good few years later.' She saw Molly's disappointment and shook her head. 'No, the last time I saw your mother, I'm pretty sure she was still working at Tommy's.'

Molly blinked. 'Tommy's? Do you mean the hospital? St Thomas's?' Had her mother been a nurse as well?

But Mrs Bridges was shaking her head with a laugh. 'I can tell you don't live round here. No, the department store, at Paddington. It's called Thompson's, but us locals call it Tommy's.'

Molly looked at her eagerly. 'And it's still there? It hasn't been bombed or anything?'

'Oh, it's still there all right,' Mrs Bridges said. 'There's not much in it, mind. I believe old Mr Thompson is having a job keeping it going with all the shortages and that.' Suddenly she brightened. 'Why don't you go and ask about your mother there?' She winked. 'Between you and me, Mr Thompson has always had an eye for the ladies. I reckon as he might remember her.'

Half an hour later, having thanked Mrs Bridges profusely and run nearly all the way to Paddington, Molly was standing in a somewhat shabby wood-panelled office at the back of Thompson's department store, staring at an elderly man in an extraordinarily old-fashioned frock coat seated on the other side of an enormous desk.

'Oh yes, indeed,' Mr Thompson was saying. 'I remember Prissy. Little Prissy Cavanagh. She worked in the gentlemen's department. Goodness, that must be twenty years ago now.' He peered at Molly through slightly rheumy eyes. 'And you're her daughter, you say? Well, well, how about that. You're darker than she was, but perhaps you get that from your father.'

'I don't know,' Molly stammered. 'I never met my father. And I don't remember my mother. That's why I came here. I was hoping you could tell me something about her.'

'Well, it was a long time ago,' he said, 'but I'll certainly try. What exactly do you want to know?'

'You're sure her surname was Cavanagh?' Molly asked. 'Not Coogan?'

'No, definitely Cavanagh. Prissy Cavanagh.' He stopped and rubbed his nose. 'Or was it Cavendish? No, no, it was Cavanagh, I'm sure of it.'

Molly hesitated. A name was something, but she needed more than that. 'And do you know anything else about her? Like where she came from?'

He tapped his gnarled fingers thoughtfully on his desk. 'She was certainly always very punctual, and very neat and tidy. I seem to recall she lived locally, but I don't remember exactly where. A nice, well-brought-up girl like that, I imagine she was still living at home with her parents.'

Molly bit her lip, disappointed. Once again she had hit a brick wall. He clearly had no idea of her mother's unfortunate history, let alone her family background. For a second, she thought of explaining where little Prissy Cavanagh had really lived, with her illegitimate baby, but she found she was reluctant to disillusion him. Or was it some odd sense of loyalty to her mother that stopped her?

'Yes,' he said. 'She was a good girl. It was a shame we lost her.'

Molly took a slow breath. 'How did she die?' she asked. 'Was it an accident?'

He blinked at her. 'She didn't die,' he said. 'She left to get married. That's why we lost her.'

It was Molly's turn to blink. 'To get married?' she gasped.

'Yes indeed,' he said. 'She married one of our customers. A slightly older man. I never met him and I don't recall his name. But he must have been well-to-do, because she had previously sold him a rather expensive double-breasted suit. That's how they had met. It was some beautiful tweed we'd had in from the Outer Hebrides. The Isle of Harris, I think. We never got it again, but it was wonderful stuff while it lasted.'

'But . . .' Molly wasn't interested in the tweed. Who cared about tweed when all her assumptions, all her preconceptions, were being blown out of the window?

In the end, though, it was the tweed that broke her heart. Mr

Thompson might not remember the date that her mother had left his employ, but he knew exactly when that tweed had been delivered, and it was a month before Molly had been admitted to the Home for Waifs and Strays.

She hardly knew how she got out of the room, let alone out of the department store. As she stood numbly in the street, she finally realised why people had warned her about searching for her past.

She had tried to prepare herself. Tried to convince herself she wouldn't mind, whatever she discovered. It was never going to be good news, after all. She had just wanted to know how she had become an orphan.

Well, now she did know. She wasn't an orphan at all.

And she'd had no idea how much it would hurt to discover that she had been dumped in an orphanage just because her mother, pretty little Prissy Cavanagh, had decided to marry a man rich enough to buy himself a Harris tweed suit.

Part Three

Chapter Eleven

Helen and Ward arrived back in London on 11 October. It had taken them much longer to get home than they had expected. The ports of Calais and Boulogne, despite having finally been wrested out of the hands of the tenaciously stubborn remnants of Field Marshal Rommel's army, were both too badly damaged to receive ships, and so they'd had to travel all the way down to Saint-Malo in Brittany before they could find themselves a passage back to England. And even then it was an uncomfortable journey, because the American loadmaster in charge of the port put them on a barge carrying German prisoners to Portsmouth, and they had to endure the sound of patriotic German marching songs echoing defiantly up from the bowels of the ship for almost the entire ten hours of the night crossing.

'They don't seem to realise they're in the process of losing their precious war,' the barge master remarked sourly as he and his first mate shared a rough-and-ready breakfast with Ward and Helen in the wardroom.

'They'll find out soon enough,' the first mate said confidently. 'When the Allies move on into Germany. It's surely not going to be long now. We'll soon have them on the run again.'

Helen glanced at Ward. She so hoped that would be true. But even though the naval officers were treating the Arnhem disaster as an unfortunate blip, she knew Ward feared that the Germans were unlikely to roll over easily.

'I know it's unpatriotic to say so,' he said to her later as they stood at the rail and watched the rising sun casting a pink glow over the tall chalky islets of the Needles on the south-west tip of the Isle of Wight. 'But after what we've seen in Paris, I reckon it's dangerous to underrate the Nazis. It might be expedient just now for them to give up France. But I figure it's going to take a hell of a lot to get them to give up Germany. Their fatherland.' He jerked his head down towards the hold. 'You only have to hear them sing "Die Wacht am Rhein".'

Helen hadn't been listening to the words. Her German was good, but not as good as Ward's. Now she concentrated more closely as the rousing voices reverberated through the vessel. 'Dear fatherland,' Ward murmured drily. 'Firm stands, and true, the Watch, the Watch at the Rhine.'

Helen felt a shiver pass over her skin. The sun had gone now, obscured by threatening clouds as the ship made its way cautiously through the marked channel into the Solent, and ahead of them mainland England looked dark and gloomy.

But their welcome at the Flag and Garter, when they finally arrived there later that evening, was about as far from dark and gloomy as it was possible to be.

For twenty minutes, as everyone crowded eagerly round them, toasting their safe return, Helen forgot that André was missing, and that she had come home close to despair. It was impossible to do anything but smile, and drink, and laugh at Malcolm coming tumbling downstairs in his rush to get to his father, and at Ward's dog, Lucky, barking in utter delight, and be grateful that she was once again among friends, and that she could have a bed for the night in Katy's cellar.

But then Molly came in. She was wearing a Red Cross uniform, and looked weary and rather wan, but she brightened as soon as she caught sight of the returnees. Seeing the eager question in her eyes as they kissed each other, Helen felt the dull ache she had carried in her heart since leaving Paris reassert itself.

'I never found André,' she murmured. 'He wasn't there.' She nodded at Katy, who was looking radiant encircled in Ward's arms. 'But don't say anything. I don't want to spoil the mood.'

She could see the dismay in Molly's eyes. More than anyone else, Molly had known how desperately Helen longed to see André again. It was Molly who had made the effort to bring news of André to Tunisia after she and Jen had escaped from France.

'What do you mean?' Molly whispered. 'What happened?'

Helen was tired; it had been a very long day, a very long few weeks, come to that, and she spoke without thinking. 'He'd gone off after a German SS officer called Hauptsturmführer Wessel,' she said. 'It was just before I arrived in France. We know he was in Grenoble, but that was the last anyone had heard of him.'

As soon as the words were out of her mouth, she regretted them. Molly was already looking pale; now she looked as though she was going to be sick. And belatedly Helen remembered Ward saying that Molly and Jen had known Hauptsturmführer Wessel in Italy. She could see from her friend's stricken expression that she was remembering too.

'Oh no,' Molly said. 'That's the man who . . . who Jen and I ran away from. We told André about him. How horrible he was. And André told us that if he met him in France, he would—'

'I know,' Helen interrupted quickly. 'Ward told me, but Molly, listen, I don't think that was why André went after him. Wessel had killed someone André knew, a girl in the resistance, and . . .' But she could see that Molly didn't believe her.

'And now André has disappeared,' Molly was muttering, almost to herself. 'Oh my God.' She looked up, and her eyes were wide with shock. 'I can even remember what Gefreiter Henniker called it.'

Helen stared at her in concern. She had no idea what Molly was talking about. 'What?' she asked. 'Who's Gefreiter Henniker?'

Molly shook her head. 'He was one of our guards. Gefreiter means corporal in English. He was the man who supervised me when I was working in the medical clinic at the camp. I asked him about Hauptsturmführer Wessel, and he told me to be careful, because it wasn't difficult for the Waffen-SS to make people disappear. He called it *Nacht und Nebel*.'

'Night and fog,' Helen translated. She felt a sickening sensation in her stomach and had to work hard to keep breathing normally. It sounded all too likely. André might not be dead, but he had certainly disappeared into an impenetrable dark fog.

'Oh Helen, I'm so sorry,' Molly whispered. 'I feel as though it's all my fault.'

'Of course it's not,' Helen said. 'It's just this beastly, horrible war.'

A burst of laughter erupted behind them. Angie was embracing Ward, and everyone clapped as she gave him a smacking kiss on the lips. Katy, meanwhile, with baby Caroline in her arms, looked on tolerantly, clearly so delighted about his safe return that she didn't mind who kissed him.

When things had calmed down again, Molly touched Helen on the hand. 'André is made of stern stuff,' she said quietly. 'I'm sure he'll be all right.'

Helen looked at her for a long moment, then opened her arms and stepped forward, folding her in a tight embrace. She was taller than Molly, so it was a bit uncomfortable. But it didn't matter. The embrace gave her comfort. 'Oh God, I hope so,' she said. 'I hope so.'

Molly didn't stay long in the pub. She could see that Helen was tired, and although she was putting a brave face on things, she was obviously finding the celebratory mood a bit of a strain. It certainly hadn't been the moment to tell her about her own shocking discovery.

As yet, Molly hadn't told anyone what Mr Thompson had said. Normally she would have confided in Katy or Jen; she knew they would be sympathetic, but somehow she couldn't bear to say the words, or to see the pity in their eyes. So she had merely told them casually that Mrs Bridges had turned out to be a dead end, and luckily neither of them had pressed her for details.

George, however, had been less easy to convince. He was disappointed that all his hard work had come to nothing. But in the end, Molly had managed to fob him off by saying that the only thing Mrs Bridges had remembered was that she had been an ugly baby.

George had looked cross. 'Well, that's just daft,' he had said. 'Because all babies are ugly.' And Molly had laughed gratefully. But actually, since her meeting with Mr Thompson, she hadn't felt like laughing at all. On the contrary, she felt as though an elephant was sitting on her head. Or perhaps even *in* her head. And now this news of André Cabillard was making her feel even worse. She knew it wasn't her fault, any more than her mother's defection was her fault, but somehow it felt as though it was. Perhaps if she and Jen hadn't run to André for help . . . perhaps if they hadn't told him about the horrible SS Hauptsturmführer . . . Perhaps if she hadn't been such an unattractive baby, her mother wouldn't have . . .

She shook her head crossly as she hurried across the dark street back to the Nelsons' house. She knew it was stupid to think like that, but sometimes thoughts took on a life of their own, and it was impossible to control them however much you tried.

It wasn't as if she had nothing else to worry about. Because she did. Tomorrow she was going to have to introduce George, Bella and Graham Powell to Professor Markov.

Molly had hoped to be finished with her own lesson before the children arrived at Mrs d'Arcy Billière's house, but in the event, she was still embroiled with the professor in the morning room when she glanced out of the window and spotted George and Bella standing on the terrace.

Despite George's reluctance to come at all, he and Bella had got there early, and Mrs d'Arcy Billière had clearly sent them through to wait in the garden. The rain had stopped and Molly could see George looking around with interest. Then, leaving Bella by the back door, he set off towards an ornate metal structure on the other side of the lawn. Molly had noticed it before; it seemed an odd thing to have in a garden, another example of Mrs d'Arcy Billière's exotic tastes, but it was rather attractive, all covered in climbing plants, with a seat inside. Molly had no idea what such a thing might be called: a pergola? A pagoda? Whatever it was, George had clearly decided it would make a suitable base from which to fire his catapult. Considerably dismayed, Molly was just leaning forward to see what he was aiming at when Professor Markov surged up from his chair, sending her tentative sketches of atomic structure flying across the floor.

'*No!*' he roared. '*Nyelzia!* Stop that!' And grabbing his stick, he was out through the French windows like a dose of salts.

George did indeed stop. And if Molly hadn't been convinced that the professor was about to lay into him with his stick, she might have laughed. She had never seen such an expression of horrified astonishment on the boy's face. Backing hastily into the honeysuckle-swathed depths of the pergola, he put up his hands as though to protect himself from a wild animal.

Molly didn't blame him. With his eyes gleaming with fury, his hair standing on end and his teeth bared with the effort of his sudden sprint across the lawn, the professor certainly looked as wild as any animal.

Snatching the catapult from George's apparently numbed fingers, he stood glaring at him murderously. 'What are you doing?'

'Professor, it's all right,' Molly said, running up behind him. She put a nervous hand on his arm. 'It's only Geor—'

But the Russian shook her off and brandished the catapult threateningly in front of George's terrified face. 'I asked what you were doing,' he snarled.

'It was only a stupid bird,' George said in a slightly trembling voice. His eyes flicked towards Mrs d'Arcy Billière's washing line. 'It was just sitting there on the line, and I thought—'

'*Only a stupid bird*?' Professor Markov repeated in a terrible voice. 'Do you even know what sort of bird it was?'

George blinked owlishly. 'No,' he muttered bravely. 'But—'

The professor grabbed his arm and hauled him out of the pergola. He pointed up at the bird, which was now swooping about unconcernedly overhead. 'That bird is a swallow,' he said. 'And the reason it is flying around like that is that it's feeding itself in preparation for a long journey to Africa, where it will spend the winter.' He glowered at George. 'Do you know how to get to Africa?'

George shook his head.

The professor raised his bushy eyebrows. 'But the swallow does,' he said. 'So who is the stupid one now?'

And this time Molly really did have to bite her lip to stop herself laughing.

To her astonishment, she saw that George was grinning. 'Me?' he said.

Then she saw the twinkle in Professor Markov's eyes as he nodded his shaggy head. 'But you won't be once you have studied with me,' he said. 'Instead of science, we will start with geography. We will look at all the countries the swallow has to pass through on its dangerous journey to Africa.'

'But why does it bother to go to Africa if it's so dangerous?' George asked, tilting his head back to look at the bird again. 'Why doesn't it just stay here?'

Molly didn't hear the professor's reply, but as she watched him and George walking companionably back up the lawn, she relaxed. Whether he had meant to or not, Professor Markov had certainly got George's attention.

A moment later, Bella fell under his spell too. The girl was still standing by the door, her heart-shaped face pale with apprehension. Molly noticed the professor's start of surprise as he caught sight of her, and realised that even he was not immune to her beauty, but he held out his hand solemnly as he approached. 'So,' he said. 'I suppose you are the girl who does not talk?'

Bella nodded nervously.

He gave her one of his very white smiles. 'Then I think we will get along fine,' he said. 'Because I like to talk all the time.' He winked. 'But you will have to be strong. You will have to learn to bang on the table if you don't understand, or if you want to write down a question.'

In the hallway, Mrs d'Arcy Billière was making laboured conversation with Graham Powell. She glanced at Molly rather desperately as they came in. While Molly made the introductions, hoping that George would heed the warning she had given him earlier and refrain from making some inopportune remark about Graham Powell's appearance or his wheelchair, the professor studied the unfortunate young man thoughtfully. But he didn't make any reference to Graham's disability, nor did he attempt to startle him into submission, or indeed to charm him, as he had with the children. He just nodded towards the room with the huge table.

'Go in,' he said. 'I will be with you as soon as I've finished talking to the children. Perhaps while you wait you could tidy up the papers on the table. And then you can tell me whether you feel Molly has drawn her atomic diagrams correctly.'

Turning back to Molly, he gave the tiniest flicker of a wink, and suddenly Molly wanted to hug him. It's going to be all right, she thought as she hurried back down Lavender Road on her way to work. She wasn't sure about Graham Powell, but George and Bella certainly seemed to have taken a shine to the professor, and he appeared to know exactly how to deal with them. Molly sighed. If only she knew as well how to deal with her own problems.

Her shoulders slumped at the thought. And as she turned the corner onto Lavender Hill, the elephant climbed back into her head.

Helen wasn't feeling particularly cheerful that morning either. She had been away from London nearly a year, and was shocked by the deterioration in the city. Paris had been magnificent in comparison. Even though people there had been suffering from lack of food and electricity, and some of the squares had been barricaded with barbed wire, all the buildings had still been intact. And instead of wearing their old clothes to death in order to help the war effort, Parisians had apparently felt it was their duty to use every scrap of new material and adornment they could lay hands on in order to deprive the Germans of it. As a result, the crowds on the boulevards in the liberated French capital had looked chic and vibrant, whereas on the streets of London, apart from those in uniform, everyone was looking distinctly grey and dowdy.

And in the offices of the SOE in Baker Street, they looked distinctly grim as well.

Helen's former boss Angus McNaughton was angry that she had stopped off in Paris instead of coming straight back to London as requested, and he was even angrier that she had been to Avenue Hoch.

'But Ward Frazer was there too,' Helen protested, 'and—'

'Frazer was there in a completely different capacity. He should have known better than to give you access to such highly sensitive material.'

'But I wanted to see if I could find out the whereabouts of André Cabillard,' Helen said.

'I know perfectly well what you were doing,' Angus snapped. 'But you had no right to be there.'

The fact that she had been given permission by General de Lattre de Tassigny annoyed him even more.

'What on earth has it got to do with him?' he said. 'How dare you let the French poke their noses into our business?'

And finally Helen realised what the problem was. The SOE bigwigs were desperately trying to cover up the evidence of their failings. They trusted Ward to keep his mouth shut about what he had found out at Avenue Hoch, but despite Helen's high security clearance, they didn't trust her, despite all she had done for them in the past.

And that annoyed her. It annoyed her so much that she lost her temper.

'You know, I'm not surprised André kept well clear of the SOE once he was back in France,' she said angrily. She pointed upstairs, to where the agent handlers had their offices. 'I wonder how many other agents and *maquisards* currently in German prisons wish that they had made sure that people here actually knew what they were talking about.'

'That's quite enough,' Angus said. 'You're becoming hysterical.

You've done good work for us in the past, and we are grateful for that, but I can see that your affection for Cabillard has clouded your judgement. I therefore think that the moment has come for us to part company.'

He stubbed out his cigarette and looked up at her coldly. 'I hope I don't need to remind you that you are still bound by the Official Secrets Act.'

Helen stared at him. 'What?' She could hardly believe it. 'Are you telling me that you've made me come all the way back from France and now you're going to fire me?'

Angus McNaughton stood up and came round his desk to open the door. 'Yes,' he said. 'That's exactly what I'm telling you.'

Helen was furious. For once her calm good manners deserted her, and she stormed out of the office and down the stairs without even seeing the astonished glances that followed her.

Back on the street, she stopped and took stock. She felt utterly betrayed. She hadn't intended to rock the boat. She certainly hadn't intended to fall out with Angus McNaughton. All she had been trying to do was find out what had happened to André, who, after all, had once been an SOE agent himself.

As she stood there seething, she felt a touch on her arm and realised that Vera Atkins was standing at her elbow. Miss Atkins was the person responsible for the well-being of the female agents. It was she who gave them their final briefings before they were dispatched to France. Helen had always thought of her as an ally, but now she regarded her with suspicion.

'I suppose Angus sent you after me to make sure I keep my mouth shut,' she said. 'To be honest, I'm surprised he didn't just shoot me there and then.'

Vera Atkins shook her head. 'I know you won't make trouble,' she said. 'You are too sensible for that. Angus knows it too.'

'Then instead of sacking me, why won't he help me?'

Vera Atkins lifted her shoulders slightly. 'Things are difficult here at the moment. Mistakes have been made. Serious mistakes. Of course, nobody wants to admit that. But I can assure you, steps are being taken to find the missing agents. André Cabillard is by no means the only one.' She paused for a second, and when she spoke again, Helen could hear the suppressed emotion in her voice. 'There are plenty of girls unaccounted for too. Girls I knew well. And I will be doing everything in my power to find out where they are and get them back safely.'

'Oh, really?' Helen snapped. 'And what if they are dead already? I assume even the SOE must have heard of the Nazi death camps by now?'

Miss Atkins ignored her sarcasm. 'Then they will have died in the service of their country. And in due course, the people responsible will be brought to account.'

Helen thought back to the American intelligence officer in France, to the hordes of German prisoners sitting disconsolately in fields behind lines of barbed wire. It was going to be a mammoth task to work out who had done what, let alone find the evidence to prove it. 'All of them?' she said sceptically. 'And in any case, by then the war will be over. We need to do something *now*. While there's a chance that at least some of our agents might still be alive.'

Vera Atkins nodded. 'I am hoping to go to France myself shortly. I will let you know if I hear anything.'

It wasn't much, but it was something. At least there was someone at the SOE slightly on her side.

As she walked away, Helen suddenly wished she could talk to her father. She hadn't seen him for ages, and she had so much to tell him. But she had no idea where he was. He had moved to America earlier in the war to act as a kind of unofficial ambassador in Washington on behalf of Winston Churchill. But he also travelled a lot, attending the various wartime conferences and summits between the prime minister and President Roosevelt.

On an impulse, instead of catching the bus back to Victoria from Marble Arch, Helen turned left onto Oxford Street, then cut down through Hanover Square and made her way onto Regent Street and into St James's, the district where most of the London gentlemen's clubs were situated. Since their substantial house in Mayfair had been requisitioned in 1941, Lord de Burrel always stayed at his club whenever he passed through London.

Helen knew the doorman at her father's club quite well. She had often called there earlier in the war, and even though he hadn't seen her for over a year, he recognised her at once. 'I'm sorry, Lady Helen,' he said. 'You've just missed him. He was here, but he left a couple of days ago.'

Helen didn't even try to hide her disappointment. 'Did he by any chance say where he was going, or when he might be back?'

The doorman shook his head. 'No, he didn't.' But then, taking pity on her, he lowered his voice. 'Putting two and two together, I reckon as he's gone somewhere with the prime minister, because he ordered a taxi to Northolt airport and that's where the PM always flies from.'

Helen smiled. So much for confidentiality, she thought. But at least it sounded as though her father might be back again in the not-too-distant future, so she left a message for him telling him where she was staying.

Later that day, when she and Katy were listening to the evening news on the wireless, it was given out that Mr Churchill had arrived in Moscow for talks with Marshal Stalin.

'That's probably where Daddy is, then,' Helen said.

'Goodness,' Katy said. 'Stalin's even more scary than Molly's professor. I wonder what your father will make of him.'

Helen shook her head. 'I can't imagine. But he's very fond of vodka and caviar, so I expect he's enjoying himself.' Unlike me, she thought. At that precise moment, it was hard to imagine ever enjoying herself again.

Perhaps hearing the wry tone in her voice, Katy glanced at her sympathetically. She had been outraged to hear what had happened at the SOE. 'That's absolutely monstrous,' she had said. 'How dare they treat you so badly?'

Ward, when he came in later, was more sanguine. 'Angus McNaughton has always been a fool,' he said. 'I expect he's worried about his own job. The way things are going, they're not going to need a French section much longer. Do you want me to see if you can come over to MI19 to help with screening the Nazi POWs? We're looking for people who can speak German. Plus it would give you a chance to keep your eyes open for any sign of Hauptsturmführer Wessel.'

Helen stared at him gratefully. 'That would be brilliant,' she said. And for the first time in weeks, she felt the tiniest flicker of hope.

Jen had been doing everything she could to avoid having to cook supper at Mrs d'Arcy Billière's. She had attended the communal evening meal several times now, and although she had never been keen on foreign food, she had realised that the standard was quite high. She might not particularly like the matzo ball soup, potato kugel or burnt *tahdig* rice Elsa cooked, but they were at least edible and clearly well made. And Mrs d'Arcy's mushroom stroganoff was delicious. Her Russian salad, despite bearing a close resemblance to vomit in appearance, was actually quite tasty too. Jen's worst moment had been when she was invited to try some of Elsa's mother's *maror*, which turned out to be made from raw horseradish and nearly blew her head off. To everyone's amusement, she had been obliged to run upstairs to the bathroom to spit it out, and had spent the next ten minutes gargling with cold water before her eyes stopped streaming.

After that, she had made excuses to be out for several nights in a row, cadging meals off Katy and Ward instead. Once, she and Molly had gone to the pictures and treated themselves to a packet of chips on the way home. But she couldn't avoid it for ever, and at breakfast that morning, it had been made clear that it was her turn.

'You don't need to shop,' Mrs d'Arcy Billière said. 'Elsa's mother has done that for you. But perhaps tonight when you come home from RADA, you can cook for us?'

'Yes, yes,' Elsa's mother agreed. 'We look forward to eating some English food for a change.'

Jen had a nasty feeling that scrambled egg on toast, even if she could lay hands on any eggs, which was unlikely, wasn't going to do the trick.

Later that afternoon, faced with a lump of some bony unidentifiable meat, ten potatoes, ten carrots and a cabbage, her courage failed her. Loading the whole lot up on a tray, she ran it down the street to her mother's house.

But to her dismay, Joyce wasn't there. She had taken Bella to see Dr Goodacre at the hospital. So in the end it was Angie who cooked the meal, and Gino who carried it back to Mrs d'Arcy Billière's house in a huge saucepan borrowed from the café.

'Angie say is called hotpot,' he said. 'And I think is right because I have burnt the finger. See, the skin, she is come away?'

'Then for goodness' sake run it under the tap,' Jen said irritably. Gino's terrible English got on her nerves. But at least she had something to serve. 'And tell Angie thank you, I'll bring the saucepan back tomorrow.'

Unfortunately, she forgot to return the saucepan, which caused her to get a flea in her ear from her mother a couple of days later. 'It's typical of you to shirk your responsibilities. Why should Angie cook for you? That's the last time you're using my equipment. I needed that saucepan yesterday. Not that you'd care.'

And Jen didn't care. The hotpot had been quite a success, so she had secretly arranged with Angie that, in return for a few drinks at the pub, next time Jen's turn came round, Angie would come and cook something for her in Mrs d'Arcy Billière's kitchen. Unless Henry came home first, in which case she would be off the hook. Because as soon as she and Henry were married, she would never have to cook for that bizarre household ever again.

Helen was worried about Molly. What with her work at the Red Cross, helping out in the pub, studying in the library and her lessons with the mad professor, she never seemed to have a moment to chat. Nevertheless, Helen could tell that she wasn't on her usual good form. At first she thought it might be something to do with Callum Frazer. She had guessed in Tunisia that Molly had fallen for him rather harder than she let on. But it didn't seem to be that, because when she asked Molly if she'd heard from him since she'd got back, Molly nodded and flushed slightly. 'Yes,' she whispered. 'But please don't tell anyone. I'm trying to keep it a secret.'

But there was something about the way she turned quickly away to wash up some glasses that made Helen suspect Callum might not be Molly's only secret.

Helen had already heard about Molly's apparently abortive attempt to find out who her mother was, but it was only when she spoke to George that she wondered if there was more to it than met the eye. Helen had got to know George when she had been a lodger at the Nelsons earlier in the war, and she couldn't believe how much he had grown in her absence. 'Goodness,' she said. 'I would hardly have recognised you. Last time I saw you, you were a grubby little schoolboy.'

George looked pleased. 'Well, I'm not a schoolboy any more,' he said. 'I have a private tutor now. A Russian professor.'

'So I've heard,' Helen said. 'Everyone says he's rather frightening. But I gather you get on very well with him. And I hear you've been helping Molly find out about her mother, too?'

George frowned. 'Yes, I have,' he said. 'And it's really annoying. Because I'm sure Mrs Bridges knew something. I just don't think Molly can have asked the right questions. But when I suggested that I went to see her again, Molly got cross and told me to mind my own business. And that's not fair, because it was me that found Mrs Bridges in the first place.'

The following day, Helen asked Molly to join her for a cup of tea in the café. 'You don't have to tell me if you don't want to,' she said quietly. 'But I can see there's something wrong. Is it something to do with what Mrs Bridges told you about your mother?'

Molly's eyes flew open. 'How did you know?' she asked.

Helen gave a slight grimace. 'George told me about her. He said

197

you'd got cross with him after you'd been to see her, and, well, that didn't sound like you.'

Molly was silent for a minute. Helen didn't push her. She knew Molly would tell her if she wanted to, and if she didn't, well, then she would know that there was something seriously wrong.

And in the end, Molly did tell her. She told her exactly what had happened at the department store. She spoke in a low voice, and in a light, wry tone, as though she didn't care. But Helen could see from the whiteness of the fingers clenched round her cup that deep down she cared very much.

'Oh my goodness,' she exclaimed when Molly had finished. 'So as far as you know, your mother is still alive?'

Molly nodded.

'But you don't want to find out for sure?'

'No, I don't,' Molly said. She shrugged. 'The fact that she put me into an orphanage shows she didn't care about me. So why should I care about her?'

Why indeed, Helen thought. 'There might be some other explanation,' she said mildly. Although she couldn't quite imagine what that might be. Clearly nor could Molly.

'No,' Molly said. She lifted her chin. 'That's the end of the road as far as I'm concerned. I'm fine as I am. I don't need a mother.'

Helen could hear the stubborn pride in her voice, but she also heard the slight choke of emotion, and her heart bled for her.

'Who needs mothers?' Helen said lightly. 'I've never had one either. At least not since I was five.' She paused for a moment, then leaned forward. 'But seriously, Molly, if you want me to help you find her at any time, just let me know.'

'Thank you,' Molly said. 'But I'd much rather help *you* find André. Don't forget, I'm part of the Red Cross now, and it's the International Red Cross who visit prison camps in Germany. I've been thinking, maybe we could give them his name and ask them to look out for him?'

It was Helen's turn to clench her fingers round her cup. 'Oh

Molly,' she said, and now it was her voice that sounded choked. 'Would you?'

Molly nodded. 'I'll ask Mr Sparrow,' she said.

Helen blinked. 'Who on earth is Mr Sparrow?'

'He's my boss,' Molly said. 'I don't like him very much. But I think that's partly because he looks like Adolf Hitler.'

Helen felt a gurgle of laughter in her chest. 'He can't do,' she said.

'No, honestly, he does,' Molly insisted.

It felt odd to laugh, Helen thought; she hadn't done it for so long, and it made her feel guilty. But just now it was a case of laugh, or cry.

'What are you two giggling about?' Angie asked as she passed their table with a tray of dirty dishes.

'I'm not quite sure,' Molly said. 'Adolf Hitler, I think.'

And for some reason, that made Helen laugh even more.

Chapter Twelve

True to his word, Ward Frazer organised an interview for Helen at MI19's Prisoner of War Interrogation Section, which, due to some judicious requisitioning of buildings, had its headquarters in the fashionable area of Kensington Park Gardens. Lieutenant Colonel Jones, the Intelligence Corps officer who interviewed her, was brisk and unemotional. He seemed impressed both with her recent work in France and with her languages. No mention was made of her untimely exit from the SOE, but the fact that Ward had recommended her clearly stood her in good stead.

'At some stage we might think about training you up as an interrogator,' Colonel Jones said. 'But currently our most pressing need is for help with administration, so as, being a girl, you presumably know how to type, I think it's best if you start at Kempton Park.'

He explained that on disembarkation at English ports, enemy prisoners were first deloused at reception centres, and then transported to what were known as command cages. These were holding facilities where the prisoners were assessed and, in some cases, interrogated for information. Due to the enormous numbers arriving every day, nine transit cages had now been established in various parts of the country, one of the largest being at Kempton Park racecourse to the west of London.

After being interviewed, and categorised in relation to the

perceived level of their support for Hitler's National Socialist philosophy, prisoners were then dispatched to appropriate permanent prisoner-of-war camps around the country.

'It's not a foolproof system,' Colonel Jones said. 'I'm sure we have made mistakes. Putting Nazi hardliners in less secure camps with politically indifferent enlisted men, and so on, but given the unanticipatedly large through-put, and the limited number of trained interrogators at our disposal, we are just having to do the best we can.'

Four days later, once again wearing her FANY uniform, Helen found herself at Kempton Park racecourse. In the distance, she could see the double perimeter fence and sentry towers that enclosed the two hundred or so tents that made up the holding camp. But the office to which she had been allocated was in the racecourse building itself. She shared it with three other girls. Their job was to compare endless lists of German prisoners' names, tick off the ones who had been interviewed, note down their grading and arrange onward transport to whichever POW camp they were allocated to.

In other circumstances Helen might have been peeved that she had been given such a monotonous job, but she was well used to the chauvinism of the British military, and in any case, it did at least give her access to the names of all prisoners who were passing through the camp. As Ward had suggested, there was a remote chance that one day the name Hauptsturmführer Wessel might pop up, and then she would be able to get someone to interrogate him about his dealings with André.

The other benefit was that, although she was required to work extraordinarily long hours, she was able to get back to Lavender Road each evening, unlike Ward himself, whose interrogation job took him to camps all over the country.

As a result, Helen rarely saw him, but she knew that he too would be keeping an ear open for any mention of André or his SS adversary. She also knew that he had asked his contacts at Bletchley Park to listen out for their names as well.

As yet nothing had borne fruit, so all Helen could do was get on with her new job, and hope that Molly would make better progress with the Red Cross.

Mr Sparrow had been pleased when Molly asked if he knew how to contact the International Red Cross in Geneva. 'Yes, of course,' he had said with self-important pride. 'In fact my wife works at the Wounded, Missing and Relatives Department in Belgrave Square. But I know they are run off their feet with enquiries at the moment, so perhaps it would be easiest if I asked her to look into it herself.' Being a stickler for detail, he carefully wrote down everything Molly knew about André, and then asked for a description.

Molly cast her mind back to the night nine months ago when she had sat in the Domaine Saint-Jean kitchen, watching André, with his two lovely dogs at his feet, plotting her and Jen's escape from France, but there was something about André Cabillard that defied description. He wasn't film-star handsome in the way Ward Frazer was; his nose was a little too large, his chin too strong, but he had a smile to die for, and a strength and vitality and masculine charm that made him one of the most attractive men Molly had ever seen.

'He's quite tall,' she had said in the end. 'About six foot. Dark hair. Strong face. Midnight-blue eyes. Long lashes. Good teeth. Charming smile. He's cool and clever, and very brave. And he speaks almost fluent English.'

Mr Sparrow had looked rather startled. 'My word,' he said. 'It sounds as though your friend has got herself quite a catch.'

The following day, he reported to Molly that his wife had cabled André's details to the International Committee of the Red Cross in Geneva. All she and Helen could do now, was wait.

And while they waited, Molly became even more impressed with Professor Markov's teaching, and the miraculous way he was somehow inspiring George to become increasingly interested in academic studies too, especially algebra and nature study. Only that morning, George had told her that a swallow weighed less than a box of matches, yet somehow managed to travel a thousand miles to Africa and back each year.

In the meantime, the Allies continued to advance towards Germany. On 21 October, after a long and bloody siege, the German border city of Aachen was taken. At first it seemed like good news, but the Allies had now come up against the heavily fortified Siegfried Line, which ran down the western German border and consisted of interconnected forts, bunkers, 'dragon's teeth' anti-tank obstacles, barbed-wire entanglements and minefields, sometimes well over ten miles deep.

It clearly wasn't going to be easy for the Allies to roll on into Germany, but at least by the end of October, the Germans had been routed from Belgium, which people hoped would mean the end of V-1 doodlebugs, and the new 'flying gas mains'.

However, that was not the case. On 6 November, just as everyone was heaving a sigh of relief, a massive rocket landed on Tooting Common, creating a huge crater. Thankfully nobody died in that incident, but two weeks later, soon after the government had belatedly admitted that these even more destructive V-2 rockets were being fired from German-occupied Holland, another landed on Hazelhurst Road, killing thirty-five people and injuring over a hundred.

Molly spent that entire day at the site. There were so many casualties that local boys were roped in to carry stretchers. Less acute cases were loaded onto converted Green Line buses and sent to outlying hospitals in order to free up space in the local hospitals for the more seriously injured.

It was a long, horrible day, and at the end of it, Molly wished she had been able to fly away to Africa with Professor Markov's swallows. She wished it even more when she arrived back at the pub to find Katy in a state of shock because she had just opened a letter from Ward's uncle, announcing he was coming to London.

'He claims to be coming on business,' Katy cried. 'But I'm sure he's really hoping to try to persuade Ward to go back to Canada.

And you know what a terrifying man he is. But I don't want to go and live in Canada.'

Molly had her own reasons to be nervous of Ward's uncle – Callum's father – but she tried to hide her sudden jolt of apprehension. 'When's he coming?' she asked.

'Sometime in December,' Katy wailed. 'He says he's hoping to see Callum, too.'

Molly gaped at her. '*Callum?*' She could hardly believe her ears. Was Callum coming to England? Her heart started thumping wildly, and it wasn't until she saw Katy looking at her oddly that she realised that, in her excitement, she had almost shouted his name.

She knew at once from the look on her face that Katy was leaping to the wrong conclusion. Or perhaps the right one.

'It's not what you think,' she said quickly. 'We're just friends.'

But Katy knew her too well. 'Molly, you dark horse,' she said. 'I knew you liked him, but I didn't know anything had happened between you.'

Molly was too tired after her long day to wriggle out of it. 'Nothing has happened,' she said weakly. 'At least not very much. But he has written to me since I got back, and . . .'

'And what?' Katy asked eagerly. 'Are we going to be cousins-in-law?'

Molly felt the last remnant of energy drain out of her. 'If only,' she said. She sat wearily down on a bar stool and put her head in her hands.

'What's the matter?' Katy asked in quick concern. 'Molly, are you all right?'

'No,' Molly mumbled through her fingers. 'I'm not. I'm madly in love with Callum, and I think he quite likes me too.' She looked up pitifully. 'But seriously, can you imagine him marrying someone like me?'

'Well, Ward married me,' Katy said stoutly. 'So I don't see why Callum can't marry you.'

Molly looked at her irritably. 'Oh come on, Katy. It's completely different. Ward's older than Callum. He was already estranged from his parents when he married you. But Callum loves his parents, and he would never want to do anything to upset them.'

She could tell from Katy's compassionate look that she knew she was right. 'I'll talk to Ward,' she said. 'See what he thinks.'

'No!' Once again, Molly almost shouted the word. 'No, Katy, please don't say anything to Ward. Or anyone else,' she added quickly. 'I'll feel self-conscious enough as it is without everyone watching to see what might, or more likely might not, be happening.'

Katy looked at her for a long moment, then sighed. 'All right,' she said. 'I'll try not to tell him. But to be honest, I don't find it very easy to keep secrets from Ward.'

'Well, you'd better keep this one,' Molly said fiercely. 'Or I'll tell Mr Maurice Frazer that it's your dearest wish to up sticks and go and live in Canada.'

At first Joyce was pleased that Bella seemed to be enjoying her lessons with the Russian professor. She had checked with her friend Dr Goodacre, Bella's doctor, whether he thought it was a good idea, and he had been highly enthusiastic.

'Oh yes,' he had said at once. 'It might be just the thing she needs. She's a bright little thing, and if she gets interested in her studies, then perhaps her subconscious mind will forget whatever private trauma it is that's currently inhibiting her speech.'

'Professor Markov is a very odd man,' Joyce had said dubiously. 'Very foreign and eccentric.'

But Dr Goodacre had just laughed. 'The Russian is a fiery species,' he said. 'A combination of the Slav, the Mongol and the Cossack. Look at the way they fight. But if Bella takes to him, then I think the mental stimulation would be beneficial.'

Bella *had* taken to him. But now, three weeks later, Joyce was worried that the girl was studying too much.

'I can't think it's good for her,' she remarked to Albert as they listened to the variety show *Monday Night At Seven*, introduced by the irritatingly jolly Judy Shirley. Angie and Gino had gone over to the pub. Bella, of course, was upstairs reading.

None of Joyce's own children had ever been remotely interested in books. Even Jen had only read the books needed to pass her school exams. The only thing Angie ever read was magazines, and Joyce doubted if any of the boys had ever read through an entire book in their lives.

'This morning I found her in the library reading a book about the Zulu war,' she said.

Albert chuckled. 'Well, I believe that's George Nelson's fault,' he said. 'I gather that Professor Markov has been teaching them about Africa, and George has become fascinated by the Zulu warriors.'

Joyce looked at him in dismay. 'Oh no,' she said. 'That boy's always been a bloodthirsty little devil. The next thing we know, he'll have painted himself black and we'll find him running about with a spear in a leopardskin jockstrap, trying to kill white men.'

Albert had been sipping at his evening mug of Horlicks, but now he gave a choke of laughter. Setting the drink down with a shaking hand, he took out a handkerchief and wiped his eyes.

'My dear Joyce,' he gasped. 'You'll be the death of me one of these days.'

Joyce looked at him affectionately. She liked making him laugh. Not that she had meant to on this occasion. She was genuinely worried about Bella, and not just because of the reading. When the war ended — which it seemed to be about to do, now that the Allies were poised on the German border — her sons would come home. Not only was there not going to be room for them in the house, but the younger two, Paul and Pete, would probably fall madly in love with Bella. It wasn't as though Joyce had a great big house like Mrs Rutherford or Mrs d'Arcy Billière. She didn't even have an indoor bathroom, let alone a cellar she could kit out with extra beds as Katy had done in the pub.

Albert had owned his own house on the other side of the road, of course. But both it and the house next door to it, where Bella and her unfortunate mother had lived, were still in ruins. As indeed was the house belonging to Ward Frazer's aunts, further up the street beyond the pub. And despite various promises of compensation and war reparations, there was no sign yet of the government stepping in to rebuild them.

Then another worrying thought occurred to her. In August, Gino had received a letter from his parents in Italy. It had been forwarded on by the Red Cross from his former POW camp in Devon. Joyce had no idea what it said, because it was written in Italian, and Gino was incapable of translating, but his delight at hearing from his family after all this time was evident. She had never seen a grown man cry before, but Gino had blubbed tears of joy for about half an hour.

'What if Angie and Gino decide to go and live in Italy?' she said now. For all she knew, there might be a house waiting for him there, and work.

She would hate that more than anything. Somewhat to her surprise, she had grown fond of Gino. He might be cack handed, a terrible cook and hopeless at English, but he was a good-hearted boy in his way. And the idea of losing Angie's companionship and her ever-ready good humour was quite awful. Not least because over the past year she had become indispensable in the café.

Albert looked startled by the sudden change of subject. 'Well, if they do, they do,' he said calmly. 'It will be their choice. But there's no need to fret about it now. It won't happen for a good while yet. Certainly not until the war is well and truly over.'

Joyce was already fretting about it, though. 'I don't want it to happen at all,' she said plaintively.

Albert reached over and patted her hand. He smiled reassuringly, and gave her a sly wink. 'Then we'd better start thinking of ways to make them want to stay,' he said.

Winston Churchill had got back from Russia in late October, but Helen's father had stopped off for diplomatic meetings in North Africa on the way home, so it wasn't until the evening of 20

November that he finally appeared at the Flag and Garter in response to the note she had left at his club.

Helen was upstairs putting Malcolm and Caroline to bed when he arrived, and when Katy called up excitedly that there was someone to see her, she almost dropped the baby. For a wild, mad second she thought it was going to be André, but her father was a good second best, and she was delighted to see him.

She had been feeling increasingly depressed and hopeless over the last couple of weeks, and a short letter from Monsieur Cabillard a couple of days ago hadn't helped. He had thanked her most kindly for writing to him from Paris and told her that, apart from that fact that the post van had been discovered just outside Besançon with a bullet hole through the window, he had no further news of André. Raoul had now returned to the Domaine to help with the grape harvest.

That night, for the first time, Helen had wept silent bitter tears into her pillow. But now, suddenly, her father's easy embrace, the warm familiar scent of him, a mixture of expensive cologne and cigar smoke, lifted her spirits immeasurably.

He had already equipped himself with a gin and tonic. 'Now, my dear,' he said as he quickly downed it. 'Where around here can we go and eat? I've been in the War Rooms all day today, and all you get down there is a dry cheese sandwich.'

Helen smiled; she couldn't envisage her father eating a dry cheese sandwich — he had always been a bit of a bon viveur — but nor could she imagine where she could take him to eat locally.

She heard Katy give a slight giggle behind her. 'Angie and Gino are doing one of their Italian evenings in the café tonight,' she murmured. 'You could go there. Angie would be thrilled.'

Helen eyed her dubiously. She had heard about Angie and Gino's pasta dinners, and couldn't believe they were quite as bad as everyone said.

'All right,' she said bravely. 'We will.'

Angie was indeed thrilled. 'Oh, I must go and tell Gino,' she said breathlessly as she showed them to a table. 'We've never had a lord in here before.'

Helen tried to avoid her father's eye. 'But Molly told me you had a Russian prince in here on your first night,' she objected.

Angie looked surprised. 'Oh, but he was a foreigner,' she said. 'Princes may be two a penny in Russia for all I know. But your father is the real thing. A real live lord.'

'It sounds as though she's had a few dead ones in,' her father murmured as he and Helen sat down at a neatly laid table for two. 'I hope that's not going to be a reflection on the food.'

That was one of the many things Helen loved about her father. He wore his rank very lightly. His languid upper-class accent and well-bred manners spoke for themselves, but he never stood on his dignity. Indeed, when Gino emerged, pink and sweating, from the kitchen, her father shook his hand with great affability, and even spoke a few words to him in Italian.

'I didn't know you spoke Italian,' Helen said when Gino had taken himself off. She knew her father spoke French, of course, and some Spanish, but she had never previously heard him conversing in Italian.

'I don't,' he said. 'But I recently spent a few days in Naples with Winnie, and it's an easy language to pick up.' He smiled as he unfolded his napkin. 'I wish I could say the same for Russian. That bugger Stalin was all smiles, and of course the interpreters told us everything we wanted to hear, but I'm convinced it would have been a different matter if any of us had been able to understand what he was really saying.' He gave a wry laugh. 'Mind you, the amount of vodka they plied us with, I'm not sure any of us would have been much the wiser anyway.'

Helen laughed. 'You should ask Molly to get Professor Markov to give you some Russian lessons,' she said. She had told him about Molly's unorthodox school on the way to the café. It was lovely to see her father, but his sudden appearance had caught her by surprise, and she felt she needed a moment to gather some emotional equilibrium before telling him about André. The last thing she wanted was to start weeping over her pasta.

Helen had been joking about the idea of Russian lessons, but to her surprise, her father took her seriously. 'Actually, that's not a bad idea,' he said. 'Unfortunately I've got to go back to the States early next week. But I'll be here again in the new year. Perhaps I'll have a go at it then.'

Helen was conscious of a stab of dismay. She had hoped he would be staying in England long enough to make some enquiries on her behalf among his friends in high places. She sat in silence as Angie plonked two plates of food in front of them.

'*Buon appetito*,' Angie intoned carefully. 'That's what Gino told me to say,' she added confidingly. She nodded at the plates. 'I know it's a bit of an odd colour, but it's nicer than it looks. And we've got some rather tasty sago for afters.'

Angie was right, the food didn't look all that appetising. The strips of home-made pasta were grey and flaccid, and the beetroot sauce was a shocking shade of pink.

Helen saw her father eyeing it dubiously. '*Buon appetito* indeed,' he said, as he took a drink of the water Angie had thoughtfully provided, and bravely lifted his fork.

Having swallowed the first mouthful with a slight wince, he looked up and caught Helen's gaze across the table.

'So,' he said meditatively. 'Are you going to tell me? Or am I going to have to beat it out of you with some overcooked tagliatelle?'

Helen wasn't ready. She tried to pretend she didn't know what he was talking about. 'Tell you what?' she asked.

'Why you are looking so sad,' he said.

In the end, she barely tasted the pasta. Afterwards she couldn't have said whether it was good or not. Her father listened to her story in compassionate silence.

When Angie had cleared away their plates, he took a silver cigar case out of his pocket and lit himself a fat cigar. 'Life is full of surprises,' he said. 'Some good, some bad. And that beetroot sauce was surprisingly good.' He smiled, and Helen couldn't help smiling back.

'That's better,' he said. He studied the tip of the cigar for a moment, then lifted his gaze, his eyes narrowed slightly against the smoke. 'The only advice I can give you, my darling girl, is to stay strong. It's clearly not good news, but you don't know yet that it's bad news. Really bad, I mean.' He drew on his cigar and exhaled slowly. 'If and when that moment comes, I give you full permission to mourn. But until then, you should try to stay hopeful. I know it's not easy. But life isn't easy, especially when love is involved.'

And now Helen's eyes did fill up. He knew what he was talking about. He had lost her mother to tuberculosis after only a few years of marriage. And even though he had always led the high life, often with a glamorous woman on his arm, he had never married again.

'Of course I will ask around,' he went on. 'But I am not optimistic. We have no dialogue with Hitler's regime. No ambassador. Nothing. Young Molly is right. Just now your best bet is the International Red Cross.'

Helen flinched, but oddly, his frank, unemotional reaction reassured her. Her father had never babied her. He had always treated her as an equal even when she had been a child. And although he had always been a good father to her, he had never spoiled her, much preferring her to learn to stand on her own two feet. So she was surprised when he leaned forward and put his hand over hers. 'I don't like the idea of you sleeping in a rat-infested cellar,' he said. 'Would it help if I got you a little flat of your own somewhere?'

For a second, Helen was tempted, but not for long. She didn't particularly like sleeping in the Flag and Garter cellar, but its subterranean austerity suited her mood, and living in the pub gave her something useful to do in the evenings, helping in the bar, or putting the children to bed. Anything to keep her mind off what might be happening to André. It wasn't exactly penance, but it wouldn't feel right living in luxury when André was almost certainly living in very different conditions, if indeed he was still alive. Letting her father find her a nice apartment would feel like giving in.

'No,' she said. 'No, I'm fine there. There aren't actually any rats. Katy and Ward's dog sees to that. But thank you. And thank you for listening.'

He smiled. 'That's what fathers are for.' He squeezed her hand. 'And now, my dear, I suggest we both brace ourselves, because here comes your young friend, and she's carrying two dishes of something that looks suspiciously like frog spawn.'

Whether it was relief of unburdening herself to her father, the starchy food, or the two brandies he'd bought her back at the pub while they talked about Aunt Isabelle, Helen slept like a log that night, and found it hard to wake up. It was only Malcolm trundling down the cellar stairs to bounce on her camp bed that finally roused her.

'Mummy says you'll be late for work,' he said.

When she got to Kempton Park, having had to run through sleety rain all the way from the station to the racecourse, she still felt heavy eyed. So when her boss, Captain Kirkwood, complained that nobody had filed away the previous three weeks' lists, Helen volunteered to do it. She knew the other girls hated filing and, afraid that she might fall asleep at her desk any moment, she was glad of the excuse to get up and walk around.

It was even more brain-numbingly boring work than usual, but Helen stuck at it, and only stopped when one of the other girls brought her a cup of almost undrinkable army coffee at elevenses time. It was as she leant wearily on one of the metal filing cabinets, wishing she was back in Paris, where if nothing else you could at least get a decent cup of coffee, that her eye was caught by a name in the topmost list of the pile still waiting to be filed.

Gefreiter Henniker.

Why did that ring a bell? It took her sluggish brain a moment to make the connection, and then suddenly her lethargy left her.

Gefreiter Henniker was the man Molly had mentioned. One of

her and Jen's captors at the POW camp in Italy. The man who had told her about *Nacht und Nebel*. The man who knew SS Hauptsturmführer Wessel, and what he was capable of. He might even know where he was.

Quickly Helen cross-checked the list with the file in the other office. Gefreiter Henniker had been captured by the Americans in the south of France as part of a German division that had recently arrived from Italy to help crush the Allied invasion. Far from crushing the invasion, the SS unit to which he had been attached had been surrounded in Nice, and ultimately forced to surrender. Shipped straight to England, he and his cohorts had passed through Kempton Park camp in late September, when he had been classified as a hard-core Nazi. He was now residing in an American-run prison in a converted barracks in Devizes.

Helen spent the next half-hour checking the lists of the other men who had arrived with him, and also those incarcerated at Devizes, but there was no mention anywhere of an SS Hauptsturmführer Wessel.

Gefreiter Henniker was a start, however. So she made her way to Captain Kirkwood's office to ask permission to contact Devizes to request an interview with him.

But when, having battled past his steely-eyed middle-aged ATS secretary, she finally gained admittance, Captain Kirkwood looked at her as though she had asked permission to strip naked and dance round his office.

'Absolutely not,' he said. 'Quite out of the question. Not at all the thing.'

Helen groaned in frustration, but she might have known. It was no accident that Captain Kirkwood had been selected to oversee the logging-in and out of the prisoners. Not only was he painstakingly meticulous, he was also fanatical about procedure and protocol.

'But he might be able to give us information about a particular Nazi officer who's known to have murdered innocent civilians.'

Captain Kirkwood looked pained. 'There are plenty of Nazis who've murdered innocent civilians,' he said. 'Just look at London.'

Helen bit back an irritable retort, and decided to try charm instead. 'Well, I know,' she admitted. 'But this was in cold blood, with bullets in the back of the neck.' She gave what she hoped was an endearing smile. 'Oh please help me, sir. It really is frightfully important.'

And to a certain extent, it worked. A signal was sent to HQ in London. Three frustrating days later, a message came back saying that the said soldier had been interviewed by a German-speaking American intelligence officer at Devizes, but had refused to confirm or deny knowledge of any SS officer, let alone the one mentioned in the request. He had in fact refused to speak at all, and it was the view of the intelligence officer that he was going to be a hard nut to crack.

After another bout of pleading from Helen, a response had been dispatched, this time asking if Gefreiter Henniker showed any reaction to the names Molly Coogan or Jennifer Carter.

This time the result was marginally more positive. Yes, there had been a definite reaction. Gefreiter Henniker had clearly recognised the names. Nevertheless, he had still refused to say a single word.

Helen stared at the yellow signal pad in dismay. 'There's only one thing for it,' she said. 'I'll have to get Molly and Jen to go down there. He might talk to them.'

Captain Kirkwood almost fell off his chair. 'I've never heard of such a thing,' he stuttered. 'It's quite impossible. You'd never get permission.'

Helen gave him a steely look. 'Nothing is impossible in this world,' she said grittily. 'Not if you want it enough.'

Chapter Thirteen

Molly was appalled by the idea of having to go and see Gefreiter Henniker. 'Oh no,' she said at once. The very thought sent shivers down her spine. 'I can't, I really can't.'

She started loading a tray with empties, racking her brain for a good excuse.

'I know you're really busy,' Helen said, following her into the small scullery. 'But I've already asked Jen, and she was absolutely adamant she wouldn't go.'

That didn't surprise Molly. It had taken Jen months to recover from their ordeal in Italy. Even now, she could scarcely bear to talk about it. She would hardly want to bring it all back by meeting one of their former guards.

Molly gritted her teeth, aware of Helen's eyes on her as she began to unload the tray into the sink. She didn't want to bring it all back either.

'Jen said you knew him better than she did,' Helen said quietly. 'She said you quite liked him.'

Molly leaned on the edge of the sink and looked into the sudsy beer-stained water. 'I didn't like him,' she said. 'I hated him. I hated all of them.'

But it was true that she had disliked Gefreiter Henniker slightly less than the rest of their thuggish captors. One of his tasks had been to supervise her sessions in the medical aid room, to make sure she didn't steal or misuse the meagre first-aid equipment she had been allocated to treat the women in the camp. Not the Jews, of course, she wasn't allowed to treat them, but the other women, expats and Italians who had made the mistake of showing their opposition to the fascist regime too openly. Once she had even treated him. He'd had a badly infected splinter in his arm and she'd taken it out. It must have hurt like hell, but he hadn't even flinched.

She hadn't asked what act of brutality had caused him to suffer the injury in the first place. She knew that he and his vicious Nazi cohorts spent most of their time rounding up Jews and young Italian deserters. But afterwards he had been marginally nicer to her. And behind his cold, unemotional gaze, the gaze of a man who had seen far too many horrible things, once or twice she even thought she'd glimpsed the faintest flicker of compassion.

'All right,' she said. 'If you get permission, I'll talk to him. But I can't guarantee he'll tell me anything useful.'

Somewhat to Molly's relief, Helen didn't get permission. As the Devizes jail fell under American military jurisdiction, it was entirely up to them to say who was allowed to visit the prisoners. However, thanks to the intervention of Helen's father, just before he went back to America, the wheels of international cooperation eventually began to turn.

In the meantime, lots was happening on the war front, and indeed on the home front too. There were celebrations in the pub when news came through that the almost brand-new German warship the *Tirpitz* had been sunk by a squadron of RAF bombers, flying a mission of 4,000 miles from their base in Scotland. There were even more celebrations a week later, when blackout restrictions were partially lifted. Angie and Gino took Bella and George up to the West End to see the lights come on in Piccadilly Circus and the Strand. The following night, cinemagoers queued for hours in icy rain in the West End to see Laurence Olivier starring in *Henry V*, the first Shakespeare adaptation to be filmed in glorious Technicolor.

And as though in response to Henry V's battle cries, two days

216

later it was announced that American troops had burst into one of Germany's most strategically vital regions, the Saar basin. General de Lattre de Tassigny's French troops had taken Strasbourg and, further north, having succeeded in breaching part of the Siegfried Line, the British were advancing towards Cologne.

Optimism was in the air, despite the fact that the weather was cold and wintry. Surely now Hitler would see the writing on the wall. Once again people started hoping that it would all be over by Christmas.

But whether Hitler could see the writing on the wall or not, he didn't hold back on his beastly V-2s. On 25 November, one hit a Woolworth's store in New Cross, killing 168 people and badly injuring at least another hundred.

Molly missed that incident as she was escorting a consignment of badly wounded servicemen from Southampton to King's College Hospital in Camberwell. Some of the other Red Cross girls didn't like working as escort nurses because it was often so harrowing, but it was handy for Molly because she was able to study on the train on the way to the south-coast ports where the hospital ships docked. But it did sometimes involve very long hours. In fact the following weekend, due to an overnight delay caused by a derailed train, she only got back to Lavender Road just in time for her lesson with Professor Markov first thing on Sunday morning.

Normally the professor taught her separately, but every now and then he combined her sessions with those of Graham Powell. Molly didn't begrudge sharing her lessons, but although she felt terribly sorry for him, she found the incapacitated Graham somewhat irritating. He was a diligent student, very well informed and clever – much cleverer than her – but it would have been nice if he had smiled occasionally. She didn't care that he virtually ignored her, although it was somewhat galling when it was because of her that he was there at all, but she felt he could at least make the effort to respond to Professor Markov's jokes. Not that the professor seemed to mind. He ploughed on regardless, and in any case, George's new-found enthusiasm more than made up for Graham's dogged melancholy.

That was certainly the case that Sunday morning. The professor was due to conduct a chemistry experiment and had invited George and Bella to come and watch. When Molly arrived at Mrs d'Arcy Billière's, straight from her night shift, there was no one in their usual room, but she could hear delighted squealing coming from the direction of the kitchen.

She could also smell burning, and it was with a sense of faint panic that she ran through the hallway and pushed open the kitchen door.

The scene that greeted her could have come from a strange futuristic movie. Standing by the gas stove, surrounded by billowing smoke, Professor Markov was drawing wild circles in the air with a wooden spill, which was burning with an extraordinary deep lilac flame, while George, gurgling in delight, was clasping another spill, this one flaming bright red.

Standing warily well back on the other side of the room were Bella and, to Molly's astonishment, Jen, who was wearing a ridiculously skimpy dressing gown and, judging from her bare legs and feet, clearly visible below the clinging fabric, not much else. Just inside the door, Graham Powell sat in his wheelchair, looking bored.

'Watch out, Professor,' George shouted suddenly. 'The tea towel's on fire!'

Swinging her startled gaze back to Professor Markov, Molly saw that his wildly flaming spill had caught the bottom of one of Mrs d'Arcy Billière's towelling tea towels, which was now burning merrily on its peg by the cooker. Indeed, as she stared in horror, the towel burnt through its loop and fell in a shower of smouldering pieces to the wooden floor, at which point the professor gave a roar of alarm and began to stamp on it like a demented bull, seemingly unaware that the spill in his hand was still showering the room with burning cinders.

'Oh my goodness,' Molly gasped. But impeded by Graham's

wheelchair, there was nothing she could do, and she clearly wasn't going to get any help from Jen, who, clutching a piece of half-eaten toast, was doubled over with laughter. The professor's precipitate experiment had clearly overlapped with Jen's lazy Sunday-morning breakfast.

Suddenly Molly heard footsteps in the hallway behind her. Thinking it might be Mrs d'Arcy Billière, she swung round in alarm.

But then she heard a voice, a male voice, with a confident well-to-do accent.

'Hello? Is anyone there? The front door was open, so . . .' A tall, khaki-clad figure loomed through the swirling smoke. 'Good lord,' he said. 'What's going on?'

It was George who broke the astonished silence. 'Look, Jen,' he shouted. 'It's Captain Keller.'

Jen didn't need telling. At the first sound of Henry's voice, the last remnant of toast had fallen from her fingers. Already her startled expression was turning into one of utter delight.

But between her and her fiancé was a floor covered in smouldering tea towel.

Molly had once seen a film about an Indian guru who claimed that the power of meditation allowed him to walk barefoot over burning coals, but the way Jen, the inadequate dressing gown flying behind her, danced obliviously across the width of Mrs d'Arcy Billière's burning kitchen floor knocked the guru's feat into a cocked hat. The power of meditation was clearly nothing compared to the power of love. Or even, Molly thought drily to herself, of lust.

Either way, Jen's reaction wasn't surprising. Last time Molly had seen Henry Keller, he had been dressed in a sleek double-breasted suit, a club tie and brogues, and had looked as smooth and unapproachable as someone off the pages of a high-society magazine. Today, in his battle-scarred Rifle Brigade uniform, unshaven and clearly travel weary, he looked about as down-to-earth and gorgeous as she had ever seen him.

'Well, well,' he said, as the half-naked Jen catapulted into his chest.

'I see you've dressed for the occasion.' He kissed her hard on the lips and then glanced round the crowded kitchen, laughter dancing in his eyes. 'If you'll excuse us,' he murmured courteously, backing away with an apologetic smile. 'I think I might have a fire of my own to put out.'

Luckily, although Molly could almost see the question forming on his lips, there wasn't time for George to ask what he meant. Professor Markov, having doused his flaming spill in the sink, was now using a rather beautiful cut-glass vase he'd found on the window-sill to throw water on the floor, and George and Bella had to leap out of the way to avoid getting soaked.

'Ha,' the professor said in satisfaction as the flames were finally extinguished. He straightened up and eyed his startled pupils sternly. 'So what did you learn from that?'

George giggled. 'That Jen Carter's in love with Captain Keller?' he suggested.

Professor Markov looked surprised. In all the excitement, he barely seemed to have noticed that Jen and Henry had vanished. Certainly he hadn't batted an eyelid when they had all quite clearly heard the rapid clip of Henry's steel-toed boots on the stairs, swiftly followed by the sound of a door closing upstairs.

'No, no,' he said impatiently. 'Not about that. About the experiment.'

Molly bit her lip. 'That it's dangerous to play with fire?' she murmured. And received a glare for her pains.

As Bella was unlikely to make a suggestion, partly due to her usual reticence, and partly because, like George, she was rapidly becoming overcome with giggles, it was left to Graham Powell to answer the professor's question.

'That the presence of potassium is indicated by a lilac flame,' he said in his usual bored tone. 'And lithium by a red one.'

It was too much for Molly. Out of respect for the professor, she had tried to control herself, but now, perhaps because she was so tired after her long night, as she glanced round the ravaged, smoking kitchen, her self-control crumbled.

'I'm sorry,' she gasped, putting a hand to her mouth. 'But really . . .' And that was all she could say. Catching George's eye, she leaned weakly against the door frame and laughed until she wept.

Sunday was usually Helen's day off, but the girl who normally did the weekend duty hadn't been feeling well all week, and Helen had volunteered to stand in for her. So she was in the office that Sunday morning when a somewhat terse signal came in from MI19 HQ authorising her and Miss Molly Coogan to visit Gefreiter Werner Henniker at Le Marchant Barracks in Devizes on Friday 8 December.

It was nearly a week away, but Helen was hardly going to complain about that.

Slumping down at her desk, she could feel her heart pumping in her chest. Her hand was shaking as she picked up her pen to sign the receipt slip for the signal. She knew it was a long shot. She knew she shouldn't hold out too much hope. But she couldn't help it. Closing her eyes, she tried to will her thoughts to reach André, wherever he was, in this world or the next. 'I love you,' she whispered. 'And I'm going to find out what's happened to you. If it's the last thing I ever do.'

A self-conscious cough in the doorway caused her eyes to fly open.

'I'm sorry, ma'am,' the corporal signaller stammered. 'But HQ are asking me if there's a reply.'

'Yes,' Helen said firmly. 'There is a reply. Please let them know that Miss Coogan and I will be at Devizes at eleven o'clock promptly on Friday.'

Jen had often wondered what it would be like to go to bed with Henry. To be honest she hadn't been entirely sure how much she would enjoy it. She fancied him all right. She always had, even though for several years she had tried to convince herself otherwise. But he had always been so cool, so well groomed and debonair, that she couldn't quite imagine him entering into the spirit of the kind of uninhibited lovemaking she had once enjoyed with her former boyfriend, the happy-go-lucky Irishman Sean Byrne, at the beginning of the war.

But today Henry wasn't at all well groomed or debonair, or indeed cool, and he had entered into it with both alacrity and a considerable amount of skill. It certainly hadn't been Jen's intention to fall into bed with him the moment she saw him, but that was what had happened. After one long kiss in the hall, he had swept her up into his arms and carried her upstairs as though she were a feather.

And as soon as he had kicked the bedroom door closed behind them, they had fallen onto the bed in a tangle of limbs, hers already naked, and his increasingly so, as she desperately tried to extricate him from his ridiculously complicated uniform.

It had been half funny, half passionate, and all the while, in between every increasingly frantic manoeuvre, Henry was kissing her as if there was no tomorrow.

But at the crucial stage, he had hesitated. 'Jen,' he had muttered against her hair. 'Are you absolutely sure about this? Do you want me to stop?'

'Yes, I'm sure,' she had moaned. 'And if you stop now, I'll kill you.'

So he hadn't stopped. And afterwards, Jen was glad he hadn't. The potentially awkward first time had been successfully accomplished. It hadn't been awkward at all. Not one bit. All her secret fears had been burnt away by the heat of their passion.

Now as they lay entangled in the bed, panting and laughing, she saw a fabulous future opening up for her. A future of glamorous opening nights, theatrical parties, maybe even film premieres. Already celebrated in his own right as a highly successful West End producer, Henry would be reassuringly at her side. And now she wouldn't be shy, she wouldn't feel outfaced by his famous, illustrious friends, because she would have the secret knowledge that when she and Henry got home, this would be waiting for her. This lovely, easy, companionable utter gorgeousness.

'Oh my God, Jen,' Henry said suddenly. 'I'm sorry about that. I got a bit carried away. I think it must have been that robe affair you were almost wearing.' Easing a leg out from under her hip, he drew her more comfortably into the crook of his arm. 'But now, you know, we really will have to get married. I'm not due back in Belgium until the weekend after next. So how about we try to fix it for one day next week? That would give us time to let everyone know, and we can treat ourselves to a proper honeymoon next time I'm home.' He grinned and kissed her. 'Not that we really need one now . . .'

By the time Jen and Henry finally emerged from the bedroom, Molly's mad professor and his extraordinary mishmash of students had gone. The kitchen floor was slightly charred, but Mrs d'Arcy Billière didn't seem to mind. Arriving back from a coffee with a friend, she was so delighted by the news of an impending wedding that instead of worrying about the floor, she got out a bottle of vodka.

Half an hour later, Jen and Henry walked up the street to Joyce's house, where, to Jen's astonishment, both Angie and her mother cried, and Mr Lorenz produced a celebratory bottle of wine. After that, they went to the pub, where Katy treated them to glasses of brandy.

Later that day, reeling from all the alcohol, Jen visited Henry's flat, which turned out to be a three-roomed bachelor apartment on the first floor of an elegant town house in Pont Street. She loved its spacious rooms, its smart, masculine minimalism, its stylish modern furniture, and was almost disappointed when Henry said that they would buy a better place as soon as the war was over.

But despite her protestations, he wouldn't let her stay there. He said it was bad luck, but really she knew he was trying to protect her from any censure from her family or friends. He was also trying to prevent her from getting pregnant. So each evening that week, after a prolonged session of carefully protected gorgeousness in his bed, he decorously took her back to Mrs d'Arcy Billière's, and each morning, she went off to RADA as normal. While she was working at her vocal technique and practising improvisation, Henry spent his time meeting friends, sorting out loose ends from his old job at ENSA and organising a wedding party.

Molly was thrilled about the news, even though Jen had almost caused her to choke on her drink one evening by confiding, in a voice Molly was sure everyone in the pub could hear, how very satisfactory things had turned out to be in the bedroom department.

But she was very much less thrilled at the prospect of having to meet Gefreiter Henniker at Devizes prison. In fact when Friday morning dawned, she felt quite sick. George, despite taking advantage of her nausea to eat her breakfast as well as his own, wasn't at all impressed by her nerviness.

'I wish I could go,' he said. 'I'd make him talk, and if he refused, I'd kick him in the face. And then when he'd told me what I needed to know, I'd kill him. And all the other Nazi prisoners too.'

Molly had felt obliged to remonstrate, once again trying to make him realise that most German prisoners were probably perfectly ordinary men caught up in the war through no fault of their own.

But when, several hours later, she and Helen arrived at Le Marchant Barracks in Devizes, it was clear that the hard-faced American major in charge of the facility did not hold quite such a benign view of his charges.

'I have no idea why you girls are here,' he said bluntly. 'But I'd better warn you that these guys we're holding are hard-line Nazi bastards. We're putting them in lockdown for the duration of your visit, but as they normally have the run of the place, that's not going to be popular, so you'd better be prepared for some verbal flak.'

'As long as it's only verbal,' Helen said, and he laughed sourly.

Molly already felt intimidated by the grim castle-like barracks with its great square red-brick towers and huge gated entrance. It was obvious just from the look of it why it had been chosen as a prison. Now she quailed even more, and hoped that the prison commander was only trying to frighten them because his earlier decision to refuse permission for their visit had, thanks to the intervention of Helen's father, been overruled.

Whether he had been trying to scare them or not, Molly definitely felt alarmed as she heard the sinister noise of hundreds of steel-heeled boots banging out an angry rhythm. And the faces she glimpsed through the metal-barred doors as they entered the main facility certainly did not look like those of ordinary soldiers. Nor did they look remotely welcoming. On the contrary, with their closely cropped hair and scornful, supercilious eyes, they reminded her all too forcefully of the thuggish guards in Italy who had made her and Jen's life at the Italian POW camp such a misery.

Gefreiter Henniker was waiting for them in a small office. He was sitting on one side of an empty table, flanked by two huge American soldiers. A third, holding a heavy black truncheon, stood threateningly behind him.

As Molly, Helen and the prison commander filed in, the German looked up. He clearly hadn't been told who was coming to see him, and his surprise was palpable. But he hid it quickly, only meeting Molly's nervous gaze for the briefest second before deliberately lowering his head, giving the distinct impression that he was much more interested in studying his hands, which lay on the table, than looking at her.

Molly felt her mouth go dry. She remembered those hands, with their blunt, scarred fingers. She remembered the awkward way he had held a pen, as every day, with stolid German efficiency, he ticked off the medical items she had used. She remembered the burly forearms too. In fact, she realised, she remembered everything about him. The bullish face, the broken nose, the clammy pale skin, and more than anything, the emotionless piggy eyes.

But those eyes hadn't looked emotionless when she'd come in.

In that brief moment, before he had recognised her, she had thought he looked distinctly fearful. She could still see that fear in the way his fingers were pressing into the table. Presumably he had been ordered to keep them there, because when he lifted a hand to his face, the soldier with the truncheon grunted a sharp admonishment.

But it didn't seem to be the American guards Werner Henniker was frightened of, because, paying absolutely no heed to the soldier, he defiantly and deliberately scratched his nose before slowly putting his hand back on the table.

The American officer waved Molly into the chair on the opposite side of the table. Molly cast an anguished glance at Helen, who nodded encouragingly. Actually Molly was glad to sit down, because her knees were in imminent danger of giving way.

'Hello,' she said. 'I think you remember me, don't you?'

She looked hopefully across the table, but Gefreiter Henniker didn't raise his eyes. Nor did he answer. Not that Molly entirely blamed him. She felt pretty tongue-tied herself. With four huge grim-faced Americans breathing down their necks, listening to her every word, and watching his every move, the set-up was hardly conducive to a friendly reminiscent chat.

Nevertheless, knowing how important this was to Helen, she persevered.

But to no avail. Gefreiter Henniker didn't even look at her, let alone respond to her increasingly inane gabble. The only time she got any reaction was when she mentioned the splinter she had extracted from his arm. Then, and only then, she thought she saw a flicker of a smile show briefly on his lips.

A minute later, Molly stood up. She turned to the prison commander. 'Can I have a word with you outside?' she said.

He looked surprised. But then, rather grumpily, he nodded to the corporal to open the door.

Outside, the noise of the thrumming feet was much louder, and an unpleasant smell of vinegar and cabbage was drifting down the corridor.

'I want to see him alone,' Molly said.

'No way,' the prison commander said at once.

'He's never going to say anything otherwise.'

The American looked annoyed. 'You don't seem to get it,' he said. 'These men are animals. How can I guarantee that he won't assault you? Or claim you as a hostage?'

Molly shook her head. 'He had plenty of opportunity to assault me in Italy,' she said. 'And he never did. So I can hardly imagine he's going to now. As for taking me hostage, well, if he does, you can just come in and shoot him, and I'll take my chances. I haven't got any family, so nobody's going to complain.'

Five minutes later, she was back in the room on her own with the Gefreiter.

And now he did look at her. But he still wouldn't talk.

Suddenly Molly thought of Bella. Maybe the poor man lost the ability to speak. Or had he lost his hearing? That was much more likely.

She reached over the table and touched his arm, deliberately pressing it at the point where she had withdrawn the septic splinter. 'Gefreiter Henniker,' she said clearly. 'Can you hear what I am saying?'

To her surprise, he nodded and leaned forward. 'Yes,' he said very quietly. So quietly in fact that she had to strain to hear him. He raised his eyes significantly to the ceiling of the room. 'But so also can the Americans.'

Molly stared at him, and then at the ceiling. 'You mean they've put some kind of listening device in here?' she whispered.

He shrugged. 'Perhaps.'

Molly felt aggrieved; surely the prison commander should have told her that. 'Even so,' she whispered, 'what does it matter? You surely aren't frightened of the Americans?'

'No.' His voice was almost a breath. 'I am frightened of the men out there. Listen to them.' He nodded towards the door, through which the sound of drumming feet was still clearly audible. 'If they find out I have talked, they will kill me.'

He saw the shocked horror on her face and lifted his broad, thickset shoulders. 'They will probably kill me anyway. Just for being in here for so long. They will not believe I have not spoken.'

The look of resentful anger in his eyes made Molly believe he was telling the truth. 'What if I arrange for other men to be questioned?' she said. 'Then, whatever happens, they won't only blame you?'

He gave a grim little gesture of acknowledgement. 'Perhaps that would help,' he said. 'But still I have nothing to tell you. I don't know where is Hauptsturmführer Wessel. The last time I saw him, it was in Nice. But he was not captured with the rest of us. I think he had already left the city.'

Molly sighed. 'What about a Frenchman, André Cabillard?' she persisted. 'He was an agent for the British secret service and then the French resistance. He was known as Renard.' As she spoke, she flinched, realising she had used the past tense. She was glad Helen hadn't been there to hear.

But Gefreiter Henniker didn't seem to notice the slip. 'I never heard this name,' he said.

Molly looked at him helplessly for a moment, then slumped back in her chair. So it was a dead end after all. The whole thing had been a waste of everyone's time, and now poor old Gefreiter Henniker would probably get killed by his beastly comrades.

Then she thought of Helen standing anxiously outside in the corridor, and made one last effort. 'Perhaps you could ask around?' she suggested. 'In case anyone else knows something. I'll come back next week and see if you have discovered anything.'

The words were barely out of her mouth when he lurched to his feet, reached over the table and grabbed her arm. 'No,' he hissed through closed teeth. 'Listen to me. You must not come here again. It's not safe.'

His fingers bit into her skin, and, stifling a scream, Molly jerked away, frightened for the first time. Now that he was standing up, she could see that he had a black circle sewn onto his uniform. She shivered. She knew that all German prisoners wore colour-coded circles, but she also knew that a black circle was only allocated to the most avid Nazis.

'Why not?' she asked shakily. 'What do you mean, it's not safe?'

He muttered an expletive under his breath. 'I don't mean anything,' he muttered 'Just don't come back next week.'

Molly stared at him. Then slowly, deliberately, she leaned forward over the table. 'I want to know what you meant,' she whispered. 'I'm not going to leave here until you tell me. As I understand it, the longer you and I stay in here, the more likely it is that your horrid Nazi friends will kill you, so you might as well tell me and get it over with.'

But once again his lips seemed to be sealed.

'Something is going to happen, isn't it?' she insisted. 'But what?' He was watching her steadily, almost as if he was willing her to guess. She frowned. 'A riot? An uprising against the Americans?'

She knew at once, from the way he clenched his jaw, that she had hit the nail on the head.

'They're planning to break out of the prison?' she whispered incredulously. 'Next week?'

He closed his eyes for a second. 'Yes,' he murmured. 'But not just from the prison camps. Also from Germany. The Wehrmacht and the SS will retake Belgium.' He saw her incredulity and shrugged. 'This war is not over yet. Whatever you and the Americans might think.'

'But . . .' Molly didn't know what to say. There was nothing she could say.

'So,' he said. 'Now I have told you. Because I do not want to bring you into danger. And now I will die, unless you can make the Americans move me to a different camp.'

Molly stood up. 'I will do what I can.'

But when ten minutes later she breathlessly told the camp commandant what the Gefreiter had said, the American just laughed in her face.

'Oh come on,' he said. 'He's lying to you. Why would he tell you something like that? He's just trying to find a way of getting himself transferred to a more comfortable camp.'

Molly gritted her teeth. 'Nevertheless,' she said. 'At the very least, you must promise to interview some other men. So he isn't the only one they suspect. I owe him that.'

In the end, very grudgingly, he did promise. But that was all. When she urged him to pass the news of a potential German counter attack to his superiors, he just laughed. 'Don't you worry your pretty little head,' he said. 'We have it covered. Nobody is getting out of here any time soon.' He laughed. 'Or out of Germany, come to that.'

'Why are men such idiots?' Molly asked Helen as they walked back to the station.

Helen laughed. 'I don't know,' she said. But she looked uneasy. And a moment later, she stopped and turned to face her. 'Molly, seriously,' she said. 'Did you really believe what Henniker said? Like really, truly believe it?'

Molly thought about it, and also about what he had said just as she left the room. 'The commandant of the Italian camp told us that you and that other girl escaped from the prison train,' he had murmured. 'I was glad. I didn't want anything bad to happen to you.' And it seemed to her that there was a look of sincerity in his eyes.

'Yes,' she said now to Helen. 'I believed him.'

Helen made a noise in her throat. 'Then it's up to us to make sure the right people get to hear of it,' she said.

Concerned that she might be disciplined for spreading defeatist rumours, Helen was careful whom she told. But in any case, nobody believed her. Lieutenant Colonel Jones at MI19 HQ was the obvious choice. But, like the Americans, he refused to take it seriously.

'Don't you think General Montgomery and General Patton would be the first to know if there was likely to be a German counter-offensive?' he asked. 'That's why we have an intelligence service. So we don't have to rely on two silly young women who have fallen under the spell of some sweet-talking Nazi. For all we know, he was deliberately spreading misinformation.'

Helen came out of the meeting spitting feathers. She had no better luck at the SOE, Angus McNaughton even going so far as to refuse to see her. Vera Atkins did at least promise to pass the information up the line, but Helen didn't hold out much hope. If only her father wasn't halfway across the Atlantic on his way back to America, she would have told him; and just when she and Molly most needed him, blasted Ward Frazer had gone swanning off to Scotland.

Jen couldn't believe how lovely it was being in love. All week she walked about in a rosy glow. Even at RADA, where she tried not to let it show, she got teased for the smile that hung on her lips, despite the fact that she was trying to convey a tragic scene. One of her tutors knew Henry and told Jen that he was going to put in a complaint. 'I've never seen such a jolly Lady Macbeth in all my life,' he said. 'As far as I'm concerned, the sooner you two get married the better. It will soon wear off then.'

Henry laughed when she told him. 'I hope it never wears off,' he said.

The wedding had been set for the following Thursday. In the meantime, they had an idyllic weekend. Quite a lot of it they spent in bed, but they also went shopping in the West End, where Henry bought Jen a belated but utterly beautiful emerald engagement ring. They also enjoyed an evening out at the swanky 400 Club with a couple of Henry's friends, one of whom turned out to be Lord Freddy Manson, the somewhat rotund but very jolly aristocrat who declared himself to be madly in love with Louise Rutherford.

As far as Jen was concerned, everything was going swimmingly. But on Tuesday morning, disaster struck.

She was halfway through an improvisation class when one of the RADA secretaries popped her head round the door and told her that she was needed urgently in the lobby. Puzzled, Jen ran down the stone staircase. Waiting in the hallway below was Henry, an agonised expression on his face.

'I've been summoned back to my unit,' he said. 'It seems there's some kind of crisis brewing, and I'm on strict orders to catch an RAF plane back to Belgium this afternoon.'

Jen stared at him in disbelief. 'But . . . ' There were so many buts, she didn't know where to start. 'But what about the wedding?'

Henry took her hands and drew her into his arms. 'It's going to have to wait until I get back again,' he said. He swore under his breath. 'My darling, I'm so sorry. If I'd known something like this was going to happen, I'd have tried to organise it for sooner.'

Jen suddenly felt very cold. 'What sort of crisis is it?' she asked. Oddly, her voice seemed to come from a long way away.

'God knows,' Henry said. 'It's probably all a big fuss about nothing. But as I can't afford to be court-martialled, I'm going to have to go. You do understand that, don't you?'

Jen understood all right. And now, suddenly, she knew exactly how to act the tragic heroine. But she didn't need to act. She could feel the anger, the misery and the bitter resentment that whatever she said wouldn't make a damned bit of difference. He had to go. He had to leave her. And God only knew when she would see him again.

Chapter Fourteen

Ward Frazer came back from Scotland later that week. He listened with obvious unease to Molly's account of what Gefreiter Henniker had told her, and the danger he was in. When she had finished, he swore softly under his breath and promised to see what he could do.

Molly didn't see him for the next couple of days, but when she popped into the pub late on Saturday evening, he drew her to one side.

'You won't hear it on the news,' he murmured, 'because it's being hushed up. But I guess you'll be glad to know that a mass escape of German POWs has been averted. It was due to happen this morning. The SS had planned a coordinated breakout from a number of camps. They were going to overpower their guards, steal weapons from nearby military bases and march on London.'

Molly stared at him aghast. 'Goodness,' she said. 'But I thought nobody had listened to us.'

'Somebody listened,' he said. 'It seems that British intelligence was already beginning to suspect something was afoot even before they got to hear what you'd discovered. So as a precaution, soldiers from the Parachute Regiment were sent to the suspect camps in full battle kit. I guess the Nazis realised that their little plan wasn't going to work.'

'What about the military breakout from Germany? Gefreiter Henniker said that was going to happen at the same time.'

Ward shrugged. 'It doesn't sound as if anyone is taking that very seriously. They seem to think it's more wishful thinking than reality. I guess the American commanders on the ground reckon they have the German border pretty much sewn up.'

Molly tried to feel reassured. 'What about Gefreiter Henniker?' she asked. 'Is he all right?'

'Yes, as far as I know.'

But she sensed his hesitation. 'What do you mean?'

'It seems he's been transferred to a prison camp in Scotland with the other ringleaders. A place called Cultybraggan. It's where they tend to send the worst of the SS and the Gestapo prisoners. The really nasty ones. The Nazi diehard fanatics.'

'But that's not fair,' Molly said hotly. 'Why did they do that? He wasn't a ringleader. I don't think he's even a proper Nazi. I told them he was in danger. Why didn't they send him somewhere well away from the others, like he wanted?'

Ward looked uneasy. 'Now that they know he's fallible, I imagine the Americans have some idea of trying to use him as an informer. To keep an eye on the hardliners and report back if there's any more trouble.'

'And they don't care if he gets killed?' Molly said. She was furious. She felt betrayed, and that she had betrayed Gefreiter Henniker. She wished now that she'd never told the beastly camp commandant what he had said.

Ward frowned. 'Molly, listen, it's out of my hands. There's nothing I can do.'

'You're just as bad as the rest of them,' she snapped. 'I almost hope the Germans do counterattack back into Belgium. Just to teach those stupid Americans a lesson.'

As soon as the words were out of her mouth, she felt guilty. Ward had never been anything but kind to her, and she knew he was on her side.

But it was indeed a shame that the Americans hadn't taken a bit more notice of Gefreiter Henniker's warning, because that very morning, the Germans launched a huge surprise assault against the Allied troops massed in the Ardennes on the Belgian border.

They began with a massive ninety-minute artillery barrage. At first the Allied commanders believed it was merely retaliation for their recent penetration of the Siegfried Line. But it soon became clear that it was in fact an attempt by Hitler to drive a massive wedge through the long multinational Allied front, with the ultimate aim of retaking the port of Antwerp and thus destroying the Allies' ability to resupply.

Over the next couple of days, as the Germans drove deeper into the Ardennes in an attempt to secure vital bridgeheads, the retreating Allied front line began to curve dramatically backwards, which soon caused the British press to refer to the sudden, unanticipated conflict as the Battle of the Bulge. They also reported that it was American forces that were taking the brunt of the action, which made Jen hopeful that neither Henry nor her two brothers would be involved.

Nevertheless, casualties were high, and it wasn't many day before Molly began finding injured soldiers from the Ardennes on the hospital ships docking at Dover, not all of them American, despite what it said in the newspapers. But as nurses were forbidden to speak about what they saw on those trains, she kept the information to herself. In any case, she didn't want to make Jen and Mrs Lorenz any more worried than they were already. Jen in particular had been distraught to discover that she and Helen had known that there was a suspected danger in Belgium.

'But that's exactly where Henry was going,' she had wailed. 'Why the hell didn't you tell us?'

Molly knew better than to try to reason with Jen when she was in this mood, but Helen was braver than her. 'Even if we had told you, there was nothing you or Henry could have done about it,' she said. And that had caused Jen to flounce off in high dudgeon.

Jen had recovered her temper since then and was now thinking of moving into Henry's flat. Her mother, however, concerned about what people would think, had forbidden her to do any such thing.

'What difference does it make?' Jen had grumbled to Molly. She fingered her engagement ring. 'Who cares what a load of old busybodies like Mrs Rutherford think? As far as I'm concerned, Henry and I are as good as married.'

'I'm sure your mother's only trying to protect you,' Molly said mildly. 'You know how people gossip.'

But Jen wasn't feeling tolerant. 'Well, I think she's being ridiculously old fashioned about it. I know you don't think so, but you're lucky you don't have a mother.'

But I do have one, Molly had wanted to scream.

For the last few weeks she had tried to put the knowledge that her mother might still be alive to the back of her mind. But it hadn't worked. It niggled at her like a sore. So far, Helen had been the only person she had told. That had been hard enough, but now she wished she had told Jen and Katy too. Because they were bound to find out sooner or later, and the fact that she hadn't said anything would make them think it was more important to her than it was.

It was bad enough that they knew about Callum. Molly had been trying not to think about him either. He had told her not to worry. But how could she not worry when she hadn't heard from him for ages? Surreptitiously she slid her hand into her pocket and touched his letter. She knew it was weedy and superstitious, but she had taken to keeping it with her at all times. Like a talisman.

Suddenly she made a decision. She wasn't going to be weedy any more. There was no point burying her head in the sand. She needed to face up to things. There wasn't anything she could currently do about Callum, but she could make a final push to find out if her mother really was still alive. After all, for all Molly knew, the poor woman might for some reason have been forced to put her illegitimate child into care. It wasn't entirely inconceivable that, instead of being relieved to have got shot of her ugly little daughter, pretty Prissy Cavanagh might have spent the intervening years wondering what had happened to her.

★　★　★

236

Joyce was feeling concerned. Christmas was nearly on them, and far from the war being over, things were now looking bleaker than ever. There was certainly very little sign of peace in the world, even less of goodwill. She and Albert had received a forces Christmas greeting card from Albert's cousin Leszek, but needless to say, she'd had nothing from any of her sons. She had no idea how, or indeed where, they were.

'Why can't the buggers just get it over with?' one of Joyce's customers had asked irritably, while waiting for a corned-beef sandwich. 'I know the Battle of the Bulge business is annoying, but even so, with the Russkies coming in from the other side, Hitler must know he doesn't stand a chance. Why does he have to spin it out with even more deaths?'

Joyce had wanted to pick up the slice of National Loaf bread she was spreading with margarine and slap the woman round the face with it.

That evening, when Albert mentioned that he was at last making progress in getting permission to have his house rebuilt, Joyce couldn't help snapping at him. 'I can't see there's any point in getting it rebuilt if the boys are going to get killed. If it's not this damn Battle of the Bulge, it will be some other beastly offensive.'

Albert had been silent for a moment. 'I know how worrying it is,' he said. 'Especially now, when it seems we are so near the end. But actually I wasn't thinking about the boys. I was thinking about Angie and Gino. If they knew that they could have a home of their own here, then perhaps they would decide to stay in London instead of going back to Italy.' Apparently unaware of her stupefied expression, he gave a bland smile and went on calmly. 'I had another idea as well. I've been wondering about Christmas presents, and as there's so little in the shops, it occurred to me that we could offer to pay for some proper English lessons for Gino. I'm sure he'd be happier here if he could understand what people are saying.'

'English lessons?' Joyce's head was already spinning at the thought of Albert rebuilding his house for Angie and Gino. 'But who on earth could teach him?'

'I thought we could ask Molly Coogan to find someone,' he said. 'She seems to have become our local education expert.'

Joyce blinked. He clearly had it all worked out. She was just wondering what Molly might think about incorporating gormless Gino into her little school at Mrs d'Arcy Billière's when the thought brought the issue of Jen into her mind.

'We can't allow Jen to live in Henry's flat,' she said abruptly. 'You know what everyone will assume, and I don't want people thinking she's a slut. I'm sure Henry wouldn't either. I can't think why he gave her the keys. Whatever else they got up to while he was here, he at least had the sense not to let her stay overnight.' She gave Albert a fierce look. 'She won't listen to me, so you'll have to talk to her.'

But Albert knew Jen's temper as well as she did. 'I can't talk to her,' he protested. 'It's not as if I'm her father. What makes you think she'd listen to me?'

Joyce glared at him. 'Because you hold the purse strings on that damn acting course of hers.'

Albert gave an uneasy laugh. 'I had a feeling that would come back to haunt me.'

'Well, it serves you right for giving her the money in the first place,' she said. 'And now that I come to think of it, Angie and Gino aren't your children either, and if you think I'm going to let you give your house to them just to please me, then you've got another think coming. English lessons are one thing; handing your house to two feckless young people is quite another.'

'I thought you'd be pleased,' he said. 'But perhaps you're right; perhaps we should just loan it out to them until they are in a position to get somewhere of their own.'

Joyce eyed him suspiciously. She realised he had led her neatly to the conclusion he had wanted all along. He was beginning to know her far too well. 'I'll loan *you* out if you're not careful,' she said. 'To women who want someone to run rings round them.'

238

He laughed and leaned over to kiss her decorously on the cheek. 'You are the only woman in the whole wide world I have ever wanted to run rings around,' he said.

It was much easier at Somerset House the second time. Especially now Molly knew what she was looking for: the marriage certificate of Miss Priscilla Cavanagh. And in spite of the ponderous officialdom of the General Register Office, she found it relatively quickly.

During the two hours it took for a copy to be made, she went to a library on the Strand, looked up the names and addresses of the various medical schools in London and drafted out a brief letter of enquiry to send to each one.

She also spent time trying to think of who might be able to teach Gino Moretti English.

Mr Lorenz had approached her in the pub the previous night, but although Molly agreed that Gino would benefit from some lessons, she couldn't for the life of her think of anyone suitable to teach him. Professor Markov was the only teacher she knew, but although his English was technically almost perfect, he spoke it with a heavy Russian accent that would almost certainly confuse the linguistically challenged Gino.

Back at Somerset House, she waited impatiently for the hand-copied certificate to emerge from the bowels of the building. But when one of the brown-coated clerks finally produced it, she could hardly bring herself to look at it.

In August 1925, less than a week after Molly had arrived at the Home for Waifs and Strays, Miss Priscilla Cavanagh, 20, shop assistant, spinster of Marylebone, London, had married Mr Clarence Wright, 38, businessman, widower of Chelverton Road, Putney.

Priscilla Cavanagh had given birth to Molly at the tender age of seventeen. Three years later, she had gone on to marry a man nearly twice her age.

Molly forced herself to study the tiny handwritten entries for more details. The two witnesses' names and signatures meant nothing to her, but in the space allocated to the bride's father was written *Gerald Cavanagh, Yew Tree House, Headley, Epsom, Surrey, gentleman.*

Which made it sound as though her mother had indeed come from a good family, Molly thought as she walked somewhat blindly across Waterloo Bridge and boarded a number 77 bus back to Clapham.

And now, for the first time, she was aware of feeling a tiny bit of compassion for pretty little Prissy Cavanagh.

That evening she lured Helen into a quiet corner of the pub.

'What is it?' Helen asked anxiously. 'What's happened?'

'Nothing's happened,' Molly said. 'It's just that I've decided I want you to find my mother after all. I've got the name of her husband and his address at the time of their marriage.' She saw Helen's eyes flicker in concern and knew she was speaking too fast. 'It's quite a smart street in Putney. I'd go myself, but I don't want to meet her. Not yet. So I need you to go and see what you can find out.'

Jen had spent a miserable week. The first couple of days after Henry's precipitate departure hadn't been too bad. Yes, of course it had been horrible having to cancel all the wedding arrangements, but everyone had been so kind, so concerned for her, that it had taken the sting out of it somehow. But once it was done, she became just one more of the many girls in London whose sweethearts were away at war. It wasn't that people weren't still sympathetic – they were – but with Christmas approaching and things going so disastrously wrong on the Continent, nobody had the energy to reassure her that it would all be all right.

The last thing Jen wanted just now was to have to put on a brave face over Christmas. All she wanted was to move into Henry's flat so she could wallow in her misery in peace. She knew her mother disapproved of the idea, and she didn't care about that. But yesterday, Joyce had set Mr Lorenz on her. He hadn't mentioned, as her mother had, that people might start thinking she had become a kept woman.

Nor had he reminded her that he had been paying her fees at RADA. Instead he had appealed to her better nature.

'Your mother needs you here in Lavender Road,' he had said. 'I know you have your own worries, but with all the boys away, your mother is feeling rather down herself. And as it's our first Christmas together, I want to make it as happy a one for her as I can. I can assure you she won't be happy if she knows you are moping around on your own in Knightsbridge.'

And looking into his kindly eyes, all Jen had been able to do was groan inwardly and agree to stay at Mrs d'Arcy Billière's at least until the new year. Mr Lorenz had smiled gently and patted her hand. 'You're a good girl, Jen,' he said. 'These are tough times for us all. But whatever happens, we'll get through it if we stick together.'

It didn't take long for Helen, a trained secret agent, to discover that Mr and Mrs Wright had left Chelverton Road many years previously. It took her slightly longer to find out where they lived now. But a chatty neighbour came to her rescue by remembering that perhaps ten years ago Mrs Wright, 'a very pretty young woman, much younger than him', had boasted that she and her husband were moving to a bigger house in Wimbledon.

Putney to Wimbledon wasn't far on the bus, and there, via a helpful lady in the post office, Helen discovered the Wrights' new address. It was a substantial, well-maintained Edwardian villa in a leafy cul-de-sac in Wimbledon village. Mr Wright, businessman, now fifty-seven years old, had clearly continued to prosper, despite the rigours of war.

Unfortunately, the discreetly affluent neighbourhood wasn't the sort of place where people loitered on street corners. Not knowing who else might be living in the house, Helen didn't want to blow her cover by knocking on the door. Instead she made a couple of casual enquiries at various shops in the high street, and learned from a woman in the greengrocer's that Mrs Wright met a small group of local ladies in the Wimbledon village café for tea every Saturday afternoon. Keen to get her on her own, Helen formulated a plan of lying in wait and waylaying her on her way home.

She couldn't help wishing that her search for André had been as easy. After the abortive interview with Gefreiter Henniker, she had been pinning her hopes on Bletchley Park. But nothing had come back from there, nor from Mrs Sparrow at the Red Cross. She hadn't lost hope, but the wall of silence was both frustrating and demoralising, and it took considerable effort to keep her increasing sense of despair at bay.

The upcoming Saturday was 23 December. Helen had already agreed to work over Christmas, so she was allowed to take the day off, but she was concerned that as it was so close to the festive season, the Wimbledon ladies might alter their routine.

'Are you quite sure you don't want to go yourself?' she asked Molly the night before, as they stood in the pantry of the pub washing glasses.

'Yes, I'm quite sure,' Molly said. She wiped a sudsy hand across her brow. 'I don't want to meet her unless she wants to meet me. Anyway, I can't go because Professor Markov has summoned me and the others to a Christmas gathering at Mrs d'Arcy Billière's. He told us to be there promptly at three o'clock. I hope it's not going to last too long, because I'm on duty at the Red Cross at six.'

'Then I'll come and find you at the first-aid post when I get back,' Helen said. She glanced at her friend. Molly was washing the glasses very diligently and didn't return her gaze. Helen felt her heart twist. But perhaps by this time tomorrow she would have good news. Christmas was, after all, a time for families and loved ones to get together. What a brilliant Christmas present for Molly it would be if she could arrange for her to be reunited with her long-lost mother.

'I hope he's got a Christmas cake for us,' George remarked to Molly the following day as they hurried, muffled up like Russian babushkas, through sleeting fog to Mrs d'Arcy Billière's house for Professor Markov's 'gathering'.

But although he had brought some Russian delicacies for their consumption, including odd little pastries shaped like reindeer that tasted of some sweet unidentifiable spice, it turned out the professor hadn't invited them to a party; he had summoned them to an impromptu exam.

He had written out individual question papers for each of his students, to test the knowledge he felt they should have acquired over the course of his tuition.

'What?' Molly cried in alarm. She glanced helplessly at George and Bella, who were both standing open mouthed. Graham, true to form, barely reacted; he just sat in his wheelchair looking as supercilious as usual.

'But it's not fair,' Molly wailed. 'You haven't given us a chance to revise.'

Professor Markov gave a gleeful laugh as he carefully positioned the papers round the huge table. 'I didn't want you to revise,' he said. 'I don't approve of students cramming in the knowledge only to forget it the next day. I intend what I teach you to remain in your minds. This is the true meaning of learning.'

Convinced that very little of what he had taught her remained in her mind, Molly turned over her paper with extreme trepidation. She had become fond of her eccentric tutor over the last couple of months, and didn't want to disappoint him. Nor did she want to disappoint herself. She had already sent off letters to the various medical schools in London enquiring about their application procedures, and it would be awful if it turned out now that she wasn't going to be up to it after all.

'No talking,' Professor Markov said sternly as George gave a sudden giggle and looked up from his paper. 'You have one hour. Then we will celebrate with a cup of tea and some traditional Russian Christmas snacks.'

For a second, as Molly stared blankly at the first question, she found herself wondering how Helen was getting on in Wimbledon. A shiver ran through her and she felt the pencil tremble in her fingers. But then she forced herself to concentrate, to be calm, to read through the questions carefully, all the while praying that there would indeed be something to celebrate.

An hour later, while George surreptitiously scoffed half a dozen pastry reindeers, Molly and Bella went off to make the tea and Graham sat disinterestedly by the fire reading *The Times* newspaper, Professor Markov sat down grimly to mark their papers.

By the time they had nervously reassembled in the morning room, he was smiling.

'Ha,' he said, his white teeth gleaming. 'So how do you think you got on?'

'Mine was easy,' George said. 'I knew all the answers.'

The professor raised his bushy eyebrows. 'Except how to spell Rhodesia,' he said. 'Last time I looked, it had an h in it. Nevertheless, I am beginning to suspect that you are not quite as stupid as I originally thought.'

George giggled, clearly delighted by the compliment. But the professor was already looking at Bella. 'You clearly knew the answers to your questions too,' he said. Ignoring her blushes, he went on calmly. 'Your description of the Zulu war was excellent. Both intelligent and concise. And *your* spelling is exemplary.'

Graham was next. He, of course, had done brilliantly too. But the bored look on his face as he listened to the professor's praise made Molly want to throw a reindeer at him.

Then it was her turn. Her mouth was already dry, and as she saw the professor's smile turn to a frown, her hands started to sweat. In spite of her early fears, like George she had found the test surprisingly easy. But perhaps that was false confidence. Perhaps she had misunderstood the questions, or misremembered the periodic table. Or, now she came to think about it, had she stupidly mixed up alkanes with alkenes? Or drawn her carbon skeleton of ethanol with three carbon atoms instead of two?

'Well, well,' Professor Markov said. His brows drew together fiercely. 'So you needed to revise, did you?'

Molly winced. 'I think I might have done better if I had,' she mumbled.

To her astonishment, he let out a roar of laughter. 'You couldn't have done better,' he said. 'You got one hundred per cent. *Otlichno*! Excellent! Not one single mistake.'

As Molly stared at him incredulously, George suddenly started applauding. Bella and Professor Markov joined in enthusiastically.

Even Graham managed a couple of claps. 'Well done,' he said. 'Especially as you have so little time to study.'

Slightly mollified, Molly smiled encouragingly at him. 'You did really well too.'

He gave a dismissive shrug. 'That's hardly surprising, is it?' he said. 'I'm a cripple. There's nothing else I can do, except study.'

Molly wanted to slap him, but as she looked into his bitter, self-pitying eyes, she suddenly had an idea. 'That's not true,' she said. 'There are plenty of things you could do. For example, how would you feel about teaching English to my friend's brother-in-law?' For once she had managed to get his attention. 'He's Italian. He was a prisoner of war, but when Italy capitulated, the authorities let him go, and now he's married to my friend's sister. He's not exactly the brightest spark in the box, but his father-in-law will pay.'

Expecting Graham to dismiss the idea out of hand, she was surprised to see a bit of colour staining his pale cheeks. But before he could speak, George had chipped in.

'Is it Gino?' he asked through a mouthful of *vatrushka*, a sticky bun filled with apple puree. When Molly nodded, he grinned at Graham. 'He's really nice,' he said. 'But he's hopeless at English. And at cooking. He makes this thing called gravyoily, and it looks just like slugs. And tastes like them too.'

Molly had to bite back a gurgle of laughter, but Graham nodded knowledgeably. 'Ravioli,' he said. 'I ate it when I was serving in Italy. I rather liked it.' He was silent for a minute, drumming his fingers on the arm of his wheelchair. 'All right,' he said. 'I'll give it a go. But I can't guarantee to be as good a teacher as Professor Markov.' He glanced patronisingly at George. 'I can't imagine how he's managed to get so much information into your thick head, for a start.'

George returned his look benignly. 'I think it's because he makes it fun,' he said. 'Like setting Mrs d'Arcy Billière's kitchen on fire and everything. None of the teachers at school ever did that.'

On the other side of the room, unwittingly living up to his reputation, Professor Markov was diving into Mrs d'Arcy Billière's drinks cupboard. 'We will drink a toast to our brilliance,' he announced, pulling out a bottle of vodka and a handful of glasses. Sloshing a generous measure into each, he gaily handed them round. Then, raising his own glass, he smiled round benevolently. '*Vyp'yem*! Let us drink! Let our wishes be realised and our dreams come true.' He downed the vodka in one, then, smacking his lips in satisfaction, gestured for them to follow suit.

Molly glanced quickly at George, but she was too late. Following the professor's example, he emptied the contents of his glass in one gulp. A second later, he was clutching his throat. 'Aaaaaargh!' he cried, and Molly was laughing so much she could hardly lift her own glass to her lips.

'Drink!' Professor Markov shouted at her. 'Drink to your dreams!'

For a second, Molly forgot that Helen was presumably even now trying to intercept Mrs Priscilla Wright on her way home from the Wimbledon café. She forgot that André was still unaccounted for. She forgot she had failed to keep her promise to Gefreiter Henniker, and she forgot that Callum's terrifying parents were due to arrive in London tomorrow.

For that brief moment, as the alcohol burnt its way down her throat, all that mattered was that she had got one hundred per cent in Professor Markov's exam, and that her ridiculous, pie-in-the-sky dream of achieving the grades to get into medical school had suddenly become a real possibility.

As Molly escorted Bella and George back along Lavender Road half an hour later, they ran into Louise Rutherford and her ghastly brother

Douglas. They were both in uniform, but so muffled up against the cold that, in the drunkenly wavering beam of George's torch, it was hard at first to make out who they were. It was with considerable dismay that Molly recognised Douglas's self-satisfied, plummy voice.

'Anyway,' he was saying, 'I can't tell you exactly what I'll be doing, because it's all frightfully hush-hush.'

'Who goes there?' George shouted at them as they approached. 'Friend or foe?'

As Molly tried to silence him, she heard Louise's distinctive laugh. 'Is that you, George? If so, we're friends.'

George, clearly still under the influence of the vodka, laughed delightedly, but Molly was considerably less enthusiastic. Louise was just about all right, but as far as Molly was concerned, Douglas Rutherford was definitely foe.

Douglas was a prat, and he'd had it in for Molly ever since she'd had to drag him off Angie Carter in the back yard of the Flag and Garter. She had met him again in Tunisia, and although she'd avoided him as much as she could, whenever they bumped into each other, he'd made it his mission to be as objectionable as possible. Helen had contrived to put him in his place a couple of times, but knowing that Lord de Burrel was a friend of Winston Churchill, Douglas was much more circumspect around her. Whereas plebeian Molly he clearly saw as fair game.

Now it seemed the nasty little brute was back in London.

Louise was pointing her torch at them now. 'Oh hello, Molly,' she said. 'Goodness, and Bella too? What are you three doing roaming the streets on such a horrid night?'

'We've been doing an exam,' George said happily. 'I spelt Rhodesia wrong, but Molly came top and soon she's going to go to medical school and become a doctor.'

'I doubt that,' Douglas murmured.

George bristled. 'She is too,' he said. He swung round to Molly, nearly losing his footing on the icy pavement in the process. 'Aren't you?'

247

Molly cringed. 'Well, I am certainly hoping to apply.' She took George's arm and tried to urge him on.

But George stood his ground, glaring at Douglas. 'Then after that she is going to marry her boyfriend and be happy ever after.'

A short silence followed this pronouncement. Then Louise giggled. 'Oh really?' she said. 'I didn't know Molly had a boyfriend.'

And now Molly remembered why she had never much liked Louise either.

'I haven't,' Molly said. 'Come on, George, Bella. For goodness' sake, it's too cold to be standing here chatting.'

'No, don't go,' Douglas said. 'I haven't been introduced to Bella yet.' He held out his hand to the girl and smiled. 'Have you got an imaginary boyfriend too? If not, can I volunteer?'

Naturally Bella didn't answer, but before Molly could intervene, Douglas had taken a step forward and was playing his torch caressingly over the girl's pretty face. 'What's the matter with you?' he asked as Bella blinked against the light. 'Cat got your tongue? Or has Molly been bad-mouthing me as usual?'

'Stop it, Douglas,' Louise said sharply.

But George was already muscling to Bella's defence. 'There's nothing the matter with her,' he said. 'Except she can't talk.'

Douglas ran his torch deliberately down Bella's slender figure. 'How convenient,' he murmured.

'And Molly's boyfriend is not imaginary,' George went on belligerently. 'He's called Callum and he's a pilot in the Royal Canadian Air Force.'

Once again there was a moment's silence, but even before Douglas gave a snort of sceptical amusement, Molly was aware of a hot wave of mortification sweeping up her body. If only she'd had a weapon to hand, she would have willingly killed George there and then. And Professor Markov too. If only the stupid man hadn't given the idiotic child that glass of vodka. If only . . .

Her throat was too tight to speak. But her anger gave her strength.

Digging her fingers deeper into George's arm, she dragged him off up the street, praying that Bella would follow.

Behind her, she heard Louise's incredulous voice. 'Callum Frazer? Ward's cousin?'

And Douglas's mocking laugh. 'In her dreams,' he said. 'I saw them together once or twice in Tunisia, but I saw him with plenty of other girls too. And all one hell of a lot better looking than that dreary, pixie-faced little witch. Good God, a chap like Callum Frazer wouldn't touch Molly Coogan with a bargepole. Nobody in their right mind would.'

Chapter Fifteen

Wimbledon was shrouded in a freezing, bone-chilling fog. From where Helen stood, partially concealed behind a tree at the corner of the Wrights' road, she could see it eerily rolling towards her over the dusk-blackened grass of Wimbledon Common. Inconveniently, there were quite a few people about, swathed in hats and scarves, hurrying homewards with carefully wrapped parcels and baskets presumably containing last-minute Christmas shopping.

Wondering how long it would be before she froze to death, Helen stamped her feet and tried to look as though she was waiting for someone. Which, of course, she was. Nevertheless, convinced that either the icy conditions or the proximity to Christmas would have caused the Wimbledon ladies to cancel their usual Saturday tea party, she was taken by surprise when the front door of the Wrights' house opened and a woman dressed in a long fur coat emerged.

Hastily Helen hurried back to the café on the high street. She had originally intended to wait outside, but she was so cold now, she changed her mind and went in. Summoned by a ping on the doorbell, a waitress in a pink pinafore materialised and showed her to a table.

Helen had barely had time to take off her hat and gloves before the door opened again and the woman in the fur came in. At once a lady at a table on the far side of the room waved her arm and called out, 'Prissy, darling, we're over here.'

Aware of a sudden acceleration of her pulse, Helen covertly watched the newcomer weave her way across the café. When she reached the table, she looked around for the waitress to come and relieve her of her coat. The girl was busy taking Helen's order of a cup of tea and a bun, but eventually she scurried over with an apology and reverentially carried the fur coat away to a cloakroom.

Helen knew from Molly that Priscilla Wright was forty years old, but, revealed now in an elegant, slightly figure-hugging jersey twinset, she looked considerably younger. Even so, Helen couldn't see any resemblance to Molly at all.

Mrs Wright was petite, blond and very attractive, in a carefully coiffured kind of way. Molly certainly wasn't tall, but you couldn't really call her petite, nor did she have her mother's peaches-and-cream complexion. On the contrary, Molly had a snub nose, shortish dark hair with a slightly uneven self-trimmed fringe, and the kind of skin that tanned easily. In Tunisia, she had been positively brown.

Nor did she speak with a slightly affected middle-class accent. From her position on the other side of the café, Helen couldn't hear exactly what Mrs Wright and her friends were saying, but she could hear their self-consciously tinkling laughs and their over-extended vowels.

Helen had drunk two cups of tea and eaten two dainty teacakes before the Wimbledon ladies looked like moving. As soon as she saw them reaching for their handbags, she stood up, put on her coat and, having already paid, exited the café, retracing her steps to the corner of the Wrights' road. It was completely dark now, and an icy mist was swirling under the recently reactivated street lamps.

It wasn't long before she saw Mrs Wright walking towards her. As the other woman approached, looming in and out of the lamp-light, the heels of her stylish, albeit well-worn, winter boots clicking rhythmically on the slippery pavement, Helen could feel her heart accelerating. This was going to be the tricky bit and, for Molly's sake, she desperately didn't want to get it wrong.

'Excuse me,' she murmured politely, stepping out of the shadow of the tree into the oncoming woman's path. 'But I think you must be Mrs Wright. I wonder if you can help me.'

Mrs Wright stopped and, taking a step back, eyed her uncertainly. She showed no sign of recognising her from the café, but perhaps reassured by Helen's well-modulated voice and tidy, well-groomed appearance, she nodded and smiled faintly. 'What can I do for you?'

Encouraged, Helen smiled back. 'My name is Helen de Burrel,' she said. 'I am a friend of . . . of someone you used to know. Quite a long time ago. Someone who is hoping to get back in touch with you.'

Mrs Wright raised her eyebrows in polite enquiry. 'Oh yes?' she said. 'And who is that?'

Helen took a slow breath. 'Her name is Molly Coogan.'

If she'd said she was a friend of the devil incarnate, she could hardly have got a more dramatic reaction. For a second, Mrs Wright's eyes looked as though they were going to pop out of her head. The peaches vanished from her cheeks, leaving her looking ashen and grey. Taking another convulsive step back, she slipped on the icy pavement, gave a strangled cry and crashed to the ground.

If it hadn't been so awful, it would have been funny. But Helen certainly wasn't laughing as she helped the poor woman back to her feet. Nor was Priscilla Wright. It had been a hard fall, and as her heel threatened to slip on the ice again, she was forced to cling to Helen's arm.

But as soon as she had regained her balance, she thrust Helen violently away. 'Leave me alone,' she hissed. 'How dare you come and threaten me. I don't know what you want, but whatever it is, you've got the wrong person. I don't know anyone of that name. I never have.'

'I have no intention of threatening you,' Helen said. 'Or of embarrassing you. That's why I didn't come to the house. I just wanted to ask—'

'No,' Mrs Wright almost shouted. 'Don't you dare come to the

252

house. My husband . . .' She stopped, wobbled slightly and put out a gloved hand to steady herself against the lamp post.

'Your husband doesn't know?' Helen suggested gently. 'Well, don't worry. I'm not going to tell him.'

Suddenly Mrs Wright started scrabbling in the handbag that was still hooked over her arm. 'What do you want? How much?'

Helen stared at her in amazement. 'I'm not trying to blackmail you,' she said. 'And nor is Molly.'

Mrs Wright recoiled again at the name. But some of the fight had gone out of her. 'How did you find me?' she muttered angrily. 'Why were you even looking? They promised they'd tell her that I was dead.'

'They did,' Helen said. 'And it's a long story. But now we have found you, surely you must want to know about her? Don't you want to know how she turned out?'

Mrs Wright stared at her as though she was mad. 'No,' she said. 'Don't you understand what I've been saying? I don't want to know anything. Whoever your friend may claim to be, she's nothing to do with me.'

Helen couldn't help uttering a slight gasp of dismay, but Mrs Wright didn't seem to notice. She was looking around rather wildly, as though afraid that someone might be listening. 'My God,' she muttered. 'If this should get out . . .' She stopped abruptly, clearly unable or unwilling to articulate the unthinkable horror of exposure. 'My whole life, my family, everything . . .' She tailed off again, and stood for a moment in silence.

Then she lifted her chin defiantly, and Helen caught a sudden glint of steel in her eye. Molly's mother might be petite, but she wasn't short on guts, or gall.

'I can't help you,' Priscilla Wright said grittily. 'Nor do I believe you can prove anything. My name is not Coogan, and it never has been. You've clearly got the wrong person. So please don't bother me again. Either of you. If you do, I'll go to the police and have you arrested.'

253

It was clearly an empty threat, but there was nothing Helen could do about it. She had tried, and she had failed. She was already wondering how on earth she was going to break the news to Molly.

Unable to think of anything else to say, she turned away. But at the corner, she stopped and looked back. To her surprise, Mrs Wright was still standing under the street lamp.

'I'm staying at the Flag and Garter pub, in Lavender Road, in Clapham,' Helen called through the swirling mist. 'If you change your mind, you can contact me there.'

Mrs Wright didn't answer. She might not even have heard. She just swung on her heel and disappeared into the darkness.

'You're late, Nurse Coogan,' Mr Sparrow said. 'You were meant to report for duty at six o'clock.'

'I know,' Molly said. 'But my landlady's son wasn't feeling very well.' She could hardly explain that what had really delayed her was trying to prevent George Nelson, still under the influence of Mrs d'Arcy Billière's vodka, running off in hot pursuit of Douglas Rutherford with the express purpose of 'punching his lights out'.

'I like Louise,' George had announced as Molly bundled him forcefully into the house, 'but I don't like that brother of hers. Even if he is an officer in the Coldstream Guards.'

But although Molly agreed with him about Douglas, she didn't feel that any further intervention by George was likely to do her much good. The damage was done, the Callum Frazer cat was well and truly out of the bag, and she was going to have to live with it. As for Douglas's comments about her, well, she knew he was being deliberately malicious. That didn't stop her feeling upset, though. Even if it was exactly what she had so often told herself. She knew Callum was hardly the type of young man to fall in love with someone like her. Nevertheless, the thought of him dating other girls left her feeling as though someone had kicked a hole in her heart.

All in all, it wasn't surprising she was late for work. And now Mr

Sparrow was expecting her to set off immediately for Southampton, where a hospital ship was due to dock later that evening.

'You're the only trained nurse I've got on tonight,' he said crossly, seeing her dismay. 'You said you didn't mind working a bit extra over Christmas.'

It was true, Molly had volunteered to work over the Christmas holiday. Mainly because she wanted to avoid being in the pub when Callum's parents turned up. She knew it was cowardly, especially as Katy needed her help, but now, even more than before, she had good reason to keep well away. Neither Louise nor Douglas were known for their discretion, and the thought of someone teasing her about Callum in front of his dour, authoritarian father didn't bear thinking about.

'There's a train at six thirty from Clapham Junction,' Mr Sparrow said. 'So you had better get your skates on.'

'Oh no,' Molly wailed. 'My friend Helen is due to call here later with some news for me, and—'

'Well, it will have to wait,' Mr Sparrow interrupted heartlessly. 'This isn't a social club. There is still a war on, you know. That reminds me. I've got a note for you here somewhere from my wife.'

Molly had been on the point of turning away. But now she swung round so fast she nearly knocked him over as he fumbled in his pocket.

'Is it about André Cabillard?' she asked eagerly.

He drew out a folded piece of paper. 'Yes,' he said. 'But I'm afraid it's not the news your friend was hoping for.'

Molly stared at him in alarm, then at the handwritten note.

Dear Miss Coogan,

Further to my enquiry on your behalf, the International Committee of the Red Cross have finally responded to the effect that they have no record of anyone by the name of Cabillard being present in any of the prisoner-of-war camps they have visited. As, under the terms of the Geneva Convention, all military prisoner-of-war camps must allow

Red Cross access, we must assume that your friend is not present in any such camp. However, on further questioning, my personal contact in Geneva has reluctantly confirmed something that some of us have suspected for some time: that there are other prison camps in existence in Germany to which, since they house so-called 'enemies of the state' – saboteurs, dissidents and so on – rather than purely military prisoners of war, the Red Cross have not been granted access. It is therefore possible that your friend is incarcerated in one of these. If, as is hoped, the Red Cross succeeds in due course in gaining access to these other camps, my contact will make further enquiries. In the meantime, I hope this information proves useful.

Yours,

Mrs P. Sparrow

Molly closed her eyes. She didn't like the sound of 'other camps', and dreaded to think what sort of conditions might prevail in such places. She knew from her own experience in Italy that the Germans used a very loose interpretation of the Geneva Convention. And now there was talk of death camps for Jews, and torture chambers too. There was even a horrible waxwork exhibit somewhere in central London showing the vicious techniques the Nazis allegedly used on their enemies. George had wanted to go and see it, but thankfully Pam and Alan had forbidden it.

Molly opened her eyes to find Mr Sparrow watching her. 'Thank you,' she said. 'Please thank your wife, too.' And feeling cowardly once again, she was almost glad she had to rush off to catch the train. She thrust the note back into Mr Sparrow's hand. 'Could you give this to Helen de Burrel when she calls by,' she said. 'Please can you explain that I've been called away, and tell her I'll come to the pub as soon I get back, to find out about . . .' She paused and took a steadying breath. 'About the other matter.'

Joyce glared at the dead chicken lying on her kitchen sideboard. Last year she had cooked a beautiful turkey for Christmas lunch. All her children had been there – except Bob, of course; the Nazis weren't much of ones for letting their prisoners go home for Christmas. But this year, there were no turkeys to be had anywhere. This piddly chicken was all she could get, and she'd virtually had to sleep with Mr Dove, the butcher, to get even that.

'A puff of wind and it will blow away,' she muttered to herself as she sat down at the table and began plucking it crossly.

She could hear Angie laughing at something in the front room. Perhaps Gino was attempting to tell her a joke, Joyce thought sourly. That would be the day. She and Albert hadn't told Gino yet about the English lessons Molly was organising. They were saving that for Christmas Day. It was an odd sort of present, but at least it was useful, although now she came to think of it, maybe some cooking lessons would have been even more useful. Gino and Angie were still getting a few customers for their Italian evenings, but they were hardly a sell-out success. Angie insisted that they needed time to educate the locals' palates in foreign food, but Joyce suspected it was Gino who needed educating, in how to cook a decent meal.

Hearing a knock on the front door, she shouted to Angie to go and see who it was, and then groaned as the draught from the opening door blew chicken feathers all over the room.

A moment later, Angie appeared in the doorway. She wasn't laughing now. But nor had she shut the front door. Joyce could hardly see her for feathers and was just about to berate her when she caught sight of the yellow piece of paper trembling in her hand.

Angie took a shaky step forward and laid the telegram on the sideboard.

Joyce stared at it. Stared at the feathers already settling on top of it. Then, very slowly, she picked it up.

Immediate, it read. *For Mrs J. Carter. Regret to inform you Private Paul Carter seriously wounded during recent action. Prognosis not good. Further information will be communicated in due course.*

'Oh Mum,' Angie whispered.

Joyce had forgotten her daughter was there. Now she looked up at her blankly. 'Where's Albert?' she asked.

'He's in the pub,' Angie said. She turned blindly towards the door. 'I'll tell Gino to fetch him.'

Joyce didn't move. She couldn't. It was as though the shock had turned her into a block of stone.

Albert was there within a minute. 'Oh my dear,' he murmured as he drew her into his arms, feathers and all. 'I am so sorry.'

He was breathing hard and his jacket was cold and damp. Joyce realised he must have run back from the pub without even stopping to put on his coat.

Behind him she heard Gino muttering something to Angie and Bella.

'Is not dead,' he said. 'Only wounded. Is possible he still be OK, no?'

Joyce wanted to scream at him to shut up. His stupid pidgin English got on her nerves. But more than that, she almost couldn't bear that flicker of hope. They wouldn't have telegrammed if it hadn't been very serious.

'I can't bear to think of him lying there in pain,' she muttered into Albert's shoulder. 'This bloody war. I hate it. I absolutely hate it. I should never have let him join up. He's only just sixteen. *Sixteen*.'

'I know,' Albert said gently. 'You did everything you could to stop him. But it was what he wanted to do. And Gino is right, you know. We can't start grieving yet. We have to stay strong and keep hoping for the best. It won't be easy, but we will bear it together, as a family.'

It was a slow journey back from Wimbledon. The wind had blown some branches onto the railway track and they had to wait until a suitable person came to clear them. It had begun to get so cold in her carriage that Helen had been tempted to get out and move the damned things herself.

When she eventually arrived at the Red Cross first-aid post, Molly wasn't there.

'I'm afraid she's been called away,' Mr Sparrow said. He coughed awkwardly and reached for something off the shelf. 'She asked me to give you this.'

Helen read the note from Mr Sparrow's wife with a sense of stunned disbelief. She had spent the whole journey worrying about how to tell Molly what had happened with her mother; she hadn't expected to receive bad news herself. However much she had told herself that the Red Cross had always been a long shot, deep down she'd been secretly hoping that they'd come back with the news that they had found André somewhere, alive and well. The disappointment was intense.

'What's the point of the International Red Cross if they don't visit all the prison camps?' she asked Mr Sparrow crossly. 'God only knows what's going on in those "other camps".'

He looked startled. 'Well, it's not their fault,' he said defensively. 'If the Germans won't give them access . . .'

'Of course it's their fault,' Helen said. 'The Germans are clearly playing them for fools. And they aren't doing a damn thing to stop it.'

Mr Sparrow bristled. 'That's all very well for you to say, but it states quite clearly in the Geneva Convention that—'

But Helen wasn't in the mood to listen to someone who looked like Adolf Hitler pontificating about the Geneva Convention. 'I don't care what it states,' she snapped. 'And I don't suppose for a moment Hitler does either.'

Mr Sparrow's eyes bulged alarmingly. 'Well, really . . .' he began.

Suddenly Helen remembered that this was Molly's boss. The last thing Molly needed right now was for her to alienate him. 'I'm sorry,' she said. 'I didn't mean to be rude. I'm very grateful to your wife for trying.' She paused and closed her eyes for a moment. What a horrible day it was turning out to be. She took a steadying breath. 'But I still need to see Molly. Do you know when she's going to get back?'

'Not until tomorrow,' Mr Sparrow said with vengeful satisfaction.

Helen groaned. 'But I won't be here tomorrow,' she said. The following day was Christmas Eve, and she was on duty at Kempton Park all day. She couldn't keep Molly waiting that long.

Awkwardly she raised her eyes to Mr Sparrow. 'Do you by any chance have a piece of writing paper and an envelope I could borrow?' she asked.

Mr Sparrow pursed his lips in irritation. 'This is a first-aid post,' he said, 'not a post office.' But eventually, with a good deal of huffing and puffing, he produced some stationery and let Helen sit down at his desk.

Dear Molly,

I know this is a ghastly way to tell you, but I'm working all day tomorrow and I couldn't leave you on tenterhooks.

I'm really, really sorry, but your mother didn't want to meet you.

She was terribly shocked about being found, and probably wasn't thinking straight, but she clearly can't bear the thought of anyone discovering about her past.

I know it's not what you wanted to hear and I wish I'd handled it better. I haven't handled Mr Sparrow very well either. I'm afraid I flew off the handle with him over André and the Geneva Convention. In fact I'd better stop now before he throws me out.

Helen x

On the envelope she wrote: *For Molly Coogan – to be opened in private.* That was the best she could do. At least that way Molly would be able to read the note, and perhaps come to terms with it, before having to face the inquisitive eyes of Mr Sparrow, or indeed of George Nelson, or anyone else in Lavender Road. Even if Helen couldn't spare her the pain of knowing that her mother didn't want to see her, she could at least spare her that.

It was late in the evening by the time Molly reached Southampton, and freezing cold. The whole place seemed bleak and godforsaken.

The city had been badly bombed over the last few years, the docks included. Icy sleet was blowing in from the sea, and Molly was glad that she had borrowed Alan Nelson's old Home Guard greatcoat, even if it looked a bit odd over her uniform. She didn't care. Rather that than freeze to death.

Inevitably, the hospital ship was late. In the end, it didn't dock until well after midnight, by which time Molly had spent three hours unsuccessfully trying to snooze in a hard chair in one of the American Transport Corps offices. The US Army 14th Major Port Transportation Corps was in overall charge of the docks. They were also in charge of the transit camp for German POWs on West Quay. And now there was another delay because the hospital ship was also carrying prisoners of war, and for some reason they had to be disembarked first.

Molly was starving, and seeing through the window that a WVS canteen van had arrived, she decided to venture outside to get a cup of tea and a sandwich.

She was standing in the long queue, stamping her feet to try to keep warm, and patiently waiting her turn, when two Americans soldiers pushed in ahead of her.

'You don't mind, do you, darling?' one of them muttered, blowing on his hands. 'It's just that those Jerry bastards will be getting off any time now and we figure this is the last chance we'll get for a cuppa.'

Molly did mind. She was cold and tired and frustrated. She could easily have left London on a later train, which would have meant that, instead of freezing to death at the docks, she could have been finding out from Helen what had happened in Wimbledon.

But she knew better than to voice her irritation. Instead she took a step to one side, and resigned herself to waiting even longer for her own much-needed cuppa. But as she slotted back into line behind them, she realised there was something vaguely familiar about the two men. Certainly they were making no secret of the fact that they were looking at her. Indeed, after a moment, one of them addressed her again.

'Hey,' he said. 'Aren't you one of the gals who came down to Devizes to interview that Kraut prisoner?'

At once, Molly remembered. They were the men who had been standing menacingly each side of Gefreiter Henniker when she and Helen had first been shown into the interview room at the prison.

The other soldier gave a short laugh. 'Hell, you sure caused a stir,' he said. 'Thanks to you, we had to move the whole shooting match up to some place in Scotland.'

'So I gathered,' Molly said drily.

The man laughed again. 'Just in time too, I reckon.' They were at the front of the queue now, and he paused to give his order to the tweedy WVS lady peering out of the hatch.

'Turns out they've been busy killing each other up there,' the other man said. 'Our CO told us this morning. Two of the bastards are dead already. One was found hanging from a rafter, and the other was kicked to death in the latrines.'

Molly felt as though he had punched her in the stomach. It was a moment before she could speak. 'Oh no,' she gasped. 'What were their names? The men that died? Please tell me it wasn't the man I spoke to? Gefreiter Henniker?'

The men were taking their coffees now. The taller of the two turned and grinned at her unconcernedly. 'Hell if I know,' he said. 'These Nazi bastards are all the same to us. Any case, what difference does it make? I figure the more of them kill each other, the better. Saves us doing it.'

And with that they were gone, leaving Molly shaken and angry. 'But they aren't all the same,' she muttered. 'Gefreiter Henniker is not the same. Please God, don't let it be him.'

The WVS lady peered at her out of the hatch. 'You poor dear,' she said. 'You look frozen to death. What you need is a nice warm cup of tea.'

Jen woke up on the morning of Christmas Eve with a sense of dread. She'd been all right until she'd heard the news about Paul last night. At just sixteen, Paul was the youngest of her four brothers, and perhaps as a result, her favourite. Like her mother, she had tried to dissuade him from enlisting. But in the end, he'd run away and joined up anyway. He was military mad and wanted nothing more than to kill Germans.

Now it seemed they had almost managed to kill him. And the news that he had been wounded in action made her even more worried about Henry. She'd only heard from him once since his precipitate departure from London, a brief note apologising for leaving her in the lurch and promising to get back as soon as humanly possible so they could reactivate their wedding plans. *My darling*, he had written, *it was agony leaving you. Especially after what we had shared.*

A pleasant frisson of remembered warmth had travelled down her spine at the words, but now, as she lay in Mrs d'Arcy Billière's guest bedroom, she began wondering why she hadn't heard from him since. Abruptly she pushed back the covers. All this worrying was making her feel sick. Almost as sick as she'd felt earlier in the week, on the last day of term at RADA, when she'd been picked to perform one of Lady Macbeth's speeches in front of the whole school. Despite her nerves, she had done it well, and the generous applause had made all the scrimping and saving she'd had to do to in order to attend the prestigious academy worthwhile. Mr Lorenz might have been paying for the course, but her rent was coming out of her rapidly dwindling savings.

She reached over to the bedside table for her engagement ring, but as she picked it up, it slipped out of her clammy fingers and skittered away over the floor. When she bent down to pick it up, she realised she felt rather more than sick; she felt distinctly dizzy as well. So much so that she had to grasp the foot of the bed to stop herself falling over.

It was as she sat on the bed clutching the ring in her hand, waiting for the giddiness to wear off, that a horrible thought crept into her mind.

Slowly, carefully, she calculated the days.

It was exactly three weeks since that day she and Henry had ripped each other's clothes off in this very bed. And well over four weeks since she'd last had the curse. She wasn't always regular, but nevertheless . . .

'Oh no,' she whispered. She couldn't be so unlucky. But the truth was that she could. All the other times Henry had used protection, but not that time. It had been too rushed, too unplanned, too overwhelmingly exciting. With a squirm of horror, Jen remembered that he had offered to stop, and she had prevented him. More than that, she had urged him on. Surely some beastly, vengeful God wasn't going to make her pay the price for that one moment of wild, unbridled enthusiasm?

Now Jen really did feel sick. She didn't want to be pregnant. She certainly didn't want a baby. She didn't even like babies. In fact she quite actively disliked them. In any case, she was too young. She had her RADA course to finish. A career to pursue.

Desperately she tried to calm her rising sense of panic. Maybe she was wrong. She could be feeling sick because of Mrs d'Arcy Billière's disgusting *pelmeni* dumplings the evening before. Or perhaps the stress of Henry's departure had affected her more than she'd realised. It wasn't as though she hadn't been late before.

Tentatively she stood up and slipped the ring onto her finger. She felt better now. Quite hungry, in fact. The dizziness had passed. There was nothing she could do about it anyway. Not until after Christmas. Not until she knew for sure.

For Molly it had been a long, horrible night. It had taken an age for the German prisoners to be escorted off the boat and into the delousing unit. And another age to transfer the wounded Allied soldiers from the boat to the train. Then, just as they had finally pulled out of the station, the train had broken down.

There was only one doctor on board and nowhere near enough nursing staff. Molly was run off her feet hurrying from one carriage to the next, trying to give as much relief as she could. Some of the soldiers had come straight from the battlefield. Many were suffering from severe frostbite. Others were covered head to toe in mud. Most were in considerable pain. There was very little water on the train, and even less morphine. The best Molly could do was wrap them in warm blankets, wipe their faces and mutter empty words of comfort and encouragement.

One young American whose legs had been blown off by a mine showed her a Christmas card he had received from General Patton. On the back was printed a prayer asking God to intervene on behalf of the Allies. 'I guess God wasn't listening,' he whispered. 'Sometimes I wonder if he ever does.'

The next time she visited that carriage, the young man had died.

They didn't reach London until ten o'clock on Christmas Eve morning. By the time the wounded had been distributed to various London hospitals, and the dead to the morgue, it was mid afternoon. Molly hadn't slept for thirty-three hours, and the last food to pass her lips had been the WVS cheese sandwich on the dock at Southampton. All she wanted to do was fall into bed, and it took every scrap of her rapidly waning willpower to drag herself back to the Red Cross post to write her report.

There she found a couple of the other girls chatting over a cup of tea. As soon as they saw her, they started giggling. 'Looks like someone had a rough night,' one of them muttered.

There was no sign of Mr Sparrow, but a sealed envelope addressed to Molly was tucked into the top of the report pad. Recognising Helen's writing, Molly felt her heart accelerate.

'Go on, open it,' one of the girls called over. 'We're dying to know what's inside.'

Molly stared at the envelope. It was going to be bad news. That much was obvious. Helen wouldn't have told her to open it privately otherwise. But after the night she had just had, she was almost past caring.

Nevertheless, having waited to open the envelope until she was on her way home, her fingers were quivering so much she could hardly hold the paper steady. And not just her fingers. Her heart was quivering too, and jolting, as though someone had got it in a vice and it was trying to escape. It was getting dark now, and there were very few people about. For a horrible second or two, Molly had a vision of passing out and being left to freeze to death on the pavement.

But she didn't pass out, even though part of her wanted to. Instead, somewhat to her surprise, a surge of hot, resentful fury jolted her back into life. How dare her mother spurn her? How dare those Red Cross girls mock her? How dare those American soldiers laugh at her concern about Gefreiter Henniker? She was fed up of being treated like a nobody. She might be ugly and inept and clearly surplus to her mother's requirements, but at least she had a conscience. A sense of justice. And before she got into bed and beat her brains out on the pillow, there was one more thing she had to do.

Determinedly, she marched up Lavender Road to the Flag and Garter, opened the door and pushed through the blackout curtain.

The fug of smoke enveloped her like a toxic cloud. The pub was busy and noisy. Katy had strung bunches of holly and mistletoe from the beams. Christmas carols were playing on the wireless. Some of the drinkers were singing along, others were chatting and laughing. The whole place looked festive and jolly. But Molly didn't feel jolly or festive. On the contrary, she felt angry and oddly unbalanced, as though she was occupying someone else's body.

She saw Ward at once. He was standing by the blazing fire, chatting to a woman wearing a smart navy suit, smiling at something she was saying.

Once upon a time that smile had curled round Molly's heart, but now she wanted to slap it off his handsome face. He didn't care. None of them did. None of the men in charge, at least. They treated this war as some kind of elaborate game, a game they were determined to win at any cost.

Somewhat to Molly's surprise, the crowd parted as she headed towards the fireplace. She was vaguely aware of people gawping at her as she stumbled past, but she didn't care. She didn't care that she was still wearing Alan Nelson's greatcoat. Or that her nurse's cap felt a bit askew. All she cared about was getting to Ward Frazer.

He had noticed her now, and as he put out a hand to steady her impetuous approach, his smile faded abruptly.

'Molly?' His lovely Canadian voice sounded concerned. 'Are you OK? You look kind of—'

'No, I'm not OK,' Molly snapped. 'Something awful has happened, and you're the only person who can help me.'

'Of course I'll help you,' Ward said promptly. 'What is it you want me to do?'

'I want you to go to Scotland.'

Ward's grey eyes widened. 'Scotland?' She saw a tremor of something like amusement cross his lips. 'What? Right now?'

Molly glared at him, wondering if perhaps he'd had a bit too much to drink. 'Yes, right now,' she said. 'It's Gefreiter Henniker. I told you he was in danger. But you wouldn't listen. Nobody would. And now—'

Ward raised his hands as though to fend off the accusation. 'I did listen,' he objected.

'But you didn't do anything about it,' Molly said. 'You didn't get him out of there. And now I think he's been killed.'

A sudden silence greeted this announcement. For some odd reason everyone else had stopped talking, and Molly was suddenly aware of a rather tinny rendering of 'Jingle Bells' playing in the background. Ward didn't seem to notice the music, but he did cast a faintly agonised glance towards Katy, who was standing rather rigidly behind the bar.

But when he turned back, instead of the expression of shock and horror that Molly expected to see in his grey eyes, she caught a glint of something else. A mixture of humour and compassion.

'I'm sure he's fine,' he said soothingly. 'I'd have heard if he had been killed. In any case, there's nothing we can do about it now. How about we talk again tomorrow when you are feeling calmer?'

267

But Molly wasn't in the mood to be fobbed off by his charm. '*No*,' she said. It came out much louder than she intended. 'I'm feeling perfectly calm and I want to talk about it *now*.'

Hearing a sudden snort of mirth behind her, she swung round to see Douglas Rutherford watching her with a look of incredulous glee on his smug little face.

'I don't know what you think's so funny,' she snapped at him. 'You've never even seen a German, let alone killed one. All you ever did in Tunisia was stand around looking pretty outside Allied head-quarters. But you're not so pretty now, are you? Not since that camel kicked you in the face and broke your nose.' She saw him flinch. 'Oh yes, you may well flush up. I know you told everyone it happened during a skirmish with natives, but I know the truth, and so do you.'

Douglas wasn't laughing now, but several other people were. Including Louise.

'What's more,' Molly went on, warming to her theme. She hadn't realised quite how satisfying it would be to tell Douglas Rutherford some home truths. 'Callum Frazer might have hundreds of girlfriends for all I care. But at least he doesn't spend his time trying to touch up underage girls.'

Suddenly Katy was at her elbow.

'Molly,' she said gently. 'I think I'd better take you home, before you—'

'I don't *want* to go home,' Molly snapped. She snatched her arm away from Katy's insistent fingers. 'I want to stay here and talk to Ward.'

Ward had apparently been amused by her assault on Douglas too. As she swung back to him, she could see a sparkle of shocked laughter lurking in his grey eyes.

'In that case,' he said, slightly unsteadily, 'perhaps I should take this opportunity to introduce you to my aunt, Mrs Frazer.' He indicated the smart navy-clad woman who was standing rock-still beside him. 'She and my uncle have just this minute arrived from Canada.'

Molly felt the ground heave under her feet.

Suddenly, in a horrible flash, reality returned. And with it a sense of horror and embarrassment so great that all she could do was turn on her heel and flee.

Once again the crowd in the bar parted for her, like Moses parting the Red Sea. But as Molly plunged through the blackout curtain, she cannoned headlong into somebody else coming in.

'Molly?' Even through her panic, Callum's voice was instantly recognisable, and she froze mid stride. As she looked up at him in numb shock, he smiled his wonderful smile.

'I've been looking all over for you,' he said. 'Where the hell have you been? I guess I should have let you know I was coming to London, but I was hoping to surprise you.'

Molly couldn't speak. She couldn't do anything except stand there and stare into his lovely eyes. Only to see them narrow in dismay. 'Hey, sweetheart,' he said. He raised a hand towards her face. 'You've got blood on your cheek. Are you OK?'

But Molly had reached the end of her tether. She had made enough of a fool of herself already. She knew that if she let his fingers touch her skin, she would be lost. 'Leave me alone,' she screamed. 'I'm not your sweetheart. And I don't like surprises.'

And with that, she pushed past him and ran out into the blessed darkness.

Part Four

Chapter Sixteen

Afterwards, everyone agreed that Christmas 1944 was the worst Christmas of the war. After expectations of an early end to the conflict, it was demoralising that the Germans were now punching back with such force. The weather was awful, icy, cold and dark. Many winter crops had failed, even potatoes were in short supply, and the banks had run out of sixpences for electricity meters.

For Helen, haunted by endless images of André being tortured in some hideous SS prison, waiting his turn to step out in front of a Nazi firing squad, or already lying somewhere in an unmarked grave, it was hard to summon up much Christmas spirit.

When she'd got back from work late on Christmas Eve, Katy had told her about Molly's extraordinary outburst in the pub. 'It was awful,' she said. 'I can't imagine what came over her. It was almost as though she was drunk or something. She came barging in, looking like the wild woman of the West, covered in blood and her hair all over the place, and in front of Callum's parents too. Oh God, it could hardly have been worse.'

It wasn't hard for Helen to guess what had come over Molly. All day Helen had been regretting leaving that note. It had been a stupidly insensitive way to impart such bad news. No wonder Molly had been in a state.

'And goodness only knows what she said to Callum,' Katy went on. 'She must have bumped into him outside. When he came in a minute later, he was very subdued. And he nearly bit his father's head off when Mr Frazer made some joshing remark about him apparently having hundreds of girlfriends.'

Helen reached for her coat. 'I'll go over and see her,' she said.

'I've already been,' Katy said. 'I went as soon as the Frazers left. But Pam said she'd gone to bed and didn't want to see anybody. Not even me.'

Helen grimaced. 'Then maybe I'd better let her sleep,' she said. 'I'll talk to her in the morning.'

But when, having been woken by an overexcited Malcolm just after seven o'clock on Christmas Day, Helen went over the Nelsons' house, armed with Christmas presents wrapped in colourful magazine covers, she found that Molly had already left for work.

'I tried to persuade her to take the day off,' Pam said. 'She looked like death this morning. But she insisted she wasn't ill.' She glanced at Helen. 'Were you in the pub last night?'

Helen shook her head. 'No, but Katy told me what happened.'

'And me,' Pam said. She sighed. 'It's hardly surprising Molly flipped. She's got so much on her plate at the moment, what with long hours at the Red Cross, and helping in the pub, as well as her studies. This extra thing about the German prisoner obviously just tipped her over the edge.'

Helen nodded, though actually she felt it was much more likely that the news about her mother had done it.

But of course she didn't say so. Instead, having handed over her gifts, and dutifully admired the *World Atlas in Colour* George had found in his stocking, she headed back over the road to the pub, where she found Katy in a state of anxiety about Christmas lunch, to which Callum and his parents had been invited.

Convinced that Maurice Frazer had come over for the express purpose of persuading Ward to return to Canada when the war was over, Katy was determined to prove what a civilised and flourishing life she and Ward led at the pub. She was therefore appalled that while she had been at the Christmas service, Lucky the dog had scoffed half of the already rather meagre Christmas pudding she'd left on the sideboard.

Callum and his parents arrived before last orders had been called, and as Katy had given Elsa the day off, they unfortunately had to wait for lunch until the Flag and Garter customers had drunk up and left.

While Katy finished in the bar and Ward tried to speed up the final stages of cooking lunch, Helen manfully tried to engage Mr and Mrs Frazer in jolly conversation. She found to her surprise that once she got used to Ward's uncle's tendency to stand on his dignity, he wasn't quite as intimidating as Katy and Molly had made out. His wife, although admittedly somewhat severe looking, was actually quite friendly, and clearly very proud of her handsome pilot son.

'I gather from Callum that you were in Tunisia too?' she said.

'Yes, I was.' Helen smiled. 'And I can assure you he didn't have hundreds of girlfriends.'

But even that effort to lighten the mood backfired, because Maurice Frazer overheard, and remarked that he would much prefer his son to play the field than make a fool of himself over someone unsuitable.

As this was clearly a dig about Molly, Helen glanced nervously across at Callum, who was sitting further up at the bar, desultorily talking to Katy. It wasn't clear whether he had heard or not. But the way he was moodily twiddling a beer mat in his fingers told her that he wasn't in the sunniest of tempers.

Nevertheless, despite the evident friction between father and son, Helen couldn't quite see why Katy was so nervous about Christmas lunch.

But half an hour later, as Ward was serving up the rather stodgy chicken pie Katy had made, Malcolm dropped a roast potato on the floor and exclaimed with considerable delight, 'Bugger!'

Callum, momentarily startled out of his bad mood, gave a choke of laughter, but his father was not at all amused. And when Katy mumbled apologetically that Malcolm must have picked the word up in the taproom, Maurice Frazer remarked that in his opinion a pub was not a fit place to bring up children.

All in all, it was a difficult Christmas Day, compounded, in Katy's view at least, by the extravagant presents Ward's parents had sent over with them for the children.

'It's bare-faced bribery,' she muttered as soon as the Frazers had finally departed. She eyed with displeasure the glossy push-along tricycle that had arrived for Malcolm. Baby Caroline had received a huge Ideal 'Mayfair' composite doll almost as large as she was, with jointed limbs, dark curly hair and rather spooky opening and closing eyes. And for her first birthday, which fell on the same day, four beautiful hand-embroidered little dresses with matching bootees.

'Oh, I don't think so,' Helen said. 'But they certainly are generous gifts.' There had been nothing like that available in England since the beginning of the war. All Helen had found for Malcolm was a flimsy colouring book, and for Caroline she'd bought a funny little metal chicken on wheels from a man selling them on the street corner in Kempton. She'd bought one for Nellie, too. For George, on Molly's advice, she'd bought a second-hand geometry set in a wooden box.

It seemed a boring gift, but when she went over later to see if Molly was home yet, George seemed to be thrilled with it. While Pam went into the kitchen to make a cup of tea, he painstakingly demonstrated the workings of the hinged metal compass, into which he had already fitted a stubby pencil. 'Now I can draw a circle of any diameter,' he said. He eyed the result with evident satisfaction. 'I bet Professor Markov will be impressed.'

Helen glanced at him with amusement. 'When did you start liking geometry so much?' she asked.

He looked a bit sheepish. 'It's only because Professor Markov makes it fun,' he said. 'It was always so dull in school. I hope Mum and Dad don't make me go back there when the war's over.'

Knowing George would certainly be expected to resume normal schooling as soon as the war ended, Helen didn't quite know what to say. But she didn't want to spoil his Christmas, so she changed the subject and asked him when Molly was due home.

He wrinkled his nose. 'She told me that if anyone asked, to say she wouldn't be back until very late. But I don't think she meant you. I think she meant Callum Frazer.'

'And did he ask?'

He nodded. 'Yes, he called by this morning before he went over to the pub. But I don't understand why she doesn't want to see him. It's not as though he's not nice. Because he is, *and* he's a Spitfire pilot, and he's probably shot down hundreds of German planes.'

Helen bit back a smile. 'Unfortunately, it's not quite as simple as that,' she said.

'But I know she likes him,' George insisted. 'Because she went all red when I told her that he'd come knocking at the door last night when she was asleep.' He fiddled with the compass for a moment, his brows together, then looked up.

'Do you think I ought to talk to him?' he suggested. 'I could tell him that she likes him really.'

Helen shook her head hastily. The thought of George and Callum having a man-to-man discussion about life and love made her feel quite anxious. 'Oh no,' she said. 'It's never good to interfere. I think you should let them sort things out on their own.'

George looked disgruntled. 'Well, I don't see how they can sort things out if Molly won't talk to him.' He clearly had more to say on the subject, but luckily Pam came in with the tea, and he was distracted by the presence on the tray of a small fruit cake with a tiny plastic model of Father Christmas perched on top.

'Oh, yum,' he said. He glanced at Helen eagerly. 'And after tea, if Molly comes back, I'm going to show you a new magic trick I've designed for Bunny.'

But Molly didn't come back, and having waited for ages, and eventually been shown on her own the rather impressive trick in which George somehow contrived to magically produce his pet rabbit out of a previously empty top hat, Helen went back to the pub to help Katy with the Christmas evening rush while Ward put the children to bed.

Molly had never felt worse in her life. Not only was she utterly mortified by her behaviour in the pub on Christmas Eve, she was still feeling angry that nobody had listened to her warnings about Gefreiter Henniker's safety. But as Helen had suspected, more than anything, she had been cut to the quick by her mother's rejection of her tentative advances. She had felt so peculiar, shaky and distracted on Christmas Day that she had begun to wonder if she was going mad. However much she told herself nothing had changed, that it made no difference to her one way or another, she knew something *had* changed. Instead of wondering vaguely what had happened to her mother, she now knew only too well. And it hurt like hell.

For two days she contrived to avoid seeing anyone apart from the Nelsons. She knew Callum had called a couple of times, but she couldn't bear to see him. Not in the state she was in. She couldn't trust herself to hide her real feelings, but she knew she had to. The alternative was to throw herself into his arms, which was clearly out of the question.

The thought of meeting Callum's parents was even worse. Her fitful sleep was punctuated with dreams of his well-dressed mother staring at her with utter astonishment in her cold blue eyes, and his proud, authoritarian father turning quite puce at the thought of anyone, let alone an impoverished, illegitimate ragbag of a nurse, having the presumption to pass comment on his precious son's romantic affairs in such a public place.

But she couldn't hide for ever, and on the day after Boxing Day, against her better judgement, George persuaded her to take him to the café to sample a magnificent chocolate cake he'd spotted on the counter.

And who should they find in there but Callum Frazer.

Ridiculously handsome in his crisp Royal Canadian Air Force

uniform, he looked like a pin-up poster from a girls' magazine, even if he was sitting alone at a table with a half-empty cup of Camp coffee.

'Oh look,' George cried. 'There's Callum!'

Something in his voice made Molly glance at him sharply. But there wasn't time to do more than that, because Callum was already getting to his feet and waving them over to join him. There certainly wasn't time to cut and run. Not without being even more crashingly rude than she had been on Christmas Eve.

But as Molly sat down awkwardly, George caught sight of Bella through the window and sped off to talk to her. Or so he said. Glancing out of the window a moment later, Molly couldn't see any sign of Bella, or indeed George. Belatedly she realised that the little blighter had set her up.

Turning back to Callum, she felt herself colouring up in embarrassment.

'I'm sorry,' she stammered. 'This is George's doing, isn't it? I'm probably the last person you wanted to see.'

Callum looked surprised. 'Of course I want to see you,' he said. 'I've been trying to get to see you for days.'

He was looking at her, but she couldn't meet his eyes. 'I know,' she mumbled. 'But I don't know why.'

'Because I guess I thought we were friends.'

He sounded reproachful, and Molly felt a twinge of anguish. But she had given him such a comprehensive brush-off on Christmas Eve, it wasn't unreasonable for him to be cross. 'I'm sorry about what I said the other night,' she said awkwardly. 'I was in a bit of a state.'

He nodded. 'That's what Katy said. She told me you'd just gotten bad news about some German guy you know.'

'Yes, that's right,' Molly said. She had momentarily forgotten about Gefreiter Henniker, but it all came back in a hot rush. 'I'm still really angry about it. I told them he was in danger, but nobody did anything about it.'

Callum was looking at her oddly. 'But you know he's OK, right? At least that's what Ward said earlier.'

Molly stared at him blankly, too flustered by his presence on the other side of the table to think straight. 'What do you mean?' she said. 'Ward hasn't said anything to me. You mean Gefreiter Henniker's not dead after all? Then why hasn't Ward told me? He knew how worried I was, and—'

'Hey, Molly, take it easy.' Callum reached over the table to stop her jumping up. 'A telegram arrived just as I was leaving the pub to come here. Ward was all set to come and tell you. I guess he must have just missed you.'

Having been convinced that she had been the cause of Gefreiter Henniker's death, Molly's main emotion was one of relief, but now she was cross that she had been put through the wringer unnecessarily. 'I wish I'd been there to talk to Ward,' she said tetchily. 'I would have been if George hadn't made me come over here.'

Callum withdrew his hand from her arm and sat back in his chair. 'Well, I'm sure sorry about that,' he said. 'Since when did talking to me become such a chore?'

Molly looked at him in despair. What was the matter with her? She seemed to put her foot in it every time she opened her mouth. 'I didn't mean that,' she said. 'It's just that I want to know if they're transferring Gefreiter Henniker to a nicer camp.'

Callum was still looking put out, however, and she realised that she needed to explain.

But even though he listened attentively to her description of her trip to Devizes, it sounded inadequate even to her ears. If only she could tell him about Douglas's hurtful remarks, and about her mother too, then her subsequent crazy behaviour might seem more explicable. But she couldn't. It was all too raw. In any case, she didn't want Callum to know. One of the main reasons for searching for her mother had been to try to equip herself with a background that might prove acceptable to his parents, and now it had turned out to be even worse than she had imagined.

'I guess you must like this guy?' he said, when she eventually ground to a halt.

Molly looked at him in surprise. It wasn't that she liked or disliked Gefreiter Henniker. But in some odd way she felt sorry for him. Despite his boorish appearance, there was something wretched about him. She couldn't help believing that underneath all that enforced Nazi brutality there lurked a nicer, kinder man.

Aware that Callum was watching her, she flushed slightly. She knew it would sound stupid if she said it. And luckily she didn't have to say it, because at that moment Angie came over to take her order.

Grateful for the interruption, Molly asked her if there was any more news about her brother. Pam had told her that Paul had been badly wounded in Belgium and she knew how worried they must all be. Not that Angie was looking unduly worried. On the contrary, she was gazing at Callum rather dreamily. But at Molly's question, she reluctantly dragged her eyes away.

'Well, he's still alive so far,' she said. 'Mum heard this morning. If he survives another few days, they're going to try and bring him back to England. So I reckon, all in all, it's good news.'

Molly thought of the American soldier who'd died on the train on Christmas Eve and crossed her fingers under the table. It didn't sound like very good news to her. But before she could think of anything reassuring to say, Angie's eyes had drifted back to Callum.

'I can recommend the chocolate cake,' she said confidingly. 'It's ever so good.'

Callum glanced at Molly and raised his eyebrows. 'We might as well,' he said. 'I guess that's why we're here, isn't it? Even if George didn't stay long enough to enjoy it with us.'

Molly winced, but Angie looked pleased. 'You won't regret it,' she said. 'It's really tasty, even if hasn't got any egg in it. Oh, and I forgot to say,' she added to Molly. 'Gino is ever so excited about the English lessons. What's this Graham person like? Do you think Gino will like him?'

Molly glanced at her uneasily. This was another disaster pending. She couldn't imagine anyone liking Graham very much. 'Well, he's rather serious,' she said tentatively. 'But that may be because he's confined to a wheelchair. He lost the use of his legs when he was fighting in Italy.'

'Oh, how awful,' Angie said at once. But then she brightened. 'Still, at least if he's been to Italy, it will give him and Gino something to talk about.'

As Angie hurried away, Molly met Callum's gaze and caught a glint of amusement in his eyes. With a painful twist of her heart, she remembered why she liked him so much. It wasn't just his good looks and his boyish smile; it was because, like Ward, he was always quick to see the funny side of life. Of course in Tunisia, where so many foreign quirky things had happened, there had been lots to laugh about. But nothing seemed very funny just now in dreary old war-ravaged London.

Nevertheless, encouraged by his questioning glance, and the arrival of the much-vaunted chocolate cake, she told him about her bizarre little school, and was gratified when she made him laugh a couple of times, particularly when she mentioned Professor Markov setting fire to Mrs d'Arcy Billière's kitchen.

'Wow,' he said. 'No wonder you're exhausted. But do you really need to study quite so hard?'

'Of course I have to,' Molly said. 'I need to get really good grades in my Higher Certificate if I have any chance at all of going to medical school. And I'm determined to do it.' She flushed slightly. 'I don't want to boast, but I got a hundred per cent in the exam Professor Markov set me before Christmas.'

Callum smiled obligingly, but there was a slight frown over his eyes. 'And how long does medical school last?'

'I think it takes about five years to qualify as a doctor,' Molly said.

He had been in the process of lifting a piece of cake to his mouth. His hand froze in mid air. 'Five years?'

Molly forced herself not to look at his fingers. She hadn't realised how hard it was going to be watching him eat a piece of cake. She couldn't help remembering the time when he had curled those fingers round hers as they danced under the stars in Tunisia. How her heart had leapt. 'I know,' she said quickly. 'It's going to be expensive, but I'm hoping there might be some kind of scholarship I can apply for, and that five years does include time working in hospitals and so on, and at least I'd get paid for that. The Nelsons charge me a very cheap rent, and Katy's keen for me to carry on working in the pub in the evenings and at weekends.'

Callum gave a strange little laugh. 'You seem to have it all figured out,' he said.

Molly looked at him uncertainly. It almost sounded as though he was mocking her. 'It's all right for you,' she said crossly. 'You've got a nice job in your father's business to go back to in Canada when the war's over. I haven't got anything like that. I need to make plans.'

He didn't answer. Instead he ran a finger round his plate to pick up the last few cake crumbs. Misinterpreting her agonised glance as he licked them off his finger, he shrugged apologetically and nodded towards Angie behind the counter.

'She's right,' he said. 'That cake is real tasty.' But his smile didn't quite reach his eyes. 'I'm sorry,' he said after a moment. 'I didn't mean to sound dismissive. I think what you are doing is great. It's just that . . .' He stopped, and his gaze dropped to his empty plate. When he looked up again, there was a wry look on his face. 'Well, it all sounds so grown-up. So serious. I guess I'm wondering what happened to the happy-go-lucky, fun-loving Molly I knew in Tunisia.'

What indeed? As she met his eyes, Molly felt her heart jolt. She would give anything to be transported back to those hot, carefree, sunny days. Camel rides in the desert, exotic picnics on the beach, swimming in warm seas, dancing under the stars in open-air clubs. It had seemed so romantic at the time. But now she wondered how many other girls he had entertained in a similar way.

Callum suddenly leaned forward eagerly. 'Talking of which,' he said. 'Are you free tonight? My parents are taking me out to dinner, and I'd like for you to come. Then afterwards, how about we go dancing in the West End.' He gave a slight grin. 'Just you and me, I mean, for the dancing. Not my parents.'

In Tunisia, Molly had never been able to resist that faintly bashful smile. But she was well able to resist it now. 'I can't,' she said at once. Much as she would like to spend the evening with him, the thought of spending it with his parents too filled her with utter horror. He hadn't witnessed the full extent of the debacle in the pub on Christmas Eve, but she could just imagine the look on Mr and Mrs Frazer's faces if she waltzed into some fancy restaurant on his arm. 'I can't possibly.' Frantically she groped around for an excuse. 'I've got to work.'

She knew from the way his eyes flickered away from hers that he didn't believe her. It occurred to her that he had probably already ascertained from George that she had a full day off today and she wished she hadn't lied. But it was too late now. Callum was already taking out his wallet. 'That's a real shame,' he said, as he waved for Angie to come and take his money. 'Because I'm heading off tomorrow. I'm only back in England to pick up a new plane. I doubt I'll be here again for a while.'

Molly's heart gave a painful jolt. He was going away. Flying away, God only knew where. Into what dangers. And judging from the look on his face, she had well and truly messed things up between them. But it was never going to work anyway. She knew that. How could it? She knew she had to let him go. For her own peace of mind, she had to let him go, once and for all.

But it was easier said than done.

Outside on the street, he turned to her and gave a regretful smile. 'I'm sorry, Molly,' he said. 'I guess I caught you at a bad time. I should have warned you I was coming. I didn't realise it would be awkward for you.'

Molly felt her throat constrict. 'It's me that should be apologising,' she muttered.

'Not at all,' he said. 'I understand.' He stepped forward and gave her a quick, hard hug.

She could hardly bear it when he let her go. 'Please write to me,' she said. 'If you have time. I'd like to know that you are safe.'

He looked surprised. 'Sure I will, if you really want me to.'

'Of course I do,' she said. She attempted a smile. 'Even if I am a complete idiot, we can still be friends, can't we?'

He hesitated for a second as if he wanted to say something else, but then apparently decided against it. A moment later he was gone, walking away without a backward glance.

George was hanging about at the corner of Lavender Road. He looked disappointed when he saw Molly coming back on her own. But he gave her a hopeful look. 'Did it work?' he asked eagerly. 'Is he your boyfriend now?'

'No,' Molly said. 'It didn't. And he's not.' Then, unusually for her, she burst into tears.

For Joyce, the last week had passed in a blur of anxiety about Paul. In church on Christmas morning, she'd had to blow her nose when the vicar prayed for all those currently in suffering or pain, and she nearly threw her hymn book at Mrs Rutherford in the churchyard afterwards when her employer made the mistake of saying how lovely it was to have Louise and Douglas home for Christmas.

In the end, it didn't matter that the chicken was so small. Nobody felt much like eating anyway, not even Angie, and especially not Jen, who seemed to have picked up some kind of stomach bug and spent most of the day either snapping people's heads off or shivering miserably in the outside lavatory. By teatime, Joyce had got fed up with her and sent her back to Mrs d'Arcy Billière's.

'Don't be too hard on her,' Albert murmured as the front door slammed behind her. 'It's not just Paul. She's worried about Henry too. You know she hasn't heard from him for well over a week.'

Joyce didn't know, and she was conscious of an extra stab of alarm.

God only knew what histrionics she would have to put up with from Jen if something had happened to Henry.

When, after Christmas, the telegram came saying that Paul was going to be sent back to England, Joyce felt marginally reassured. Then, at the beginning of January, just as it started to snow, she received a telegram saying he was actually on the way.

By a lucky chance, Molly was on Red Cross duty the night Paul's hospital ship docked at Southampton. Paul was unconscious, but recognising the name on the label pinned to his chest, Molly persuaded the doctor in charge to assign him to the Wilhelmina Hospital in Clapham Junction, which meant he'd be near his family. It also meant that he fell into the enthusiastic hands of Dr Goodacre.

Paul had been shot in the stomach by a German sniper. That was bad enough, but as he'd lain bleeding on the ground, he'd also been run over by a Leichter Panzerspähwagen, a German reconnaissance vehicle, which had broken his ribs and caused his guts to spill out onto the road. According to the notes that accompanied him on his journey back from Belgium, it was only the prompt action of some other British soldiers that had prevented him from dying where he lay. One of them had contrived to shove his intestines back into the cavity in his abdomen, and having bound him up as best they could, they had somehow got him back to an Allied medical post, where he had eventually been stitched up.

For a few days Paul's life had hung in the balance, but thanks to excellent nursing and the miracle drug penicillin, gradually he had seemed to be on the mend. But then he had unexpectedly taken a downward turn, and by the time he arrived at the Wilhelmina on 8 January, he was in a very bad way indeed.

Joyce was only allowed to see him for a few seconds that first day, but that was enough to give her the shivers. Even though Paul's eyes had been wide open, he clearly didn't recognise her. And the lines of pain etched on his apparently lifeless young face made her want to weep.

286

But the jovial Dr Goodacre seemed undaunted. As Joyce staggered out of the intensive-care ward, he was almost rubbing his hands with glee. 'I believe what we have here is some kind of traumatic hypovolemic shock,' he said. 'Hypoxia is evident in the blueness on the extremities. It was probably missed in earlier diagnoses, due to the extensive bruising.'

'Oh my goodness,' Joyce gasped. 'That sounds bad.'

'Oh, it's extremely bad,' Dr Goodacre agreed. 'I suspect internal bleeding is causing an inadequate delivery of oxygen to one or more of the vital organs.'

Joyce felt short of oxygen herself. But Dr Goodacre was nodding happily. 'The first thing is to open him up and have a look inside,' he said. 'I'll have a word with the anaesthetist now. Rest assured we'll do what we can.'

Joyce didn't feel remotely assured. Nor did she think she would ever rest again. Assuming the interview was over, she picked up her handbag with shaking fingers. But as she went to turn away, Dr Goodacre glanced at her enquiringly. 'How is young Bella these days?'

Bella? Joyce stared at him incredulously. Who cared about Bella when Paul was about to be 'opened up'?

'She's all right,' she said. 'As far as it goes.'

'Still not talking?' Dr Goodacre tapped his fingers together thoughtfully as though he had all the time in the world. 'That's a pity. I'd hoped resuming her education might help. But elective mutism is an odd phenomenon; it's impossible to predict when or if the sufferer will revert to normal speech.' Brightening suddenly, he gave her a beaming smile. 'Never mind, she's in the best possible place with you, my dear Mrs Lorenz. A secure, happy home is exactly what she needs.'

The eighth of January was the start of the spring term at RADA, and by then Jen knew she must be pregnant. Not only had she failed to bleed, she still felt sick, and her bosoms were swollen and uncomfortable. Having witnessed Katy go through two pregnancies, she knew the signs, and the faint hope that her unsettled stomach might have been connected to all the spicy food she had been forced to eat at Mrs d'Arcy Billière's house faded.

As the reality of the situation sank in, she felt increasingly panicky. The last thing in the world she wanted was a baby. It wouldn't have been quite so bad if Henry had been there, because they could have decided together what to do about it. But Henry wasn't there. She had written to him, of course, nervously telling him what she suspected, but so far she hadn't heard anything back.

So it was with considerable relief on Monday morning, as she set off to RADA, that she spotted the solemn-looking Rifle Brigade officer who had previously brought her good news of Henry coming up Lavender Hill towards her.

Eagerly she ran to meet him. 'Please tell me you're bringing me news of Henry,' she said.

It was bitterly cold and the man's face was pinched. His voice was tight and slightly hoarse. 'I was just coming to see you, Miss Carter,' he said. 'I'm sorry to have to tell you that Henry Keller went missing just before Christmas. He was operating with a small troop independently of the rest of the regiment. As you can imagine, the situation in Belgium is rather difficult at the moment, so hope was not lost. But efforts to locate them have failed. I'm afraid he is now being listed as missing, presumed dead. His commanding officer asked me to let you know before you saw it in the paper.'

Chapter Seventeen

The Red Cross were holding a walk-in clinic that Monday morning, and as Molly headed down Lavender Road on her way to work, she knew she had a busy day in front of her. She was glad about that: the busier she was, the less she thought about Callum. It was already two weeks since she'd seen him. Which meant she had two weeks to come to terms with what an idiot she had been to turn down his offer of a night out. OK, she would have had to endure an excruciating dinner with his parents first. But looking back on it, she had begun to think that it might have been worth it. Surely anything was worth the chance of spending a few hours dancing in Callum's arms.

For a while she had been unable to think of anything except what a terrible Christmas she'd had, but gradually she had begun to realise that, even though there was no doubt that she'd made a complete fool of herself in the pub on Christmas Eve, nobody seemed to hold it against her.

Nobody except Douglas Rutherford, at least. He of course took the first opportunity he got to accuse her of slandering his good name. Oddly, it wasn't her accusation about underage girls that had piqued him, it was her all-too-public revelation that, despite all his fighting talk, he'd never actually come face to face with a German.

'I'll have you know that I've been brought back to England for a very important mission,' he said. 'I can't tell you what it is because it's top secret. But if I ever catch you maligning me again, there'll be trouble.'

Ward Frazer, on the other hand, had apologised for doubting her. Two Germans had indeed been murdered by their SS comrades at the Scottish prison camp on suspicion of leaking information about the breakout, but not Gefreiter Henniker. He was now being transferred to a different camp for his own safety.

Unfortunately, Ward had also asked her if there might be room at her little school for Malcolm. 'He's too smart for his own good, and I don't like him hanging around the bar all day long, because he picks up on every damn thing he hears. But what with the pub and the baby and all, Katy simply doesn't have time to give him the attention he needs.'

Unable to resist the smile that accompanied the request, Molly promised to see what she could do. But her heart had sunk. She was already worried about Gino. His first lesson with Graham was scheduled for later in the week, and she couldn't imagine it was going to be a success.

She shivered and began to walk a bit faster. She was already in Mr Sparrow's bad books, and didn't want to annoy him further by being late.

But as she rounded the corner onto Lavender Hill, she heard a scream, and was just in time to see Jen collapse to the ground at the feet of a tall young infantry officer.

Running forward, she saw the look of shock on the officer's face. 'What happened?' she shouted at him. 'What have you done to her?'

'I haven't done anything,' he said, clearly aggrieved. 'I was asked to come and tell her that her boyfriend has been reported missing, and she passed out.'

'Oh no,' Molly whispered. Crouching, she lifted Jen's head off the icy, snow-caked pavement and patted her cheeks gently. But Jen didn't respond. Molly looked up at the man. 'Give me your coat,' she said. 'We need to keep her warm.'

Obligingly he began unbuttoning his greatcoat. 'Do you know her?' he asked.

Molly nodded. 'Yes, I do. And I know Captain Keller too.'

She took the proffered coat and, with a quick apologetic glance at the officer, laid it on the snow, carefully rolling Jen onto it in the recovery position and wrapping the rest of it over her.

'Perhaps we should try and get her to the hospital?' the officer suggested uneasily.

Molly knew how much Jen hated anything medical, but they clearly needed to get her into the warm as soon as possible. The obvious place was the café a little further down the road. It wouldn't be open yet, but Joyce would almost certainly be there by now, getting things ready, and with any luck she would already have the tea urn on the go.

Nevertheless, Molly hesitated for a moment. It was unlike Jen to faint. Despite her theatrical, prima-donna-ish ways, she was surprisingly tough. She never would have survived their shared ordeal in Italy otherwise. But she was also impulsive, and madly in love with Henry Keller. Madly being the operative word. Molly couldn't help remembering her boasting how satisfactory things were in the bedroom department, and felt a flicker of unease. But she couldn't worry about that now.

She looked doubtfully up at the officer. 'Do you think you can lift her?' she asked.

When Jen came round, she found herself lying on her side on a painfully hard floor, having her hands chafed by Molly.

For a second she couldn't imagine where she was, but then she realised she didn't care.

'Henry's missing,' she mumbled as she struggled to sit up.

Molly slid her hand under her shoulders to help her. 'I know,' she murmured. 'I'm so sorry, Jen. What horrible news. No, don't get up. Not yet. Just take it easy for a minute. Your mother's making you a cup of tea. That'll make you feel better.'

Suddenly the full extent of her predicament rushed back into Jen's mind. Already she was nauseous again. Any sudden movement seemed to bring the sickness on.

'Nothing will make me feel better,' she said. Feeling a sudden tension in Molly's supporting arm, she glanced up at her, saw the look in her eye and groaned. 'You've guessed, haven't you?'

Molly nodded. 'I think so. You're pregnant?'

Jen nodded. 'But for God's sake don't tell my mother.'

But she was too late. Joyce was coming out of the kitchen and had clearly heard every word. The tea almost spilled out of the cup as she jerked back in horror.

'Oh Jen,' she gasped. 'You're not. How could you? That's all we need.'

Hearing the shocked condemnation in her mother's voice, Jen flared up at once.

'Is that all you can say?' she snapped. 'For God's sake. I've just heard that Henry's missing, presumed dead. Don't you care about that?' To her annoyance, her voice came out like a sob. 'I thought you liked him. Obviously I was wrong. Because it seems to me that all you care about is that I don't embarrass you by giving birth to an illegitimate child.'

'That is not all I care about,' Joyce said. 'I care very much about Henry. I just can't imagine how you could be so stupid as to get yourself up the duff. There are ways to avoid that happening. I'd have thought you were old enough to know that.'

'Of course I know that,' Jen said through gritted teeth. She was damned if she was going to cry. 'We got carried away, that's all.' And now she heard herself shouting at Molly and the young officer. 'Why did you have to bring me here? Why couldn't you have taken me somewhere else?'

She saw Molly recoil, and knew she was being unreasonable. But she couldn't stop. She was so angry, with her mother, with Henry's friend for bringing her such awful news, and with Henry himself. How dare he go missing, just when she needed him so badly?

More than anything, she was angry with herself for getting

pregnant. How could she have been so stupid? Furiously she struggled to her feet and flung off the officer's coat. Having been freezing
cold just a moment ago, she was baking hot now.

'Well, don't worry,' she spat at her mother. 'I don't want it either.
So I'll get rid of it. I'm sure there's some means of doing that. In
the meantime, as my presence here is clearly going to embarrass
you, I shall go away.' She turned to the Rifle Brigade officer, who
was staring at her goggle eyed. 'If you have any further news, please
bring it to me at Henry Keller's flat in Knightsbridge, because that's
where I'm going to be living from now on.' And with that, she flung
open the door and marched out into the street.

But there she hesitated. She couldn't go to RADA. Not today.
She was too upset. So in the end she turned back to Lavender Road.
She would go and talk to Katy. Surely she would know what to do.

Somehow Joyce managed to get rid of the Rifle Brigade officer.
Afterwards she couldn't remember what she had said to him; she
hoped she'd thanked him and apologised for Jen's behaviour, but
she wasn't sure. She got rid of Molly Coogan too. Molly had been
all set to go after Jen, but Joyce had dissuaded her. 'I should leave
her for now,' she'd said. 'You know what she's like when she gets
into a mood. She'll only bite your head off. Better to wait till
later, when she's calmed down.'

So Molly'd gone off to the Red Cross, leaving Joyce to mop up
the spilled tea and move the tables back into their normal positions.

Leaning weakly on the mop, Joyce closed her eyes for a second. She
felt guilty for not being a bit more sympathetic, but it seemed so typical
of Jen to choose such a disastrous moment to get pregnant, and her
daughter's histrionics had always got on her nerves. You'd think the way
Jen went on that she was the only person suffering in this war. That
nice Helen de Burrel's fellow had been missing for months on end,
and you didn't see her having tantrums, and when Ward Frazer had
been missing earlier in the war, Katy had still managed to run the pub,
give birth to Malcolm, and goodness knew what else, at the same time.

Hearing the door clang behind her, Joyce jerked upright and swung round to find Angie and Gino bumbling in. For the first time in her life, she was glad that they were always late getting to work.

'What's happened?' Angie asked. 'Why are the tables all out of place?'

'Nothing's happened,' Joyce said quickly. 'I spilled some tea, that's all, and I'm just clearing it up.'

Angie would be bound to find out sooner or later, Joyce thought. But later would be better than sooner. Maybe morals were looser in the theatrical world and people didn't care about such things, but round here people were still very strait-laced, and whatever she said, Jen would hate being gossiped about, possibly even cold shouldered. Until they had formulated some sort of plan, her condition needed to remain a secret. Because Joyce was certain that when it came to it, Jen would never get rid of the baby. She was far too squeamish for anything like that. Or at least Joyce hoped she was, because much as Jen got on her nerves, she certainly didn't want her falling into the hands of some grubby back-street abortionist. Joyce took a long breath. No, if Jen really was pregnant, they would have to cope with it, as a family. But it would make life a lot easier if the stupid girl didn't fly off the handle every time she tried to speak to her.

Molly had intended to go up to Mrs d'Arcy Billière's to see Jen as soon as she left work. But just as she was about to come off duty, the Red Cross telephone rang with news that a V-2 bomb had landed on the corner of Clapham High Street and medical help was urgently needed.

Molly had been due to work at the pub that evening, but she knew Katy would understand that she was needed elsewhere.

Amazingly, considering the power of the blast, and the size of the crater, there were no fatalities, but there were lots of injuries, and the damage to the surrounding buildings was extensive. By the time Molly left the scene, it was too late to call at Mrs d'Arcy Billière's.

But seeing that the lights were still on in the pub, she popped in there to apologise for missing the evening session. Katy and Helen were in the scullery, washing glasses, but Ward was in the bar, busy upending the chairs onto the tables.

'Hey, Molly,' he said. 'I've got some news for you. Your friend Henniker has arrived in a new camp in Kent.'

'He's hardly my friend,' Molly said. 'But I do feel oddly responsible for him, so thank you. I'm really pleased.'

'Well, I'm sure glad about that,' Ward said. 'Because there's another thing. He's asked to see you.'

'To see *me*?' Molly said. 'But why? Oh my goodness, do you think he might have some information about André?'

Ward shrugged. 'I don't know. It's possible. On the other hand, he might just want to thank you for getting him moved.'

Molly glanced towards the kitchen. 'Have you told Helen?'

He shook his head. 'No. I thought I'd better talk to you first, in case you didn't want to go. I know you found it kind of tough last time.'

Molly stared at him incredulously. Had he gone mad? 'Of course I want to go,' she said. 'I must go.'

But when was another matter. Her schedule was so tight, she had no spare time at all until the weekend. And even then, she had already promised to help Katy in the pub, as Ward was due to be away and Helen was working.

But when she told Helen the news a few minutes later, she realised she couldn't possibly delay visiting Gefreiter Henniker until the weekend.

'Oh my God,' Helen whispered. 'I'm not going to be able to sleep until I know. How soon can you go?'

Molly glanced at Ward. 'I suppose I could go tomorrow morning,' she said doubtfully. 'If it's not too far.' It would mean missing a lesson with Professor Markov, but she could nip back up the street now and leave a note for him in Mrs d'Arcy Billière's letter box. He'd be cross, but least it wouldn't be a wasted journey for him, because he was teaching George and Bella later on.

It was only as she was sitting on the train to Kent early the following morning, with Ward's letter of authorisation in her hand, that she realised not only that she had forgotten about Jen, but also that this was the day Gino was due to have his first lesson with Graham.

Jen was wishing she hadn't snapped at Molly, because now she wanted to talk to her.

Katy hadn't been helpful at all. 'I think there are people who do things like that,' she had said doubtfully when Jen announced that she wanted to terminate the pregnancy. 'But I have no idea where. Jen, are you sure that's what you want to do? What if Henry's still alive?'

Jen bit her lip. 'I'm sure Henry wouldn't want a baby any more than I do.' Suddenly she couldn't bear it. 'Oh Katy,' she muttered. 'What on earth am I going to do?'

But Katy had no more idea than Jen had, and having sworn her to secrecy, Jen left the pub feeling worse than she had before. Perhaps in due course she would get more news from Henry's regiment. Not knowing for sure what had happened to him was somehow almost worse than being told he was dead. That little bit of hope niggled constantly at her mind.

In the meantime, she would continue at RADA, even it was the last thing she felt like doing, and at the weekend she would move into Henry's flat. At least that would save her money. Not just her rent and keep at Mrs d'Arcy Billière's, but also the cash she had to dob out to Angie for cooking a stand-in dinner for her once a week.

But telling Mrs d'Arcy Billière and the others that she had decided to move out proved quite difficult. They might be mad foreigners, but they had been kind to her, and had accepted her into their midst with easy-going tolerance. She had even got used to the food, or at least some of it. There were certain things, like Mrs d'Arcy Billière's prized meat jelly, and Elsa's mother's horseradish *maror*, that she'd be happy never to see again.

She didn't tell them about the pregnancy, of course, but unlike her mother, their sympathy and compassion about Henry was overwhelming. They all knew what it was like to lose friends and family, of course. They had all been refugees at one time or another, Mrs d'Arcy Billière from the Bolsheviks, the others from the Nazis. Not that they ever talked about it. They were much more intent on forging new lives for themselves in England.

Aaref had confided to her one evening that his ambition was to provide a home for the entire family, Elsa's sister and parents and all. 'It was very kind of Mrs d'Arcy Billière to take us all in,' he said. 'But we cannot live on her hospitality for ever.'

'So what will you do?' Jen asked.

'I don't know,' he said. 'Perhaps we will try to buy a house. But even here in England it is not so easy for Jews.'

Jen had looked at him doubtfully. She didn't know anything about buying houses, but it was bound to involve deposits or mortgages or some such thing, and she had a feeling that regardless of his race, banks wouldn't look very kindly on Aaref's wheeler-dealer under-the-counter business, or indeed the meagre wages Elsa earned at the pub.

Nevertheless, she had been impressed that he and Elsa wanted to stand on their own feet. It was more than you could say for Angie and Gino. They seemed perfectly happy to have free accommodation in her mother's house, and Joyce paid them for working in the café too.

It wasn't fair that Angie and Gino got preferential treatment, Jen thought resentfully, as she sat glumly on the Tube on the way up to RADA that morning. Joyce was happy to bend over backwards for them, but she wouldn't lift a finger for Jen. Oh no. She had always been expected to fend for herself.

Emerging at Goodge Street station, Jen caught sight of a newspaper stand. *Germans routed again. Belgium Bulge territory regained.* For a second, she felt a surge of optimism. Perhaps Henry had got trapped behind enemy lines, and now that the Allies were advancing again, he would emerge unscathed.

Due to her ever-present need for frugality, she didn't normally buy a newspaper, but today she did. She quickly regretted it. Not only were the descriptions of the Allies' valiant if somewhat chaotic efforts to repulse the enemy graphically gruesome, it was clear that many of the clashes had been fought in almost blizzard conditions. Even if Henry and his troop had been listed missing just because they'd got cut off from their unit, by now they'd have probably frozen to death anyway.

She flung the newspaper in a nearby litter bin in angry despair.

A second later, she was accosted by an irate man in a bowler hat. 'Eh, you,' he said. 'What do you think you are doing? You can get fined for that. Paper is a precious commodity. There is a war on, you know.'

He had chosen the wrong person to admonish.

A red mist came down over Jen's eyes. 'I'll give you a precious commodity,' she snapped. Reaching into the bin, she yanked out the newspaper, rolled it up and thrust it into his gloved hands. 'You can stick it up your arse for all I care.'

Gefreiter Henniker's new POW camp was situated in the grounds of an enormous Jacobean Mansion called Somerhill House near Tonbridge. Unlike the menacing, fortress-like prison at Devizes, POW Camp 40 consisted of row upon row of neat wooden huts with shiny corrugated-metal roofs. Admittedly the whole place was surrounded by a high wire fence, but it was guarded by British soldiers instead of American ones, and they were considerably more friendly, the staff sergeant on the main gate going so far as to both salute Molly and call her 'love', before shouting, in a stentorian bellow that nearly blew her eardrums out for someone to escort her at the double to the commandant's office.

Major Withers, the camp commander, would have been a good-looking man if it hadn't been for the livid scar across his right cheek. He was also missing his right hand, which presumably explained why he had been given the job of looking after prisoners of war, instead of commanding troops on the battlefield. Molly thought briefly about Graham, and wondered if this man was equally bitter and resentful about his impairment.

But Major Withers made no mention of his missing hand, merely using the other one to wave her with easy courtesy to a chair and offering her a cup of tea.

'I gather you have previous knowledge of one of our new inmates,' he said as he took his own seat behind his desk.

His unruffled manner and languid upper-class accent made Molly suspect he belonged to one of the posh Guards regiments. Normally she found such people intimidating, but Major Withers had none of the smug superciliousness of Douglas Rutherford, or indeed the arrogant, toffee-nosed doctors she had sometimes come across during her nursing career, and he listened with apparent interest to her brief account of her dealings with Gefreiter Henniker.

At some stage the tea arrived, which to Molly's astonishment was served in bone china, from a silver teapot. It was accompanied by ginger nut biscuits, which she hadn't seen since before the war. 'My batman hails from Glasgow,' Major Withers explained in his Home Counties drawl. 'One of his relatives works at the McVitie's factory there.'

To Molly's astonishment, he proceeded to dip his biscuit in his teacup, and, catching her startled expression, indicated that she should follow suit. 'Only way to eat 'em,' he said with a blasé wave of his hand. 'Trick is not to leave them in too long.'

Molly had a sudden memory of being severely told off for dipping biscuits in tea at the Home for Waifs and Strays. Her punishment had been to stand in the corner for an hour, balancing a plate on her head. Even now she found it hard to override that ingrained inhibition.

She wondered briefly if some teacher at Eton or Harrow had ever forced Major Withers to stand in the corner with a plate on his head. It seemed unlikely. Or if they had, he clearly didn't care. Nonetheless, he was clearly intrigued by her mission. 'I've seen the chap you're talking about,' he said. 'Seems a surly, brutish sort of fellow to me. Not surprised he was originally categorised as a hardliner.' He uncrossed his legs unhurriedly and stood up. 'But from what you say, he's not as bad as he looks. So let's go and find him, see what he wants to tell you.' Picking up his hat and an ivory-topped swagger stick, he opened the door and politely held it for Molly to pass through first. 'Fingers crossed it's something useful,' he said. 'If it is, and if he behaves himself over the next few weeks, we might let him join one of our working parties.' He gave a short laugh. 'In my experience, these Germans chaps like to keep busy.'

As they strolled across a kind of inner enclosure towards a hut on the far side, Molly heard someone ahead of them barking out a command. It was the staff sergeant who had been on the gate. 'Lady and officer approaching,' he bellowed. 'Prisoner, STAND!'

Biting her lip to stop herself laughing, Molly stepped inside, and once again came face to face with her former captor.

This time Gefreiter Henniker was wearing a dark brown uniform with a large yellow circle sewn on the trousers. Last time she had seen him, he had looked strained and pale. This time he just looked pale.

As she came into the room, he stood up and clicked his heels together in a very German gesture.

There was a moment's confusion when the staff sergeant looked as though he was determined to stay, but luckily Major Withers caught his eye and, to Molly's relief, they both withdrew.

Nervously she waved Gefreiter Henniker to a chair. But to her dismay, instead of sitting down, he took a step towards her. 'I think it is because of you that I am here, yes?'

For an awful moment Molly thought he was going to embrace her but, noticing her recoil, after a brief awkward pause he sat down, with his hands, perhaps from habit, on the table in front of him.

'So,' he said. 'You save my life. Because of this, I wish to give you some information. It concerns your friend, André Cabillard.'

Suddenly it seemed very quiet. The room they were in was gloomy and bleak. There was nothing in there except the table and two chairs. All Molly could hear from outside was the faint sound of a generator, and the distant murmur of men's voices.

'One of the SS I met in Scotland worked closely with Hauptsturmführer Wessel,' Gefreiter Henniker said. 'He remembered him talking about the Frenchman, Renard.'

Molly realised she was holding her breath. She sat forward, willing him to go on.

'Wessel knew that the Frenchman was coming after him. He had by then learned his true identity, so he instructed his men to find him and capture him so he could be tortured to reveal what he knew, and then, of course, killed.' He heard Molly's agonised gasp, and gave a small shrug. 'But your man was clever. Every time they came close, he evaded them. And now Wessel is in a hurry because your Allies are advancing north from Toulon very fast. Nobody likes to retreat. Especially, I think, men like Hauptsturmführer Wessel. Perhaps, also, he is frightened his crimes will, how you say, catch up with him. So to save time, he has his remaining prisoners shot and withdraws further north.'

'But what about André?' Molly asked.

'He was unlucky,' Gefreiter Henniker said. 'Or perhaps lucky, I don't know. He had commandeered a vehicle from the telephone company of France. And this vehicle was stopped by a routine Wehrmacht patrol. I do not remember the name of this place. Perhaps Besançon? Your friend could not produce the correct papers, so they took him in. Wessel's men hear of this, but in confusion of retreat they were not able to come for him. So instead, they instruct that he should be killed.'

Molly gaped at him in horror. 'But surely that's against the Geneva Convention?'

Gefreiter Henniker was silent. He looked down at his hands. 'There was an order from the Führer,' he said very quietly after a moment. '"The Kommandobefehl". Perhaps you would call it the Commando Order. We all knew of it, but it was forbidden to speak of it. Not even to each other. It was issued by Adolf Hitler himself maybe two years ago. It stated that captured Allied spies and commandos were to be killed immediately and without trial. Failure to comply with this order would be punishable under German military law.' He looked up. 'But by now, with the Allies approaching, some of the Wehrmacht officers, it seems, begin to be a little less obedient to the Führer's command.'

Molly was finding it difficult to breathe. 'So André wasn't killed? What happened to him?'

Gefreiter Henniker's expression was not reassuring. 'My informant believes he was dispatched to a prison camp in Germany.'

'So he is still alive?'

'Perhaps.' The German seemed reluctant to go on. 'But these camps,' he said. 'Some of them aren't just prisons, you understand?'

Molly frowned. 'No, I don't understand.'

'These camps are run by the SD and the Gestapo.' He hesitated. 'And they have never been slow to carry out the Führer's orders.'

Molly realised he was referring to the same 'other' camps that the International Red Cross had mentioned. As the implication of his words sank in, she felt a shiver pass down her spine. It was already well known that the Nazis were intent on massacring Jews; that was bad enough, but nobody had suggested they were deliberately killing anyone else. But if what Gefreiter Henniker said was true . . .

The room was very cold. She shivered. She couldn't imagine how on earth she was going to impart this news to Helen. 'But there must be thousands of people like André,' she asked. 'They surely can't kill everyone?'

The Gefreiter didn't answer. And his silence made goose bumps break out on Molly's skin.

'Is there any way you can find out more?' she asked. She glanced out of the small window, at the lines of neat huts stretching away beyond the wire fence. 'Perhaps from someone who has worked at these . . . these camps?'

He looked doubtful. 'Nobody likes to admit to knowing things,' he said. 'They fear that if we lose the war, they will be held to account.'

'And so they bloody well should be,' Molly said hotly. She saw him flinch and remembered that he probably had some nasty skeletons in his own past. Abruptly she stood up. 'Thank you,' she said coldly. 'Thank you for telling me this. And if you do find out more, please ask the commandant to let me know.'

Gefreiter Henniker stood up too. He made a small appeasing gesture with his hand. 'We were only acting on orders,' he said. 'All of us.'

Molly stared at him. At his blank, unemotional face. 'Orders, my foot,' she said. 'That's no justification for doing things that are blatantly wrong. More than wrong. Immoral. Criminal. Evil.' She stopped, frustrated. 'I don't even have the words to make you understand how wrong.'

Angrily she went to the door. But there she stopped and swung round. 'I do know one thing,' she said. 'We are going to win the war. And then, hopefully, bastards like SS Hauptsturmführer Wessel will find out what it's like to be at the other end of the bullet.'

'Ah, there you are, Mrs Lorenz,' Dr Goodacre said, striding into the lobby of the hospital, where Joyce had been waiting in a state of anxiety for over an hour. 'I hope I haven't kept you waiting, but Matron wanted to have a word, and, well,' he winked and gave a roguish laugh, 'it would take a better man than me to defy a command from Matron.'

But Joyce wasn't in the mood for jolly hospital banter. 'I came to ask about Paul,' she said.

'Ah yes, of course,' Dr Goodacre said, sobering alarmingly. He rubbed his hands together pensively. 'It was just as I thought,' he said. 'Internal haemorrhage, caused, I imagine, by the crushed ribs rather than the bullet wound. The military medics did their best in the circumstances, but my exploratory laparotomy showed that they had unfortunately overlooked a small rupture in one of the blood vessels of the inferior vena cava.'

It was impossible to tell from his tone whether this was good news, or very bad news indeed.

'However,' he went on, 'I have removed the resulting haemotoma and I believe I have successfully sutured the guilty party.'

Realising that he was looking at her expectantly, Joyce took a hesitant breath. 'Is he going to survive?'

'Survive?' Dr Goodacre looked astonished. 'Of course he will survive. He won't feel up to much for a few days yet, but he's a tough young fellow, and I have every expectation that in time he will make a full recovery.'

Chapter Eighteen

Molly had been dreading the moment when she had to tell Helen what Gefreiter Henniker had said. But Helen took the news surprisingly well. 'After reading Mrs Sparrow's letter, I'd prepared myself for the worst,' she said. 'This sounds bad, but at least we now know André's not lying dead in a ditch in France. What's more, until someone tells me he is definitely dead, I am going to do everything I can to find him.'

Molly didn't like to mention that she had lost her temper with the Gefreiter. She regretted it now, worried that even if he did discover something else, he wouldn't bother to tell her.

But it turned out that she had misjudged him. A few days later, she received a brief note from Major Withers asking if she had a photo of André Cabillard. *Your fellow Henniker seems to feel it might be useful,* he wrote. *Although the blighter wouldn't tell me why. Nevertheless, in an attempt to sweeten him up, I've put him on a work detail at a local market garden.*

Helen only had one photograph of André, and she was reluctant to let it go. It was the picture of the two of them standing in front of a tree. Molly had seen it before, but that didn't stop her heart twisting because you could see in their eyes how much in love they were. She understood why Helen didn't want to lose it.

But in the end, Helen felt it was worth the sacrifice. So Molly dispatched the photograph to Major Withers with a request for Gefreiter Henniker to take good care of it and to return it as soon as possible.

Once again, all they could do was wait.

In the meantime, Molly had plenty to be getting on with, as she suddenly found herself inundated with requests for people to join her little school. Word had got out about George and Bella's success in the Christmas exams, and a friend of Pam's now wanted to enrol her sickly ten-year-old twin daughters. Another woman produced two little boys of four and five she felt would benefit from lessons as they would be starting proper school as soon as the war was over. On top of that there was Gino, Malcolm and, rather bizarrely, Helen's father, Lord de Burrel, who, back once again from America, had appeared in the pub one evening asking if Molly could organise some Russian lessons as he was shortly due to accompany the prime minister to a conference in the Crimea.

When Molly consulted Mrs d'Arcy Billière to see if she would mind accommodating extra students, she seemed delighted. 'I love to see the house full of lively young people,' she said. 'To hear laughter. This war has made us all too dull and sad.'

But Professor Markov, despite being gratified that his reputation had spread, was unexpectedly reluctant to take on too many extra students. 'My wife,' he explained. 'She is complaining that she never sees me now. Perhaps you find another teacher to help me, yes?'

Molly's only other possible teacher was Graham, but his first lesson with Gino had not been a success. 'He kept going on about verbs and nouns,' Angie said, 'and other things that Gino didn't know about.' She looked at Molly hopefully. 'But perhaps he'll make it simpler next time.'

'I'll have a word with him,' Molly said. But Graham had not been very receptive to her suggestion that he limit himself to teaching Gino some easy, useful phrases and a bit of everyday conversation.

'But what about grammar?' he had asked. 'That's the basis of language, after all.'

'Well, yes,' Molly agreed. 'But I'm not sure Gino is going to be very interested in grammar.'

'He didn't seem very interested in anything,' Graham said huffily. 'I don't think he's got two brain cells to rub together.'

Molly gritted her teeth. 'Perhaps you should try talking about food next time,' she suggested. 'He's interested in that.'

She had a more pressing problem than Gino, and that was what to do about Helen's father. Lord de Burrel had been very kind to her in the past, not least introducing her in Tunisia to Winston Churchill's private physician. Helen always said it wasn't what you knew that mattered, it was who you knew, and Molly was hoping that if and when she managed to secure a place at medical school, Lord Moran might be persuaded to recommend her for a scholarship.

Professor Markov, however, was much more interested in teaching the children, and in the end it was Mrs d'Arcy Billière who volunteered to take on Helen's father. 'Well, why not?' she said. 'I speak Russian, and it would be a great pleasure to speak it with a friend of Mr Churchill. Perhaps I will be able to persuade Lord de Burrel not to trust this madman Stalin, who is, I think, a great deal more dangerous now than Adolf Hitler.'

'Ha!' Professor Markov gave one of his barking laughs. 'Plus if he is travelling to the Crimea, he might bring you back some vodka and some caviar.'

Mrs d'Arcy Billière laughed delightedly. 'That also would be a pleasure,' she said.

Then even more help came from an unexpected quarter: Louise Rutherford, who was in London for a night.

'My friend Susan Voles is a brilliant teacher,' she said. 'She taught me the maths I needed to get through artillery training. She's going to be demobbed next month and she loves kids. I'm sure she'd be happy to help.'

When Molly met Susan Voles the following weekend, she liked her immediately. Having expected her to be posh and very sure of herself like Louise, it was a relief to discover that she had a broad Yorkshire accent and was actually quite shy. Susan was hoping to train as a teacher after the war and thought that running an informal kindergarten would be good experience. She promised to start as soon as she was demobbed.

In the meantime, Molly had twice managed to see Jen. The first time was when she helped her move her stuff up to Henry's flat. The second was when she called there on her way home from a Red Cross escort duty one afternoon the following week.

On the first occasion Jen had been grimly determined to find a way to get rid of the baby. But by Molly's next visit, she was having second thoughts. An expensive consultation with a pompous, disapproving GP in Knightsbridge had revealed that it was not only illegal but also dangerous to terminate a pregnancy. Jen realised that to find some suitably qualified person to undertake such a procedure off the record would be extremely costly, and she simply didn't have the cash to pay for it.

'I've been trying to think who might help me out,' she said as she boiled Henry's smart little kettle to make Molly a much-needed cup of tea. 'Mr Lorenz has money, but I can hardly ask *him* to pay.'

Molly shivered and wondered if Prissy Cavanagh had gone through the same thought process when she was in a similar predicament twenty-two years ago.

'And I can't ask Ward,' Jen continued. 'He's such a friend of Henry's and . . .' She stopped and shuddered. 'Oh Molly, what am I going to do? I'm terrified of medical things, especially things like that. But without Henry, there's no way I can afford to bring up a baby on my own.'

'But you wouldn't have to do it on your own,' Molly said stoutly. 'If the worst came to the worst, we'd all help you. Me and Katy and Helen. Maybe even Louise. I'm sure we can sort something out. We could take it in turns to babysit, and . . .' She tailed off awkwardly. They both knew that if Henry really was dead, Jen was going to need a lot more than babysitting. 'And I'm sure your mother would help you too.'

'Huh.' Jen gave an angry snort. 'I doubt that. Even if she did, there isn't room for me to live in her house, let alone with a baby, not with Angie and Gino sitting in there like two fat cuckoos.'

Molly frowned. There was no doubt Jen was in a terrible fix, but she couldn't help wishing she hadn't fallen out with her mother. It made everything so much more difficult.

'But what about the baby?' she ventured. 'It's Henry's child too, don't forget.'

She was dreading Jen saying that the best thing would be to give birth then offer the baby up for adoption. Molly knew that if it was her who had got unexpectedly (and miraculously) pregnant with Callum's baby, she would move heaven and earth to be able to keep it.

But Jen wouldn't reply. Or perhaps she couldn't. It was clear that the double disaster, the pregnancy coupled with Henry's disappearance, had knocked her for six. What was worse, she was obviously in no fit state to make a decision.

Molly didn't like her being all alone in Henry's flat, plush and comfortable though it was. Jen wasn't at all practical. Molly was worried that she wouldn't eat, or that she would fall into a depression, or do something rash.

Molly wished she could stay here with her, but she knew she couldn't. She had too much on her plate already. In any case, Jen wouldn't want her. She'd already said she liked being on her own. That it was a relief after years of communal living.

So in the end Molly had to leave her to it. No matter what she or anyone else thought, it was going to have to be Jen's decision. 'Whatever else,' she said as she left, 'please promise me you won't do anything without letting me know first. If it comes to it, I'll come with you, and I'll look after you afterwards.'

Despite the brave face she had put on to Molly, Helen was tortured by the thought of André being incarcerated in a horrible Gestapo prison camp. Every night as she settled down on her makeshift camp bed in the pub cellar, with Lucky the dog on the floor beside her, she made a point of praying that the war would be over before they got round to killing André.

Quite often in her dreams Helen found herself rushing to rescue him even as the firing squad took up their positions. Each time, when she woke, heart pounding, she felt a renewed terror that she was going to be too late to save him. Once or twice she had been trembling so much that she had invited Lucky into the bed with her, and lay with her face pressed close up against his reassuringly warm fur.

Even though Helen didn't really believe in portents or premonitions, gradually she came to wonder if her dreams were telling her something, and she began to start looking for ways she might be able to get back to France, and perhaps even to Germany.

When she heard that boat trains were now occasionally running between London and Paris, she immediately applied for a ticket. Only to be refused. Seats were reserved for people on government business. A few days later, she read in the paper that General de Lattre de Tassigny's troops had been involved in renewed fighting near Colmar. For a brief moment she wondered if she might be able to contact the French general to ask for his help, but the chances of him ever receiving such a letter were slim. Instead, she cabled André's father, telling him about Molly's interview with Gefreiter Henniker and asking him to send her a more recent photo of André if he had one.

On 17 January, news broke that the Red Army, which was now advancing fast across central Europe, had taken Warsaw, the capital of Poland, from the Nazis.

Shortly after that, on the 27th, they came across a place called Auschwitz. Despite the Nazis' efforts to hide the evidence, including the forced march of thousands of inmates to other camps, it was obvious to the Russians that it had been the scene of murder on an unprecedented scale.

But even though news of the shocking discovery filtered through to MI19, for some reason the British press barely mentioned it. They were much more interested in the rapid Russian advance, and speculating as to the effect it would have on the forthcoming summit of the three Allied leaders, Roosevelt, Churchill and Stalin, in Yalta, during which, it was rumoured, plans would be agreed for the carving-up of post-war Germany.

Whether that was true or not, Lord de Burrel was certainly taking steps to prepare himself for the negotiations. When Helen enquired how his first session with Mrs d'Arcy Billière had gone, he told her that they had got on like a house on fire and that he was already looking forward to trying out his new linguistic skills on Marshal Stalin's staff.

The next time they met, he asked Helen if she would like to go to Yalta with him. 'Winnie's bringing Mary,' he said. 'So I don't see why you shouldn't come if you want to. God knows what sort of accommodation the Russkies will lay on for us, but I'm sure you could share with her if necessary.'

Helen had only met Winston Churchill's daughter once or twice, but she was pretty sure that Mary Churchill wouldn't relish sharing a room with someone she barely knew. In any case, interesting though the trip might be, it wasn't going to be any help to André.

In the end, Helen was glad she had refused, because the day her father left, she got wind of a possible means to get to Germany. According to Ward Frazer, the horrific discoveries at Auschwitz had caused certain senior members of the security forces to start worrying about what treatment might be meted out to Allied prisoners of war when the final push into Germany took place. One scenario imagined them being killed; another that the camps would simply be abandoned and the prisoners might starve. They were therefore discussing the idea of setting up teams of special agents who could be parachuted in near POW camps to intercede in the event of any observed untoward actions being directed against prisoners.

Helen was not a keen parachutist; nevertheless, it seemed too good an opportunity to turn down on such a flimsy excuse, and she asked Ward to put her name forward. He of course had already volunteered.

'Oh no,' Katy wailed when she got to hear of it. 'I thought he was enjoying being here with me and the children.'

'He is enjoying it,' Helen said. 'But you know what he's like. He's always been one for a bit of excitement.'

'I know,' Katy said. 'And I know he's not going to want to settle down to running the pub when the war's over. If he survives that long.' She sighed. 'To be honest, I'm not all that keen to do it either. It's such long hours, and I want to have time to spend with the children. But I don't want to go to Canada.'

Helen was troubled to hear the slightly desperate note in her friend's voice. Katy and Ward had such a good relationship, she didn't know why this issue was causing Katy such grief. 'Have you told Ward you don't want to go to Canada?' she asked.

'Yes,' Katy said. 'He knows. He doesn't want to go either. But everyone is saying how hard it's going to be to find work after the war is over, and there's a good job waiting for him there in his father's aeronautics business. His uncle made that perfectly clear when he was here. And even though Ward doesn't get on with his father, I'm worried he might be tempted, because so far he hasn't made any effort to look for anything here.'

'I'm sure something will turn up,' Helen said. 'After all, none of us know what we'll be doing when the war's over. Look at me. God knows what I'll do if André never comes back. And Louise is going to be demobbed soon, and she's certainly not going to want to go back to that ghastly factory she worked in before she was called up.'

'And goodness only knows what's going to happen to Jen,' Katy agreed. She shook her head and gave a rueful grimace. 'No, Molly's the only one who has it all worked out. She'll go to medical school and become a doctor, and leave the rest of us wondering where we went wrong.'

★　★　★

The trouble with families, Joyce thought, was that no problem was ever really a new problem. It was always a version of a previous problem, and came with all the memories of the strife that had accompanied it in its previous incarnation. It would be so much easier if you could start each time from scratch.

Like now, for example, it would be nice if she and Jen could sit down and discuss the various options rationally and calmly. But because of all the rows and upsets they'd had in the past, that was impossible.

Experience had taught Joyce that the only hope of reconciliation was to give Jen time to cool off. She knew that Albert thought she was being unduly unsympathetic, but he hadn't had years of dealing with Jen's moods. He didn't know just how touchy and intransigent she could be.

'We must go and see her,' he said. 'We can't just leave her all on her own up in town. The poor girl must be worried to death.'

But when, having got her new address from Katy, they sent a short, carefully worded message to Jen suggesting they meet up to discuss things, they got a brief note back saying that she was perfectly fine and there was nothing to discuss.

'Oh dear,' Albert said. 'I wonder what that means.'

'I don't know,' Joyce said grimly. 'But I don't like the sound of it.'

But, before they could pursue matters further, things got even more complicated.

Three days after Dr Goodacre's emergency operation, Paul came off the danger list but, owing to his weakened state, it wasn't until the following weekend that he was deemed strong enough to sustain anything more than a very brief visit.

On Saturday, Joyce was finally allowed to sit with him for half an hour. Previously he had been too heavily sedated to do more than smile weakly and mutter a few incoherent words of greeting, but today he was looking significantly more perky.

'I didn't think I was going to make it,' he said when Joyce told him how much better he was looking. His voice was husky from lack of use, and slow from the sedative. But his words were perfectly distinct, and his rueful grin looked much more like that of the old Paul, the fifteen-year-old boy who had gone off to war with such gung-ho excitement.

'Well, you *are* going to make it,' Joyce said bracingly. 'Dr Goodacre says you're going to be right as rain in no time.'

'How long have I been here?' Paul asked.

'It's the twentieth of January today,' Joyce said. 'You've been back in London for over a week.'

'Blimey,' Paul said. He was silent, and after a moment, his eyes drifted shut. Thinking he was going to sleep, Joyce sat back in her chair. But then his eyes suddenly flickered opened again. He shook his head as though to clear his thoughts, and a slight frown creased his forehead. 'What about Captain Keller?' he asked. 'Is he all right?'

Caught unawares, Joyce stared at him blankly. Who had told him that Henry was missing? Jen? Angie? But then she realised it couldn't be, because nobody apart from her had been allowed in.

'What do you mean?' she asked. 'What about Captain Keller?'

Paul looked confused. 'I thought you'd know,' he said. 'I thought he would've told Jen.'

Joyce frowned. 'Told her what?'

'That it was him who saved me,' Paul said. 'His troop had just gone past us into the woods when my patrol came under fire. We had no idea Jerry was there, otherwise we wouldn't have been in the open like that.'

He paused briefly and moistened his lips with his tongue. 'I saw the others go down, then I copped it too, right there in the road. I remember it being really quiet for a minute or two. There was snow everywhere and it was all hushed like it is with snow. Then I heard a vehicle, and they drove this damn great truck right over me. I could hear them Jerries laughing up on top while they did it.'

Once again his eyes started to close, and Joyce saw him fighting to hang on to his thread. 'Then the next thing I knew, Captain Keller was kneeling beside me on the icy road. I couldn't speak, but I know he recognised me because he said my name. Anyway, he rolled me onto some kind of stretcher and told three of his men to get me to a medic as soon as possible.'

Paul took a laboured breath. 'They told me afterwards that he'd picked the three married men to do it. That was the last I saw of him. I don't know what he was doing there, but they were obviously moving forward into enemy-held territory, and I've been wondering if he was OK, because without those three men, his troop must have been pretty thin on the ground.'

Joyce didn't know what to say. Paul was already having to cope with extreme physical injuries, as well as mental and emotional trauma. She didn't see any need to add guilt into the mix. But nor did she want to lie. So she just patted his arm vaguely. 'I don't think Jen's heard from Henry recently,' she said. 'But I'm sure he's OK. I'll make sure she thanks him when she next writes to him.'

Thankfully, Paul's lashes drooped again. This time he really was asleep, leaving Joyce with a brand-new dilemma. Whether to tell Jen what he had said, or not.

Before she could make up her mind, another bombshell fell.

Arriving back at the café, she found Angie and Gino fidgeting about in the kitchen.

'How was Paul?' Angie asked at once.

'He's much better,' Joyce said. 'He could talk today, and—'

'Thank goodness for that,' Angie cut in. 'Because Gino and me have got something to tell you, but we didn't want to say anything until we knew Paul was going to be OK.'

As she looked at her younger daughter's rosy face, at the gleeful excitement in her eyes, Joyce was aware of a sinking sensation in her stomach. They're going to tell me they want to go and live in Italy, she thought.

But she was wrong.

Grabbing Gino's hand, Angie took a big breath and, with a peal of delighted laughter, announced that she was eight weeks pregnant.

The news could hardly have been delivered in a more contrasting way to Jen's resentful announcement the previous week, but oddly, Joyce felt almost as shocked. Her immediate thought was to wonder what on earth they were going to live on. But this time she managed to hide her dismay under a valiant gasp of amazed delight. In any case, Angie had second-guessed her.

'Now that the government has lifted the ban on making ice cream, Gino thinks it would be a good idea to start an ice-cream business,' she said. 'He says Italian ice cream is the best. His mother is going to send him the recipe. So we'll be able to provide for the baby and everything.'

Joyce had a vague memory of the stop-me-and-buy-one Italian ice-cream man who used to come round on his bicycle during the hot summers before the war. It had indeed been delicious, but . . . She couldn't help glancing out of the window. Sleety snow was billowing down the street. Nobody in their right mind would want to eat ice cream in the middle of a British winter. And surely it would require all sorts of expensive equipment . . .

'*Gelato*,' Gino murmured. 'Is very nice. And very nice news about the baby, no? I hope you are pleased, Mrs Lorenz, yes?'

'Oh yes,' Joyce said faintly. 'Very pleased.'

Angie poked him in the side admonishingly. 'Of course she's pleased,' she said. 'Everyone loves babies. So anyway,' she went on, 'we've asked Mr Lorenz if he will give us a loan to buy a refrigerator. And a churning pail, and—'

'Wait a minute,' Joyce interrupted sharply. 'You've already discussed this with Albert?'

Angie looked at her in surprise. 'Oh yes,' she said. 'He popped in for a cup of tea while you were at the hospital and we asked him then.'

'What did he say?' Joyce asked.

'He said he was very pleased for us,' Angie said with a giggle.

Joyce glared at her. 'About the ice cream, I meant.'

Angie wrinkled her nose. 'He said we'd have to ask you. But I think he thought it was a good idea.'

'Did he indeed?' Joyce said grimly.

Later, when she took Albert to task in the privacy of their bedroom, he was unrepentant.

'Well, a refrigerator would be a useful addition to the café,' he said.

'And a baby? Another baby? Is that a useful addition?'

He laughed fondly and sat down on the edge of the bed to take off his shoes. 'It never rains but it pours,' he said. 'I just hope Bella doesn't suddenly announce that she is pregnant too.'

Joyce gaped at him in horror. 'Don't say such a thing. At least Angie and Gino are married. Nevertheless, I can't imagine how they are going to cope financially. I hardly think making a few ice creams is going to do the trick.'

Albert was untying his shoelaces. 'The war will be over soon, and everything will be easier then.'

'What about Jen?' Joyce asked sarcastically. 'Will it be easier for her?' She groaned as she unbuttoned her cardigan. 'If Henry doesn't come back, we'll have to offer to accommodate her and all. She won't like it. But she'll come round. She's not daft. She knows she won't be able to support a baby on her own. Not with that acting lark.'

Albert straightened up and smiled at her. 'Then you'll be pleased to hear that the council has finally decided to start giving permits for rebuilding. Although finding a builder will be easier said than done. And the weather's not on our side. I don't suppose we'll get it sorted out until the summer.'

Joyce groaned. 'We're going to need to do something sooner than that. What will happen to Paul when he comes out of hospital? He can hardly share a room with Bella. And for all we know, Pete and Mick will reappear too. Even if they're not demobbed straight away they're bound to get leave when the fighting's over.'

'And Bob,' Albert said. 'Don't forget him. He might be first back. They're saying the POWs will be brought home as soon as their camps are liberated.'

Joyce didn't want to think about Bob. She had never told Albert that her eldest son disapproved of their marriage. That was one worry she had managed to shove right to the back of her mind. And she wasn't going to bring it out now. She would cross that bridge when she came to it.

But there was another one to cross first.

'You'll have to go and see Jen,' she said. 'She'll only fly off the handle if I go.'

For a moment Albert looked as though he was going to protest, but then he nodded slowly. 'All right,' he said resignedly. 'Maybe it would be for the best. What do you want me to say to her?'

'Well, you'll have to tell her about Angie,' Joyce said. 'And what Paul said about Henry. But whatever you do, don't give her money for an abortion. Tell her we'll muddle through somehow.' She grimaced as a thought occurred to her. 'I suppose there's a lining to every cloud. She must be about eight weeks too, so they should give birth around the same time. If necessary, Angie will have to pretend she's had twins.'

Jen felt as though she was living a weird, secret double life. On the surface things were relatively normal: she went to RADA each day, took notes in lectures, worked on her performance pieces, wrote an essay on production techniques, had coffee with her classmates, and even twice went to the pictures with them in the evening.

But underneath that veneer of confident, ambitious young actress, she was living a completely different existence, one of indecision, procrastination and utter terror. Neither of the options facing her was remotely appealing. Either she had to put herself through a gruesome operation, or she had to face up to getting fat and bloated, and even more uncomfortable than she was already, and eventually giving birth to an illegitimate baby.

317

She suddenly felt very alone. Her friends had done their best to support her. Both Molly and Katy had been up to see her. Both of them had been kind. But there was a limit to the number of times they could come traipsing up to town, and a limit as to what they could do to help her.

The beastly weather didn't help her mood either. Pretty as Sloane Square looked under a drift of fresh snow, the surrounding pavements were either frozen solid and slippery, or sloppy with melting slush. Twice she had got home from college with wet feet, and eventually, in desperation, she had started wearing a pair of wellington boots she had found lurking at the back of Henry's coat cupboard. They were far too big for her, but padded with three pairs of his thickest woollen socks, they did at least keep her feet warm and dry. Even if she did feel like a right idiot clumping around fashionable Chelsea and Knightsbridge looking like a country bumpkin.

Luckily there was no one there to recognise her. Exclusive, elegant Pont Street was a much less gregarious place than Lavender Road. Most of its wealthy inhabitants either sensibly stayed indoors in their huge centrally heated homes or, if they had to go out, hopped straight into waiting taxis. It was only impoverished people like her who were forced to battle with the blizzard conditions on a daily basis.

Or so she thought. Waddling home in her wellies late one evening, huddled in her coat and scarf and lost in her gloomy thoughts, she nearly jumped out of her skin when someone coming in the opposite direction suddenly stopped in his tracks and spoke her name.

'Jen? It is you, isn't it? My word, what a lovely surprise.'

Peering through her frosted eyelashes, under the dim light of the street lamp at the corner of Pont Street, Jen saw the beaming face of Henry's aristocratic friend Frederick Manson.

If anything, Lord Freddy looked even more extraordinary than she did. Admittedly his navy overcoat was clearly of excellent quality, but round his neck he sported a bright-red knitted scarf topped with a multicoloured bobble hat, the sort that children wore in picture books for skating on the village pond.

'Ha,' he said. 'I thought I recognised that pretty face. I assume this means that Henry's home? The old dog, why hasn't he let me know?'

Jen wanted to reply. She wanted to explain. She wanted to be brave. Above all, she wanted to be calm and rational. After all, she barely knew Freddy; she had only met him once before. But there was something about the way his jovial smile was already fading from his kindly face as he looked at her with mounting concern that made the words impossible to find.

Despite his jaunty winter attire, Lord Freddy's nose and cheeks were bright red, and Jen could see his breath freezing in the cold air. Ridiculously, as her eyes welled up, she found herself wondering if her tears would freeze too. Or would they be too salty? Madly she had the thought that that was probably something Molly would know, with all her new-found scientific knowledge.

'Oh my dear girl,' Freddy said suddenly. 'What a bloody fool I am.' He took her arm and steered her gently on towards Beauchamp Place. 'What's more, you're clearly frozen to death. Let's go and find you a nice warming snifter at the Grove. Then you can tell me all about it.'

Chapter Nineteen

The previous time Jen had met Lord Freddy, at supper with Henry, she had thought he was a bit of a buffoon. This time she discovered that his hearty upper-class geniality concealed a heart of gold.

Not only that, but he was a surprisingly good listener, muttering interjections of sympathetic shock and encouragement at exactly the right moments. To her surprise, as she wasn't much of a one for trusting people with her confidences, Jen found herself pouring out her sorry tale, warts and all.

It didn't seem to occur to Lord Freddy to censure her for having jumped into bed with Henry, although he did go a bit pink when she got to that part of the story.

'Quite understandable in the circumstances,' he mumbled, taking a fortifying slug of his beer. 'Don't blame you at all, or him come to that. After all, you were on the brink of getting married.'

As to her current plight, he clearly understood how she had come to fall out with her mother. 'Well, people are funny about these things,' he said. 'It's the fault of the Church, of course. The sanctity of marriage and so on. Lot of nonsense, of course, but I suppose it helps keep society on the straight and narrow. Nevertheless, if dear old Henry doesn't reappear, I can see you are going to be in a bit of a fix.'

Jen felt she was going to be in considerably more than a bit of a fix, but a glass of warming brandy and a spam sandwich had done much to restore her equilibrium, and somehow, with Lord Freddy nodding at her benevolently on the other side of the small table, things suddenly didn't seem quite so desperate.

'I'd offer to marry you myself,' he said meditatively. 'But it might be a bit awkward if Henry does come back. Although I expect he would understand.'

Awkward? Jen spluttered over her drink. Awkward was the least of it. She thought he must be joking, but realising that he looked perfectly sincere, she bit back the laugh that sprang to her lips. 'That's terribly kind,' she said. 'But I couldn't possibly ask you to do that. Anyway, I thought you wanted to marry Louise Rutherford?'

At once he coloured up. 'Oh, I do,' he said. 'More than anything in the world. And I wrote to tell her so after the first time we met. But unfortunately I haven't managed to see her since then. She's always so busy with her ATS duties. Between you and me, I'm beginning to wonder if she's trying to avoid me ...' He gave a slightly forlorn laugh. 'Of course I'm not very good with the ladies, so it's perfectly understandable.'

At that moment Jen could have kicked Louise. It was mean of her to keep poor Freddy dangling. Jen was sure it was only because he wasn't very good looking.

'Well, she won't be busy for much longer,' she said. 'Because she's being demobbed soon. And then she'll be living back in London again.'

Lord Freddy brightened up at once. 'Really?' For a second he looked like an eager puppy with his eye on a tasty bone. Then he shook his head determinedly. 'But this isn't about me and my hopeless aspirations, my dear Jen, it's about you. And if you want my opinion – which I don't suppose you do for a moment, because after all, what does a blithering idiot like me know about anything? – I think you should go on with this baby. Be a shame to lose it. Henry's got plenty of friends, and I'm sure between us we can help you out. Certainly not going to leave you in the lurch, anyway. So don't worry about that.' He smiled reassuringly, then hesitated. 'But in the meantime, I can't help thinking that you might feel more comfortable if you could find a way to make it up with your mother.

A girl needs her mother at times like these. No, please,' he added hastily. 'I shouldn't have said that. Please don't start crying again. I'm not good at dealing with tearful women.'

Even though her eyes were indeed filling up again, Jen couldn't help giggling. 'I think you're very good at it,' she said. 'In fact I think you're a lot better with women than you think. And if you want my opinion, which you probably don't because I'm such a stupid cry-baby, I think Louise would be a fool to turn you down.'

Half an hour later, having learned to his horror that due to her inadequate cooking skills Jen was living mainly on toast and Bovril, Lord Freddy had arranged to take her out to dinner later in the week, and made her promise to summon him from his own nearby home in Cadogan Place should she need him before that.

Having always felt rather nervous at the idea of getting to know Henry's posh friends, Jen was unaccountably reassured by Freddy's unstinting offer of support, and it was with a lighter heart that she made her way down to Clapham the following afternoon after college with the intention of making peace with her mother.

An icy wind was sweeping across Clapham Common as she walked along from the Tube station, and feeling in need of a warming cup of tea, she decided to call in on Mrs d'Arcy Billière and her former housemates first. But just as she turned the corner onto Lavender Road, she bumped smack into Louise's mother.

'Oh my goodness,' Mrs Rutherford cried, flailing slightly in an attempt to keep her footing on the frozen pavement. 'Oh it's you, Jennifer, I didn't recognise you all swaddled up like that. How nice to see you. I suppose you've come down to celebrate the exciting news.'

Startled by her unaccustomed friendliness, Jen blinked. 'Exciting news?'

Mrs Rutherford chortled merrily. 'Didn't you know? We're all terribly excited. We're going to hear the patter of tiny feet in the café. Angie has just announced that she's going to have a baby.'

Jen stared at her blankly. 'No,' she said. 'I hadn't heard.' Good God, she thought. Angie and Gino having a baby. Patter of tiny feet indeed.

If Angie was anything to go by, she would more likely give birth to a trumpeting elephant. What was more, Angie and Gino were even more penniless than Jen herself was. She gave a sour laugh. 'What does my mother think about that?'

'Oh, she's thrilled,' Mrs Rutherford said. 'Absolutely over the moon. We've all just been celebrating in the café. And as luck would have it, permission came through this morning for Mr Lorenz to have his house rebuilt, so that's where Angie and Gino are going to live. It couldn't be better, could it?'

Even though she knew Mrs Rutherford was looking at her expectantly, Jen was unable to reply. Suddenly she was almost incandescent with anger. But much as she longed to let rip, she knew if she opened her mouth she would say something she would regret.

Despite her remarkable self-control, something must have shown in her face, however, because Mrs Rutherford started fussing uneasily with her handbag. 'Oh well,' she said. 'I'd better hurry on. I've got a WVS meeting this evening. Oh, and Jen, I haven't had a chance to say so before, but I was so sorry to hear about Henry. How horrid for you. He's a lovely man. I know Louise is upset about it as well. What a beastly war this is. I don't suppose you've heard any more . . .?'

Now, finally, Jen was able to speak. 'No,' she said tightly. 'I haven't heard any more.' With that, she nodded as politely as she could, and crossed the road to Mrs d'Arcy Billière's house.

For once, Molly had been having a quiet day. With Bella curled up in a chair in the corner of Mrs d'Arcy Billière's morning room reading a book, Molly was taking advantage of a couple of hours' free time to write her letters of application to various London medical schools.

Earlier, Malcolm had had his first session with the professor, and to Molly's relief it seemed to have gone well, which actually wasn't surprising as it mostly seemed to have involved romping about in the garden building a snowman.

'Is important to make learning fun for him,' the professor said rather shamefacedly when they eventually came in with their cheeks glowing from the cold. He then proceeded to hide some tiny peppermints he had brought with him in the gaps in the ornate wooden frieze of Mrs d'Arcy Billière's amazing table. The idea was that Malcolm would be allowed to look for one each time he got his numbers right. As Ward had already taught him his numbers up to ten, he was soon awash with peppermints, and by the time Ward arrived to collect him, he was easily able to recite up to twenty.

'Wow, that's great,' Ward said. He smiled at Mrs d'Arcy Billière, who was standing in the hallway. 'It's kind of you to do this. You have a beautiful home. I have to admit, I'm envious. Especially of the back yard. It's great the kids can play out there.'

'It's not a back yard, it's a garden,' George said. 'With trees and bushes and everything.'

'And it's got a pergiola,' Malcolm said proudly.

'Is that right?' Ward laughed and tousled his hair. 'And what do you know about pergiolas?'

'I know they're good for hiding in,' Malcolm said. 'I wish we had one. And a great big table with sweets in it.' He looked up at the professor with a winsome smile. 'I wish I could come again tomorrow.'

Ward was smiling too, and not for the first time Molly thought how alike they were. Father and son, both with those lovely grey-blue eyes and irresistible smiles. So like Callum, too.

'Not tomorrow, but perhaps one day next week,' Professor Markov said. He winked at Malcolm. 'Soon we'll have another lady to help us, and then you can come more often.'

'Thank you, Molly,' Ward said as he helped Malcolm on with his coat. 'This is going to be great for him. Oh, and Helen was looking for you. Shall I tell her you're here?'

'Don't worry,' Molly said. 'I'm just writing some letters. I'll pop down to the pub when I've finished.'

But to her surprise, five minutes later, Helen appeared. Molly heard her voice in the hallway, talking to Mrs d'Arcy Billière, who had answered her knock on the door. When Molly emerged from the morning room, Helen was telling Mrs d'Arcy Billière how much her father was enjoying his Russian lessons, but Molly could tell from her friend's quick meaningful glance that whatever she had to tell her was important.

She was right. 'I've had a note from your mother,' Helen whispered as Molly led her into the garden.

Molly almost tripped down the step.

Helen looked at her in concern. 'She wants to meet up,' she said. 'But . . .' She handed over a folded piece of notepaper. 'I think you'd better read it yourself.'

Dear Miss Burrel,

I imagine you will be surprised to hear from me. I have thought about what you said, however, and I find I am indeed curious to know how our mutual friend has turned out. I suggest we meet at the Lyons Corner House in Oxford Street at eleven o'clock on Thursday 1 March. If she is not there, I will assume it is not convenient. Either way, please do not respond to this letter. I wish to make it clear that although I am prepared to meet her on this occasion, I am not intending it to become a regular occurrence.

Yours sincerely,

Mrs Priscilla Wright

Molly's first reaction was stunned disappointment. 'She sounds ghastly,' she said.

Helen bit her lip. 'I told you she was anxious about it all,' she said. 'But I agree it could have been a bit warmer.'

A bit warmer? Molly stared at her incredulously. If she hadn't been so shocked, she might have laughed. That was an understatement if she had ever heard one. She hadn't expected her mother to welcome her with open arms, but this was completely the other end of the scale.

'She's not exactly in a hurry, is she?' she said. 'The first of March is over a month away.'

'Maybe she's going on holiday or something,' Helen said. She lifted her shoulders in an elegant shrug. 'Or maybe she just thought it was best to give plenty of notice.'

'What, so I didn't feel the need to contact her to change the day?' Molly said sarcastically. She looked at the letter again, then folded it crossly and put it in her pocket. She could feel Helen's sympathetic eyes on her and made an effort to smile. 'Thanks for bringing it,' she said. 'I will go and meet her, even though she sounds like a right madam. It obviously hasn't occurred to her that I might not want it to become a regular occurrence either. After that letter, she's lucky I'm prepared to even go once.'

Helen laughed and seemed reassured. 'I'd better go back to the pub,' she said. 'I promised Katy I'd man the bar while she and Ward put the children to bed.' But at the front door she paused, her eyes narrowed slightly in concern. 'Molly, are you sure you're OK?'

Molly nodded. 'I'm fine. I'll just finish my application letters and then I'll come and give you a hand.'

But back in the morning room, Molly found she couldn't concentrate on the letters. If Bella hadn't been still there, reading quietly by the light of a table lamp, she would have put her head in her hands and wept. Or better still, banged her brains out on the table. The see-saw of emotions was such that she didn't know if she was angry or upset.

Either way, she felt far too preoccupied to think of suitably convincing reasons as to why she wanted to train as a doctor. So she was glad a few minutes later when she heard the front door open again. Hoping it might be Aaref, who had always been a good friend to her, she went out to see who it was, and found Jen in the hallway angrily kicking off a pair of oversized wellington boots and looking as though steam was about to come out of her ears.

'Jen?' Molly regarded her with alarm. 'Are you all right? What on earth's happened?'

'What's happened?' Jen spluttered in fury, following her back into the morning room. 'I'll tell you what's happened. Mrs busybody

326

Rutherford and my bloody mother have happened.' Pulling out a chair, she slumped down at the table. 'I ask you, when so many bombs have fallen in London, why the hell hasn't one of the beastly things fallen on them?'

'I don't know,' Molly said. 'I certainly wish one would fall on *my* blasted mother.'

Seeing that Jen was shivering convulsively, she turned towards the fireplace to kick some life into the smouldering logs, and found herself face to face with Bella, who had leapt to her feet, sending the book she had been reading skittering across the floor. It was clear from the girl's anguished face that she was trying to shout something, but her voice was husky with disuse and the words came out as a low rasp.

'No!' Her eyes were wild. 'You mustn't say that! That's what I said to my mother and the next day she died.'

Jen, who clearly hadn't even noticed the girl was in the room, nearly jumped out of her skin. 'Good God,' she said, swivelling round in astonishment. 'What the . . .?'

But Molly quelled her with a warning look. Slowly, carefully, she took a step towards Bella, who was standing wide eyed and trembling, as though she had seen a ghost. Desperately trying to remember what she knew about Bella's condition, Molly took her arm and steered her gently across to the table.

Joyce had told her Dr Goodacre's diagnosis: selective mutism or *aphasia voluntaria*. Molly had subsequently looked it up in the library. But although the medical dictionary had indicated that it was generally caused by some kind of physical or psychological shock, it had failed to advise on what to do when the sufferer suddenly, unexpectedly, started talking again. Molly's experience of shock, however, had taught her that there was one remedy that generally seemed to help.

'Jen?' she murmured. She nodded meaningfully towards the kitchen. 'Is there any chance you could go and make us all a nice cup of tea? Then can you go and fetch your mother?'

As soon as Jen had gone, Molly sat down calmly beside the shaking girl. 'It's OK,' she said. 'Jen and I didn't mean what we said. And I'm sure you didn't either.'

'But I did,' Bella whispered. 'I hated her. I hated the men that came to the house. I hated what she did with them. The noises they made, and the way they looked at me. But she wouldn't stop. And I got angry and I told her I wished a bomb would land on her. And then the next day it did.' She looked up at Molly with staring eyes. 'I made it happen. And it nearly killed Mr Lorenz and George and Louise too.'

Molly felt a shiver run up her spine. She had been in Tunisia when the V-1 had landed in Lavender Road, but she knew it had been a horrific incident. Not only had Bella's mother and several other people died, but Mr Lorenz, Louise and George had all been trapped for hours under the wreckage. 'No you didn't,' she said. 'Hitler made it happen. Look at all the other bombs that have fallen. People haven't wished for those. It was just a horrible coincidence. It wasn't your fault.'

'But I've wished for things before,' Bella said. 'And they have come true too.'

'I think that happens to all of us, to a greater or lesser degree,' Molly said. 'That's why they call it wishful thinking.'

Bella looked unconvinced. 'But sometimes I know things are going to happen,' she said.

'What sort of things?' Molly asked tentatively. She didn't really want to know, but she instinctively felt it was important to keep Bella talking. The last thing she wanted was for her to clam up again.

'I knew as soon as I heard the explosion that my mother was going to be dead,' Bella said.

And now Molly remembered Katy saying that Bella had stopped speaking the instant the bomb hit. Hours before Mrs James's body was discovered. She shivered again and glanced at the fire, but it was burning merrily now and the room was warm.

'And I knew ages ago that Angie was going to have a baby.'

Molly smiled gently. 'Well, that wasn't so difficult to guess,' she said.

'But I know that Jen is going to have a baby too,' Bella said rather desperately. 'And I know that Mr Keller is still alive. Just like I knew Paul was going to be all right. And I know things about you too. Like that the London medical schools are going to turn you down. And that Ward's cousin, Callum, is going to . . .'

And now, suddenly, desperately, Molly wanted to shut her up again. To her relief, at that moment she heard footsteps and the clinking rattle of cups and saucers in the hallway. Quickly she stood up and opened the door.

'Here comes Jen with the tea,' she said. 'That will make us all feel better.'

A moment later she was handing round the cups, and Jen was murmuring that Mrs d'Arcy Billière had gone to find Joyce.

And then Joyce was there, and Mr Lorenz, and Bella seemed pleased to see them, and Mrs d'Arcy Billière was asking them if they would like a cup of tea too, and Jen was casually asking Bella what book she had been reading, and everyone was careful not to show any surprise or relief when she responded quite naturally that it was *Rebecca* by Daphne du Maurier.

'Ah yes,' Mr Lorenz said easily, picking it up off the floor. 'An excellent book. I read it when it was first published and enjoyed it enormously. I particularly liked the scene at the ball when . . .'

And Bella had liked that scene too.

Suddenly, from one moment to the next, it was all normal again. Or almost normal. Because despite the warmth in the room, Molly still had the shivers.

That night as she lay in bed, she still felt cold. She tried not to think about what Bella had said. Because it couldn't be true. The girl couldn't possibly have second sight. It was a ridiculous thought. In any case, surely not all the medical schools would turn her down.

Most especially she tried not to think about Bella's final remark just as Jen carried in the tea tray. *And that Ward's cousin, Callum, is going to . . . ask you to marry him.*

Or had she misheard those last few words under the clinking of Mrs d'Arcy Billière's elegant tea-service china? Restlessly Molly turned over in the bed and plumped her pillows, trying to get comfortable. Had that really been what Bella had said? Or was it she who was indulging in wishful thinking? Either way, that night she found it impossible to sleep.

Jen didn't stay long at Mrs d'Arcy Billière's house. It seemed somehow typical that just when she wanted to have a blazing row with her mother, something more important had got in the way. Much as she was pleased that Bella was talking again, it was frustrating that for the sake of normality, she had had to button her lip and pretend everything was sweetness and light.

In the end, she had barely exchanged two words with her mother. But Mr Lorenz had done his best to make things up with her. In fact he had contrived to take the wind right out of her sails by kissing her on the cheek and saying how pleased he was to see her. According to him, he had literally just been about to set off to Knightsbridge to come and talk things through with her.

'We obviously won't be able to do it now,' he said in a low voice. 'I think young Bella will have to take priority this evening. But I want you to know that your mother and I will do all we can to help you, Jen. Whatever that involves. We are all on the same side, you know.'

Jen didn't know whether to believe him or not; nevertheless, she had felt mildly mollified. But she wasn't going to let her mother off the hook as easily as that.

'That's just you saying that,' she said. 'Mum's certainly not on my side. She made it perfectly clear that I'm an embarrassment to her. Unlike darling Angie, who can't put a foot wrong.'

Mr Lorenz gave a slight smile. 'Ah,' he said. 'So you have heard the news, have you? Well, I'm sure it won't surprise you to know that your mother is somewhat concerned about that too.' He tilted his head, and for a brief second she caught the twinkle of complicit amusement in his eyes. 'But we will find a way to support them, just as we will you. After all, that's what families are for. To support each other in our hour of need.'

'Huh,' Jen said sourly. 'That's hardly been the case in my family.' But as she went to turn away, he put a hand on her arm.

'There's one other thing, Jen,' he said. 'Something else you ought to know.'

Alerted by the sudden serious tone in his kindly voice, she swung back at once. Drawing her away from the others with a slight pressure on her arm, he told her that Paul had seen Henry in Belgium. That in effect, Henry had saved her brother's life, and in so doing had almost certainly put his own at additional risk.

Jen heard him out in silence, then, on the muttered pretext of fetching some more hot water for the teapot, she left the room. It was either that or scream the place down, and even she knew that would be unacceptable in the circumstances. For a brief second, as she stood in the hallway, she toyed with going to the pub. But the thought of coping with everyone's well-meaning enquiries about Henry was more than she could bear. Let alone any celebratory chit-chat about Angie's pregnancy. So instead, she pulled on her coat and scarf, and Henry's over-large wellies and, letting herself out of the house, plodded her way along the edge of dank, dark, foggy Clapham Common back to the Tube station.

On 1 February, the barrage balloons were lowered for the last time in Regent's Park. Helen watched the small ceremony on her way back from her preliminary interview for the new Special Allied Airborne Reconnaissance Force.

The discussion had gone well. The officer in charge had seemed interested in her and her SOE background. 'We can't formally sign anyone up until we are given a mandate,' he said. 'But we expect to start training in March. Or earlier if our boys in France manage to advance into Germany sooner than expected.'

Helen was frustrated by the delay, but at least the Allies were pushing on. Not only was the controversial blanket bombing of German cities proceeding apace, but almost all the territory the Allies had lost during the German counterattack in the Ardennes was in the process of being retaken.

Further south, French troops were even now mounting a massive attack on the city of Colmar on the Franco–German border. The Nazi occupiers put up fierce resistance, but eventually the city was taken together with a huge number of German prisoners. A week later, it was announced that the west bank of the Rhine, from the Swiss border right up as far as Strasbourg, was in Allied hands, and Helen started hoping that the final push into Germany might indeed come sooner than expected.

In the meantime, the Yalta Conference was over, and it was being reported that Roosevelt, Churchill and Stalin had come to a successful agreement over the future organisation of Europe. The British press were ecstatic. But the outcome of the conference didn't please the Germans, who claimed that the unwarranted severity of the agreement, and the excessive partiality shown to Russia, had released Germany from all its moral scruples.

'What moral scruples are those?' Helen asked Ward bitterly.

But when her father reappeared in London the following week, it seemed the Germans weren't the only ones dubious about Russia.

Due to the extraordinarily rapid advance of the Red Army, and the fact that his troops were now within forty miles of Berlin, Marshal Stalin had been in a strong bargaining position.

'It wasn't so much us asking him to agree to things,' her father said. 'It was more him telling us what he was prepared to accept. He did at least promise not to impose communism on the countries he's currently occupying. But he's a slippery devil and my guess is that he will renege as soon as we turn our backs. Even with my limited Russian, I could tell he was playing us. And I think Winnie could too. Still, the conference had its advantages. The food was spectacular. And we were able to get hold of plenty of vodka and caviar to bring home with us.'

Some of which, according to Molly, had already made its way to Mrs d'Arcy Billière. 'I think he's getting rather keen on her,' she said to Helen. 'He brought her flowers yesterday and she went all pink.'

But Helen had more urgent things to think about than her father's relationship with Mrs d'Arcy Billière. At long last she had received a letter back from Monsieur Cabillard enclosing a photograph of André. It was a much clearer image than the previous one she'd had. This one showed André standing in front of the vineyard delivery van, holding up a bottle of wine and smiling for the camera. At his feet were two dogs. One of them Helen recognised from her recent visit; the other, she realised sadly, was the one that had been killed by the departing SS. In the background, slightly out of focus behind the van, and probably unaware that he was even in the frame, was the familiarly impassive figure of Raoul.

But it was the faintly ironic expression on André's handsome face that made Helen's heart jolt painfully in her chest. It was such a long time since she had last seen that lovely smile, and now she couldn't help wondering if she would ever see it again.

Reluctant to let another precious photograph of André pass out of her hands, with some difficulty, and at vast expense, she had it copied. She sent one of the copies to Mr Sparrow's wife at the Red Cross; another was dispatched to Major Withers for Gefreiter Henniker. The rest she handed out to the interrogating officers at MI19 in the hope they might show them to any SS or SD POWs who passed through their hands.

Once again it was a long shot. But she didn't want to leave any stone unturned.

She could tell from Monsieur Cabillard's letter accompanying the photo that he was trying everything he could too. He had even contacted General de Gaulle himself, but to no avail.

Then, on 18 February, four days after 800 RAF and USAAF Lancasters and 400 B-17 bombers had left the German city of Dresden a smoking ruin, with suspected casualties of up to 100,000 people, Molly received a note from Major Withers to say that Gefreiter

Henniker had requested a visit. *Reckon latest photo must have done trick. Tried to get your friend to give the info to me, but no luck. Let me know suitable date and I'll have him (and ginger nuts) ready and waiting.*

Most of the other patients on Paul's ward were GIs, and as some of them had friends stationed in or near London, they got plenty of gum-chewing, candy-toting American visitors. But recently, incensed by finding numerous pieces of discarded gum stuck to her precious pristine floor, the ward sister, Sister Morris, an old friend of Joyce's, had implemented a gum ban on the ward. To that end she had placed a warning notice and a litter bin outside the ward's swing doors.

For a few days, visiting GIs had dutifully discarded their gum before entering, but when Joyce arrived at visiting time on the third afternoon since the notice had gone up, she was amused to see that, instead of using the bin, the resourceful Americans had instead started to stick their gum on the corridor wall under neatly pencilled initials, presumably ensuring that they could reclaim the correct piece on their exit from the ward. Joyce wondered what Sister Morris would think of that, and decided it certainly wasn't going to be her that told her.

'I've got a joke for you,' Paul said as Joyce drew up a chair by his bed. 'What do you call a man who smokes twenty fags a day, eats chocolate and smells of onions?'

'I don't know,' Joyce said. 'What do you call him?'

'A millionaire.'

Joyce laughed obligingly. It was a pretty feeble joke, but it was a relief to see Paul looking so much better. And actually the joke wasn't so far off. Since Christmas, things in London had got very short. Last time she had been to the grocer's, there'd been no toothpaste, no soap powder, no knicker elastic and no lavatory paper. There were certainly no onions.

Nevertheless, despite the privations, Joyce was aware of feeling a bit better about everything. Paul was on the mend, Bella was talking again, Gino was at last making progress with his English, and Albert had somehow managed to smooth things over a bit with Jen. She wasn't exactly friendly, but she had at least been civil when they met last week. On top of all that, the weather was better. Yesterday, after the interminably long, cold winter, the temperature in London had soared to well over sixty degrees.

'About time too,' Mrs Rutherford had remarked. 'Because we are almost out of coal, and Greville has found it impossible to get any more.'

Joyce had been out of coal for weeks and, nervous that there might be another cold snap, decided to go up to the common to see if there were any fallen branches or twigs she could use for kindling.

Albert was at home when she called to pick up a basket, and she was touched when he offered to come with her to see what they could find. Which wasn't much. They weren't the first household to run out of fuel, and plenty of people had been there before them. It was surprising the trees themselves were still standing. Goodness knew how the Dutch were coping, Joyce thought. It had said in the paper yesterday that there was hardly a speck of food or fuel left in Holland. Their German occupiers had taken it all. The report said that the Dutch had resorted to eating their famous tulip bulbs to stay alive.

'I hope Hitler gets his comeuppance,' Joyce said as she and Albert began to make their way back towards Lavender Road. 'I'd like to stuff a tulip bulb down his throat and watch the flowers grow out of his you-know-what.'

Albert laughed. 'I'd like to do much worse than that,' he said. 'I'd like to . . .'

But before he could say exactly what he'd like to do, he stopped abruptly.

'Joyce, look,' he said. He pointed towards the far corner of the common. 'I can't quite see from here, but isn't that Jen?'

Joyce's eyesight was better than his. And yes, in the low reddish light of the setting sun, she could quite clearly see her elder daughter pelting along the top of the common as though wolves were after her.

'Yes, it is,' she said. 'But what on earth's she doing haring about like that in her condition? If she's not careful, she'll lose that baby.'

But Albert didn't answer. Because he was no longer standing beside her. He was already running forward to intercept Jen.

'Jen?' he shouted. 'Stop! What's the matter?'

Joyce saw Jen falter. Then abruptly she changed direction and came pelting across towards them, weaving her way through the allotments. Albert hastily put down the basket he was carrying, and a second later Jen collapsed into his open arms. And now Joyce saw that clutched in her daughter's hand was a yellow telegram. She must have carried it all the way from Pont Street.

'Jen, for goodness' sake,' she shouted as she ran towards them. 'What is it? What's happened?'

Jen raised her head and looked at her over Albert's shoulder.

'It's Henry,' she gasped. 'Oh my God. He's alive. And he's coming home.'

Chapter Twenty

Gefreiter Henniker put his hands on the table. 'One month ago, your friend Cabillard was in a prison camp called Konzentrationslager Buchenwald, near Weimar,' he said. 'If he is still alive, this is where he will be.'

Molly took a breath. They were in the same room as before. It was warmer than last time. A shaft of sun caught the corner of the table that stood between them. Outside the window, along the edge of the wire surrounding the prisoners' section of the camp, Molly could see a line of daffodils. They looked incongruously pretty against the stark outline of the huts. She wondered if there were daffodils at Konzentrationslager Buchenwald, and rather doubted it.

Despite the warmth of the room, she shivered and glanced back at Gefreiter Henniker. 'How do you know this?'

He shrugged his heavy shoulders. 'There is a man who came here last week who was captured at Colmar. Before this he had worked on the trains. He recognised the photo. He remembers your friend being at the transfer camp at Saarbrucken. He remembered him because he was French and very handsome, not a Jew, and also because he kept asking about SS Hauptsturmführer Wessel. He wanted to know if Wessel was still alive, or if he had been taken prisoner by the Allies.'

Molly wondered if Henniker was telling the truth. But it sounded plausible. It certainly sounded like André, and it matched what Major

Withers had said earlier. As he had walked her over to the interview hut, he had nodded to a group of POWs digging over some kind of plot behind the wire 'We've just taken in a lot of Germans captured at Colmar,' he had said. 'And there's plenty more on the way. God only knows where we are going to put them all. I've got those chaps working on the foundations of a new dining block. At this rate we might end up having to use it for accommodation.'

Whatever the new building was going to be used for, the prisoners seemed to be enjoying the work. Even now Molly could hear the distant sound of spades clinking on stony ground and the occasional burst of laughter.

It was all right for them to laugh, she thought crossly. With nice Major Withers to look after them. And a brand-new dining block on the way.

Becoming conscious that Henniker was watching her, she dragged her resentful thoughts back to the matter in hand. 'When was this?' she asked sharply. 'When did this man see André?'

He shrugged again. 'Not so long ago. I believe sometime before Christmas.'

'But André went missing in August,' Molly said. 'Where had he been in the meantime?'

'This I do not know.'

'So how does your contact know where he was sent after Saarbrucken?'

Gefreiter Henniker had been answering her questions promptly, but now he hesitated. 'He was on the same train,' he said. 'This was his job. I don't know how you say it – going with the prisoners to the camps.'

'Escorting them?' Molly suggested. Although judging from her own experience in Italy, that was almost certainly far too mild a name for it. She was pretty sure that Gefreiter Henniker would know that too.

But he just inclined his head. 'So. Because of this escorting, he knew the guards at the Konzentrationslager. He had admired your

338

friend. They spoke of him. The last time my contact was there was one month ago. They told him that he was still alive.'

Molly could feel her hands shaking and clasped them on her lap. 'Who is this man? Give me his name. I want to speak to him.'

'He won't speak to you.'

'But why not?'

A flicker of impatience showed in his eyes. 'Because he wants to go back to Germany when the war is over. This camp, Buchenwald, is not a good place. You understand? If he admits to knowing things that happen there, he may become witness to what you British now call war crimes and will be kept in prison for a long time.'

Molly gritted her teeth. 'We don't just *call* them war crimes,' she said. 'They *are* war crimes.'

He was silent, his eyes impassive again, and she decided it was pointless to pursue it. 'You said André asked about Wessel,' she said. 'Did your man know where he was?'

Gefreiter Henniker shook his head and looked down at his hands. Molly saw that his nails were broken and dirty. Perhaps he had been on the digging detail before she arrived. In any case, she could see from his sudden withdrawal that she had annoyed him. The interview was clearly coming to an end. But despite his silence, she was convinced that he knew something more.

She leaned forward slightly. 'Tell me,' she said. 'Tell me what you know. Please.'

He pursed his lips in an oddly feminine gesture. 'SS Hauptsturmführer Wessel was seen withdrawing from Colmar,' he said. 'So I believe he is still alive. But I also know that he does not wish to leave witnesses to his crimes. Which perhaps is not good news for your friend.'

If he was right, it certainly wasn't good news. Once again, as Molly trundled back to London on the train, she wondered how Helen was going to react.

But Helen was made of resilient stuff.

'We've got to get André out of there,' she said. 'Before Wessel gets to him. I just hope to God it's not already too late.'

339

'But I can't see how,' Molly said. 'You've done everything you can.'

'Now we know where he is, we can try the Red Cross again. Surely they can't refuse if we have the actual name of the camp where he's being held.'

But the Red Cross did refuse. The International Red Cross in Geneva had no knowledge of a camp called Buchenwald. Even if such a place existed, they had no access to it.

Nor did Helen and Ward's efforts to alert the SOE to the danger André was in bear any fruit.

'Good God,' Maurice Buckmaster said when they eventually bearded him in his den at Baker Street. 'There are more than two hundred thousand British and Commonwealth POWs being held in over two hundred German POW camps. How can we expect anyone to pay attention to one Frenchman?'

'Nobody seems to be paying attention to anyone,' Helen snapped. 'What about all the British agents who have gone missing. Girls, too? What are you doing about them?'

'There's nothing we can do at the moment. Once we advance into Germany, then of course we will do everything we can to get them back safely.'

'If they're still alive,' Helen said grimly. But there was no point in getting angry. Maurice Buckmaster might be burying his head in the sand, but there was very little he could do, even if he wanted to.

She knew from her father, who had also been trying to make representations on André's behalf through his own high-level channels, that the government was far too concerned about the safety of British POWs in general to worry about the fate of a few missing agents.

The Allies were on German soil now, and as they began to advance towards the Rhine, the fear was growing that Hitler might well take revenge on all his prisoners of war, not just those who fell under the so-called Commando Order.

But that clearly wasn't going to stop the advance. On 27 February, the Allies took Mönchengladbach. The Rhine cities of Krefeld, Cologne and Bonn were all under attack, and suddenly things began moving fast, both abroad and at home.

Helen and Ward were advised that they had been selected for operational work with the newly formed Special Allied Airborne Reconnaissance Force.

And Henry Keller finally reappeared in London.

Having received a telegram to say that Henry would be back sometime that day, Jen had cut her lessons at RADA and was waiting for him at the flat in Pont Street. She felt shaky and sick. Because instead of the rapturous welcome he was presumably expecting, the first thing she was going to have to tell him was that she was pregnant. He clearly didn't know, otherwise surely he would have mentioned it in the letter she had received the day before yesterday.

My dearest Jen,

I am so sorry. I hear the idiots told you I was missing, and I can imagine how worried you must have been. But I'm absolutely fine. Nobody seemed to realise that the Germans had planned such a massive counterattack into Belgium, and we found ourselves on the wrong side of the front line, that's all. Because we'd lost communications we had very little idea what was going on, but we had some good luck and found somewhere to hide out while we did what we could to disrupt Jerry's progress. Thankfully he didn't get far. He's in retreat again now, and the day before yesterday we finally came across some friendly forces. I'm back at my HQ now. They're sending me home for a bit of R and R. I'll probably be back almost as soon as you get this letter. I hope this time we'll manage to get married!

With all my love as always,

Henry

PS I came across your brother Paul a while back. He was pretty badly injured. I've been trying to find out if he's OK, but all I can gather is that he's been sent back to England.

341

Even though she had obviously been extremely glad to know that Henry was indeed safe, for some reason that letter had irritated Jen. It had been so casual. So bright and breezy. From what Paul had told her yesterday, when she had finally been allowed to visit him, it sounded extremely unlikely that Henry's ordeal has been anywhere near as easy as he made out.

'Blimey,' Paul had said. 'God knows how they survived. There was three feet of snow on the ground the day I was injured, and those Jerries weren't pussyfooting around.'

In any case, Jen had been way beyond mere 'worried'. Henry might have known he was all right, but she hadn't. What was more, she had been lumbered with his blasted baby. Now she was going to have to break the news to him, and God only knew what he was going to say about it.

Hearing the front door of the building opening and shutting below her, Jen stood up. Then sat down again. Then stood up again. For a second she thought she was going to have to rush to the bathroom. It would serve him right if he caught her throwing up just at the moment he arrived home.

But then his key was in the door and there he was, as gorgeous as ever, standing in the lobby, looking at her with a smile dawning on his handsome face.

'Oh my darling,' he said, dropping his kitbag on the floor and stepping forward, holding out both his hands. 'I am honoured. I was all set to come over and prise you out of RADA.'

Then his hands were on her, and he was drawing her slowly towards him, looking at her. And the smile was fading. 'Jen? What's happened?'

Over the last twenty-four hours, Jen had planned a million ways of tactfully breaking the news, but now, suddenly, she couldn't remember any of them. All she could think about was the exciting things she had hoped to do when they were married and the war was over. The glamorous parties, the outings, the holidays, the big fancy theatrical productions with her in the main role, and lots of long lovely nights of uninhibited lovemaking. And now they wouldn't be able to do any of it.

Henry was frowning. 'Sweetheart, what's the matter?'

She couldn't look at him. Instead she bit her lip and dropped her gaze to her feet.

'I'm pregnant,' she said.

She heard his sudden indrawn breath and felt a faint tremor of shock pass through his hands.

'I'm so sorry,' she mumbled.

There was a pause, during which she didn't dare look up at him. She couldn't bear to see the disappointment in his eyes.

But when he spoke, he didn't sound disappointed. He sounded absolutely shattered. Slowly he drew her across to the sofa and lowered her on to it, releasing her hands.

'Jen,' he said. 'Look at me.' When she obediently turned her face up to him, he took a long breath. 'Tell me why you are so sorry.' For someone who normally spoke with such laid-back ease, his voice was unusually tight.

Jen grimaced. 'Because I imagine the last thing you want is to be saddled with a baby,' she said bitterly. 'Especially when it must have been that one time at Mrs d'Arcy Billière's house, when you came home last time. It seems so unfair.'

She expected him to nod or to agree, but instead he gave a kind of choked groan and sat down beside her, putting his face in his hands.

'Oh my God,' he said through his fingers. A second later, he looked up, saw her startled expression, gave a slight gasp of laughter and leaned over to kiss her on the lips. 'I'd forgotten about that,' he murmured against her mouth. 'For a horrible moment there I thought you were going to tell me it was someone else's.'

Jen pulled back at once. 'Of course it's not,' she said hotly. 'Who else's could it possibly be?'

'Nobody's, I hope,' he said sternly. But he was smiling. 'It was just your expression; you looked guilty, so remorseful.'

343

'I'm not guilty,' Jen said crossly. 'But I am remorseful. I didn't want to be pregnant. I hate the thought of being fat and ugly. Let alone giving birth. And I was sure you wouldn't want . . .' Catching the gleam of denial in his eye, she stopped abruptly. 'Oh my God. Are you really saying you don't mind?'

He tried to draw her back into his arms. 'My darling, of course I don't mind. Selfishly, I'm delighted. I can't think of anything nicer. I know it's a bit sooner than we might have planned, but . . .'

Jen started at him incredulously. *A bit sooner than we might have planned*? She had never planned to have a baby at all. Such a thing had never crossed her mind.

Already Henry was sobering. He took her hands and raised them to his lips. 'But you really do mind, don't you?' he said. 'And I'm sorry about that. Now *I* feel guilty. And remorseful. Because it was entirely my fault. I should have taken precautions. But you are just so unutterably desirable . . .'

He groaned, and then suddenly she was in his arms and he was kissing more than her hands; he was kissing her hair, her face, her neck, her mouth. And Jen was responding. And suddenly the baby was forgotten.

Later, as she lay decadently in his arms in bed at three o'clock in the afternoon, he brought the subject up again. 'Jen, listen.' He raised his head up on one hand so he could look at her. 'I do understand. And if you really don't want a baby just now, I'm sure there are ways to . . . to deal with it. That's not what I want, but it's your body, and if you—'

'But there aren't any ways to deal with it,' Jen wailed. 'At least there are, but not very nice ones. I've already looked into it. What's more, it's illegal and terribly expensive.' She made a face. Suddenly, wrapped in Henry's arms, things didn't seem quite as bad as they had before. 'I even thought of asking Lord Freddy to pay.'

'Freddy?' Henry sat up abruptly. 'Good lord, what on earth has he got to do with it? Don't tell me he's been sniffing around while I've been away. I'll have to have a few words with him.'

Jen giggled. 'He's been terribly kind,' she said. 'He said he'd marry me if necessary.' She looked up at him demurely. 'And of course he is awfully rich.'

Henry laughed. 'I'll definitely be having words with him.'

Jen shook her head and pulled him back down beside her. 'No,' she said. 'I don't think that's necessary. But we must ask him to our wedding. And Louise Rutherford too. I'm determined to make her marry him.'

But when they bumped into Louise in the pub a few days later, after they'd been to see Paul in hospital, she seemed reluctant to even meet Lord Freddy, let alone marry him. 'I don't want to be rude about your friends,' she said to Henry. 'But he simply isn't my type.'

'You mean he's not good looking,' Jen said. 'But what does that matter?'

'Exactly,' Katy agreed, leaning over the counter. 'Looks don't matter. It's niceness that's important.'

Louise rolled her eyes. 'Well, that's all right for you two to say,' she said. 'You've got Ward and Henry.' She giggled and gave Henry a coy look under her lashes. 'By any standards, two of the best-looking men around.'

Not so long ago, Louise had made a play for Henry, and at that time Jen would have taken extreme exception to such blatant flirting, but now she just thought it was funny.

'Well, that's as may be,' she said smugly. 'All I'm saying is that looks aren't everything.' She nodded across the bar to where Angie was using the excuse of a bit of swing music on Katy's wireless to get Gino into a rather intimate clinch. 'Look at my sister. You could hardly say Gino was good looking. And it hasn't stopped her.'

Louise laughed. 'Well, no,' she said. 'Clearly not.'

'And Freddy is tremendously rich,' Henry put in helpfully.

Jen glared at him. She didn't want Louise to marry Lord Freddy for his money. She wanted her to fall in love with him. 'The important thing is that he's incredibly nice,' she said. 'Can you believe it,

he offered to marry me himself when I told him I was . . . Oops.'
She stopped abruptly, realising her mistake. Out of respect for her
prudish mother's wishes, she and Henry had agreed to wait until
they were well and truly married before letting anyone know about
the baby. Katy knew, of course, but Jen had deliberately kept the
news from Louise.

Always on the alert for gossip, Louise at once pricked up her ears.
'You're not!' she said. 'Ooh, you naughty things.'

She was a fine one to talk, Jen thought, exchanging a wry glance
with Katy. Louise had had several steamy affairs in the past.

'You're not to tell anyone,' Jen said. 'Especially not your mother.
And even more especially not your ghastly brother. He treats me
and Molly like dirt already. I don't want to make it any worse.'

Louise waved her hand reassuringly. 'My lips are sealed. I couldn't
tell Dougie anyway, because apparently he's away on an ultra-top-
secret, highly dangerous mission. It sounds unlikely to me, but
Mummy and Daddy are frightfully impressed.'

They all laughed. Douglas Rutherford had a reputation for enlarg-
ing on the truth, or even reinventing it altogether. In his father's eyes,
he could do no wrong. Anything Louise did was always second best.

'Your father would be even more impressed if you married Lord
Freddy,' Katy murmured. 'Douglas would have to assassinate Hitler
single-handed to come anywhere close to matching that.'

Louise found that hilarious. But she at least agreed to try and get
time off to come to the wedding, which had been arranged for
eleven o'clock that Thursday, 1 March, just two days away.

'I'm not waiting around this time,' Jen had said when the registrar
suggested it might be more convenient to go for a later date. 'I don't
care if nobody can come at such short notice. I just want to get
married as soon as possible, before something else gets in the way.'

Molly had been distraught when Jen had told her the wedding date.
'Oh no,' she had wailed. 'That's exactly when I'm meant to be
meeting my mother.'

Jen was disappointed. 'Surely you can meet her another time?'

But because of Prissy Wright's refusal to communicate, it was impossible to rearrange. Molly's only other option was to stand her mother up. It would serve her right for being so unnecessarily stand-offish. But if she did that, she might never get another chance to meet her, and she didn't want to spend the rest of her life regretting the missed opportunity.

Molly hadn't yet told George about her mother's surprising reincarnation, but as the meeting approached, she felt obliged to take him into her confidence. Inevitably he was agog.

'Cor,' he said, his eyes round with excitement. 'I knew she was going to be alive. Bella did too. I'm sure she'll be nicer than you think. Perhaps she'll be really rich and give you a million pounds.' But then suddenly his face fell. 'You're not going to go and live with her, are you? I don't want you to do that. Who would organise my lessons with the professor, and help me train Bunny and practise magic tricks with me if you weren't here?'

Molly was touched. 'No,' she said firmly. 'I'm not going to live with her. And even if she did offer me a million pounds, which she won't, I wouldn't take it. Not after how she's treated me. No, I'm going to meet her this one time, that's all. Just to see if she really is as ghastly as she sounds.'

But having felt quite blasé about the upcoming encounter earlier in the week, when Molly presented herself at the Lyons Corner House in Oxford Street and enquired if a Mrs Wright had already arrived, she was feeling extremely nervous. This was something she had never expected to happen, and although she told herself she didn't have high hopes for the encounter, she was terrified of making a mess of it.

As the nippy waitress led her across to a table where a dainty, refined-looking woman was already sitting alone, she felt her heart sinking. The woman was staring at her as she approached in the wake of the waitress, and the expression on her face was distinctly unfriendly.

'Here we are,' the nippy said brightly. 'This is the young lady you are waiting for.' She looked at the woman expectantly, but, receiving no thanks for her pains, let alone a tip, she shrugged and withdrew, leaving Molly facing her mother for the first time in twenty years.

As she stood there awkwardly, looking down at the woman, who hadn't made any effort to stand up to greet her, Molly didn't know what to do. All her life she had had the importance of good manners and decorum drummed into her, but as far as she knew, there was no established etiquette for meeting your long-lost mother. Should she offer her hand? Or just nod a polite how-do-you-do? In more promising circumstances a hug might have been appropriate, but that seemed absolutely out of the question.

In the end, in the absence of any clue as to what her mother expected her to do, she just smiled rather grimly, said, 'Hello, I'm Molly,' and sat down uninvited in the chair on the other side of the table.

Her mother's eyes narrowed sharply. It was almost as though Molly's slight south London accent told her everything she needed to know. She then proceeded to glance covertly around the restaurant, presumably to check that there was nobody there who might recognise her.

Molly gritted her teeth. But before either of them could speak, the nippy was back, wanting to take their order.

With her constant need to save money, it was a rare treat for Molly to visit a Corner House, and assuming that her mother would be paying, she had been looking forward to one of their reputedly delicious cakes. For some reason she didn't fancy one now, so she settled for a cup of tea.

While her mother ordered, also a cup of tea, Molly studied her covertly. She was undoubtedly a good-looking woman. Mr Wright of the Harris tweed suit had made a good choice. Pretty little Prissy Cavanagh had aged well: her hair colour seemed natural, her nails were neatly manicured and her teeth, under her perfectly applied lipstick, were white and even, unlike Molly's, one of which had got chipped when she had fallen off a rope ladder into a lifeboat after the ship carrying her to Tunisia had been torpedoed.

In the face of her mother's elegance, Molly was glad she had worn her best suit. She had even got Pam to trim her hair for the occasion. But though she had done her best to look as nice as possible, she felt clumsy and unattractive in comparison with Prissy Wright's delicate, well-bred appearance.

Suddenly she wished she hadn't come. Looking across the table, she caught her mother's cold gaze and felt her temper spark. 'I've missed the wedding of one of my best friends to come here today,' she muttered. 'The least you could do is say something.'

Priscilla Wright raised her neatly plucked eyebrows. 'What do you want me to say? If I recall correctly, it was you who wanted to meet me. Not the other way round.'

Now Molly wanted to hit her. It was too much. For her entire life she had laboured under the impression that her mother had died a tragic early death. And here the blasted woman was, dressed to the nines, sitting on the other side of the table, as cool as cucumber, as though nothing untoward had happened.

Molly took a slow breath. 'I want you to tell me why you felt it necessary to dump me in an orphanage and never make any effort to contact me again.'

Priscilla Wright flinched, and Molly realised that she wasn't cool at all. For all her show of indifference, her mother was wound up tight as a spring. Her voice was suddenly strained. 'You don't under-stand.'

Molly raised her own, unplucked, eyebrows. 'Don't I?' Clenching her fingers together under the table, she tried to speak reasonably. 'Then why don't you tell me your side of the story?'

'All right,' Priscilla Wright said. 'I will.'

But before she could start, the nippy came back with the tea. Having laid the cups and saucers, teapot and milk jug neatly out on the white tablecloth, she asked if they wanted her to pour. Priscilla waved her away and did it herself, and Molly couldn't help noticing that she did it the way the King and Queen – according to a magazine one of the nurses had left at the Red Cross post – took their tea, with the milk in second.

'This is not an easy story for me to tell,' Priscilla said, using the tiny silver tongs to pick up a lump of sugar. 'You need first to understand that my parents were strict churchgoers. They were well-to-do and had quite a position in the local community. I was their only child and they wanted me to be the perfect daughter.'

Trying not to think what an entirely different childhood she herself had had, Molly glanced longingly at the sugar bowl. She liked sugar in her tea too, but she had a nasty feeling that if she attempted to use the tongs, the sugar lump would ping off across the restaurant, and now that her mother had finally started talking, she didn't want to put her off with some untoward gaucherie.

'I was sent to a very strait-laced, old-fashioned school near where we lived in Epsom,' Mrs Wright went on. 'And I did well. I enjoyed it and was often top of the class. But I was very sheltered. Although some of the girls at the school had brothers, we were all very innocent, and none of us had boyfriends or anything like that.'

She paused and took a dainty sip of tea. As she swallowed it, Molly saw an expression of pain flit across her face. 'Then one day my parents' gardener brought his son to work with him to help with some heavy digging. Terry, he was called.' She gave a low, humourless laugh. 'It was ridiculous, of course. I had no idea about anything. Nor had he. He was even younger than me, sixteen, and common as muck. I don't think he had ever properly been to school, and his family hadn't two beans to rub together. I suppose to him I was a beautiful, rich goddess, and I was bowled over by the sight of him digging my father's compost heap without his shirt on. I'd never seen anything like it.' She made a dismissive gesture with her hand. 'Of course, looking back on it, he was nothing special. Just a typical local lad.'

She glanced across the table. 'I suppose that's where you got your snub nose and dark hair. Anyway, you can imagine what happened.

I'm not going to give you the gory details. It only happened once and it was a dreadful mistake in every way, one I have regretted all my life. Of course I had no idea then what the outcome might be.'

She stopped again and picked up her teacup. But then, without drinking from it, she put it down again. 'A couple of months later, it became obvious that I was pregnant. And that was the end of everything. Certainly the end of life as I had known it. My parents basically threw me out. My father drove me to London and left me on the pavement outside a mother-and-baby hostel, telling me he never wanted to see me again.'

Molly didn't want to feel sorry for her, but she couldn't help it. 'And did you see them again?' she asked.

Priscilla shook her head. 'No, I never did. I did go back once, but my mother refused to let me in.' She shrugged. 'Shortly after that, they died in a car accident. I discovered then that they had written me out of their will.'

Molly stared at her. She sounded completely unconcerned. Unemotional. Not bitter. Not angry. Not even sad or regretful. Nothing. Either she really didn't care, or she had taught herself to hide her feelings.

'What about Terry?' she asked. 'What happened to him?'

Priscilla looked surprised at the question. 'Goodness, I don't know. My father sacked his father, of course, but I don't suppose he told him why. I have no idea what became of any of them after that.'

Molly took a careful breath. 'So what happened when you got to London?' she prompted. This was the bit she really wanted to know about. Her own birth and early life.

But Priscilla seemed keen to gloss over that. 'I can't tell you how horrible that place was. They were meant to be helping us, looking after us, but they made us work like skivvies, scrubbing the floors and doing the laundry until our hands bled. I think it was a kind of punishment for what we had done, getting ourselves pregnant out of wedlock. You can imagine what it was like for a girl like me, who had been brought up with housemaids and gardeners. Anyway,

I was one of the lucky ones. I found a job in a local department store, and then I met a man who wanted to marry me.'

'Mr Wright,' Molly said.

She nodded. 'He was one of my customers. He was quite a bit older than me, but he was clearly affluent. And it was a dream come true. Except for one thing.'

She paused and Molly looked at her. She knew what was coming so she decided to say it first. 'He didn't want me.'

But to her surprise, Priscilla shook her head. 'No. I never told him about you. I haven't to this day. I just couldn't. I didn't want to spoil the one chance I had. You have to understand how desperate I was. I had to get away from that place.'

'So you sacrificed me,' Molly said. 'You gave me a different name and dumped me in a children's home. Then, having abandoned me to my fate, and secure in the knowledge that I'd never try to look for you because I thought you were dead, you casually waltzed off to marry Mr Wright.' She knew it was blunt, but that was how she felt. She had been cast out so that pretty little Prissy Cavanagh could regain the comfortable, privileged lifestyle she'd been brought up to expect as her due.

Priscilla looked annoyed. 'If you must know, Coogan was your father's surname. That's why I gave it to you.' Now she did drink her tea, and put the cup back on the saucer with a distinct clink.

'I knew this was how you would react,' she said. 'That's exactly why I didn't want to meet you. But now that I have, I want you to know that I didn't *abandon* you to your fate. I honestly thought you'd be happier living with other children. And when you were finally adopted, I found out from one of the staff at the children's home where you were living and I saved up my housekeeping and sent money to your new parents for your education. I never had any other children. Mr Wright didn't want any. Nor did I. So I felt you might as well benefit from money I might otherwise have spent on them.'

'What?' Molly could hardly believe her ears. Her adoptive parents had known her mother was alive all along? It seemed inconceivable. But not as inconceivable somehow as Priscilla Wright paying for her schooling. 'I don't believe you,' she said.

'You can believe what you like,' her mother said irritably. She glanced at an elegant watch on her wrist and lifted her hand to summon the nippy. 'But if it hadn't been for me, you'd have left school at fifteen.'

It was true. Molly had stayed at school much longer than normal for someone of her class, long enough at least to enable her to enrol as a nurse when her adoptive family was killed during the Blitz.

'When I heard that everyone in that block of flats had been killed by a bomb, I naturally assumed you had died too,' Priscilla went on implacably. 'That was partly why I was so shocked when your friend came to see me.'

But she hadn't been as shocked as Molly was now. Molly had been all set to hate her mother, and now she found she had cause to be grateful to her. If it hadn't been for those last two years at school, she would not now be thinking of going to medical school. For a fleeting second she considered asking for more financial help. She was certainly going to need it. But then she dismissed the idea. She was damned if she was going to ask this cold-hearted woman for anything. But she did let her pay for the tea.

Priscilla was already standing up and putting on her jacket. The meeting was over, and so far she hadn't asked Molly one single question.

Perhaps realising the omission, she paused as she put her handbag on her arm. 'So what are you doing with your life now?' she asked. She glanced at the third finger of Molly's left hand. 'I can see you aren't married yet. So how do you support yourself?'

With enormous difficulty, Molly wanted to shout at her. She wanted to tell her just how difficult it had been. She wanted to tell her how she had scrimped and saved for years just to keep her head above water. But even more than that, she wanted to shock her. For a second she even considered telling her about her experiences in

Italy, about the torpedo attack in the Mediterranean, about the hideous prison camp, about SS Hauptsturmführer Wessel and her escape from the train. More than anything, she wanted to wipe that bored little smile off her mother's face.

But in the end, she didn't even try. There was no point. She was never going to get what she wanted from this woman. Someone had once said to her that you could choose your friends but you couldn't choose your family. Suddenly that seemed all too true.

'At the moment, I'm nursing for the Red Cross,' she said. 'But in the autumn I'm hoping to go to medical school to train to be a doctor. It's going to be expensive, but don't worry. I'm not going to be knocking at your door. Or at least not unless you or Mr Wright are taken ill one day and I happen to be on duty.'

She shrugged on her coat. 'So I'll say goodbye. Thank you for agreeing to meet me. I hope it wasn't too difficult for you to spare the time. I would hate to cause you any inconvenience after all you have done for me.' And gratified by the flash of irritation in her mother's pretty eyes, with a final dismissive smile and an over-polite thank-you for the tea, she turned on her heel and walked out of the restaurant.

Chapter Twenty-One

Molly wasn't the only person unable to make Jen and Henry's wedding ceremony. Ward and Helen missed it too, as they had both been summoned to the new Special Allied Airborne Reconnaissance Force HQ at Sunningdale golf course in Wentworth, Surrey for a preliminary briefing by Brigadier Nichols, the British officer who had been appointed commander of the recently formed organisation.

SAARF's aim was to set up and train what the Brigadier called 'contact teams', each composed of three people – two officers and a radio operator – who would be dropped into Germany ahead of advancing Allied troops to attempt to make contact with the commanders of POW camps to try to prevent any last-minute Nazi atrocities being wrought on Allied prisoners.

Most of the hundred and fifty or so volunteers had been drawn from the various airborne and parachute divisions of the British, American, Free French, Polish and Belgian armies, while the rest were former SOE, OSS and SAS operatives. Several were girls Helen knew from the SOE. But, conscious that she needed to be discreet, she refrained from telling them she had seen their names on the wall of Sturmbannführer Hans Kieffer's office all those months ago at the SD HQ in Paris. Nor did she tell them about Hitler's Commando Order authorising German units to kill foreign agents on sight.

Nevertheless it seemed that the security chiefs were taking this last threat seriously. Brigadier Nichols made a point of saying that the contact teams would be issued with leaflets written in German containing a strong warning that any executions of SAARF personnel by Nazi forces would be considered a war crime and dealt with harshly when hostilities came to an end.

Catching Ward's eye as this was announced, Helen grimaced. It wasn't a hundred per cent reassuring, but it was at least a step in the right direction.

Those volunteers who were not already airborne qualified were sent to the RAF Parachute Training School at Ringway in Cheshire. The rest were told to report again on 15 March to start training.

Mercifully, because Helen had jumped successfully once before, she was excused the training, and as she and Ward set off back to the station, in the hope of getting back to London in time for Jen and Henry's wedding lunch, she was aware of a surge of excitement. Even if did mean a parachute jump, at least she would soon be going to Germany. It might be dangerous, but she didn't care. She was prepared to do anything to try to rescue André from whatever hideous fate might even now be awaiting him.

Despite the short notice, a surprising number of people had managed to make it to Chelsea Town Hall in time to see Jen and Henry take their vows.

Even though it was considered unlucky for the bride and groom to see each other on the happy day prior to the ceremony, Jen had adamantly refused to spend the night apart. Now that Henry was back, she was determined to keep him at her side until the knot was tied.

When that had been done, in a brisk little service that thankfully took no longer than fifteen minutes, she had to pose for photographs on the steps of the town hall in the lovely white dress Henry had borrowed for her from the costume department at Drury Lane. It was all very fancy and nice, but Jen would actually have much preferred to disappear straight off to the hotel Henry had booked in Oxford, because she was dreading the buffet lunch he had organised at the fashionable, exclusive Draycott Hotel.

The reason for that was that she was once again feeling terribly sick. Whether it was nerves, excitement or morning sickness, the effect was the same. The only thing she had been able to face in the way of food for the last two days was Marmite sandwiches, and they certainly weren't on offer at the Draycott. All she really wanted to do was lie down. She certainly wasn't in a fit state to exchange pleasantries with people like Ivor Novello and Laurence Olivier, let alone the ghastly forces sweetheart, Janette Pymm, who had been after Henry for years.

Adding to Jen's discomfort was her fear that the Lavender Road contingent would be completely outfaced by Henry's sophisticated friends. Prior to the party she'd had a vision of them huddling awkwardly together at one side of the room, but oddly that didn't seem to have happened.

Even as Jen struggled to maintain a conversation with one of the directors of ENSA, behind her she could hear Angie making John Gielgud guffaw with laughter at some story she was telling him about Gino's newly purchased ice-cream-making equipment.

'Mum's furious because the refrigerator takes up far too much room in the café kitchen,' she was saying. 'And then there's the churner. You have to wind the handle round and round for bloody ever. When I took a turn the other night, I thought my arms were going to fall off.'

Over by the door, Joyce and Mr Lorenz were chatting away merrily with Vivien Leigh. Malcolm and Lord Freddy were inspecting the pudding section of the buffet together, while Louise, looking unusually demure in a neat little navy-blue suit, watched them warily from the other side of the room, ready to move away if poor old Freddy headed in her direction.

Suddenly Jen noticed Molly standing in the doorway talking to Katy, then Helen and Ward were there as well, and, instead of coming over to rescue her, the four of them were now engrossed in conversation.

Feeling a hand on her waist, Jen swung round and to her relief

357

found Henry at her side. With a murmur of apology to the ENSA director, he drew her over to the window.

'Are you all right?' he asked. 'You're looking very pale.'

Jen could tell he was enjoying the party. She had watched him moving round the room looking unbelievably handsome and gorgeous in his smart service dress uniform, chatting and laughing, charming everyone with his easy smile, accepting their congratulations. I love him, she thought. I completely love him. But she wasn't going to tell him that. Not here, at least.

'No, I'm not all right,' she said, with a wry laugh. 'Not only do I feel sick, I feel a complete fraud wearing this dress.'

Henry drew her to him. 'You may feel a fraud,' he murmured against her hair, 'but you look absolutely beautiful in that dress. In fact I don't think I've ever seen you looking more ravishing.'

'I won't look quite as ravishing if I'm sick all over it,' Jen muttered.

He laughed and kissed her neck. 'Oh my poor darling,' he said. 'I'm sorry it's such an ordeal, but it has to be done. I don't want anyone to think it was shotgun wedding.'

And deep down, Jen knew he was right. The London theatre world might not be as prudish as the Clapham WI, but it was even more prone to gossip. It had probably already raised eyebrows in certain quarters that Henry had married someone so far beneath him both socially and theatrically. It would make it doubly difficult for her to be accepted among his friends and colleagues if they thought she had forced him into it.

Henry took her hand and kissed it. 'We're married,' he said. 'At last. All the time I was stuck in that damned forest in Belgium, I was living for this moment. It's probably what kept me alive.' He looked at her over her fingers and gave a faint rueful smile. 'Nevertheless, I promise you I'll get you away just as soon as possible.'

He was as good as his word. And as they left, Jen suddenly remembered her matchmaking intentions and contrived to throw her bouquet into Louise's arms. As she did so, she noticed Henry murmuring something to an unusually despondent-looking Lord Freddy.

'What did you say to him?' she asked as the taxi pulled away.

Henry laughed. 'I told him Louise had always fancied going to the Embassy Club, and suggested he invited her and Ward and Katy and maybe one or two others to go there tonight as an extra celebration.'

Jen stared at him. 'But Louise has been avoiding him all afternoon.'

'I know,' he said. 'That's why I thought we needed Ward and Katy to go too. She can hardly refuse if they're going to be there as well.'

'But Katy will never do that. What about the pub and the children?'

'Elsa and Aaref are in charge of the pub today, and Molly and Helen are helping out tonight. We all agreed it would do Ward and Katy good to have a night out. That blasted pub is going to drain the life out of them if they aren't careful.'

He sat back in his seat and drew her into his arms with a sigh of satisfaction. 'So I reckon between us we've done the best we can to further our friends' happiness. And now, my darling new wife, my aim is to further yours. You've had a horrible couple of months, and for the next few days we are going to do *exactly* what you want, even if that involves you lying in bed and me serving you Marmite sandwiches.'

Molly had indeed agreed to babysit. She certainly wasn't in the mood to go dancing, and she too felt Katy needed a night off.

Since the beginning of the war, Katy had been the lynchpin of Lavender Road. Through thick and thin, in all their various comings and goings, their highs and lows, Katy had always been there, offering cups of tea, reviving brandies, and a bed if needed. As well as providing unstinting support to her friends, she had done a brilliant job building up the pub to the thriving enterprise it was today. When Ward had been away, carrying out his secret derring-do activities with the SOE, or as a prisoner of the Germans, Katy had needed the income, and had been glad of the hard work to keep her mind off her fears for his safety. But a cramped, smoky and often rowdy pub was no place to bring up children, and it was becoming clear that they were soon going to need somewhere better to live.

'I really don't know why Katy is worrying so much,' Helen said now. 'Ward's war record and his family background will make him highly employable.'

'Ah yes,' Molly said drily. 'The all-important family background.' Picking up a cloth, she began to polish a glass. She knew her own family background now. And already she was half wishing she didn't. Maybe it would have been better to let sleeping dogs lie after all. It would certainly have been easier not to have known that she stemmed from such ruthless and cold-hearted people.

Now that she had had time to think about it, there was a cruel irony there too. Or perhaps it was just that history had a tendency to repeat itself. Like her father, she too had fallen head over heels in love with someone well out of her league on the social scale. She couldn't quite imagine that Callum's parents would have deliberately caused her to lose her job if the worst had happened, but they certainly wouldn't have welcomed her into their privileged little fold, any more than Mr and Mrs Cavanagh had welcomed the unfortunate Terry into theirs.

Suddenly Molly's hand froze on the glass she was holding. She had been so fixated on finding her mother that she had barely spared a thought for her father. But now, not only did she know who he was, she actually knew his name. Terry Coogan.

Even as a shiver of excitement coursed through her, she quailed. Oh no, she thought. Do I really want to go through all this again? Terry Coogan had probably forgotten all about that one hot-blooded moment in the Cavanaghs' garden in Epsom. By now he would surely be happily married with numerous other snub-nosed, dark-haired children.

'Molly?' Helen was looking at her with concern. 'What's the matter? You look as though someone's walking across your grave.'

Molly put the glass down on the counter. Then she turned her head to look at her friend. 'I want to try and find my father,' she said.

She had already given Helen the low-down on her meeting with her mother. Now, as she saw Helen's eyes widen in protest, she rushed on quickly. 'No, listen. I don't want to meet him. I just want to find out what he's like. Even if he is common as muck, he might still be nice. I just want to know. I might even have half-brothers and sisters by now.'

'But Molly—' Helen began.

'He can't be more than forty,' Molly said. 'Which means he's probably in the forces. Surely it wouldn't be too hard to find out?' She didn't wait for Helen to reply. 'Then once I find out, I promise I'll stop. That will be the end of it. After that, I'll try and forget all about it.'

And about Callum too, she added to herself. She'd had enough of pain and heartache. She would make this one final attempt and then she'd put her hopes and dreams aside and get on with her studies. Ward wasn't the only one who needed a new career. Medical school was going to be her salvation, and that hinged on her getting top grades.

But putting her romantic hopes and dreams to one side proved difficult, because two days later she received a letter from Callum.

As promised, here is my letter to say I'm safe. I can't tell you exactly where I am, but if I tell you I'm currently stationed not a million miles away from a pretty large river, maybe you can figure it out. Judging from the build-up going on around here, the end of dear old Adolf and his nasty little friends can't be too far away. It seems strange, doesn't it, that all this rumpus will soon be over. Sometimes I think it's all a weird dream and we will all suddenly wake up and find that none of it ever happened. To be honest, some of it I'd be glad to let go, but there have been other bits that I don't want to forget. Like some of those sunny days in Tunisia. Or maybe that was a dream too.

In any case, it was good to see you when I was back last time,
even though it wasn't quite the same. It's not looking likely that I'll
be in London again any time soon, and once the war is over, I guess
I'll be heading back to Canada and civilian life. In the meantime,
let's hope that we all get through this last stage safely.
  All good wishes to you and everyone in Lavender Road.
  Callum

She knew what he meant. That interlude in Tunisia had been like
a dream for her too. But she could tell from the tone of his letter
that that was all it was ever going to be. It hadn't been the same in
London and, like her, he had clearly come to his senses. The letter
read almost like a goodbye, and she couldn't believe how much that
made her heart ache.

But it didn't stop her worrying about him.

When she bumped into Helen in Lavender Road later that evening,
she showed her the letter. 'It's not like him to sound nervous,' she
said. 'He's always been so gung-ho up to now.'

Helen frowned. 'However confident Monty and Patton are about
this final push they keep talking about, it's probably not going to
be quite as easy as they make out. Callum can probably tell that
from what he sees when he's flying over the Rhine. I suppose we
have to face the fact that, unless by some miracle Hitler surrenders,
people are going to go on dying until the bitter end.'

Molly had crossed her fingers and hoped that those people
wouldn't be anyone she knew. Because despite the Allies taking the
western sections of the Rhine-straddling cities of Cologne, Bonn
and Koblenz, there was no sign that the Germans were thinking of
surrendering. On the contrary, they had made a strategic withdrawal
back across the river, blown up all the bridges, and were busy
strengthening their defensive positions on the other side.

'You'll never guess who came into the café last night,' Angie said
to Joyce.

'I don't know,' Joyce said. In her opinion, anyone who went to one of Angie and Gino's pasta evenings needed their heads examined. They certainly needed to have a strong constitution. 'Adolf Hitler?'

Angie roared with laughter. 'No,' she said. 'Mrs d'Arcy Billière and Helen's father, Lord de Burrel.'

'And are they still alive?' Joyce asked.

'Of course they are,' Angie said indignantly. 'They loved it. Gino did spaghetti bollynaysie, which Mrs d'Arcy Billière said was just as good as she'd once had in Venice or Vienna or some such place. And Lord de Burrel adored our new jelly arto ice cream. He said he thought we might have a hit on our hands.' Catching the sceptical gleam in Joyce's eye, she lifted her chin. 'I took some to Paul in the hospital yesterday afternoon and all, and he loved it. And the two poorly American soldiers each side of him did too.'

'Did they indeed?' Joyce said. 'And what did Sister Morris say about that?'

Angie giggled. 'Well, to be honest she wasn't best pleased, especially when it melted and dripped all over their sheets. But I gave her a taste, and even she thought it was good. And Dr Goodacre nearly went berserk over it. He said he'd come in today for a bit more.'

And to Joyce's astonishment, he did. 'Oh yes,' he said, standing at the counter rubbing his hands together. 'It's absolutely delicious, and just the thing for convalescent patients. Smooth and cool on the throat, and very easy to digest.' He smiled happily at Joyce. 'Talking of which, your boy is getting up today for the first time. He's made a marvellous recovery. I told you he was a strong lad. He'll be ready for duty again in a week or two.'

Joyce nearly dropped the teapot she was holding. 'Ready for duty?' she repeated. 'But surely you can sign him off for longer than that?'

Dr Goodacre made a face. 'Normally I'd recommend at least two or three months' light duties after injuries such as those he sustained. But the problem is that he's determined to get back to the front line as soon as possible. He told me this morning that he'd kill himself if his unit crosses the Rhine without him.'

'And what did you say?' Joyce asked.

Dr Goodacre laughed delightedly. 'I said it wouldn't be the first time he'd killed himself, because that's pretty much what happened in Belgium.'

Joyce put the teapot down carefully on the counter. She was extremely fond of Dr Goodacre, but sometimes she wished he would take things more seriously. 'But surely you can explain that it's far too soon?'

'I can explain whatever I like,' Dr Goodacre said. 'But he won't take any notice. If we try to stop him, he'll only wait until we aren't looking and sneak off anyway. To be honest, I can't blame him. If I was a younger man, I'd want to be doing my bit too.'

Joyce looked at him incredulously. Men, she thought. Sometimes they seemed to come from a different planet.

Two days later, Paul was discharged from the Wilhelmina and sent home to rest and recuperate. Gino and Angie had spent the previous evening heaving the spare bed from Bella's room down the stairs to the front room, but there was very little sign of Paul resting. On the other hand, he was certainly recuperating. Mr Poole, the builder, had finally started work on Albert's old house on the other side of the road, and Paul spent most of his time over there helping to lug out the remaining rubble. When he wasn't doing that, he was either eating, or falling in love with Bella.

It was exactly what Joyce had been worried about. The blasted girl was too pretty for her own good. Now that she was talking again, it was even more difficult to keep her out of harm's way. Angie and Gino often took her to the pub with them, or to the pictures, and of course as soon as Paul reappeared in the house, they started taking him too.

Unlike Jen, who despite apparently thoroughly enjoying her honeymoon was still moaning about feeling sick, Angie was entirely unaffected by her pregnancy. On the contrary, she was brimming over with what Albert called *joie de vivre*, and seemed determined that everyone else should share her high spirits.

When Joyce told her off for leaving Bella and Paul alone in the house together one evening, Angie just laughed. 'Oh, but it's all completely innocent,' she said.

'It bloody better had be innocent,' Joyce said grimly to Albert later in the privacy of their bedroom. 'That girl is only sixteen and we don't need any more babies coming along just at the moment.'

The only advantage as far as she could see was that Paul's infatuation with Bella might make him think twice about returning to his unit sooner than he had to.

But she was wrong. Unfortunately Paul's bloodlust proved stronger than his puppy love. On 15 March, a small platoon of American troops, in a daring, high-risk manoeuvre, managed to capture the Ludendorff Bridge at Remagen. As it was one of the very few remaining intact bridges across the Rhine, it was a significant breakthrough, and as soon as Paul heard about it, he announced that he was going to rejoin his unit.

'I can't sit it out,' he said. 'I want to be there for the big push. I want to kill as many Germans as I can while we still have the chance.'

But there was one thing Paul wanted to do before he left, and that was to give Douglas Rutherford a black eye.

Ward and Helen had left the previous weekend for the SAARF training course, and Douglas, once again back in London for a few days, had taken advantage of their absence to start making a nuisance of himself in the pub with Bella.

'I know he's an officer and that,' Paul had muttered grimly to Molly one evening as Douglas, catching Bella's arm as she walked past his chair, pulled her down onto his lap. 'But if he's not careful, I'm going to deck him.'

'Oh, please don't,' Molly said nervously. She didn't like Louise's brother any more than Paul did, and in other circumstances she would have been delighted for him to get his just deserts, but unfortunately Douglas's father was Katy's boss, and the last thing Katy needed just now, with Ward once again about to risk his life overseas, was to lose the lease on the pub.

It would have been helpful if Louise had still been around. But after spending what, according to Katy, had been a surprisingly convivial evening with Lord Freddy at the nightclub after Jen's wedding, Louise had disappeared back to her unit, and was not on hand to control her oversexed brother.

To Molly's relief, Douglas's inappropriate ardour that evening had been thwarted by Lucky, who, woken from a comfortable sleep in front of the fire by Bella's squeal of dismay, leapt immediately to her defence with a ferocious bark, causing Douglas to throw her off his lap in terror. The incident had caused a lot of amusement in the bar, and for the next night or two Douglas had been more circumspect, merely murmuring teasing endearments to Bella when he squeezed past her, or offering to buy her drinks.

But on the night before Paul's departure, he made the mistake of pinching Bella's bottom, and that was enough for Paul. If there was one thing Paul had learned in the army, it was how to land a good punch.

Douglas went down on the floor of the pub like a sack of potatoes.

'Oh my God,' Katy whispered.

There was a moment's shocked silence, then everyone started laughing. One or two people even clapped.

'Good on yer, lad,' someone shouted from the bar as Molly put her hand on Bella's arm and quickly drew her out of the way. 'Nasty little toff deserved that.'

'That lad's got a handy bunch of fives,' someone else remarked.

Douglas was less impressed. As he staggered angrily to his feet, he pointed a shaky finger at Paul.

'I'm an officer, you know,' he snarled through a rapidly thickening lip. 'And I'll have you court-martialled for that.'

'Oh, come off it,' the first man shouted. 'Nobody would take any notice of a twit like you.'

Douglas swung round angrily. 'I'll have you know that I'm currently engaged in extremely dangerous top-secret work.' But unfortunately his words were blurred by a gush of blood from his nose.

'Yeah, yeah, yeah,' the man said. 'Pull the other one.'

Clearly sensing that things were getting out of control, Katy took a step forward. 'That's enough,' she said. 'I don't allow fighting in here. Paul, even though I understand why you did it, I'm afraid I'm going to have to ask you to leave. As for you, Douglas, it was entirely your fault. As an officer, you should know better than to harass an underage girl.'

'Quite right,' the wag at the bar shouted. 'Don't you go telling no tales to Daddy neither. We know who you are, and if you want to keep the rest of your teeth in your gob-hole, you'd better not make trouble.'

Bella, meanwhile, was looking very shocked. For a horrible second Molly wondered if she was going to stop talking again. 'It wasn't your fault,' she murmured. 'Listen to what they're saying. Douglas Rutherford is a stupid idiot, and it's best to keep well clear of people like that.'

'I know,' Bella said. 'And I'm grateful to Paul. I'd have liked to punch him myself, but I didn't know how to.'

Molly laughed. 'Perhaps we should get Professor Markov to teach us,' she said. 'It would probably be more useful in the long run than chemistry.'

George, when he heard about it the following day, was ecstatic. 'I wish I'd punched him,' he confided to Molly the following day as she helped him with some homework Professor Markov had set him. 'I'd like to punch his horrid father too.'

Molly couldn't help laughing. She didn't like Mr Rutherford either, but she had never actually been tempted to punch him.

'Why?' she asked. 'What's he ever done to you?'

She was expecting him to say that Mr Rutherford had caught him stealing eggs, or carrots for his rabbit, or that he had told him off for driving his go-cart too fast in the street. But George was looking uncomfortable, as though he was regretting making the comment at all. He fiddled with his protractor, then stabbed the point of his compass into the paper a few times, as though wishing it was Mr Rutherford's head. Watching him, Molly began to feel alarmed that his new-found antipathy towards his father's employer might stem from something more serious.

'George,' she said sternly 'Tell me, what have you done?'

'I haven't done anything,' he said, looking aggrieved. He hesitated for a moment, then spoke with a rush. 'It's just that I heard Mummy and Daddy talking in bed last night.'

Molly began to feel uncomfortable. 'It's naughty to eavesdrop,' she said.

'I wasn't eavesdropping,' he said. 'I just needed to go down to the lav, and when I went past their door, I heard them talking. And they were talking about me.'

'So you stopped to listen?'

He flushed slightly, and his gaze dropped to his geometric diagrams. 'Only for a minute.'

Molly looked at him uneasily.

'They were talking about me going back to school,' he said.

'Oh,' she said. Pam had told her just the other day that she had received a letter from the education authority saying that George's school would soon be returning to London. Molly knew how badly George didn't want to go back there. She didn't blame him. He had been bullied and the teachers had failed to do anything about it. Nor, unlike Professor Markov, had they managed to interest him in his classes.

'Mum was saying she wished they could afford to send me to a better school,' George went on in a low voice. 'She sounded cross with Dad because Mr Rutherford hadn't given him a pay rise for all the extra responsibilities he'd had to take on at the brewery while Mr Rutherford was away with the Home Guard.' He looked up. 'But that's not Dad's fault, is it? It's Mr Rutherford's fault, and . . .' His voice faltered. 'Anyway, I don't like it when they argue.'

Molly felt her heart twist. On the surface, George seemed lively and spirited, but underneath he was still an adopted child, with all the added insecurities that brought with it.

'It must be hard being a parent,' she said. 'Because you desperately want to do the best you can for your children, but sometimes the best is more than you can afford.'

George kicked the table leg a few times. He looked disgruntled. 'I know Professor Markov can't teach me for ever,' he said. 'But it's unfair that Mr Rutherford paid for Louise's stupid brother to go to an expensive boarding school, and he won't even pay Dad enough for me to go to Clapham College or Emanuel.'

'Life isn't fair,' Molly said. 'Especially for those of us who weren't born into wealthy families.' She shook her head. 'All we can do is work as hard as we can, and hope one day we'll get a lucky break.' She picked up the protractor and prodded him in the arm with it. 'Talking of lucky breaks, if you finish this homework in the next ten minutes, I'll treat you to one of Gino's ice creams at the café.'

Paul Carter wasn't the only soldier returning to the front. As it became obvious that a massive push across the Rhine was imminent, all military leave was cancelled, extra ships were laid on to take returning troops back across the Channel, and soldiers currently stationed in the UK were put on twenty-four hours' notice to move, presumably in case reinforcements became necessary.

So once again Jen found herself saying goodbye to Henry. She could hardly believe it. His leave had been far too brief, and the honeymoon far too gorgeous. Nevertheless, she tried to be brave.

'I'll miss you even more this time,' she said as she lay on the bed watching him pack his kitbag. 'Because now I really know what I'm missing.'

He laughed and leaned over to kiss her. 'Me too,' he said. 'But when this damned war is over, you and I are going to have a wonderful time.'

Sitting down on the bed, he laid a gentle hand on her stomach. 'And so is whoever is in there.'

He paused, and his smiling gaze wavered slightly. 'Oh, and sweetheart, I want you to know that I've written a will. That's what I was doing yesterday when you were shopping. I wanted to be sure that whatever happens, you and the baby will be OK. I've asked Freddy to be my executor, so he would deal with everything and make sure it all gets sorted out quickly.'

Catching Jen's instinctive recoil, he took her hands and kissed them, then tried to change the subject. 'Talking of Freddy, he seemed to think it had gone rather well with Louise the other night.'

But Jen didn't want to talk about Lord Freddy. Not did she want to talk about wills. Not at all. And after Henry had gone she wished he hadn't said anything about it. Because she knew that if he didn't come back, she would be very far from OK, however quickly Lord Freddy sorted things out.

Even though it was physically demanding, Helen was enjoying the SAARF training. Every day that first week they had done fitness runs, gym work, map-reading exercises and orienteering. It wasn't dissimilar to the SOE selection training she had done in the wilds of Scotland earlier in the war. It was tough and brutal, intended to sort the men from the boys, or, in the girls' case, the ones who could hack it without crying, or complaining they had broken their nails.

Helen certainly wasn't going to cry. She wanted to be fit. She wanted to be ready. She had a purpose, and that was to pass the programme and get to Germany as soon as possible. Everyone knew the Allied commanders were making final preparations for a Rhine crossing. And once that happened, surely the SAARF teams would spring into action.

Whatever their private reasons for volunteering for SAARF, most of the other girls seemed equally committed to the project. None of them were new to this business. They knew what had to be done, and were determined to prove they were just as keen and capable as the men.

So it was a nasty surprise when they were summoned for a girls-only meeting with Brigadier Nichols.

'I know you are going to be disappointed,' he said. 'I can assure you it's no reflection on your abilities. But a decision has been taken not to include females in the contact teams.'

The girls immediately started to protest, but he held up his hand and they quietened obediently. The tone of his voice was apologetic but firm. 'Despite the explanation leaflets the teams will be carrying, it is felt that the risk of retribution is very high, and that young women like yourselves would be particularly vulnerable.' He glanced round the room placatingly. 'As I say, I know you will be disappointed, but I'm sure you will understand.'

Oh yes, Helen thought. She understood all too well. The people who ran the security services had finally realised it wasn't a game. That all their missing agents and saboteurs were probably not sitting safely in POW camps waiting for the war to be over, but had most likely been tortured for information and then killed. So now, at this late stage, having already sent hundreds to their deaths, they had finally decided it was too dangerous for girls.

Nervously, she put up her hand and waited for Brigadier Nichols to give her permission to speak. 'But what if we are prepared to take that risk?' she asked. She glanced at the other girls and they all eagerly nodded assent.

But Brigadier Nichols was not the kind of man to be swayed by a bunch of women. 'I'm sorry,' he said stiffly. 'The decision has been made at a very high level.'

And of course that was that.

Some of the girls agreed to stay on to help behind the scenes. The rest, including Helen, left that afternoon.

So that was it, she thought angrily, as she walked up the hill from Clapham Junction station to Lavender Road. Another door had been slammed in her face.

But as so often in life, as one door closed, another opened. In this case, it was the door of her father's taxi, which had just pulled up on the opposite side of the road.

Her father was leaning out of the window. 'Helen?' he called, beckoning her across. 'What are you doing here? I thought you'd gone off on some training course.'

'I had,' she said, and getting into the cab, she told him what had happened.

Her father was dutifully sympathetic. 'My dear girl, what a pity,' he said. 'Although selfishly I must admit I'd rather you didn't put yourself in unnecessary danger.'

He leaned forward and tapped on the driver's window. 'Drop us at the pub, would you? Yes, the one just up here on the right.' He smiled easily at Helen. 'I am actually on my way to Mrs d'Arcy Billière's for a Russian lesson, but why don't we have a quick snifter first?'

But once they had got out of the taxi and he had paid off the cabby, instead of going into the pub, he put a hand on her arm.

'I could see that fellow's ears were flapping,' he said. 'And I didn't want him to hear what I'm going to say. Just between you and me, there's a plan afoot for Winnie to pop over to Europe in a day or two to watch old Monty crossing the Rhine. He's asked if I'd like to go with him. Shall I see if you can come too? It would only be for a couple of nights, but you've had a bit of a tough time of things recently, and it might do you good to have a little holiday.'

Part Five

Chapter Twenty-Two

It seemed a long wait, but on the morning of 21 March, Helen received a short note from her father confirming she was to be included on the proposed trip to Europe. *Could be any day now*, he wrote. *So stand by, and I'll let you know where and when to present yourself as soon as we get the green light.*

At once her life went into a whirl of activity.

'Blimey,' Katy said when she went down to the cellar and found Helen squeezing a packet of biscuits, three cans of sardines and two chocolate bars into a kitbag that was already bursting at the seams. 'I thought your father said you'd only be away a couple of days.'

Caught red handed, Helen sat back on her heels guiltily. 'He did.'

Due to security considerations, Helen's father had warned her not to tell anyone where they were going, or that the prime minister was going to be in the party. Winston Churchill's movements were always kept top secret. Nobody wanted some pre-primed German sniper to take a potshot at him over the Rhine. But as Lord de Burrel himself had told Katy that he was hoping to take Helen away for a couple of days on the continent, and as the newspapers were full of speculation about the forthcoming Rhine crossing, it hadn't been hard for her to guess the purpose of their visit.

Now, catching sight of the map of Germany spread out on Helen's camp bed, Katy's eyes widened. 'Oh my goodness,' she gasped. 'You're going to try to find André, aren't you?'

Helen nodded. 'Yes, I am. This is my best chance. If it's possible, I'm going to try to stay on and join the push into Germany.' She nodded at the sardine tins. 'These are just emergency rations in case I can't immediately find some suitable unit to get myself attached to.'

She saw Katy shudder and felt a chill flicker over her own skin. Suddenly she had a terrible premonition that she was going to be too late. She could see in Katy's eyes that she thought so too.

But the following morning Katy thrust some rations coupons into her hand. 'Use these to get what you need,' she said. 'Is there anything else I can do to help?'

Helen shook her head. She was grateful for the coupons, but there was nothing more anyone could do now. She would just have to keep her fingers crossed and hope Winston Churchill wouldn't have second thoughts about including her in his party.

In the meantime, two days ago, she had called on a girl she knew who worked in military records to ask if she could find any information about someone called Terry Coogan. Now she needed to go back to see if her request had borne fruit.

But it hadn't. 'No,' the girl said. 'There are plenty of Coogans – it's quite a common name – but I can't find any records of a forty-year-old Terry, Terrence or any other T, I'm afraid.'

Helen groaned to herself. Now she would have to ask someone at MI5 to check civilian records, which was more problematic because her contact there might know that she was no longer employed by SOE and therefore not authorised to ask for such information.

But even though she got over that hurdle quite easily, there was no luck there either. 'I can't find any trace of the fellow,' the man said. 'Whoever he is, he doesn't have a ration card, or a criminal record.'

Helen frowned. 'What does that mean?' she asked.

'It probably means he died some time ago. Some people do slip through the net, of course, change their names and so on, but even so, they generally pop up somewhere in the records. As it was you asking, I've checked back a good ten years, but there's not a squeak about this chap, nothing.' He saw her grimace of disappointment and shrugged. 'The only thing I can suggest is that since you know his father once worked in Epsom, you go down there and ask around. It's possible someone might remember the family.'

But much as she wanted to help Molly out, Helen simply didn't have time to go to Epsom. The call from her father could come at any moment, and she couldn't miss her one chance of getting over to Europe.

Molly didn't have time to go to Epsom either. Mrs d'Arcy Billière had come up with the idea that Molly and her fellow pupils should prepare an evening's entertainment for a few of her friends. The idea had found favour not only with Professor Markov and the new teacher, Susan Voles, but also with George.

'I could do some magic tricks,' he had said eagerly to Molly. 'Bunny's got really good at waiting in the top hat, and if you help me, we can do the trick where we turn him into a pack of cards.'

Professor Markov had been even more enthusiastic. 'Yes, yes,' he said. 'It is good for students to learn to perform in public. It builds confidence.'

After the bruising encounter with her mother, and having not yet heard back from any of the teaching hospitals she had applied to, Molly felt her own confidence was in need of a bit of building, but she didn't feel that trying to conceal a rabbit up her jumper in front of Mrs d'Arcy Billière's aristocratic friends was going to be the best way to do it. She certainly didn't relish the idea of all the extra work that putting on such a show would inevitably entail.

But unfortunately, nor did she feel she could refuse the request. If it hadn't been for Mrs d'Arcy Billière, she would never have met Professor Markov, never have felt able to apply for medical school. And if it hadn't been for Professor Markov, George would probably have run riot and been hauled up by the police instead of becoming interested not only in Zulu warriors, but also in his other studies.

The professor had even begun teaching him Latin. If only George's earlier education hadn't been so poor, he might have stood a chance of getting a scholarship to one of the local fee-paying schools, as Aaref's two younger brothers had.

'What about putting it on at the beginning of May?' Mrs d'Arcy Billière suggested, consulting the calendar on her desk. 'That would give you six weeks to get it ready.' She looked up and smiled encouragingly. 'And if by any luck the war is over by then, we'll call it a victory show.'

Weakly, Molly heard herself agreeing. But on the way home, she wished she'd held out for a later date. She couldn't imagine how she was going to marshal her motley troops into the kind of show Mrs d'Arcy Billière clearly expected in six weeks, or even at all. She had no experience of theatrical productions, and nor had Susan Voles. Typically, Graham Powell had already set his face against the whole idea, and although Professor Markov was full of wild ideas about staging a series of exciting experiments to demonstrate his students' skills and knowledge, he was hardly the most suitable person to organise it. Or at least not unless Mrs d'Arcy Billière was prepared to have her house burned down in the name of dramatic art.

No, Molly thought, as she pushed open the Nelsons' front door. The person they needed was Jen. She must know how to stage a decent show by now. Glancing at her watch, she wondered if she had time to go up to town to ask her. She had an hour and a half free before she was due back at the Red Cross. It wasn't enough time to go to Epsom, but with a bit of luck she might be able to get to Pont Street and back. She ought really to use the time to do the homework the professor had set her, but she hadn't seen Jen since Henry had left, and she wanted to know how she was getting on without him.

But even as she turned to leave the house again, George came hurtling down the stairs.

'Have you seen?' he said. 'Look. Some letters have come for you.

One is stamped University College Hospital. Do you think they're from the medical schools?'

All thoughts of visiting Jen flew straight out of Molly's mind. This was the moment she'd been waiting for. Who cared about some stupid theatrical production when her entire future might hinge on the contents of those letters?

If just one of them offered her the chance of a scholarship, then all her worries might be at an end.

Her fingers were shaking as she tore open the envelopes.

They were indeed from the various teaching hospitals she had applied to. St Mary's, St Thomas's, University College and the Royal Free.

But none of them mentioned a scholarship.

None of them even offered her a place.

St Mary's just turned her down flat. St Thomas's and University College had the courtesy to explain that they did not accept applications from women, and the Royal Free thanked her for her application but regretted that although they did accept female students, unfortunately their allocation for the forthcoming year had already been filled.

George was outraged. 'That's just stupid,' he said. 'Why won't the others accept women? Women are just as clever as men. You're just as clever as Graham.' Becoming aware of her silence, he glanced at her uneasily, then hastily looked away and kicked the hall table crossly. 'Surely you applied to more places than that?' he said after a moment.

But when three more letters arrived over the next few days, it was the same story.

Guy's Hospital, St George's and Westminster Medical School were all unable to further her application as they were not currently accepting women on their courses.

Molly had expected to be rejected if she failed to reach the academic standard required, but it had never occurred to her that she would be turned down flat due to her gender.

That evening, she finally got to see Jen, who had come down to the pub. Jen was extremely sympathetic about the rejections, but that didn't stop her refusing point blank to help with Mrs d'Arcy Billière's 'evening's entertainment'.

'Good God,' she said. 'I can't think of anything worse. I'm an actress, not a producer. Anyway, I'm not good with children.'

Molly hadn't the strength to argue. It was disappointing, but nowhere near as disappointing as being refused the chance of training to be a doctor.

'Oh Molly, I'm so sorry,' Helen said as they cleared up in the pub that night. 'I know how much you were pinning on it. And we all know you'd make a fantastic doctor.'

Molly had tried to smile bravely, but she felt her lip tremble and quickly turned her attention to some glasses that needed washing.

'What about Callum?' Helen asked after a moment. 'Have you heard from him again?'

Busy with the glasses, Molly shook her head. 'No,' she said. Callum hadn't written to her since that last letter, the one that had sounded so final. Now, with a pang of grief, she wondered if she would ever hear from him again. She would know what happened to him, of course, via Ward and Katy. She tried to tell herself that she would be happy to hear that he had come through the war safely and gone back to Canada. She'd even try very hard to be happy for him if, in due course, she heard he had got married.

'I'm sorry about that too,' Helen said quietly. Molly could feel her friend's eyes on her and doggedly stuck to her washing-up.

Helen picked up a cloth and began to dry the glasses. 'I had hoped that you and he might . . .' she began, then stopped abruptly as Elsa appeared at the door.

Molly looked up too. And saw that Elsa had a telegram in her hand.

It was for Helen. It was short and to the point. *Be at Northolt at 9.30 tomorrow morning. Daddy.*

Helen put her hand to her mouth. 'Oh my God,' she whispered. 'This is it.'

For a moment Molly forgot her own troubles. She knew where Helen was going, and what she intended to do. Turning round and catching the look of trepidation on her friend's pretty face, she gave her a brief, rather soapy, hug. 'I'm sure you'll be all right,' she whispered. 'I'm sure you'll find him. And I'm sure he'll be OK.'

But even though Molly tried to put conviction into the words, she wasn't sure at all. She wasn't sure of anything any more. For nearly six years she had longed for the war to be over, and now that it looked as though it was finally coming to an end, everything seemed to be going wrong.

Jen hadn't meant to be grumpy with Molly. But Molly wasn't the only one having a bad time at the moment. Jen had thought she'd feel better now that she was married. But actually she felt worse. Smart and convenient though Henry's apartment was, she was lonely, and even though Lord Freddy took her out a few times, once to supper in a frightfully posh restaurant, and twice to the cinema, she began wishing that she was still living in Lavender Road. She didn't like coming home to an empty flat. She found herself missing the easy camaraderie of Mrs d'Arcy Billière's unconventional household. She even missed the food. She was a hopeless cook, but even she was beginning to get bored of Marmite sandwiches. To make things worse, she still felt ropy most of the time. It wasn't so much that she felt sick, although she did, especially in the mornings, but she also felt weary and lacking in energy, and that was making things hard for her at RADA.

So far she had successfully concealed her unwanted pregnancy from her tutors and fellow students, but she was now finding it increasingly difficult to cope with the gruelling physical side of the course. Twice she had been told off for lacklustre performances, and that morning she had almost fainted in the middle of the improvisation class when she'd been pretending to pick up something from the floor.

'I'm sorry,' she'd muttered, holding her swimming head. 'I'm feeling a bit under the weather today. Do you mind if I sit down for a minute?'

Her drama teacher had waved her impatiently to a seat at the side. 'It's not just today, is it?' he had snapped. 'It seems to me you've been away with the fairies all week. If you don't pull your socks up, you'll be off this course. I've no time for slackers.'

But when he came to sit next to her a few minutes later, he was rather more conciliatory. 'I know your husband's gone back to the front,' he said. 'I know that will be hard for you when you're so recently married.' He looked at her speculatively for a second, then lowered his voice. 'But I'm beginning to wonder if there might be another reason why you are below par?'

After two terms of training, Jen should have been able to simulate a blank, puzzled look, but before she could even think of improvising her reaction, traitorous colour had rushed into her cheeks.

'I see,' her tutor said drily. 'Well, in that case, my dear, you have a decision to make. You're already a good actress, and you're going to be even better. But you're not going to get through this programme unless you're able to give it your all.' He saw her shocked expression and shrugged. 'This term is nearly over. If you can, I should stick it out. But if you are still feeling "under the weather" after Easter, then I don't think you should come back next term.'

Now, as she lay in Henry's bed, Jen felt again the awful sinking feeling in her stomach that she had experienced in response to the drama teacher's words.

'But that means I won't get the diploma,' she had whimpered. And she had been hard pushed not to cry. Even now, tears were welling in her eyes. But the awful truth was that she knew he was right. If she had been Angie, bubbling over with exuberant health, she could have coped, but feeling as she did, alternately lethargic and light headed, it would indeed be impossible.

'You can always come back later on,' her tutor had said as he stood up to resume the class. 'Not everyone completes the course in one go.'

But how would she ever be able to go back? Once the blasted baby was born, she would be breastfeeding, and she couldn't imagine RADA would be very happy if she had to keep breaking off from her classes to suckle some horrible squalling brat.

Oh God, she thought. I'm not ready for motherhood. I wanted to have a career. I wanted to be a star.

Joyce was also in bed, waiting for Albert to come upstairs. He seemed to be taking a long time, and she hoped he hadn't somehow got locked in the outside lavatory. Gino had been locked out there one evening a couple of weeks previously, and had almost frozen to death by the time any of them heard his pitiful shouting.

But Albert had mended the catch since then, and in any case, the weather was warmer now. Even Monty the tortoise had woken up. While it had been cold he had been hibernating in a crate of straw in the corner of the Anderson shelter, but when Joyce had checked on him last week he had blinked at her, and now he was up and about again, patrolling the back yard for new shoots of dandelion leaves and gobbling up the little bits of fruit and veg she was able to smuggle out of the café. Wartime regulations prohibited the use of human food for pets, but unless some nosy food inspector took it upon himself to strip-search her on her way home, nobody was ever going to know. In any case, Monty needed to put on weight after his winter fast, and he was partial to a nice tender cabbage leaf.

Tomorrow she would ask Bella to go up to the common to gather some weeds for him. Bella loved Monty and would do anything to make him happy. Not that Monty showed happiness very readily. But if you held him up to your ear and stroked the back of his leathery old head, he gave contented little puffs of air, and if you watched him carefully when you offered him a dandelion leaf, you could almost think he was smiling.

Joyce certainly hadn't been smiling when she'd found out about Paul knocking Douglas Rutherford down in the pub.

'It was a brilliant punch,' Angie had said. 'Poor old Douglas went down like a sack of potatoes.'

'Poor old Douglas?' Joyce had stared at her daughter incredulously. 'Good God. He deserves to be whipped, not punched.'

But afterwards she began to worry about what Mrs Rutherford would say. It would be very awkward if she took it badly. But, always one to know which side his bread was buttered, it turned out that Douglas had fed his parents some cock-and-bull story about intervening in a dispute between a drunk and his wife on his way home from the pub.

'He couldn't see who it was because it was too dark,' Mrs Rutherford said. 'But at least he showed the man that you can't treat women like that, even if he did receive a black eye for his pains. I must say, it was plucky of him.'

'Oh, very plucky indeed,' Joyce agreed, ignoring Angie's choked giggle from the other side of the café.

'How long is Douglas home for?' Joyce had asked. She wanted to know how long she'd have to keep Bella out of his way.

But it seemed that the 'chivalrous' young officer had already gone back to his secret unit. Mrs Rutherford had lowered her voice conspiratorially. 'We have no idea what he's doing. All we know is that it's vital to the war effort and very hush-hush. We just hope it's not too dangerous.'

Joyce had wanted to say that her boys were doing work vital to the war effort as well, and that theirs was definitely dangerous. Not Bob, of course, but even he had done his bit in North Africa before he was taken prisoner.

Joyce moved restlessly in the bed. Bob's latest letter, which she had received this afternoon, had been just as angry about Albert as the one before. What was more, he had addressed it to Mrs Carter rather than Mrs Lorenz, as she was now. Luckily Angie, Gino and Bella had stayed on late in the café this evening making a new batch of *gelato*, so for once Joyce had been first home, and had therefore been able to read it and hide it under the mattress before Albert came in. She didn't want him hurt by Bob's ridiculous loyalty to his deceased father, or by his stupid anti-Semitic attitude.

She shivered and pulled the eiderdown up closer under her chin, then jumped as Albert appeared in the doorway. She had been so lost in her thoughts, she hadn't heard him come upstairs.

He peered at her in concern. 'My dear Joyce, are you feeling quite all right? You look cold. I hope you aren't sickening for something.'

Joyce levered herself up in the bed. 'I'm all right,' she said. 'I think I just got a bit chilled in the lavvy. I expect you have too if you've been out there all this time.'

To her surprise, he sat down on the edge of the bed and took her hand. His fingers were indeed very cold. 'Ah,' he said. 'Yes, I'm sorry. I have been rather longer than usual, but that's because I found a small frog in there, and while I was trying to get it out, I had a sudden idea.'

Joyce sat up straighter and eyed him apprehensively. 'What sort of idea?' she said. The outdoor toilet was hardly the place for creative thinking. In and out as quickly as possible had always been her policy. Frog or no frog.

He smiled. 'Well,' he said slowly. 'It occurred to me that as we are rebuilding my house over the road, we could put in a proper bathroom upstairs. And maybe add an extra room on the back too. We could certainly make the kitchen larger, and install central heating, and some other modern conveniences. Then, if you were agreeable, instead of Angie and Gino going over there, you and I, and Bella, could move in and have the benefit of the new facilities, while Angie and Gino and the boys stay on here.'

As she stared into his eager, kindly face, Joyce was aware of her jaw dropping. Suddenly she wasn't cold any more. On the contrary, a tremor of hot excitement ran through her. Central heating? Smart new facilities? It was a marvellous idea. More than marvellous. It would be like having a brand-new house. All clean and shiny and

full of mod cons. She could hardly believe it. Her, Joyce Carter –
Joyce Lorenz – living in a house with a proper indoor bathroom.

'Oh Albert,' she breathed.

He looked at her anxiously over his glasses. 'What do you think?'

She pulled him towards her and kissed him on the lips. 'I think
you are the best husband in the world,' she said. 'And if anyone ever
says otherwise, I'll get Paul to give them a black eye.'

Helen had a long wait at RAF Northolt. As per instructions, she had
got there promptly at 9.30. But there had been no sign of her father
or indeed anyone else apart from the aerodrome staff, and in the end,
having negotiated the security detail at the gate, she had to kick her
heels in a very small waiting room for the best part of the day. While
she waited, she composed a telegram to André's father informing him
that she was travelling to the Rhine area, and that she hoped to be
able to send him further news in due course. This she was able to
dispatch at the RAF station post office, but after that, all she could
do was sit and wait for the prime minister and his entourage, who
finally arrived at four in the afternoon.

Thanks to her father's friendship with the great man, Helen had
met Winston Churchill several times before; nevertheless, she was
gratified when he remembered her name. His big round face was
glowing under his colonel's forage cap as he clambered out of the
staff car, and he seemed to be in fine fettle, showing an almost
childish excitement at the prospect of witnessing what everyone
now hoped would be the decisive battle of the war.

Normally the prime minister flew in a specially modified Douglas
C-54 Skymaster, but on this occasion, owing to the short runway
at General Montgomery's HQ at Venlo in Holland, near the German
border, today they were flying in a Dakota. The flight was uneventful,
and after a bumpy ride in a convoy of open-topped Jeeps that had
been waiting for them at the landing strip, they eventually arrived
at a small clearing in a forest where Montgomery's tactical HQ was
set up.

After an early supper, they were invited to the map room, where the general explained his grand plan of attack. Grand it certainly was. The sheer numbers of troops involved was mind-blowing.

Starting that very night, 80,000 men were to cross the Rhine at ten different points, supported by an aerial operation that would be the largest of its kind during the entire war, larger even than D-Day, utilising nearly 2,000 air transports, 1,500 gliders and hundreds of escort fighters, with the aim of delivering over 22,000 airborne infantry into the battlefield on the other side of the mighty river.

That night, under cover of darkness, using amphibious vehicles, boats and landing craft, all of which had been transported by the Royal Navy the whole way across France, the first of Montgomery's divisions crossed the river. As it began to get light, the prime minister's party took up a position at a vantage point high above the Rhine at Ginsberg.

Helen had thought the invasion of the south of France spectacular, but it was nothing compared to this. Already they could hear the sound of aircraft approaching from the west, and now the sky became black with planes, many of them towing gliders, a continuous moving blanket of aircraft that lasted for over two hours. She was aware of a surge of emotion, and several times had to bite her lip hard to stop tears filling her eyes. It really was an incredible sight. At one point, led by the PM, the watching dignitaries broke into spontaneous applause.

Oddly, despite the deafening roar of aircraft engines, somewhere in the background, tinkling out of one of the vehicles that had brought them to the viewpoint, Helen could also hear the tinny sound of American forces radio, and perhaps embedded there by the extraordinary scene she was witnessing, she found she had the tune of 'String of Pearls' on her brain for the rest of the day.

There was so much haze and smoke from the relentless German anti-aircraft fire that it was impossible to see the actual landing of the airborne forces on the other side of the river, but she could see their parachutes floating down and the hawsers whipping away as the gliders were released. She could also see quite clearly that quite a few of the gliders were instantly blown out of the sky by German gunners. Others clearly crashed on landing.

Nobody was clapping now.

Soon the tow planes began to return. Many of them were clearly in trouble too, several in flames. Twice debris fell in the vicinity of their observation post, wafting the assembled company with the unpleasantly acrid smell of burning oil. When a Dakota, struggling low over the recently evacuated town of Xanten, crashed in a ball of fire at the bottom of the hill, just below where the prime minister's party stood, they were bundled off to a different viewpoint.

After enjoying a substantial picnic lunch in the new location, the PM announced his desire to cross the Rhine himself, but neither Eisenhower nor Montgomery was prepared to let him put his life in danger. The following morning, however, as soon as the American general had left on other business, Churchill pointed to a nearby landing craft and insisted that no harm would come of him paying a brief visit to the other side.

To everyone's surprise, Montgomery capitulated, and before Helen knew it, they were all packed onto the landing craft and nosing out into the fierce current.

A featureless meadow greeted them on the other side. The fighting had already swept forward way beyond the riverbank, and apart from the distant booming sound of gunfire, they might for all the world have been standing in some English field next to the Thames.

After ten minutes of looking around rather aimlessly, they crossed back over and went to examine a damaged bridge at Wessel. There, to the PM's evident gratification, they came under some sporadic shellfire and had to beat a hasty retreat.

Lord de Burrel found the whole thing highly amusing, but Helen was getting anxious. It was becoming obvious that it was going to be nigh-on impossible for her to stay behind when the PM's party left for England following day. When she had ventured to ask Montgomery's ADC if he thought the general might allow her to tag along with his camp, he had looked at her in amazement. 'Good lord,' he said. 'Not in a million years. It's astonishing he allowed you to come at all. I'm afraid General Montgomery is rather old fashioned in that way; he believes women should confine their activities to the home front, not the battlefield.'

Despite herself, Helen didn't entirely blame him. She had found the sight of those burning planes extremely disturbing. She knew that young men died in battle, of course they did, but there was something unutterably horrible about them dying before they even reached the ground.

The shattered, ruined towns and villages they had driven through that day had shocked her too. Where possible, the population had been evacuated prior to the assault. Nobody knew yet whether the Germans had shown equal compassion on the other side of the river, but the bleak, devastated ghost towns on the western bank were enough to send shivers up her spine. It was much worse than anything she had seen in France. She had no idea what state the rest of Germany would be in, but this section of the country had been bombed and shelled almost out of existence.

In light of what she had already seen, and without the support of the military, the task she had set herself seemed daunting in the extreme, and as she tossed and turned on her uncomfortable camp bed that night, for the first time she wondered if she was up to it.

Chapter Twenty-Three

The news that General Montgomery's troops had finally crossed the Rhine caused great excitement in the Flag and Garter on Sunday night. All the regulars had poured in to celebrate. 'Three cheers for Monty!' one man shouted. 'Next stop Berlin.'

Without Helen there to help, Katy, Molly and Elsa were rushed off their feet. Ward had been back in London for the weekend, but as soon as the news about the Rhine crossing came through, he had disappeared back to SAARF in case he was called upon to set off for Germany. But he had been home long enough to discuss his and Katy's future and, to Molly's surprise, she found it involved her.

As soon as the clearing-up was done and Elsa had gone home, Katy poured two small brandies and carried them over to the threadbare armchairs by the dying fire. 'Ward and I have made a decision,' she said. 'We've definitely decided to give up the pub when the war is over.' She took a sip of her brandy and glanced hesitantly at Molly. 'But we still have two years' lease to run, and, well, we wondered if you'd like to take it on?'

Molly had slumped down in the chair beside her, weary after an entire day on her feet, but now she jerked forward so fast she nearly spilt her drink. She stared at her friend in astonishment. The flickering firelight made Katy's face look unnaturally pale. Probably as pale as her own.

A couple of years ago, Katy and Ward had invited her to join them in the business, but they had never previously suggested she take on the whole thing.

'But . . .' she began. 'But . . .' She didn't know where to start.

Katy gave a slight grimace. 'It's only a thought,' she said. 'I'd never have suggested it if you hadn't been so disappointed about the whole medical school thing.' She hesitated. 'Or if things had worked out between you and Callum.' Catching Molly's wince of pain, she rushed on. 'I know it's hard work and everything, but it's quite a good business, and it would give you somewhere to live.'

'But would Mr Rutherford let me take over the lease?' Molly asked. Louise's father was an out-and-out chauvinist. And it wasn't just women Greville Rutherford disapproved of. His prejudice included blacks, Jews and anyone else he considered to be inferior to himself. The only person who managed to escape his snobbish intolerance was his ghastly son. Though everyone else thought Douglas Rutherford was a nasty little git, for some extraordinary reason he had always been the apple of his father's eye.

Katy shrugged. 'I don't know. He let me take it on when my father died, and that was before I married Ward, so I don't see why not. We can but ask. But only if you are interested. I don't want to rattle his cage unnecessarily.'

Was she interested? Molly tried to think about it rationally. But the offer had taken her completely by surprise. She had always enjoyed the camaraderie of working at the pub. In the absence of any family, it had given her a kind of base, a focus, somewhere she belonged and felt at home. And her friendship with Katy and Ward meant a lot. But was it really what she wanted to do longer term? The answer to that was no. On the other hand, she might be mad to turn it down. The London medical school doors had already been slammed in her face. She was still waiting to hear from some of the regional universities, but soon there might not be many doors left. With all the National Service soldiers presumably soon to be demobbed and expecting to get their former jobs back, it was obvious that, despite their manful war work, women would once again be

391

shunted to the back of the queue, or more likely back into the home.

'But what would *you* do?' she asked Katy. 'Where will you go? Surely not to Canada?'

Katy shook her head. 'If Ward can find a decent job, we'll stay here. He wants to buy a house with a garden for the children and Lucky.' She gave a slight grimace. 'Somewhere big enough for my mother to live with us, and maybe his aunts too, because he thinks they're getting too old to be on their own. It would be lovely to find somewhere near here, but it's not going to be easy, not with so many houses destroyed by the bombing.' She gave an uneasy laugh. 'It sounds so grown-up, doesn't it? Buying a house with a garden? I can't really believe it will happen.'

Molly smiled reassuringly. 'If Ward's got anything to do with it, it'll happen,' she said. She had every faith in Ward Frazer. Not only was he one of the most competent men she had ever met but, like Callum, he came from one of the richest families in Canada, and despite his determination to be independent, she was sure that, if necessary, for the sake of Katy and the children, he'd find a way to gain access to some of that Frazer wealth.

'I wish it *had* worked out between you and Callum,' Katy said suddenly. 'Because then—'

'No,' Molly cut in at once. 'Please don't say it. I don't want to think about what might have happened. I have to look forward, not back.'

Aware that her voice was shaking, she took a steadying breath. 'But I don't think I can take on the pub. It's really kind of you to offer it, but it wouldn't be the same without you here. I don't think I could do it on my own. I've seen how tough it's been for you, and you're much stronger than me.' She shook her head as Katy tried to interrupt. 'No, it's true. Look how brilliantly you dealt with Douglas Rutherford that night. I'd never have managed that.'

Katy was silent. She looked disappointed. But Molly had already had a better idea, even if it did close off the opportunity for her. 'Why don't you offer it to Aaref and Elsa?' she said. 'It would suit them down to the ground. They're looking for a business, and they know this one inside out.'

Katy nodded. 'I'd thought of that,' she said. 'But I wanted to offer it to you first.'

The following morning, when she mentioned the idea to Elsa and Aaref, they couldn't believe their luck. It was their dream. The perfect solution to their own worries about work and accommodation. So Katy said she would speak to Mr Rutherford as soon as she got the opportunity.

In the meantime, Molly received another blow. That Monday morning she had got a letter back from her old mentor, Dr Florey in Oxford, saying she had made enquiries at the Radcliffe Infirmary on Molly's behalf, but that they too were reluctant to take girls as they were already finding it difficult to get placements in other hospitals for the few female students already on their course. *I'm so sorry, Molly*, she wrote. *But I did warn you of the chauvinistic attitude of the British medical profession. I had hoped the war would change all that, but if anything it's made it worse.*

Molly closed her eyes. She knew Oxford was fiercely competitive, but it had been worth a try. Perhaps luckily, she didn't have time to dwell on it, because that morning she and Susan Voles were going to work out what on earth sort of show they could put on for Mrs d'Arcy Billière.

All they had so far was a hopeless hotchpotch of ideas: George's conjuring tricks, Malcolm counting to twenty in four different languages, English, Italian, French and Russian, Gino explaining how to make *gelato* in his still-far-from-perfect English, Bella reciting a poem she had learned by heart, the kindergarten children singing a nursery rhyme in their squeaky, slightly out-of-tune voices and Professor Markov demonstrating one of his less dangerous experiments. It didn't add up to much, and Molly and Susan were trying to think of ways of stringing it all together when Graham arrived, wheeling himself laboriously into the morning room in preparation for a session with Professor Markov.

He was clearly in one of his gloomy moods, and when Susan made the mistake of asking him if he'd thought about what he could do in the show, he nearly bit her head off.

'I'm not going to do anything,' he snapped. 'How can I, stuck in a wheelchair? The whole thing is a ridiculous idea anyway. I don't know why you are bothering with it. It's just a waste of everyone's time.'

As Susan flushed scarlet and looked down at her shoes unhappily, Molly felt a surge of anger. Susan wasn't the most confident person in the world, and the last thing she needed was Graham taking his frustrations out on her.

'We're bothering with it because Mrs d'Arcy Billière has asked us to bother with it,' Molly snapped. 'And I'm sorry if you feel we're wasting your time. But if it wasn't for Mrs d'Arcy Billière, none of us would be here.'

If he had looked apologetic, or responded more positively, she might have stopped there, but he didn't; instead he gave a faint derisive snort as though she had said something stupid, and looked away. And that really got her goat.

'It may surprise you to know that you aren't the only person who feels hard done by,' she said crossly. 'Think what it's like for me. At least you're a man. *You're* not going to have doors slammed in your face because of that, even if you are stuck in a wheelchair at the moment. And even if you are stuck in it for ever, which I personally doubt, at least you're alive. The papers this morning are saying the casualty figures for the new offensive at the Rhine are lower than expected, but they are still casualties. Deaths. Thousands upon thousands of young men who will never see another day. So instead of feeling sorry for yourself and griping all the time, why don't you start showing a little compassion for other people for once in your life? It would certainly make a nice change.'

She hadn't meant to say it. She hadn't meant to say anything. But it was too late. She grabbed Susan's arm and, dragging her to her feet, hustled her out of the room.

'Oh my God,' she whispered as they reached the relative safety of the hallway. 'What have I done? I'm so sorry, Susan. I don't usually lose my temper. But really, he is an arse . . .'

To her surprise, Susan giggled. 'Well, at least it solves the problem of what part he might play in the show,' she said. 'After that, I don't suppose we'll ever see him again.'

Molly groaned and was about to reply when the front door flew open and George and Malcolm surged into the hallway.

'Look, Miss Voles,' Malcolm shouted, brandishing a jar. 'I found a butterfly asleep in the cellar.'

'It's not asleep,' George said. 'I told you, it's hibernating. I looked it up in the library and I think it's a red admiral. They come here from central Europe in the spring and—'

'Well, wherever it's come from, and whatever it's doing now, I think we'll go and look at it in the garden,' Susan said, ushering them hastily through to the back of the house.

Equally hastily, Molly let herself out of the front door. She knew she should go and apologise to Graham, but she couldn't bring herself to do it. Nevertheless, she felt bad as she hurried away down Lavender Road.

How could she have been so blunt? So brutally heartless? What was worse, she had done exactly what Graham himself had done: taken her own frustrations out on someone else. Now either Graham would storm off, never to be seen again, or he would complain to Professor Markov. Either scenario would be awkward and embarrassing. She groaned. She had tried so hard. Why was everything going so badly wrong? She only hoped Helen was having better luck in Germany.

Helen wasn't having better luck. On the contrary, she was having no luck at all.

Unsatisfied with the previous day's efforts, that morning the prime minister had made a second crossing of the Rhine, across a pontoon bridge that the sappers had just finished constructing at Xanten. On the other side they found a number of captured German soldiers who had been herded into a barbed-wire enclosure. Some of the prisoners recognised Churchill and gaped at him in utter astonishment, especially when he waved his cigar at them benignly.

The Highland Division soldiers who were guarding them seemed equally amazed to see the prime minister, but his presence appeared to raise their morale, which had been lowered by the death of their commander during the crossing the previous night, and by the fact that the regimental bagpipes had also suffered a fatal bullet wound, which had prevented the piper from piping his comrades ashore.

The Rhine crossings had been declared a great victory by Montgomery and Eisenhower, but it didn't look like it from the ground. The whole area was littered with smoking pieces of flak, spent cartridges and shell casings. Helen's father had lent her a pair of binoculars, and everywhere she looked, there were crashed gliders, most of them with their cargo still on board. She could see mangled Jeeps, guns and other unidentifiable vehicles spilling out of the broken fuselages onto the scorched and pitted grass. Although the injured and dead had been cleared away, she couldn't imagine that the men on board had fared much better than the equipment.

The PM was invited to travel back across the river in an amphibious vehicle, which he thoroughly enjoyed. But for Helen, it was a moment of despair, because before she could even think of an excuse to break away from the group, General Montgomery had packed them all into cars with instructions to the drivers to get them back to Venlo before nightfall. He was clearly fed up with his visitors now and didn't want them staying another night.

Obediently the driver of the lead car set a furious pace, but even so, the sun was low in the sky by the time they reached the airfield, where the Dakota was standing ready on the apron with its steps down. As the PM's party straggled wearily across to it, Helen was already kicking herself. She had been utterly pathetic. Hopeless. She had completely failed to find any means of staying on, and not only did she feel she had let herself down, she had let André down too.

'Are you all right, my dear?' her father asked, coming up behind her and taking her arm. 'You seem rather quiet. Mind you, I'm not surprised after that hair-raising journey. I feel rather queasy myself.'

As Helen turned her head to answer him, she caught sight of an American Air Force corporal hurrying across towards them from the gate.

'Excuse me, ma'am,' the man called, saluting as he approached. 'But are you Miss de Burrel?'

Startled, Helen nodded. Assuming he had a message for the PM or one of his entourage, she glanced towards the Dakota. But no, it was her he wanted. He shuffled his feet rather awkwardly and gestured back towards the entrance to the airfield. 'It's just that there's a rather odd Frenchman at the gate asking for you. I tried to get rid of him, but he was insistent.'

Helen felt her heart accelerate like one of Montgomery's cars. 'A Frenchman?' Wildly she swung round to stare in the direction of his pointing finger. And there, to her utter astonishment, on the other side of the security barrier, looking as drab and grimly unemotional as ever, was Raoul.

She waved, but he didn't wave back because he was busy rolling a cigarette. Instead, true to form, he just jerked his head slightly in acknowledgement.

'Who is it, my dear?' her father asked, squinting against the setting sun. 'Good God, I hope that's not André?'

Letting out an involuntary gasp of amusement, Helen swung back to him. 'No,' she said. 'But it is one of his men.' She grasped his arm. 'Daddy, listen. I'm going to stay here. No, please. I've got to do this. I've got to try and find André.'

Her father was shaking his head, but he knew her too well to put up more than a token objection. 'I had a feeling this was what you had in mind,' he said. 'But I hoped you would realise it was impossible.'

Helen smiled and squeezed his arm. 'It might be impossible, but I have to try,' she said. 'And you're right, it's what I wanted to do all along, but it was all so ghastly at the Rhine and I couldn't see how I was going to manage without transport or rations. Raoul will help me. He will know what to do.'

'So where has this damn fellow sprung from?' her father asked, frowning back at the gate. 'How on earth did he find you?'

Helen laughed and reached up to kiss him on the cheek. 'I have absolutely no idea,' she said. 'But now that he has, I can't let the opportunity pass.' Turning back to the startled corporal, she smiled. 'Please could you arrange for my kitbag to be taken off the plane,' she said. 'I'm not going to be joining the flight after all.'

Having become resigned to the fact that she was going to have to give up RADA, and determined not to fall into a gloom, Jen had taken the bull by the horns and composed a polite note to Mrs d'Arcy Billière to ask if she could come back and stay for a few weeks, at least until such time as Henry came home. Mrs d'Arcy Billière had responded by return of post.

> *My dear Jen,*
>   *Of course you can come back. I can't think of anything more delightful, and I'm sure Molly would relish some help from an expert with the show she and the students are putting on. Let me know when you'll arrive and I'll make sure your room is ready.*
>   *With all best wishes,*
>   *Lael*

Jen had groaned. But if helping Molly with her daft little project was the price for returning to the cosy comfort of Mrs d'Arcy Billière's house, so be it. After all, she wouldn't have anything else to do, apart from hang around the place feeling sick and lethargic. Even the thought of dragging her things back to Lavender Road made her feel weary.

When she told Lord Freddy she had decided to go back to Clapham, he seemed disappointed. 'It's been nice having you as a neighbour,' he said. But over the regulation five-shilling dinner at Bailey's Hotel in Kensington on Saturday evening, he rallied, and came up with a suggestion. 'I tell you what,' he said. 'It's the Easter holiday next weekend and I've got plenty of petrol coupons, so why don't I dig out the old motor and we'll pop your bits and pieces in the back? Save you lugging everything on the Tube. Oh, and while we are at it, maybe we could pick up Louise and take a run out into the country. To Windsor, perhaps. Somewhere like that. She might like to see the castle.'

Jen laughed. 'Ha. I might have guessed you had an ulterior motive.'

'Not at all,' he said. 'Not at all.' But he hadn't been able to disguise the flush on his round cheeks. 'It would be a pleasure to drive you down to Clapham. I just thought . . .'

'I know exactly what you thought,' Jen said. 'And the last thing I want is to sit in the back of the car like a gooseberry while you and Louise take a romantic drive out to some scenic spot in the country.'

'But I don't think she'd come with me on her own,' he said plaintively. 'She's very correct.'

Jen was hard pushed not to laugh. Correct? Louise! Little did he know. But if that was the way Louise was playing it, who was she to disillusion him?

In any case, he was already leaning forward eagerly. 'I know,' he said. 'Why don't you bring a friend too? There's room for four in the Alvis. If it's a nice day, we can have the top down. We'll take a picnic and some wine and make a day of it. What could be more jolly? We'll say we're celebrating the breaching of the Rhine.'

Swayed by his enthusiasm, Jen found herself traipsing down to Lavender Road on Sunday evening to see if she could persuade Louise and Molly to join her and Lord Freddy on a jolly day out in the country on Easter Saturday.

'Oh no,' Louise wailed. 'I can't believe he's still after me. I swear I haven't given him any encouragement.'

'I don't think he needs any encouragement,' Jen said. 'And I can't think why you are being so mean. He's a lovely man. If it wasn't for Henry, I'd marry him myself. Especially as it now turns out that he has some fancy sports car as well as everything else.'

Louise giggled. 'Oh all right. But only if you promise not to leave us alone for a millisecond. I don't want him proposing all over again.'

Molly was even less enthusiastic. 'I was going to go to Epsom on Saturday,' she said. 'To see if I can find out anything about my father's family who used to live there. I really don't have time to—'

But Jen was damned if she was going to act as chaperone to Freddy and Louise on her own. 'Epsom's in the country, isn't it?' she said. 'Well then, we'll go there. I'm sure Freddy wouldn't mind. He'd be happy to go to Nazi Germany if he thought Louise would come along for the ride. Oh go on, Molly, please. If you come, I promise I'll help you with your damned show.'

So Molly capitulated too, and of course Freddy didn't mind the change of plan. 'Epsom?' he said. 'I've been to the races there, of course, but I've never explored further than that. But I believe the Epsom Downs are very pretty.' He nodded in satisfaction. 'Lots of space to walk and so on. So while you and Molly are making enquiries in the town, Louise and I can look for a nice spot for a picnic. It couldn't be better.'

It turned out that Raoul had set off from the south of France within two hours of Monsieur Cabillard's receiving Helen's telegram. With the vineyard van packed to the gunnels with petrol, tinned food, bottled vegetables, numerous crates of wine and a box of homing pigeons, he had driven non-stop for nearly thirty hours.

'But how did you know where I would be?' Helen asked.

He gave one of his negligent shrugs. '*Alors*. You said you were travelling with your father. Monsieur Cabillard knew that your father was a friend of Monsieur Churchill, so when I heard that Monsieur Churchill was at the Rhine, it was not so hard to know where to look. But when I arrived this afternoon they said Monsieur Churchill had already left for Venlo. So I came here, in case you needed my help.' He nodded towards the Dakota. 'But it is no problem if you wish to go back to England, I can find Monsieur André on my own.'

There was an accusatory look in his eye, and Helen bristled. 'I didn't want to go back to England,' she said. 'I wanted to find André, but I realised I couldn't do it on my own.' She glared at him. 'I do need your help.'

Glancing back towards the airfield, she saw the USAAF corporal struggling across the grass with her kitbag. The Dakota's propellers were already turning. Gradually the blades became a blur and the plane shuddered into motion and lumbered off in a slow wide circle towards the runway. Helen watched in silence as it paused, presumably waiting for the go-ahead from the control tower. Then all at once it was off, jolting along the rough tarmac towards the trees that fringed the aerodrome. She held her breath, digging her fingernails into her palms, because it looked as if it would never get off the ground.

But it did; it lifted cleanly, and roared away over the trees into the orange glow of the sunset.

Letting out her breath, Helen smiled ruefully at Raoul. 'You'll have to help me now,' she said.

He didn't smile back. He just picked up her kitbag and thrust it into the back of the van.

'Tonight we stay near here,' he said. 'Tomorrow we try to cross the Rhine.'

But crossing the Rhine proved impossible. The loadmasters of the various troop-carrying ferries, Bailey bridges and makeshift pontoons were stubbornly intransigent. Orders were orders, and none of them were prepared to let an unauthorised civilian vehicle across, however much wine it had on board.

So each evening, in the absence of anywhere else to stay, Helen and Raoul were forced to return to the small *gasthuis* they had found on that first night near Venlo. Holland had had a bad time over the winter. Much of the country was still occupied by the Germans and in the grip of famine. But Venlo had been liberated several weeks before and, despite continuing privations and a lack of hot water, the owners of this shabby little guest house were taking advantage of their proximity to the airfield to try to get their business going again.

Only Helen actually slept there. Raoul bedded down in the van to guard the wine. When Helen offered to take turns, he shook his head. 'No,' he said. 'It is not right.'

Helen had laughed. 'Goodness, I have slept in worse places than a wine van. For the last few months I've been sleeping in a mouse-infested pub cellar.'

But he had been adamant. 'No,' he said again. 'Monsieur André would not like it.'

He was prepared to sit in the *gasthuis* bar with her of an evening, however, and it was on the evening of their fourth frustrating day that a group of USAAF pilots from the Venlo base came in and took up what was clearly a regular position at a table at the far end of the room.

It was obviously a night off for them, and they were determined to have a good time. But as they got increasingly rowdy, and Raoul increasingly irritable, Helen began to wonder if she might be wise to call it a day and go up to bed. She was sitting with her back to the pilots, but she could tell from the tenor of their conversation that her presence in the bar was causing interest, and the last thing she wanted was Raoul suddenly deciding to weigh in to defend her honour.

It was only as she stood up that she realised they weren't all Americans. Through the fug of smoke that was now filling the bar, she saw that some of them were wearing the uniform of the RCAF, the Royal Canadian Air Force. Even as she took in that fact, she saw one of them do a double-take. The next minute he was on his feet and walking slightly unsteadily towards her.

'Helen? What are you doing here?'

And blinking through the smoke, Helen realised that she was

staring into the unmistakable, if somewhat unfocused, grey-blue eyes of Callum Frazer.

'Oh my goodness,' she said. 'I might ask you the same thing. But I suppose it's obvious.'

The other pilots were delighted by this turn of events, and Helen had to raise her voice over their catcalls to make herself heard.

'Let's go outside,' Callum said, gesturing rather drunkenly towards the door. 'We're never going to be able to talk in here.'

But Raoul had other ideas, and it took Helen some minutes to persuade him that Callum wasn't about to ravish her at the roadside.

'Good God, who is that guy?' Callum asked when they eventually managed to escape.

By the time she had explained that she and Raoul were on their way to see if they could find André, they were already some distance from the bar. A big yellow moon had come up now, and as Callum politely murmured vague words of hope, she could see the shocked sympathy on his face.

Helen felt a cool breeze whisper across her skin, and as they stood in silence for a moment while a cloud passed briefly over the moon, Callum raised a hand to brush a lock of hair off his forehead.

He really was ridiculously handsome. It was easy to see why Molly had fallen for him so hard. With his film-star looks, his appealing smile, and the smart blue uniform that so perfectly matched his eyes, he could easily have just stepped off a Canadian Air Force recruitment poster.

'So you only left England a few days ago?' he said.

His voice was casual, but Helen could sense a sudden tension in him and had a nasty feeling she knew where this was going. She was right.

'How was Molly?' he asked. 'What's she up to?'

At once Helen realised she was in a tight spot. She had no idea what Molly would want her to say.

Sensing her reluctance, he gave a light laugh. 'It's OK. You don't have to pussyfoot around me,' he said.

'I'm not pussyfooting,' Helen said. 'I just don't quite know what to say.'

'Oh come on, Helen.' He scuffed the toe of his boot on the ground. 'I know she was keen on some German prisoner when I was there.'

Helen stared at him. It was the last thing she had expected him to say. 'Gefreiter Henniker?' she said incredulously. 'You must be joking.' But seeing his sceptical expression, suddenly she began to wonder. It was true that Molly had been exceptionally protective of the German. But surely that had just been because she wanted him to help them. 'No,' she said firmly. 'She's not remotely keen on him. I've met him and he's not at all her type.'

Callum smiled faintly. But he had noticed her hesitation. 'I didn't know Molly had a type,' he said. And once again Helen realised she was on dodgy ground.

Her loyalties lay with Molly, but she liked Callum too. 'Oh God,' she said. 'You're putting me in a really difficult position here, Callum. All I know is that Molly was mad on you when you were in Tunisia, and that she was really upset over whatever happened between you at Christmas. But she's OK. She's tougher than she lets on. She can cope. And even though things have gone really badly for her recently, she's still coping.'

His brows snapped together at once. 'What do you mean? What's gone wrong?'

Helen sighed. 'Well, all the London medical schools have turned her down, because of her being a girl, and then there's this business about her mother, and . . .' She stopped, wondering how much Molly had told him. The two of them had been very close in Tunisia, but perhaps . . .

'What about her mother?' Callum asked. 'I thought she died when Molly was a child and that's why Molly was brought up in a children's home.'

So Helen felt obliged to tell him that Molly's mother hadn't died at all. But she was reluctant to give him all the gory details, and in the end she didn't have to, because suddenly there was a commotion back at the *gasthuis*.

'Hey, Casanova,' an American voice shouted. 'We're heading back to base. You coming? Or will you be canoodling out there all night?'

Callum grimaced. 'I guess I'd better go,' he said. 'I'm back on duty first thing tomorrow and I don't want to miss my lift.' He turned back towards the *gasthuis*. 'I'm coming,' he shouted. 'Just give me two seconds to say goodbye.'

A rude wolf-whistle greeted this request, and Callum smiled apologetically. 'Sorry about that,' he said. 'It's been a tough week, and I guess the guys are letting off steam.'

'Were you involved in the Rhine crossing?' Helen asked.

He nodded. 'Fighter escort,' he said. 'But to be honest, most of the trouble came from the ground.'

'I know,' Helen said grimly. 'I saw.' She looked at him and wondered how these young men coped. For years now, month after month, week after week, they had been witnessing death and destruction. One day had been bad enough for her.

But Callum's thoughts were already back on Molly. 'Do you really think she was keen on me in Tunisia?' he asked.

'Of course,' Helen said. Perhaps that was how they coped, she thought. By thinking of other, pleasanter things.

But Callum was frowning now. 'Then why didn't she say? Why did she always draw back?'

Helen looked at him. If she'd been in Molly's shoes, she wouldn't have drawn back. 'I honestly don't know,' she said, but then she hesitated. 'Although part of it may be because she's convinced she's not good enough for you.'

'Not good enough?' Callum gasped. 'My God, Molly's worth a million of me.'

Helen smiled. 'I don't know about that, but you have to admit that your circumstances are somewhat different.'

He looked surprised. 'Who cares about that?'

'Molly,' Helen said drily. 'And maybe your parents?'

He gave a slightly sour laugh. 'I guess,' he said. He looked thoughtful for a moment, then suddenly he leaned over and kissed her on the cheek. As the wolf-whistles started up again, he rolled his eyes. 'I'm real glad I saw you,' he said. 'And I sure hope you find your guy.'

Helen smiled. 'I hope so too.' Outside the *gasthuis* a vehicle engine fired noisily into life. She put a hand on Callum's arm as he moved away. 'Please be careful. We don't want any accidents at this late stage.'

He laughed as the driver revved pointedly. 'I'll do my best. And hey, Helen, if you come this way again, stop by the base and I'll show you some proper Royal Canadian Air Force hospitality. We are much more civilised than those damn Yanks.'

Chapter Twenty-Four

Lord Freddy's car was indeed a smart affair. Jen had never in her life travelled in such a snazzy vehicle. She had in fact rarely travelled in a private car of any description. Mr Rutherford was the only person in Lavender Road to own a car. Ward Frazer had occasionally appeared in one earlier in the war, but neither his borrowed Ford, nor Mr Rutherford's staid old Wolseley, were a patch on Lord Freddy's Alvis Speed 20 SD Drophead Coupé. It was a deep, shiny blue and had an enormously long bonnet, on the front of which, over a fearsome-looking grille, were stuck four silver headlamps.

Lord Freddy drove with considerable panache and, as they roared through central London, heads turned to watch them pass. With a fancy wicker picnic basket strapped to the boot, her suitcase in the back, the emerald engagement ring glinting on her finger and her hair blowing loose in the slipstream, Jen felt like a film star on the way to some glamorous assignment.

Even Louise seemed impressed. She had heard the throaty growl of the Alvis from Cedars House and came tripping over the road just as Freddy was helping Jen carry her things indoors. Louise might claim not to relish Lord Freddy's attentions, but Jen was amused to see that Miss Fancy-Pants Rutherford hadn't spared any effort to look as elegant as possible for the occasion. Her hair was curled into a stylish chignon, her neat little summer suit had clearly come from one of London's top fashion houses, presumably at the cost of numerous clothing coupons, and her silk stockings shimmered alluringly as she walked up the steps towards them. So much so that Lord Freddy took one look at her and dropped Jen's suitcase on his foot.

'Oh my word,' he stammered. 'How lovely. To see you, I mean. I'm so glad . . .'

But already Mrs d'Arcy Billière was coming into the hallway to greet them and, to Jen's surprise, Helen's father, Lord de Burrel, was there too. He didn't seem remotely embarrassed to have been caught taking a cup of coffee with his Russian tutor at such an early hour of the morning, and when he learned that the new arrivals were friends of Helen's, he greeted them warmly, explaining that he had recently arrived back from Germany.

'I expect you know I took Helen over there with me,' he said, bringing out a case of cigars and genially offering one to Lord Freddy. 'Well, she insisted on staying on in the hope of finding this Frenchman of hers. I'm afraid she's going to be disappointed. From what I hear of Nazi methods, the poor fellow's most likely been shot months ago. But hats off to her for trying.'

By the time they left the house, a small crowd had gathered round the Alvis. Louise had not been the only person who had heard its arrival in Lavender Road. Among the awed onlookers were George and Malcolm, and recognising Lord Freddy from Jen's wedding, Malcolm immediately began clamouring to be allowed to sit inside.

Lord Freddy laughed delightedly. 'I think we can do better than that,' he said. 'If you like, I'll take you for a quick spin.' Then, as the boys immediately began arguing about who was going to sit in the front, he turned anxiously to Louise. 'That's if you don't mind waiting for a moment? I was only thinking of a couple of laps round the common?'

Since the boys were already clambering in, having decided to both squeeze into the front passenger seat, Louise didn't have much choice. Nevertheless she waved her hand graciously. 'No, no,' she said. 'We're in no hurry. In any case, Molly's not here yet.'

'How fast will we go?' Malcolm squeaked excitedly as the car roared into life.

Lord Freddy chuckled as he let in the clutch. 'Well,' he said. 'If we're lucky, we might get her up to sixty on the straight.' And with a blast of exhaust fumes and a shriek of tyres, they were off.

As the smoke drifted away, Jen saw Molly hurrying up the road towards them, wide eyed with horror. 'Oh my goodness,' she said. 'I hope he doesn't kill them.'

Louise laughed. 'I hope he doesn't kill *us*,' she said. 'I told you he was bonkers.'

'He's not bonkers,' Jen said crossly. 'He's sweet. And he's a good driver. We didn't hit anything on the way down here.'

That made Louise laugh even more. But when the Alvis eventually reappeared, her concerns for her admirer's sanity didn't stop her choosing to sit in the front. Nor, Jen noticed with satisfaction, did it stop her flirting prettily with him all the way to Epsom.

Louise wasn't the only person feeling somewhat uneasy about the outing.

Molly hadn't met Louise's aristocratic admirer before. She had seen him of course at Jen's wedding reception, but they hadn't been properly introduced, and she had been feeling uncomfortable at the thought of him using his precious petrol ration on her behalf, especially as it would almost certainly prove to be a wild goose chase. But as soon as she made Lord Freddy's acquaintance that morning, she realised that everything Jen had said about him was true. He really was sweet. She only had to see how kind he had been to the boys to know that. George and Malcolm had come back from their spin round the common in a state of ecstasy. It was obvious that Lord Freddy had become their new hero.

Nevertheless, Molly still felt the trip to Epsom was a bit of an imposition on his good nature, and she was therefore, like Jen, relieved to see that he was clearly enjoying the opportunity to impress Louise with his fancy car. And despite all her supposed misgivings, Louise, sitting gracefully in the front like Lady Muck, with her sleekly stockinged legs crossed demurely, and a fashionable headscarf over her beautifully styled hair, seemed to be lapping it up.

As they passed through Wandsworth, they were held up briefly by traffic lights right underneath one of the government's huge *Is Your Journey Really Necessary?* posters. Louise gave a coy giggle and glanced at Freddy under her lashes, 'Is *our* journey really necessary?' she asked.

'Absolutely essential,' he responded promptly as he accelerated away again. 'Good lord, how else would I have persuaded you to spend the day with me?'

Louise threw him a provocative glance and recrossed her legs. 'I thought the main aim was to find Molly's father,' she said.

Lord Freddy swerved slightly, and had to make a hasty evasive manoeuvre to avoid hitting a bus coming in the other direction. 'Yes, yes, of course,' he said. Colouring slightly, he turned his head to wink apologetically at Molly over his shoulder. 'That's right. Absolutely. Finding your father is our first priority.'

But first priority or not, right from the start things went wrong.

Molly had memorised the address of her mother's deceased parents from the wedding certificate. Yew Tree House, Headley, Epsom. But far from being a suburb of Epsom, as Molly had assumed, Headley turned out to be a village four miles away, in the middle of the country.

'I'm so sorry,' she muttered, as she climbed back into the car after enquiring at the Epsom post office.

But Lord Freddy waved her apology away with an airy hand. 'No problem,' he said. He cast a rather regretful glance at the hotel on the corner. 'I was just about to suggest we stop for a quick snifter at the Spread Eagle, but we can easily motor on to Headley instead.'

But that wasn't so easy, because most of the signposts were still missing, having been taken down at the beginning of the war due to concerns about spies from Germany parachuting into the Home Counties. When they did eventually find Headley, the post office there was closed for lunch.

It was Jen's bright idea to ask at the pub, and although none of the patrons of the Wheatsheaf knew of any Coogans living nearby, they were able to direct them to Yew Tree House, the site of Prissy's downfall.

While Lord Freddy equipped Louise with a sherry and himself with a pint of bitter, Jen and Molly went off to investigate. After a couple of wrong turnings, they eventually found it. There was no sign of the yew tree that had presumably given the property its name, but the house itself was a substantial turn-of-the-century building, with what looked like stabling behind it. To one side of the long driveway was a sloping lawn, and on the other a small orchard and two herbaceous borders.

'Blimey,' Jen said, clearly impressed. 'I had no idea you were going to turn out to be so posh.'

Molly rolled her eyes. 'Hardly,' she said. 'Don't forget my father was the gardener's son.'

Concerned about breaking Jen's promise to Louise by leaving her alone with Freddy, they didn't linger, but when they got back to the pub, they found their travelling companions looking very relaxed, sitting on a bench in the sun. As there were no angry glares from Louise, Jen and Molly left them there and went back to the post office.

The woman behind the counter was quite elderly. 'Coogan,' she said thoughtfully. 'No, there's never been anyone of that name living in this village. Not that I recall.'

'It would be about twenty years ago,' Molly prompted her. 'Mr Coogan was a gardener. He worked for the Cavanaghs who lived at Yew Tree House.'

The old lady frowned. 'Well now, let me think. I knew the Cavanaghs, of course, very hoity-toity people they were. I seem to recall the daughter went off to live in London. And the parents died in a car accident some time later.' She brightened suddenly. 'I know who you should speak to. Mrs Rogers. She worked at Yew Tree House around that time. She might remember.'

411

'Oh, that's brilliant,' Molly said eagerly. 'Where does she live?'

'She used to live in the village,' the postmistress said. 'But she moved to Epsom a couple of years ago.' She reached under the counter for a pencil. 'I'll give you her address.'

Molly groaned. 'Oh no,' she said. 'We've just come from Epsom.' She glanced at Jen. 'I can hardly ask Freddy to go back again.'

'There'd be no point anyway,' the postmistress said, handing over a slip of paper. 'Because I happen to know Mrs Rogers is away visiting her sister in Wales. She won't be back until later in the month.'

And that was that. The postmistress couldn't think of anyone else who might have known the Coogans, and in any case, Molly didn't feel she could delay Lord Freddy's picnic any longer.

She was bitterly disappointed, but oddly so was Freddy. 'Oh what a shame,' he said. 'I had hoped you would be coming back with good news. Still, at least you've got a lead and perhaps in due course this Mrs Rogers will point you in the right direction.' He smiled consolingly. 'In the meantime, we are going to enjoy ourselves. The gentleman at the bar tells me there is a fine picnic spot at a place called Box Hill; what do you say we pop down there?'

Somewhat to Molly's surprise, she did enjoy herself. For once the war seemed a long way away, and it was hard to resist Freddy's enthusiastic good humour. He had certainly pushed the boat out with his picnic, which was as sumptuous as a wartime picnic could possibly be, with smoked salmon specially sent by a friend of his from Scotland, sandwiches made with Gentleman's Relish, and choc-olate biscuits from Fortnum & Mason, all washed down with a bottle of champagne, apparently procured from his club.

Molly had never seen or tasted anything like it. Even Jen with her faddy pregnancy tastes enjoyed it, and Louise sparkled almost as much as the champagne. When they walked down to the stepping stones across the stream at the bottom of Box Hill, she even went so far as to let Lord Freddy hold her hand to steady her, even though presumably she had jumped across much more difficult obstacles during her military training.

'What do you think?' Jen whispered to Molly under cover of the throaty roar of the Alvis's engine as they headed back to London. She nodded meaningfully towards the front of the car. 'Do you think she's warming to him?'

Molly could only see the side of Louise's face, but she could tell that she was smiling with what looked like genuine amusement at something Freddy was saying. She had never been all that keen on Louise, but even she had to admit that the army had improved her. She didn't seem to be anywhere near as spoilt and stuck-up as she used to be. She had been good company today, funny and lively. She had certainly been friendly towards Lord Freddy. But whether her new-found tolerance would overcome her reservations about his florid, rather jowly puppy-dog looks was anyone's guess.

'I have no idea,' she whispered back. 'I think the sherry and the champagne might have helped. And the picnic. And the car.' She glanced quizzically at Jen. 'You're turning into a right little match-maker. Is that what happens when you get married? You want all your friends to get married too? When are you going to turn your attentions to me?'

She thought Jen would laugh, but she didn't. 'I still think you could have had Callum Frazer if you had played your cards right,' she said.

Molly was aware of a stab of pain in her heart. 'I couldn't,' she said after a moment. 'I know he was keen on me, but not that keen. Not enough to defy his parents. Reality would have kicked in sooner or later, and I couldn't bear the thought of that.'

'So what *are* you going to do?' Jen asked, grasping her armrest as Lord Freddy put his foot down coming out of a bend. She had to raise her voice over the noise of the engine.

It was a good question and one to which Molly didn't have the answer. Professor Markov had been absolutely furious when he'd heard that the medical schools had turned her down. 'This is monstrous!' he had shouted. 'But you will come about. I am sure of this. Between us we will make sure you achieve the very best marks in the examinations, and then they will be forced to reconsider.' But although Molly was grateful for his confidence, she was nowhere near as optimistic.

'God knows,' she shouted back to Jen, as the Alvis once again surged forward alarmingly.

Molly was already clinging to her own armrest for dear life. Perhaps the end would come on a sharp corner, she thought, and put her out of her misery. 'But I can tell you one thing. If we get back alive, I'm going to hold you to your promise to help with Mrs d'Arcy Billière's show.'

She needed Jen more than ever now, because, as it turned out, Graham had not stormed off after their altercation earlier in the week. On the contrary, when they next met, he had apologised, albeit rather grudgingly, and offered to write a script, which had left Molly feeling even more nervous than before.

Jen groaned. 'Oh all right,' she said. 'But I warn you, I'm not good with grumpy men, or with children. Frankly, I have very little patience with anyone at the moment.'

Helen was rapidly running out of patience too. It had taken her several days to convince Raoul that her innocent night-time stroll with Callum Frazer had been just that. She had explained countless times that Callum was the former boyfriend of a friend in London. The stupid Frenchman had even met Molly when she and Jen had taken refuge at the vineyard after escaping from Italy, but he still looked disbelieving and resentful, and in the end she had given up. It was no skin off her nose if he wanted to converse only in monosyllables, although it did make the days of waiting to cross the Rhine seem even longer and more frustrating. But at least she now knew that his grumpiness stemmed from a deep-seated concern for André.

'For God's sake,' she had said on the third morning. 'I wouldn't be prepared to risk life and limb looking for André if I was busy having an illicit affair with someone else, would I?'

But Raoul had just grunted, and she had turned away in irritation, because of course she wasn't risking life or limb.

That morning, on her suggestion, they had driven all the way down to Mannheim, where the French troops were reported to be stationed, in the hope that they would be more helpful. But after an interminable journey they found, to their dismay, that without the naval resources available to the British, or the military might of the Americans, General de Lattre de Tassigny's troops had so far found it impossible to cross the Rhine. The Germans weren't helping. Determined not to allow yet another breach of their sacred river, they were firing back so many shells at the French troops that Helen and Raoul weren't even allowed anywhere near.

That night, owing to the almost total destruction of the nearby towns, they were unable to find anywhere to stay, and for the first time Helen had to doss down in the wine van with the homing pigeons, which clucked and cooed all night, while Raoul slept under a blanket on the ground outside. They had parked by a small lake, and the only consolation was that they were able to freshen up in the morning with a quick dip in the ice-cold water.

The following day, Easter Sunday, they heard that some of General de Lattre de Tassigny's troops had finally managed to cross the river, but only in small boats under cover of darkness. Clearly there was no way the vineyard van was going to be able to get across, even if it did have plenty of tasty wine on board.

In despair, they decided to use up yet more of Raoul's dwindling supply of fuel and head back north. Perhaps by now the efficient British and American engineers might have repaired a bridge or built a usable one of their own. The problem was that without proper access to the military it was hard to get the latest news of what was happening at the front. None of the displaced German civilians who filled the roads with loaded carts and small herds of animals knew anything at all, nor did the American soldiers who were marshalling a long column of surrendered German soldiers marching west away from the river. And the information Helen managed to glean from the military units now occupying and administering the miserable towns and cities they passed through was normally already out of date.

A French military policeman in Grünstadt told her that he'd heard it was possible to cross the Rhine in Worms, which was now occupied by the Americans, but when they made their way into the shattered city, they found the promised crossing point was just a small river boat that served foot passengers only.

'*Merde.*' Raoul leaned on the steering wheel and swore under his breath. '*Quelle perte de temps.*' Resignedly he ground the van into reverse and started to back up the narrow rubble-filled street. They both knew there was no point crossing the Rhine without a vehicle.

Helen didn't blame him for his irritation. At this rate the war would be over before they crossed the blasted river. What they needed more than anything was a bit of luck, and it was at that moment that they got it, albeit in a somewhat unexpected guise.

'Wait,' Helen said as Raoul started to manoeuvre the van past a huge pile of bomb debris. 'There's a bar open over there. Let's at least treat ourselves to a cup of coffee, if they have any. Look, there are tables outside so we can keep an eye on the van. And . . .' She stopped with a gasp of astonishment.

For, emerging from the bar, with a bottle in one hand and his pith helmet in the other, was the familiar figure of Colonel Izzard-Lane.

'Good lord,' Helen said.

For a naughty second she toyed with asking Raoul to drive away before the eccentric colonel saw them, but then her better nature got the better of her, and leaving Raoul to park the van, she got out and went across.

Colonel Izzard-Lane was absolutely delighted to see her. More than delighted. After a few incoherent phrases and a violent handshake, he even went so far as to kiss her on the cheek.

'My dear girl, how lovely. What a pleasant surprise.'

Helen was touched. Hoping Raoul wasn't watching, she greeted him warmly in return.

'I would offer you a glass of wine,' the colonel said, politely holding a chair for her so she could sit down. 'But unfortunately they haven't got any. Glasses, that is. There's plenty of wine. Although I'm afraid it's rather sweet.'

Helen smiled as he sat down beside her. 'We have glasses in the van,' she said, and seeing Raoul checking the lock on the back doors, she caught his eye and called across for him to bring some over.

Colonel Izzard-Lane leaned forward eagerly. 'You have a van?' he asked. 'How marvellous. I wonder if you could give me a lift. I'm meant to be with the American Third Army but I seem to have got left behind. I managed to catch a ride with a BBC radio unit, but they rushed off earlier to cover some story about Jerry not bothering to dig bomb victims out of the rubble in Bonn and I haven't seen them since.'

Helen eyed him with affectionate exasperation. Clearly not much had changed since she last saw him. She wondered how the poor old soul had managed to get even this far.

'Well, I'm afraid we are a bit stuck too,' she prevaricated. The thought of letting the colonel loose in the back of the van with all the delicious Cabillard wine was not one she felt Raoul would relish, especially as the two of them hadn't exactly seen eye to eye on their previous encounters. She nodded down the road towards the river, where the small passenger ferry was now battling across diagonally against the current. 'With all the bridges destroyed, we can't find any way of getting the van over to the other side.'

'Oh, that's easy enough,' Colonel Izzard-Lane said casually. 'The Yanks have put up a nice little floating bridge just up the river at a place called Boppard. I know the men there. Shared a few beers with them a couple of days ago. Nice fellows. I'm sure they'll let us across.'

Sure enough, the American engineers at Boppard greeted the colonel like an old friend, and Helen could only assume that he

417

had treated them to more than just a few beers. A couple of barrels would probably be more like it. He had already admitted he found it hard to work out the value of the Allied Military deutschmarks he had been issued.

As there were only two seats at the front of the van, and they needed Colonel Izzard-Lane to sweet-talk their passage across the Rhine, Helen had been obliged to take up a position in the back among the crates of wine and the increasingly restless pigeons. It was an odd experience crossing a floating bridge without being able to see anything except the back of Colonel Izzard-Lane's slightly balding head through a small hatch behind the passenger seat. Nevertheless, as Raoul drove carefully across the narrow, wobbly pontoon, Helen felt a surge of optimism. At last they were on their way.

Unfolding her map, she spread it out across the top of the pigeons. By her calculations it was only about 250 miles from Boppard to Weimar, the town where Gefreiter Henniker had told Molly the horrible-sounding Konzentrationslager Buchenwald was situated. If they had a free run, it probably wouldn't take them more than five or six hours to get there. But of course there was not a chance in hell of a free run, because not only were the invading Allies in the way, but also whatever remained of the German army.

However bruised they felt by the breaching of the Rhine, the Nazis soon made it clear that they were intending to defend their country to the last man. Raoul had driven only ten or so miles when they came up behind the rear convoy of one of the American divisions. As they crawled slowly up and over the crest of a hill, they could see ahead of them that hundreds of troop carriers and tanks were blocking the road, and over the sound of idling engines and US forces radio they heard the distant crump of missiles.

'Jerry's got artillery in one of the forests ahead,' the driver of the vehicle in front of them said when Helen emerged from the back of the van to enquire what the hold-up was. Apart from a quick admiring glance and a sketchy salute when he saw the pips on her shoulder, he didn't seem particularly surprised at being approached by an English girl wearing FANY uniform, and Helen guessed that by this point he had seen so many different uniforms he probably never gave any of them a second glance. He lifted his shoulders in a typical American shrug and offered her a cigarette. 'Some of our boys have gone ahead to rootle him out.'

As Helen walked back to the van, Raoul wound down his window. 'It's going to take ages,' she said. 'Maybe we should go back a few miles and see if we can find somewhere to stay for the night.'

'*D'accord,*' Raoul replied. He jerked his chin towards the colonel, who was taking a quick nap in the passenger seat beside him. 'But how long do we have to keep him with us?'

How long indeed? Helen wondered with a slight groan. It was perfectly clear that the two men disliked each other, although the colonel was too polite to show it. It didn't help his cause that, still apparently unable to speak a word of French, he insisted on addressing Raoul in overloud, hearty English as though he was some mentally deficient lackey. Raoul on the other hand was not polite at all and pretended not to understand anything the older man said.

'Well, he's no trouble,' Helen said in French. 'And to be fair, he did get us across the Rhine.'

In reply, Raoul gave a hostile grunt and muttered something about not letting him get his hands on the Cabillard wine.

But an hour later, the colonel proved useful once again. When they arrived in a small town a couple of miles back the way they'd come, he at once demanded of the sentry at the checkpoint to be taken to the occupation commander, who turned out to be a rather portly American lieutenant. Unlike Raoul, the lieutenant seemed impressed by the colonel, and on his requesting accommodation for the night offered them a house recently vacated by some Nazi bigwigs.

A few minutes later, they found themselves being ushered into a spacious German family home. There were four bedrooms equipped with vast pillows and huge feather quilts, a laundry cupboard neatly stacked with brand-new sheets such as had been unseen in English homes since linen was rationed and 'make do and mend' had become the norm, a well-appointed bathroom with hot and cold running water, a surprisingly stylish kitchen, and a large *Wohnzimmer* with a beautifully framed picture of Adolf Hitler in prime position above the fireplace.

'Ha,' Colonel Izzard-Lane said happily, relaxing into a comfortable leather armchair and crossing his ankles on a footstool. 'Jolly good show. Now what do you say we crack open a bottle of that rather tasty-looking wine you have in the back of the van?'

It didn't take Molly long to regret asking Jen to help with the play.

The first group meeting to discuss it was a complete disaster. George, who had insisted on being allowed to come, kept suggesting he teach everyone magic tricks, Jen told Graham that his proposed script was boring, and Susan Voles was too much in awe of Jen to speak at all. The only thing Molly could think of to calm everyone down was to suggest they all have another think about it and meet again later in the week.

By then Molly and Susan had also agreed that Graham's script wouldn't work. 'What we need is lots of little short skits and performances, all held together by some kind of overall structure,' Molly said, and it was then that Susan suggested running it like a radio variety show, with a compère to introduce the various elements.

Jen looked dubious. 'I still think it would be dull,' she said. 'Just one stupid act after another and none of them likely to be any good.'

'Well, then why don't we make the compère be part of the play?' Molly suggested. 'Make a proper script for them and everything. Better still, why don't we have two compères and make them funny in some way?'

Jen raised her eyebrows. 'Funny? Who are you going to get to write the jokes? Graham?'

Molly giggled. 'No, I don't mean jokes. More like if the two announcers didn't like each other and kept bickering with each other in between acts.'

Jen gave a sour laugh. 'Like me and Graham the other night?' she said. 'I suppose that might work. It might even be funny. But who's going to script it?'

'We'll have to ask Graham,' Molly said. She heard Jen's groan and grimaced. 'No, I can't just ignore him, not now he's offered to help. I know he's annoying, but I'll explain exactly what we need, and whatever he comes up with we'll have to try to adapt it as tactfully,' she glared at Jen, 'as we can.'

'I don't mind asking him,' Susan piped up. 'I actually quite like him. Gino invited him to the pub the other night after his English lesson, and with a couple of drinks inside him he got quite jolly.'

Molly stared at her in astonishment. '*Jolly*? Graham?'

Jen burst out laughing. 'In that case, you'd better get some drinks inside him before you ask him to write the new script,' she said.

Molly laughed too. 'But not too many,' she added hastily, remembering what had happened with the first teacher she'd hired all those months ago.

She never found out exactly how many drinks Susan had plied Graham with, but when he presented his revised script at the second of Molly's meetings, they all agreed that it had the potential to be quite funny.

'This could work,' Jen said. 'But it will depend on who the compères are going to be.'

'I was thinking Susan and Molly,' Graham said.

'I know you were,' Jen said. 'You make that obvious in the script. But I think it would be better if it was a man and a woman. Like, for example, you and Molly.'

Molly stared at her in horror, but it was Graham who spoke first. 'Don't be ridiculous,' he said. 'I can't be in it.'

'Why not?' Jen retorted. 'What? You mean because of the wheel-chair? Well, who cares about that? You'll both be sitting down anyway, at one side of the stage. So the spotlight can be on you while we change the sets for the various acts.'

Molly blinked at her, aghast. 'Stage?' she gasped. 'Spotlights? Sets? Jen, for goodness' sake, we're not going to have all those things. We're doing it in Mrs d'Arcy Billière's drawing room.'

Jen shrugged. 'I thought you wanted to put on a decent show,' she said huffily. 'And that's why you wanted me to help.'

'Oh, but we do,' Susan chipped in at once. 'It's going to be brilliant. I'm sure we can find some lighting. I can always get the children to paint the sets.'

Molly was feeling rather faint. 'Well, it won't be brilliant if I'm in it,' she said. 'For one thing I'll never find the time to learn my words. So you'll have to be the other compère, Susan. That's all there is to it.'

Of course that wasn't all there was to it. The new format seemed to have breathed fresh life into the project, and for the next few days every time Molly arrived at Mrs d'Arcy Billière's house she found the would-be playwrights noisily discussing the proposed script in one or other of the rooms. Unable to find any peace and quiet for her studies, she eventually took refuge in the public library. Bella had had the same idea, and it was there one afternoon that Molly found herself asking the girl about the day she had recovered her voice.

She hadn't meant to bring up the subject. But in light of her recent disappointment, that odd conversation had been preying on her mind. So when she saw that the librarian was temporarily absent from her desk, she deliberately sat down at Bella's table.

Bella looked up, surprised.

'You know that day?' Molly whispered after a moment. 'When you started talking again?'

At once she saw a wary expression cross the girl's face. But she nodded slightly.

'How did you know the medical schools were going to turn me down?'

There was a long pause, during which, to Molly's dismay, the librarian loomed into view at the end of one of the bookshelves.

Bella saw her too and waited until she had moved away again. 'Sometimes I just know what's going to happen,' she murmured awkwardly. She looked at Molly for a fleeting second, then down at her book, causing Molly to marvel at the length of the girl's curling lashes. 'Mummy didn't like it,' Bella went on. 'She always told me it was wrong to say. I think she thought people would think I was mad, or a witch or something. I shouldn't even have told you, but I wasn't thinking straight that day, and . . .' Suddenly she raised her head in alarm. 'You haven't told anyone, have you?'

'Shh!' the librarian hissed from her desk.

'No, of course not,' Molly muttered. 'I wouldn't dream of it. I think that was good advice your mother gave you. Some people are so stupid, they might misunderstand.'

The combination of Bella's unfortunate parentage and her beauty already made her a talking point. The thought of what would happen locally if word got out that she could see into the future made Molly feel quite faint. In addition to all the unpleasant attention Bella already received, the poor girl would be plagued with people wanting her to predict their fortunes.

But having agreed with Bella's deceased mother, Molly now found it difficult to ask the subsidiary question. The one she really needed to know the answer to. She suddenly felt stupid herself, and wished she had never brought the subject up.

'But when you do have those thoughts,' she said tentatively, 'are you always right?' She caught the librarian's beady eye on her, and lowered her voice even more. 'I mean, does what you think always come true?'

Once again Bella threw her a brief sideways glance, and equally quickly looked away again. This time the pause was even longer. A tinge of colour crept into her cheeks.

'I know what you want to know,' she whispered eventually. 'It's what I said about you and Callum.' She nibbled her lip with dainty white teeth. 'I shouldn't have said it. I thought it was true when I said it. But now I don't know.' She looked up and her eyes were apologetic. 'Perhaps that's what my mother really meant. Perhaps talking about it makes it all go wrong.'

In the end, they stayed in the Nazi house for three nights. As Colonel Izzard-Lane pointed out, there didn't seem to be any point in struggling on at a snail's pace behind the battle when they could be whiling away the time in relative luxury in a comfortable house.

'We can catch up again when the Yanks have cleared the way forward,' he said, and proceeded to ask Helen if she knew how German washing machines worked. 'Not used to mod cons,' he said. 'Had a dhobi wallah to deal with all that kind of thing in India, don't you know.'

But Helen had no idea how to operate the washing machine either. In the end, it was Raoul who got the thing going by fitting the hoses to the taps.

To make the place even more salubrious, they turned Hitler's face to the wall, and brought in some of the provisions – including wine – from the van so they could cook up meals on the handsome stove.

The other thing they did was to release one of the homing pigeons with a message to Monsieur Cabillard telling him in the tiniest writing that they had crossed the Rhine and were slowly making their way towards Weimar.

But when they got back into the van the following day, the progress was far from slow. The Americans had pushed forward much faster than they had expected. The only thing holding them up now as they raced in hot pursuit were the Allied ambulances and empty supply vehicles coming in the opposite direction. There were also columns of captured German soldiers being marched briskly to various holding camps, and gaggles of foreign workers brought in by the Germans as slaves in their factories and now waiting helplessly for someone to tell them how to get back to their countries of origin.

But there was no one to tell them anything. The front line had moved on too swiftly. By the time the Cabillard wine van caught up with the rear echelons of the American Third Army, they had already taken Kassel and were moving on towards Leipzig. And it was on the road to Leipzig that Helen stumbled across the American intelligence officer she had worked with in France the previous year. A temporary Third Army HQ camp was being set up by the side of a wide highway, and in the general melee Helen and Colonel Izzard-Lane were able to walk right in past the guards. Helen spotted the officer carrying a cup of something out of a mess tent.

He recognised her at once. 'Wow,' he said. 'What are you doing here?'

'I'm still trying to find my fiancé,' Helen said. 'André Cabillard. I have reason to believe he is in Buchenwald concentration camp, near Weimar, which isn't all that far from here.'

The intelligence officer's brows snapped together. 'How in God's name do you know that?'

'It's a long story,' she said. 'But what I need to know is, are any troops being sent in that direction? I need to get there as soon as possible. It's what the Nazis call a death camp, you know, people are being killed there all the time.'

He looked at her through narrowed eyes. 'I know,' he said slowly. 'Some of our boys came across a similar place further north. At Ohrdorf. I can't even begin to tell you what horrors they found there.'

Helen tried to suppress a shudder. 'Please tell me you are sending troops to Weimar.'

He lifted his shoulders. 'Some of the 9th Armoured Division guys are heading that way. But the Nazis are putting up stiff resistance. It's going to take our boys a while to get there.'

That night the colonel found a billet in the camp, Helen slept in the van and Raoul once again slept on the ground under a tarpaulin. The following morning they hung around the camp waiting for news.

It came just after midday.

Helen was sitting on an empty jerrycan, staring restlessly at the canvas door of the HQ map tent, wondering if they would murder her if she went over yet again to ask about progress, when the flap swung open and the intelligence officer emerged.

Even from that distance she could see that his face looked grim, and she felt her hands go suddenly cold and clammy even as her heart started pounding in her chest. Her legs suddenly felt so weak, she could barely stand up.

'What is it?' she asked breathlessly as he approached. 'What's happened?'

The officer clamped his teeth for a moment. 'We just picked up a Morse message from Buchenwald. Sounded like one of the prisoners has fixed up some kind of ham radio transmitter.'

'What did it say?' Helen asked.

He took a long breath. 'Are you sure you want to know?' Slowly he took a piece of paper from his jacket pocket. '"To the Allies",' he read. '"To the army of General Patton. This is the Buchenwald concentration camp. SOS. We request help. The SS wants to destroy us."' He looked up and winced slightly at her expression. 'The text was repeated several times, in English, German and Russian.'

'Oh my God,' Helen whispered. 'Were you able to reply?'

The officer nodded and glanced down at his notes. 'We sent this a few moments ago. "KZ Buchenwald. Hold out. Rushing to your aid. Staff of Third Army."'

Chapter Twenty-Five

'I'm afraid I have some bad news for you, Miss Coogan,' Mr Sparrow said. 'Now that the bombing has stopped, it has been decided the local Red Cross posts are surplus to requirements.'

Molly was in the middle of rolling bandages. 'So what does that mean for us?' she asked.

'It means we are being disbanded. I have been instructed to give you six weeks' notice.'

As Molly stared at him in horror, the bandage she had been holding slipped from her fingers. Numbly she watched it unravel as it rolled away over the concrete floor.

'Oh no,' she whispered. 'Surely they can't do that. What about the hospital trains? Won't they still need nurses for those?' But then she realised they wouldn't. When the war was won, there wouldn't be any need for hospital trains either.

'It's all right for you,' Mr Sparrow said crossly. 'You're a trained nurse. You can get a job back at the Wilhelmina. But what am I going to do?'

Molly closed her eyes. She knew he was right. But she didn't want to go back to full-time nursing. She didn't want to be back on the wards at the beck and call of the horrible nursing sisters. She had wanted more than that.

It was with a heavy heart that she called at the pub on her way home later that afternoon. Ward Frazer had finally set off on a

SAARF mission to Germany the previous day, and she suspected that Katy would need moral support. If not, she was certainly in need of some herself.

But to her surprise when she pushed open the door she found Katy brimming over with excitement.

'You'll never guess what's happened,' she said as soon as she caught sight of Molly pushing through the blackout curtain. 'Mrs d'Arcy Billière has just been in and . . .' She stopped and put a hand to her cheek. 'I can hardly believe it. Lord de Burrel has asked her to marry him. I had no idea, did you? Apparently she's intending to move to America with him after the war and she came in to ask if Ward and I would be interested in buying her house.'

It was so sudden, Molly couldn't quite take it in. 'But what about Aaref and Elsa and—'

'Well, they'll come here,' Katy interrupted eagerly. 'That's why it's so perfect.' But then she paused, and sobered. 'Well, that's assuming that Mr Rutherford agrees. I wrote to him last week explaining the situation, but I haven't heard back yet.'

Before Molly could respond, Malcolm came running into the bar from the back yard, with Lucky in hot pursuit. 'Mummy says we're going to live in Mrs d'Arcy Billière's house,' he shouted at Molly as he raced past her towards the playpen where Caroline was currently ensconced. 'I love Mrs d'Arcy Billière's house. I specially love the big table and the pergiola in the garden. And Lucky will love it too.'

Molly caught Katy's eye and laughed. 'Then let's hope Mr Rutherford gives you the go-ahead,' she said.

But he didn't. Two days later, Katy received a curt note from the property agent at the Rutherford and Berry brewery saying that transfers of title were only allowed with the permission of the brewery and in this case that permission had been refused. The terms of the lease were quite specific. As no break clause had been written into the contract, as far as the brewery was concerned there was still two years to run.

'But why would he be so mean?' Molly said when she heard the news.

Katy made a face. 'I asked Louise that, and she said he's been grumpy ever since the Home Guard was disbanded. He loved lording it about as the local commander.' She hesitated. 'She also thinks it's because Aaref and Elsa are Jewish.' Taking a cloth, she wiped the counter angrily. 'If it's true, it makes you wonder what we've been fighting for, doesn't it? All this talk of tolerance and equality, and when it comes down to something like this, it turns out we're no better than the Nazis.'

She was clearly bitterly disappointed.

'Can't Louise persuade him to change his mind?' Molly asked.

Katy shook her head. 'She's already tried,' she wailed. 'So has Alan Nelson. I even asked Joyce to ask Mrs Rutherford about it, but it was no good. Apparently Mr Rutherford is determined to hold me to the contract, and that's that. I know it's nothing in the big scheme of things, the war and all that, but I've been a good tenant all these years, and this is the first thing I've ever asked him for.'

Molly heard the despondency in her voice and wished she could help in some way. It had all seemed so perfect. Such a good solution. There would have been room in Mrs d'Arcy Billière's house for Katy's mother, and maybe even Ward's aunts too. Now they were all back at square one. 'It's a shame we didn't know last weekend when Lord Freddy was here,' she said. 'We could have arranged for him to run Mr Rutherford over with the Alvis.'

'If only,' Katy said with a weak smile. 'If Ward was here he'd probably put a bullet in the back of the blasted man's head.'

But Ward wasn't there, and for all they knew, he might even at that moment be jumping out of a plane somewhere behind the Nazi front line. And that made it all seem much worse.

The city of Weimar surrendered to the Americans on 12 April, but it took two more days for troops to reach Buchenwald.

Helen and Raoul arrived there on the 15th, in the wake of the 80th Infantry Division, who had been tasked with taking over the administration of the camp.

Helen's first glimpse of the *Konzentrationslager* sent shivers up her spine. There was something awful about the perfection of the barbed-wire fence that ran round the perimeter of the camp. At least fifteen feet high, it was obvious that no expense had been spared in its design or construction. Each one of the thirty or so taut, vicious strands was perfectly aligned to the wires above and below, and every one was fixed to the high angled concrete posts with meticulous precision. Tall, sinister watchtowers were dotted along inside the fence leading to the Bauhaus-style entrance. It all added up to an impression of ruthless German efficiency.

But inside the camp, it was very different. The first thing that hit her was the smell. A horrible, evil odour of putrid flesh and ordure, a ghastly, almost zoo-like stench that seemed to stick to her skin.

Helen had tried to imagine what the interior of a concentration camp would be like, but it hadn't been anything like this. She hadn't imagined that she would see hundreds of naked corpses stacked outside the crematorium because in the last few days the camp had run out of fuel. Nor had she imagined the ghastly living throng of pitifully skeletal figures, with sunken eyes and shaven heads. Mostly barefoot, some were wearing remnants of tattered uniforms; others were clad in obscene striped pyjamas. All were clearly in need of urgent medical attention.

Those were just the ones able to walk. Despite the best efforts of the military medical teams who were now pouring into the camp, thousands more prisoners, too weak even to lift their heads to greet their liberators, were still crammed in overcrowded accommodation huts in unbelievably unsanitary conditions. One building, a stable that would previously have housed perhaps eighty horses, had been home to 1,200 men, five to a bunk.

Helen quickly realised that the only way she could cope was not to look. Not to think. To try to prevent the horrors around her becoming part of her. She even found herself trying not to breathe. But she knew the things she saw that first day would haunt her for ever more.

She heard an American sergeant briefing a platoon of young soldiers just outside the gates.

'Remember this,' he shouted at them. 'Whatever state they are in now, the people inside this camp are still human beings. The Nazis seem to have forgotten that. But don't you forget it. Whoever the prisoners are — political dissenters, foreign agents, politicians, Jews, intellectuals, gypsies, homosexuals, communists, women — they are all people, and they all have hopes and dreams and feelings like anyone else.'

Helen couldn't fault the American soldiers for their efficiency or their compassion. Many of them were younger than her, and she could see the shock and disbelief on their faces. It was obvious that whatever they had witnessed in battle paled into insignificance compared to this hellish place.

'It's beyond comprehension,' the intelligence officer said as he led her and Raoul across to the former camp offices. Even he looked shaken. 'According to the documents the SS left behind in their rush to get away, at least thirty-five thousand people have been systematically killed here over the last few years.'

Helen was conscious of feeling numb. He was right. It was impossible to take in death on such a scale. But sickened and appalled as she felt, the only thing she really wanted to know was if André was still there somewhere.

She already knew that some of the prisoners had been forcibly marched away by the SS guards, but when the radio message from the Americans had been received, another group of inmates had stormed the watchtowers, killing the remaining guards with a motley selection of weapons they had secretly been assembling for the purpose. As a result, the Nazis had failed to complete the evacuation, and Helen was hopeful that André, if he was alive, would still be in the camp.

But the intelligence officer shook his head. 'He definitely *was* here,' he said. He hesitated, then pushed a neatly annotated document across the table. 'We know that because his name is on this week's

431

list for execution.' He heard Helen's gasp. 'But he's not listed as having been killed. Yet nor is he here, I'm sure of that. We've announced his name several times over the megaphone, and surely he would have come forward by now. I'm afraid he must have been one of the men marched away.'

But they soon discovered that wasn't the case. It was Raoul who found out. Somehow he managed to seek out the men who had overthrown the guards. Neither he nor Helen were surprised to learn that André had been one of the instigators. But according to one of his former comrades-in-arms, as soon as the insurrection was over, André had left the camp.

Helen stared at Raoul's informant in dismay. The man was a Russian, speaking in German, and for a moment she thought she had misunderstood. 'Left?' she said. 'But he knew the Americans were so close . . .'

The Russian shrugged his emaciated shoulders. 'On the day we sent the radio message, there was an SS officer visiting the camp. André knew this man from before. It was this man who put his name on the list for execution. We tried to kill him, but he escaped.'

'I don't believe it,' Helen whispered. But she could see from the man's angry, glittering eyes that he was telling the truth.

'Are you telling me André has gone off after him?' she said. She glanced out of the window at the throng of pitiful humanity outside. 'But how on earth . . .?'

'We broke into the stores,' he said. 'He took clothes and shoes. And money.'

'What about transport?'

For the first time since coming into the office, the man smiled, showing a set of gruesome blackened teeth. 'By this time, the SS were in a hurry,' he said. 'They destroyed the vehicles they left behind them, but there was a motorbike in the repair shop. We fixed it up, and André took that.'

'But where has he gone?' Helen asked.

The Russian shrugged again. 'This I do not know. You must

understand. It was all so quick. Somewhat chaos, yes?' He waved a bony hand towards the window. 'So many people. One minute he is there, and the next he is gone.'

'I can imagine,' Helen said drily. She glanced at Raoul and knew that he had understood what the Russian had said. But she could also see the relief in his eyes, and realised that, even though the news was frustrating, it meant André was alive. Or at least that he had been four days ago. Not just alive; clearly in sufficient health to speed away on a stolen motorcycle.

Suddenly, unexpectedly, she felt her knees start to shake.

At once she felt Raoul's hand under her elbow. '*Eh bien*,' he said. 'We will find him.'

She looked at him gratefully and took a steadying breath. 'But how? We have no idea where he might have gone. And what if SS Hauptsturmführer Wessel finds out that André's after him.'

'He knows this already,' the Russian chipped in helpfully. 'André shouted it to him through the wire as the SS drove away.'

'Oh my God,' Helen said.

The intelligence officer frowned. 'We have a few of the SS guards in custody,' he said. 'They are not in great shape, but I guess we can ask them if they know where Wessel might have gone.'

But despite the beatings they had received from the prisoners, or perhaps because of them, or due to some other misplaced loyalty, the captured guards claimed they had no idea where Hauptsturmführer Wessel might have gone. One of them, a young SS officer with fractured ribs and a recently broken nose, refused to speak at all, merely clicking his heels and holding his arm up painfully in the Nazi salute.

'You leave me alone with him a few minutes,' the Russian suggested darkly. '*Svolochnie niemtsy*. I make him talk, yes?'

'No,' the intelligence officer said. 'I can't allow that. Not that I'm not tempted. But we have to prove that we are better than them.'

'Where would you go?' Helen asked. 'If the situation was reversed?'

The intelligence officer thought about it. 'I guess I'd go home,' he said. 'Wessel surely knows that the game is up, and my guess is that he'll go home to collect some things. He may have a wife and children, for all we know. And then he'll disappear.' He took a breath and blew air out from his cheeks. 'Or maybe not. I guess there are going to be plenty of German soldiers who just slip quietly back into civilian life. Wessel may feel he's covered his tracks sufficiently to make any accusation of war crimes untenable.'

Helen gritted her teeth. 'So the first thing we need to do is find out his home address.'

But the Buchenwald guards were equally unwilling to divulge that information, even if they knew it. In the end, Helen realised that there was only one course of action open to her. Somehow, and goodness only knew how, she was going to have to get a message to Molly. There was a remote possibility that Gefreiter Henniker might know where Hauptsturmführer Wessel hailed from. Even if he didn't, he might be able to find out.

Jen was glad she had made the decision to move back to Clapham. She was even glad she had offered to help with Molly's show. She found she was rather enjoying putting her new-found RADA knowledge into practice. After a rocky start, the production was beginning to shape up quite well. What with trying to find all the props and other bits and pieces she needed, she hardly had time to worry about Henry. It also took her mind off the baby and her disappointment about giving up RADA. It also stopped her tearing her hair out with all the constant speculation about the progress of the war.

Things were moving so fast now, it was actually quite hard to keep up with which German cities had or hadn't fallen to the Allies. The Germans had finally been cleared out of Holland, and the French were busy fighting for Stuttgart. On the Eastern Front, the Soviet army had not only liberated Vienna, but were already beginning an assault on Berlin.

Now, among it all, poor old President Roosevelt had died, and the residents of Mrs d'Arcy Billière's house were worried that Winston

Churchill would go the funeral and leave the country unattended just at the crucial moment.

But Lord de Burrel, now a regular guest at dinner, was able to reassure them. 'Good lord, no,' he said eyeing a radish on his fork with some surprise. It clearly wasn't something he expected to find in a chicken stew. 'Winnie's decided to stay put. Reckons he can't afford to turn his back in case that bugger Stalin snaffles the whole of Germany, as well as Poland and Romania and all the other countries he's got his greedy little fingers on already.' He laughed sourly and pushed the radish discreetly to one side of his plate. 'Anyway, between ourselves, Winnie had rather taken against Roosevelt recently. Thought he was putting too much faith in Stalin's promises.'

'He was,' Mrs d'Arcy Billière said. 'And now Europe will pay the price.' She picked up the ladle and waved it in her future husband's direction. 'More stew?'

'No, no.' Lord de Burrel shook his head rather urgently. 'Absolutely delicious, though.' Catching Jen's eye on him, he gave her a quick, sly wink before turning his attention back to his intended. 'I must give the recipe to my housekeeper in Washington when I get back.'

'I didn't know you were going back to America so soon,' Jen said. 'I hoped you'd still be here for Molly's show.'

Lord de Burrel looked a bit dubious and she guessed amateur dramatics were not his thing. But before he could think of an excuse, Mrs d'Arcy Billière leaned across and put a possessive hand on his arm. 'Of course you will,' she said. 'It is your chance to meet all my friends. I am inviting everyone I know.'

Oh lord, Jen thought. She had understood from Molly that their audience was going to be an intimate gathering, easily able to fit in the drawing room. Now it sounded as though they would have to pray for good weather and put the damn thing on in the garden, and goodness only knew where they were going to get enough lighting for that.

Molly was at the café when Helen's telegram arrived. Luckily she had told George where she was going, and he took the opportunity of accompanying the post girl, clearly agog to know what it contained.

'Oh my goodness,' Molly said.

'What does it say?' George asked.

She pushed it over to him.

'"MOST URGENT stop",' he read out. '"Need Wessel home address stop Pls ask Henniker stop Respond plus description asap stop Send response c/o Colonal Izzard-Lane stop Thnx Helen."'

'What does it mean?' he asked, looking up, puzzled.

Molly took a breath. 'It means I'm going to have to go to the POW camp in Tonbridge tomorrow, to see if Gefreiter Henniker knows where SS Hauptsturmführer Wessel lives in Germany.'

George frowned. 'But I thought we were going to Epsom to find the lady who knew your father.'

Molly groaned. She had promised to take George with her to Epsom. He had been pretty good recently, and she thought he deserved a treat. She remembered the beneficial effect he had had on the woman at the church in Marylebone, and thought his angelic looks and innocent winsome smile might also help in her attempt to elicit information from the as-yet-unknown Mrs Rogers.

'We were,' she said. 'But we won't be able to now. This is much more urgent, although I can't imagine why Helen needs Wessel's address. And why doesn't she say whether she's found André?'

'Perhaps SS whatever-he-is Wessel killed André, and now Helen's going there to kill him,' George suggested. 'Or maybe—'

But Molly didn't want to hear any more. 'George, for goodness' sake shut up,' she said sharply.

He grinned. 'All right. But only if I can come to the POW camp with you.'

'No,' Molly said at once. 'It's out of the question.'

'Pleease, Molly,' he wheedled. 'I've never met a German person. I've never even seen one properly. Only in films. And I did bring you the telegram.'

Unable to resist that smile, Molly felt herself weakening. 'Oh, all right then. But I warn you, seeing one is the nearest you are likely to get. There's no way Major Withers is going to let a precocious, bloodthirsty brat like you loose on any of his prisoners.'

Actually, perhaps inevitably, it didn't take George long to win over Major Withers. The camp commander had looked mildly surprised at Molly's unscheduled appearance, and even more so that she had seen fit to bring a schoolboy with her, but it didn't stop him inviting them both into his office. Clearly awed by his upper-class accent and languid demeanour, at first George was unusually shy and polite. He even, on Molly's stern instruction, managed to avoid looking too closely at the major's empty sleeve. But when the tea and biscuits were brought into the office, he was unable to hide his excitement.

'Ha,' Major Withers said. 'So you like ginger nuts too, do you?'

'Yes, sir,' George responded promptly. He gave Major Withers his most appealing smile. 'Especially if I'm allowed to dunk them in my tea.' And that of course got them off to an excellent start. The only problem was that Gefreiter Henniker wasn't at the camp.

'Gone off on a work detail,' Major Withers said. 'If you'd let me know you were coming, I'd have held him back.' He glanced at the watch on his good arm. 'But they're due back any time now, so if you'd like to wait here, I'll leave a message at the guardroom for the lieutenant who's escorting them.' He looked speculatively at George. 'I daresay Miss Coogan will want to talk to him alone, so what do you say we take a tour of the camp in the meantime and I'll introduce you to one or two of the prisoners? Have you ever met a German?'

'No, sir,' George said, sliding a gleeful glance at Molly. 'But I'd very much like to. As long as they don't try to kill me.'

Major Withers laughed. 'Not much danger of that. Not here, at least. God knows what they might have got up to if they'd met you on the battlefield. But no, whether they like it or not, the war's over for these chaps, and I think you'll find they are perfectly decent fellows.'

George looked extremely doubtful about that, but he went off quite happily and, glancing out of the window a few minutes later, Molly saw them entering the first compound deep in conversation.

She didn't hear the prisoners' transport come back. So the first she knew of the return of Gefreiter Henniker to the camp was when someone knocked on the door of the office.

The door opened and a young officer came in and saluted sharply. 'We're back, sir, and the prisoner you requested is waiting for your visitor in the . . .'

Suddenly becoming aware that his commanding officer wasn't in the room, he stopped abruptly with an incoherent gurgle of shock. Molly, for her part, burst into astonished laughter.

For standing there, looking as if he wished the ground would open up and swallow him whole, was Douglas Rutherford.

Molly was the first to recover. 'Oh,' she said. 'What a surprise.' Making no effort to hide her gleeful amusement, she raised her eyebrows. 'So this is the highly dangerous top-secret job your parents are so proud of you doing?'

Douglas's mouth opened and closed a few times, but he seemed unable to respond. His face was scarlet now.

'Oh dear,' Molly said. 'Cat got your tongue?' She stood up. 'Well, in that case, if it's not too dangerous for you, perhaps you would escort me to see Gefreiter Henniker.'

Douglas's eyes were almost popping out of his head. 'But what are you doing here?' he stuttered. 'Why . . .?'

But Molly just smiled sweetly as she brushed past him in the doorway. 'I'm afraid I can't tell you why I need to see him,' she said. 'It's rather confidential.'

Douglas didn't move. He seemed to be rooted to the floor.

'It's also rather urgent,' Molly added sharply. 'So I'd appreciate it if you'd put your obvious dismay about being caught out in a bare-faced lie to one side and take me to him right now.'

There were quite a few military personnel milling about in the compound outside, and that prevented Douglas from speaking. But

438

as they approached the interview hut, he stopped suddenly and took her arm.

'It's not what you think,' he muttered. 'I wanted to fight. I really did. It's not my fault I got sent here instead.'

There was so much sincerity in his voice, Molly almost felt sorry for him, but not quite.

'I'm not blaming you for not fighting,' she said. 'But I am blaming you for spinning a pack of lies.' She laughed sourly. 'Not that anyone believed you. Generally people who do top-secret work, like your sister, for example, don't feel the need to blab it all around the local pub.'

He had the grace to flush. 'Molly, listen . . .' he began as she moved impatiently away towards the interview hut.

'Listen?' she said incredulously. 'Why should I listen? In fact, after this, I'm never going to listen to you again.'

'Please,' he said. 'Promise me you won't tell anyone. I only did it because my father kept asking when I was going to have a chance to fight. He was desperate for me to get a combat medal, and it was driving me mad, and—'

But Molly was bored of him now. 'Oh for goodness' sake,' she said. It was on the tip of her tongue to tell him that his secret was safe with her, when an idea occurred to her.

'All right,' she said. 'I won't tell anyone, but only if you do something in return for me.'

He looked suddenly suspicious. 'What?'

'Katy wants to hand over the Flag and Garter to Aaref Hoch and his wife,' she said. 'But your father refuses to amend the lease. However, for some mad reason, he thinks the world of you. So if you can persuade him to change his mind, then I promise not to spill the beans.'

Douglas spluttered. 'That's downright blackmail,' he said.

Molly shrugged. 'It's up to you. That's the deal. Take it or leave it.'

He was silent, and she raised her eyebrows. 'Oh, all right,' he said angrily. 'I'll have a go. But you must know that my father isn't an easy man. For all I know, he'll fly into a pet.'

Molly looked at him. 'Having a go isn't good enough,' she said.

'There's a war on, you know. And that means that from time to time people are expected to show a bit of guts and resilience.' With that, she pushed open the door of the interview hut.

Gefreiter Henniker was waiting for her in the usual room. Buoyed up by her encounter with Douglas, Molly greeted him warmly. The German looked surprised, and she remembered that they had not parted on very good terms last time.

'How are you?' she asked. 'I hope they are treating you as well as possible.'

He gave a slightly twisted smile. 'For a prison camp, is not so bad,' he said. 'The other men are OK. And now I work a little, it, how you say, relieves the boredom.'

Molly nodded. Working in the medical room at the prison camp in Italy had certainly relieved the boredom there.

'Good,' she said. 'I am glad that you are happier here, because I need another favour.'

But he had no idea where in Germany SS Hauptsturmführer Wessel came from.

Molly was disappointed. 'Can't you tell from his accent?' she said suddenly. 'Like I could if someone was Glaswegian or Liverpudlian.'

Gefreiter Henniker thought about it. 'I only heard him speaking a few times,' he said. 'Like many officers, he always used what we call Hoch Deutsch. Proper German. But even so, I would say he came from the north. Even Hoch Deutsch speakers from the south sometimes use a local word from perhaps Swabian or Bavarian. I never heard that.'

Molly nodded encouragingly. That wasn't going to be much use to Helen. But at least he was trying to help. She just needed him to do a bit more. 'Would anyone else know?' she asked. 'Anyone else here in the camp? Your friend who worked on the trains, perhaps?'

For a moment, as his gaze dropped away from hers, she thought he was going to refuse. But then he looked up again. 'It is important, yes?'

'Yes,' Molly said. 'My friend, the girl you met before – André Cabillard's fiancée – is in Germany now. She sent me a telegram yesterday asking me to find out. I think it must be very important.'

He inclined his head. 'Then I will try to find out.'

Molly heaved a sigh of relief. 'Thank you.' She looked at him eagerly. 'How soon do you think . . .?'

'It may take a small while,' he said. 'Some men are out of camp working.'

'OK, but if you find out something, you must give the information to Major Withers.'

But now he looked reluctant. 'I would rather give it to you,' he said. He gave a sudden awkward smile. 'I enjoy when you come to see me. I don't know how to say, but you make like a small light in my life.'

Ridiculously, Molly felt herself colouring. 'Gefreiter Henniker, I . . .' she began.

But he held up his hand. 'I do not mean romantic. I know is impossible,' he said, and now he was flushing too. 'I never ask, but I am expecting that you already have very nice boyfriend, yes? I hope so, because a girl like you, you deserve the very best.' He smiled self-consciously. 'But I wish you to know that you have made me think. Perhaps even to be a better man. You have shown me that there is still possibility for kindness in this dark world. And for this I am grateful.'

Molly felt unexpectedly choked. She had no idea how to respond. All she could do was stand up and offer her hand. 'Thank you,' she said, smiling nervously as he grasped it warmly in his own. 'I have enjoyed our meetings too. I am very grateful for your help.'

Gefreiter Henniker nodded. 'You know, we were always taught in Germany that our misfortunes were the fault of someone else, Jews, communists, foreigners. I now understand that this is not the case. It is our arrogance that has caused our downfall.' He released her hand and clicked his heels. 'I hope perhaps we meet again one day, Fräulein Molly. Also please to tell me if you succeed to find your friend Cabillard. I would like to know this.'

Outside in the yard, Molly found George and Major Withers waiting for her. There was no sign of Douglas and, thinking how awkward it would be if George caught sight of him, she quickly started saying her goodbyes.

But George had other ideas. 'We can't go yet,' he said. 'Not until Major Withers gives us the light.'

Molly's mind was still on Gefreiter Henniker. She stared at George blankly. 'What are you talking about? What light?'

'For our show,' George said eagerly. 'I told him all about it, how we were going to have to do it outside because Mrs d'Arcy Billière had invited so many people, and . . .' He glanced anxiously at Major Withers. 'You did say we could borrow one, didn't you, sir?'

Major Withers saw Molly's astonished expression and laughed. He gestured airily around the line of watchtowers that surrounded the camp. 'Well, the one thing we aren't short of is floodlights,' he said. 'I'm sure we can spare one or two for a good cause.'

Half an hour later, Molly and George found themselves sitting on the train in the company of two enormous spot lamps. They were so large they took up the entire seat opposite.

'I did well, didn't I?' George said, eyeing them with smug satisfaction.

Molly nodded. 'You certainly did.' Although she couldn't quite imagine how they were going to lug the lights from Clapham Junction station all the way up to Lavender Road.

'So, did you enjoy the visit?' she asked, settling back in her seat.

'Oh yes,' George said at once. 'Thank you so much for taking me.'

She had been ready to return to her own thoughts, but there was something in his voice that made her look at him more closely. She realised he was fidgeting with suppressed excitement, rather more than the procurement of the lamps perhaps warranted, and she eyed him uneasily.

'The German prisoners weren't scary at all,' he said. 'They were just like normal people.' For a second he sounded a bit disappointed, but then he produced a small carved animal from his pocket. 'Look. One of them gave me this. I'm going to give it to Malcolm because it looks a bit like Lucky.'

Dutifully Molly took the carved dog. But even as she admired it, she could sense George's mind was elsewhere.

'Did you see anyone else?' she asked suspiciously as she handed it back. 'Apart from Germans.'

George put the dog back in his pocket. 'I saw some guards,' he said. He gave her a bright smile. 'One of the staff sergeants taught me how to do an about-turn.'

But Molly knew that wide-eyed innocent expression too well.

'George?' she said threateningly. 'Tell me who you saw.'

'Oh, all right,' he said. 'I saw Douglas Rutherford.' He gave an unruly giggle. 'I'd already seen him talking to you, but I thought he was going to have a fit when he saw me. Major Withers thought it was funny that we knew each other. But Douglas didn't. He got me alone a bit later and made me promise not to tell anyone in Lavender Road that I'd seen him.'

'And did you promise?'

George nodded. 'Yes, I did. But only because he told me you had. And only after I'd made him promise me something first.'

Molly frowned. This was sounding unnervingly familiar. 'What did you make him promise?'

'I told him the only thing that would stop me telling was if he made his father give Dad a pay rise,' he said. 'Because then I might be able to go to a proper school.'

Molly choked. 'That's blackmail,' she said.

'I know,' George said happily. He sat back in his seat, clearly feeling that he had had a very satisfactory day.

Molly eyed him sternly. 'Then you'd better make sure you don't tell anyone,' she said.

George looked incensed. 'Of course I won't.'

'But you've just told me,' Molly pointed out.

He giggled. 'Oh well, you don't count. You knew anyway.' He looked at her fiercely. 'Don't you dare tell anyone either. Otherwise my blackmail won't work.'

Chapter Twenty-Six

'Molly!'

Molly blinked as Professor Markov's irritable voice cut through her thoughts. 'Why don't you concentrate?' He glared at her from under his bushy eyebrows. 'It is the show, no? I wish it had never been suggested. Everyone talk show, show, show, and nobody concentrate on what I teach. As far as I'm concerned, the sooner it's over and done with, the better.'

Molly rather agreed with him. Preparations for the forthcoming entertainment were taking up far too much of her time. What with Mrs d'Arcy Billière adding extra people to her invitation list, Jen now proposing an outdoor production in the garden, Graham constantly wanting her to read his revised script, and Gino suggesting he and Angie serve ice cream in the interval, she barely had a moment to think about anything, let alone her studies.

Nevertheless, she felt bad for letting her attention wander. It was very rare that Professor Markov got annoyed with her. But he was right, she hadn't been concentrating. Although on this occasion, it hadn't been the show that had distracted her, but the fact that she had as yet received no message from Major Withers, and she was beginning to worry that Gefreiter Henniker had been unable or unwilling to help after all.

'I'm sorry,' she said. 'It's just that . . .'

Hearing someone running up the steps to the front door, she

paused mid sentence. The next moment, George burst into the room.

'A letter's just come,' he gasped, thrusting an envelope into her hand. 'And it's military post.'

Ignoring the professor's gasp of outrage, Molly ripped it open.

Your man has come up with an address for the SS officer. You'll see it's in Hamelin, which seems appropriate since, as I recall from my childhood, that is where the Pied Piper's rats came from. He also remembers that the fellow is left handed, although why you might need to know that I can't imagine.

Best regards to you and your young friend. Nice little chap, I thought.

Yours,

Withers

She stood up abruptly. 'I'm sorry, Professor,' she said. 'I'm afraid we'll have to abandon the lesson. I've got to go to the post office.'

The professor looked shocked. 'Well,' he huffed angrily. 'Really, it's too much . . .'

'Perhaps I can stand in for her,' George said eagerly. 'I was doing my homework and I got stuck, and I want you to explain how to . . .'

But Molly didn't hear what he wanted the professor to explain, because she had left the room and was already running off down Lavender Road.

In Germany, the military situation was changing rapidly. In some places Wehrmacht troops had taken up tough defensive positions; in others they were surrendering in droves. There was fierce fighting to the east around Leipzig, and to the north of Buchenwald in the Harz mountains. As a result, the Allied divisional HQs kept moving, which made Helen concerned that Molly's response to her message might not get through, even though she had Colonel Izzard-Lane standing by in Weimar to receive it.

445

In the meantime, she and Raoul went back to Buchenwald to offer what assistance they could. There was so much to be done, so many wretched people needing help. Not just men. Women and children too. Some pitiful little babies had even been born there. Although it was also a horrible truth that many of the former prisoners were beyond help. Already in the last stages of disease and malnutrition, more than four hundred of them had died since the camp had been liberated.

Because she had no official status, to Helen's secret relief she was not allowed to help with the dead or dying. Instead, while Raoul was set to assist in the building of new medical huts, she was given another job altogether.

One of the most shocking things about Weimar was that the local population denied all knowledge of the camp. According to them, they had never heard of such a thing as a *Konzentrationslager*. Even the men and women tending the lush rolling fields within view of the place claimed to have had no idea what was going behind the menacing barbed-wire fence.

Their casual indifference had infuriated General Patton when he visited the camp, so much so that he had left orders that a couple of thousand local residents, of all ages and sexes, should be brought in to see what had been going on right on their doorstep. Helen's language skills meant that she was one of the people given the unpleasant task of showing the unwilling visitors around.

Things had been cleared up a bit by now. There were no piles of pitifully emaciated corpses waiting for fuel to feed the incinerator, the only smoke now was coming from the burning of the prisoners' lice-infested clothes. The bodies hanging on the whipping stalls were no longer human beings, but dummies made of sacking. Nor were there any prisoners literally dying at their feet. Nevertheless, Helen could see the shock and distress on some of the German visitors' faces when she tried to recount what she had seen on that dreadful first day. Others made her blood boil by refusing to look or listen.

A few even went so far as to imply that the whole thing had been set up as some kind of elaborate Allied propaganda.

Loathing her new role, and increasingly anxious about André, she was heartily relieved when two days later Colonel Izzard-Lane appeared at the camp bearing Molly's response to her telegram. The colonel had refused to set foot in the *Konzentrationslager* previously, claiming he wasn't good with illness, or indeed starvation. 'Saw too much of it in India, don't you know.' But thankfully, on this occasion he'd put his aversion to one side.

'Had a devil of a job getting someone to bring me,' he complained. 'All the transport is busy taking people up to the front.'

He looked even more disgruntled when Helen, having had an urgent consultation with Raoul, told him that she and the Frenchman were going to leave for Hamelin that very afternoon.

'But what about me?' he said, his moustache bristling in horror. 'You can't leave me here.'

'Well, we can't very well take you with us,' Helen said. 'Surely you need to get to the front?'

But the colonel seemed dubious about that. 'No,' he said. 'I think on balance I'd be more use coming with you. Much more fun too, probably.'

Catching Raoul's horrified expression, Helen tactfully tried to dissuade him, but the more she tried, the keener he seemed.

'*Non*,' Raoul insisted angrily in French when he saw her begin to weaken. 'The last thing we need is to carry this imbecile with us.'

But Helen was beginning to wonder if having a colonel with them might actually come in handy. She hadn't forgotten the ease with which he'd rustled up accommodation on their earlier journey.

An hour later, having collected the colonel's trunk from his comfortable lodging in Weimar, they set off, with Raoul driving, Helen map-reading and Izzard-Lane perched on a box in the back of the van in the company of the two remaining pigeons.

'*Merde*,' Raoul had muttered as he slammed the door on him. '*Quel idiot!*'

447

But Helen's faith in the colonel was vindicated when, after a slow journey through a countryside of wooded hills and wide fertile plains, criss-crossed by long Allied supply convoys and dotted with distant fairy-tale castles and tiny jewel-like villages, they arrived in Hamelin.

Expecting the town to have suffered almost total devastation like so many of those they had passed through since arriving in Germany, they were surprised to find it intact, with almost no sign of bomb damage at all. On the contrary, the quaint narrow streets and wooden-framed houses with their pastel plasterwork looked as though they had come straight out of a children's picture book, although the pretty little town seemed far too clean and neat to harbour anything as grubby as a rat. If it wasn't for the resentful expressions on the citizens' faces, the Nazi posters that still adorned some of the buildings and the large numbers of occupation troops patrolling the streets, one might have thought the war had passed Hamelin by.

But as with all the other surrendered towns, there was a new administration in place. Colonel Izzard-Lane, having been briefed by Helen, immediately brought his authority to bear on the recently appointed American commander, and before long they found themselves in a comfortable house with a convenient garage in which they could hide the van. The last thing they needed was for SS Hauptsturmführer Wessel to get wind of their presence and do yet another disappearing act.

Here in Hamelin, Eisenhower's policy of no fraternisation was strictly in force, but that didn't stop the colonel sauntering out in search of a beer later that evening while Helen and Raoul discreetly reconnoitred the area in the vicinity of Wessel's home, which stood in a quiet residential street on the outskirts of the town.

The commander had warned them that without a legal warrant, he had no authority to take a German officer into custody, whatever atrocity he had committed. But they still felt their best hope of finding André was to find Wessel, so having ascertained from the requisitioned records that the house was still registered in the SS officer's name, they looked for some inconspicuous place from where they could keep it under observation. What they found was an empty cow byre at the corner of a field on a small incline just beyond the edge of town. The byre wasn't ideal because it was dirty and damp, but it had the benefit of being accessible from an adjacent wood, which meant they could come and go without attracting suspicion. Better still, with the aid of the strong binoculars Raoul had brought with him from France, it offered an uninterrupted view of the Wessel house from its fly-stained window.

'Ça va,' Raoul said, looking around with satisfaction. Wedging his knee into an old wooden manger, he leaned against the grimy wall and raised the binoculars to his eyes. 'Now we wait and watch. If Wessel is here, this is where Monsieur André will come.'

But Helen was no longer quite so sanguine. Nearly a week had already passed since André had left Buchenwald. His Russian comrade-in-arms had told her that he had been in better health than most of the prisoners, partly because he hadn't been there as long, and partly because he had forced himself to exercise every day. Nevertheless, having seen for herself the hideous watery slop the prisoners had been expected to live on, Helen couldn't imagine that André would be in great shape physically. As for his psychological state, God only knew. Such barbaric conditions and the daily presence of death would surely have an effect on any man, even one as tough and well balanced as André.

The town commander had never heard the name Cabillard, which presumably meant that André had not made contact with any of the Hamelin occupation troops. Nor had there been any report of the murder or disappearance of one of the Hamelin residents. Now Helen was beginning to worry if in his weakened condition André might have fallen off that stolen motorbike, and was even now lying dead in a ditch somewhere between Weimar and Hamelin.

★   ★   ★

449

On 23 April, the British government announced that the threat of any further bombing was officially over, and that as a result all remaining blackout restrictions were to be lifted.

'Hurrah!' Susan said to Jen. 'So that'll mean we can definitely hold the play in the garden. Nobody's going to complain about the floodlights now.'

Jen laughed at her enthusiasm, but deep down she was pleased too. Considerably to her surprise, the show was beginning to come together. After a few annoying rehearsals when nobody seemed capable of doing what she told them, she had started thinking about how Henry had managed things earlier in the war when he had produced an ENSA show she was in. He certainly hadn't ranted and raved, but nor had he tolerated poor performances. By praising what people had done well, and calmly suggesting different ways of approaching the bits they did badly, he had contrived to bring out the best in everyone. As soon as she began to emulate his technique, things had definitely started to go a bit better.

Thanks to Susan and Bella, the children now knew the words of the songs they were going to sing. All they needed was a few more sessions with Jen on the piano. Bella had practised the poems she was reciting so often that even Jen knew them by heart. George had perfected his patter for his rabbit trick, and for the suction experiment with the hard-boiled egg which he and the professor were going to carry out. They hadn't actually performed it yet, because of the shortage of eggs, but their dummy runs had gone smoothly. Gino, to show off his new-found language skills, had opted to give a short talk on ice-cream making, which would be followed up by *gelati* being served in the interval. Last but not least, the script that Graham and Susan had created to link the various acts together was actually quite amusing. If she could just get them to improve their projection and timing a bit, Jen thought it was remotely conceivable that Mrs d'Arcy Billière's friends might even raise the occasional smile.

'How many people has Mrs d'Arcy Billière invited?' Susan asked. 'Do you know?'

'I'm not sure,' Jen said. 'About fifty, I think.' But when she asked Mrs d'Arcy Billière the same question later that morning, she was horrified to discover that the numbers had already grown to nearly a hundred.

'A hundred?' she gasped.

Mrs d'Arcy Billière laughed. 'Well, now that we can hold it in the garden, it seemed a shame not to invite a few more. With the war nearly over, people are in the mood to celebrate.'

'But what if it's raining?' Jen wailed. 'Even if it's not, where's everyone going to sit?'

Mrs d'Arcy Billière looked startled. 'Oh, I hadn't thought of that. Perhaps you'd better ask your mother if we can borrow some chairs from the café.'

But when Jen called at the café, her mother wasn't there. 'She's gone to look at the new house,' Angie said.

'What are you talking about? What new house?'

Angie rolled her eyes. 'Oh all right, it's not a new house, it's Albert's old house, the one Mr Poole is rebuilding. But anyway, Mum and Albert have decided that when it's ready, they're going to have that one, and me and Gino will stay in Mum's house.'

Jen blinked. It was the first she had heard of it. But that wasn't the only thing that surprised her. 'Since when did you start calling Mr Lorenz by his Christian name?' she asked

Angie gave an airy wave of her hand. 'Well, calling him Mr Lorenz seemed so formal,' she said. 'And it seems a bit odd to call him Dad, especially as he's so much nicer than our real dad ever was, so he suggested Albert. But I don't think it's his Christian name,' she gave a sudden giggle, 'because he's Jewish.'

Jen smiled dutifully, but she was aware of feeling slightly piqued that Mr Lorenz hadn't invited her to call him Albert too. And that her mother hadn't bothered to tell her about their change of plan regarding the houses.

As she walked back up Lavender Road, she realised that the rebuilding of Mr Lorenz's old house was quite a bit further advanced than it had been last time she had passed by. It had a roof now, and even though there were no windows or doors, and only a ladder to serve as a staircase, progress was obviously being made.

It wasn't quick enough for her mother, of course. Jen found Joyce standing in what was going to be the kitchen, glaring through a cavity in the back wall at the sight of Mr Poole and his men sitting on a pile of bricks in the back yard enjoying a leisurely smoke in the sun.

'Oh dear,' Jen murmured. 'On a go-slow again?'

Joyce swung round. 'Goodness! You made me jump. What are you doing here? I thought you were far too busy up at Mrs d'Arcy Billière's to waste time coming to see us.'

Jen bristled. 'I am,' she said. 'But I wanted to ask you if I could borrow some chairs. And to see how your new house was coming on.'

But Joyce didn't seem to notice the sarcasm in her tone. She nodded towards the workmen. 'It would be coming on well if they didn't take so many breaks,' she said.

Jen remembered the efforts she had made to spur Mr Poole on to repair her mother's house last year and felt a stab of irritation. All the thanks she had got was to be deprived of her bedroom.

But she manfully refrained from mentioning it, and a few minutes later, as Joyce began showing her round the reconstructed house, she was glad she hadn't said anything, because she had never seen her mother so animated. As she listened to her waffling on about the design for her new indoor bathroom, and the newfangled electric twin-tub washing machine Mr Lorenz had offered to buy her, Jen surprised herself by thinking, perhaps for the first time ever, that her mother was actually rather sweet. Mr Lorenz certainly knew the way to her heart, she thought in amusement. What was more, Joyce had become a different person since marrying him. A happier, more relaxed person who no longer bit everyone's head off as soon as look at them.

But as soon as her eye fell on the inactive builders again, Joyce abruptly lost her enthusiasm. 'I was so hoping it would be finished before the boys came back,' she said.

'But they won't be back for ages,' Jen said, puzzled by her anxious tone. 'Even if the war is over soon, it'll take months for them to be demobbed. They're hardly going to send them all home straight away.'

Joyce looked at her for a moment before answering. 'No,' she said. 'But they are sending Bob home. I got a letter this morning. His camp was overrun by Monty's troops earlier in the week.'

'Blimey,' Jen said. She had barely given her POW brother a thought for months. 'That's good news.'

'Oh yes,' Joyce said. But she didn't look very convinced, and Jen was surprised, because Bob, the eldest of the family, had always been her mother's favourite, despite the fact that he had also been the one most like their late, and for her at least, unlamented father. Work-shy, arrogant and a bit too keen on the drink.

'Why do you say it like that?' she asked. 'Is it that after three years in a Nazi prison, you think he won't be able to keep his hands off the booze?' She laughed. 'Or are you worried he'll have a go at Bella?'

But her mother didn't seem amused. For a long moment she didn't say anything; then she frowned. 'I'm more concerned about him having a go at Albert.'

'Why on earth would he do that?'

A hint of colour crept into her mother's cheeks. 'I don't know,' she said, avoiding Jen's curious eye. 'I suppose because he feels a certain loyalty to your father.'

Finally Jen understood. It wasn't just in his addiction to drink that Bob resembled his father. He held the same prejudices too. 'Oh my God,' she said. 'It's the Jewish thing, isn't it?' She saw the stricken look in her mother's eyes. 'Have you told Mr Lorenz?'

'No,' Joyce said. 'I didn't want to upset him.'

Jen shrugged. 'I don't think you need to worry. Bob might be a fool, but he's not a complete idiot. When he sees how happy you are, he'll forget all about his stupid prejudices.'

'Do you think so?'

'I'm sure of it.' Jen grinned. 'And knowing Mr Lorenz, he'll have poor old Bob eating out of his hand in no time.'

Joyce gave a little laugh. 'You like him, don't you? Albert, I mean. Not Bob.'

'I adore him,' Jen said. 'He's the best thing that's ever happened to this family.'

Joyce stared at her. 'Oh Jen,' she mumbled. 'I never thought . . .' But then she tailed off, apparently too overcome to speak.

Embarrassed by her emotion, Jen gave her an awkward smile and began to sidle towards the door.

She was already in the street when she heard her mother's voice behind her.

'How many chairs did you say you wanted?'

Jen laughed as she turned round. 'All of them,' she called back. 'And I hope you and Mr Lorenz can come to the show. Mrs d'Arcy Billière has told us to invite anyone we want.'

Her mother smiled with pleasure. 'We'd love to. I was hoping you'd ask us. Bella is so excited about it, and Gino too, in his way. It's kind of you to let him and Angie serve the ice cream, although goodness knows what people will think of it. Oh, and Jen,' she added, as Jen went to turn away, 'I think we've had enough of the formality now. I know Mr Lorenz would much prefer you to call him Albert, like the rest of us.'

Helen and Raoul took it in turns to watch Hauptsturmführer Wessel's house.

At first there was very little activity. There was certainly no sign of André, or of Wessel himself, but they did occasionally catch a glimpse of a woman they assumed to be Wessel's wife.

The following morning, at about 10.30, Mrs Wessel emerged from the front door and headed off in the direction of the town centre, reappearing half an hour later with a basket of provisions. That was the only time she left the house, but two or three times during the day she opened the back door, which they could only just see from their vantage point, to let a large Alsatian dog out into the small back garden.

They had agreed to do shifts of three hours each, day and night, but by the end of the second day even Raoul realised that keeping up that level of concentration with so little sleep was impossible. So with considerable reluctance, they asked Colonel Izzard-Lane if he would consider taking a turn too.

He seemed pleased to be asked, and although they didn't feel they could leave him alone in the cow byre, his presence on the binoculars meant that whoever was up there with him could doss down in the corner on a pile of blankets they had brought from their requisitioned house to try and catch a few winks of extra sleep.

In practice, however, perhaps because he was unsuited to this type of patient surveillance work, or any kind of work, come to that, Colonel Izzard-Lane tended to keep up a running commentary on what he was seeing.

On the third afternoon, Helen was trying to doze when he suddenly remarked, 'Have you noticed, my dear, that there is one window in the house where the curtains are always closed?'

'Really?' Helen scrambled to her feet and took the binoculars. For a moment she thought he must be looking at the wrong house, but then she noticed that at the back of the Wessel house, slightly recessed into the wall above the back door, there was indeed another window. Because of the angle, it was very difficult to see, but now, perhaps because for the first time since they had begun their vigil the sun had come out from behind the clouds, Helen realised that the colonel was right. The curtains were closed.

She felt her heart jump in her chest. 'Oh my goodness,' she whispered. 'You surely don't think they're holding André prisoner in there?'

Colonel Izzard-Lane looked astonished. He clearly hadn't been thinking any such thing. 'No, no,' he said. 'Just thought I should mention it, that's all. Thought it seemed a bit odd to have the curtains closed in the middle of the afternoon.'

Helen was staring at the house through the binoculars. 'Maybe that's why she stays indoors all the time with that dog,' she said. 'Because they're guarding him.'

Handing the binoculars back to the colonel, she sat down on the blankets to think. If only Raoul was there, she thought. Then they might be able to come up with a plan. If nothing else, he had weapons and other equipment in the van that might prove useful if they felt the need to break into the house.

Even as she had the thought, the colonel gave a grunt of surprise. 'No, I don't think so,' he said. 'Because she's coming out, and she's got the dog with her on a leash. It's got a muzzle on. Looks like she's taking it for a walk.'

Once again Helen jumped to her feet. Sure enough, the woman was marching off down the street, the muzzled dog prowling obediently along beside her.

Helen was aware of a sudden prickling sensation in the palms of her hands. 'I'm going to go down there,' she said. 'I need to see what's in that room.'

'What?' Colonel Izzard-Lane reeled back as if he'd been shot. 'You can't do that. You can't break into someone's house.'

'I have to,' she said. 'It might be our only chance.' But at the door of the byre, she hesitated. 'I just wish I had a weapon.' All the weapons Raoul had brought from France were locked in the van in the garage of the house.

To her astonishment, Colonel Izzard-Lane struggled his own enormous old-fashioned revolver out of a concealed holster on his belt. 'Then you'd better take this,' he said, thrusting it towards her. 'Better safe than sorry.'

For a second, Helen was tempted, but then she shook her head. The weapon was too big, too unwieldy. It would be impossible to conceal such a thing under her FANY uniform. Her best chance of success was to be as inconspicuous as possible, and she certainly wouldn't be that if she was seen carrying a weapon that looked like it had last been used for hunting tigers in India.

Seeing his concern, she smiled reassuringly. 'Keep watching,' she said. 'And if anything bad happens, go straight back to the house and wake Raoul. He'll know what to do.'

Then she was climbing over the fence beside the barn and running down the shadowed fringe of trees to the small unpaved road that ran past the back garden of Wessel's house.

When Helen had first been selected as a possible SOE agent, she'd been sent to a remote training school in Scotland. The instructors there had taught her how to be inconspicuous. They had also taught her map-reading, surveillance and tracking, escape and evasion, techniques for resisting interrogation, weaponry and unarmed combat.

What they hadn't taught her was how to break into a house belonging to an SS murderer without knowing for sure that he wasn't inside.

Whatever she was going to do, she knew it would have to be quick. Even under an unwelcome occupation, the German people had proved to be extremely law-abiding. The town commander had told her that his new rules and curfews had been accepted and adhered to with rigid obedience. He believed that long years of punishment for the smallest violation of Nazi edicts had sapped the local population of their free will. But it had also made them all too willing to curry favour with the authorities by reporting any crimes or infringements.

On the streets of occupied Hamelin, Helen's FANY uniform was relatively unremarkable, but she was quite certain that if anyone caught sight of her lurking about in the back garden of the Wessels' house, they would be straight on to the police.

Taking temporary refuge among the leaves of a large glossy-leaved shrub with bright red flowers that she thought might be a camellia, she looked back up the hill at the cow byre and gave a quick wave. She couldn't see Colonel Izzard-Lane, but she felt marginally safer knowing that he had his binoculars trained on her.

From where she was crouched, she could clearly see the curtained window above the back door. She listened carefully but couldn't discern any sound coming from within, just the faint swish of the breeze passing through the branches of the blossom-laden cherry trees that fringed the little road on the other side of the garden fence.

There was a faint smell of dog in the yard. A small bucket and spade by the back door showed what happened to the Alsatian's excrement, and a large well-chewed bone lay on the patchy grass of the lawn.

The only odd note in the otherwise neat and tidy garden was a flowerpot containing an old, straggly lavender plant, which stood against the back wall of the house. Slowly Helen edged along the fence towards it. It occurred to her that it would be a sensible precaution for any household with a family member serving in the forces to keep a spare key hidden somewhere in case of last-minute unannounced visits home. To her satisfaction, she was right. Lying on the bare earth under the pot, which had obviously recently been disturbed, was a brass key.

Two seconds later, without pausing for further thought, she had fitted it into the lock in the back door, and was stepping silently into the Hauptsturmführer's kitchen.

Again she paused to take stock. And to listen. Somewhere, on the other side of the kitchen door, she could hear a clock ticking but, apart from that, the house was silent.

Slipping off her shoes, she moved across the tiled floor and gently pushed open the door. A short corridor led straight through to the front door. Quickly, she tiptoed along it, checking the rooms on either side.

To the left was a comfortable sitting room, with the inevitable picture of Hitler above the fireplace; to the right was a formal dining room with a polished wooden table and four ornately carved high-backed chairs. Under the stairs by the front door was a smaller latched door behind which she found several home-made racks containing a considerable amount of wine.

She was half tempted to check to see if any of the bottles bore Cabillard labels, but instead she closed the door quietly, slid the latch back to its original position and nervously began to climb the stairs.

Still there was no noise, just the faint creak of the wood as her weight caused the treads to flex away from the banister.

Upstairs, leading off the landing, were four closed doors. She opened the front two first. Both were bedrooms, one double, clearly in recent use, the other a rather bare-looking single. A small bathroom lay behind the third door. That left just one more. The door at the back.

Worried that she was being too slow, she took a breath and tentatively tried the handle. And found to her surprise that it opened easily, revealing a bright, pleasant room set up as a study, with a floor-to-ceiling bookcase on one side and a desk and chair on the other. From one moment to the next, her heart rate increased tenfold. Because against all expectation, the curtains were wide open.

For a fleeting second, as panic swept through her, she thought there must be someone else in the house after all, and swung round in alarm, ready to flee.

Then logic reasserted itself. This window did indeed face out over the back garden, but it wasn't recessed. This was the window they could see clearly from the cow byre. So where was the other one?

The only place it could possibly be was behind the bookshelves. How long did it take for someone to walk a dog, Helen wondered anxiously, as she ran her eyes over the tightly packed books. And how long did it take someone to find a door in a false wall covered in shelving?

Her hands were shaking as she fingered the books, easing them out slightly in small batches, looking for some kind of latch or join in the wall behind.

It seemed like an age before she found it, a small handle concealed behind a well-thumbed copy of *Mein Kampf*. She might have guessed that would be the book the Hauptsturmführer would choose.

She thought back to the tales of priest holes and secret passages she had enjoyed as a child. In those nail-biting stories, at some special pressure on the handle, whole sections of medieval panelling rotated on eerie, squeaking hinges to reveal dark tunnels shrouded in cobwebs and lined with skulls or disembodied suits of armour.

The Hauptsturmführer's secret door was more prosaic. The entire bookcase swung back perfectly easily, exposing a small square room. The only light was that filtering in around the closed curtains at the small window. Even so, Helen could see at once that nobody was hiding here, nor indeed being held prisoner. And never had been. The tiny room was filled with so much jumble and so many boxes, there was barely room to stand up in it.

But as her heart rate subsided slightly and her eyes acclimatised to the darkness, she realised that her initial impression was wrong. The contents of the room might look like jumble, but it was far from being junk. Stacked neatly against the right-hand wall were numerous pictures, and not just any old pictures; these were paintings in fancy gilded frames, clearly of some considerable quality.

Screwed to the wall on the other side was yet another shelving unit, containing several loosely wrapped porcelain figurines, a silver tea service and half a dozen or so ornate jewellery boxes.

On the table under the window were piles of banknotes, weighed down by other ornaments, and in one case, a small carved wooden bowl brimming with what looked like curious misshapen gold nuggets. Helen had stared at them for several seconds before she noticed the tooth attached to one of them, and finally, with a gasp of horror, realised that they were gold fillings, presumably extracted from the prisoners at one of the death camps.

It was as she recoiled in revulsion, the gorge rising in her throat, that she heard the distinctive, reverberating crack of a gunshot.

She knew at once that it had come from the direction of the cow byre. She was in such a state of shock that her first reaction was a flash of fury. Who on earth had the idiotic colonel shot? Hopefully not Raoul, she thought wildly, or indeed himself. Or had someone taken a potshot at him? Either way, the stupid old fool had almost certainly compromised their position.

Then, belatedly, a more likely explanation presented itself. Perhaps he wasn't such a fool after all. Perhaps he had fired his weapon as a warning that Mrs Wessel was on her way home.

At once a cold hand clasped Helen's heart. Swiftly she backed out of the gruesome hidey-hole and swung the bookshelf closed. Then she sped to the door and, having checked that all the other doors were as she had found them, ran lightly down the stairs. Already she could hear the dog snuffling at the front door, and rapid footsteps, and now a sharp female voice. Mrs Wessel's voice.

'*Was ist los, Wolf?*'

Because she pronounced the dog's name in the German way, *Volf*, it took Helen a second to translate, but even as she fled down the corridor to the kitchen, she remembered reading somewhere that Hitler also had a dog called Wolf.

As the door from the passage to the kitchen had been open when she arrived, she didn't dare close it now. Nor did she waste time putting on her shoes. Knowing the dog had picked up her scent and would be running through the house the instant Mrs Wessel got the front door open, she scooped them up and let herself out into the garden, managing to get the back door closed behind her just as Wolf's huge face appeared at the glass.

He wasn't wearing a muzzle now.

Crouching to one side, she hastily tried to relock the door, but her fingers were sweating so much, the key slid out of her hand.

The Alsatian was growling and pawing at the door, and as she scrabbled on the ground, Helen was finding it hard to keep her cool. As she picked up the key and once more tried to insert it into the lock, she caught sight of the animal's ferocious teeth and had a vision of him bursting through the glass and grabbing her by the throat. She wouldn't stand a chance.

But this time she managed to get the key to turn, then, having thrust it back under the pot of lavender, she was over the fence,

461

fumbling on her shoes and sprinting as fast and as silently as possible round the corner and across the road into the trees, out of sight.

Raoul was furious. He had also heard the shot and had hurried immediately to the cow byre, arriving there only a minute or two after Helen. '*Putain d'enfer*,' he muttered when she explained what had happened. '*Comment pourriez-vous être si stupide?*' He nodded towards the still-shaking colonel. 'It is only thanks to that imbecile that you were not caught. Now we must leave this cowshed at once, and not come back. People will have heard the shot.'

'Well, I wasn't caught, was I?' Helen snapped back. 'OK, it may have been a bit rash, but I wasn't being stupid. For all we knew, André was in the house, and now we know he isn't. Nor is Wessel, but he's definitely been there very recently. There were two men's shirts folded neatly on the ironing board.'

Raoul swore again. 'He must be hiding somewhere else. Now she will warn him that there has been someone in the house, and he will disappear.'

'But she won't know there has been someone there,' Helen retorted. 'I left everything exactly as I found it, even his beastly gold.'

'What about the dog?' Raoul said. 'He knew you were there.'

'So what? He can't talk, can he? For all she knows, he smelt a fox in the garden.'

Unable to understand the argument, but clearly aware that he was in disgrace with Raoul, the colonel had moved surreptitiously back to the window. Now he picked up the binoculars again.

'I say, chaps,' he said, jerking in surprise. 'You'll never believe it. The damned woman is leaving the house again. This time without the dog. But she's carrying a basket, and she looks like she's in a hurry.'

Raoul swung accusingly on Helen. 'Maybe the dog *can* talk,' he said sarcastically.

Helen gritted her teeth. But she didn't have time to argue. 'We must follow her,' she said urgently. 'If she is going to warn him, she will lead us straight to him.'

462

But Raoul had other ideas. '*I* will follow her,' he said.

'Oh, for goodness sake, Raoul,' Helen groaned. 'Don't be so *fâché*.'

'No,' he said. 'You are too conspicuous in that uniform. It will have to be me.'

Deep down Helen knew he was right. She also knew how good he was at making himself invisible. If anyone could tail Frau Wessel without her knowing, it was Raoul.

In any case, he was already gone.

Helen could hardly believe it. She had only turned her head away for an instant. But like a wraith, from one second to the next he had completely disappeared.

'Can't say I'm sorry he's taken himself off,' Colonel Izzard-Lane remarked from the window. 'Temperamental buggers, these Frogs, aren't they? Don't know what you see in them myself.'

Putting down the binoculars, he smiled conspiratorially. 'Anyway, since he's no longer here to shout at us, what do you say we pop into town? There's a nice little bar just opposite the Rathaus. I don't know about you, dear girl, but I could do with a brandy after all that excitement.'

Part Six

Chapter Twenty-Seven

'I think Mummy's cross with me,' Malcolm confided to Molly when she came into the pub that afternoon to get ready for the evening shift.

'Oh dear,' Molly said. 'Have you been naughty?'

Malcolm's little face twisted in thought. 'I don't think so. I did give Caroline a ride on Lucky and she cried. But it wasn't my fault. I thought she'd like it.'

Molly had to hide her smile. Malcolm had always been an intrepid child. Just like his father, he seemed unaware of the concept of fear. He was nearly three and a half now, but even at Caroline's age, taking a ride on a dog would have been his idea of fun. His sister, on the other hand, took more after Katy. She was friendly and sociable, but not adventurous. She had only just begun to think about walking, and much preferred to sit in the safety of her playpen, humming indistinguishable tunes to the magnificent doll Ward's parents had given her for Christmas, or playing peek-a-boo with any passing adult with time on their hands.

'Poor Caroline,' Molly said. 'You know she doesn't like that sort of thing, so it was naughty. But I'm sure Katy's not still cross about it.'

'Well, she's cross about something,' he said. 'Because she didn't laugh when Lucky chased the brewery horse up the road, and it was really funny.'

Although Molly privately doubted Katy would ever think that

was funny, actually Malcolm was right. Katy had been subdued all week. She was still upset about Mr Rutherford's refusal to let her transfer the lease of the pub to Aaref and Elsa, and she was worried about Ward, Helen, and increasingly about André.

A few days ago, there had been a radio broadcast by a reporter called Richard Dimbleby, who had been present at the liberation of a Nazi death camp called Belsen by the British 11th Armoured Division. Molly had been working at the Red Cross that day, so she hadn't heard first-hand about the terrible atrocities that had been discovered, but Katy had clearly been shocked to the core.

'I just can't believe it,' she had whispered. 'I can't believe anyone could be so cruel.' She had looked at Molly with fear in her eyes. 'Surely this Buchenwald place can't be as bad as that?'

Molly hadn't known what to say. There had been no mention of Buchenwald in the British media, and she felt cross with Helen for not letting them know what was happening. Surely she must realise how worried they all were.

But in other ways, things were looking up. The newspapers had been reporting that the Russians had Berlin more or less surrounded, and even though the professor and Mrs d'Arcy Billière were furious that Stalin had been allowed to steal a march on the Western Allies, surely the fact that the capital of Germany was on the brink of collapse meant that the war would soon be over. Nobody knew exactly where Hitler was, but even he must realise by now that his days as Reichsführer were numbered.

Today, though, Katy's concerns were closer to home.

'Louise was in earlier,' she said, as she and Molly carried a keg up the cellar steps. 'Apparently that blighter Douglas is home on leave for a few days from his special top-secret unit.'

Molly had been wondering if she'd have time to go to Epsom the following day to see the woman who might have known her father, but at Katy's words she looked up eagerly. 'Oh, that's good,' she said.

'*Good*?' Katy nearly dropped her end of the keg. 'What's good about it? Last time he was in here, he nearly caused a punch-up. At the very least, we'll have to warn Mrs Lorenz to keep Bella out of his way.'

Molly quickly tried to cover her mistake. 'Sorry,' she said. 'I was just thinking about something else. I actually meant good*ness*. How awful. But perhaps he won't come in here after last time.'

She felt Katy's eyes on her, but luckily, as they heaved the keg onto the counter, George came sidling into the bar. Concerned that he too might have discovered that Douglas was back in London, Molly eyed him warily. The last thing she wanted was for him to spill the beans and mess up her plan. 'What are you doing here? You're meant to be at Mrs d'Arcy Billière's this afternoon.'

'Jen needs Malcolm for a rehearsal,' George said. 'So I said I'd come and fetch him.' He smiled winningly at Katy. 'But I wondered if I could have a lemonade first.'

Katy glanced at Molly and rolled her eyes. 'Oh, all right,' she said, reaching for the bottle opener. 'But if Jen needs you, you'd better drink it pretty sharpish.'

Thankfully, whether he knew about Douglas being in London or not, he didn't mention it, and by the time the boys had gone off, Katy had forgotten about their earlier conversation.

But Molly hadn't, and when Douglas Rutherford came into the pub with Louise a couple of hours later, she prepared herself for a confrontation.

As he approached the bar, Molly eyed him steadily. 'I'm surprised you dared to come in here,' she murmured under cover of the wheezing noise of the beer pump. 'Or have you come to tell me you've spoken to your father?'

Angry colour flooded into his cheeks. 'I haven't had a chance yet,' he said.

Molly blew the froth off his beer. 'Well, *make* a chance,' she snapped. 'Nothing in life happens by itself. Sometimes you have to show a bit of guts and make things happen.'

He looked for a moment as though he was going to snap back,

but then he saw Katy coming past with a tray of empties and, picking up the two glasses, he carried them over to Louise, who was talking to Jen by the fireplace.

Seeing him approach, Jen quickly made her excuses and came to the bar. 'I've been trying to persuade Louise to invite Lord Freddy to the show,' she said.

'Is she going to?' Molly asked.

'I'm not sure. She wouldn't commit herself. So I'm going to invite him anyway.' Jen glanced at Katy. 'I hope you're coming.'

Katy had been keeping a wary eye on Douglas Rutherford, but now she turned her attention to Jen. 'Of course I'm coming,' she said. 'I wouldn't miss it for the world.'

When Jen had gone, Katy glanced at Molly. 'Jen seems surprisingly excited about this show,' she said. She nodded across the room to where their friend was now flirting with Mr Poole the builder. It sounded as though she was inviting him to the show too. Katy shook her head. 'I'm glad it's given her something to think about other than worrying about Henry and the baby, but I hope she's not expecting too much. Most of them are only kids, after all.'

Molly felt her heart sink. Katy was right. For all their efforts, it was perfectly possible that the show would be a complete fiasco. 'I know,' she said. 'But there is one good thing. At least the audience won't get wet; Jen's asked Mr Lorenz to see if he can lay hands on a tarpaulin.'

Molly didn't get back to the Nelsons' until quite late that night, and was just climbing into bed when George crept into her bedroom.

'Molly,' he whispered into the darkness. 'Are you still awake? I wanted to tell you that Douglas Rutherford is back. I saw him as I was coming back from Mrs d'Arcy Billière's with Malcolm and Bella.'

'I hope you didn't say anything,' Molly said, turning on the light. 'Not in front of them.'

George shook his head. 'Of course I didn't. But I gave him a look.'

'A look?'

'Yes. I gave him the look the professor gives me when he sets my homework. The sort of look that makes it clear that he means business.' He grinned. 'I didn't quite understand it at first. But I do now.'

Molly bit her lip. 'And do you think Douglas understood your look?' she asked.

He nodded confidently. 'Oh yes. His face went all pale and he scurried off as though wolves were after him.'

Raoul didn't reappear until late that evening. By that time Helen had almost given him up for lost.

'Where've you been?' she asked crossly, emerging from the sitting room where she had been playing cards with the colonel. 'I've been worried to death. Especially as Frau Wessel got back ages ago.'

'How do you know that?' Raoul asked sharply.

'I went back to the barn,' Helen said. She saw his face darken and quickly held up her hands. 'I know you said we shouldn't go back there again. But I was very careful. Nobody saw me. But I saw her, and I could see that she no longer had the basket.'

'That is because she gave it to him,' he said.

Helen stared at him. 'To who?'

Raoul shrugged. 'To Wessel. He is in a monastery, some distance from here.'

'You followed her all the way?'

He looked surprised. 'Of course. It was not so difficult. She took a bus and she did not notice me sitting at the back. It was a long walk from the village where we got off, but I could follow in the woods above the road.'

'And you actually saw Wessel?' Helen could hardly keep the incredulity out of her voice.

Raoul lowered his lips and jerked his chin up slightly in a typical Gallic gesture. 'C'est vrai. I needed the binoculars. He was wearing a religious habit, brown, with a hood. Perhaps it is called a cowl. But I am sure it was him. I could see a scar on his face, and he took the basket with his left hand.'

471

Helen was impressed. She wasn't sure that she would have noticed that detail. She suddenly felt rather breathless. 'But you didn't see any sign of André?'

'No. But I am sure he is there.'

Helen stared at him. 'How can you be so sure?'

Raoul raised his hands. 'Where else can he be?'

A million places, Helen thought. Not least in a ditch somewhere between here and Weimar. Or indeed in an unmarked grave somewhere in the nearby woods. But she knew better than to say it. She had learned by now that Raoul had infinite faith in Monsieur André, and any doubt on her part just made him even more sullen and unhelpful. 'So what do we do now?' she asked.

Raoul glanced at the fine ormolu clock that their absent Nazi hosts had left on the mantelpiece. Helen was surprised to see it was already nearly midnight.

'We sleep for a few hours,' he said. 'Then we go to watch the monastery.'

This time they didn't take Colonel Izzard-Lane with them.

'It is not suitable,' Raoul said firmly. Instead he brought his two remaining pigeons into the house and instructed the colonel in their care.

Colonel Izzard-Lane had been woken from a deep sleep and was not in a good mood. At first he listened attentively to Helen's translation of Raoul's detailed instructions about food and water. But when he cottoned on to the fact that Raoul was intending to let the pigeons loose in the house, he began to object.

'I can't have birds flying about in here,' he said. 'For one thing it'll be a damned nuisance, and for another it's not hygienic.'

Privately Helen rather agreed with him, but Raoul was adamant that his birds needed exercise. 'They have been confined too long,' he insisted stubbornly. Reaching into the crate, he carefully drew out one of the roosting pigeons and stroked its grey plumage tenderly. 'When we find Monsieur André, we will need these birds to inform his father. It will be no use sending them if they are too weak to fly.'

In the end, Helen brokered a compromise by suggesting that the elegant spacious dining room might be sufficient for the pigeons' needs. None of them cared about the mess they were likely to make in there. If the Nazis ever got their house back, Helen thought as the pigeons took up a comfortable position on the glass candelabra that hung above the impressive dining table, then they could deal with it. Serve them right.

When she and Raoul arrived at the forest that surrounded the monastery, it quickly transpired that the reason Raoul had been so late home was that he had been scouting around for the best vantage points. He had also found a suitable place to hide the van, at the end of what looked like a logging track.

Once the vehicle was wedged into the thicket of fir trees at the edge of the small clearing, and the tyre marks scuffed over, it would be virtually invisible to any but the most zealous observer. Once again Helen was impressed by Raoul's thoroughness. And when, after a fifteen-minute scramble through the woods carrying a bag of supplies and equipment, they reached the place he had decided on for their surveillance, she knew he had chosen that well too.

Knowing they could use binoculars, he hadn't gone too close to the monastery. The spot he had found, in a patch of undergrowth in a shallow depression near the top of a small incline, was perhaps three hundred yards away from the nearest section of the high protective stone wall that encircled the monastery complex. It was also well angled, so that sunlight wouldn't reflect on the lenses of the binoculars, giving away their position.

Provided they kept low to the ground, a small outcrop of boulders shielded their movement from any observers below. It gave them perfect cover to observe both the gated main entrance and the interior courtyard and cloisters, which formed a covered passageway running from what looked like an accommodation building on the left-hand side to the small white chapel with a rather unusual domed bell tower on the far right.

The only area not enclosed within the high perimeter wall was the monastery's vegetable garden, which the monks accessed from the courtyard via a small metal door sunk into the stonework. In the thin dawn light, Helen could make out one or two monks already at work, raking over the soil of a bare earth bed. She had no idea what type of monastery it was, but it clearly wasn't a silent order, because even from three hundred yards' distance and perhaps a fifty-foot elevation, she could hear the men exchanging the odd remark as they worked.

'I thought the Catholic Church disapproved of the Nazis,' she whispered to Raoul. 'So what on earth is Wessel doing here?'

But Raoul wasn't interested in discussing the monks' motivation in offering refuge to a Nazi war criminal; he was too busy preparing their stake-out. Once again he was nothing if not meticulous. While Helen kept the monastery under observation, he carefully cut the branches off the couple of bushes that impeded their view and used them to make a hiding place for the bag he had brought with him. Then he dug a long, wide indentation in the leaf mould under their feet, and gathered the debris in two long piles so they could quickly lie down and conceal themselves if the need arose.

So far so good, Helen thought. But then she heard a scuffling noise and turned to see him unfolding a large tarpaulin from the bag. With some alarm, she watched him fitting it carefully into the area he had dug out. After all the time they had spent together, she had developed a certain respect and affection for the surly Frenchman, but their relationship wasn't sufficiently advanced for her to feel comfortable sharing what in effect was a sleeping bag, particularly as Raoul's personal hygiene left rather a lot to be desired.

But thankfully it seemed that Raoul was intending them to take it in turns. One on watch, and the other resting in relative warmth and comfort between the waterproof folds of the tarpaulin.

474

However, during that long first day neither of them wanted to rest, and as they lay at a discreet distance from one another, peering down at the monastery, Helen noticed that when it was Raoul's turn on the binoculars, he wasn't always focused on the monks going about their business. Instead he spent ten minutes or so of every watch scrutinising the scrubby, wooded slopes that bordered the monastery walls. She knew exactly what he was looking for.

'Do you really think he's here?' she murmured.

Raoul shrugged as he reached over to hand her the binoculars. 'If he is, I doubt we will see him. Monsieur André is too clever to show himself too soon.'

All day they watched the comings and goings both inside and outside the monastery. Several men visited the place that day, and one or two women too. But not once did they see anyone even remotely resembling André Cabillard.

But they did see Wessel.

To Helen's astonishment, at dusk, just after the monastery bell had rung out for some kind of evening service, and the monks had all scurried into the chapel, he appeared through the side gate and took a slow walk round the vegetable garden.

It wasn't Helen's turn on the binoculars, but there was little doubt it was Wessel. The cowl of his habit was thrown back as though to enjoy the cool evening air, and his blond hair gleamed in the reddish glow of the evening light. When Raoul handed her the binoculars for a better look, Helen saw the fat pink lips Molly had described in her telegram, and the scar running up his cheek.

The man's obvious confidence gave her the shivers. He didn't seem to be remotely afraid. He certainly didn't look as though he was expecting to come under attack from a former adversary. On the contrary, he was calmly smoking a cigarette, tapping the ash negligently on the vegetable beds as he sauntered past. She could see the tip of the cigarette glowing each time he drew on it.

Lowering the binoculars, Helen turned to Raoul. 'Surely he wouldn't be showing himself like this if he thought he was in danger,' she whispered, and she could see from the tension in the Frenchman's shoulders that the SS officer's insouciance had made him uneasy too.

Then abruptly Wessel was gone.

Tossing the stub of the cigarette on the path, he ground it out with his shoe and let himself back into the courtyard through the side door, leaving Helen even more worried than she had been before.

'Perhaps he's not allowed to smoke inside the monastery,' she said. 'Perhaps that's why he came out.' But she knew she was clutching at straws. She sensed Raoul thought so too. But typically he didn't make any comment, just jerked his chin towards the tarpaulin.

'You sleep first,' he said. 'I will wake you at midnight.'

Jen had wanted Molly to go to a rehearsal with her entire cast the following morning, but instead Molly went to Epsom. She just couldn't put it off any longer. She wanted to know if this Mrs Rogers really did remember her father.

But as she walked along Epsom's main street, past the tall clock tower, with a set of rather convenient public lavatories at its base, and the Spread Eagle Hotel where Lord Freddy had wanted to have a drink, she felt her steps slowing.

There was very little traffic on the wide street, but the shops all had their awnings up and the whole place was bustling with life. But Molly wasn't bustling. Half of her even wondered about turning tail and going back to London. However much she told herself it had been ridiculous to be so upset about how things had turned out with her mother, she couldn't deny that it had hit her hard, and now, for all she knew, she might be about to lay herself open to yet another disappointment.

But if she was, she couldn't have found a nicer person than Mrs Rogers to give it to her.

'Oh, what a treat to have a visitor,' the elderly woman said at once when Molly started to explain her errand. 'Do come in, dear. I have just made some nice rice-flour buns and I was wondering who to share them with.'

Having settled Molly in a comfortable chair in her tidy little front room, she rushed off to the kitchen.

'Yes, I was at Yew Tree House in the early twenties,' she said as she carried in a tea tray with a plate of rather solid-looking buns. 'I was Mrs Cavanagh's housekeeper. So who was it you wanted to ask about, dear?'

Molly took a careful breath. 'It was a family called Coogan. Mr Coogan was the Cavanaghs' gardener. I'm looking for them because I think they might be distant relatives of mine.'

It wasn't a lie, of course. Mr Coogan, if he was still alive, would be her grandfather. But as with her mother, Molly didn't want to embarrass anyone by making what the woman at the adoption society had called an importunate approach.

But Mrs Rogers was smiling as she poured the tea and offered Molly a bun. 'I thought you reminded me of someone,' she said. 'As soon as I clapped eyes on you. Yes, of course I remember Mr Coogan. I knew him well. He was a lovely man, and his wife—'

'And they had a son?' Molly cut in rather breathlessly.

Mrs Rogers nodded. 'Terry,' she said. 'Yes, indeed. He was a fine young man.' But then her face clouded slightly. 'It was such a shame what happened.'

Molly's bun almost fell off her plate. It was lucky she hadn't already taken a bite because she would certainly have choked. 'What did happen?' she asked.

Mrs Rogers put down her cup. 'It was that Mrs Cavanagh,' she said. 'I don't like to speak ill of the dead, but she was a funny woman. If she took against one of the staff, that was it. They were out straight away. That's what happened with young Terry. Not that he was staff precisely. But he had helped his dad out once or twice. Then out of the blue, Mrs C accused him of stealing something from the house.' Mrs Rogers looked shocked at the very thought. 'She was wrong, of course. The Coogans were honest as the day is long. But,' she sighed, 'well, you know how it is with posh people like the Cavanaghs. Nobody was going to argue with them.'

Molly gave a slight grimace of agreement, but actually she knew that Mrs Cavanagh's accusation wasn't so wide of the mark. Terry Coogan had indeed stolen something. He had stolen her daughter's virginity.

'So Mrs Cavanagh sacked him?' she said grimly.

'Yes.' Mrs Rogers nodded. 'And his father. Not only sacked him, but refused to give him a reference. And things were tight at that time, and Mr Coogan's wife wasn't well, and well, it was a terrible blow. And so unfair.'

'What happened?' Molly asked. 'What did they do? And what happened to Terry? Do you know?'

Mrs Rogers looked surprised. 'Yes, of course I know,' she said. 'The first thing was that Terry had to leave school. They couldn't afford that no more, not with his dad out of work. But with that slur on him, there was no way a young lad like him was going to find work. Not around here at any rate. So in the end he joined the merchant marine. It was the only thing he could think of.' She smiled fondly. 'And he did well. He's a sea captain now.'

Molly's heart missed a beat. 'Do you mean you're still in touch with him?' she asked rather breathlessly.

Mrs Rogers picked up her teacup again. 'Not in touch, precisely, but I hear news of him from time to time from his mother.'

Molly felt her mouth fall open, and hastily closed it again. 'So Mrs Coogan is still alive? I understood from what you said earlier that . . .'

'Oh yes. She's still alive. And Mr Coogan too. We've always kept in touch. Christmas cards and that.'

Molly leaned forward expectantly. 'So you know where they live?'

Mrs Rogers nodded. 'They live in the same town as Terry. I'll find you the address in a moment.' But instead of getting up, she reached over and put a gentle hand on Molly's arm. 'Don't get too excited, dear. I'm afraid you are going to be disappointed.'

Molly felt a flicker of unease. 'Why?' she said. 'What do you mean?'

She wasn't remotely disappointed. On the contrary, she was getting more and more excited. The Coogans sounded really nice. Not rich and posh maybe, but just the kind of people she'd like to have as relatives.

But Mrs Rogers was looking at her in kindly concern. 'I mean that it's not going to be very easy for you to meet them.'

'Why not?' Molly asked.

Mrs Rogers gave an apologetic shrug, then calmly delivered her bombshell.

'Because they live in America.'

Molly stared at her. '*America*?'

Mrs Rogers pursed her lips in a sympathetic little moue. 'I knew you were going to be disappointed. That's why I didn't tell you straight away. I could see how much it meant to you. But as I say, Terry did well in the merchant navy. Then on one shore leave in America, he met a girl and fell in love. He sent money for his parents to go over for the wedding, and they loved it so much, they stayed there and never came back.'

Giving Molly another kindly pat on the arm, she stood up and went to an old-fashioned bureau that stood under the window. Pulling back the lid, she rummaged through one of the small inside drawers, and came back holding a Christmas card.

'Here we are,' she said. 'That's it. Funny sort of name. Sounds Spanish to me. San Diego, California.' She looked up with a regretful smile. 'They were nice people, them Coogans. It's a shame they live such a long way away. I looked into the idea of visiting once. But even with the savings my husband left me, it was far more than I could ever afford.'

The second day in the forest seemed to be even longer than the first. There were few visitors to the monastery, and very little else to look at, and after a cold, uncomfortable night under the slithery tarpaulin, with hardly any sleep, Helen struggled to keep herself awake and alert.

To make things even worse, a light drizzle had begun to fall.

479

It was almost a relief when the vespers bell rang again, signifying that the interminable day was almost over.

'It was this time last night that Wessel came out,' Helen murmured.

Even as she said it, out he came again. He looked just as relaxed as he had the evening before. Once again he was smoking, but perhaps because of the rain, this time his cowl was up, and his other hand was tucked into some kind of pocket in the habit.

As she watched him through the binoculars, Helen suddenly felt goose bumps break out on her skin. Something was nagging at her subconscious. But she couldn't think what it was. The only thing different about the SS officer this time was that he looked a bit more bulky. As though he was wearing extra clothes under the habit. But it was no colder tonight, despite the rain. If anything, the cloud cover had made it warmer.

Next to her, Raoul was watching too. 'If I had a rifle, I could kill him from here,' he muttered.

Helen nodded. 'He must be mad. Why else would he show himself like this?' But even as she spoke the words, another possibility occurred to her. Suddenly her hands started to tremble. Lowering the binoculars, she turned to Raoul.

'What if he's doing it on purpose?' she said. 'What if it's a trap?'

Raoul took the binoculars. She could see the sceptical expression on his face as he raised them to his eyes.

But Helen was thinking fast now. 'Those men we saw yesterday,' she said. 'The ones visiting the monastery. What were they doing? Maybe Wessel was briefing them, or giving them weapons. I know we saw them leave again, but they might not have gone far. For all we know they are here now. In the woods. Waiting for André to show himself.'

Then, belatedly, she realised what had been bugging her earlier.

'I think Wessel's wearing protection under his habit,' she said. 'Like the flak vests that pilots wear. Just in case his plan goes wrong. And, oh my God, Raoul, look. He's holding the cigarette with his right hand. Wouldn't it be more natural for a left-handed person to hold it in his left hand? But his left hand is inside the habit. That's why he seems so casual. What if he's got a gun in there? Maybe that's what Frau Wessel brought him in that basket. Guns.'

And now, at last, she could feel that Raoul was taking notice.

For a second he was still, then, grunting at her to keep well down, he reached forward and took a smallish stone from the outcrop in front of them. Easing himself into a crouch, he drew back his arm and flung the stone as hard as he could out over the rocks.

They didn't see it land, but they heard it. A dull thud as it hit a tree, and then a scuff of leaves as it ricocheted to the ground.

It was an old trick, but on this occasion it worked. For a second there was silence, then they heard another sound. The crack of a twig as someone or something moved on the hillside directly below them.

Helen grasped Raoul's arm.

She was certainly alert now.

Slowly Raoul brought up the binoculars again. She saw him swing them in a slow, careful arc over the terrain beneath the outcrop, but even as she began to relax again, he gave a slight start, and the binoculars froze where they were.

'What is it?' she breathed. 'What can you see?'

'A man,' he murmured. For a second Helen felt a surge of hope, but then he spoke again, so quietly she almost missed it. 'No, two men.' Then a moment later, 'They're armed and they are coming this way.'

And now she could indeed hear the soft crunch of footsteps in the undergrowth below their position. Whoever it was, they were moving slowly, cautiously. Too slowly for woodsmen. Probably too slowly even for poachers.

They could hear the men's breathing, shallow and slightly laboured as they advanced up the side of the steep slope. A flash of torchlight briefly lit the back of the rocks.

A pistol had miraculously appeared in Raoul's hand, but Helen shook her head urgently, and as one, as silently as they could, they wriggled back down onto the tarpaulin, carefully drawing the piles of damp leaves that Raoul had prepared the previous day over their prostrate bodies.

As she pressed her face into the cold canvas, Helen could feel her heart hammering in her chest and very much hoped the approaching men couldn't hear it too.

Then, to her horror, through the ground, she felt the vibration of other footsteps, this time behind them, and the murmur of low guttural voices. Her heart sank. Two on two, she and Raoul might have stood a chance, but two on four was impossible.

It was almost dark now, so there was still a chance that the men might pass by without noticing the strategically placed outcrop.

Three of them did pass by. Perhaps because of the steepness of the slope immediately below the stone, the two men approaching from below veered off to the right of their position. Of the pair coming in from behind, one carried straight on through the clump of trees just yards behind them.

But, unfortunately, the other decided that he needed to relieve himself, and, with a grunt of explanation to his partner, he pushed through the shrubby undergrowth into the small clearing where Helen and Raoul lay concealed.

Helen realised now why she had been worried about the tarpaulin. Yes, it was warm and waterproof, but it was also noisy. One rustle or swish of canvas would instantly give them away. As the man began to urinate copiously only a yard or so from her head, she prayed that he wouldn't step on it. Or indeed on her.

In the event, as he gave a sigh of satisfaction and took a step back, it was Raoul he stepped on.

Raoul was up on his feet in a flash.

It wasn't clear if it was the sight of the Frenchman rising from the leaf mould like some kind of hideous mythical monster or the noise of his boots on the tarpaulin that startled the intruder more, but one or the other caused him to drop the torch he had carefully wedged under his arm in order to do up his track, which gave Helen the perfect opportunity to hunker back on her knees and head-butt him hard in the groin.

He went down at once with a scream of pain.

Instantly they heard the crash of foliage as his colleague began to retrace his steps.

Raoul grabbed the bag from its hidey-hole in the ground, then picked up the man's torch and thrust it into Helen's hand.

'*Allez*,' he hissed, pointing to the animal track that led into the forest on the right-hand side of the outcrop. 'Run! *Vite*. We meet back at the van, *d'accord*?'

And without waiting for her reply, he melted away into the darkness.

Helen ran.

At first she had no idea which direction she was going in. It didn't matter. All that mattered was putting distance between her and the Germans. But even as she stumbled along the narrow path, holding one arm in front of her face to shield her from any overhanging branches, she could hear more voices, ahead of her this time, the crashing of branches, and once, a shot.

Heart pounding, she struggled off the track between a couple of fir trees, and doubled over, trying to catch her breath. There was no point in pelting headlong into a tree, or indeed into the next group of men.

She didn't dare use the torch, but she held it ready as a potential weapon in her other hand.

Gradually her breath came back, and now, as she forced herself to calm down and take stock, she could taste blood on her lip from where a sharp twig or perhaps a bramble had snagged her.

Deep in the trees, it was hard to work out where she was. But gradually, with the help of the moon and a brief glimpse of the silhouette of the hill that lay behind the monastery, she got her bearings, and began to work her way round the contour of the hill until she found what she thought was the track they had driven along when they first arrived.

Checking that the coast was clear, she ran across into the deep shadow of the trees on the other side. A bird clattered away from under her foot. She had no idea what it was. A nightjar? An owl? Whatever it was, it had made her jump, and she suddenly found herself thinking of Raoul's two pigeons perched on the candelabra at the house in Hamelin. She wished she was back there, safely tucked up in bed. She wondered if Raoul was all right. Had the German hunters shot him? Or caught him? For all she knew, they might even now be torturing him for information.

As she slunk along the edge of the dark track, she realised that this had always been a hopeless quest. How could she possibly hope to find one man, in a hostile country, in the middle of a war? The whole thing had been a stupid waste of time and energy.

But already ahead she could see the trees thinning out. Was this the clearing where they had parked the van?

It was, and despite her sudden despondency, Helen hadn't forgotten her SOE training.

It was perfectly possible that if he had been caught, Raoul might have been forced to divulge the location of the van. Or maybe the Germans had found it for themselves, and were even now waiting to pick up anyone who approached it.

Slowly, silently, she skirted the clearing. Then abruptly she stopped again. The moonlight had caught something, a brief flicker of metal. A gun? A buckle? There was definitely someone there by the fir trees.

Hastily she took a step back, moulding herself to the shadowy tree trunk behind her.

But it wasn't a tree trunk.

It was a man, and even as he moved, and the scream rose in her throat, a hand clamped harshly over her mouth. An arm gripped her from behind, pinning her tight against her assailant's hard body.

For a terrified second her entire mind went blank, and her limbs turned to jelly. She was unable to think, let alone struggle. But thankfully, she could still hear.

And what she heard was a low, heart-tinglingly familiar voice in her hair. 'Hélène, *c'est moi*. Please don't kick me. And whatever you do, don't scream.'

Helen hadn't heard that voice for two and a half years. And she couldn't believe she was hearing it now. Gradually she felt his arms relax, and swinging round, still half in his embrace, she stared incredulously up into his face. But they were deep in the trees, and it was too dark to see him properly.

'André?' she gasped. 'Is it really you? But how . . .?'

At once his finger was on her lips. 'They are very close,' he murmured.

She shook her head, trying to clear her befuddled brain. Trying to make sense of his miraculous reappearance. Trying to stop her reaction to his sudden unexpected proximity. He felt thinner than before, but no less strong, and she could feel her heart pumping as though there was no tomorrow.

'Raoul was with me,' she said.

'I know,' he said. 'He's waiting by the van.'

So it was Raoul she had seen in the clearing.

For a moment, they stood in silence, clasped together, unmoving.

'What happened?' she whispered. 'Did we make a mistake?'

He shook his head. 'No,' he said. 'I did. Wessel must have seen me and sent his men to flush me out. If it hadn't been for you throwing that stone, they would have got me. They were only yards away.'

'It was a trap,' she said.

She felt a tremor of amusement run through him. 'I know that now.'

He was laughing. She couldn't believe it. After all he had been through. After all *she* had been through. All he could do was laugh?

But then he wasn't laughing any more. '*Ma chérie*,' he murmured. 'I am so happy to have you in my arms again.'

Once again she tilted her head up, and now her eyes had acclimatised to the darkness and she could see under the growth of beard how thin his face had become. How gaunt. His thick dark hair was shorter than she had ever seen it, but even though there were deep shadows under his eyes, it was the same face, with its strong nose and sensual mouth. But to her dismay, as she smiled up at him, she saw an agonised look creep into his eyes. Abruptly he shook his head and looked away. 'I want to kiss you,' he said. 'But I daren't. God knows what I might have picked up in that awful camp. The place was rife with disease.'

'I don't care,' Helen whispered.

'But I do,' he said. 'I would never forgive myself if I passed something on to you.'

Even as he spoke, she felt a convulsive shiver run through him.

'Oh my God,' she said as he swayed slightly, grasping her shoulder for support. 'Do you really think you've caught something?'

'I hope not.' He clasped his spare hand to his stomach, and she saw his teeth clench as he bit back a groan of pain. As the spasm wore off, he gave a slightly self-conscious laugh. 'But I've certainly felt better.'

Suddenly Raoul was there beside them. 'We must leave,' he said. 'There are too many of them. They have moved away now, but they will find us if we stay, and Monsieur André is too weak to fight. In any case, it is Wessel we want, not his lackeys.' Ignoring André's objections, he guided the two of them to the van. The back doors were already open, and within seconds he had pushed André inside, helping him to lie down, putting the bag under his head as a pillow and covering him with a rug.

Helen wanted to climb in with him, but Raoul shook his head. '*Non*,' he said sharply, urging her to the front. 'It is better if he is alone. And if they pursue us, then I may need you to read the map.'

486

Chapter Twenty-Eight

It was late when Molly got back to London. After leaving Mrs Rogers, she had made her way blindly back to the station, hardly even noticing that the weather had turned and a sleety rain had started to fall. By the time she had been sitting on a bench at the station for over an hour, waiting for a train, she was frozen to the core.

When the train did eventually come, it was crowded with people all taking advantage of the lifting of the blackout restrictions to go up to London for a night on the town. The last thing Molly felt like was listening to endless chit-chat about their gleeful plans for their evenings' entertainment, and in the event the potential revellers might as well have held their breath, because the points on the track froze and they were stuck for almost the entire evening in the middle of the pitch-dark countryside somewhere between Stoneleigh and Worcester Park.

Not only had Molly missed her afternoon's lesson with the professor, she had also missed an entire evening's work at the pub.

And for what? To discover that her father lived so far away that her chance of ever meeting him was about as likely as flying to the moon.

As she sat on the dark train, listening to her fellow passengers grumbling about their wasted evening, she felt like shouting at them to shut up. After all, what was one lost evening compared to all the frustrating setbacks she had endured over the last few months? She felt as though she had been jinxed at every turn. But conscious that her friends had warned her that the additional quest for her father might not have a happy outcome either, she made a pact with herself not to show the full extent of her disappointment. After all, they had their own problems too. There was no reason why she should burden them with her stupid self-inflicted misery. She certainly didn't want to put a downer on Mrs d'Arcy Billière's show. On the contrary, she was increasingly feeling that in order for it not to be a total disaster, it was going to need every ounce of optimism and enthusiasm she could throw at it.

The lights were still on in the pub, and expecting to find Katy wearily clearing up after a busy evening with insufficient bar staff, Molly was astonished to find, when she went in to apologise for her absence, that things were still in full swing. Last orders hadn't even been called.

Katy was standing at the bar looking so unusually bright eyed and bushy tailed that for a second Molly wondered if she might have been at the brandy bottle. Or perhaps the war was over and nobody had thought to tell the people on the train.

'Molly!' Katy screamed across. 'Where on earth have you been? You'll never guess what's happened. Ward's fine. I had a telegram this afternoon. He's going to be home as soon as he can. *And*,' she shook her head rather dazedly, as though she couldn't quite believe what she was about to say, 'Mr Rutherford has changed his mind. Aaref and Elsa can have the lease after all.'

And that of course meant that if Ward agreed and thought they could afford it, he and Katy would in due course be able to buy Mrs d'Arcy Billière's house.

It was indeed wonderful news, and Molly was happy for them all. She really was. Especially as she suspected that she had been instrumental in bringing it about.

Later, when she eventually escaped back to the Nelsons', she discovered that George's blackmail had paid off too.

She found Pam and Alan sitting rather glumly in the front room, with a cup of Horlicks each.

'Alan's had a pay rise,' Pam said.

'Oh, that's good news,' Molly said. She looked from one to the other. 'Isn't it?'

Pam nodded. 'Well yes, of course,' she said. 'But we are a bit worried George might have had something to do with it.'

Molly felt herself colouring. 'Really?' she asked. 'Why do you think that?'

'Because he asked if we could afford for him to go to Emanuel School now,' Pam said. 'And we hadn't even mentioned the pay rise.'

Alan sighed. 'But the thing is, even with the pay rise, we can't afford it. Not unless he got some sort of a scholarship, and I don't think that's very likely, do you? I know that he's enjoyed his lessons with the professor, but, well, he was always at the bottom of the class in school before, and I can't think he's changed that much.'

At breakfast the next morning, George seemed very despondent. 'After all that,' he said indignantly to Molly when Pam was upstairs getting Nellie dressed. 'It's not fair. I don't see why a prat like Douglas Rutherford should have been able to go to a fancy boarding school, and I can't even go to Emanuel.'

Molly knew how he felt. It wasn't fair. *Life* wasn't fair. 'You're turning into a communist,' she said. 'Don't let Mrs d'Arcy Billière or the professor hear you, or they'll have your guts for garters.'

George laughed and took a mouthful of toast. 'As soon as the play's over, I'm going to make the professor and Miss Voles teach me all the things I'd need to know for a scholarship exam,' he said as he chewed. 'And maybe Mrs d'Arcy Billière too, if I need to know French.' He wrinkled his nose. 'Or perhaps Helen can teach me when she gets home.'

Molly smiled manfully. 'That's the spirit,' she said. But there was no sign of Helen getting home. No word from her at all.

★ ★ ★

The first thing André wanted to do when they got back to the house was have a bath. He was almost too tired to climb the stairs, but he insisted that he had to get clean before he slept. While he was upstairs washing off months of grime, Raoul released his last but one pigeon, with a message from André tucked into a little cylinder on its leg telling Monsieur Cabillard he was safe.

Helen and Colonel Izzard-Lane, in the meantime, went to find the Hamelin occupation commander, who promised to send a military doctor to the house but said there was nothing he could do about Wessel being at the monastery.

'He's well beyond my remit there,' he said. 'Even if you had a warrant, we're not allowed to set foot in religious institutions. In any case, he's probably using an assumed name. That's what a lot of these Nazis bastards are doing, you know, claiming they are displaced persons and getting new documents and international transit papers from the Red Cross. All it takes is a signature from a priest.' He saw Helen's incensed expression and shrugged. 'I guess the Pope doesn't want to see too many people standing trial for war crimes.'

He was rather more interested in their suggestion that there might be a cache of looted goods hidden in a secret room in Hauptsturmführer Wessel's house. 'Wow,' he said. 'I won't ask how you found that out, but I'll sure pass that news up the line. There's bound to be some special team dealing with that kind of thing.'

In return, he brought them up to date with the progress of the war. The British were still fighting to take Hamburg in the north, but Stuttgart in the south of the country, where the Germans had also continued to put up fierce resistance, had finally fallen to the French. The Russians, advancing rapidly from the east, had Berlin almost surrounded. And in Italy, after a massive Allied assault on their doggedly held positions in the north of the country, all remaining Nazi and fascist troops were now in retreat.

'It's kind of weird to think of this damned war being over,' he said as he showed them out of his office, with a polite farewell salute to Colonel Izzard-Lane. 'But I guess it's not going to be too long now.'

★　★　★

André slept on and off for nearly twenty-four hours, and if Helen had found Raoul annoying before, she found him absolutely infuriating now. He insisted on being the one to look after André's needs, and would hardly let her in the room.

'Monsieur André needs to rest,' he said.

'I know he does,' Helen said crossly. 'I'm not going to wake him up. I just want to look at him, that's all.'

'It is better not,' Raoul said.

Once the doctor had been, it was even worse, because as well as diagnosing severe malnutrition and exhaustion, he had also mentioned the words typhus and tuberculosis and, having extracted copious samples of André's blood, had taken them away for analysis.

'I'm so sorry, my darling,' André said with a groan. 'But Raoul's right. I can hardly bear to say it when I see you standing there looking so unutterably beautiful, but until that damn doctor gives me the all-clear, it really would be safer if you don't come too close to me.'

'When will he know?' Helen asked. She certainly didn't want to keep away from him. She wanted to get as close as possible. Ideally she wanted to climb into bed with him and lie in his arms from now until eternity. Even with his prison haircut, with the dark rings under his eyes and dressed in one of Colonel Izzard-Lane's extraordinarily old-fashioned nightshirts, André Cabillard was the most gorgeous and desirable man she had ever seen.

Catching the quizzical smile that curled onto his mouth as he returned her look, she hastily took a calming breath. After all, his health was more important than anything. If he had stayed in the camp, he would have received the same medical treatment as the other ailing prisoners, but he had spent two cold, wet weeks out in the open since then, sleeping rough, with hardly any food or drink. It wasn't surprising that he was close to collapse. It was a miracle he had survived at all.

She looked at him anxiously, worried by his unusual pallor. 'Perhaps we should take you to a hospital,' she said. 'Even if there aren't any

Allied military hospitals near here, there must be a German hospital we can get you to.'

But André didn't want to go to hospital. 'I can't let Wessel get away,' he said. 'I'm going to go back tomorrow and finish the bastard off once and for all.'

'But that's madness,' Helen objected. 'You're not well, for goodness' sake. Anyway, after the other night, Wessel will surely know you're not alone, and he'll be even more on guard.'

But André shook his head. 'Oh, I don't think so. There's no reason he should think that. For all he knows, his men surprised a couple of lovers on a secret tryst in the woods.'

Helen doubted that. Lovers surprised on a secret tryst might have been mildly embarrassed to be stumbled upon by hunters or woodsmen, or whatever those men had been, but they would hardly have been likely to head-butt them in the privates. But she could see there was no point in arguing about it. André was not himself. He had a feverish look in his eye, and in any case Raoul was already coming into the room with a tray.

One of André's problems was that he found it extremely painful to eat. After months of starvation, his stomach cramped as soon as he swallowed anything. Helen remembered the thin but nutritious soup that the medics had fed the pitifully emaciated survivors at the camp, but when she had suggested to Raoul that she could make something like that, he shook his head.

'Monsieur André would not like it,' he said.

'I don't want him to like it. I just want him to eat it.'

But Raoul had a different solution to the problem, and when Helen glanced at the tray that he had brought into the room now, she recoiled in horror. '*Wine?*' she gasped. 'You can't give him wine.'

André gave a guilty laugh from the bed, but Raoul just lifted his chin. 'It is the best thing for him,' he said sullenly.

To Helen's irritation, Colonel Izzard-Lane agreed. 'Oh yes,' he said, suddenly appearing in the doorway. 'Just the ticket. Nice glass of Cabillard red. Best thing for him. Very health-giving. And as I saw the bottle was open downstairs, I hope you don't mind, but I took the liberty of taking a small glass myself.'

Astonishingly, the wine did indeed seem to have a beneficial effect on André's health. The following morning when Helen went into the sickroom, he said he was feeling better and asked her to bring him some clothes so he could get up.

'Raoul said he'd washed them,' he said. 'I got them from the officers' stores at Buchenwald. I don't like wearing Nazi clothes, but at least they are warm and well camouflaged.'

Determinedly Helen went downstairs and bearded Raoul in the kitchen, where, with considerable distaste, he was preparing André a cup of K-ration coffee from one of Colonel Izzard-Lane's ration boxes.

'It is too soon for him to get up,' Helen said. 'For goodness' sake, he can barely drag himself to the bathroom.'

Raoul was watching the water in the saucepan. 'If Monsieur André wants to get up, it is not for me to stop him.'

Helen glared at him. 'Well, it's certainly too soon for him to go chasing about in the woods after Wessel.'

'That is for Monsieur André to decide,' Raoul said.

'No,' Helen said firmly. 'It is not for Monsieur André to decide. Monsieur André is not capable of deciding anything just now. *I* am going to decide, and I do not want him to risk his life trying to capture Wessel.'

Raoul's lip curled. 'I do not think he is intending to capture him.'

Helen swallowed. 'I don't care what he intends to do to him,' she said. 'I don't want him doing it. I love him and I don't want to lose him again.'

There was a long pause. Then the water in the pan began to boil. Raoul took it off the heat and poured it onto the coffee granules. 'Monsieur André will never be safe while Wessel is alive,' he said.

With a horrible sense of shock, Helen knew he was right. But nor did she want André to kill Wessel. Not just because she feared for André, but because she didn't want to think of him as a killer.

Yes, of course, she knew he had killed before. If nothing else, he had killed the SOE double agent who had tried to kill her. But that was in the heat of the battle for Toulon harbour. This was something completely different. This was premeditated, cold-blooded revenge.

For a second as Raoul met her eyes, she thought she saw a glimmer of understanding, but then it was gone, and he turned his attention back to the coffee.

Helen didn't hear him leave the house, but at lunchtime when she defiantly took some K-ration instant soup up to André's room, Raoul wasn't there.

André had been snoozing, but he roused himself as soon as he saw her. 'My darling,' he said. 'You don't have to serve me. That's Raoul's job. Talking of which, why hasn't the damned fellow brought me my clothes?'

Helen smiled. 'Poor Raoul. It's mean of you to call him a damned fellow when he clearly worships the ground you walk on.'

André laughed as he levered himself up in the bed. 'I don't know about that, but he certainly worships you.'

Helen almost dropped the bowl of soup. '*Me?* You must be joking. He hates my guts.'

André looked surprised. 'Well, that's odd, because he clearly adores you.'

'I don't believe you.'

André took the soup and eyed it warily, before looking up at her with a smile. '*Alors*, maybe not in so many words, but he certainly said that I had chosen well for my wife, and I think that amounts to the same thing, *n'est-ce pas?*'

Helen felt ridiculously pleased. Nevertheless, she didn't tell André that Raoul had gone out. Instead she sat on the end of the bed and, at his request, began to tell him what she had been up to for the last six months. Concerned about tiring him, or upsetting him, she deliberately underplayed the emotional agony she had been through, and instead tried to focus on the funnier side of things. But André

494

wasn't fooled, and when she had finished, he leaned weakly back on his pillows.

'*Mon Dieu*,' he said. He gave a low groan, and a look of pain crossed his handsome face. 'My darling, I am so sorry. You shouldn't have had to go through all that. It's my fault. I should have stayed and waited for you to come. But I just couldn't bear to let that bastard Wessel get away with what he had done. I still can't bear the thought of it. That's why I have to do what I have to do.' He stopped and shook his head, as though in despair. 'But, *ma chère* Hélène, I know much I owe you. I also know how much I love you, and as soon as that damned doctor gives me the all-clear . . .'

Seeing the sleepy, sensual look in his eye, Helen felt a shiver of excitement pass through her body. But his voice was drowsy now, his words slurring as he struggled to stay awake. 'And then,' he murmured in French, 'my beautiful, brave darling girl, if after all this you still want to, we'll get married, and be happy for ever after.'

There were so many things Helen wanted to say in reply. But she felt too choked to say any of them. After six months of worry, it was impossible to express what she felt now. The only thing she really wanted to do was throw herself into his arms, and cry with relief.

But she knew she couldn't. In any case, André's thick dark lashes were already flickering down over his eyes.

A moment later, he was asleep, the smile still on his lovely lips.

At least he had eaten the soup without apparent pain. After watching him for a minute, she reached over and eased the empty bowl gently out of his hand. Then she stood up and tiptoed out of the room.

It was Monday morning, and in the café Joyce was already busy baking. But even though Mrs Rutherford had brought in half a dozen eggs from her chickens, which meant Joyce could be more adventurous than usual in her cake-making, for once her heart wasn't quite in it.

The war was nearly over. Or so everyone assumed. With Holland now clear of Germans, a huge relief operation was under way to provide food to the millions on the brink of starvation there. The Russian and American armies had finally met each other on opposite banks of the river Elbe. Berlin was completely surrounded. And military transport coming back to England from Germany was full to the brim of newly released British and American prisoners of war.

It was ridiculous to be worried about your long-lost son coming home, Joyce told herself as she put her first batch of cakes in the oven, and began beating the eggs into the flour for the second batch. Nevertheless, she was getting increasingly jumpy, and when the door of the café banged open, causing the warning bell to clang wildly, she swung round so fast she almost knocked her mixing bowl, with its precious eggy cake mix, off the table.

But it was only Angie and Gino. Normally at this time of day they were sleepy and lethargic after a heavy night of lovemaking, but today they were brimming with news.

'Mum, have you heard?' Angie was bellowing before she was even through the door. 'Mussolini has been killed, and the Germans in Italy have surrendered.'

'Oh my goodness,' Joyce said, as she hastily steadied the bowl. That poor baby, she thought, it would probably be deafened before it was born. When she looked up again, Angie and Gino were in the kitchen, and to Joyce's astonishment she saw that Gino was weeping.

'Italy, my beautiful country, is free,' he mumbled, wiping his face on his sleeve. 'Oh Mrs Lorenz, it make me so happy. Now, *finalmente*, I can take Angie home to my village.'

Joyce had been about to give him a celebratory hug, but now she froze in alarm. Suddenly she almost felt like crying herself. After all this time, despite the plans she and Albert had made about the house, and all her hopes for their future . . .

'You want to take Angie to Italy?' she said faintly. 'But I thought . . .'

But Angie and Gino never heard what she thought, because at that moment there was another commotion at the door of the café. A van had pulled up outside and the delivery boy was unloading a pile of what looked like very heavy boxes. ''Ere,' he shouted as he lumbered in with the first one, making the bell clang again. 'Where do you want me to put these crates?'

Joyce wiped her hands on her apron and hurried through. 'They can't be for us,' she said in consternation. 'I haven't ordered anything.'

But she was interrupted by a peal of laughter from Angie. 'Oh, it must be the ice,' she said. She punched Gino gleefully on the shoulder. 'Go on, cry-baby,' she said. 'Help the man unload it.'

'Ice?' Joyce stared at her in astonishment.

Angie nodded eagerly. 'Me and Gino ordered it the other day. It's for the ice cream for Molly and Jen's show.'

Joyce started at the growing pile of crates on the pavement. 'But we haven't got room for all those boxes in here,' she said.

Angie giggled nervously. 'It does seem rather a lot. But we'll never be able to keep a hundred portions cold without it. There's nowhere near enough room in the fridge.'

'A hundred portions?' Joyce said faintly. She couldn't begin to imagine how much of her precious sugar and milk allocation they would need for that.

'Well, that's what Mrs d'Arcy Billière thought,' Angie said. 'But Jen says it might be even more, and we don't want people to be disappointed.'

Joyce groaned. Perhaps it was better that they did go to Italy, she thought suddenly. At least they wouldn't be able to ruin her business from over there. But then, as she lowered her eyes, she caught sight of Angie's growing bump bulging out between the flaps of her coat, and another wave of misery overcame her. She and Albert had been looking forward to having grandchildren. It was bad enough that Jen would soon be moving away, but she had been hoping that Angie and Gino would settle in Lavender Road.

'Mum?' Angie was staring at her in concern. 'What's the matter?

You can't start crying just because Gino has ordered a bit too much ice. Katy's having a whip-round for sugar in the pub, and we don't have to pay for the milk powder because according to Aaref Hoch it fell off the back of a lorry.'

'I'm not crying because of that,' Joyce said. 'I'm crying because I don't want you to go to Italy.'

For a second Angie looked puzzled. Then she let out one of her enormous laughs. 'Gino only wants to take me to meet his mum,' she said. 'He doesn't want to stay there. Not for ever. He loves it here now, especially as his English is getting so good. If we can just get the ice-cream business going properly, he reckons we can make a good living for ourselves and all.'

Helen didn't hear Raoul return to the house. But when she woke up in the early morning and crept into André's room to see if he was awake, Raoul was already there, laying out André's newly washed clothes on a chair. He had clearly been up all night, and when Helen threw him a questioning glance, he gave a slight nod.

But not so slight that André didn't notice. '*Qu'est-ce que c'est?*' he asked at once. He seemed much more alert today. 'What are you two up to?'

'We aren't up to anything,' Helen said.

But Raoul straightened up and turned to André. His expression was bland. 'Alas,' he said. 'There was an unfortunate accident in the night. I'm afraid Hauptsturmführer Wessel fell into the river and drowned.'

Both Helen and André stared at him. André was the first to speak. 'So that's where you were last night! You deliberately went behind my back and . . .'

He stopped and turned angrily to Helen. 'You knew, didn't you? You told him to do it.'

But Helen was looking at Raoul. 'How?' she asked, aghast. 'How did it happen?'

Raoul gave a negligent shrug. 'I don't know why,' he said, 'but he chose last night to go for a drink in town. Perhaps when his men failed to find Monsieur André in the forest, he thought the danger was over. It was an easy thing to follow, and when he needed to go outside to relieve himself, he found himself a little too close to the bridge, and *pouf, quel dommage*, he fell in.'

Helen wasn't quite sure what *pouf* meant exactly, but the gesture that Raoul used to accompany his words made it clear that Wessel had been dead before he hit the water.

She put a shocked hand to her mouth. 'Oh my God,' she said.

André was staring at Raoul. '*T'es un salaud*,' he said.

But Raoul didn't seem put out by the crude insult. If anything, he looked rather pleased, but he quickly sobered. 'There is one small problem,' he said. 'His body may be found.'

'That's not my problem,' André laughed.

'People may start asking questions,' Raoul said. He jerked his head in Helen's direction. 'She has made it known to the authorities that we were searching for him.'

'I had to,' Helen said crossly. 'We needed to know if he was still registered at that address.'

Raoul looked away. 'Nevertheless . . .'

There was a pause, then André pushed back the covers on the bed.

'He's right,' he said to Helen. 'We don't want to get involved in post-mortems.' He grinned suddenly at Raoul. 'Even if it was just an unfortunate accident.' He swivelled his legs to the floor and stood up rather shakily. 'Comfortable though it is here, we can't stay for ever. So let's pack up the van and get on the road.'

'But where are we going to go?' Helen said, averting her eyes hastily from his half-naked body. 'What about the doctor? We haven't got your results yet. And what about the colonel? We can't just leave him here.'

'*Pourquoi pas?*' Raoul muttered under his breath.

André laughed. He spread his hands. 'Let's go home,' he said. 'To France.'

Helen at once began to object. 'But you're not well enough for

499

such a long journey,' she said. 'Not in the van. Even if you haven't got typhoid, you need to rest and . . .'

To her relief, she saw that Raoul was also shaking his head.

'We do not have enough fuel,' he said, and for the first time since Helen had known him, he sounded apologetic. '*Je m'excuse*. I brought all I could from France, but there is not very much left. Not enough for that, and just now it is not easy to find more.'

'Then where can we go?' André asked.

Raoul didn't have a suggestion. He was clearly too mortified at having let Monsieur André down. But then Helen had an idea. She glanced at Raoul. 'I suppose we could go back to Venlo.' But even as she spoke, she realised that what she really wanted to do was to go back to London, so she could hug Molly and Ward to bits. If it hadn't been for them, she would never have seen André again.

In the circumstances, though, Venlo was a good second best. It wasn't all that far away. At least they knew a nice place to stay, and they would be able to send telegrams to Molly and Katy from the airbase to let them know that all was well.

Raoul inevitably started shaking his head, and Helen groaned. 'Oh for goodness' sake,' she said impatiently. She knew exactly what was bugging him. 'I am hardly about to run off with Callum Frazer when I've got André with me, am I?'

André glanced up at her through narrowed eyes. 'And who, may I ask, is Callum Frazer?'

'He's Ward's cousin,' she said. 'And he's not remotely interested in me. But I'm sure he would find us some fuel and a doctor.'

So Venlo was where they went. With Raoul driving, André in quarantine in the front with him, and Helen and Colonel Izzard-Lane, who refused to be left behind, in the back.

And when, four hours later, having crossed back over the Rhine on a temporary American bridge near Duisburg, they finally arrived at the airfield, they found not only Callum Frazer, but, to Helen's delight, Ward too.

While Callum took André to see the camp medical officer, and

Raoul went off to the motor pool to try to scrounge some fuel, Ward brought Helen up to date with what he had been doing for the last week or so.

Having, in the end, been part of one of the very few 'contact teams' to enter Germany, he had liberated a group of senior British officers from the prison camp he'd been allocated and escorted them all the way back across Germany to Venlo, only to discover that there were nowhere near enough troop transport planes to take them all home. Thousands of other Allied POWs had converged on the small airport from all directions. Most had been liberated by the advancing troops; others, discovering that their German guards had fled, had just walked out of their camps. They were all hungry and weary and desperate to get back to England.

'It's all happened so fast,' Ward said. He waved a hand at the hordes of thin, scruffy men milling around the airfield. 'I guess no one had time to work out exactly how many of these guys there were going to be. The RAF are doing what they can, but obviously the POWs have to take priority. There's no way I'm going to get a seat for a good while yet, which is a damned shame, because it's Molly's show tonight and I was real keen to get back in time to see it, especially as Malcolm has a starring role.'

With all that had been going on, Helen had completely forgotten about the show.

'Oh my goodness,' she said. 'I must send them a telegram. They don't know yet that I've found André.'

'It might not go tonight,' the signals clerk said when, after a long wait, she finally reached the counter. 'I've got a hundred or so POW messages to send as well. So keep it brief.'

It was as she came out of the signals office that she saw Callum sprinting across the tarmac, alone. At once a frisson of fear ran through her.

'Callum?' she shouted, running to meet him. 'What's happened? Is it André?'

He screeched to a halt in front of her. 'No,' he said. 'André's fine. They've taken him in to run some tests. They'll know more tomorrow.'

'Then why were you coming back so fast?'

'Because of Adolf Hitler.'

Helen stared at him. 'What about Hitler?'

To her astonishment, Callum started laughing. 'He's dead. It's just been given out on German radio. They're saying he was killed in battle, but nobody believes that. Anyway, who cares how the bastard died? He's dead. Gone to join Mussolini in hell, I hope.' He saw Helen's surprise. 'You surely knew Mussolini was dead?'

'No,' she said. 'I didn't. We're obviously a bit behind on the news. When did that happen?'

He shrugged. 'I don't know. A couple of days ago?'

All over the airfield Helen could hear the rumble of excited voices, then over by the hangars, a great cheer went up. Her eyes swimming with tears, she turned back to Callum.

'Does that mean the war is over?'

He shook his head. 'No,' he said, sobering slightly. 'Apparently Admiral Dönitz is now in charge. He says they're going to fight on to the last man.'

'It's going to be a disaster,' Jen said. 'I'd completely forgotten that we'd need stage hands.'

Molly stared at her in dismay. They were standing in Mrs d'Arcy Billière's dining room, up to their ears in props, costumes and home-made scenery. There was only an hour to go before the curtain, one of Mrs d'Arcy Billière's largest bedspreads, was due to go up.

Already the first of the numerous guests were arriving. Mrs d'Arcy Billière, wearing a scarlet robe with a matching turban, was, in the grand manner, waiting in the hallway to greet them, while in the drawing room, Lord de Burrel was dispensing liberal amounts of vodka from a crate of bottles Aaref had produced from one of his nefarious sources. Because Gino's ice boxes had taken up all the space in the cloakroom, Mrs d'Arcy Billière had co-opted George to take people's coats up to one of the spare bedrooms, and he was already scurrying up and downstairs like a yo-yo.

Now he popped his head round the door and grinned at Molly. 'That prince has arrived,' he said. 'The one that put Angie's ravelioli in his pocket.'

'Oh my God,' Jen said. 'That's all we need. A Russian prince who's probably more used to seeing the Bolshoi ballet than a hopeless ragtag of idiots trying to be funny.'

George looked incensed. 'We aren't idiots,' he said. 'And it *is* funny. Even Graham laughed once yesterday.'

Molly caught Jen's eye and tried to smile. 'I'm sure it will be all right on the night,' she said.

'But this is the night,' Jen wailed. 'And nothing's all right. There's a million things to be done and nobody to do them because they're all busy getting ready. What's more, it's perishing cold and windy out there. The last thing anyone's going to want in the interval is ice cream. The tarpaulin's come loose and is flapping about all over the place, and the spotlight we fixed to the pergola, the one that's focused on Susan and Graham, is jiggling around so much it's going to make everyone feel sick. And talking of feeling sick, I'm so nervous I might throw up at any moment.' She gave a dramatic groan and clutched her stomach. 'How could I be so stupid as to think I could make it work?'

'Bunny's feeling nervous too,' Malcolm said suddenly, emerging from behind some scenery and peering into the cage that George had brought in earlier. 'I'd better get him out and give him a stroke.'

'No!' Jen screamed. 'Whatever you do, don't let him out.' Turning back to Molly, she rolled her eyes. 'The blasted creature's already escaped once today. Bella found him eating Mrs d'Arcy Billière's spring lettuces.'

Molly laughed, but at the same time she could feel her heart sinking. She felt guilty for not being there earlier to help, but she had been needed at the Red Cross. Now she gave Jen a reassuring smile. 'What can I do to help?'

Jen slumped down on a chair and put her head in her hands. 'Tell everyone to go home,' she said. 'Or tell Lord de Burrel to get them so drunk they don't know what they're seeing.'

But Molly didn't do either of those things. It wasn't like Jen to fall at the last hurdle, and guessing that she hadn't eaten or drunk anything all day, she went into the kitchen to make her a cup of sweet tea.

'Come on, Jen,' she said when she brought it out to her. 'You can't give up now. I know it's not ideal, but everyone's here now – your mother, Mr Lorenz, Katy, Pam and Alan, even Louise and Lord Freddy – and they are all happy to help. For goodness' sake, just tell us what needs to be done, and we'll do it.'

Chapter Twenty-Nine

An hour and a half later, Jen was standing in Mrs d'Arcy Billière's kitchen eating one of Gino's ice creams.

It was the interval, and Jen was feeling rather stunned. Not just because Gino's ice cream was absolutely delicious, although that was surprising enough, but because the show wasn't a disaster.

On the contrary, the audience was loving every moment. And they weren't freezing to death after all. Prior to the curtain going up, on Molly's instructions, George had given everyone back their coats, and Joyce and Pam Nelson had scurried up and down Lavender Road gathering as many blankets as they could to drape over people's legs. Thanks to some remedial action by Aaref Hoch, the tarpaulin had kept the worst of the rain off and, so far at least, none of Jen's motley selection of performers had missed their cues.

The children in fact had been word-perfect, and thanks to Molly and Pam's last-minute efforts in the dining room, they had all appeared on stage looking as cute as pie. Malcolm had looked particularly sweet, standing in the middle of the stage all on his own. His solemn recitation of his numbers in Russian, French and Italian had generated such enthusiastic applause that Katy, who was hovering in the wings in case he lost heart halfway through, had glowed with pride. The slightly risqué interplay between Graham and Susan Voles, the two presenters of the show, was quite simply hilarious. Thanks to Jen's hastily written instructions, Alan Nelson had proved to be a dab hand on the curtain, and the two spotlights provided by the POW camp had been a triumph, mainly thanks to Mr Lorenz, who, despite his fingers nearly falling off with cold, had spent the entire first half clinging to the one attached to the roof of the pergola to stop it wobbling in the wind.

Finishing the ice cream, which, since Gino and Angie had forgotten to provide any suitable receptacles, had been served on Mrs d'Arcy Billière's best French china, Jen took a deep breath. There were still plenty of pitfalls ahead, of course, but if she'd got her timings right, in three quarters of an hour's time it would all be over, and she would be able to go to bed.

Exactly three quarters of an hour later it was indeed over. George and Molly had magically produced Bunny from what a minute previously had been an empty top hat; Bella had made everyone cry with her shy but moving rendering of Alfred, Lord Tennyson's 'The Charge of the Light Brigade'; the professor had succeeded in reproducing his flaming torches experiment without setting fire to the curtain, the tarpaulin, or indeed anyone in the audience; and the children had all sung their songs very sweetly, and surprisingly in tune.

Having got carried away with their success in the first half, Susan and Graham had embellished their roles by pretending to be in the middle of a romantic embrace each time the spotlight fell on them. Or perhaps they hadn't been pretending. Jen had no idea. Either way, it had been very funny, and when, knowing that Graham wouldn't be able to get his wheelchair onto the stage for a bow, Jen waved to Mr Lorenz to turn the spotlight on them once again, the applause was tumultuous.

Now, suddenly, Molly was at her side. 'I think we ought to thank everyone, don't you,' she whispered.

'Go on then,' Jen said, nodding at the stage.

Molly looked appalled. 'I can't do it,' she said. 'I'm hopeless at that sort of thing. I'll go all red and get my words muddled, and I'll be bound to forget someone crucial.'

There was no time to argue about it; the last curtain call was already taking place, and the audience would think it was all over if they didn't get a move on.

So, with a final glare at Molly, Jen stepped up on stage.

As she began to run through the list of people who needed to be thanked – Mrs d'Arcy Billière, the professor, Susan Voles, the cast – she realised that somehow, she had no idea how, she and her strange little cast had pulled it off. Oddly, as the audience cheered and clapped each name, her sense of satisfaction exceeded even the thrill she had felt on the various occasions when she had received equally enthusiastic applause for her own performances.

'And we mustn't forget everyone who helped behind the scenes,' she went on. 'All our friends in Lavender Road leapt valiantly into the breach tonight. It is only thanks to them that the show was able to go on.' She laughed as the applause swelled again. 'I have a special thank you for my wonderful new stepfather, Albert Lorenz, who spent the whole evening standing on a chair in order to keep the spotlight steady . . .' But as she squinted into that very light and raised her hand to her mouth to blow him a kiss, she realised that Albert wasn't there. His place on the chair had been taken by an officer in Rifle Brigade uniform.

And that was the end of her speech.

With an incoherent shout of joy, she jumped off the stage and ran down the garden. Seeing her approach, Henry hastily abandoned the light and was back on the ground in time to catch her in his arms.

'Oh Henry,' she gasped. 'How long have you been here?'

He smiled down at her. 'Long enough to see that if you ever decide to give up acting, you'll have a bright future ahead of you as a theatrical producer.'

Jen felt a surge of delight. Praise from Henry was praise indeed. Before joining up, he had been one of the most celebrated producers in London. 'It was just about all right, wasn't it?' she asked.

'It was more than all right. It was a triumph, and according to Mr Lorenz, it was all down to you.'

Jen looked around vaguely. 'Where is Mr Lorenz?' she said.

Henry laughed into her hair. 'He's gone indoors. By the time I arrived, the poor man was frozen to death. So I offered to take over. And now I'm frozen to death too.' He wasn't joking. His fingers, as he cupped her face for a kiss, were indeed icy cold.

Not that Jen cared about that. She was warm enough for both of them. But before his cold lips could touch hers, Katy was suddenly there, tugging at her arm.

'I'm so sorry to interrupt,' she muttered, flushing in embarrassment. 'But your brother Bob has just turned up.' She glanced anxiously over her shoulder towards the house. 'And I think you'd better come and talk to him.'

Jen groaned. 'Katy, can't you see I'm a tiny bit busy at the moment . . .'

'I know,' Katy said. She smiled awkwardly at Henry, who smiled politely back. 'But the thing is, he's just asked me if he can stay at the pub.'

But Jen was hardly listening. Henry was pulling her close against him, and . . . 'Katy, for goodness' sake go away,' she hissed.

'But Jen, listen,' Katy insisted. 'The reason he wants to stay in the pub is because he refuses to sleep under the same roof as Mr Lorenz and Gino. And I'm pretty sure he told your mum that too, because I just saw her leaving and she looked really upset.'

'What!' Disengaging abruptly from Henry's embrace, Jen swung round. 'The little bugger,' she muttered grimly.

She was already two steps away when she stopped again. Glancing back at Henry, she held up her hand. 'Stay there,' she said. 'Don't move. I'll be back in two seconds.'

She found her brother standing by the stove in Mrs d'Arcy Billière's crowded kitchen, cradling a large tumbler of vodka. He looked thin and tired, and a little more lined than she remembered, but otherwise he was clearly the same old Bob. He certainly had the same pleased-with-himself expression on his face, and it was somehow typical that, even though everyone else was frozen to the

508

bone after sitting in Mrs d'Arcy Billière's garden for two hours, it should be him who was hogging the warmth of the stove.

Feeling her blood starting to boil, Jen pushed her way through to him.

'Hello, Bob,' she said. 'I'm glad you've turned up, because you and I need to have a little chat. I know you've been stuck in a POW camp, and I know you've probably had a pretty rough time. But it's not been all that easy for us either.'

She took an angry breath. 'What I'm trying to say is that things have changed around here, and if you think you can come back and start making trouble for Mum and Mr Lorenz, then you've got another think coming. I know you've always been full of stupid ideas. But that's what they are. Stupid. Just like our stupid father who gave them to you. Good God, don't you realise that the whole point of this bloody war was to get rid of that bigoted bastard Adolf Hitler and all his stupid prejudices about race and religion?'

A flash of anger had crossed Bob's face when she mentioned their father, but he hid it behind a supercilious laugh. 'Oh come off it, Jen,' he said. 'Don't pretend you approve of Mum marrying old Lorenz. Let alone Angie marrying that Eyetie.'

'I don't have to pretend,' Jen said. 'Because I do approve.' She saw his sceptical expression and gritted her teeth. 'OK, maybe at first I wasn't sure. But I am now. Yes, Gino may be Italian, but he is one of the sweetest people you could ever hope to find. As for Mr Lorenz, he has made Mum happier than she has ever been in her life. And if you begrudge her that, then you are even more of a selfish bastard than I thought you were.'

The previously noisy kitchen had fallen silent. But as Jen glared angrily at her brother, someone by the sink shouted, 'Bravo!' and started clapping. Immediately others joined in, and suddenly the room was full of noisy applause.

'Bravo indeed,' someone murmured behind her and, turning round, Jen saw Henry standing in the doorway, looking at her quizzically.

'I thought I told you to stay where you were,' she muttered crossly.

'You did,' he said. 'But it was a bit cold.'

Jen flushed. 'I'm sorry,' she said. 'But I felt I had to . . .'

'I know,' Henry said. 'I heard.' He glanced at Bob, who was still standing by the stove. But he had lost his smug expression, and now looked more as though he had just been slapped round the face with a dead fish.

'Hello,' Henry said, extending his hand. 'Welcome home. I'm Henry Keller, Jen's husband.'

Now Bob's eyes nearly popped out of his head, and Jen wondered if her mother had failed to tell him about Henry. Or perhaps she had just failed to mention that Henry had joined up, and instead of being the effete theatrical type Bob had perhaps imagined, he was, for the time being at least, a rather muscular-looking officer serving in the prestigious Rifle Brigade.

Bob muttered some incoherent greeting, but as they shook hands, Henry fixed him with a steely eye. 'I don't want to get off to a bad start with you,' he said quietly. 'But as Jen said, things have changed around here. I am part of your family now. And if you ever upset my wife like this again, or indeed my mother-in-law, I'm afraid you are going to have me to answer to.'

Dropping Bob's apparently lifeless hand, he smiled easily and draped a casual arm round Jen's shoulders. 'Now, my darling wife, I think the time has come for us to treat ourselves to one of Lord de Burrel's vodkas.'

Having left André in the care of the RAF medics, and having celebrated Hitler's demise with a round of drinks in the officers' mess, Helen, Ward and Colonel Izzard-Lane decamped to the *gasthuis* where Helen had stayed before. Somewhat to her relief, Raoul, who had driven them there, had opted to go back to the airbase in case André needed him.

The rest of them made an odd little party that night at dinner, but Helen's fear that conversation would be somewhat laboured was not realised. At some stage during the afternoon Colonel

Izzard-Lane had discovered that Ward came from an aeronautical family in Canada and had learned to fly when he was ten years old.

'My dear old brother is rather keen on aeroplanes,' the colonel said as he tucked into his third glass of wine. 'Must introduce you sometime. I think he'd like you.'

'That's very kind, sir,' Ward had responded politely. 'I'd be interested to meet him too.'

He had caught Helen's eye as he said it, and she had choked on her noodle soup.

Nevertheless, the colonel had clearly taken a shine to Ward, and indeed, it soon transpired, to André.

'Shame he's not well,' he said. 'He seems surprisingly civilised for a Frenchman. Not like that other surly fellow who keeps foisting himself on us. Between you and me, I'm rather glad he's taken himself off tonight. Frankly, I hope that's the last I see of him.'

But it wasn't the last he saw of him, because the following morning, just as Helen, Ward and the colonel had sat down to breakfast in the hotel dining room, Raoul reappeared. And with him were André and Callum.

Having assumed that André would be incarcerated in the RAF hospital facility for several days, Helen could hardly believe her eyes. Especially as he was suddenly looking very chic in grey flannels and a high-necked navy sweater, which she later discovered he had borrowed from Callum.

'Oh my goodness,' she gasped, transfixed in her chair on the other side of the table. 'Does this mean you're OK?'

André laughed. 'That might be a matter of opinion. But I've been given a clean bill of health, if that's what you mean. I apparently have some vitamin deficiency and a little muscle wastage here and there, but that's all.'

Ward stood up and offered his hand. 'Hey,' he said. 'I'm real pleased for you. From what I've heard about those camps, I guess you've been lucky.'

André gave a rueful smile. 'You can say that again. In so many ways.'

The two men had met before when they were working for the SOE, but only very briefly. Now, as they shook hands, Helen could see them sizing each other up, and was pleased to see that they both seemed satisfied with what they saw.

But then André turned his smile on her, and at once her legs turned to jelly.

'So what are we going to do now?' she asked.

André walked slowly round the table towards her. 'Well, the first thing I need to do,' he said, 'is to kiss you.'

Helen looked up at him as he reached her chair. 'What? Now?'

He nodded and held out his hand. 'Yes.'

She could feel the heat in her cheeks, but on the pressure of his fingers, she stood up obediently. Expecting him to lead her out of the room, she was startled when instead he drew her into his arms.

'What are you doing?' she muttered. 'Surely you don't mean now, this minute?'

But André just smiled down into her eyes. 'I mean now, this second,' he said, and proceeded to kiss her right there at the table, in full view of the entire dining room.

'Good lord,' Colonel Izzard-Lane said in shock. If he had worn a monocle, it would certainly have fallen from his eye.

As she melted into André's embrace, Helen felt a tremor of amusement course through his body. 'My darling,' he whispered against her lips, 'I'm sorry to embarrass you, but I can't tell you how much and for how long I have wanted to do this.'

Seeing that Helen was incapable of speech, Ward swung into action, pulling up chairs and summoning the waitress to bring extra coffee and some more breakfast buns.

'No, but seriously,' Helen said, once they were all settled down again round the table. 'What *are* we going to do now?' She was still feeling flustered, but was trying hard not to show it. The fact that Ward and Callum were both grinning like Cheshire cats didn't help.

Nor did the shocked expression on Colonel Izzard-Lane's face. She spread her napkin neatly back on her lap and glanced at André, who was now sitting beside her. 'I know you want to go home, but do you really feel well enough to drive all the way down through France?'

André took her hand and kissed it. 'It's not just about me. You've had a hell of a time too, my darling. It occurred to me last night that you might prefer for us to go to London.' Catching the flicker of grateful surprise in her eyes, he leaned back in his chair. 'The war's going to be over any day now, and you'll want to celebrate with your friends.' He smiled. 'I would certainly like to thank Molly for all her help. I'd probably be dead now if it wasn't for her. And,' he put on a more serious face, 'it also occurred to me that I really ought to do the right thing and ask your father for your hand in marriage.'

'Quite right,' Colonel Izzard-Lane agreed, eyeing him with slightly renewed enthusiasm. 'Correct etiquette is very important in these matters.'

Once again Helen saw the laughter sparkling at the back of André's eyes.

'But with all the POWs waiting to go home, we'll never get a flight,' she said.

André shrugged. 'Then we'll take the van.'

Helen was aware of a frisson of excitement at the thought of spending a few days alone on the road with André. 'Really?' She stared at him for a second, then turned to Raoul. 'But what about you?' she said. 'Would you mind?'

Raoul lifted his chin. 'It is Monsieur André's van,' he said. 'It is for him to decide.'

Helen bit her lip.

But André was looking at Ward and Callum. 'Do you reckon we'd be able to ship the van across the Channel? A civilian vehicle?'

Ward shrugged. 'I guess so. Not from Holland yet, or Calais, but maybe from one of the ports in Brittany. I know the dockmaster at Caen. I could give you his name.'

Helen turned eagerly back to André. 'If we're going to Caen, then maybe we could stop off in Paris on the way.' She looked at him through her lashes. 'I'd like to get my aunt's approval too.'

She could see at once from the look in André's eyes that the idea of a few romantic nights in Paris certainly met with his approval. She knew what he had in mind and felt a shiver of anticipation. But it wasn't just romantic nights that she was thinking about. It was the shops, too, and the fashion houses: Schiaparelli, Molyneux, Dior. Knowing the style-conscious Parisians, the couturiers would surely all be back in business by now, and what a delight it would be to treat herself to some new clothes after five years of austerity.

But her gleeful anticipation was short lived.

'In that case,' Colonel Izzard-Lane chipped in, 'perhaps you could take me with you. Not much more for me to do here, after all.'

As Helen swung round in dismay, she caught Ward's amused expression. 'While you're at it,' he said, 'can I cadge a lift too? It's going to take an eternity if I have to wait for the RAF.'

Helen glared at him, but André was already laughing. 'Why not?' he said. 'The more the merrier.' Noticing that Raoul didn't look very merry, he grinned at him. 'Don't worry,' he said. 'You don't have to come all the way to England. We'll put you on a train in Paris, if they are running again, and you can go home to your lovely wife.'

Helen stifled a gasp of astonishment. It had never occurred to her that Raoul might have a wife.

'But what about your father?' she said suddenly to André. 'He'll be terribly disappointed. He must be desperate to see you.'

André smiled. 'He'll understand. Assuming that damn pigeon got there, he knows I'm safe. Raoul can give him all the gory details.'

So that was it. It was decided. They would go to Paris.

Helen glanced round the table. Everyone seemed happy with the plan. Everyone, that was, except Callum, who was staring pensively into his coffee cup. She wondered if it had been André's casual mention of Molly's name that had spoiled his earlier high spirits.

514

She leaned over and touched him on the arm. 'Why don't you come too?' she whispered.

Callum looked up, startled. 'I can't,' he said. 'We're still operational. The war's not over yet.'

'Surely you could get a few days' leave?'

He took a breath. 'I dunno.' Lowering his eyes, he fiddled with the coffee cup for a moment, then looked up again. 'Even if I could, do you think it's worth it? Do you think she . . .?' He stopped and looked away.

Helen felt her heart twist. She had been away from England for several weeks and had no idea what Molly might be feeling by now.

'Have you heard from her?' she asked.

He shook his head. 'No.'

Helen sighed. 'Then I don't know. All I can say is that sometimes in life you have to fight for what you really want.'

Callum was silent for a long moment, then suddenly he leaned forward across the table. 'Hey, André?' he said. 'I don't know when you were thinking of leaving. But can you give me a couple of hours? If I can get permission from the wing commander, I'd like to come too.'

'I'm glad the show was a success,' George said. 'But the best bit for me was when Jen let rip at her brother in Mrs d'Arcy Billière's kitchen.' He grinned at Molly through a mouthful of toast. 'I was hoping Captain Keller was going to punch him and all. But he didn't.'

Molly laughed. 'I should think not,' she said. She had heard about Jen's outburst last night and was slightly disappointed not to have witnessed it herself. But she had been too busy receiving acclaim from Mrs d'Arcy Billière's multitude of guests.

Ward's elderly aunts, who had come up to London for the occasion with Katy's mother, were over the moon. 'It was all so professional,' they said. 'And wasn't Malcolm adorable?'

Lord de Burrel had been most complimentary too. 'Just like

something you'd see in the West End,' he said. 'Now, my dear, let me get you another vodka.'

Lord Freddy wanted to congratulate her and George on the rabbit trick. 'I still can't work out how you did it,' he said.

Louise, who was standing next to him, giggled. 'Let's have another vodka. Then it might all become clear.'

And Professor Markov had barely been able to contain his excitement. 'I couldn't be more proud of you if you were my own daughter,' he said. '*Maya doch*. It was magnificent. Everyone says how much they enjoyed it. What a shame we didn't choose to put it on for more than one night.'

The thought of doing it all again made Molly feel quite faint, and however much she tried to pass the credit on to Jen, nobody was having it.

'No, no, it was your idea,' Mrs d'Arcy Billière said. 'I know Jen helped a lot, but without you, it would never have happened.'

In any case, Jen wasn't there to accept the praise, because she and Henry had surreptitiously disappeared upstairs, armed with a bottle of vodka.

Of all the post-show compliments, one of the most gratifying moments for Molly was when she was cornered in the hallway by Graham's mother.

'Oh there you are, Miss Coogan,' Mrs Powell said. 'I've been looking for you everywhere. I wanted to thank you for all you've done for Graham. He's been a different boy these last few weeks. When I saw him tonight, being so funny and gay, it was almost like he was his old self again. It made me want to cry.' She gave a little choked laugh. 'I am crying now. Bringing him to you was the best thing I ever did.'

A few minutes after that, just as Molly was saying goodbye to some of Mrs d'Arcy Billière's grand Russian friends, Dr Goodacre had loomed into view.

'Well, well,' he said. 'I had no idea I was in for such a treat. And to see little Bella reciting her poems so beautifully, well, you'd never think she'd had a problem earlier in the year, would you? This school of yours has been the making of her. Now tell me, what's the news on your medical training?'

Suddenly all the excitement went out of the evening. 'There isn't any,' Molly said. 'None of the medical schools will take me.' She put on a brave smile. 'It's beginning to look as if I'll have to go back to nursing.'

'Well, that's monstrous,' Dr Goodacre exclaimed, and she realised he had probably had a couple of vodkas too many. For a moment he looked quite brought down, but then he squeezed her arm encouragingly. 'I'm sure a clever girl like you will find an opening sooner or later. If you want me to put in a word somewhere, you know I'd always be happy to do it.'

Molly had smiled gratefully. He was a kind man and it was a kind offer. But where? There was nowhere left to ask.

'There is something you could do for me,' she said. 'I expect you noticed the young man in the wheelchair? Well, his doctors have told him that it's unlikely he'll walk again. But I've seen him rubbing his legs, which must mean he has some feeling there, and I'm sure I've read somewhere that if there's some residual sensation, then there can occasionally be a chance of recovery.'

Dr Goodacre had brightened at once. 'Yes indeed,' he said. 'Not much of a chance, I'm afraid, especially if time has elapsed, but definitely a chance nevertheless. Physiotherapy might well help, or possibly even surgery. It would definitely be worth exploring. Especially if he's got a positive attitude, and judging from his sparkling performance this evening, he certainly seems to have that.' He rubbed his hands together happily. 'That's him over there, isn't it? Talking to Jen's sister? Perhaps I'll go and have a quick word with him now.'

For a moment, Molly had almost felt like rubbing her own hands together in glee. If anyone could convince Graham to have further medical explorations, it would be the combination of Dr Goodacre and Angie Moretti.

But now, this morning, after all the excitement of the previous night, Molly was conscious of a sense of anticlimax.

She tried to tell herself that her unexpected malaise probably wasn't unusual. Jen had often told her how exhausted she felt the day after a big performance. But this wasn't just tiredness. This was something else. A strange feeling of emptiness. As though she had been drained of all emotion. Drained of everything, in fact, especially of all her former hopes and expectations.

Later, as she and George and Pam were setting off to begin the clear-up operation at Mrs d'Arcy Billière's house, a brief telegram arrived from Helen. *Found André stop Long story but safe in RAF hospital now stop All thanks and love stop Helen.* But even then, Molly couldn't summon up quite the enthusiasm she felt the news deserved.

George, however, was absolutely over the moon. 'Coo,' he said. 'That's brilliant! I can't wait to hear the long story, can you? Do you think it was Helen and André who killed Hitler?'

'Of course it wasn't,' Molly said.

'How do you know?' George asked. 'It might have been.' He giggled and cast her a sidelong glance. 'Or maybe it was Callum Frazer. Maybe he flew his Spitfire over Berlin and dropped a bomb right on top of him.'

But Molly wasn't in the mood for jokes. 'Oh for goodness' sake, George,' she snapped. 'Just shut up.'

It took them seven hours to get to Paris. André, Raoul and Ward took it in turns to drive.

When André drove, Helen took the position next to him in the passenger seat, and when he didn't, she lay cuddled up against him in the back. Despite the noisy, rattling discomfort of the van, the residual smell of pigeon guano and the occasional disapproving glances from Colonel Izzard-Lane, she had never enjoyed a journey so much in all her life. Callum had indeed managed to get a week's leave, and whether it was his infectious delight at his sudden unanticipated freedom, or just the general feeling that the war was nearly over, the atmosphere in the van was one of excited exuberance. It was almost as though they were children who had broken out of school and were now absolutely determined to enjoy their unexpected truancy.

Callum had had the forethought to bring some snack rations, and those, combined with the last of the Cabillard wine, kept them all well fortified, and in a high state of merriment, for the entire journey. He had also brought a pack of cards, which endeared him to Colonel Izzard-Lane, who proved to be a dab hand at cribbage. In fact it was lucky they weren't playing for cash, because otherwise the colonel would have cleaned them all out by the time they arrived at the Belgium border, near Mons.

As they crossed into France, André took the wheel again, and it was as the light gradually faded that Helen realised they were going to arrive in Paris far too late to inflict themselves on her aunt.

'What are we going to do?' she asked André. 'Where are we all going to stay? None of us has any money on us, not francs, at least.'

'Don't worry, my darling,' he said. 'I bank in Paris. We can get money tomorrow. As for tonight, I suggest we stay at the George V. I'm known there. That's where I always stay when I'm in Paris. Or at least I used to. Not while the Boches were in town, obviously. Then of course I stayed in Avenue Foch, courtesy of the Gestapo. Nevertheless, I'm sure the manager of the George V will remember me.' He glanced across at her with a smile in his eyes. 'Before the war, they used to serve Cabillard wine in the restaurant.'

Helen smiled back at him. She would have been attracted to André Cabillard even if he had been a pauper. It was his rugged good looks, his humour and his unbelievable courage that had made her fall in love with him. The fact that he was also the kind of man who stayed at the George V in Paris was the icing on the cake.

And of course the manager of the fashionable George V hotel did remember him, falling upon him like an old friend. 'We are very busy since liberation,' he said. 'But for you, Monsieur André, we always have a room. And for your beautiful fiancée.' He bowed graciously to Helen, and then, rather less enthusiastically, glanced over André's shoulder at the ill-assorted group of men standing behind him. 'And for your friends also?'

'If possible,' André said.

'Of course,' the manager said. 'Excuse me one moment while I just check the register.'

Colonel Izzard-Lane was hugely impressed. 'Well, this is more like it,' he said, glancing around the elegant Galerie. But when André, to help the manager out, tentatively suggested that the colonel might be prepared to share a room with Raoul, he adamantly refused.

'Good lord. You must be joking,' he expostulated. 'The man would probably cut my throat in the night.'

So in the end Callum shared with Raoul, and Ward shared with the colonel.

Helen, of course, shared with André.

'It is one of our best suites,' the manager said. He lowered his eyes decorously. 'I hope you will find it satisfactory.'

It was, in fact, much more than satisfactory, and two hours later, as Helen lay in the enormous bed, watching the soft light of the street lamp outside glinting on the chandelier above her head, she wondered if she would ever feel as happy again. It wasn't just the passion, although that had been intense; it wasn't the touch of André's fingers, the almost shocking, sensual pleasure of his lips on her skin; it wasn't even the knowledge that these last terrible months had all been worthwhile.

No, it was something much more fundamental. Much more lasting. A feeling of total and utter ease, of understanding, of confidence, of contentment. A sense of being completely in tune.

She turned her head on the pillow to look at him. He too was lying on his back. His eyes were closed, his long lashes casting faint shadows over his high cheekbones, but there was a smile on his lips. A smile of bliss and fulfilment that exactly mirrored her own. On his bare chest he held her right hand, clasped in both of his. She

520

could feel the warmth of his body all the way down her right-hand side.

'I know you are looking at me,' he murmured.

'I can't help it,' Helen said. 'I have to keep checking that you're really there.'

He turned his head and his eyes opened. 'I am really here,' he said. 'And I am very much hoping to be at your side for ever more.'

Helen felt she could almost drown in that look of love, but just for the moment she resisted it. 'That's good,' she said. 'Because there is something I want to ask. Something I've been meaning to ask you ever since I found you.'

His eyes opened wider, and a faint frown creased his forehead. 'What?'

She smiled. 'Not what. Why. Why did you go running off after Wessel? The invasion was already under way. You must have known I would come.'

André was silent a long moment, then he lay back and stared at the ceiling. 'He had done terrible things,' he said. 'He had murdered too many people. I couldn't let him get away with it.'

'I know,' she said. 'But they've all done terrible things. Why him? Why just then?'

This time the silence was even longer.

And now, as she studied his strong, handsome profile, she suddenly wished she hadn't asked the question, because she saw the muscles tense in his jaw as he clenched his teeth.

'He shot my dog,' he said. 'He could have shot me, but instead he shot my dog, and he laughed as he did it.'

A tremor of emotion passed over his lips as he turned to face her again. 'I'm sorry, Hélène, but I couldn't let him get away with that.'

'Oh André,' Helen said. She rolled over and buried her face in his chest. And at that moment, she knew she loved him more than life itself.

Chapter Thirty

Joyce was still upset about her scene with Bob the previous evening. The applause had barely died away when Bob had materialised beside her. Before she could even greet him, let alone hug him, he'd started ranting about Albert.

'Oh Bob,' she had pleaded. 'Please don't be like that. Look, we can't talk about it here. Let's go home and make a nice cup of tea and . . .'

But he had shaken his head. 'I don't want a cup of tea. I'm not coming home. I'm not coming to the house. Not with that bloody Jew in there.'

'Don't you dare call Mr Lorenz a bloody Jew,' Joyce had said hotly.

'I'll call him what I want,' Bob snapped back. 'You've betrayed Dad's memory, that's what you have done . . .'

But Joyce had heard enough. And she couldn't bear to hear any more.

Pushing him out of her way, she had stumbled into the sitting room. Ignoring all Mrs d'Arcy Billière's grand guests, she had told Albert she had a splitting headache, and asked him to take her home.

She hadn't told Albert what had really happened. She couldn't do that to him. She just prayed that somehow in the light of day, it wouldn't seem quite so bad.

But unfortunately, it actually seemed worse. A cowardly little voice in her head told her to bury her head in the sand, to pretend she was ill. But she couldn't do that because Albert was already worried enough about her headache.

'How do you feel this morning?' he asked solicitously as he brought her a cup of tea in bed. 'Do you want me to call the doctor?'

Then to her dismay, half an hour later, just as Albert was putting on his coat ready to go down to his shop, there was a knock on the front door, and when she went to open it, who should be standing there but Bob.

He still looked surly and resentful, and Joyce felt her heart jump in her chest. Angie and Gino and Bella were upstairs, but she could hear Albert coming along the passage behind her, and she suddenly wished that Mr Poole hadn't done such a good job of restoring the house, because at that moment she would have been quite happy for it to collapse on top of her. On top of them all.

'What do you want?' she hissed at Bob. 'I thought you'd said your bit last night.'

She fully expected him to fire up again, but he didn't. He just flushed slightly, then lowered his gaze.

Then Albert was at her side, with his hand on her arm, smiling pleasantly at the newcomer, and Joyce had never felt so awkward and flustered in her life.

'Oh Albert,' she said. 'Look, here's Bob. Oh my goodness, because of the show and all I forgot to tell you. But he got back last night. There wasn't room here, so he stayed over at the pub, and I know he could have slept on the mattress in the sitting room, but . . . Anyway, I expect you remember him from the old days, and—'

'Yes indeed,' Albert said. 'Of course I remember him.' He turned courteously to Bob, and Joyce held her breath, praying he wouldn't try to shake hands. She couldn't bear the thought of Bob snubbing him.

But, somewhat uncharacteristically, Albert didn't offer his hand. He just nodded politely. 'I used to see you in the pub,' he said. 'And of course I watched you grow up from across the road. I often used to speculate how you would turn out.' Grasping Joyce's hand firmly in his own, he lifted it briefly to his lips. 'But with a mother like yours, how could you go wrong?'

Joyce was standing there aghast, waiting for the explosion. But it didn't come. Nor did Albert turn to glance at her, not even for a second. He just squeezed her hand gently, and continued to look steadily at Bob. 'I'm sure Katy was glad to have you over at the pub,' he said after a moment. 'I worry about her being there on her own at night. But her husband will be home soon, and when that happens, I hope you will come to us.'

Bob didn't reply, and Albert inclined his head. 'We might be a little cramped for a week or two, but I expect your mother told you last night that we are rebuilding my house over the road, so in due course we will have plenty of room for everyone.'

Joyce had dug the nails of her spare hand into her palm, waiting for a sharp retort from Bob, but it didn't materialise. To her astonishment, he just looked down at the ground.

'Thank you,' he mumbled. 'I might take you up on that.'

'Good,' Albert said brightly. 'In that case, I'd better get off to work.'

Bob threw a slightly sheepish glance at Joyce and began to back away. 'I reckon I'll go back to the pub to see if Katy needs a hand,' he said.

Dumbfounded, Joyce watched him cross the road, then turned to stare at Albert. Catching his brief, fond glance as he stepped past her into the street, she realised that he had known all along. The wily old bird. He had known what Bob was going to be like. He had known she had been worried about him coming back. And somehow he had known that Bob had made a fuss and a half last night. But how?

She was about to call him back when he paused at the gate. He smiled and lowered his voice. 'Oh, and I forgot to tell you, my dear, that when I popped out for the paper earlier, I bumped into Henry Keller at the newsagent's. I gather that Jen had a word with Bob last night, and she and Henry are hoping he might have begun to see the error of his ways.' He gave a small, complicit wink. 'So providing we don't make too much of it, perhaps in due course we'll all be able to rub along quite happily.'

The extraordinary thing was that he was right.

Twenty-four hours had elapsed since then, and although Bob hadn't precisely apologised, he had at least made some effort to reintegrate himself into the Lavender Road community. He had helped Katy shift some barrels in the cellar of the pub. He had helped Angie and Gino carry the ice crates back from Mrs d'Arcy Billière's house. He had even helped Molly and Aaref dismantle the stage in the garden. And now, it seemed, he had offered to help Mr Poole work on Albert's house.

'Oh, that was my idea,' Angie said airily when Joyce expressed her astonishment at seeing Bob hard at work on the site on her way to open up the café. 'I know Jen's been trying to persuade Mr Poole to get a move on, so when I saw how handy Bob was with the stage, I thought he might be able to give him a hand.'

So in the end it had all been down to Jen. Joyce felt absurdly touched.

But when, half an hour later, Jen came into the café for elevenses with Henry, she laughed off Joyce's thanks. 'It was a pleasure,' she said. 'Bob's a bully. Just like Dad was. But if this damned war has taught me anything, it's that you have to stand up to bullies.' Leaning back against Henry, who stood behind her, she made a wry face and patted her stomach. 'Anyway,' she said, 'I wanted to get back in your good books, because in due course – in about six months' time, to be precise – I'm rather hoping you and Albert might be on for quite a lot of babysitting.'

And Joyce had to turn away, because her eyes were suddenly welling up. 'Of course we will,' she said gruffly as she busied herself with the tea urn. 'We can hardly wait.'

The French trains were running again. In fact the Gare de Lyon was incredibly busy. It was as though the whole of Paris was on the move. But after a prolonged visit to the bank, André managed to secure Raoul a ticket to Toulon, and suddenly the moment came for them to say goodbye.

Ward and Callum seemed genuinely sorry to see him go. Even Colonel Izzard-Lane managed a handshake.

Then it was Helen's turn. As she looked at Raoul, she realised how fond she had become of André's stolid, impassive henchman. But she also knew that the last thing Raoul would want was an excess of emotion. Nevertheless, quickly, before she could change her mind, she stepped forward and hugged him. '*Je suis pour toujours dans votre dette,*' she whispered in French. 'I cannot thank you enough. Without you, this would not have had a happy ending.'

To her surprise and gratification, Raoul patted her awkwardly on the shoulder. 'Nor without you, *mademoiselle,*' he murmured. 'Monsieur André is a lucky man.'

Stepping back, she blinked away the threatening tears. 'Please pass my best regards to your wife,' she said. 'And thank her for sparing you for all this time.'

He nodded. 'She will look forward to meeting you.'

Then André was gripping his hand. '*Merci, mon brave.*' He clapped Raoul on the elbow. '*Bon voyage.* Give my good wishes to my father and tell him we will be home soon.'

'*Bien sûr,*' Raoul replied.

And then he was gone, melting into the crowd, and Helen was rounding on André angrily. 'Is that it?' she said. 'Is that all you could say? After all he's done for you.'

André looked surprised. 'I've known Raoul all my life. He knows how I feel. I don't have to spell it out.'

All Helen could do was laugh. Men, she thought. They were a different species.

The next stop was her aunt.

When they arrived in Avenue de Camoëns, Helen was pleased to see that things had improved enormously since her last visit six long months ago. The doorbell worked. There was a new concierge, and the lift carried the five of them easily to her aunt's floor.

Tante Isabelle had put on weight, and was wearing an elegant gown. Her hair was neatly permed and she could not have been happier to see them. There was no likelihood of her fainting this time.

'*Oh là là*, Hélène,' she laughed delightedly as she drew them into the apartment. 'I thought you were looking for one man. You seem to have found four.' She gave a coy smile. 'And if you don't mind me saying so, very handsome ones at that.'

She knew Ward, of course, and greeted him as an old friend, kissing him twice on each cheek, whereas Callum and Colonel Izzard-Lane only got one on each side. Even so, that was enough to turn the colonel quite pink. Then she took André's hand.

'So you are the one,' she said softly in French, standing back a fraction to look at him. 'I hope you are worthy of her.'

'I hope so too,' André said promptly, returning her quizzical look with one of his most charming smiles. 'I will certainly try to be.'

That seemed enough for him to warrant four kisses too. But a few minutes later, as she busied herself in the kitchen making coffee for her unexpected guests, Isabelle cast Helen a sly glance. 'I think it is already too late to ask for my approval, *non*?'

When Helen blushed, the old lady gave a nod of satisfaction. 'I thought so. I could see it in his eyes. Nevertheless, I think you have chosen well. If I was forty years younger, I would have chosen him myself.' She gave a coy giggle. 'Although I must say the two Canadians are also *très beaux*. As for the other one, the English colonel, *sacré bleu*, where did you find him? In the Ark?'

But despite her aunt's less-than-flattering impression of Colonel Izzard-Lane, she actually got on with him like a house on fire, and when a little later the colonel suggested that he take them all out to lunch, she seemed delighted. The meal at the Café de Paix was such a success that they followed it up with an equally jolly dinner at the George V.

In between, Helen and André did some thoroughly enjoyable shopping. Ward went off to meet some old resistance friends, and Callum manfully escorted Tante Isabelle and Colonel Izzard-Lane by bicycle rickshaw to the Louvre gallery.

'It's like old times,' Tante Isabelle gushed. She winked roguishly at the colonel. 'In my youth, I had all the handsome men at my feet.'

'It's like old times for me too,' Izzard-Lane replied, eyeing the rickshaw with approval. 'We used to ride in these all the time in Calcutta.'

The next night, invited by a friend of Ward's whom he had bumped into on the Champs-Elysées that afternoon, they dined at Maxim's. Decorated in the extraordinary art nouveau style, for the last few years Maxim's had served as the hub of Nazi society in Paris. Now it had become the city's British officers' club.

It was there that they discovered that a German capitulation was imminent. General Montgomery had already accepted the surrender of German troops in the British sector two days before; now the whole Allied military machine was holding its breath, waiting for the Russians to announce that they too had accepted the German admission of defeat.

It came that night. Feeling it might be wise to take Tante Isabelle home before things got too lively at the officers' club, Helen and André left the others there and hired a horse carriage to take them back to Passy. They then went back to the hotel and straight to bed, only to be disturbed in the early hours of the morning by Callum banging on the door.

'It's over,' he shouted. 'Helen, André, wake up. The war's over. The Germans have signed an unconditional surrender. The news just came through.'

As it happened, Helen and André were not asleep, and as André shouted at them to go away, Helen, with a slightly hysterical laugh, pulled on a silk dressing gown she had bought earlier that day, and opened the door to find their three travelling companions standing outside, each clasping a bottle of champagne and a couple of glasses.

'It's over,' Ward said rather unsteadily as they surged into the room.

'We gathered that,' André remarked drily from the bed. 'But are you sure? Or are you just drunk?'

Ward laughed. 'Both, I guess. But the war's definitely over. In Europe, at least.'

'Yes, indeed.' Colonel Izzard-Lane said, jumping with alarm as Ward popped the cork on his bottle. 'Jolly good show. What's more, we won.' He raised his glass to Helen. 'Thanks to you, my dear girl, it's been the most enjoyable war I've ever had the pleasure of serving in.'

And now they could hear noises outside in the street. Cars sounding their horns, people shouting excitedly. Somewhere in the distance they could even hear someone bashing out 'La Marseillaise' on a piano.

Helen glanced at André. 'It really is over,' she whispered. 'They're right.'

Ward thrust a glass of champagne into André's hand. 'Of course we're right. That's why we figured we'd better wake you lovebirds up. If we don't get on the road pretty damned soon, we'll miss the celebrations in London.'

The news of the German surrender hit London later that morning. Albert heard it on the wireless as he made Joyce's early-morning cup of tea. In his haste to get back upstairs to tell her, he spilled the tea all over the bed, and hearing his cry of dismay, Angie and Gino emerged from their bedroom.

'What's happened?' Angie said in alarm.

'The war's over,' Albert replied, and Joyce could hear the emotion in his voice. Hearing it himself, he gave a self-conscious laugh. 'And to celebrate, I poured tea all over your mother.'

Then Bella was there too, and they were all sitting on the bed and laughing and crying, and Joyce was laughing and crying too, and also hoping and praying that Paul, Pete and Mick were all right, and that none of them had, by some horrible twist of fate, perished in the final throes of the conflict. She knew that Albert's young cousin Leszek was safe because he had written only a couple of days ago saying that his regiment had been withdrawn from Germany to help with the relief operation in Holland. But of course she hadn't heard a squeak from her own boys.

Eventually she shooed Angie, Gino and Bella away. But as she got up and made breakfast, the feeling of anxiety grew. And when she and Albert left the house together an hour later, and she saw the post girl bicycling fast up Lavender Road towards them, she grasped Albert's hand in alarm.

'Oh no,' she whispered. 'Oh no, please no.'

Albert squeezed her hand reassuringly. 'She may not be coming to us,' he said.

But she was.

Delving into her shoulder bag, she produced both a telegram and a letter. Joyce's fingers were shaking too much to open either of them. So Albert tore open the telegram.

It was from Mick. *Just leaving US port. Home soon on leave. Met a nice girl in Liverpool last time back. Might bring her too. Love Mick.*

Albert smiled. 'It sounds as though our family might be about to get even bigger,' he said.

Joyce couldn't read the letter because her eyes were swimming in tears. Funny little Mick, with his freckles and his big ears, had met a nice girl.

The letter was from Paul, and had been written three days previously.

Hi Mum and Mr Lorenz,

I expect you've heard by now that Jerry has surrendered. So we've had to lay down arms. Shame really as I was hoping to get a few more of the Nazi blighters first. I wanted to go to Berlin and all. But we're not allowed to as the Russkies are in charge there now. Anyway I knew you'd want to know I was safe. Pete's all right too. I saw him yesterday in a place called Hamburg, trying to repair a bridge. It was

where Jerry made his last stand, and blimey, you should have seen it,
all bombed out and the poor old locals grubbing about in the gutters
for food like rats.

Hope you are OK, give my love to everyone, especially Bella!
Love, Paul

'Oh Albert,' Joyce said. 'They've done it. They've survived.' And she suddenly realised that, despite all her fears, she was one of the very few lucky ones. While so many mothers had lost sons, and indeed daughters, all her children were still alive.

Albert was hesitating. 'I'm afraid there's a PS,' he said.

Joyce blinked. 'What does it say?'

He made a face and looked back at the letter in his hand. '"I'm thinking of volunteering for the Far East now. It would be fun to have a go at the Japs. What do you think?"'

Joyce knew exactly what she thought. But she couldn't worry about that now. Not today. That could be left until later. She was fed up of worrying. She had done so much of it over the last six years. Just now, she wanted to celebrate.

So, it seemed, did Albert, because he drew her into his arms and kissed her.

'*Albert!*' she hissed. 'The neighbours! What are you doing? What if someone sees?'

'Let them see,' he murmured against her lips. 'I'm not ashamed of my joy that the war is over. I'm certainly not ashamed of anyone knowing how much I love you.'

It was announced later that morning that the following day, 8 May, would be a national holiday, to be known as Victory in Europe Day. Licensing laws would be suspended, the King and Queen would appear on the balcony at Buckingham Palace and Winston Churchill would make a speech. Suddenly, all over London, Union Jack flags and red, white and blue bunting miraculously began to appear, and people began planning impromptu parties.

531

Wandsworth Council announced that there would be a bonfire on Clapham Common in the evening, and a dance band would play on the bandstand, but the residents of Lavender Road felt they wanted something more than that, something of their own. But what?

It was Jen who suggested a picnic. Henry had gone to the Rifle Brigade HQ to discuss his demobbing, and she had come down to Clapham to see how everyone had taken the news of victory. The truth was that they were all a bit stunned. After such a long, bloody and relentless ordeal, nobody could really believe it was over. Nor could they decide on how to celebrate.

When Jen arrived in the pub, she found Molly, Katy and Pam racking their brains over a cup of tea, while George and Malcolm and the two little girls wrapped Lucky in bunting, then screamed with laughter as he ran round the pub like a mad thing trying to shake it off.

'I've been saving a couple of tins of peaches for a victory supper,' Pam said.

Katy giggled. 'I think we're going to need a bit more than that.'

Then Jen remembered the day out in Epsom with Lord Freddy, and they all agreed that a picnic seemed like the perfect solution.

Those that wanted to would go up to town to join in the celebratory parades, and to see the King and Queen on the balcony, and then they would all congregate back on Clapham Common for tea.

It didn't have to be formal. It didn't even have to be organised very much. All they'd have to do was spread the word, then set up a kind of Lavender Road HQ on the common with drinks from the pub and whatever bits and pieces of food they could lay hands on; perhaps they could even club together for some sandwiches, cake and ice cream from the café.

'Please can we go to town?' George said. 'I want to see the King.'

'So do I,' Malcolm said at once. 'I want to see the King too.'

'King,' little Caroline cried in agreement. 'See King.'

Katy rolled her eyes. 'No, sweethearts,' she said. 'I'm sorry, we can't. I've got far too much to do here.'

Molly wanted to see the King too. Even though her own dreams hadn't come to fruition, she still wanted to join in the celebrations. More than anything, she wanted to see the joy and relief on people's faces. However disappointed she felt personally, she couldn't be churlish about victory. Even if she did have to go back to nursing at the Wilhelmina, at least she would no longer be in fear of her life from bombs or rockets, or dealing with gangrenous bullet wounds, amputations and burns.

But she also knew what she had to do. 'You take them if you want,' she said to Katy. 'I'm perfectly happy to stay here and get things ready.'

But Katy wouldn't hear of it. 'Good God, Molly,' she said. 'I'm not going to let you miss the celebrations. You've had a bad enough year of it as it is. Anyway,' she added with a hopeful smile, 'Ward is bound to get home any day now, and I want to be here when he arrives.'

Molly could see from her expression that she meant it. Having Ward back safe and sound was the only thing Katy wanted, the only thing she really wanted to celebrate.

'Then let me take Malcolm and Caroline,' Molly said. She glanced at Pam and then back at Katy. 'If we all go together, we'll be fine. It is a huge day, after all, and it would be nice for them to see the parade. They'll remember it for the rest of their lives.'

In the end Helen and André, and their three travelling companions, didn't leave Paris until late that morning. Even though she was keen to get back to London, Helen wanted to say goodbye to her aunt. She also wanted André to get some rest before the long drive.

He was much stronger now, but even though he covered it well, once or twice she had seen a kind of weariness come over him. Faint lines would suddenly crease his forehead, his skin lost some of its colour, and his lovely smile became a little strained. It might have been fatigue, the remnants of his exhaustion, or it might have simply been the memory of what he had been through creeping into his mind. He hadn't wanted to talk about the last six months, not in detail at least. But she had discovered scars on his body that hadn't been there before, and there were probably psychological scars too that were going to need time to heal.

But even though they had all managed a few hours' rest, by the time André had driven out of Paris through the Bois de Boulogne, past the famous Longchamp racecourse and across the Seine, the three passengers in the back of the van were fast asleep.

They slept all the way to Rouen, where they had a brief stop for a snack, and then Ward took over the driving. With Helen map-reading, and André now snoozing with Callum and the colonel in the back, they set off again.

As they crossed the winding Seine once more, and began to head south towards Brittany and the coast, Ward glanced across at Helen. It was the first time they'd been alone together since Venlo.

He jerked his head towards the back of the van and grinned. 'I guess you're pretty happy, huh?'

'Oh Ward, I can't tell you how much.' She turned her head to look at him. 'To be honest, I still can't quite believe it. I don't think I've thanked you enough for your help. If you hadn't got me into MI19, I never would have found Gefreiter Henniker, and . . .' She stopped and turned her face away. The thought of how very different the result could have been was almost too much to bear.

As she stared blindly out of the window, she felt him touch her arm. 'My advice?' he said. 'Don't think about it. It's over. We won. You won. André's a great guy. Now you have the future to look forward to. We all do.' He grinned suddenly, glanced over his shoulder and lowered his voice. 'And I'm kind of hoping your crazy colonel is going to sort out mine.'

Jerked out of her daze, Helen stared at him in astonishment. 'Colonel Izzard-Lane?'

Ward laughed at her tone. 'I discovered last night that his dear old brother who is "rather keen on" aeroplanes is actually one of the directors of BOAC, and he's on the lookout for experienced pilots to forge new routes, to India, the Far East and maybe even Australia. That would be kind of cool, huh?'

Hearing the boyish excitement in his voice, Helen gave a despairing laugh. She didn't know what Katy would think about it, but nothing would be more perfect for Ward.

But then, suddenly, they nearly didn't have a future at all. Happy or otherwise.

Ward was an excellent driver, and despite the revelries of the night before, of all of them he was the most alert, which was lucky because at that moment, one of the tyres blew, and without his speedy reactions and his firm grip on the wheel, the van would have plunged off the side of the road into a deep gulch.

He swore violently and then, as they came to a shuddering halt, glanced apologetically at Helen. 'Sorry about that,' he said. 'Are you OK?'

'I'm fine.' Luckily she had been able to grab the door handle to stop herself flying through the windscreen. Straightening up, she turned to peer anxiously through the small hatch. The passengers in the back hadn't fared quite so well. André, who had been fast asleep when the accident happened, had ended up sprawled half on top of Callum, and the colonel had gashed his forehead on one of the crates.

At least it had woken them up. While Helen bathed and dressed the colonel's wound, the others set about changing the wheel. But unfortunately, although Raoul had equipped the van with both a first-aid kit and a spare wheel, unaccountably there was no jack. Nor was there any other vehicle on the road that might have been able to help them. Empty countryside stretched in all directions.

There was only one solution. With André muttering darkly about what he would do to Raoul when he saw him next, the four men lifted the offending corner of the van and, with a considerable amount of muffled swearing and grunting, especially from the injured colonel, held it up long enough for Helen to change the tyre.

Then they were on the road again. But it had delayed them, and it was early evening by the time they reached Caen.

At first, as everyone on the busy military dock sucked their teeth and shook their heads, it looked as if none of them was going to be allowed to travel at all, let alone with the van. But then Ward tracked down the man he knew – the dockmaster – and suddenly things began to look more hopeful. It wasn't clear why the man was so keen to help, but he clearly felt he owed Ward a big favour.

'Sure,' he said. 'I reckon we should be able to winch it over onto the SS *Liberty*. She's a useful little ship. It only takes her seven hours to reach Portsmouth.'

There was just one slight problem. The SS *Liberty* wasn't scheduled to sail until three o'clock in the morning.

VE Day in London dawned with a massive thunderstorm. For an hour or so, as torrential rain poured down, it looked as though the victory celebrations were going to be washed out. It certainly looked as though any kind of picnic was going be out of the question.

But then gradually the rain lessened, and by the time Molly arrived in central London with Malcolm and Caroline, Pam, George and Bella to take part in the joyful victory celebrations, the clouds were beginning to lift. From time to time a thin sunshine glinted on the plethora of flags and bunting that had appeared overnight.

It wasn't all joy, of course. For most people the celebrations were bittersweet. So many loved ones had been lost. Nobody wanted to dwell on that, not today, but even among the little Lavender Road party, almost everyone had lost at least one family member or friend. Bella had lost her mother, Molly had lost her adopted family, Pam had lost her best friend, George's mother. George had lost both his parents and his brother.

But all that was forgotten as they squeezed through the cheering crowds to watch Winston Churchill lead a procession of MPs to a victory service at St Margaret's Church in Westminster.

'Winnie, Winnie!' everyone shouted, and the prime minister raised a hand in acknowledgement as he stumped along.

Later, to everyone's delight, he appeared on the balcony of the

Ministry of Health building wearing a siren suit and a homburg hat.

'Were we downhearted?' he shouted, and the Londoners yelled back, 'No!' And within seconds the shouts turned into 'For He's a Jolly Good Fellow', and that was followed by 'Land of Hope and Glory'.

Outside Buckingham Palace, the crowds were even larger. 'We want the King,' people were chanting, while others filled the time by hokey-cokeying round the statue of Queen Victoria. A red London bus adorned with the painted slogan *Hitler missed the bus* caused much hilarity as it edged its way through the crowds.

When the King and Queen eventually emerged with the two princesses, Elizabeth in her frumpy but patriotic ATS uniform, and Margaret much more glam in electric blue, the roar was even louder.

For Molly, struggling to give the children the best view possible, terrified that she was going to lose one or other of them, the whole morning passed in a weird kind of blur. But it had been worth the effort. George and Malcolm had absolutely loved it, though the two little girls had found the crowds scary and the cheering incomprehensible. But at least in years to come they would all be able to say that they had been there, on the amazing day when peace finally returned to Europe.

Chapter Thirty-One

Two hours later, Molly, Pam and the children were back in the relative peace and quiet of Clapham. But although Lavender Road itself was almost deserted, the tea party up on the common was already in full swing.

Katy and Joyce had surpassed themselves. Not only had they set up a tea table, a drinks table and a sandwich table within striking distance of the bandstand, but they had roped in all the help they could find, and as though by magic, rugs and chairs had appeared from all quarters. The enormous tarpaulin that had previously covered the stage in Mrs d'Arcy Billière's garden had been laid out on the damp ground and was now itself covered with cushions. Gino and Angie had been up all night making red, white and blue ice cream for the occasion, and from some dark recess of his shop Mr Lorenz had produced an enormous Union Jack, which was fluttering from one of Mr Poole's scaffolding poles.

Everybody had come, even people who didn't actually live in Lavender Road. Lord Freddy had given Jen and Henry a lift down in the Alvis; Professor Markov had brought his surprisingly dainty wife; Susan Voles had appeared with Graham Powell; Dr Goodacre and Sister Morris had escaped for the afternoon from the Wilhelmina, and Mr Poole, having taken the opportunity to down tools for the day, had brought his entire workforce, including Bob Carter.

It had taken a while to get everyone equipped with drinks and sandwiches, but now the rush on the drinks tables had subsided and people had settled into little groups, some on chairs, others sprawled on the cushions and rugs.

As she looked around at all these people she had come to know so well, Molly felt a surge of affection for them. They had been through so much. But they'd been through it together. The nightmare was over. And now, at last, the future beckoned.

Leaving the drinks table, where she had been helping Katy, Molly sat down on a cushion next to Bella. And as she leaned back against the flagpole and closed her eyes, she suddenly felt that she, like Bella, could see into that future. She could see Malcolm and Caroline chasing Lucky round Mrs d'Arcy Billière's garden. She could see Katy and her mother serving tea to Ward's aunts in the pergola. She could see Jen and Henry attending glamorous theatrical parties in the West End, accompanied by an adorable, and adored, little baby. She could see Aaref and Elsa breathing new life into the Flag and Garter.

Louise would marry Lord Freddy and become Lady Bountiful. Angie and Gino would turn the café into a flourishing ice-cream parlour. Bella would go to college and become the sweetest, prettiest teacher anyone could hope for. Graham would walk again. And somehow, by hook or by crook, George would wangle his way into a better school.

Molly sighed and lay back on the rug, letting the laughter, the voices and the distant music from the bandstand wash over her. It was easy to see what would happen to her friends. It was less easy to see what might happen to her. Her future didn't look quite as bright as theirs. But she would survive. She always had, and surely she would again.

Beside her, Bella gave a sudden gasp.

Reluctantly dragging her eyes open, Molly sat up and eyed her in alarm. 'What is it? What's the matter?'

But Bella was shaking her head. 'Nothing,' she said. 'At least, I'm not sure. I—'

'Molly!' Jen's sudden scream jerked Molly's head round the other way. The sun was in her eyes, and for a second she couldn't see what Jen was pointing at. Then, to her astonishment, she saw a large van bumping slowly across the grass towards them.

Even without seeing the writing on the side of it, she recognised it. She knew that van. She and Jen had travelled in it several times, hidden in the back among wine crates, when they had sought refuge at André's vineyard after fleeing from Hauptsturmführer Wessel in Italy.

And now here it was again. Here in Clapham.

Or was she dreaming? Was she imagining it?

No, she couldn't be, because everyone else was staring at it too.

Then she heard George shouting something from the other side of the tea table. 'It's Helen!' he yelled.

It was indeed Helen. And André. And then, as the back doors opened, it was Ward Frazer too. And another very odd-looking man wearing what looked like enormous jodhpurs.

Then someone else was getting out, and stretching, and now Molly really did think she was dreaming. Her heart knew at once who it was, before he even turned round.

He didn't see her. Not straight away. There were too many people surging towards them. Katy was there first, screaming with delight, running across with little Caroline bumping on her hip, and then Jen and Henry, and George and Malcolm.

They were all hugging and kissing and shaking hands, and Malcolm was on Ward's shoulders, and little Caroline in his arms, and Katy was clinging to him, while Lucky leapt around them, barking his head off, desperately trying to get at his beloved master.

Then the whole group was coming back over.

Somehow Molly was on her feet, and Helen was coming towards her with outstretched arms.

'Molly,' she cried. 'Oh Molly.'

But Molly was too panic-stricken to return her hug. She just stood there, somehow both rigid and shaking, glaring at Helen accusingly. 'Why didn't you warn me?' she hissed.

Helen knew exactly what she meant. 'Because I thought you might run away,' she said.

She was right. If Molly had known that Callum was going to appear, she would certainly have run away. She wanted to run away now, but she couldn't, because now he was coming over too.

'Molly,' he said.

Then he seemed to run out of words. And Molly certainly hadn't got any. She could barely stand. Let alone speak. And suddenly she hated Helen for doing this to her. She could have wept.

If only she had known he was coming, she could have prepared herself. Built up her resistance. Built up her courage.

It had taken her weeks to get over that debacle at Christmas. Weeks of grief and agony. And now she was going to have to go through it all over again.

'Oh damn,' Helen suddenly exclaimed. 'I've left my bag in the van. Callum, would you be a love and fetch it for me? I brought some little gifts from Paris for the children.'

But instead of turning away obediently, as Molly had hoped, Callum hesitated. 'Sure,' he said. 'But only if Molly comes with me. There's a couple of things I want to ask her.'

But Molly couldn't move. It was as though she had become rooted to the ground.

She heard Bella's soft voice beside her. 'I think you should go, Molly,' she said.

'No,' Molly whispered back. 'I can't. I can't.'

But somehow she did. She followed him back to the van.

It was only perhaps twenty yards away, but it seemed like miles. By the time she got there, she was quite breathless.

Once again, Callum seemed lost for words.

When he did finally speak, it wasn't at all what she was expecting. 'Helen told me the London medical schools had turned you down,' he said.

Molly nodded. This is a nightmare, she thought. I'm not over him at all.

He waited for her to speak, but when she didn't, he gave a diffident shrug. 'Well, I knew how disappointed you must be. I was trying to figure out if there was anything I could do. And, well, there's a real good medical college near where I live back home in Montreal. It's called McGill.'

Molly stared at him. Even she had heard of McGill University, it was one of the best in Canada, but . . .

'The thing is,' he went on carefully, 'my mother knows the dean there, and if you want, he'll give you a place.' Catching her gasp of surprise, he shrugged apologetically. 'I guess you'd have to meet the entry requirements, but . . .'

Molly knew now that she was definitely dreaming. '*Your mother?*'

He nodded.

She stared at him aghast. 'But why would she do that?'

He looked surprised. 'I guess she wanted to help. I told her ages ago that you were hoping to go to college, and when Helen told me what had happened, I wrote her and—'

'But I've never met your mother,' Molly stammered. 'Not properly.' That awful encounter at the Flag and Garter had haunted her dreams for months. It was haunting her now.

He was clearly thinking about it too. 'I know,' he said. 'I wanted to introduce you at Christmas, but, well, it didn't work out. I was stupid. I thought you were keen on that German guy, and I—'

'What German guy?' Molly stared at him aghast. 'Gefreiter Henniker? But I never . . .'

'I know that now,' he said. 'But you know what it's like when you're madly in love with someone; you can't think straight, and you say stupid things.' He flushed slightly and looked away. 'Or maybe you don't know, but anyhow, I wasn't thinking straight that night.' He saw her recoil, and swore under his breath.

'Of course I know,' Molly muttered crossly. She was rather enjoying this dream now, and it was annoying to think that in a minute she was going to have to wake up. 'I haven't been thinking straight ever since I met you.'

542

He looked at her eagerly. 'You haven't? But you always seemed so sensible and in control.'

'Sensible?' Molly stared at him incredulously. 'In control? I'm about as out of control as you can get.'

He grinned and reached for her hand. 'In that case, I'm going to risk it and ask you to marry me. Then we can be out of control together.'

At once the dream was over. 'No,' Molly said, snatching her hand away. 'I can't marry you. And I certainly can't come to Canada. You live in a different world to me. A rich, successful world. I'm a complete nobody. I'm quite sure your parents have somebody much better in mind for you.'

He grimaced and ran a hand through his hair. 'Helen told me that's what you thought. But you're wrong.' He saw her sceptical expression and shrugged. 'Well, OK, I guess maybe they did at one time. But all they want now is for me to be happy, and to come back to Canada. What they don't want is me saying I'm going to stay in London with you.'

Molly wanted to believe him. She wanted to so much. But she couldn't. 'But they don't know my history. I was born out of wedlock. It's true my mother was quite posh, but she was only seventeen when she got pregnant. Her parents threw her out. She kept me for a couple of years, and then she shoved me into an orphanage so she could marry someone else. And now she doesn't want to have anything to do with me.'

'Well, I guess that's her loss,' Callum said. He frowned. 'What about your father? Helen said you were looking for him too. How does he feel about it all?'

Molly groaned. 'He was the gardener's son. I have no idea how he feels, because he lives a million miles away in San Diego.'

Callum brightened. 'San Diego is a nice place. Maybe I'll fly you down there for our honeymoon, and we can check him out. We could go on to Mexico afterwards. That would be fun, wouldn't it?'

Molly stared at him. He obviously hadn't been listening to a word

543

she had said. 'Your parents would hate me,' she said. 'In any case, you're far too young and far too gorgeous to get tied down to someone like me. I can't marry you. I just can't.'

He laughed. 'Sure you can. We don't care about all that class nonsense in Canada. I know you think I'm too young, but I love you, Molly. I've loved you since the moment we met. I know you think I've dated other girls, and it's true, I have. But only because I was trying to get you out of my system. And it didn't work.'

He paused, and for a moment he seemed to lose confidence. 'But I don't want you to feel you have to marry me just so you can go to medical college. That offer's there whether you marry me or not. I promise I wouldn't put pressure on you.' He hesitated again, and looked at her doubtfully. 'Maybe you want some time to think about it?'

And there was something in that anxious, hopeful look that broke Molly's resistance. She simply couldn't hold out a moment longer. If it was a dream, so be it. She would enjoy it while she could.

'I don't need time to decide,' she said. She gave a nervous laugh and felt the heat flood into her cheeks. 'If you really are serious, I don't need even a millisecond.'

She saw his eyes light up. The incredulous smile on his lips.

'Oh my God,' he whispered, and then he was stroking her face. Staring at her in wonder. In disbelief. Then he was laughing too, and kissing her, and this time, for the first time, his kisses weren't at all chaste.

Molly was leaning back against the side of André's van, and the wheel hub was digging into her thigh, but she didn't care. She could take the pain. She was glad of it. Because her knees had finally given way in delight, and without that wheel hub she would almost certainly have collapsed to the ground in a dead faint.

'I can't believe it,' she whispered. 'Are you sure it's not a dream?'

But it wasn't a dream. Because in a dream, there was no way George would have come sauntering round the back of the van just at that point.

544

'Yuck,' he said. 'I guessed something like this would be going on. Can't you do it later? Helen said she'd got us gifts from Paris and I want to see what they are, and I want to ask Callum about the war, and how many German planes he shot down.'

Callum was laughing again. 'I promise I'll tell you everything I know,' he said. 'But only if you leave us alone for a couple of minutes so I can kiss Molly again.' He slanted her a wry grin. 'I guess then we'll have to go and tell everyone that we're engaged.'

But they didn't have to tell anyone anything, because by the time they emerged from behind the van, George had already spread the news, and as they walked self-consciously back to the group, hand in hand, everyone started clapping and cheering.

In the background, behind all the noise, Molly could hear Winston Churchill's voice blaring out of the wireless that Mrs Rutherford had brought with her. 'Our gratitude to our splendid Allies goes forth from all our hearts within these islands and throughout the British Empire,' he was saying, but for once nobody seemed to be listening.

Helen was the first to congratulate her. 'I'm so thrilled for you, Molly,' she said as she hugged her. 'Do you forgive me now?'

As soon as Helen released her, Katy was there, and Ward, and Pam and Alan, and Professor Markov and Dr Goodacre, and even Sister Morris.

Molly had never had so many hugs and kisses in all her life.

Finally, when all the toasts and congratulations were over, she turned to Bella. 'This is what you saw,' she whispered. 'Isn't it?'

Bella nodded. 'But I was really worried I'd made it go wrong.'

It hadn't gone wrong, though. It had gone right. It couldn't have gone more right if it had tried.

Suddenly Molly realised that the clouds had disappeared. The sun was bright. The sky was blue. And her future was clear.

At a stroke, all the confusion, all the blur, had gone. Her struggles were over. Maybe she and Callum would go to San Diego. But then again, maybe they wouldn't. It no longer seemed to matter. She didn't need a family. Perhaps in time she and Callum would make their own. In the meantime, she had friends. They might not always be together, but they would always be her friends. And there would be visits, letters, holidays . . .

Jen was grinning at her. 'Are you happy now?' she asked.

'Yes,' Molly said. 'I am.' She *was* happy. So happy she could almost cry.

But then George was shouting something, and pointing urgently up into the sky. At once a shiver of fear ran through her. She was aware of the others falling silent too.

'Look,' George shouted. 'Molly! Professor! It's those birds. They're back. Back from Rhodesia.'

At once, the frisson of alarm that had passed through the group faded again. People laughed self-consciously. It wasn't a Messerschmitt or a Junker, or indeed a rocket. With any luck, it never would be again. As Molly followed George's pointing finger, she saw them too. Four swallows, swooping high above them.

It seemed fitting that they should reappear today. The swallows weren't worried about territorial disputes, about nationalism, about religion. They were the ones that were truly free.

Professor Markov was too emotional to respond, but letting go of Callum's hand for a moment, Molly poked a finger into George's arm. 'How do you spell Rhodesia?' she asked.

George giggled, and put on a superior expression.

'With an H,' he said. 'Everyone knows that.'

Author's Note

Researching and writing the six Lavender Road novels has been a long and immensely satisfying project for me, and it was therefore quite a poignant moment when I eventually arrived at VE Day and found myself writing the final scene of the series. If you are one of my many loyal readers, and have read all the books in the series, you might be interested to know that by the time you have finished *Victory Girls* you will have read over one million words! I sincerely hope you have enjoyed the experience, and I'd like to take this opportunity to thank you for taking the wartime journey with me, and for all the wonderful messages you have sent me by email and on social media.

Bringing a book like *Victory Girls* to fruition takes a lot of input from a lot of people and I am immensely grateful to everyone who helped me, in whatever way, especially my literary agent, Anne Williams, my editor, Marion Donaldson, and all the publishing team at Headline Books, without whom it might not have happened at all.

Although based on real history, *Victory Girls*, like the other Lavender Road novels, is of course a work of fiction, and I hope my various informants will forgive me for any occasions when, for the sake of the story, I have felt the need to simplify, invent or adapt things slightly.

I don't have the space here to thank everyone who helped me

with my research, but I would like to thank the extraordinarily obliging staff at Battersea Local History Library, the Imperial War Museum, and RADA. Special thanks too, to Elizabeth Cherhal-Cleverly for her wonderful hospitality during my research trip to the Vercors, to Lally Porter for driving in such adverse conditions, and to Jean-Claude Cherhal for sharing his knowledge of wartime France, and for showing me round the Musée de la Resistance in Grenoble. I am also extremely grateful to Maria McCarthy for her insights into the adoption process and for all the invaluable information she gave me on that subject. Ian James was a fount of wisdom on war-time ice-cream making, and two clever young women, Alex Chaffey and Lucie Ferguson, helped me enormously both with Molly's science curriculum and by suggesting suitable experiments for Professor Markov to perform. Susanna Capon provided me with a range of fascinating Russian expressions, and it was lovely to be able to incorporate into the book my mother's memory of American servicemen sticking their chewing gum on the wall outside her hospital ward to avoid the fury of a ferocious Nursing Sister.

Of course, none of my Lavender Road books could have been written without all the people who lived and died during the Second World War. That amazing wartime generation lived through the kind of terrible and tumultuous times that thankfully most of us have never had to experience, and hopefully never will. Their well-documented courage, stoicism and dogged resilience continues to give me hope that when things get very dark, people do have the capacity to rise to the occasion and are able to show tolerance and compassion, even against all the odds.

I salute them.
Helen Carey

Further reading:

Barry Turner, *Countdown to Victory*

Jacques Robichon, *The Second D-Day*

Wynford Vaughan-Thomas, *How I Liberated Burgundy*

Anthony Glees, *The Secrets of the Service*

Nigel West, *Secret War: Story of SOE*

Antony Penrose (ed.), *Lee Miller's War*

Gavin Mortimer, *Stirling's Men*

Damien Lewis, *The Nazi Hunters*

Gerald Pawle, *The War and Colonel Warden*

Sarah Helm, *A Life in Secrets*

Virginia Nicholson, *Millions Like Us*

Philip Ziegler, *London at War*

A Q&A with Helen Carey

Victory Girls **is the final novel in your much-loved Lavender Road series. What was your original inspiration for the series?**

I was living in London at that time. My car had broken down and I was waiting for a bus. At the bus stop I fell into conversation with a wonderful old lady called Laura who had lived in Clapham all her life, including the war years. She told me some stories of her wartime experiences and pointed out the sites of the old air raid shelters and the anti-aircraft emplacements on the common, all of which are now covered over with grass. That was the first of many conversations (Laura and I became close friends) but her descriptions that day had conjured up a different era, and even as I sat on the bus I thought how interesting it would be to write a novel about what it was like to live in south London during the war.

Is Lavender Road based on a real street in south London?

It is a mixture of streets. I didn't want to choose a real street because I thought it might spoil it for local people if they knew who had really lived in particular houses. But for readers who know the area it is quite easy to locate my fictional Lavender Road as running more or less parallel to the existing Jedburgh Street, running from Lavender Hill up to Clapham Common.

What did you find fascinating about writing about the Second World War years?

I hardly know where to begin! It was an extraordinary period of history. So much happened in a relatively short time and that caused unprecedented social upheaval. As well as struggling to cope with the danger and deprivation of war, people often found themselves doing things they never would previously have imagined. There are perhaps two key themes that really caught my interest. The first was the concept of people dealing with adversity and rising to the occasion. The second was the determination to overcome intolerance and prejudice. I know these both strike a chord with many of my readers too, particularly in our current troubled times.

There is a huge amount of historical detail woven into the stories. How did you do your research for the novels?

When I was first commissioned to write this series I remember saying airily to my editor that I was sure there would be plenty of material to draw upon. I had no idea then how much I would find! Initially I haunted the Imperial War museum, my local history library and various Second World War exhibitions. I read countless history books and novels, watched all the war films I could find, and spent days on end following leads through Google. The problem was knowing when to stop. The issue is that everyone nowadays knows so much about the war years. So gradually my aim became to seek out information and incidents that perhaps weren't quite so well known. For example, the invasion of the South of France in *Victory Girls*, which is much less documented than the Normandy D'Day landings.

Did you draw on any real-life accounts of women during the war when creating your characters and their stories?

Yes, indeed. Many of Helen de Burrel's stories were drawn from the unbelievably brave women who volunteered to work for the SOE, putting their lives on the line for the sake of their country. For Helen's role in *Victory Girls* I also drew on the extraordinary accounts of the American journalist Lee Miller, who followed the advance right through Europe to the final capitulation. Katy and Molly's nursing experiences are mostly based on stories told to me by my mother and her friends who were nurses during the war. A neighbour who served in the ATS was the inspiration for Louise's military adventures in *The Other Side of the Street*, and the wonderful wartime singer and dancer Mary Morland gave me so much amazing information I could probably have written six books just about Jen's acting ambitions.

Who were your favourite Lavender Road characters to write about, and why?

The five main girls, Katy, Jen, Helen, Molly and Louise, were obviously my favourites and I loved creating problems for them to overcome. But I have always had a soft spot for Joyce and Mr Lorenz, and was so pleased that I could finally get them married off in *Victory Girls*! I liked to include a bit of humour whenever I could, and it was often the children and animals that gave me that opportunity. As a result I became quite fond of Miss Taylors' dog, Winston, and Ward Frazer's dog, Lucky, and indeed Monty the tortoise. And talking of Ward Frazer, I know my readers have their own views about who is the most all-round gorgeous man in the books, but for me it has to be Ward Frazer!

The stories in the six novels show us the lives of a large group of women through the years of the war. They're connected, but each book stands completely alone. How did you make sure that each book worked independently of the others?

I plotted the books very carefully. I wanted to make sure that each one had its own unique story. Although all the girls are present in all the books, you will have noticed that each book is principally focussed on one or two specific girls. That meant finding key historical incidents that would work as a story structure with those girls' pre-existing interests and abilities. So, for example, the Winston Churchill penicillin story in *London Calling* called out for Molly as a nurse. And the hazardous trek across Europe in *Victory Girls* to the liberation of Buchenwald was ideally suited to Helen de Burrel. Then to bind the books together as a series I had other ongoing stories and relationships that moved from one book to the next, such as Jen's turbulent relationship with Henry Keller, and the ongoing dramas at the Flag and Garter.

What did you find difficult, and enjoyable, about writing a series?

Writing over a million words takes a lot of blood, sweat and tears! The most difficult thing perhaps was spending so much time at my computer, at the expense of my lovely husband and dogs.

The most enjoyable is the feeling that, in some small way, I have been able to create a story that acts as a tribute to the resilience and fortitude of all the ordinary people who lived through such dramatic and savage times.

Have you read all of the novels in the Lavender Road series?

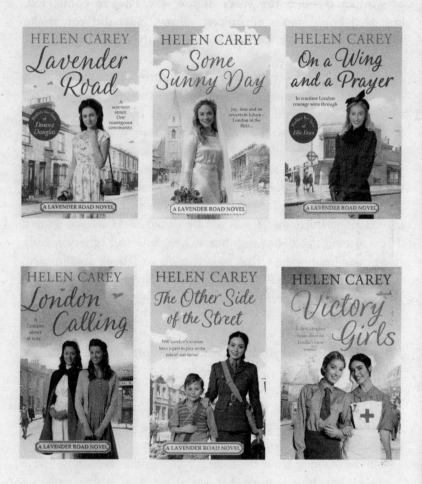

All available to buy in paperback and download in ebook.

www.headline.co.uk
www.helencareybooks.co.uk